STEPHEN JONES is the winner of two World Fantasy Awards, two Horror Writers Association Bram Stoker Awards and The International Horror Critics Guild Award as well as being a ten-time recipient of the British Fantasy Award and a Hugo Award nominee. A full-time columnist, television producer/director and genre movie publicist and consultant (the first three *Hellraiser* movies, *Night Life, Nightbreed, Split Second, Mind Ripper, Last Gasp* etc.), he is the co-editor of *Horror: 100 Best Books, The Best Horror from Fantasy Tales, Gaslight & Ghosts, Now We Are Sick, H.P. Lovecraft's Book of Horror, The Anthology of Fantasy & the Supernatural, Secret City: Strange Tales of London* and the *Best New Horror, Dark Terrors, Dark Voices* and *Fantasy Tales* series. He has written *The Illustrated Vampire Movie Guide, The Illustrated Dinosaur Movie Guide, The Illustrated Frankenstein Movie Guide* and *The Illustrated Werewolf Movie Guide*, and compiled *The Mammoth Book of Terror, The Mammoth Book of Vampires, The Mammoth Book of Zombies, The Mammoth Book of Werewolves, The Mammoth Book of Frankenstein, The Mammoth Book of Dracula, Shadows Over Innsmouth, Dancing With the Dark, Exorcisms and Ecstasies* by Karl Edward Wagner, *The Vampire Stories of R. Chetwynd-Hayes, Dark of the Night, James Herbert: By Horror Haunted, Clive Barker's A–Z of Horror, Clive Barker's Shadows in Eden, Clive Barker's The Nightbreed Chronicles* and *The Hellraiser Chronicles*.

Also available

The Mammoth Book of Vintage Science Fiction
The Mammoth Book of New Age Science Fiction
The Mammoth Book of Fantastic Science Fiction
The Mammoth Book of Murder
The Mammoth Book of True Crime
The Mammoth Book of True Crime 2
The Mammoth Book of Short Horror Novels
The Mammoth Book of True War Stories
The Mammoth Book of Modern War Stories
The Mammoth Book of the Western
The Mammoth Book of Ghost Stories
The Mammoth Book of Ghost Stories 2
The Mammoth Book of Astounding Puzzles
The Mammoth Book of Terror
The Mammoth Book of Vampires
The Mammoth Book of Killer Women
The Mammoth Book of Historical Whodunnits
The Mammoth Book of Werewolves
The Mammoth Book of Erotica
The Mammoth Book of International Erotica
The Mammoth Book of Battles
The Mammoth Book of Astounding Word Games
The Mammoth Book of Mindbending Puzzles
The Mammoth Book of Historical Detectives
The Mammoth Book of Victorian & Edwardian Ghost Stories
The Mammoth Book of Dreams
The Mammoth Book of Symbols
The Mammoth Book of Brainstorming Puzzles
The Mammoth Book of Great Lives
The Mammoth Book of Pulp Fiction
The Mammoth Book of The West
The Mammoth Book of Love & Sensuality
The Mammoth Book of Chess
The Mammoth Book of Fortune Telling
The Mammoth Book of Dracula
The Mammoth Puzzle Carnival
The Mammoth Book of Gay Short Stories
The Mammoth Book of Fairy Tales

THE
BEST NEW HORROR
VOLUME EIGHT

Edited and with an Introduction by
STEPHEN JONES

Carroll & Graf Publishers, Inc.
NEW YORK

Carroll & Graf Publishers, Inc.
19 West 21st Street
Suite 601
New York
NY 10010–6805

First published in the UK by Robinson Publishing 1997

First Carroll & Graf edition 1997

Collection and editorial content
copyright © Stephen Jones 1997

All rights reserved. No part of this publication may be reproduced in any form or by any means without the prior written permission of the publisher.

ISBN 0–7867–0474–8

Printed and bound in the United Kingdom

10 9 8 7 6 5 4 3 2 1

CONTENTS

ix
Acknowledgements

1
Introduction: Horror in 1996
THE EDITOR

49
Walking the Dog
TERRY LAMSLEY

86
Mussolini and the Axeman's Jazz
POPPY Z. BRITE

109
An Eye For An Eye
NORMAN PARTRIDGE

124
Underworld
DOUGLAS CLEGG

138
The Curse of Kali
CHERRY WILDER

154
The Film
RICHARD CHRISTIAN MATHESON

CONTENTS

160
Of a Cat, But Her Skin
STORM CONSTANTINE

175
Hopscotch
DONALD R. BURLESON

187
Ghost in the Machine
STEVE RASNIC TEM

193
The Moon Never Changes
JOEL LANE

204
Butcher's Logic
ROBERTA LANNES

215
Kites and Kisses
D.F. LEWIS

222
Last Train to Arnos Grove
MARNI GRIFFIN

231
The King of Rain
MARK CHADBOURN

258
Hardball
IAIN SINCLAIR

269
Gas Station Carnivals
THOMAS LIGOTTI

286
Ghost Music
A Memoir by George Beaune
THOMAS TESSIER

CONTENTS

305
That Blissful Height
GREGORY FROST

340
Skin Deep
NICHOLAS ROYLE

357
Hell Hath Enlarged Herself
MICHAEL MARSHALL SMITH

382
Unforgotten
CHRISTOPHER FOWLER

401
A Plague on Both Your Houses
SCOTT EDELMAN

435
Final Cut
KARL EDWARD WAGNER

443
The Break
TERRY LAMSLEY

489
Necrology: 1996
STEPHEN JONES & KIM NEWMAN

510
Useful Addresses

ACKNOWLEDGEMENTS

I would like to thank Kim Newman, Gordon Van Gelder, Ellen Datlow, Bill Congreve, Mandy Slater, Sara Broecker, Stefan Dziemianowicz, Steve Rasnic Tem, John Douglas, David Pringle, Stuart Hughes, William K. Schafer and Michael Stearns for their help and support. Special thanks are also due to *Locus*, *Science Fiction Chronicle*, *Variety*, *Screen International* and all the other sources that were used for reference in the Introduction and the Necrology.

INTRODUCTION: HORROR IN 1996 copyright © 1997 by Stephen Jones.
WALKING THE DOG copyright © 1996 by Terry Lamsley. Originally published in *Conference With the Dead: Tales of Supernatural Terror*. Reprinted by permission of the author.
MUSSOLINI AND THE AXEMAN'S JAZZ copyright © 1996 by Poppy Z. Brite. Originally published in *Dark Destiny Proprietors of Fate*. Reprinted by permission of the author.
AN EYE FOR AN EYE copyright © 1996 by Norman Partridge. Originally published in *Gahan Wilson's The Ultimate Haunted House*. Reprinted by permission of the author.
UNDERWORLD copyright © 1996 by Douglas Clegg. Originally published under the title 'Underground' in *Phantasm* No.3, Spring 1996. Reprinted by permission of the author.
THE CURSE OF KALI copyright © 1995 by Cherry Wilder. Originally published in *Interzone* 103, January 1996. Reprinted by permission of the author.
THE FILM copyright © 1996, 1997 by Richard Christian

Matheson. Originally published in a slightly different version in *Rage* No. 6, January 1997. Reprinted by permission of the author.

OF A CAT, BUT HER SKIN copyright © 1996 by Storm Constantine. Originally published in *Twists of the Tale: Cat Horror Stories*. Reprinted by permission of the author.

HOPSCOTCH copyright © 1996 by Donald R. Burleson. Originally published in *Terminal Fright*, Issue #11, Spring 1996. Reprinted by permission of the author.

GHOST IN THE MACHINE copyright © 1996 by Steve Rasnic Tem. Originally published in *Bloodsongs*, Issue 7, 1996. Reprinted by permission of the author.

THE MOON NEVER CHANGES copyright © 1996 by Joel Lane. Originally published in *Peeping Tom* 24, January 1996. Reprinted by permission of the author.

BUTCHER'S LOGIC copyright © 1996 by Roberta Lannes. Originally published in *Lethal Kisses*. Reprinted by permission of the author.

KITES AND KISSES copyright © 1996 by D.F. Lewis. Originally published in *Peeping Tom* No.22, April 1996. Reprinted by permission of the author.

LAST TRAIN TO ARNOS GROVE copyright © 1996 by Marni Griffin. Originally published in *The Urbanite* No. 7: *Strange Transformations*, 1996. Reprinted by permission of the author.

THE KING OF RAIN copyright © 1996 by Mark Chadbourn. Originally published in *Squane's Journal*, Issue Three, 1996. Reprinted by permission of the author.

HARDBALL copyright © 1996 by Iain Sinclair. Originally published in *A Book of Two Halves: New Football Short Stories*. Reprinted by permission of the author.

GAS STATION CARNIVALS copyright © 1996 by Thomas Ligotti. Originally published in *The Nightmare Factory*. Reprinted by permission of the author.

GHOST MUSIC: A MEMOIR BY GEORGE BEAUNE copyright © 1996 by Thomas Tessier. Originally published in *Dark Terrors 2: The Gollancz Book of Horror*. Reprinted by permission of the author.

THAT BLISSFUL HEIGHT copyright © 1996 by Gregory Frost. Originally published in *Intersections: The Sycamore Hill Anthology*. Reprinted by permission of the author.

SKIN DEEP copyright © 1996 by Nicholas Royle. Originally published in *Twists of the Tale: Cat Horror Stories*. Reprinted by permission of the author.

HELL HATH ENLARGED HERSELF copyright © 1996 by Michael Marshall Smith. Originally published in *Dark Terrors 2: The Gollancz Book of Horror*. Reprinted by permission of the author.

UNFORGOTTEN copyright © 1996 by Christopher Fowler. Originally published in *Lethal Kisses*. Reprinted by permission of the author.

A PLAGUE ON BOTH YOUR HOUSES copyright © 1996 by Scott Edelman. Originally published in *A Plague on Both Your Houses*, Halloween, 1996. Reprinted by permission of the author.

FINAL CUT copyright © 1996 by Karl Edward Wagner. Originally published in *Diagnosis Terminal: An Anthology of Medical Terror*. Reprinted by permission of the estate of the author.

THE BREAK copyright © 1996 by Terry Lamsley. Originally published in *Conference With the Dead: Tales of Supernatural Terror*. Reprinted by permission of the author.

NECROLOGY: 1996 copyright © 1997 by Stephen Jones and Kim Newman.

USEFUL ADDRESSES copyright © 1997 by Stephen Jones.

*In recognition of shared adventures
and interesting restaurants, this one has to be for Ramsey –
indefatigable friend, colleague and mentor.*

INTRODUCTION

HORROR IN 1996

IN JANUARY, BRITAIN FINALLY EXTENDED copyright duration to life plus seventy years for all literary, dramatic, musical, film and artistic works, as per a European Union Directive. Copyrights which had previously expired were revived.

The bottom finally began to fall out of the publishing field for games companies such as Wizards of the Coast, creators of the card game *Magic: The Gathering*, and White Wolf. Wizards of the Coast fired more than thirty people, including the entire publishing division in December 1995 to return "to core business", while White Wolf laid off around fifteen people and remaining staff took a 15 per cent pay cut in January. This was apparently the result of both companies expanding too quickly.

In the spring, Salman Rushdie toured the world to promote his latest adult novel, *The Moor's Last Sigh*, despite being sentenced to death by an Iranian *fatwa* in 1989 for his book *The Satanic Verses*. "They tried to silence a writer, and it didn't work out," he told journalists.

Savoy Books lost its High Court appeal in July/August for the right to a jury trial to decide whether material (including copies of *Lord Horror*, *Hard Core Horror* and *Meng & Ecker*) seized in a raid by Manchester police in 1991 and ordered destroyed was obscene. The appeal depended on an assurance by law officers to Parliament that "serious publishers of literature and art" would receive a jury trial if they requested one. According to some reports, the Crown Prosecutor revealed in court that he didn't want the case heard before a jury because he would have stood little chance of winning. Meanwhile, Savoy published Dave Britton's hardcover follow-up to *Lord Horror*, *Motherfuckers: The Auschwitz of Oz*, set in a brutal alternate Britain.

In America, Zebra Books announced that it would be discontinuing its entire horror line, cancelling a Hallowe'en reprint programme and dropping a number of authors. Around the same time, Britain's Penguin/Signet also cancelled its Creed horror imprint after only two years.

It was the Summer of Stephen King. Each subsequent volume of King's six-book, Bram Stoker Award-winning paperback serialization, *The Green Mile*, was simultaneously released in bookstores across America on the day it was published. In the US the series was supported by a thirty-second TV commercial, featuring the author himself, and a letter from King to booksellers, explaining how the project came about.

Set in the Deep South during the Depression in the 1930s, the series of thin volumes detailed the characters and events in and around Cold Mountain Penitentiary and included several fantasy elements, including a psychic healer and an intelligent mouse.

All six volumes were on the *New York Times* paperback bestseller list at the same time and resulted in other publishers considering the multi-part novel format.

King also had two major novels published simultaneously last year, one under his own byline and the other under his old alias "Richard Bachman" (who supposedly died ten years ago of "cancer of the pseudonym"). King's chunky *Desperation* was set in the small Nevada mining town of that name, where something horrific came out of the abandoned copper mine and a maniac cop was possessed by an age-old evil. A limited, slipcased edition of 4,000 copies and a signed, numbered and traycased edition of 2,000 copies (at $175.00 apiece) were also produced by publishers Donald M. Grant.

When "Bachman's" widow reputedly found a box of unpublished manuscripts, the result was *The Regulators*, a novel which shared some themes, settings, characters and situations with *Desperation*. It was set in the little Ohio town of Wentworth, where random violence inspired by TV cartoons exploded on a summer afternoon. In Britain, both books were also published together in a signed, slipcased edition of 250 copies costing £125.00.

For those who bought both *Desperation* and *The Regulators* in America, Penguin apparently made available in November a 64-page mini-book of the first two chapters from King's next novel, *The Dark Tower IV: Wizard and Glass*. The complete book was not scheduled for publication until mid-1997. And for a reissue of the omnibus of four novels, *The Bachman Books*, King contributed a new introduction entitled "The Importance of Being Bachman".

In a welcome change of pace for the author, Dean Koontz's *Ticktock* was a mixture of screwball comedy and horror, about a writer who had until dawn to elude a soul-sucking monster that emerged from a Vietnamese doll. Also from Koontz, *Santa's Twin* was a short Christmas story in rhyming verse about Santa's evil brother, illustrated by Phil Parks.

And the latest volume in Terry Pratchett's seemingly endless Discworld series, *Hogfather*, was also an unusually dark Christmas fable.

Anne Rice's *Servant of the Bones* involved a university professor who encountered an ancient Babylonian spirit named Azriel. Over a period of forty-five days, the author promoted the novel by visiting forty cities in the US and Canada in the "Ricemobile", a customized tour bus with sleeping berths. The tour concluded with a Hallowe'en signing in a Florida cemetery. Meanwhile, Knopf reissued Rice's classic 1976 novel *Interview With the Vampire* in a special signed, boxed and reset 20th anniversary edition.

Clive Barker's *Sacrament* was about a gay wildlife photographer who was attacked by a polar bear. While in a coma, his mind travelled back to his past and encountered a pair of strange dream-beings. Barker also published *Forms of Heaven: Three Plays*, a second collection of his theatrical work that included "Crazyface", "Paradise Street", and "Subtle Bodies".

James Herbert's *'48* was an alternative-history novel, set three years after a 1945 in which Adolf Hitler unleashed a deadly plague called the "Blood Death" on Britain. Peter Straub's *The Hellfire Club* cleverly combined a fifty-eight year old literary mystery and monstrous serial killer Dick Dart, who kidnapped the wife of a publishing heir.

V.C. Andrews'® *Tarnished Gold* was a prequel to, and the fifth volume in, the Gothic horror "Landry" family series, while *Melody* was the first in a new series. Both books were still probably written by Andrew Neiderman for the late author's estate. And Marion Zimmer Bradley's contemporary dark fantasy *Witchlight*, about a woman with amnesia who experienced poltergeist activity, was a sequel to her 1995 novel *Ghostlight*.

After having problems finding a publisher for it, Poppy Z. Brite's *Exquisite Corpse* was an extremely graphic and erotic horror novel about a pair of serial killers. Ramsey Campbell continued the grand tradition of the haunted house novel in *The House on Nazareth Hill* (aka *Nazareth Hill*), and Dennis Etchison's *Double Edge* involved a series of murders surrounding a TV movie about the life of Lizzie Borden.

Brian Lumley continued to fill in the missing chapters in *Necroscope: The Lost Years Volume II* (aka *Necroscope: Resurgence*), and *Titus Crow* was the first omnibus edition of the author's 1970s Lovecraftian novels *The Burrowers Beneath* and *The Transition of Titus Crow*.

From the writing team of Douglas Preston and Lincoln Child, authors of the bestselling *Relic*, came another commercial thriller, *Mount Dragon*, about a genetic engineering experiment that went disastrously wrong. Helped by an option sale to Steven Spielberg's DreamWorks SKG, Michael Marshall Smith's second novel, *Spares*, about the horrific harvesting of cloned replacement limbs and organs, was guaranteed plenty of attention on both sides of the Atlantic. Brian Hodge's *Prototype* involved genetic horrors and the next step in human evolution.

Tanith Lee's *Louisa the Poisoner* was a macabre novella first published by the Science Fiction Book Club, while in the same author's *When the Lights Go Out*, a teenager ran away to a strange seaside town. Kathe Koja's *Kink* was a non-supernatural horror novel dealing with erotic obsession and sexual manipulation, and Lisa Tuttle's *The Pillow Friend* was a complex psychological tale about a young girl whose wish for a magical doll turned into a nightmare.

In *The Tooth Fairy* by Graham Joyce, a boy who glimpsed the title character discovered he was cursed for life. *Somewhere South of Midnight* was the latest from Stephen Laws, and a pharmaceutical company was hiding a deadly secret about its fertility drug in Peter James' *Alchemist*. *Mr. Bad Face* by Mark Morris involved the return of a neighbourhood bogeyman, apparently burned to death years before, and in Chaz Brenchley's *Dispossession*, an amnesiac needed the help of a fallen angel against a killer.

Rachel Pollack's dark fairy tale *Godmother Night* was about two lesbian lovers who encountered the angel of death of the title, and Storm Constantine's *Scenting Hallowed Blood* was the second volume in her Grigori trilogy, about a race of fallen angels. *Neverwhere* was Neil Gaiman's first solo novel and an improvement over the disappointing BBC-TV series he created, set in an alternate underground London filled with monsters and saints, murderers and angels.

In Richard Laymon's *Body Rides*, a bracelet enabled those who possessed it to enter the bodies of others. Robert Holdstock's *Ancient Echoes* was about a scientist who used his strange visions to enter the realms of the "Mythagos" on a quest to save his daughter's soul. A reality-altering drug opened a gateway between dimensions to soul stealers in *The Rare Breed* by Ben Leech (aka Stephen Bowkett), and Mark Laidlaw's *The 37th Mandala* combined New Age beliefs with Lovecraftian horrors when a cynical charlatan learned about the mandalas that spawn a sickness of the soul.

Dark Cathedral by Freda Warrington concerned a battle for the female spirit of Earth. *Witch-Light*, the second (and apparently last) collaboration between Melanie Tem and Nancy Holder, was an erotic reworking of Mexican legends, while Tem's solo *Tides* was a ghost story involving a series of fatal accidents in the eponymous nursing home.

A couple moved into a haunted house in *The House That Jack Built* by Graham Masterton and, from the same author, *Rook* was the first in a series about Jim Rook, a teacher with occult powers. Steve Harris's *Black Rock* concerned a manuscript sent from a haunted house, and a family became involved with a fugitive fleeing the supernatural in *Darker* by Simon Clark.

The Eternal by Mark Chadbourn was a cursed immortal who arrived in an idyllic English village bringing death, destruction and zombies. *Escardy Gap* by Peter Crowther and James Lovegrove strayed into Ray Bradbury territory with its tale of a dark carnival that visited the fictional town of the title, and in his sequel to *Rockabilly Hell*, William W. Johnstone's *Rockabilly Limbo* featured hellish events triggered by old 1950s songs.

Ed Gorman's *The Cage of Night* was about voices from a well that urged the inhabitants of a small town to commit violence, while *Runner in the Dark* was another of the author's dark horror/suspense novels.

Steven Barnes' *Blood Brothers* involved modern sorcery in Los Angeles. *The Bowl of Night: A Bast Mystery* by Rosemary Edghill (aka eluki bes shahar) was the third in the series featuring a modern-day white witch. In Robin Wayne Bailey's *Shadowdance*, a witch's spell that forced a crippled man to dance every night led to dark desires. Charles West's *The Tenant* was a variation on the brain-swapping theme, and *Cruelty Games* was a first horror novel by children's and historical writer Wendy Robertson.

In *Walking Wounded* by Robert Devereaux, a woman with the power to heal by touch was stalked by a serial killer. Officers from Scotland Yard were on the trail of a serial killer and an ancient evil in Camille Bacon-Smith's *The Face of Time*, and in George Foy's *The Shift*, a killer from 1850s New York escaped from virtual reality into the present.

A Tibetan cult and the secrets of the Vatican were entwined in *The Burning Altar* by Frances Gordon (aka Bridget Wood). A group of nuns protected an unholy secret in *Moonfall* by Tamara Thorne, while in *Breath of Brimstone* by Anthea Fraser, a young girl was seduced into evil. *Stolen Angels* by Shaun Hutson was about Satanic child abuse.

The Devil's Churn by Kristine Kathryn Rusch featured a man who returned from death fifty years after he was drowned. *The Rosewood Casket* by Sharyn McCrumb was a mystery set in Appalachia with ghosts, and Elizabeth Ann Scarborough's *Carol for Another Christmas* was a sequel-of-sorts to Charles Dickens' novel, set in contemporary America and featuring Scrooge's ghost.

In the Bram Stoker Award-winning *Crota* by Owl Goingback, a sheriff and a shaman teamed up to confront an ancient monster from Native American folklore released from hibernation by an earthquake. *The Wishing Tree* by James Buxton revolved around a series of horrific events that led a young couple into the dark mysteries of Epping Forest, and in *Lord of the Dark Lake* by Ron Faust, an archaeologist was forced to re-enact the story of the minotaur. A teacher from Harlem encountered a Greek lamia in *A Fling With a Demon Lover* by Kelvin Christopher James, the mythical ghost ship gave its name to *Dutchman* by

Richard Knaak, and *The Undine* by Michael O'Rourke was an erotic horror novel based around the aquatic myth.

Zombie was the latest in the "Special X Unit" series written by two Canadian lawyers under the pseudonym "Michael Slade". *Killjoy* by Elizabeth Forrest involved the US government sending a covert operation into Haiti to discover a zombie-making formula, and in *Last Rites* by David Darke (aka Ron Dee), a group of high school misfits reunited to raise the dead. *Leanna: Possession of a Woman* by Marie Kiraly (aka Elaine Bergstrom) was about voodoo, set in New Orleans,

The vengeful spirit of Madeline Usher haunted Edgar Allan Poe in *Madeline: After the Fall of Usher*, also by "Kiraly"/Bergstrom, while *Return to the House of Usher* was a contemporary reworking of the original written by Robert Poe, apparently a distant relative of Edgar Allan. *The Darker Passions: The Picture of Dorian Gray* by Amarantha Knight (aka Nancy Kilpatrick) was an erotic retelling of Oscar Wilde's original, and C. Dean Anderson reworked Mary Shelley's classic from the viewpoint of the creator and his creation in *I am Frankenstein*.

House of Echoes by Barbara Erskine involved a curse that killed the male members of any family who lived in an old mansion. Judith Merkle Riley's *The Serpent Garden* featured supernatural incidents in the court of Henry VIII, and in Mickee Madden's *Dusk Before Dawn* the Scottish ghosts of the author's *Everlastin'* returned for the sequel. A successful woman had forgotten she had sold her soul to Satan in Jane Heller's *Infernal Affairs*, and there were more devilish doings in *Repossession* by Nicola Thorne (aka Rosemary Ellerback).

Dead Things was the last in Richard Calder's much-hyped trilogy, and there were also new novels by Joe Donnelly (*Incubus*), Simon Maginn (*Methods of Confinement*), John Douglas (*Hard Shoulder* and *Zoo Event*), Guy N. Smith (*Dead End* and *Water Rites*), Clare McNally, (*Good-Night, Sweet Angel*), Sheila Holligan (*Bridestone*) and Gary Goshgarian (*Rough Beast*).

A cut from an antique mirror turned a lawyer into another kind of bloodsucker in Michael Cadnum's impressive *The Judas Glass*. Jonathan Aycliffe (aka Denis MacEoin/Daniel Easterman) served up an unconventional twist on the vampire theme through extracts from journals, letters and historical records in *The Lost*, a slim novel about a Cambridge teacher who travelled to modern-day Romania and discovered his hidden heritage. And Jay Russell (aka Russell Schechter/J.S. Russell) also attempted something different with the genre in *Blood*, as Los Angeles street gangs slaughtered each other for an addictive drug with terrifying side-effects.

Chelsea Quinn Yarbro's vampire Count Saint-Germain travelled to 17th century Peru in *Mansions of Darkness*, *Lord of the Vampires* concluded Jeanne Kalogridis' trilogy of "The Diaries of the Family Dracul", and Fred Saberhagen continued his long-running Dracula series with *A Sharpness on the Neck*.

Laurell K. Hamilton extended the exploits of Anita Blake, Vampire Hunter, with her fourth adventure, *The Lunatic Cafe*, a Christmas story about a feud between vampires and werewolves. The character was back with a new assistant in *Bloody Bones*, this time attempting to raise 200-year-old zombies and investigating a bizarre series of teenage killings. The titular amnesiac investigator turned vampire found he was suspected of the ritualistic slaying of his ex-wife in *Raven* by S.A. Swiniarski (aka S. Andrew Swann), and in Stephen Spruill's *Daughter of Darkness*, a sequel to *Rulers of Darkness*, a vampire cop who destroyed others of his kind had to face his own family.

Dance of Death was the fourth volume in P.N. Elrod's romantic series about vampire Jonathan Barrett. Nancy Kilpatrick's *Child of the Night* was a prequel to her *Near Death*, and Tom Holland's *Supping with Panthers* was a semi-sequel to his *The Vampyre* (aka *Lord of the Dead*).

In Richard Laymon's *Bite*, a teenager asked for help against her new boyfriend, a vampire. A ghostly, vampiric twin haunted the amnesiac heroine of Louise Cooper's *The King's Demon*. In *The Time of Feasting*, Mick Farren's New York vampires discovered they could survive for nearly seven years on blood stolen from blood banks before they needed to drink the real stuff, and a series of baby kidnappings in California were the result of a subculture where blood was offered as the ultimate aphrodisiac in Jonathan Nasaw's *The World on Blood*.

A crippled rock star lived with a female vampire in *Stainless*, the second novel by Todd Grimson. The titular character went on a luxury cruise in Michael Romkey's *The Vampire Princess*, a man who didn't believe in vampires discovered he was one in Mark Wm. Simmons' *One Foot in the Grave*, a backwoods family resurrected their vampiric Great-Grandpa in *Blood Kin* by Ronald

Kelly, and a family of incestuous, gender-changing vampires were the subject of *Blood of Mugwump* by Doug Rice.

There was also *Thirst* by Michael Cecilione, *Immortal* by Jason Nickles (aka T. Lucien Wright), *Kindred* by John Gideon and *Nightlife* by Jack Ellis, while in a humorous twist on the theme, aliens were convinced that vampires really existed in Robert Frezza's *The VMR Theory*.

Set in 1939, an American couple fleeing Berlin encountered a sexy pair of Romanian vampires in *The Kiss* by Kathryn Reines. *Eternal Kiss* by "Anastasia Dubois" was a sexually explicit vampire novel and a sequel to *A Slave to His Kiss*, and more erotic undead turned up in *Vampire Desire* by Eva Linczy and *Demonia* by Kendal Graham.

Pat Murphy's *Nadya: The Wolf Chronicles* involved a nineteenth-century frontierswoman from Missouri who discovered she was a first-generation werewolf, while one reviewer summed up Katherine Eliska Kimbriel's dark fantasy *Night Calls* as "*Little House on the Prairie* with werewolves, vampires and magic."

In Tracy Briery's *Wolfsong*, an LAPD detective hunted a werewolf serial killer, and Denise Vitola's *Quantum Moon* featured a lycanthropic detective investigating a political killing. *Prince of Shadows* by Susan Krinard was a romantic sequel to the author's previous werewolf novel *Prince of Wolves*, William W. Johnstone's *Prey* was a sequel to his earlier werewolf novel, *Hunted*, and a family of were-panthers were the subject of *Shadows* by Kimberly Rangel.

Evil Seeds of the Father was James Tatham's attempt to create a werewolf story out of Australian bush legends. *Howl-O-Ween* by Gary Holleman involved voodoo and a bodyguard who was bitten by a werewolf, and Brett Davis' *Hair of the Dog* was a another humorous werewolf novel.

Celestial Dogs by Jay Russell (aka Russell Schechter/J.S. Russell) was an audacious first novel combining a down-at-heel private eye, the Hollywood movie industry and ancient Japanese demons. Rock star Greg Kihn revealed his love of old horror B-movies in his début novel, *Horror Show*, and a struggling actor found a wicked new agent in *The Short Cut* by Mark Pepper.

Marian Veevers made her novel début with *Bloodlines*, a complex story about three women separated in time but drawn together across the years by a curse involving Lady Macbeth. A writer's son became involved with a supernatural horror novel in *Scare Tactics* by Elizabeth Manz, and in Ken Delo's first novel, *The Frozen Horror*, the cryogenically frozen dead attacked Los Angeles.

Kevin J. Anderson took over the successful book franchise with his novel *The X Files: Ruins*. When FBI agents Mulder and Scully travelled to Mexico to investigate a lost Mayan city, the result was a bestselling if not particularly well-written book. The young adult series of *X Files* novelizations continued with *Tiger, Tiger* by Les Martin and *Squeeze* by Ellen Steiber.

For anyone who needed to update their episode guides, there was a choice between *The X Files Declassified: The Unauthorized Guide to the Complete Series* by Frank Lovece, *X Files Confidential: The Unauthorized X-Philes Compendium* by Ted Edwards, and *Trust No One Out There: The Official Third Season Guide to the X Files* by Brian Lowry. Meanwhile, *Deny All Knowledge: Reading the X Files* edited by David Lavery, Angela Hague and Maria Cartwright was a collection of academic essays about the popular TV series created by Chris Carter.

Chet Williamson novelized the disappointing sequel movie *The Crow: City of Angels*, based on a screenplay by David S. Goyer. *Godzilla King of the Monsters* by Scott Ciencin and *Godzilla Returns* by Marc Cerasini were the first two books in a new series of young adult novels based on the Japanese movie series, with dustjacket art by Bob Eggleton.

Elvira: Transylvania 90210 by Elvira and John Paragon was inspired by the adventures of the campy horror film host. *Countess Dracula* was a welcome reissue by Redemption Books of Michel Parry's 1971 novelization of the Hammer Film, with an added eight pages of stills and a new introduction by the author.

American Gothic: Family was W.T. Quick's novelisation of the dark TV series. Published in the *Missing Adventures* series, David McIntee's *The Shadow of Weng-Chiang* was set in 1930s Shanghai and a sequel to one of the best *Doctor Who* stories. Streamline Pictures' *Twilight Zone: Scripts & Stories* contained eleven stories and teleplays by George Clayton Johnson.

With *Tarzan: The Lost Adventure*, co-author Joe R. Lansdale expanded and adapted a previously unpublished story by Edgar

Rice Burroughs. *Mirage* by F. Paul Wilson and Matthew J. Costello was developed by the authors as a simultaneous CD-ROM game, and *King of the Dead* by Gene DeWeese and *To Sleep With Evil* by Andria Cardarelle were both based on the TSR *Ravenloft* dark fantasy role-playing game.

As previously mentioned, White Wolf went through a number of "reorganizations" in 1996, including changes to its editorial department and a split of publishing responsibilities. However, under its various imprints, it still managed to put out quite a number of books of varying worth:

Saint Vitus Dances Eternity: A Sarajevo Ghost Story by Stuart von Allmen was a large-size hardcover from White Wolf's Borealis imprint containing the novelette with simultaneous text in Bosnian translated by Aida Musanovic, who also contributed the illustrations. With afterwords by the author and Michael Moorcock, all proceeds from the sale went to the New Bosnia Fund supplying humanitarian aid for victims of the war.

Book of the Kindred by Mark Rein-Hagen, Don Bassingthwaite, Lawrence Watt-Evans and others was a sourcebook for the game *Vampire: The Masquerade*. And Bassingthwaite teamed up with Nancy Kilpatrick for *As One Dead* which, along with *Blood Relations* by Doug Murray and *Blood on the Sun* by Brian Herbert and Marie Landis, was based on the same role-playing game. Also set in The World of Darkness, *A Dozen Black Roses* marked the return of Nancy A. Collins' vampire heroine Sonja Blue, who came into conflict with the Kindred. *The Unbeholden* by Robert Weinberg, also based on *Vampire: the Masquerade*, was the third and final volume in his 'Masquerade of the Red Death' trilogy.

Call to Battle by Doug Murray was the first book in new series based on the card game *Rage*, *Hell-Storm* by James A. Moore was based on the role-playing game *Werewolf*, and Jackie Cassada's *Shadows on the Hill* and *The Court of All Kings* were the second and third volumes in her 'Immortal Eyes' trilogy set in The World of Darkness.

Beyond the Shroud was a Jack the Ripper-inspired novel by Rick Hautala, based on the game *Wraith: The Oblivion* as was *The Ebon Mask* by Richard Lee Byers, the first volume in another new series.

According to Baltimore physician R. Michael Benitez, it now

appears that Edgar Allan Poe died of rabies. Poe, who died on his fourth day in Washington College Hospital in 1849, was admitted suffering from hallucinations and had difficulty drinking water. According to another doctor, who supported the view, Poe "had all the features of encephalitic rabies" and almost certainly did not die from the effects of alcohol, as had been previously reported.

And while in the classics department, *The Transition of H.P. Lovecraft: The Road to Madness* continued Del Rey's deluxe reissue programme of all Lovcraft's short fiction. This latest volume contained twenty-nine stories and fragments, a new introduction by Barbara Hambly and illustrations by John Jude Palencar.

Terrors of the Sea, published by Donald M. Grant, was a new collection of fourteen stories by William Hope Hodgson with a preface and article by Sam Moskowitz. Apparently ten of the stories were not previously published, and it was easy to understand why.

For the Blood is the Life and Other Stories was a welcome paperback reissue by White Wolf's Borealis imprint of F. Marion Crawford's 1911 collection *Wandering Ghosts* (aka *Uncanny Tales*). This edition included an extra ghost story, "The King's Messenger", and a new introduction by Darrell Schweitzer.

The Ghost-Feeler: Stories of Terror and the Supernatural by Edith Wharton was a collection of nine tales, many appearing for the first time since their original magazine publication, edited and with an introduction by Peter Haining. *The Masterpieces of Shirley Jackson* was an excellent omnibus of *The Haunting of Hill House*, *We Have Always Lived in the Castle* and the collection *The Lottery* with a new introduction by Donna Tartt.

Barnes & Noble published Louisa May Alcott's *A Whisper in the Dark*, a collection of twelve Gothic stories edited by Stefan Dziemianowicz with an introduction by Susie Mee, and "The Definitive Edition" of Bram Stoker's *Dracula*, which included the missing chapter "Dracula's Guest", an introduction and notes by Marvin Kaye, and illustrations by Edward Gorey.

Meanwhile, yet another edition of Stoker's novel from Oxford University Press featured a new introduction, bibliography and notes by Maud Ellmann. Also from OUP, *The Castle of Otranto: A Gothic Story* was a reprint of the 1798 text of Horace Walpole's 1764 novel, edited by W.S. Lewis with notes by E.J. Clery.

Parachute Press and R.L. Stine (who was reportedly under contract to produce a book for Scholastic every two weeks!) continued to exploit their young adult "Fear Street" titles with the first in a new series featuring the Fear family, *Fear Street Sagas: A New Fear*. The series continued with *Fear Street Sagas 2: House of Whispers*, *3: Forbidden Secrets* and *4: The Sign of Fear*, although according to the copyright pages, the latter two may have actually been written by Brandon Alexander and Cameron Dokey, respectively.

In Stine's *Fear Street: The Perfect Date*, a teenage boy was haunted by his dead girlfriend, and in *Fear Street: Night Games* a dead boy wanted revenge. There was also *Fear Street Super Chiller: Goodnight Kiss 2* and a new trilogy about a haunted amusement park, *Fear Street: Fear Park 1: The First Scream*, *Fear Park 2: The Loudest Scream* and *Fear Park 3: The Last Scream*.

Joan Aiken's dark fantasy *The Cockatrice Boys* was set in a Britain overrun by strange monsters and involved an attempt to bring food by train to a besieged Manchester. *Getting Wired!: A Techno Terrors Story* was the first children's book by Peter James, and *Bruce Coville's Chamber of Horrors 4: Waiting Spirits* was a revised and updated version of the 1984 novel about a summer island getaway invaded by ghosts.

Robert Swindells' *Jacqueline Hyde* was a variation on the R.L. Stevenson theme. The ghosts of Jewish children killed in World War II were the subject of *After the Darkness* by Michael Smith, and a Druid curse was behind *The Bog Spell* by Mike Sackett. Raised by floods, a terrible evil was released from *The Coffin* by Barbara Steiner, and in Don Whittington's *Dark Charm*, a blind hillbilly boy used his special powers to battle the supernatural.

Land developers disturbed the ghost of a Viking warrior in Garry Kilworth's *The Raiders*, while the same author's *A Midsummer's Nightmare* was a magical modern reworking of Shakespeare's characters and themes.

In *When Darkness Calls* by Janet E. Gill the new girls discovered that the school clique were Satanists, and a teen called up demonic powers while seeking revenge against another popular clique in *The Sending* by Robert Hawks. *The Dreamer* by L.D. Pierce (aka Linda Piazza) involved a teenager suffering nightmares sent by a demon.

Two teenage witches fell in love with the same boy in *Nightworld: Spellbinder*, while *Nightworld: Dark Angel* was about a girl who had a near-death experience, both by L.J. Smith. A group of teens met nasty ends while exploring a haunted house in Jesse Osburn's *He's Waiting For You*, and the same author's *Only Child* was about youngsters mysteriously disappearing at a seaside resort. A girl teamed up with the shade of a pirate in *The Ghost of Grania O'Malley* by Michael Morpurgo, and Pam Conrad's *Zoe Rising* was a sequel to her *Stonewords* and involved ghosts and time travel.

The latest titles in the *Horror Scopes* series included *The Knowing* by Andrew Matthews and *The Gravediggers* by J.H. Brennan. *Blood Dance* marked the welcome return of author Louise Cooper, and other young adult titles included *Blood Sinister* by Celia Rees, *Transformer* by Philip Gross, *The House of Death* by Patricia Windsor and *The Mummy* by Barbara Steiner.

Christopher Pike's *Phantom*, *Evil Thirst* and *Creatures of Forever* were the fourth, fifth and sixth volumes respectively in *The Last Vampire* series. The twins encountered a mesmerizing blood-drinker in *Tall Dark and Deadly*, *Dance of Death* and *Kiss of a Killer*, the new *Vampire* trilogy in Francine Pascal's hugely popular *Sweet Valley High* series.

Song of the Vampire by Carmen Adams (aka Carol Anshaw) was a sequel to *The Band*. *Nightworld: Secret Vampire* was the first in a new series by L.J. Smith about a secret society of vampires, werewolves and witches, while *Nightworld: Daughters of Darkness* involved a pair of vampire sisters who found love with humans.

In *The Blooding* by Patricia Windsor an au pair in England became involved with werewolves, and an ancient shapeshifter menaced a teenager and his father in *Human Prey* by L.D. Pierce.

Scary Stories from 1313 Wicked Way by Craig Strickland featured ten stories dating from the eighteenth-century to the present and set in a haunted house. *MindQuakes: Stories to Shatter Your Brain* collected ten original young adult stories by Neal Shusterman, and eleven stories of fantasy and horror by Anne Mazer appeared in *A Sliver of Glass*.

A Nightmare's Dozen: Stories from the Dark edited by Michael

Stearns contained fourteen original young adult dark fantasy stories by Jane Yolen, Nancy Springer, Steve Rasnic Tem, Nina Kiriki Hoffman and Bruce Colville, amongst others, nicely illustrated by Michael Hussar.

Future Fright: Tales of High-Tech Terror edited by Don Wulffson was an original anthology of six SF/horror stories. *The Young Oxford Book of Supernatural Stories* edited by Dennis Pepper featured twenty-four stories, nine original, and *Night Terrors* edited by Lois Duncan included eleven young adult horror stories by Joan Aiken and others.

Joan Aiken, Margaret Mahy and Robert Swindells were among the eighteen authors featured in *A Treasury of Ghost Stories* edited by Kenneth Ireland. *Classic Ghost Stories* edited by Molly Cooper contained six ghost stories by such familiar names as Bram Stoker, Oscar Wilde and Charles Dickens, amongst others, and from the same editor came *Classic Vampire Stories: Timeless Tales to Sink Your Teeth Into*, featuring half-a-dozen tales by F. Marion Crawford, E.F. Benson and others, including an extract from Stoker's *Dracula*. Both books were illustrated by Barbara Kiwak.

Joyce Carol Oates's short novel *First Love* was about a woman being physically and emotionally abused by a relative. The book was illustrated with woodcuts by Barry Moser and published by Ecco Press.

William Peter Blatty's *Demons Five, Exorcists Nothing* was a satire of the Hollywood system, while Todd Grimson's darkly witty first novel, *Brand New Cherry Flavor*, was the tale of a woman's revenge in Hollywood involving dark magic, psychic tattoos and zombie bikers.

Another début, *Dark Debts* by television scriptwriter/producer Karen Hall, put a contemporary spin on *The Exorcist*, with a trendy Los Angeles newspaper reporter heroine, a handsome Jesuit priest facing a crisis of faith, and a man who just might be turning into a demon. It received a 150,000 first printing in hardcover and has already been optioned by Paramount, with Hall retained as the screenwriter.

Along the same lines, Joe de Mers' *The Return* was about a priest who had to prove that the Second Coming was a fake.

The Journal of Antonio Montoya by Rick Collignon featured a female artist who shared her house with various dead relatives who continued to interact with her life. In *Tex and Molly in the Afterlife*, Richard Grant's two aging hippies continued to remain as ghosts in the small Maine coastal town where they had lived for many years. Literary ghosts floated through *Revenance* by Terence Blacker, and *Black Night* by S.J. Strayhorn (aka Sharon K. Epperson) was a contemporary ghost story and murder mystery set in rural Kansas. Anne Billson's *Stiff Lips* was another modern story of girls, ghosts and glitterati.

Following his bizarre first novel, *The Unnatural*, David Prill's *Serial Killer Days* was set in the small mid-western town of Standard Springs, where the inhabitants annually celebrated more than twenty years of murders in the community. Nicholas Royle's *Saxophone Dreams* combined jazz music, collective dreams and suspicious organ transplants, and with *Shangri-La*, Eleanor Cooney and Daniel Altieri had the temerity to write a sequel to James Hilton's classic *Lost Horizon*.

Quicker Than the Eye was a welcome new collection of twenty-one stories (nine previously unpublished) by Ray Bradbury. It included "Another Fine Mess", featuring the ghosts of Laurel and Hardy, and other supernatural stories by one of the finest stylists of the twentieth century.

Just an Ordinary Day collected fifty-four unpublished or previously uncollected stories by Shirley Jackson, edited and introduced by Laurence Jackson Hyman and Sarah Hyman Stewart. *Voice of the Fire* by Alan Moore was a remarkable collection of dark human history that formed a novel linked by the same geographical location and spanning 5,000 years.

Edgeworks 1, a handsome collection containing ten stories and thirteen essays from *Over the Edge* and *An Edge in My Voice*, was the first in White Wolf's planned twenty-volume series of the collected Harlan Ellison. It was followed by *Edgeworks 2*, an omnibus of the crime novel *Spider Kiss* and the collection *Stalking the Nightmare*, with a new introduction by the author. Also worth reading, if only for his comments on Gene Roddenberry, was the definitive edition of Ellison's *The City on the Edge of Forever: The Original Teleplay That Became The Classic Star Trek Episode*, with afterwords by a number of the original cast members.

The double Bram Stoker Award-winning *The Nightmare Factory* by Thomas Ligotti was a very welcome omnibus of *Songs of a Dead Dreamer*, *Grimscribe* and *Noctuary*, plus a sequence of six new stories. It also included an original introduction by the author and a foreword by Poppy Z. Brite.

Jonathan Lethem's *The Wall of the Sky, the Wall of the Eye* included seven quirky stories, two previously unpublished and several others revised since their first publication. S.P. Somtow's *The Pavilion of Frozen Women* was an excellent collection of ten of the author's best stories, while Somtow's omnibus volume *The Riverrun Trilogy* contained the novels *Riverrun*, *Armorica* and the previously unpublished *Yestern*, each following the exploits of the cursed Etchison family and their battle against the forces of darkness.

The Invisible Country collected nine stories by Paul J. McAuley, including "The Temptation of Dr. Stein" and "The True History of Dr. Pretorius", with an introduction by Kim Newman. Diana Wynne Jones' *Minor Arcana* contained six reprint stories and a novella, and *Distant Voices* by Barbara Erskine collected thirty stories, several of them involving ghosts and the supernatural.

Blood Waters was an overdue first collection of ten horror and crime stories by Chaz Brenchley, published by Flambard. Mike McCormack's literary collection *Getting it in the Head* included horror and fantasy elements. *Spectral Snow* by Jack Snow contained eight dark fantasy tales, including an Oz story, from Hungry Tiger Press, and *Faces of Fear* by Graham Masterson also collected eight stories.

First published in Portugal in 1915, *The Great Shadow (and Other Stories)* appeared from Dedalus and collected the stories of Mário de Sá-Carneiro, who committed suicide in 1916 at the age of twenty-six.

The Mortal Immortal: The Complete Supernatural Stories collected five stories by Mary Shelley with a "narrative introduction" by Michael Bishop. It was published by Tachyon in a limited paperback edition of 900 copies and a 100-copy deluxe hardcover signed by Bishop.

Twists of the Tale: Cat Horror Stories edited by Ellen Datlow was one of the most consistently satisfying anthologies of the year. It featured twenty-three stories involving frightening felines by such authors as Michael Marshall Smith, Gahan Wilson, Nicholas Royle, Douglas Clegg, Michael Cadnum, Storm Constantine, Joel Lane, Tanith Lee and reprints from Stephen King and William S. Burroughs. And despite its terribly sexist cover, Datlow's *Lethal*

Kisses was another major anthology containing nineteen stories of sex, horror and revenge by Caitlín R. Kiernan, Thomas Tessier, Terry Lamsley, Roberta Lannes, Michael Marshall Smith and Ruth Rendell.

Dark Terrors 2: The Gollancz Book of Horror was edited by Stephen Jones and David Sutton and featured stories by Clive Barker, Peter Straub, Harlan Ellison, Ramsey Campbell, Brian Lumley, Dennis Etchison and others. From the same editorial team, *The Giant Book of Fantasy Tales*, an omnibus volume selected from the Robinson paperback series, was only available in Australia.

Diagnosis: Terminal edited by F. Paul Wilson included fourteen stories of medical terror by Chet Williamson, Matthew Costello, Thomas F. Monteleone, Ed Gorman, Karl Edward Wagner and others.

Gahan Wilson's The Ultimate Haunted House was loosely based on the artist's work, with contributions by consulting editor Nancy A. Collins, T.E.D. Klein, Kathe Koja, Norman Partridge, Gregory Nicoll and Lucy Taylor, amongst others, and an introduction and original illustrations by Wilson.

The Sandman: Book of Dreams was an original anthology edited by Neil Gaiman and Edward E. Kramer, based on Gaiman's popular comic book character. Among the authors who contributed the eighteen stories were Gene Wolfe, Tad Williams, Barbara Hambly, Caitlín R. Kiernan and Nancy A. Collins. It also included story introductions by Gaiman, a frontispiece illustration by Clive Barker, a preface by Frank McConnell and an afterword by Tori Amos. Kramer also edited *Dark Destiny III: Children of Dracula*, a collection of twenty-two vampire stories by David Bischoff, S.P. Somtow, Rick Hautala, Esther M. Friesner and others, very loosely based on White Wolf's World of Darkness role-playing game and illustrated by Berni Wrightson.

Dante's Disciples edited by Peter Crowther and Edward E. Kramer was an original anthology of twenty-six stories inspired by Dante's Inferno from Gene Wolfe, Harlan Ellison, Douglas Clegg, Nancy Holder, Brian Lumley, Ray Garton, Steve Rasnic Tem, Brian Aldiss and others, with an introduction by James O'Barr, creator of *The Crow*. *World of Darkness: Strange City* edited by Stanley Krause and Stewart Wieck was an original anthology of fourteen stories loosely based around the White Wolf role-playing games.

Intersections: The Sycamore Hill Anthology edited by John Kessel, Mark L. Van Name and Richard Butler was a collection of stories by writers who attended an author's workshop at Sycamore Hill in 1994. These included Carol Emshwiller, Karen Joy Fowler, Gregory Frost, Nancy Kress, Jonathan Lethem and Bruce Serling, amongst others.

Otherwhere edited by Anne Laura Gilman and Keith R.A. DeCandido contained fifteen original stories of lycanthropic transformation by Nina Kiriki Hoffman, Esther M. Friesner and others. Meanwhile, editor Pan Keesey's *Women Who Run with the Werewolves* also featured fifteen stories, twelve original, about female lycanthropes.

American Gothic Tales edited by Joyce Carol Oates was an anthology of nearly fifty stories by such authors as Anne Rice, Harlan Ellison, Stephen King, Peter Straub, William Faulkner and Edgar Allan Poe. Giles Gordon chose thirteen classic tales for *Selected Ghost Stories*. From Oxford University Press, *Tales of Terror from Blackwood's Magazine* edited by Robert Morrison and Chris Baldick collected seventeen Gothic tales from *Blackwell's Edinburgh Magazine*.

Editor Michael Cox collected thirty-three stories by such authors as Fritz Leiber, M.R. James, Angela Carter and E. Nesbit in *The Oxford Book of Twentieth-Century Ghost Stories*. *New Masterpieces of Horror* was an instant remainder anthology from Barnes & Noble edited by John Betancourt and featuring twenty-four reprint stories by Peter Straub, Joyce Carol Oates, S.P. Somtow and others.

Although an anthology of new football short stories, under the editorship of Nicholas Royle *A Book of Two Halves* included fiction by M. John Harrison, Stephen Baxter, Conrad Williams, Iain Sinclair, Graham Joyce, Michael Marshall Smith, Mark Morris, Kim Newman and Christopher Fowler, amongst others.

From Masquerade Books' Rhinoceros imprint came *Sex Macabre*, an anthology of twelve so-called "erotic horror" stories edited by "Amarantha Knight" (aka Nancy Kilpatrick) that sometimes bordered on the pornographic, with stories by Poppy Z. Brite, Gregory Nicoll, Tina L. Jens, and a novel extract by Nancy Holder and Melanie Tem. The volume was also somewhat inappropriately dedicated to Vincent Price! From the same editor, *Seductive Spectres* included eleven original erotic ghost stories by such authors as John Mason Skipp and Nancy Kilpatrick.

Noirotica edited by Thomas S. Roche was published by the Rhinoceros imprint and collected new and reprint erotic crime stories by such authors as Poppy Z. Brite, Nancy A. Collins, John Shirley, Maxim Jakubowski and Nancy Kilpatrick, amongst others. *The Hot Blood Series: Fear the Fever* edited by Jeff Gelb and Michael Garrett contained seventeen "erotic" horror stories by such authors as Graham Masterton, Alan Brennert, J.N. Williamson, Tom Piccirilli, Lucy Taylor, a collaboration between Edward Lee and Jack Ketchum, and the Bram Stoker Award-winning "Metalica" by P.D. Cacek.

The incredibly prolific Martin H. Greenberg teamed up with Norman Partridge to edit *It Came from the Drive-In*, an original anthology of eighteen stories inspired by "B" movies that included Rex Miller, Gregory Nicoll, Ed Gorman, Steve Rasnic Tem and Karl Edward Wagner.

Greenberg and Ed Gorman collected twenty-two stories of terror in *Night Screams*, including reprints by Clive Barker, Lawrence Block, David Morrell and Ray Bradbury; and cashing in on an election year, the same team put together sixteen stories about US Presidents by Graham Masterton, Brian Hodge, Peter Crowther, J.N. Williamson and others for *White House Horrors*.

Greenberg and P.N. Elrod edited *The Time of the Vampires*, an anthology of eighteen historical bloodsucker stories by Elrod, Lois Tilton, Tanya Huff, Nancy Kilpatrick and others. Greenberg and Richard Gilliam edited *Phantoms of the Night*, an original anthology of twenty-eight stories about ghosts, and he also teamed up with Charles G. Waugh to edit *Supernatural Sleuths*, a disappointing reprint collection of fourteen fantastic crime stories that "borrowed" its title from a much better Peter Haining anthology.

For *Miskatonic University*, Greenberg and Robert Weinberg joined forces to edit an original anthology of thirteen Lovecraftian stories, with an introduction by Stefan Dziemianowicz.

The same triumvirate was also responsible for *Virtuous Vampires* and *Rivals of Dracula*, two instant remainder anthologies from Barnes & Noble featuring stories by Ray Bradbury, Robert Bloch, Roger Zelazny, Suzy McKee Charnas and others, along with *100 Astounding Aliens* and *100 Tiny Tales of Terror*, the latter two collecting short shorts by such eminent authors as Ramsey Campbell, Manly Wade Wellman, Dennis Etchison,

Poppy Z. Brite, T.E.D. Klein, Kim Newman, Joel Lane, Hugh B. Cave, Ambrose Bierce, Joe R. Lansdale, Andre Norton and Philip K. Dick.

Isaac Asimov's Vampires edited by Gardner Dozois and Sheila Williams collected eight stories that originally appeared in *Asimov's* magazine by such writers as Tanith Lee and Pat Cadigan, and *Sons of Darkness: Tales of Men, Blood and Immortality* collected thirteen stories about gay male vampires edited by Michael Rowe and Thomas S. Roche. *Erotica Vampirica* edited by Cecilia Tan contained ten original erotic stories of the undead.

The Vampire Hunter's Casebook edited by Peter Haining collected fifteen stories and excerpts, plus stills from various vampire movies, and Haining's *Ghost Movies II: Famous Supernatural Television Programmes* contained ten reprint stories which were used as the basis for TV adaptations.

Slightly more unusual, in *The Tiger Garden: A Book of Writer's Dreams* edited by Nicholas Royle, numerous authors (including Joan Aiken, Peter Atkins, Poppy Z. Brite, John Burke, Ramsey Campbell, Dennis Etchison, Neil Gaiman, Roberta Lannes, Kim Newman, Jay Russell, Michael Marshall Smith, Peter Straub, David Sutton, Lisa Tuttle, F. Paul Wilson, Douglas E. Winter and nearly 200 others) described their most memorable dreams. All royalties from the book went to Amnesty International.

Bonescribes: Year's Best Australian Horror Stories: 1995 edited by Bill Congreve and Robert Hood included ten stories and a recommended reading list, published by MirrorDanse Books. *The Year's Best Fantasy and Horror: Ninth Annual Collection* edited by Ellen Datlow and Terri Windling boasted thirty-five stories, eleven poems, and various summaries by the editors and Edward Bryant plus obituaries by James Frenkel. And *The Best New Horror Volume Seven* had a successful title change in America to *The Mammoth Book of Best New Horror* and included twenty-six stories along with an extensive overview of the year, a necrology for 1995 and a list of useful addresses.

After nine years and 230 books and magazines, Dean Wesley Smith announced the end of Pulphouse Publishing in February. *Pulphouse: A Fiction Magazine* was cancelled and the company sold off its backstock of books so that Smith could get back to writing and golfing.

Brian Stableford's *The Hunger and Ecstasy of Vampires*, published by Mark V. Ziesing, was an expanded version of the novella which appeared in *Interzone* and the previous volume of *The Best New Horror*.

Rick Hautala's *The Mountain King*, a boxed, limited edition from CD Publications, had a cover and interior illustrations by Steve Bissette and involved a tribe of Sasquatch-like creatures living in the New England wilderness.

Del Stone Jr's *Dead Heat*, published by Mojo Press, featured a rotting zombie biker hero battling crazed scientists and a golem to save the world. It was illustrated by Dave Dorman and Scott Hampton.

W. Paul Ganley reprinted Brian Lumley's "Titus Crow" novel *In the Moons of Borea* in its first hardcover edition, with illustrations by Jim Pianfetti. *The Lovecraft Papers* was a welcome omnibus of Peter H. Cannon's wonderfully witty Wodehouse-Lovecraft parody *Scream for Jeeves* and his Holmes-Lovecraft pastiche *Pulptime*.

Peter Crowther's atmospheric novelette *Forest Plains* combined a fourteen year-old murder mystery with touches of fantasy and was published as a attractive slim hardcover by Hypatia Press, limited to 140 numbered copies.

Shards by Tom Piccirilli was a dark mystery published in hardcover by Write Way Publishing. Set in a city that has never existed, *Dradin in Love* was a surreal novella by Jeff VanderMeer, illustrated by Michael Shores and published by Buzzcity Press. From the same author, *The Book of Lost Places* collected nine stories with an introduction by Mark Rich and artwork by Rodger Gerberding, from Dark Regions Press.

The Bighead was another grossout novel by Edward Lee about rape, murder and brain-eating, from Necro Publications. A wrestling-horror novella involving a serial killer who mutilates young women, *Goon* was a collaboration between Lee and John Pelan, from the same publisher.

George Gutheidge's *The Bloodletter*, from Northwest Publishing, was an historical western novel with supernatural elements, and *Roadkill* by Richard Sanford involved two travellers battling an ancient beast of prey in the Oregon foothills, published by Write Way. *The Parasite* by Neal L. Asher and *Eyelidad* by Rhys H. Hughes were two new novels published by Tanjen.

Arte Publico Press's *Shango* by James Roberto Curtis was a first novel about voodoo set in Miami.

Cardinal's Sin, published by Llewellyn, was the second book in Ray Buckland's occult "The Committee" series, in which a group of psychics battled demons raised by an insane cardinal. Also from Llewellyn, D.A. Heeley's *Lilith* was the first book of the "Darkness & Light" sequence, in which magicians summoned the queen of demons, while *Visions of Murder* by Florence Wagner McClain dealt with stolen occult artifacts that resulted in murder.

A newly corrected, definitive edition of *The Girl Next Door*, an "extreme" novel about madness and abuse by Jack Ketchum (aka Dallas Mayr), was published as an expensive hardcover by Overlook Connection Press boasting an introduction by Stephen King, plus essays and appreciations by Christopher Golden, Lucy Taylor, Edward Lee and Philip Nutman, and an interview with the author by Stanley Wiater.

The first American hardcover of Dennis Etchison's *Darkside*, with the author's preferred text corrected and restored, a new introduction by Ramsey Campbell and new afterword by the author, was co-published by American Fantasy/Airgedlámh Publications.

Gauntlet Press issued a handsome slipcased edition of Richard Matheson's classic haunted house novel *Hell House*, limited to 600 copies, with introductions by Dean Koontz and Matthew R. Bradley and an afterword by the author's son, Richard Christian Matheson.

Fedogan & Bremer's *Time Burial* collected twenty stories (two previously unpublished) by overlooked pulp author Howard Wandrei, with a fascinating introduction by editor Dwayne H. Olson and illustrations by the author. Under its new Mystery imprint, F&B also published Wandrei's *The Last Pin*, a collection of eleven spicy and hardboiled pulp detective stories, again edited and introduced by Olson, along with *Saith the Lord*, a limited edition chapbook containing three stories by Wandrei.

Also from Fedogan & Bremer, *Before...12:01...and After* collected twenty-three stories by Richard Lupoff, with an introduction by Robert Silverberg and illustrations by George Barr, and the indefatigable Robert M. Price edited *The New Lovecraft Circle*, a collection of twenty-five stories, three original, set in the Cthulhu Mythos with a preface by Ramsey Campbell and dustjacket illustration by Gahan Wilson.

As a follow-up to Terry Lamsley's 1994 World Fantasy Award-nominated début, *Under the Crust*, Barbara and Chris Roden's Ash-Tree Press published the author's latest collection, *Conference With the Dead: Tales of Supernatural Terror*, in a handsome 500-copy hardcover. With an introduction by Ramsey Campbell and more than half the stories original to the volume, this was one of the most satisfying supernatural collections of the year.

Ash-Tree's other titles for the year included *Nine Ghosts* by R.H. Malden, a reprint of the 1943 collection limited to 300 copies with a new introduction by David Rowlands; *Sleep No More* by L.T.C. Rolt was limited to 400 copies and expanded the 1948 edition with a new introduction by Christopher Roden; *Randalls Round* by Eleanor Scott (aka Helen Leys) reprinted the 1929 collection with a new introduction by Richard Dalby; *The Executor and Other Ghost Stories* by David G. Rowlands collected forty stories, three original, in an edition of 400 copies; *Old Man's Beard* by H.R. Wakefield reprinted the ten ghost stories from the 1928 edition along with a new introduction by Barbara Roden in a 300-copy edition; *Ghosts in the House* by A.C. and R.H. Benson was edited by Hugh Lamb and limited to 400 numbered copies, and *The Occult Files of Francis Chard: Some Ghost Stories*, the second volume in Ash-Tree Press's four-book set of supernatural stories by A.M. Burrage, was ably edited by Jack Adrian in an edition of 500 copies. *The Stoneground Ghost Tales* by E.G. Swain and *A Book of Ghosts* by S. Baring-Gould rounded off a very productive year for the small press publisher, now relocated in Canada.

Calabash Press, a new spin-off imprint from Ash-Tree Press, was launched with *The Musgrave Ritual: The Casefiles of Sherlock Holmes* edited by Barbara and Chris Roden. This was a collection of essays and articles by various people concerning the Sherlock Holmes story, and the first in a planned publishing programme of around sixty similar books over the next few years.

London's Durtro Press published *Studies of Death*, a handsome little cloth-bound hardcover of 300 copies collecting the stories of Stanislaus Eric, Count Stenbock (1860–1895), a member of the Decadent movement of the late nineteenth-century.

The Convulsion Factor by Brian Hodge contained twelve stories, three original, plus an introduction by Philip Nutman, from Silver Salamander Press. Wayne Allen Sallee's *With Wounds Still Wet*, from the same publisher, collected twenty-three stories with an introduction by Kathe Koja and illustrations by H.E. Fassel.

Subterranean Press published Norman Partridge's *Bad Intentions* as a hefty hardcover collection of fourteen stories, many reprinted from *Cemetery Dance*, with an introduction by Joe R. Lansdale and story notes by the author. And seventeen stories by *Cemetery Dance*'s editor, Richard T. Chizmar, were collected in *Midnight Promises*, published by Gauntlet Publications in a signed edition of 500 copies. It included two collaborations (with Norman Partridge and Barry Hoffman) and an introduction and afterword by Ed Gorman and Ray Garton, respectively.

Beyond the Lamplight: Stories from the Dark contained thirty-four tales by Donald R. Burleson, eleven previously unpublished, with an introduction by Ramsey Campbell, from Jack O'Lantern Press. *Will You Hold Me?* from The Do-Not Press collected ten stories, six original, by Christopher Kenworthy. *Tales of Titillation and Terror* by Mel D. Ames contained fifteen stories of the macabre and the erotic plus introductions by Peter Sellers and Don Hutchison, published by Canada's Mosaic Press.

Although nominated for a World Fantasy Award *last* year, *High Fantastic: Colorado's Fantasy, Dark Fantasy and Science Fiction* was a beautiful-looking anthology of stories, poems and essays edited by Steve Rasnic Tem that was belatedly published in 1996 by Ocean View Books.

Leviathan: Into the Gray, edited by Jeff VanderMeer and Luke O'Grady, was a literary paperback anthology published by Mule Press and The Ministry of Whimsy. *Darkside: Horror for the Next Millennium* edited by John C. Pelan was an original hardcover anthology of thirty stories from Darkside Press, with contributions by Thomas Ligotti, Brian Hodge, D.F. Lewis and Yvonne Navarro and illustrations by Alan M. Clark.

Night Bites: Vampire Stories by Women was an original anthology of sixteen stories edited by Victoria Brownworth for Seattle's Seal Press, and *Screams* was an Australian anthology of erotic horror by women writers, edited by Madelaine Kinhill and published by AMS Ironbark Publications.

Chaosium's *The Dunwich Cycle* edited by Robert M. Price featured ten stories set in or around H.P. Lovecraft's cursed town. From the same editor and publisher, *The Cthulhu Cycle* collected thirteen stories of Lovecraftian horror by all the usual suspects, and *The Necronomicon* contained fourteen stories and three essays about H.P. Lovecraft's damned book by such authors as Robert Bloch, Lin Carter, Robert Silverberg, John Brunner, Frank Belknap Long and HPL himself.

Mythos Tales & Others was a chapbook of eleven original Lovecraftian stories, two essays and eleven poems, edited by David Wynn and published by Mythos Books, and Clark Ashton Smith's *A Prophecy of Monsters*, from Virginia's 13th Hour Books, reprinted the 1954 Lovecraftian short story as a chapbook with an introduction by Paul A. Roales.

Wraiths & Ringers was a self-published chapbook of ten ghost stories by A.F. Kidd. *Forgotten Ghosts: The Supernatural Anthologies of Hugh Lamb*, edited by Barbara and Christopher Roden and featuring an introduction by Mike Ashley and bibliography, was a useful, if overpriced anthology of five stories in card covers from Ash-Tree Press in an edition of 350 numbered copies.

Firefly. . .Burning Bright from Gauntlet Press collected four horror stories by Barry Hoffman, one previously unpublished, with illustrations by Harry O. Morris and an introduction by Ronald Kelly. It was limited to 350 signed copies. *Dancer for the World's Death* by Storm Constantine was the third chapbook from Inception, The Storm Constantine Information Service. Published by the author's own Night Dreams Editions, Kirk S. King's *Booger* was an "extreme" horror novella in a chapbook edition.

Only months after going to quarterly publication, *Omni* owner General Media International announced the cancellation of the magazine's print form version, laying off forty members of staff. The magazine was relaunched in its electronic format on the Internet in June and during the year fiction editor Ellen Datlow published stories by Robert Silverberg, Harlan Ellison, James P. Blaylock and a rediscovered novella by the late Fritz Leiber.

David Riley, editor of the British newsstand magazine *Beyond*, continued to insist that issue 4 would appear, despite returning all non-contracted stories. He blamed "misleading sales/returns reports from distributors", the W.H. Smiths chain destroying copies upon receipt due to a "move to centralize their warehousing", and "some creative accounting whereby more copies were reported returned (that is, thrown away) than were actually sent."

The entire assets of the Dell Magazine Group, which included such titles as *Analog Science Fiction & Science Fact* (formerly *Astounding*), *Asimov's SF Magazine*, *Alfred Hitchcock's Magazine* and *Ellery Queen's Mystery Magazine*, were sold by Bantam Doubleday Dell to Penny Press in March.

As usual, David Pringle's *Interzone* produced a full year's worth of excellent issues, with stories by Kim Newman and Eugene Byrne, Ian Watson, John Brunner, Cherry Wilder, Simon Ings and M. John Harrison, J.G. Ballard, Terry Dowling, Ed Gorman and Garry Kilworth, plus interviews with Peter James, Joe R. Lansdale, Darrell Schweitzer and Kim Newman, articles on Leigh Brackett and John Brunner by Brian Stableford, and all the regular columns and reviews. The December 1996 issue was guest edited by Nicholas Royle.

The Magazine of Fantasy & Science Fiction continued to flourish under editor Kristine Kathryn Rusch with fiction by, amongst others, Ray Bradbury, Harlan Ellison, Alan Brennert, Lisa Tuttle, Nina Kiriki Hoffman, Kathe Koja, Tanith Lee, Ed Gorman, Gene Wolfe and Michael Bishop, plus book reviews by Charles de Lint and Robert K.J. Killheffer. However, Rusch announced that she would be leaving the job after nearly six years to pursue a full-time writing career and would be replaced in the new year by Gordon Van Gelder.

With its colourful combination of film, TV, video, book, comic and toy news, reviews and interviews, Britain's *SFX* firmly established itself as the leading media magazine in the genre with features on *The X Files*, *Star Trek*, *Babylon 5*, Troma films and *Neverwhere*, plus interviews with Terry Gilliam, Richard Matheson, Christopher Lee, Michael Marshall Smith, Wes Craven, Neil Gaiman, Graham Joyce and James Herbert, amongst many others.

Despite apparently being obsessed by *The X Files*, Visual Imagination's *Starburst*, also covered all the popular shows and movies and included interviews with Melinda Snodgrass, Terry Gilliam, Robert Rodriguez and Harlan Ellison. Its companion horror magazine, *Shivers*, also published anything to do with *The X Files*, but still found space for features on *The Wolf Man*, the UK episodes of *Tales from the Crypt*, *From Dusk Till Dawn*,

Boris Karloff, Ingrid Pitt, witchcraft in the movies and a Horror Top 50. Visual Imagination's other magazine titles included *Cult Times*, *TV Zone* and *Xposé* (the latter devoted to the unexplained and extraordinary, and you know which TV show . . .).

The always-excellent *Cinefantastique* kept to its monthly schedule under editor Steve Biodrowski. Along with the usual special issues devoted to *Star Trek* and *The X Files*, there were in-depth articles on Terry Gilliam, Dario Argento, Disney's *Hunchback of Notre Dame*, The 50 Most Powerful People in Science Fiction and the 30th anniversary of *Dark Shadows*. Meanwhile, companion magazine *Femme Fatales* continued to combine flesh and fantasy with features on *Peeping Tom*'s Pamela Green, Pam Grier, The 50 Sexiest Figures in Science Fiction and *Vampirella*.

Forrest J Ackerman resigned as editor of the revived *Famous Monsters of Filmland*, which he founded in 1958. This was the result of various disputes with current publisher Ray Ferry. Under editor Anthony Timpone, *Fangoria* continued to put out monthly issues with features on Clive Barker, Wes Craven, Jean Rollin, Antonio Margheriti, Stephen King, Christopher Lee, Lucio Fulci, Peter Jackson, John Carpenter and Deborah Hill, James O'Barr, Richard Stanley, John Astin and much more.

In a burst of creative energy, Tim and Donna Lucas published six issues of the indispensable *Video Watchdog*, with cover features on French director Jean Rollin, Lon Chaney Sr. and Tod Browning, David Lynch's (and others) *Dune*, Clive Barker, Ken Russell's *The Devils* and David Cronenberg, plus all the usual video and laserdisc news and reviews.

Al Shevy's *The World of Fandom* continued to appear with some interesting multi-media features, including an interview with Stephen King. *Worlds of Fantasy & Horror*, edited by Darrell Schweitzer, managed two issues in 1996 with fiction by Tanith Lee, Thomas Ligotti, Chet Williamson, Lord Dunsany, R. Chetwynd-Hayes and Ian Watson, plus interviews with Joe R. Lansdale and Peter Straub.

The September issue of *Alfred Hitchcock's Magazine* included a reprint of A.N.L. Munby's "The Tregannet Book of Hours", and Ray Bradbury's "Free Dirt" appeared in the October 15th issue of American Airlines' *American Way* magazine.

The October 30th edition of the London listings magazine *Time Out* was billed as a 'Halloween Special' and included an original round-robin ghost story written by Will Self, Michael Marshall Smith, Dennis Etchison, Christopher Fowler, Peter Straub, Kathy Acker and Neil Gaiman. Not surprisingly, the contributions by the horror writers worked best.

Charles N. Brown's *Locus*, the newspaper of the science fiction field, continued into 29th year of publication. Regular monthly issues were packed with news and reviews and interviews with Robert Holdstock, K.W. Jeter, Ray Bradbury, Jack Williamson and others. However, *Science Fiction Chronicle* didn't do so well, with editor Andrew Porter only managing to get three issues out in 1996.

The World Fantasy Award-winning *Cemetery Dance* returned after a year's hiatus due to editor Richard T. Chizmar's illness. It published four issues featuring new fiction by Jack Ketchum, Peter Crowther, Brian Hodge, Al Sarrantonio, Ed Gorman, Hugh B. Cave, William F. Nolan, Richard Laymon and Melanie Tem, plus interviews with Gorman, Ketchum, Laymon, David Morrell, Dan Simmons and David J. Schow.

Stephen Mark Rainey's *Deathrealm* also published four issues, including a special William F. Nolan edition, plus interviews with Nolan, F. Paul Wilson, Poppy Z. Brite, Clive Barker, Tom Piccirilli and Stephen Jones.

Along with its bi-monthly *Newsletter*, which included regular columns from Nicholas Royle and Tom Holt, the British Fantasy Society also published two issues of *Chills*. Featuring stories by Ben Leech, D.F. Lewis, David Sutton, Michael Marshall Smith and Mark McLaughlin, they marked the end of Peter Coleborn and Simon MacCulloch's dark fiction magazine after ten years. *Outsiders* was BFS Special Booklet No.22, a somewhat self-opinionated essay on horror icons Frankenstein, Dr. Faustus, Dracula and Beowulf by John R. Oram. Special Booklet No.23 was *Silver Rhapsody*, a nicely illustrated chapbook edited by John Carter and Jan Edwards commemorating the 25th anniversary of the Society. Contributors included David Sutton, Stephen Jones, Ramsey Campbell, Jo Fletcher, Mike Wathen, Brian Lumley, Andrew Porter, Storm Constantine, Joel Lane, Nicholas Royle and Graham Joyce.

The Ghost Story Society's thrice-yearly journal *All Hallows*, edited by Barbara and Christopher Roden, continued to be packed with fiction, news and reviews. For vampire fans, The

Vampire Society published *Velvet Vampyre*, while Thee Vampire Guild offered its members *Crimson*, both filled with news, views, reviews and reports of members' activities.

The overview of the British horror scene in *The Scream Factory* 17, edited by Bob Morrish, Peter Enfantino and John Scoleri, was one of the best ever published on either side of the Atlantic. It included five historical articles by Richard Dalby, Mark Valentine, Mike Ashley, Chris and Pauline Morgan and Joel Lane, and David Sutton, plus profiles of R. Chetwynd-Hayes and Guy N. Smith and articles by Kim Newman and Mike Wathen, all wrapped up in a suitable cover by Martin McKenna. For the following issue, the next to last of the magazine, the focus was on Canadian horror in fiction and films, plus articles on the work of Howard Wandrei and snakes in horror, along with all the usual columns and reviews.

Dark Regions Press became the new publisher of *Horror Magazine* and improved both the layout and the contents, helped by an impressive list of contributing editors drawn from the small press. Issue 7 featured interviews with Clive Barker and Brian Lumley.

Andy Cox's near-professional looking *The Third Alternative* included fiction by Rick Cadger, Allen Ashley, James Miller and Conrad Williams, along with an interview with Chris Kenworthy and a profile of Geoff Ryman. Originally announced as simply *Bones* and subject to a last-minute title change, *Bones of the Children* was the first and last issue of a new small press horror magazine edited by Paula Guran, with fiction by John Shirley, Steve Rasnic Tem, Yvonne Navarro and an interview with and novel excerpt by Poppy Z. Brite. Plans are to change the title to *Wetbones* in 1997.

The Silver Web put out a very impressive, perfect-bound issue with fiction by Jeff VanderMeer and others, and the annual issue of *Heliocentric Net* edited by Lisa Jean Bothell included stories from Edward Lee, D.F. Lewis, Mark McLaughlin and Sue Storm.

Dead of Night magazine indefinitely suspended publication, but *The Urbanite* continued with a "Strange Transformations" issue. Joel Lane was the featured writer, along with M.R. Scofidio (aka Marni Griffin), Jessica Amanda Salmonson, Don Webb, Andy Cox and poetry by Lawrence Schimel.

Michael Andre-Driussi's *Abberations* published three issues, featuring interviews with Neil Gaiman and Jack Vance, and Joseph K. Cherkes' *Haunts: Tales of Unexpected Horror and the Supernatural* also managed three editions, including a 10th anniversary issue. Peggy Nadramia's *Grue Magazine* 18 featured fiction by Wayne Allen Sallee and Darrell Schweitzer, and Rod Heather's *Lore* 3 and 4, subtitled *The Quarterly Digest of Maddening Fiction*, included Lovecraftian stories by Donald L. Burleson, Peter H. Cannon and Robert M. Price.

Peeping Tom, edited by Stuart Hughes, managed its usual four issues with fiction by Steve Harris, Simon Clark, Joel Lane, Guy N. Smith, Ben Leech, D.F. Lewis, Ian Watson, Brian Lumley and David Riley. Issue two of Simon Wady's *Squane's Journal* was a special Mark Morris volume, with an introduction by Nicholas Royle and an interview and novel excerpt by the author, along with new fiction by Simon Clark and another novel extract by Peter James. Issue three featured fiction by Mark Chadbourn, articles by Simon Clark and Steve Harris and reviews by Chaz Brenchley. Cover art on both was by Jim Pitts. Graeme Hurry's *Kimota* 4 and 5, published twice yearly by The Preston Speculative Fiction Group, was another nicely-designed magazine with fiction by Gary Kilworth, Simon Clark, Chris Kenworthy, Stephen Bowkett, Suzanne J. Barbieri, Joel Lane and Mark Chadbourn.

White Knuckles published three issues with contributions from D.F. Lewis, Yvonne Navarro and James S. Dorr. Kirk S. King's *Nightdreams* 5 and 6 featured stories by Peter Tennant, D.F. Lewis, Neal Asher and others. The seventh issue of *Plot* was billed as a "Special Horror Issue" and contained thirteen scary stories, and the first issue of *Vampire Dan's Story Emporium* featured fiction by Ken Wiseman, Chris Centore and John DeCarlo, plus a free cut-out bookmark.

The third issue of *Phantasm*, edited by J.F. Gonzalez and Debbie Smith, featured Douglas Clegg, William F. Wu and Robert Deveraux, amongst others. *Fantasy & Terror* 15 (a poetry special) and *Fantasy Macabre 17: The Pearl of Lackme & other high fantasies* were both edited by Jessica Amanda Salmonson and published by Richard H. Fawcett. *Dreams of Decadence: Vampire Poetry and Fiction* edited by Angela Kessler, included a story by Gary Bowen. *Not One of Us* celebrated its tenth anniversary with issue 16, and Canada's *TransVersions* 5 and 6 both had colour xerox covers and featured fiction by

Jeff VanderMeer, Nancy Kilpatrick, Michael Coney and Tom Piccirilli. Also from Canada, *Dreams & Visions* was subtitled *New Frontiers in Christian Fiction*.

Australia's *Bloodsongs* managed to put out a seventh issue that included articles about Nick Cave and Storm Constantine, and fiction by Steve Rasnic Tem, and Mark McLaughlin and M.R. Scofidio. Another Australian magazine reaching its seventh issue was *Skintomb*, which published reviews of books, magazines, comics and videos along with variable fan fiction. *Severed Head*, the quarterly Journal of the Australian Horror Writers included news, features, reviews and a letters column.

From Necronomicon Press, *Necrofile: The Review of Horror Fiction* edited by Stefan Dziemianowicz, S.T. Joshi and Michael A. Morrison published its usual four issues that included Ramsey Campbell's regular column and guest articles by Steve Rasnic Tem, Dan Clore and Chet Williamson. Dziemianowicz's *Other Dimensions* Number Three, a journal of multimedia horror, included articles on vampire music by Brian Stableford, the *Alien* trilogy, Frank Belknap Long and David Wickes' *Frankenstein*. Joshi's *Studies in Weird Fiction* 18 and 19 featured articles on Clark Ashton Smith, Stephen King, Robert Aickman and Dennis Etchison, plus three "uncollected stories" by Ambrose Bierce.

For those who thought there was nothing more to say about an author who had been dead for nearly six decades, there was still minutiae to be unearthed in *Lovecraft Studies* 34 and 35, both edited by S.T. Joshi, and its spin-off title *The New Lovecraft Collector* 16. Joshi's chapbook *Caverns Measureless to Man: 18 Memoirs of H.P. Lovecraft* collected reminiscences by August Derleth, Fritz Leiber, E. Hoffman Price and fifteen other authors.

With issue 92, *Crypt of Cthulhu* edited by Robert M. Price went over to all non-fiction, with issue 94 being a special August Derleth edition. Meanwhile stories and poetry moved to *Cthulhu Codex*, which published three issues also edited by Price. He also revived *Tales of Lovecraftian Horror* with a fourth issue of fiction and poetry, and Price's *Midnight Shambler* 3 and 4 were the first issues of a new series from Necronomicon Press and included a reprint story by Ramsey Campbell.

Clark Ashton Smith's *The Book of Hyperborea* was a welcome trade paperback of fourteen related stories and fragments set in the pre-Ice Age fantasy world, edited by Will Murray. *The Sealed*

Casket and Others was the second Necronomicon collection of Richard F. Searight's Lovecraftian-style stories and poems, and other chapbooks from the publisher included *Far Away & Never*, a collection of seven heroic fantasy stories, one original, by Ramsey Campbell, with cover art by Stephen E. Fabian; *Bitter/Sweet*, which collected two new stories by veteran pulpster Hugh B. Cave, and *Demon and Other Tales*, a collection of seven macabre stories, two original, by Joyce Carol Oates. The latter two were both illustrated by Jason C. Eckhardt.

Borgo Press's *The Work of Stephen King* by Michael R. Collings was an expanded version of the 1986 *Annotated Guide to Stephen King*, updating the author's work through 1994.

After having previously published several volumes about King, George Beahm moved on to *The Unauthorized Anne Rice Companion*. Meanwhile, Michael Riley's presumably authorized *Conversations with Anne Rice* (aka *Interview with Anne Rice*) collected a series of interviews by a personal friend with a biographical chronology.

Frederick S. Frank's *Guide to the Gothic II: An Annotated Bibliography of Criticism 1983-1993* took a critical look at recent Gothic literature, from Stephen King and Joyce Carol Oates to Vampirism and Werewolfery. *A Dark Night's Dreaming: Contemporary American Horror Fiction* edited by Tony Magistrale and Michael A. Morrison was a critical examination of Stephen King, Anne Rice, Peter Straub, William Peter Blatty, Whitley Strieber, Thomas Harris and other modern horror writers, published by the University of South Carolina Press.

As usual, Greenwood Press published a number of reference works of varying quality: *Writing Horror and the Body* by Linda Badley was a critical examination of contemporary horror and bodily transformation, subtitled *The Fiction of Stephen King, Clive Barker, and Anne Rice*.

In Greenwood's *A Critical Companion* series there were books on *Stephen King* by Sharon Russell, *Dean Koontz* by Joan G. Kotker, *V.C. Andrews* by E.D. Huntley (which included a chapter comparing Andrews' work with that subsequently published under her name by Andrew Niederman), *Anne Rice* by Jennifer Salt, *Mary Higgins Clark* by Linda C. Pelzer, and *John Saul* by Paul Bail. Each volume included a bibliography of its subject.

S.T. Joshi's Bram Stoker Award-winning *H.P. Lovecraft: A*

Life, from Necronomicon Press, was a major revisionist biography of the author written by the world's premier Lovecraft scholar. Meanwhile, Barnes & Noble published a low-priced reprint of L. Sprague de Camp's controversial 1975 biography, *H.P. Lovecraft*.

Robert Louis Stevenson: Interviews and Recollections edited by R.C. Terry featured more than forty recollections and interviews with people who actually met the author.

Barbara Belford's *Bram Stoker: A Biography of the Author of Dracula* also included a selected bibliography. David J. Skal's *V is for Vampire* was subtitled *The A-Z Guide to Everything Undead*. Although not up to the standard of some of the author's previous books (such as *Hollywood Gothic* or *The Monster Show*), thanks to Skal's expertise it was better than most of the other vampire knock-offs being churned out.

Editor Douglas Robillard collected essays by Brian Stableford, S.T. Joshi, Sam Moskowitz and five others for *American Supernatural Fiction: From Edith Wharton to the Weird Tales Writers*, from Garland Publishing. Don Hutchison's *The Great Pulp Heroes*, published by Canada's Mosaic Press, was a history of such characters as Doc Savage, The Shadow and Tarzan. Meanwhile, James Van Hise's *Pulp Masters*, from Midnight Graffiti, included a series of articles on pulp characters and authors.

Vanessa D. Dickerson's *Victorian Ghosts in the Noontide: Women Writers and the Supernatural* examined the way supernatural fiction reflected "women's spirituality in a materialistic age", from the University of Missouri Press. And from publisher A. & C. Black came *Writing Horror Fiction*, a how-to manual by the prolific Guy N. Smith.

Undoubtedly the most impressively researched film book of the year was *The BFI Companion to Horror*, ably edited by Kim Newman with a foreword by the ubiquitous Ramsey Campbell. A handsomely illustrated A–Z guide from 'Bud Abbott' to 'George Zucco', it was a book no serious horror film fan could afford to be without.

Despite numerous typos and minor errors, Michael J. Weldon's *The Psychotronic Video Guide*, a long-awaited follow-up to his 1983 volume *The Psychotronic Encyclopedia of Film*, was the most indispensable film reference book of the year, covering more than 9,000 movies.

The Bram Stoker Award-nominated *The Illustrated Werewolf Movie Guide* was the fourth in Stephen Jones' occasional series and included an introduction by Curt Siodmak, creator of *The Wolf Man*.

Steven Puchalski's *Slimetime* was subtitled *A Guide to Sleazy, Mindless, Movie Entertainment*. Puchalski knows his stuff, and this book of A–Z reviews also included three genre essays revised and updated from their original appearance in *Shock Xpress*. *The Mystery Science Theater 3000 Amazing Colossal Episode Guide* was aimed at those who enjoyed the infantile TV series.

Nightmare: The Birth of Horror by Christopher Frayling was a companion volume to the author's entertaining four-part BBC-TV series in which he traced the genesis and after-life of Mary Shelley's *Frankenstein*, Bram Stoker's *Dracula*, Robert Louis Stevenson's *Strange Case of Dr. Jekyll and Mr. Hyde* and Arthur Conan Doyle's *The Hound of the Baskervilles*.

Sacred Monsters, subtitled *Behind the Mask of the Horror Actor*, was a fascinating examination of cinema monsters and the men who played them by actor Doug Bradley, while *Men, Makeup and Monsters* by *Fangoria* editor Anthony Timpone looked at Hollywood's masters of make-up and special effects. Both books had (different) introductions by Clive Barker.

Although not actually a continuation of the *Shock Xpress* series (no matter how much the publisher tried to make it appear so), Stefan Jaworzyn's eclectic *Shock* covered much the same ground with chapters on Italian director Massimo Pupillo, necrophilia in the movies, an interview with Traci Lords and the making of *Blood on Satan's Claw* and *Freaks*, with contributions by David Kerekes, Lucas Balbo, Anne Billson, Kim Newman and David McGillivray, plus an hilarious look at spanking films by Ramsey Campbell!

Fragments of Fear: An Illustrated History of British Horror Films was Andy Boot's welcome, if error-filled study from Creation Books. From the same publisher, *Necronomicon Book One* edited by Andy Black was subtitled *The Journal of Horror and Erotic Cinema* and included chapters on *The Texas Chainsaw Massacre*, *Daughters of Darkness*, *The Evil Dead*, *Witchfinder General*, Jean Rollin, Alfred Hitchcock, Barbara Steele, H.P. Lovecraft, Dario Argento and others.

Loris Curci's *Shock Masters of the Cinema* contained twenty-six brief interviews with such cult filmmakers as Jean Rollin, Don

Coscarelli, Antonio Marghereti and . . . Ramsey Campbell? From McFarland, *It Came from Weaver Five: Interviews with 20 Zany, Glib and Earnest Moviemakers in the SF and Horror Traditions of the Thirties, Forties, Fifties and Sixties* was an enjoyable reprint collection of Tom Weaver's excellent interviews with directors, actors and other film-makers. Dr. David Soren updated his controversial study, *The Rise and Fall of the Horror Film*, for Midnight Marquee Press.

On a lighter note, Stephen J. Spignesi's *The Gore Gore Galore Video Quiz Book* contained 800 movie trivia questions and puzzles, while Herbie J. Pilato's *Bewitched Forever: The Immortal Companion to Television's Most Magical Supernatural Situation Comedy* was a guide to the 1960s TV series starring Elizabeth Montgomery, with a foreword by the show's creator William Asher.

In July, eleven artists won a law suit against *Starlog* magazine for breach of copyright and unfair competition in respect to a set of forty-two trading cards published without their permission in 1993. The artists, who included David A. Hardy, Chesley Bonestell and Rick Sternbach, received $30,000 from the publisher which, after attorney's fees, resulted in them each getting around $400 per card.

Dragon's World/Paper Tiger, who had been publishing excellent art books for many years, suspended business owing money to printers and artists and was put into liquidation in October with debts totalling £2.2 million. Collins & Brown assumed the company's assets, but not its liabilities, and planned to continue publishing under the imprint.

Spectrum III: The Best in Contemporary Fantasic Art edited by Cathy Burnett and Arnie Fenner with Jim Loehr was the latest in a series of superb yearbooks published by Underwood Books and featuring full-colour reproductions of more than two hundred pieces of artwork, selected by a jury, plus The Chesley Award winners.

Michael Whelan's *Something in My Eye*, published in poster format by Mark V. Ziesing Books and also edited by Arnie Fenner and Cathy Burnett, contained seventeen full-colour reproductions of the Hugo Award-winning artist's horror work which could be removed and framed.

J.K. Potter's *Neurotica: Images of the Bizarre* was the second collection of the photo-artist's work published by Paper Tiger, with text by Potter and an introduction by artist and model Lydia Lunch.

Gahan Wilson's *Even Weirder* collected numerous macabre cartoons by the master of horror humour. *The World of Edward Gorey* by Clifford Ross and Karen Wilkin was an extensive biography that included an interview with the artist, bibliography, chronology and numerous illustrations, twenty-four in full colour.

A beautiful hardcover tribute to the EC comic book and TV series, *Tales from the Crypt* by Digby Diehl was packed with over a thousand illustrations, many in full colour, including reprints of classic comic strips and covers and a complete guide to the TV show and movies. As the dustjacket said, this was the coffin table book to die for!

H.R. Giger's designs for the silly SF movie were showcased in *Species Design*, while *H.R. Giger's Film Design* included reproductions of the artist's efforts for every film and video he had worked on, with an introduction by Ridley Scott. *Mars Attacks! The Art of the Movie* by Karen R. Jones was a colourful behind-the-scenes look at the Tim Burton movie.

Hannes Bok Drawings and Sketches from Nicholas J. Certo's Mugster Press collected seventy pieces, much of it previously unpublished, by the famed pulp artist (who died in 1964), with a brief introduction by Ben P. Indick. It was limited to a paperback edition of 350 copies plus forty hardcovers with a colour plate and original sketch by Bok tipped in.

The Encyclopedia of Fantasy and Science Fiction Art Techniques by John Grant and Ron Tiner was a nicely illustrated how-to volume with examples by Jim Burns, Les Edwards, Ian Miller, Chris Achilleos and many other artists.

In December, The Marvel Entertainment Group, which includes Topps Trading Cards, filed for Chapter 11 bankruptcy protection and laid off a third of its workforce. Blamed on the waning boom in comic books and trading cards, and rival takeover bids by billionaire owner Ronald Perelman and major investor Carl Icahn, Marvel's stock plummeted during 1996 and trading was finally halted with the company citing assets of $229.6 million and liabilities of $693.2 million.

Mojo Press's *Atomic Chili: The Illustrated Joe R. Lansdale* was a bumper collection of the author's stories and images adapted into the graphic format by various writers and artists.

Godzilla King of the Monsters, from Dark Horse Comics, benefitted from some excellent cover paintings and interior art by Bob Eggleton. Dark Horse also launched *Harlan Ellison's Dream Corridor Quarterly*, containing comic strip adaptations of various Ellison stories.

Described as "a tale of vampire chic", *Dhampire: Stillborn*, a one-shot from DC Comics' prestige Vertigo imprint was written by Nancy A. Collins and Paul Lee. For the monthly series, Collins was teamed with Ted Naifeh. Meanwhile, Catwoman teamed up with Vampirella to solve a series of brutal slayings in *The Furies*, a one-shot written by Chuck Dixon and illustrated by Jim Balent and Ray McCarthy.

From Titan Books, *Batman Collected* was a lavish, heavyweight guide to Batman collectibles by Chip Kidd, packed with full colour photographs and including a do-it-yourself limited edition Batman novelty figure.

Hammer Horror was a new series of trading cards from Cornerstone Communications featuring stills and poster art from the horror studio's best-known productions. And from Kitchen Sink Press, *Universal Monsters of the Silver Screen* was another series of trading cards which featured beautifully reproduced photographs from the classic horror movies.

While still awaiting certification by the British Board of Film Classification (BBFC), David Cronenberg's award-winning version of J.G. Ballard's *Crash* became the first film to be banned from cinemas in London's West End. Following pressure from National Heritage Secretary Virginia Bottomley and moral outrage by some national newspapers that recalled the hysterical "video nasties" witch-hunts of the past, the local council gave the film an "interim prohibition", requesting that three scenes be cut. It was eventually passed without any cuts by the BBFC in March 1997. Meanwhile, in America, Ted Turner intervened to ensure that the film's release was delayed there as well.

The 68th annual Academy Awards were presented in Los Angeles in March. Mel Gibson's *Braveheart* won five awards, including best picture and best director, out of ten nominations. Genre films made a poor showing, with just two Oscars for *Apollo 13* (for editing and sound), while *Babe* won for best visual effects.

Kirk Douglas and Chuck Jones received well-deserved honourary Oscars, and the award for Special Achievement went to director John Lasseter for Disney's *Toy Story*. In an emotional speech, paralysed actor Christopher Reeve asked Hollywood to continue to tackle difficult and controversial subjects.

Science Fiction ruled the box office with three of the year's biggest movies involving evil aliens attempting to conquer the Earth. In Roland Emmerich's epic *Independence Day*, US President Bill Pullman led an all-star ensemble cast against tentacled invaders who decimated the capital cities of the world. Tim Burton's disappointing comedy *Mars Attacks!* was based on a series of bubblegum cards from the 1960s and featured US President Jack Nicholson leading an all-star ensemble cast against big-brained invaders who decimated the capital cities of the world. At least Patrick Stewart's stalwart Captain Picard had to travel back in time in *Star Trek First Contact* to stop the Cenobite-like Borg from assimilating the Earth. Co-star Jonathan Frakes sat in the director's chair and, helped by Alice Krige's sexy Borg Queen, ensured it was the darkest entry yet in the movie series.

Released at the tail end of 1996, *Scream* was a hugely successful spoof on slasher films that revitalized the flagging careers of director Wes Craven and star Drew Barrymore.

Despite a number of much-publicized reshoots, Stephen Frears' downbeat *Mary Reilly* was still a boxoffice flop. Based on the bestseller by Valerie Martin, Julia Roberts gave a strong performance as the Irish maid who discovered that her employer Dr Jekyll (John Malkovich) transformed into a younger, murderous Mr Hyde. Much more successful, unfortunately, was the heavy-handed remake of *The Nutty Professor* with Eddie Murphy.

Quentin Tarantino's first script, *From Dusk Till Dawn*, was transformed by director Robert Rodriguez into a fast-paced, violent action movie as bank robbing brothers George Clooney and Tarantino fled across the border to Mexico and ended up at a bar run by shape-changing vampires. Also set in a strip bar and featuring vampires, *Bordello of Blood* was a disappointing second *Tales from the Crypt* movie which starred Dennis Miller as a detective on the trail of vampire queen Lilith (Angie Everhart).

Originally scripted as a *Tales from the Crypt* movie, Peter Jackson's surprisingly dark comedy *The Frightners* starred Michael J. Fox as a psychic con-man in league with a pair of ghosts. The irritating Jim Carrey also showed off his dark side as the titular stalker in *The Cable Guy*.

In *The Craft*, a quartet of girls at a Catholic school dabbled in witchcraft with devilish results, while Arthur Miller adapted his own stage play of *The Crucible* starring Daniel Day-Lewis and Winona Ryder.

Based on a story by Philip K. Dick, *Screamers* failed to make a big noise at the boxoffice, while David Twohy's *The Arrival* didn't go anywhere either.

Family man Michael Pare turned into a werewolf in *Bad Moon*, and Spanish director Alex de la Iglesia's *Day of the Beast* was an inventive spoof of movies like *The Omen*.

When original director Richard Stanley was replaced by John Frankenheimer, *The Island of Dr. Moreau* turned into a beastly mess, not helped by eccentric performances from stars Marlon Brando and Val Kilmer. After a long delay and finally arriving with an infamous "Alan Smithee" director credit (actually Kevin Yagher and Joe Chappelle), the episodic *Hellraiser Bloodline* only came alive when Doug Bradley's eloquent Pinhead was on screen. Bradley also turned up briefly in Bob Keen's *Proteus*, based on the novel *Slimer* by Harry Adam Knight (aka John Brosnan, who scripted).

Directed by Tom Holland and scripted by Michael McDowell, *Thinner* was based on the Richard Bachman/Stephen King novel, but despite a gorier new ending added after test screenings it still proved to be a lightweight at the boxoffice.

Director Dario Argento continued his downward plunge with *The Stendhal Syndrome*, in which a mentally disturbed police detective (played by the director's uninteresting daughter Asia) was obsessed with catching a sadistic serial rapist. Sharon Stone and Isabelle Adjani co-starred in a redundant remake of Henri-George Clouzet's *Diabolique*.

The best thing about John Landis's comedy *The Stupids*, based on a series of children's books, was a great fantasy sequence with Christopher Lee as the evil sender (to whom letters are returned to). Although a huge hit, Disney's animated musical of *The Hunchback of Notre Dame* wasn't quite the blockbuster everybody expected, probably due to the story's more adult nature.

Roald Dahl's twisted tales of childhood were adapted for the screen in Henry Selick's underrated stop-motion fantasy *James and the Giant Peach* and Danny DeVito's *Matilda*.

Based on Lee Falk's classic comic strip, Billy Zane was perfectly cast as *The Phantom* in Simon Wincer's film, attempting to stop a megalomaniac millionaire (Treat Williams) from combining three magic skulls into a powerful weapon. *Baywatch*'s Pamela Anderson didn't want anyone calling her "babe" as comic character *Barb Wire*, while another star of the TV show, Nicole Eggert, played the leather-clad zombie avenger battling psycho gang leader Richard Grieco in *The Demolitionist*.

Ted Danson went looking for a monster in *Loch Ness*, while *Gamera Guardian of the Universe* was a throwback to the giant Japanese monster movies of the 1960s. Although not quite as much fun as its 1989 predecessor, *Tremors II: Aftershocks* still managed to deliver the thrills. *Theodore Rex* starred Whoopi Goldberg and an animatronic dinosaur and became the most expensive film ever released directly to video.

Rumpelstiltskin and *The Pinocchio Syndrome* were more failed attempts to create a new horror movie franchise, while down among the also-ran sequels were *The Crow: City of Angels, Lawnmower Man 2, Sometimes They Come Back ... Again, Beastmaster III The Eyes of Braxus, Darkman III Die Darkman Die, Carnosaur 3 Primal Species* and *Amityville The Dollhouse*, while *Campfire Tales, The Vampire Journals, Head of the Family, Cupid, The Grave, Dark Breed, Within the Rock, Donor Unknown* and *The Maddening* were among the numerous titles consigned to the video shelves.

Given a very limited release, *Whole Wide World* was about the life of Conan creator Robert E. Howard (played by Vincent D'Onofrio). Alfred Hitchcock's overrated *Vertigo* got the restoration treatment in Vista-Vision, and the 1929 reissue version of *The Phantom of the Opera* starring Lon Chaney Sr. was shown in a specially restored print featuring a music score by Carl Davis and beautiful new tints.

On TV, one of the year's biggest disappointments was *Trilogy of Terror II*, director Dan Curtis' belated cable movie follow-up to his 1975 film. The awful Lysette Anthony played three roles in adaptations of Henry Kuttner's "The Graveyard Rats" and Richard Matheson's "Bobby", plus "He Who Kills", which again featured the murderous Zuni doll.

Based on the popular comic strip character created by Forrest J Ackerman, the long-awaited *Vampirella* finally turned up as a low budget cable TV movie executive produced by Roger Corman and directed by Jim Wynorski. The flat-chested Talisa Soto starred as the title character battling Roger Daltrey's embarrassingly bad Vlad. Even cameos by Angus Scrimm and John Landis couldn't save it.

Much more fun was a four-hour adaptation of Peter Benchley's *The Beast*, filmed in Australia, in which William Petersen and Larry Drake were menaced by a monstrous giant squid. Corbin Bernsen killed off his patients in a variety of nasty ways as *The Dentist* in director Brian Yuzna's cable TV movie.

Robert Bierman's two-hour adaptation of Wilkie Collins' *The Moonstone* for BBC-TV featured Greg Wise and Antony Sher caught up in the hunt for a cursed Hindu diamond. Based on the novel by Dennis Danvers, Ben Bolt's three-hour adaption of *Wilderness* starred Amanda Ooms as a sensuous university librarian who got naked in her basement once a month and turned into a werewolf.

Despite disappointing ratings, Paul McGann made an impressive seventh *Doctor Who* in the American-made TV movie, trying to stop the Master (Eric Roberts) from stealing his body and destroying space and time. Based on the Marvel comic book, *Generation X* was a pilot TV movie about six squabbling teenage mutants using their powers to battle Matt Frewer's computer genius, who had invaded the dream dimension. Even worse was the pilot movie for *Tarzan the Epic Adventures: Tarzan's Return*, directed by Brian Yuzna. Filmed in South Africa, Tarzan (Joe Lara) discovered a lost portal to Pullicidar, where he encountered unconvincing dinosaurs and shape-changing warrior women.

Premiered on Cinemax, *Blonde Heaven* was a near-hardcore erotic vampire movie with Julie Strain and Michelle Bauer, and the Sci-Fi Channel's *Mr. Stitch* featured Rutger Hauer in a bland reworking of the Frankenstein story.

Co-producer Patrick Stewart was perfectly cast as the 400-year-old ghost in the ABC-TV movie of Oscar Wilde's *The Canterville Ghost*. Although aimed at children, *Shadow Zone: The Undead Express* was an atmospheric cable TV movie based on the book series by J.R. Black, in which a young boy (Chauncey Leopardi) encountered a vampire (Ron Silver) on the New York subway. Even Wes Craven turned up in a cameo role.

In the multiple Emmy Award-winning *The X Files*, David

Duchovny and Gillian Anderson continued to investigate the weird and bizarre in such stand-out episodes as "Piper Maru", "Jose Chung's 'From Outer Space'", "Tunguska"/"Terma" and the stunning "Home" – one of the series' most intense episodes, about an inbred family of psychopaths living in the American heartland.

Anderson and Duchovny also voiced cartoon versions of their characters when FBI agents Dana Scully and Fox Mulder travelled to Springfield to investigate a glowing alien seen by Homer Simpson in *The Simpsons* episode, *The Springfield Files*, hosted by Leonard Nimoy.

From *X Files* creator Chris Carter, *Millennium* starred the excellent Lance Henriksen as retired-FBI agent Frank Black, a member of the secret Millennium Group who used his psychic powers to enter the minds of killers. Despite Henriken's powerful performance and each episode reportedly costing more than $1.5 million, this quickly turned into a serial killer-of-the-week show.

After a shaky start, Showtime's *Poltergeist The Legacy*, which had nothing to do with the movie series, settled down as Derek de Lint, Helen Shaver and other members of a secret society protected the innocent from supernatural evil.

Set during the 1960s, Eric Close and Megan Ward played a Washington couple who discovered that a top secret government organization existed to combat body-possessing alien slugs in *Dark Skies*. In *Them*, meteorologist Scott Patterson and his young nephew Dustin Voigt battled more alien invaders.

Kindred: The Embraced was a thankfully short-lived series based on the White Wolf game, *Vampire: The Masquerade*, in which a San Francisco cop made an uneasy alliance with the head of the shape-changing vampire Clans to battle the evil Kindred. And after four years, Gerrint Wyn Davies finally had to hang up his fangs as the vampire cop hero of *Forever Knight*.

The Burning Zone was an *X Files*-like series that didn't really get off the ground, due to a major cast change mid-season. The bio-crisis team battled everything from a Lovecraftian-like dimension of evil to the Devil himself (Rene Auberjonois) before the show was cancelled. Other new series with a touch of the fantastic included *The Profiler*, *The Pretender* and even the revamped *Baywatch Nights*!

Neil Gaiman's six-part *Neverwhere*, a dark fantasy quest set in a bizarre underground London, needed better actors and a bigger budget than the BBC was obviously willing to spend on it.

At least *Sabrina the Teenage Witch* succeeded because it had a sense of humour. Melissa Joan Hart starred as the eponymous Archie Comics heroine who discovered she had inherited magical powers on her sixteenth birthday, and guest stars included Deborah Harry, magicians Penn and Teller and even Raquel Welch!

Executive produced by Sam Raimi and filmed in New Zealand, both *Hercules the Legendary Journeys* and *Xena Warrior Princess* either took their respective characters (played by Kevin Sorbo and Lucy Lawless) into the Underworld or had them battling a variety of computer-generated monsters. Unfortunately, Ed Naha's *The Adventures of Sinbad*, filmed in South Africa, was only a pale imitation.

Also executive produced by Raimi, *American Gothic* starring Gary Cole as the demonic sheriff Lucas Buck became a cult favourite on both sides of the Atlantic before coming to a reasonably satisfying conclusion. Still introduced by the irritating Crypt Keeper, the 1996 season of HBO's *Tales from the Crypt* was filmed in the UK. *Babylon 5* continued to be one of the darkest SF shows on TV as the war with the Shadows escalated in the third season, but the initially interesting *Nowhere Man* ended up going nowhere and was cancelled after just one season.

Based on the series of books by Betsy Haynes and Daniel Weiss, *Bone Chillers* featured four teenage students who attend the Edgar Allan Poe High School. The Frankenbeans Monster, Count Fangula the vampire, Mums the mummy and Wolfgang the werewolf turned out to be the real stars of the superhero series *Big Bad Beetleborgs*.

Hanna-Barbera revived a teenaged Johnny and Hadji in the animated *Johnny Quest the Real Adventures*, with George Segal and Robert Patrick amongst those supplying the vocal talents. And The Harvey Entertainment Company relaunched *Casper* in a new series of nice-looking cartoons based on the recent big-budget movie.

Biography: Peter Lorre the Master of Menace was an hour-long show about the life and career of the Hungarian-born actor, from the A&E Network. Film historian David Skal, director Vincent Sherman and co-stars Andrea King, Barbara Eden and Hazel Court were among those interviewed.

Although the clips and trailers were of variable quality, *100 Years of Horror* was one of the most fascinating TV shows to début in 1996. First broadcast on the Sci-Fi Channel in Europe, each half-hour episode was hosted by Christopher Lee and included interviews with the likes of William Alland, Roy Ward Baker, Turhan Bey, Ray Bradbury, John Carpenter, Roger Corman, Robert Cornthwaite, Hazel Court, Joe Dante, Richard Denning, Nina Foch, Freddie Francis, Pamela Franklin, Beverly Garland, Don Glut, Hugh Hefner, Bela Lugosi Jr., Mark McGee, Dick Miller, Caroline Munro, Lori Nelson, Fred Olen Ray, Jimmy Sangster, Gloria Talbott and Robert Wise, amongst many others.

For fans of Professor Bernard Quatermass, Andrew Kier recreated the character on BBC Radio 3 in *The Quatermass Memoirs*, a five-part drama-documentary by Nigel Kneale.

The 1996 World Horror Convention was held in the scenic Valley River Inn, near Eugene, Oregon, over the weekend of May 9–12th. Guests of Honour were Clive Barker, artists Don Maitz and Janny Wurts, Nina Kiriki Hoffman, Charles de Lint and Tim Powers. Both the *Deathrealm* and International Horror Critics Guild Awards were announced on the Saturday night, while the Grand Master Award went to Dean R. Koontz.

The 1995 Bram Stoker Awards for superior achievement were presented by the Horror Writer's Association at a banquet held at the Warwick Hotel in New York on June 8th. Guest speaker Tom Doherty, Publisher and President of Tor Books, gave an impassioned speech about book distribution in the United States. The award for superior achievement in Novel went to Joyce Carol Oates' *Zombie*, *The Safety of Unknown Cities* by Lucy Taylor was awarded First Novel, and Stephen King's silly "Lunch at the Gotham Café" won the Novelette award (despite rumours, the author predictably didn't show up to collect it). Jonathan Carroll's *The Panic Hand* picked up the award for Collection and *The Supernatural Index* by Mike Ashley and William G. Contento won the Non-Fiction award. Harlan Ellison (only a few weeks after he underwent quadruple heart bypass surgery) was on hand to collect the Short Story award for "Chatting With Anubis" and the Life Achievement Award.

Necon 16, held over July 19th–21st in Rhode Island, had Joe R. Lansdale and Nancy Holder as Guest Authors, Douglas

Beekman as Guest Artist and Elizabeth Massie as Toastmaster.

FantasyCon XX was held in London over October 4–6th, with Guests of Honour Christopher Fowler and Tom Holt, and Kim Newman as Master of Ceremonies. The winners of the 1996 British Fantasy Awards, presented on the Saturday evening, were Mike O'Driscoll and Steve Lockley, who won the Special Award for organizing the Welcome to My Nightmare convention; Josh Kirby for Best Artist; *The Third Alternative* edited by Andy Cox for Best Small Press; Michael Marshall Smith's "More Tomorrow" (from *Dark Terrors*) for Best Short Story; *Last Rites & Resurrections* edited by Andy Cox for Best Collection/Anthology; and Graham Joyce's *Requiem* was presented with the August Derleth Award for Best Novel.

The Twenty-Second World Fantasy Convention, celebrating The Many Faces of Fantasy, was held in Schaumburg, Illinois, over October 31st–November 3rd with Guests of Honour Katherine Kurtz, Joe R. Lansdale, Ron Walotsky and Ellen Asher, and Brian Lumley as Toastmater. The 1996 World Fantasy Awards were presented on the Sunday afternoon. The Special Award – Non Professional went to publisher Marc Michaud for Necromonicon Press. Jo Fletcher accepted the Special Award – Professional on behalf of the late Richard Evans, for editing. Gahan Wilson's award for Best Artist was collected by Tor Books' Melissa Ann Singer, Gwyneth Jones received the Best Collection and Best Short Fiction awards for, respectively, *Seven Tales and a Fable* and "The Grass Princess" from the same collection. *The Penguin Book of Modern Fantasy by Women* edited by A. Susan Williams and Richard Glyn Jones won the award for Best Anthology, collected by Laura Gillman; Michael Swanwick's "Radio Waves" (from *Omni*) was voted Best Novella, collected by Ellen Datlow; and John Clute accepted the Best Novel award on behalf of Christopher Priest's *The Prestige*, while the Life Achievement award went to Gene Wolfe.

Perhaps somewhat predictably, Stephen King was named the Most Collectable Author of the Year for 1996 in California dealer Barry R. Levin's 9th Annual Collectors Awards. Dutton's numbered and lettered state of King's *The Regulators* (published under the "Richard Bachman" pseudonym) was voted Most Collectable Book of the Year, while John L. Clute was given the special

Lifetime Collectors Award for his work in codifying the history and bibliographic knowledge of the science fiction field.

In America during 1996, book sales increased 4 per cent over the 1995 total, reaching more than $20 billion for the first time. However, this was the result of higher cover prices, not increased sales.

Overall, there was a decrease in the amount of genre material being published last year on both sides of the Atlantic. But when compared to science fiction and fantasy, the number of horror books dropped considerably – particularly in the young adult market, which finally seemed to have reached saturation point. When Scholastic announced a slowdown in sales of its phenomenally successful *Goosebumps* YA horror series, shares in the company fell by 40 per cent on the stock market.

Yet despite all the cries of doom and gloom about the current state of horror from the publishers and, perhaps more importantly, from those within the genre itself, the field continues to thrive and grow. A quick glance through the above essay will attest to the fact that there is still a huge amount of material being produced every year that can be termed "horror", whether it is labelled as such or not.

As the professional publishing houses have continued to cut their horror lines (especially those new authors and mid-list titles), the smaller presses have stepped in to fill the void, and this is where some of the most interesting and cutting-edge work in horror fiction is now appearing.

Having participated in numerous panels and talks about this subject throughout 1996, my own sense is that the horror field is on the brink of a resurgence again. Since the slump of the early 1990s, much of the inferior material that was being produced has gone and those publishers and authors who jumped on the commercial bandwagon have been forced to move on to other genres. We are starting to see exactly the same thing happen with the young adult and gaming imprints now that those successful publishing markets have also become glutted. Horror may never again be as big as it was during the boom years of the 1980s, but the best material has survived the culling and the field is all the stronger for it.

I believe that horror fiction is set for a renaissance as the new millennium approaches. All publishing booms are cyclical and the wheel has nearly turned full circle again for horror. It has always survived and flourished in one form or another, and for those of us who continue to work in the genre, it remains as viable and vibrant a form of literature and communication as ever.

People are talking about horror once more, and there is a whole new generation of writers, artists, editors and publishers who are beginning to make themselves heard. This is hardly indicative of a dying field. Perhaps we have just been waiting for everybody else to catch up with us again . . . ?

The Editor
June, 1997

TERRY LAMSLEY

Walking the Dog

TERRY LAMSLEY WAS BORN in the South of England but has lived in the North for most of his life. He likes it there.

His first collection of supernatural stories, *Under the Crust*, was published in a small paperback edition in 1993. Originally intended to only appeal to the tourist market in Lamsley's home town of Buxton in Derbyshire (all six of the collection's stories are set in or around the area), its reputation quickly grew, helped when Ramsey Campbell and myself and the late Karl Edward Wagner included stories from the book in our annual "Year's Best" anthologies.

It was Wagner who brought the book to the attention of the World Fantasy Award judges, and Lamsley's debut collection was subsequently nominated for no less than three prestigious awards: Best Collection, Best Short Story ("Two Returns") and Best Novella ("Under the Crust"). The book won the award for Best Novella; Ramsey Campbell accepted it on the author's behalf, and Lamsley's reputation as a writer of supernatural fiction began to grow.

Ash-Tree Press has recently reissued *Under the Crust* as a handsome hardcover. It is limited to five hundred copies and is certain to become as sought-after as the long out-of-print first edition. In 1996, Ash-Tree also issued a second, equally remarkable collection of Lamsley's short stories, *Conference With the Dead: Tales of Supernatural Terror*, from which the following story is taken.

"'Walking the Dog' is a story I'd been trying to get around to writing for a number of years," explains the author. "For so long, in fact, that I can't remember how or when the idea first came to me. The long gestation period must have been good for it," he adds, "as it seems to be one of my most popular tales . . ."

O PENING A TIN OF cat food in the dark can be difficult and dangerous. Steve had cut the big muscle at the base of his thumb on a lid the first time he had tried, eleven days before. Now he was more experienced and knew the moves to make, he had one open in seconds. Nevertheless, he was careful how he went about the task. He'd learned the hard way that preparing an animal's supper could be hazardous work.

He sliced the contents of the tin of liver-flavoured "Purrfect" with a fork and sprinkled the nauseating mess over the lawn. He still could not believe that hedgehogs could eat such stuff, but each night something did.

The hedgehogs, a whole family of them, were the obsession of an elderly couple who had gone on holiday for a month and who were scared the creatures would desert their garden if they were not regularly fed during their absence. They were paying Steve well to do the job. Easy money, as he had to pass the house at that time anyway, on his way home from his other engagements.

Tonight though, it was not his last task of the day, as he had taken on an extra commitment for which, by his standards, he would be paid fabulously well. The hours were strange, from eleven at night until one-thirty in the morning, but he didn't care about that. It was regular, permanent work and, with what he would get from it and his other jobs, he would just about make enough to live on. For the first time since he'd left school almost three years ago, he'd be independent of his parents. He would no longer be a burden. They wouldn't be able to give him such a bad time at home, and make him feel so useless and depressed.

He slipped the tin-opener into his leather jacket, dropped the empty can on a heap of others exactly like it in the wheely-bin by the side of the house, then stood for a few moments watching the vacant lawn.

So far, he had not seen one hedgehog! He had a suspicion they had taken off anyway, perhaps because their admirers were no longer there to make a fuss of them. Still, it wasn't his problem; he was doing what he was paid to do; it wasn't his fault if the ungrateful little buggers had upped and gone.

Something moved in the flower-beds surrounding the lawn, rustling the dry leaves of the dying annuals planted there. He watched and waited. The soft sounds continued, but nothing appeared. It was too dark to see much anyway.

It's next door's moggy, he thought, waiting for me to go away.

He dug his hands into his pockets and strode off.

He was due at his new job at Seaton House, on the other side of Buxton. Mr Stook, his new employer, had asked him to get there early, "to receive instructions". The man spoke like that a lot; like a form from the Social Security. It worried Steve. He liked to get on well with the people he worked for. He hoped Stook wasn't going to be an awkward customer.

Steve had never been to Seaton House before. Mr Stook had interviewed him at Steve's parents' house for some reason. He had asked a lot of probing questions, mostly about how fit and strong he was, and insisted on references from previous employers. It seemed a lot of fuss to make to hire the services of an animal-minder, which is what Steve called himself in the advertisements he put in the *Buxton Advertiser*.

He walked past the house twice before he found it. It was completely hidden from the road by a five-foot wall backed by a hedge of tall black conifers.

It was a huge house. Steve knew nothing about architecture, but it looked old to him; older than most of the others surrounding it. It was enclosed in what amounted to a small wood. Only the silhouette of the roof and a number of chimneys, vaguely showing against the dimly moonlit clouds, made it visible at all. There was no knocker on the door, and Steve had trouble finding the bell. He discovered it by touch in the end; a big, old-fashioned button set in a circle of polished wood about six inches in diameter. He could feel letters cut in it under his fingers and guessed the order PRESS was written there. He pressed.

The door opened almost at once, which surprised him, but then he remembered he was expected.

A young woman looked down on him from the height of two

steps. She clicked her tongue. The way she did it made it sound interrogatory, like a question.

"Steven Cave," Steve explained.

"The pet sitter?"

"Mr Stook asked me to get here early."

"That's right," the girl agreed. "He did. Come in." As she walked away, he noticed she limped badly. She had trouble getting her right foot flat on the ground.

He stepped into the hallway. The girl preceded him up stairs that were steep and wide. The carpet was in tatters in places and he tripped and almost fell.

The girl said, "Watch your step," which was easier said than done, as the bulbs above him gave nowhere near enough light for him to see his feet. He clung cautiously to the banister rail and thought, "Stook is some kind of miser, in spite of the money he's paying me."

She opened a door on the first floor and walked into a pitch-dark room. He followed her a little way, feeling suddenly uneasy, afraid he might bang his knees against something. The girl became quite invisible, then she must have found a switch, as her face suddenly appeared in a beam of pallid illumination that shone up from the circular aperture at the top of a shaded lamp. She glanced at him (confirming what he had suspected, that she looked odd, but attractive), said, "Wait here, he won't be long," and slipped out, closing the door behind her.

Steve dropped into an armchair and tried to relax. Not easy. The chair was covered in old, bone-dry black leather as hard as wood. There were no cushions. He stretched out his legs, and almost slid off. He pulled himself upright, and looked around. He was in a large, high-ceilinged room, sparsely furnished with big, blunt, graceless furniture. Not antique and interesting, like he'd seen in shops; just old, ugly and depressing.

He sensed there was something wrong with the room, but it took him a couple of minutes to work out what. Then he noticed there was not a single picture on the walls or ornament on the surface of the tables and cupboards. Acting on a hunch, he went and opened one of the cupboards. It was empty. They all were.

He got down on his knees and peered inside one. As he did so he felt a sensation on the back of his neck, as though something had jumped on it. For a moment, a sharp pain jabbed down his spine. He swore, stood up, and rubbed the affected area. A crick in the neck, he thought, whatever one of them is.

The pain quickly receded to almost nothing, but he still felt uncomfortable.

He returned to the leather chair and sat waiting.

Somehow, the ugly furniture had a looming, brooding presence; it too seemed to be anticipating something. Steve glared round at it, but found it was more powerful than he was. Put out of countenance by a lot of dead wood, he looked away, down at his own crossed legs.

There were sounds out in the house somewhere, and footsteps passed by in the corridor.

Once he thought he felt a movement up behind the back of his head as if something was forcing its way between him and the chair. He swatted the area with his hand and jumped up. The chair was empty. He looked behind it. Nothing there.

He shook his head, and immediately felt a slight constriction round his throat, as though his shirt collar had tightened. He took off his jacket and rubbed his neck furiously, wagging his head up and down as he did so. To his relief, after a few seconds, the sensation subsided.

He put his jacket back on and sat down again, feeling worried and slightly foolish.

Five minutes went by.

He remembered he had his Walkman in his pocket. He stuck the plugs in his ear and turned up "Happy in Hell" by The Christians very loud. At once he felt armed and ready to deal with the intimidating atmosphere about him in the room; the furniture shrank back, as well it might, and the place even seemed a bit brighter. He shut his eyes and sank into the music. When he pulled the tape out of the cheap machine to play the other side, he realized he was not alone any more.

Mr Stook had joined him.

His employer was sitting at the table near the lamp, reading through a handful of documents. Steve recognized a CV he had put together and guessed the other papers were his references. He pulled out the ear plugs, switched off the hissing Walkman, and pretended to clear his throat. Stook stiffened slightly at the sound, but made no other response. He kept on reading. When he moved his head slightly, as he turned his attention to the next item in his hands, the light glistened and sparked on the silver frame and dark orange-tinted lenses of his spectacles. His face had a fuzzy, unfocused look. His features seemed to blend into each other with a smoothness that gave them an unfinished appearance, like a clay model awaiting the sculptor's final touches.

At last he finished reading, turned to Steve, and said, "Ah, there you are; the successful applicant." He hissed as he spoke, as though he had someone else's false teeth in. His voice had a querulous edge, suggesting he was not quite sure he had made the right choice. It was soft and barely audible. Steve thought if he was sitting a couple of feet further away, he would not have been able to understand what the man was saying. He found himself leaning forward, twisting slightly in his seat to point an ear towards his employer. He was suddenly alert, like a rabbit that had sniffed the scent of fox.

"Thank you for attending early as requested," Stook continued, "I appreciate your compliance." He stood up, moving carefully, as though he was afraid he might break. He was at least a foot shorter than Steve, who was five eleven. He stooped from a point low down his back, forcing him to hold his head well back to look the boy in the eye. Because of the lack of definition in his features his face looked young; even, in a rather unpleasant way, infantile. In his tinted shades, he resembled a junky baby. His little mouth was cherubic, enhancing this impression. The hands he held clasped together across his chest were thin to the bone. He was dressed in an oddly cut suit with a tight fit that clung to his scrawny body. Steve guessed the man weighed about seven stone at most. He felt he could pick Stook up and throw him in the air, but behind this thought was the conviction that something very nasty would happen to him if he did. Stook appeared capable of looking after himself, in spite of his slender corporality. He had a startling, powerful presence.

"Now, if you will accompany me downstairs, I shall introduce you to your colleague," Stook murmured, moving with slow, awkward steps across the room.

As he opened the door, light from the landing outside shone full on his face, and Steve saw Stook's flesh was covered in a fine, silvery, almost invisible down, as fluffy as the feathers of a newly hatched chick. That explained why his features looked blurred. Steve had not noticed it before, when Stook had visited his house, because the man had worn a black trilby hat pulled down almost to the bridge of his nose, and had anyway kept his distance. The sight of the down was so peculiar, Steve found himself staring blatantly at what he could see of Stook's profile.

Stook must have realized this, because he turned, pulled back his lips, and bared his teeth slightly. It wasn't a smile; Steve didn't know what it was; it was not an expression he had seen before on any other face. It startled and confused him. He blushed.

Back on the ground floor, Stook led him through a succession of barely furnished rooms to the back of the house. The final room they went through was a kitchen containing a stone sink with a wooden draining board, a dented zinc wash-tub, and a large and ancient stove. There was no sign of any plates or food, and no cupboards to store such things. All was spotlessly clean. The air was sharp with disinfectant.

They went out into a large, dark, cobbled yard. In the distance, twenty yards away, a solitary light glowed over a door to an out-building.

Stook made towards it, moving slowly and with a peculiar, heavy-footed gait, as though he were wading through water. At times they hardly seemed to be making any progress at all, but if Steve stepped ahead his employer made an irritable snatching motion in the air with his hand, ordering him back.

When they reached the door, Stook rapped on it with his knuckles. The sound was dry, like bone on bone. A bolt was drawn back inside and the door was opened by the girl who had let Steve into the house. They walked into a bare, tiled room containing a long, scrubbed bench built over a drain, a selection of electric saws and knives hanging from hooks on the wall, a hose pipe Jubilee-clipped to a tap, and not much else. The atmosphere was cold, as though refrigerated in some way. Steve saw his own breath in front of his face.

The girl was wearing a white apron over her skirt and blouse. Steve noticed there were russet stains on the apron, that could have been dried blood. The girl's face was without expression or makeup, but her lips were bright red as were, to a lesser extent, her eyes. She looked as though she had been crying, or peeling a lot of onions. She looked wasted, as if she existed on coffee and cigarettes, or gin and ecstasy. She was beautiful in a hard, macabre way that Steve found attractive, but the sight of her depressed him. These people are loonies, he thought, and they've got a bloody Rottweiler or a panther to exercise. They're going to make me earn my money.

"I know you two met briefly before," Stook whispered, "but it is necessary that you be properly introduced. You will be spending a lot of time in each other's company." He waved a finger in the air between them. "This – is Mr Steven Cave and this – is Miss Amanda Osmond." Steve nodded, and the girl moistened her lips and blinked.

"Please," Stook insisted, urging them closer together with a gesture, "shake hands."

Steve held his hand out and the girl slipped hers into it. Steve grasped her fingers, waggled them up and down, looked into her face, and smiled hopefully. He felt no response against his palm, but the girl did look him in the eye briefly. She gave no sign she liked what she saw.

"Time, now, for one more introduction," Stook said, with a certain relish. He seemed to like introductions. "I regret *I* must leave you Mr Cave, but if you would be so good as to follow Miss Osmond . . . ?" He stepped back and gave a farewell wave.

Suddenly, Steve had a hundred questions needing answers. The first was: could he go away and think if he really wanted the job? He wasn't sure he could handle it.

But the man was going, almost gone.

"Oh, by the way," Stook said, "I want you to realize that Miss Osmond is your senior. I hope you will work in happy partnership, but she will be, at all times, in charge." He stopped, waiting for an answer.

"Yes," Steve said, "of course."

And felt a sudden twinge of pain at the top of his back; a return of the sensation he had experienced when he had opened the cupboard in the house. He rubbed his neck vigorously, giving it the treatment that had proved partly successful before.

"Good," said Stook, "that is *most* satisfactory," and made his exit.

Steve realized Amanda was watching him with a strange expression on her face. He read it as a mixture of pity, distaste, and maybe something else, like fear. She said, "What's wrong?" but sounded incurious, as though she knew the answer.

"What?"

"With your neck?"

"Nothing, just a crick."

"You think that's nothing?" she said. "Well, you just wait and see." She tossed her head, gazed up at the ceiling, and echoed again, "Nothing . . ."

Steve was seriously confused. He seemed to have upset her, but couldn't think how.

Anyway, the pain in his neck had gone again.

Amanda didn't seem in a hurry to get on with the introduction. She stared out of a window into the yard for a minute or so. She looked tired and bored, as though she was waiting for something not very interesting to happen. She made Steve nervous. He wanted to break the silence, to ask some of his questions, to quell his doubts and anxieties, but he sensed small talk would get short shrift from her. Perhaps he ought to keep his mouth shut as much as possible until he knew her better. He wondered if she was a bit . . . disturbed.

Working with Amanda, he decided, was not going to be easy. She was a chilly number.

Even so, he fancied her.

Then, suddenly, as though a bell had rung, the girl became active. She had a bunch of keys in her hand. She set about unlocking a complicated mechanism on a door at the rear of the room.

When it opened, Steve saw it was four inches thick and faced with steel on the inside.

They walked through it into a little closed-up cage. The girl shut the heavy door behind them and, as she did so, a section of the cage, on some automatic mechanism, swung up and out. They entered a room even colder than the last. It was lit by clumps of peculiar shell-shaped lamps along the walls that gave an illumination like none Steve had come across before; a sharp, pearly-pink glow that seemed to hover round its source, rather than spread wide. It reminded Steve of dentists' surgeries, or operating theatres, for some reason, though it certainly would not have been suitable for either kind of establishment. The room itself summoned up images of instruments used in such places; scalpels and drills and suchlike.

Before Steve had a chance to take in details of the tidy, clinical, but dingy room something big, an animal, rose up from the floor. It was mostly charcoal grey, with dark green stripes, and had short hair over its head, back and tail. Its legs and underside were naked greenish flesh. It was almost four feet high. It had a flat face, with eyes that looked forward. It had, Steve saw at once, oddly beautiful, expressive eyes, but expressive of what? He had no idea. The creature stared at him frankly, and seemed to be trying to see into his head.

It's giving me the once over, he thought. It's trying to read my mind. It looks as though it could, too. God knows what it is! They can't expect me to walk a thing like that.

"That's not a dog," Steve objected.

"Obviously. Did Mr Stook mention a dog?"

Steve couldn't remember that he had, during his interview, but somehow he had assumed that was what he was being asked to deal with. He shook his head.

"He's dog-like, though, as you can see. Out at night, in the dark, he is easily mistaken for a dog. You don't have to worry about that."

She must have misinterpreted the expression of doubt on his face, because she said, "He's harmless most of the time. He won't hurt you. Touch him; put your hand on his head."

Steve looked from the animal to Amanda. She was watching him very closely, with a slight smile that could have been the start of a sneer.

He stepped towards the thing and scratched between its ears. It had little round ears. It made a gurgling noise in its throat, perhaps indicating contentment.

"What's its name?" he said.

"It hasn't got one." Amanda brushed her hands together briskly, impatiently. "And now we'd better get going," she added decisively.

Something touched the back of Steve's leg. The animal. It was looking up at him with its strange eyes. Its irises were a pattern of tiny black and white diamond shapes, like a harlequin's costume. The outer parts were sea-green, a very deep sea-green.

It was, on the whole, an ugly bugger, but not unfriendly.

So why didn't it have a name? The anonymity seemed pointless, heartless. People even gave their pet goldfish names!

He decided he would christen it; but what to call it?

He'd have to think about that.

"Okay," he said, "let's go walkies. Show me the ropes, Amanda."

"We go in the van," she said.

"Is this it?" Steve said, looking out at the black night all around.

Amanda lit her third cigarette in half an hour and killed the lights and engine. "It's as far as we go tonight." The windows were shut and the front of the van was full of stale smoke.

Steve opened the side door and stuck his head out. A skeletal moon hung precariously above him, washing the landscape with a pale, sick lumination.

"Are we anywhere in particular?"

"In the middle of the moors north of Leek." She stretched wearily, then clambered out of the van, lowering herself carefully onto her damaged foot.

Steve joined her at the back of the vehicle and helped push the sliding door open. A light in the sealed-off rear compartment came on automatically, revealing the creature sitting on a water bed. Steve had asked about the bed and Amanda told him it was full of cold water. It helped to keep the temperature down. Steve had said "Ah," and thought, "It's a bloody cold night anyway".

Earlier, they had loaded the "dog" on board without any trouble. It had been placid and cooperative. It had made a few noises that had alarmed Steve at first, but the girl had ignored them.

He was beginning to think that the job might be easy after all.

Amanda pulled a set of steps down out of the back of the van and said something incomprehensible to the animal. It approached them, reversed itself and, to Steve's astonishment, descended backwards. Its co-ordination was nothing like that of any animal he had ever seen. He noticed it had long, crudely prehensile claws that it used to grip the steps one at a time. It looked clumsy in motion, but seemed sure-footed enough. Once on the ground it sniffed eagerly about, like a cartoon pooch tracking game.

Amanda flung her cigarette end away and lit up another.

"You trying to burn your lungs out with those?" Steve asked.

"Perhaps."

"Mr Stook won't let you smoke in the house?"

She shrugged.

"He probably worries about your health."

For the first time, he heard her laugh. It was a painful, hacking sound that turned into a cough. When it finished she said, "He certainly likes to keep his employees going as long as possible," then coughed again. Steve thought he could hear other sounds in her chest, something glugging and gurgling. He was about to ask her if she was okay, but she gave him a look that shut him up.

The animal croaked softly, as though to draw attention to itself.

"Right," Amanda said, "this is where you do your bit." She clipped an extending lead on a collar round the creature's neck and handed Steve the other end. The lead was slightly luminous, emitting a weird green light. "So you can see where it's gone," she explained.

"Okay, beast-master," she said, climbing back into the van, "get walking. Have you got a watch?"

"Yes."

"Time?"

"Almost midnight."

"You give it an hour."

"But where do I take it?"

"Where it wants to go."

She said a mumbo-jumbo word to the animal, and it was off. It jerked the lead, nearly pulling Steve over. As he stumbled after it he heard her say, "Your eyes soon get used to the dark, and there's plenty of starlight. It's easier if you give it plenty of lead. Just press the button to run it back. Keep it tight or it gets snagged."

And Steve's nightmare began.

The thing trotted off fairly slowly at first. It moved in a peculiar way, pawing the ground like a high stepping pony with its front legs, but somehow trotting with its back ones. Steve seemed to remember seeing poodles in ballet skirts making similar motions in a circus. Right from the start he had to walk fast to keep up, but the creature soon accelerated, and he found himself running. He let out more lead and tried to slow down but his charge had other ideas. He saw the grey shape ahead of him getting smaller and smaller on the end of its thin strip of green light.

The ground underfoot was uneven and dangerous, riddled with rabbit holes and lumps of sharp rock. He fell after five minutes, without harming himself, then got up and plunged ahead again. The thing had paused when he tripped, but only for seconds.

The rest of the hour was hell. After twenty minutes he called out to the creature to slow down, even though he didn't think it understood orders in English. If it did hear him, it ignored him.

It found something to interest it at one point, and began snuffling frantically. As soon as he realized it had stopped, Steve flopped to the ground flat on his back, wound in some of the lead, and gazed up at the stars, gasping for air while his chest heaved almost to bursting point. His heart beat like the bass at a Guns 'n' Roses concert. After just a few minutes a small animal, probably a rabbit, screamed with pain again and again, as though it was being dismembered slowly. Steve looked in the direction of the sounds and saw his charge up on its back legs against the curtain of stars, seemingly dancing. It was hurling some misshapen lump of a living creature into the air, catching it in its jaws, then tugging at it with its paws. Hence the screams. The thing was obviously enjoying itself.

It soon wanted to move on, however. Too soon for Steve, who needed more time to get his breath back. He hauled on the lead, yelled at the creature, and refused to get up. The thing pulled hard, and started jerking at the lead. It was very strong. Steve found himself being dragged along in spite of his considerable weight. He tried to dig his heels into the bracken but failed to get a grip. He slid uncomfortably for a few yards until he came up against a large boulder. He managed to get his end of the lead round the rock in a loop which held. The thing stopped. It made angry, frustrated noises, like the cawing of a giant rook. Steve hung on, feeling triumphant. He had scored a point. It was finding out who was boss.

Then he felt a painful stab in the back of his head. The skin at the sides of his neck was drawn forward, as though something was reaching round towards his chin. Whatever it was grasped the flesh above his breast bone and began to crush his wind pipe. At the same time his head was being pulled up and back. It was impossible to breathe.

He was holding the lead with both hands but he let go with one of them to feel around his neck for whatever was strangling him. There was nothing there, that he could touch. There were indentations in his skin where the pain was greatest, however, as though something invisible was digging in.

He let go of the handle of the lead altogether and jumped to his feet. He saw the glowing green stripe slipping away from him like an electric snake. The animal, realizing it was free, became silent.

Steve hung onto his head as though he feared it might be torn off his shoulders. He was in agony, and quite unable to get air into his lungs.

Out of the corner of his eye he saw the creature come prancing swiftly towards him. It stopped a few feet in front of him and stared at him. It reared up on its hind legs and, as it did so, the pain Steve was experiencing became, for a second, much more intense. Then the thing took a leap in the air and sank down onto its belly.

At once, Steve felt himself released. The constriction round his neck was no longer there; the cause of pain had gone. He gasped air, and fell to his knees. He was violently sick. He found himself on all fours. He closed his eyes, and moaned. His whole body was quaking with spasms of nausea.

When he opened his eyes again, he found the creature had moved closer. They were almost nose to nose. The thing's remarkable eyes were inches from his.

It was looking straight into him, or seemed to be. It moved a fraction closer and blinked. For an instant, the pain flashed on and off in the back of Steve's head. Then the animal turned, trotted off a little way, and sat down, obviously waiting.

Steve understood.

Meekly, he went and found his end of the lead.

He looked at his watch. It was almost one, time to get back to the van.

Then he realized he had no idea where he was. He was completely disorientated.

He staggered about lost for three or four minutes, while the creature trotted calmly behind him, almost at heel. Then, not very far away, the van's headlights flashed twice.

When he reached it, the girl was standing at the back with the door open. She slipped the collar and lead off the creature's neck, and it jumped on board.

They got into the van.

"How did it go?" Amanda said.

"A few problems." Steve's neck was so sore, it hurt to speak.

"Yeah, so I heard. You two fell out?"

"That sort of thing."

"You won't do *that* again, will you?"

"I won't have anything to do with it again," he said angrily.

"Oh yes, you will." She lit a cigarette, started the engine, and turned to look at him. "It won't let you go."

"We'll see about that."

She started driving cautiously back, with the headlights dipped. "You don't understand, do you? You're hooked. You've got a monkey on your back."

Steve didn't answer.

They drove back in silence.

Steve had too much on his mind to notice how cold it was.

"I don't understand. Why do I have to walk it anyway?"

"I used to take it," Amanda said, "but my legs got broken once too often, and they won't heal properly any more. Then we got another girl to do it . . ."

"No," Steve insisted, slightly embarrassed at causing her to mention her game legs. "I mean, how come we have to take it out at all?"

"It needs exercise. Can you imagine letting that creature out the back door to roam around for the night? To wander round town on its own?"

"But why do I have to walk *with* it? Why can't we just take it somewhere and leave it to run for an hour?"

"It gets lost. It's got no sense of direction. And it's short-sighted. I don't think it can see more than a few yards."

"Even with those amazing eyes?"

"Perhaps it sees things with them we can't see. Maybe, where he comes from, he can see perfectly."

"And where do you think that is?"

She paused, lit a cigarette from the last half inch of her previous one, and said, "Who knows? Another dimension? Another planet? Hell? Your guess is as good as mine. One thing's certain, it's not part of the indigenous population."

They were driving out for Steve's fourth night on the job. Each time, they went to a different spot, just in case they'd been seen the night before, and someone was waiting for them to return. There had been articles in the local papers about a strange animal in the district during recent weeks, and a couple of eye-witness descriptions had been close to the mark. Mr Stook had got to hear about them, and had not been pleased with Amanda. She'd been disciplined, she told Steve. She didn't say how, but her "monkey" had played a part in the procedure, so now she was selecting the sites for the creature's exercise with particular care.

On their second trip out, she'd explained that she had a "passenger" on her back, the same as he did. It wasn't really a monkey, but the phrase "a monkey on the back", used by junkies back in the '40s and '50s as a euphemism for addiction, seemed to describe their own predicament exactly.

Even then, in spite of the evidence of his experiences on the first evening, Steve couldn't quite believe her; he thought it was more likely there was something wrong with *him*.

That was what he wanted to believe.

When he'd tried to stay at home on the second night, when it was time to go to work, and the pains had started at the top of his spine, and had only eased when he had left his parents' home and set off in the direction of Seaton House, he had clung to the idea that it might be due to something that was wrong inside his head. He knew nothing about psychology, but was aware that the mind could make you do strange things.

Whatever it was, however, it hurt. It forced him to get to the job on time.

The next evening, at ten, he'd jogged as far and as fast out of Buxton as he could.

His "monkey" had almost throttled him by the time he'd gone two miles, and he'd had to turn back. At home again he had run up to his room, stripped off his shirt, and looked in the mirror. At the front of his neck, just above his breast bone, were bruise marks the shape of two little three-fingered hands. The fingers had dug in deep enough to draw blood.

He'd gone to work then – in a hurry.

The fourth night, tonight, he had turned up on time: in fact, he'd been early.

The creature had not given him too many problems after their first trip out together, though walking it was still hard work. Instead of running wild for an hour, and dragging him after it, it had conformed to more dog-like ways for some of the time, trotting a few yards ahead of him at a reasonable speed and sticking mostly to sheep tracks and established paths. Steve was glad to find the thing ignored sheep. He had half expected it to kill and eat one every night for supper.

Amanda had explained when asked (she hardly ever volunteered information) that his first evening on the job had been the creature's first outing for months, so it had had a lot of steam to let off. It never went out between the start of June to the end of September because it couldn't stand the hot nights.

"It sort of hibernates in reverse in the room we collect it from. It's air-conditioned. It gets as cold as a witch's tit in there sometimes."

As to sheep for supper? "It eats when we get back, after you've gone. Stook sees to that. He's in charge of the pantry."

"What does he feed it?"

"Don't worry about that," she said. "Believe me, you don't want to know."

He mentioned the rabbit it had caught on the first night.

"It must have been a very stupid rabbit," she said, "or a sick or injured one."

"I don't think it ate it; just pulled it apart."

She nodded. "You won't see rabbit on its menu," she said. "It's a big game gourmet."

They reached some God-forsaken place and stopped. Steve opened the rear door of the van and stood aside as the thing stuck its backside out and reversed down the steps. Not for the first time, he wondered what his monkey would to to him if he gave the creature a kick in the rump. Something very painful, he was sure.

He still thought of the animal as "it". He had dropped the idea of giving it a name. Anonymity seemed to suit it.

So things continued for some months.

Stook told Steve to learn to drive, and paid for lessons.

The money Steve was earning was ridiculous, enough for him to be able to drop most of his other jobs. His standard of living soared. He started buying clothes to spruce up his image.

He had always had trouble with girls. They didn't seem to see him. Steve stared at girls a lot, he couldn't help it; but somehow, for some reason, they never so much as glanced back. It was as if he was invisible. They just looked through him.

He spent a lot of time in front of the mirror, trying to work out why. He thought he was handsome enough. Okay, he had a slightly podgy face. But his features, considered in isolation, were good. He looked . . . reasonable. Lots of worse-looking men his age were walking about with delicious girls on their arms, were sleeping with them. Steve's sex life was almost non-existent, with the few girls who were attracted to him. For some reason, these were never girls *he* fancied. Something was wrong, he felt; he wasn't getting across to the right women.

So he started buying show-off clothing and having expensive haircuts. He thought girls would be more likely to notice him. He'd be more obvious.

But his new look wasn't having much effect.

Certainly not on Amanda.

She attracted him a lot. But she was an enigma; hard to get on with, and difficult to know. She didn't reveal much about herself.

He dreamed about Amanda.

They were foolish dreams, with him as a sort of white knight, saving her from the evil Stook.

The trouble was, in reality, she didn't seem to realize she needed saving. She put up with what Steve perceived to be an abject, slavish existence.

And she always had her guard up. She had a weary, cynical attitude and way of speaking that somehow put her away at a great distance, out on her own. Steve felt she was beyond him, he couldn't reach her, though sometimes he thought she was beginning to thaw out towards him just a little.

He was not sure how she spent her days, but he suspected she acted the skivvy for Stook and the creature, as the place where it lived was kept ultra-clean, as though scrubbed and scoured by a germ-phobic fanatic. The air around the house always stank of disinfectant, dust never seemed to get to settle on any surface in the outbuilding where the thing was "kennelled", and you could see your face in the gloss paint and polished tiles on the walls.

The inside of the house, though furnished with ancient and in some cases worn and dilapidated items, was also kept fastidiously neat and clean, and Steve was sure Stook didn't do the work himself.

So it had to be Amanda.

Steve began to think of her as a kind of doomed Cinderella. Cinderella with a monkey on her back.

His own monkey didn't trouble him much. For days, he forgot it was there. Then he'd do something wrong when he was out with the creature, and it would give him a tweak, a jolt of pain that knocked him rigid, and he would remember.

And, often, he felt strangely tired. In recent weeks a lassitude was creeping over him, as though his energy was draining away through the soles of his feet. Things that had once been easy were getting difficult. He'd been a body builder for almost two years, and had got himself very fit. But suddenly it was a strain to lift weights. He kept away from the gym because he was finding it harder and harder to keep up with his friends down there, and his shorts and T-shirts were starting to hang loose on him. People noticed, and made comments.

Also, he'd been sleeping like a dead thing recently, was getting up later and later, and still he wasn't feeling refreshed.

And he was eating like a pig! His appetite was getting out of hand; his mother told him he must have worms.

Steve had a suspicion it was something worse than worms. A couple of times, in the mirror, he had caught an expression on his face that he had seen on Amanda's. A look that he was beginning to understand.

Frequently Amanda seemed to be trying to warn him about something; her conversation, sparse and elliptical as it was, was full of hints and allusions, suggested as much by her tone of voice as the meaning of the words she used. At times, when he thought she was trying to get through to him at some subliminal level, her normally blank, expressionless face would almost come alive. Feelings of frustration, fear, despair, and a terrible isolation would register briefly behind her eyes and in the lines at the corners of her mouth, to be wiped away at once by a grimace of pain, as though she had been whipped.

Reading between the lines of what she said, Steve came to understand that her monkey could somehow read her mind, even control her thoughts to some extent. Only occasionally, perhaps when it was dozing or otherwise occupied, could she communicate obliquely some of what Steve wanted to know. He got the impression she had been its victim for a long time and it had almost total mastery over her, and that he would end up in the same condition. His own monkey was growing into him. It was getting to know him, to understand him. It had command of his body; one day it would have his soul. Or so Amanda seemed to be saying. From all this he deduced that he was still, to some extent, free to think and act in ways that she was not. Perhaps there was some way he could get the monkey off *his* back and then help Amanda deal with hers. Perhaps.

But there was also Stook to contend with. Steve wished he

knew more about his employer. He became obsessed with a need to find out just what kind of eyes the man hid behind the impenetrable orange-tinted spectacles that always masked his out-of-focus face. He hardly ever had contact with Stook except at the end of each week, when he went to receive his pay. That, in itself, he found disturbing. And he realized he had never seen the man and his pet (if that was what the creature he took for nocturnal rambles was) together, not even once. Also, Stook never asked about its welfare or showed any concern about it at all, which was not natural. Steve was used to being questioned closely about the animals he cared for by their owners, as though the creatures were their own flesh and blood.

A suspicion evolved in Steve's mind that the dog-thing he exercised was just that, however; Stook's own flesh and blood!

"What does Mr Stook do all day?" he asked Amanda one evening, as they drove to some remote, chilly location. It was almost Christmas, and a couple of inches of snow had fallen on top of a skim of frozen rain during the day. The girl was driving with greater concentration than usual.

"Goes out," she said from behind the cigarette that waggled at the side of her mouth. "Every day. In the van."

"Are you sure? Where to?"

"Looking for food to feed – it," she jerked a thumb over her shoulder towards the creature in the back compartment.

"And that takes all day?"

"It can do."

"You never did tell me what it eats," he said.

She shook her head and glanced sideways at him. For a few moments she was silent, then said, apparently apropos nothing, "Every day, you know, people go missing. Particularly kids. It's a sign of the times."

"That's right," Steve agreed, unsure where the conversation was leading. "You read about it in the papers."

"All the time. It's surprising how many of them never do get found."

"Perhaps no one bothers to look for a lot of them."

"Someone does."

Steve grunted encouragingly, thinking he was perhaps beginning to understand. "And when he finds them, they stay missing?"

"Definitely. And sometimes, if he has to, he makes them go missing in the first place," she said, and turned the van off the road along a dark track to nowhere. "If he can't find what he wants, he takes what he can find. He's a good hunter. He knows how to set traps."

The full meaning of Amanda's words skipped over the surface of Steve's mind for a while, refusing to sink in. But what he was hearing, what he thought she was saying, did not come as a total surprise. It was a bit like remembering fragments of an old nightmare. He had formulated wild theories and fantasies about Stook and his "pet" at least as disgusting as the girl's story.

After another short silence he said, "And the thing eats every day?"

"It has to have very fresh meat four or five times a week at least."

"*Very* fresh?"

"Lively. Still on the hoof. It likes to do its own slaughtering, though it will take the pre-butchered option if it has to."

For once, she seemed to be able to speak relatively freely, perhaps because her monkey knew if it gave her a jolt, she might loose control of the van on the snow and ice.

Suddenly, extrapolating, Steve understood something more. "So the meal is made to walk into the cage, then out into the room, is that it?" he said, trying to sound casual and inconsequential. "The cage opens automatically. It's a feeding hatch! The metal plating on the inside of the door is to stop dinner, not the creature, escaping?"

She nodded too hard, and set herself off coughing. Her cigarette fell from her lips to the floor. A stink of burning drifted up into the van. Steve bent down to find and extinguish the little fire, prodding around with the heel of his right shoe. Amanda slowed speed to a crawl. As he fumbled he said. "Did you ever see Stook and that thing together in the same place?"

Then his own monkey woke up. He felt pain screw across the back of his eyes. He went blind. It was as though his eyes had been put out; there was that much pain. Black anguish filled his mind for an instant. He jerked back into his seat in one great spasm. He heard Amanda say something like "Drop it," or maybe, "stop it", then he passed out.

He came to. He had a searing headache, but he could see again.

The van had stopped. Amanda, looking grey-faced and ill, had got out and opened the door at his side. Fluffy snow was blowing in and setting on his face. The girl was shaking him by the shoulder. He heard a noise behind him, slightly muffled, like the cry of a monster crow trapped in a sack. The thing in the back was getting impatient.

He dragged himself through the door down onto the frozen ground. Amanda gave him the lead and opened the rear door.

The creature was angry. It snarled at him before it reversed out. It charged off as soon as he got its collar on, dragging him behind.

Then it led Steve a grotesque and terrible dance.

It was a bleak place they had come to. The murky night sky was veiled by drifting nets of wet, swirling snow. He slipped on iced-over puddles a number of times in the dark. Once, he landed awkwardly on his left arm and felt something give in the wrist. His hand went numb, then started to pulse with pain. He couldn't move the fingers of his left hand, and was forced to hang onto the lead with only his right. The creature dragged him along sideways, causing him to stumble and fall a dozen times.

He felt like a sailor, sinking in a storm and sighting a lifeboat when, at last, he saw the van lights flash.

He got Amanda to drop him off at the Cottage Hospital on the way back to Seaton House. She was very reluctant to do so. She would not, or could not, stop the van, and insisted he jump out while she cruised slowly past the drive that led up to the Accident Unit.

He caught a glimpse of her contorted features as she leaned across the passenger seat to slam the door behind him. Her monkey, he guessed, was going to give her hell when she got back.

Steve woke up shortly after noon next day. He opened his eyes and saw his left arm, in plaster up to the elbow, rising and dipping on his chest. He'd spent most of the night in hospital. X-rays had revealed chipped and broken bones in his hand and wrist. The radiographer had told him it could be months before he got full use of the hand again.

When he *had* finally got to bed, he had not been able to sleep for thinking about how the accident would affect his prospects with Stook. Strangely, he was anxious he might lose his job. It somehow seemed like a desirable occupation to him, in spite of the fact that most of his working hours were a walking nightmare. Maybe he had become addicted to money or, more sinisterly, perhaps his monkey was influencing his thinking. Either way, like it or not, he was worried.

He dragged himself out of bed. He dressed slowly, like a sleepwalker, then went to the kitchen and chomped through a breakfast of three bowls of Shredded Wheat, a fry-up big enough to hide most of the surface of a dinner plate, half a loaf of toasted bread, and a pint and a half of milk. Then he felt tired again, and was tempted to return to bed for a few more hours, as he often did. But today he had urgent things to do. He had to let Stook know about the condition of his hand. The man was not on the phone, or was ex-directory, so Steve would have to pay him a visit. The idea appealed to him. He had been looking for an excuse to call at Seaton House during daylight hours for weeks!

A lot more snow had fallen. Probably for reasons of economy, the roads had not been salted, and traffic was sparse. Everywhere was eerily quiet; all sound was baffled, trapped in the banks of drifting white flakes. The town had a deserted feel, as though the population had been lured away overnight by the saucer-people.

Steve walked slowly, picking his way with care, not wanting to fall and damage his arm still further.

The first thing he saw when he trudged up Stook's drive was the van, parked where it was never left, at the front of the house. The front end was caved in from some considerable impact. The left tyre was in shreds, and the windows were smashed. There were traces of an extra set of wheels nearby in the snow, suggesting the vehicle had been towed home.

He rang the door bell and shouted through the letter box, got no response, and wandered around to the back of the house.

The rear courtyard was surrounded by two-storeyed out-buildings and a wall eight feet high. The one door, bolted on the inside, was impenetrable without the aid of a battering-ram and a rugby team to operate it. On his own, with a duff hand, there was no way Steve could force an entry. He didn't even bother to try. He went among the trees all round the house, aware that he was leaving an obvious trail of prints in the snow, and snooped in the windows. He learned nothing about Stook's way of life, however, as all the rooms he saw were barely furnished and looked unused. He came to the conclusion that Stook chose to live at Seaton House because the building was well hidden, yet close to the centre of town, rather than because he needed a big establishment. It was probably easier to remain incognito, concealed in the community, than it would be if he inhabited some remote place where his activities, or lack of them, would become the object of speculation for farmers and other country dwellers, who commonly possess an insatiable curiosity about their neighbours' doings. Steve had been brought up on such a farm, and the same instinctive nosiness was born in him.

He wandered back into town, called the local hospitals from a telephone box to see if an Amanda Osmond had been admitted anywhere, and got negative replies from all of them. Then he sat in a pub for a couple of hours drinking lager, doing the quizzes on beer-mats, and listening to the barmaid's conversation. She was telling one of the customers (in fact, the only other customer), a sullen, silent man she seemed inordinately fond of, about her various Grand Guignol relationships. She obviously had lots of boyfriends. Steve thought she was beautiful. He fell in love with her. He normally never drank alcohol, but kept on drinking so he could stay and look at her. He thought, if he downed enough quickly, he might pluck up the courage to get talking to her himself. He stared at her shamelessly for minutes on end. She didn't seem to notice him, even when he went to the bar, even though he was dressed in one of his coolest, cost-a-packet outfits.

"I'm invisible," he thought. "I don't register with her. I suffer from negative charisma."

Then, suddenly disgusted with himself, he gulped down the last of his drink and got up to go. On the way out he walked to the bar, set his empty glass down in front of the object of his lust, and almost shouted, "See ya, then!"

"Ta, duck," she said, without turning. The customer in receipt of her monologue glanced askance at him, and raised an eyebrow.

"They think I'm pissed," Steve thought. "Perhaps I am, after five (or was it six?) pints of Special."

When he got outside and found his feet flailing about in the snow, he realized how drunk he was. Not far from the pub he slipped, fell on his backside, and bounced back up. "Ah ha," he thought, "I feel no pain!" and wanted to laugh. He stumbled back to Seaton House, lighter and happier than he had been for weeks.

When he got there he saw a new set of footprints leading up the drive. A woman's; almost certainly Amanda's. They stopped at the front door, and whoever had gone in was still there. There were no prints going back out.

He rang the bell, waited, then hammered with his fist. After a while the door opened slowly about six inches. It was on a chain. Round the edge of the door, thin, dry, scaly fingers appeared, clutching the wood with a crab-like pincer movement. Above them, a slice of Stook's furry face, half hidden behind one lens of his dark orange-tinted spectacles, pressed forward into the gap.

Partly through shock (he had been sure Amanda would answer the door) and partly because he did not want to waft lager-polluted breath towards his employer, Steve stepped backwards. He nearly fell off the step. He regained his balance, but not his composure. He could not think of anything to say. Stook broke the silence.

"Why are you here at this time?" he asked, in a tight, tiny, snarling voice. "What do you want?" His fussy manner of speech and fastidious politeness had deserted him.

"He looks like an insect," Steve thought, "with that fuzzy face and those shades. He even sounds like one. A giant house fly, or a bluebottle. He wants swatting!"

"I had an accident last night. Perhaps Amanda told you." Steve held up his plastered arm. "I fell over when I was walking the . . ."

"I know all about it," Stook snapped. "It doesn't matter."

"Oh, and I forgot to tell you, I passed my driving test the day before yesterday."

Stook grunted; a sound that may have expressed satisfaction. Steve suddenly felt stupid with drink. His brain became confused, then blank.

"I don't want you here now," Stook said.

"But what about tonight?"

"Come at the usual time."

"I've broken my arm."

"That doesn't concern me."

"I've got to rest it; take things easy."

"You've got a job to do. You'll be here on time."

"But what about the van?"

"That's my problem." Stook glared at him for a few seconds, during which Steve felt contempt emanating from the man like a powerful smell.

"I want to speak to Amanda," Steve said at last.

"Why?"

"Well . . ." Steve inwardly cursed the lager that seemed to have anaesthetized his tongue.

"She's not here," Stook said, in what could have been a taunting tone.

Then he hissed, "Go away," and shut the door.

Steve stood looking at the varnished wood in front of his nose and became very, very angry. He hardly ever was angry, about once or twice a year, but when he was, it made up for all the times he wasn't, and should have been.

He kicked the door, hurt his toe, and shouted, "You bastard, you know how I broke my wrist last night because *you were there when it happened.* I've got you worked out, you and your bloody 'pet'."

Then he felt something stirring at the back of his neck. A dull, wavering ache moved out of his spine and across his shoulders. His monkey was trying to push and punish him, and not making a good job of it. He could feel its hands groping to reach round to his throat, but they had no strength, and seemed to fumble. At one point, they lost hold altogether, as though the monkey had fallen backwards.

Gleefully, Steve recognized, in the parasite's powerless confusion, a reflection of his own drunkenness.

"It's more pissed than I am," he thought. "It feeds off me, and somehow it's got alcohol in its system, and it can't take it. It's got a weak head. It's rat-arsed; legless! It can't hurt me."

Finding himself truly free for the first time for months, Steve felt bold.

And he was still angry, deep inside.

And he was still very drunk.

"Time to get things sorted," he mumbled, as he started plodding through the snow to the rear of Seaton House. "Bugger the money. I'll not work for that *thing* any more. And I'll find Amanda, and tell her to get her monkey drunk. That's the way to beat it. Then Stook can go and take himself for a walk."

He had noticed, during his prowl through the miniature woods growing around the perimeter of the house earlier in the day, a tree, growing close to the wall, whose branches reached out above the courtyard. Then, it had not occurred to him that he might be able to use it to get over the wall, especially as he only had the use of one arm; now, thanks to alcohol, it looked an easy climb.

Steve rose up the trunk, branch by branch, as though he was ascending a ladder, using the weight of his plastered wrist as a balance. He stepped out along an overhanging branch with all the confidence of a champion tango dancer leading his partner onto a ballroom floor. The branch dipped gracefully lower as Steve moved along it. When, after he had got the wall behind him, it snapped, depositing him in a drift of snow that had formed inside the courtyard, he didn't so much feel he was falling, as flying! He was so relaxed when he hit the ground, he was able to roll over onto his feet in one unbroken movement.

It was dank and dark in the courtyard. The snow, caught in eddies of wind trapped by the surrounding buildings, spun in frantically ascending circles around him.

Looking about he saw a vertical strip of light at the edge of the door leading into the outbuilding where the creature had its "kennel". There was a sound, a high, grinding, mechanical whirring, coming from behind the slightly open door, that had been muffled by snow and the wall when he had been in the garden on the other side.

A beam of light stretched across the snow towards him from the slightly open door. He walked along its diminishing width warily, as though he were walking the plank. The noise continued, rising to a shear metallic screech, then sinking back to an even, angry snarl.

When it was at its loudest, Steve gave the door a shove and peered round it into the room.

Then drew back at once in horror.

Stook was in there, naked except for a pair of green Wellington boots and a brick-red rubber apron that almost formed a tube around his body. In it, he looked more than ever like some kind of bug. He had his back to Steve. He held an electric saw in his hands and was using it to cut up a carcass stretched out on the long wooden bench in front of him. The top end of the corpse had been jointed into unidentifiable chunks of meat. It was headless, but something heavy, about the size of a head, hung in a plastic Marks and Spencer's bag from a nail driven into the edge of the bench. The lower section of the cadaver, partly concealed under a sheet of thick plastic, was untouched and obviously human. Two feet, lolling apart at the ankles at an angle of forty-five degrees, stuck out from under the sheet and over the end of the bench.

And Steve thought he had seen a hand on the floor by Stook's boots. The hand was moving, sliding down a gutter near the bench, caught in the jet from a hose pipe that was snaking restlessly from side to side under the pressure of water it was ejecting.

The shock of what he had seen, far from sobering Steve up, flung his mind into a debilitating stew of incredulity, revulsion and blind anger. He wanted to act, to strike against Stook, to *swat him down*, but he didn't do anything of the sort. He stood rooted to the spot, gasping and howling, softly but passionately, along with the sighing of the wind, frozen in an enchantment of disgust and revulsion. He remained like that for a couple of minutes, long enough for the snow to settle as a light crust on his shoulders and head, and for his feet to start to freeze in his sodden canvas trainers.

Then a new sound came from inside the outhouse. The deeper, harsher grinding of a bigger saw. His employer was getting down to work in earnest, making the final cuts. Presumably, soon, the meal would be ready, and the creature would eat.

The thought was enough to break the icy spell that Steve was under. He turned back, pushed open the door, and walked determinedly into Stook's private abattoir. Stook did not hear him enter; he would not have heard if Steve had shouted his name, against the noise of the machine.

Wondering if he might need a weapon, or something to defend himself with, Steve looked about for something heavy he could swing. As he did so, his monkey roused itself and tried, ineffectually, to cause him pain. It seemed to be sprawling inside his head, scratching at the back of his eyes with blunted talons, and gnawing his cerebellum with toothless gums. It was desperate, but almost helpless. Steve ignored it.

He got to within a couple of feet of Stook's back when he saw something hanging on the wall that brought him up short.

There was a row of hooks for overalls and waterproofs that he and Amanda took with them when they went out on wet nights. Stook's clothing had been flung over one of these and next to it hung the skirt and blouse that Amanda had worn the previous night, when Steve had broken his wrist in the snow. The girl's clothing was covered in blood stains, and there were streaks of red down the wall below.

Previously, dominated as he was by alcohol enhanced emotions, Steve had not given a thought to the possible identity of the cadaver Stook was dismembering.

But his main motivation for invading his employer's domain had been to locate Amanda, and somehow to rescue her, as he had many times in his dreams. Now, it seemed he had found her, but too late.

He glanced again at the corpse. It was about the right size, what remained of it. The proportions were Amanda's. The hand, that was now spinning in a whirling current of crimson water outflowing down the drain, was narrow and delicate, like Amanda's. He even thought he could see nicotine stains on the fingers.

Then Stook must have become aware that he was no longer alone. He switched off the screaming saw and turned awkwardly around. He was crouching low, bent forward in his habitual stance, with his chin jutting up almost in line with his breast bone. He looked absurdly sinister and repellent with his wasted, grey, downy arms swinging ape-like by his sides, and his knotted knees showing in the gap between the tops of his boots and the bottom of his apron. He still held the electric saw in his right hand, and he whipped the tip of the blade back and forth in a tiny arc, in a tense, threatening movement. His eyes, invisible behind his tinted shades, nevertheless drove into Steve's like corkscrews.

Stook said something in a language Steve couldn't understand. It sounded like a question. Stook's tone was demanding, querulous, mystified. As if in answer, Steve felt his monkey stir again; vague waves of discomfort pulsed weakly through his brain.

Stook moved a few inches closer to Steve, and spoke again. Now he sounded angry.

But Steve's monkey seemed to give up. It faded out. Steve thought it might have gone to sleep.

Stook raised his feeble voice and mouthed more incomprehensible words.

"It's no good shouting," Steve said. "Your little mate's passed out. He's sleeping it off."

"You're drunk," Stook observed.

"Right," Steve agreed. "And I'm going to stay drunk."

Stook's lips curled, but he didn't speak.

"That way, we're more or less equal," Steve said, feeling more confident by the second. He had begun to sober up, but now he felt a surge of elation, like a shot of spirit, from the certainty he had disarmed Stook and his minion. "I don't work for you any more, Stook. I know what you are, and I'm going to do something about you. I'm going to destroy you. Christ knows where you came from, but I'm going to send you to a worse place."

Stook made a buzzing noise with his tongue against his teeth, like an insect at a window. He sounded more impatient and irritable than scared. Hearing him, Steve experienced a moment of self doubt, of anxiety that he had, perhaps, underestimated his employer, and assumed victory too soon.

Stook straightened up a little, and seemed to turn away almost derisively.

Thinking he was going to walk off, Steve was about grab him, by the throat perhaps, when Stook struck. He swung up his right arm, switching on the saw as he did so, and lunged forward at Steve's chest. The little man moved with unexpected agility. The saw blade bit something, and shrieked as it cut.

Steve thought he had been hurt, but felt no pain. He staggered back and, as he did so, Stook moved quickly forward to strike again. Then Steve understood *why* he felt no pain. He had automatically held up his left arm to protect himself, and the saw had hit the plaster close to his elbow and lopped off a slice. He had raised the injured arm defensively high above his head, out of the way, and it was still there, poised, waiting to be brought down. It felt very heavy.

Perhaps Stook recognized the danger because he snarled, adjusted his position, and side-stepped hurriedly. He lost his balance, and was on one foot when Steve's plaster-of-Paris club landed just above his right ear. The saw, on a dead-man's switch, went off.

There was a crack as Stook's neck broke, and he flew back against the bench sideways, smashing his head on its wooden top as he did so. His skull cracked open like an egg. Inside it, there were things Steve had not expected to see. There was no blood or brain. Instead, Stook's head was stuffed with what looked like dust, ashes and blackened, shapeless objects that could have been lumps of charcoal, the remains of an ancient fire that had long ago gone out.

Steve stood motionless over his employer's body, staring incredulously as the contents of the man's head crumbled in a miniature landslide onto the surface of water splashing around it from the nearby hose. The ash-like substance floated swiftly away in dark, swirling streaks towards the drain.

Stook's dark glasses had stayed on in the struggle, as though welded to his nose. Steve reached down to remove them.

As he bent forward, someone grasped him by the shoulder and said, "For God's sake, what have you done?"

It was Amanda's voice. Steve jerked upright and turned slowly, dreading what he was about to see. He half expected to find behind him a dismembered corpse, hastily reconstructed perhaps, and topped by a dead but talking head.

Amanda looked battered and bruised. She had a bandage around her head, and a long, stitched-up cut across her forehead. Her face, where it was visible, was dove grey, and her skin had the texture of tightly stretched shiny paper.

"You're alive," Steve said, and looked across at the lumps of flesh on the bench. "I thought that was you. I saw your clothes; the blood stains . . . ?"

"I smashed the van last night, soon after I'd dropped you at the hospital. I got hurt."

"Then who has Stook cut up?"

"The girl who used to do your job. She didn't last long. She fell into a quarry in the fog one night. She died. Stook made me bring her back. He put her in the freezer as emergency rations for the creature. He couldn't get out today so . . .

"She's still not thawed out, or there would be a lot more blood everywhere. The tools Stook used made a mess of a fresh corpse."

"Anyway, *Stook* is dead," Steve blurted tipsily, as though to reassure himself. "That animal will have died with him. And the monkeys can't hurt you if you get drunk. I've worked it all out. We're free of the lot of them."

"What do you mean, 'the animal will have died with him'?" she said.

"Christ, you must know *that*. You *must* have realized? Stook and that creature were one and the same. Stook was a werewolf, or something of the kind. It's bloody obvious."

The girl gave Steve an agonized look that made his heart sink into his gut. She shook her head. "He was just a man, or what was left of one. As to the creature . . ."

"Oh, *come on*, Amanda. You never saw the two of them together, ever, because they were the same thing in different forms." He gestured towards the sprawling corpse with the toe of a soggy trainer. "And you can't tell me *that* is just a man. His whole body is covered with hair, and see what he's got in his head! It looks like the inside of an oven after somebody burnt the dinner. And let's take a look at his eyes . . . !"

The girl stooped and removed Stook's tinted shades.

To reveal two red but human eyes set in dark tunnels deep behind the man's brow.

"I thought his eyes would be like the creature's," Steve said. "I was sure of it."

"He couldn't stand bright light, that's all. He *was* a man," Amanda insisted. "An incredibly old one, but that," she pointed into Stook's now half-empty skull, "is what happens to you when you have been preserved, kept alive for a very long time."

"From the look of him, he was in his seventies at most!"

"Stook was over two hundred and fifty years old. He was born in 1741."

"I don't believe it."

She glared angrily at him and snapped, "Tell me then; what age do you think I am?"

"Late twenties. No more."

"I *was* twenty-five, when Stook first employed me."

"When was that?"

"In 1926."

Steve slapped his head with his right palm. "It hurts me to say it, Amanda, but I think you're very confused. I've noticed before. You've got a real problem."

She almost laughed. "I've got plenty of them, and so have you. Even more, now Stook is dead."

"Exactly; so he can't harm us, or make us do anything we don't want to. And like I said, if you get pissed, the monkeys . . ."

"Forget that. You may be drunk now, but can't stay drunk for ever. You will have to sleep, and then, when you've sobered up, your monkey won't repeat the same mistake. Alcohol was something new, something it hadn't come across before. But it won't ever let you near drink again."

"Why should it bother with me, now Stook's gone? There's no one to work for. And I tell you; that creature *will* have disappeared. I *know it*."

Amanda sounded at the edge of her patience. "What makes you think the monkeys worked for Stook? He had his own monkey. It must have got him when he was middle-aged, over two hundred years ago.

"I found out a lot about him. He was famous once, and very rich, born into a family of fabulously successful merchants. He stayed in the business, and twice went exploring in Asia, looking for rare spices, and anything else he could sell. On the first voyage, he did well. On his second trip, an expedition to Tibet and God-knows-where beyond, he must have found more than he bargained for, or it found him, because he came back with that creature and, unknown to anyone but himself, a monkey on his back.

"The animal itself was a seven day wonder. There were all manner of strange things turning up in England then, in 1783; animate and inanimate items brought back to civilization from all over the world, and Stook's companion was just another outlandish oddity among many. Nobody knew about its peculiar appetite then, or perhaps someone *did*, as, shortly after his return, Stook faded from the limelight, retired to the country, and became a recluse. He vanished. And there's no record anywhere that he ever died. I'm sure of that; I've looked. So I know what I'm talking about. I know my man."

Steve frowned. The implications of what Amanda was saying were beginning to sink in. She knew what she was talking about. It all sounded true. Suddenly, she didn't seem crazy at all. And he was sobering up fast. And getting scared.

"But I thought Stook was in charge," he said. "You're telling me he was just a slave," he pointed to the bolted door at the end of the room, "to that *thing*?"

"Just like you and me; you've got there at last," said Amanda, bleakly ironic. "The creature runs the monkeys, and the monkeys run us. It's what's known as a symbiotic relationship and, from one point of view, it works almost perfectly."

"The creature's?"

"Well, it's not ours." She put a cigarette between her lips and lit it awkwardly, her lighter wavering in an unsteady hand. She smoked it quickly, in silence, while Steve absorbed what she had told him.

Then the creature in the room beyond began to howl, and Amanda's monkey gave her neck a jolt that threatened to tear her head off.

She went out of the room and came back immediately, pushing a stainless steel trolley. She rolled up her sleeves and began loading hunks of Steve's predecessor onto the trolley. He watched her limping painfully around the butcher's bench. She banged against the bag with the head in it, causing it to swing on its nail like the pendulum of some squat, cumbersome clock. He tried to find the courage to go and help her, but his mind was full of horror and a descending, impending monster headache. He was sober now, and feeling very bad. He remembered why he had always avoided drink; because he got terrible hangovers.

"Any moment now," he thought, "my monkey will wake up. It's going to feel sick too, and it will want to make me suffer. It's time to get out of here while I can. I need more drink to keep the monkey quiet while I work out what to do next."

He explained his plan to Amanda, who did not respond. Her face had twisted into a grotesque mask of pain. Blood seeped from the cut across her forehead, and her movements were jerky and uncoordinated. Steve guessed her monkey was giving her a hard time, pushing her faster than she could go in an effort to get the creature fed quickly.

He wondered if there was any way the hungry thing, locked in the room where it lived, could get itself out. He doubted it. How long would it take to starve in there? Amanda had said it *had* to have fresh meat four times a week. Perhaps, like certain rodents, it consumed energy very quickly! It might burn itself out in a few days.

If he and Amanda could both stay drunk for a week or more, they would have a chance . . .

"Amanda," he shouted. "We have to get out of here now."

She gave no indication she had heard, and seemed to be struggling to work even faster. Most of the joints of human meat were on the trolley. Suddenly, she started to wheel it to the door that let into the creature's room.

Steve ran towards her. "I'm taking you out of here," he yelled, "if I have to carry you. Your monkey will hurt you, but don't try to stop me. Try to relax."

She had her back to him when he reached her. He grabbed her right shoulder with his good arm, and attempted to pull her round. As he touched her, two small hard hands grasped the top of his jacket, and something invisible jumped from her onto him and began clambering up his chest.

At the same moment, the monkey lodged within him jerked awake. It squawked like a mad macaw inside his head. For the first time, an image of its face: savage, alien, birdlike, with a blunt but serrated-edged beak instead of jaws, and tiny, cold, furious eyes, projected onto the screen of his mind's eye.

It began to thrash and peck and kick. It hit with its fists at the back of his eyes as though it were trying to punch them out. It reached down with its back legs towards his heart to grasp it, to stop it beating.

And the one on his chest had him by the throat. It was digging its taloned fingers into the flesh, forcing his head ever further back, threatening to snap his spine.

Steve could do nothing about the two monkeys that were tearing him apart from within and without, but somehow he got his arm around Amanda's waist and lifted her off her feet. She would not, or could not, co-operate. She squirmed and twisted as he lurched towards the door with her under his right arm. She weighed next to nothing and her struggles were weak, but even so, Steve found he couldn't hold her. The monkey in his head, that seemed to be trying to hack its way out through his eye sockets, was blinding him. Also, it was affecting his balance. It somehow twisted his brain like a steering wheel, so he lost all sense of direction. It got to the point where he was unable to differentiate between up and down. The room seemed like a huge sphere that he was trapped in. Then he realized he no longer had hold of Amanda, and that he was falling. He thought he had walked off the edge of a cliff. The thing in his head gave a scream of triumph.

And something hit him in the belly, like a kick from a vast boot.

And then: nothing!

Amanda swayed back as the dismembered head in the plastic shopping bag bounced off Steve's stomach. She had snatched the bag off the nail at the end of the bench and swung it at him hard, in desperation. There was no other weapon in the room she could have used except the electric saws, and she might have killed him with them. She wanted to keep him alive.

As Steve doubled forward, clutching his middle, Amanda swung the head again, battering Steve's own face with it. He slumped forward like a shot deer, and landed face down in the drain near the bench. She knelt down and tugged his right shoulder up, to twist his nose and mouth up out of the water. He mustn't drown. She checked that he was still breathing, then sat down next to him in the wet.

The creature in the next room was calling for food with its harsh, crass, rook-like call.

Amanda's monkey, that had jumped back off Steve and onto her when the boy had been trying to carry her away, sent a stab of pain down her spine, to urge her to make one last effort to get up and push the trolley through to its master. But Amanda couldn't even get to her feet. She was breathless, and all her energy was spent. Her monkey, that had known and preserved her for more than sixty years, understood, and allowed her a brief respite to regain some strength.

Amanda fumbled in her pockets, found a battered packet of cigarettes, stuck one in her mouth, and lit up. She drew as much smoke as she could into her diseased, rotten lungs, exulting in the self-damage she was doing, in the knowledge that her ruined, broken body could not take much more abuse. She knew the creature and its servants, the monkeys, would keep her going as long as she was at all useful to them, or until she fell apart.

As it was, she was only just able to get around on her legs, they contained so many badly mended broken bones, souvenirs of the years she herself had spent walking the "dog". Now, she was barely able to drive the van. The accident the night before had been her fault. She had been too weak and clumsy to control the vehicle. Anyone else would have been able to avoid the accident. Unfortunately, she had not been killed in the smash.

Anyway, soon, when his wrist had healed, Steve would be able to drive the van.

Then, presumably, she would not be needed. They would let her die.

The creature beyond the door croaked again impatiently.

She got to her feet, pushed Steve's unconscious body over onto its back, and flicked her cigarette end into the drain.

She looked down at the boy for a moment, then said aloud, "Congratulations Steve, you've been promoted. You'll have to advertise to get someone to replace you. You've got Stook's job. You're the hunter now. Tomorrow, the van will be repaired, and I'll have to drive you out to look for game. The creature will need fresh meat, and heaven help you if you don't come back with some."

Briefly it occurred to her that if Steve *was* unsuccessful, she might be on the menu herself.

Then her monkey gave her mind a tweak. She pushed the meat trolley to the door, and started to open the locks.

POPPY Z. BRITE

Mussolini and the Axeman's Jazz

POPPY Z. BRITE WAS BORN in 1967, in New Orleans, where she currently lives with her husband Christopher, a chef and food writer.

She has worked as an artist's model, a mouse caretaker, a stripper and (since 1991) a full-time writer. She has published three novels to date, *Lost Souls*, *Drawing Blood* and *Exquisite Corpse*. Her short stories and articles have appeared in numerous periodicals, including *Rage*, *Spin* and *The Village Voice*, and her fiction has been collected in *Wormwood* (aka *Swamp Foetus*).

She is also the editor of the anthologies *Love in Vein* and *Love in Vein II* and her most recent project is the biography *Courtney Love: The Real Story*, published by Simon & Schuster in America and Orion in Britain.

About the following story, the author reveals: "It was written for a White Wolf anthology and had to include one or more of their gaming creatures (Wraiths, Mages, Vampires, and Werewolves). Since Harlan Ellison's story in a previous volume had only a sort of green mist oozing in at the end, I figured I could interpret pretty broadly. I began with the true story of New Orleans' only known serial killer, threw in some conspiracy theory, and went from there . . ."

SARAJEVO, 1914

STONE TURRETS AND CRENELLATED columns loomed on either side of the Archduke's motorcade. The crowd parted before the open carriages, an indistinct blur of faces. Francis Ferdinand swallowed some of the unease that had been plaguing him all day: a bitter bile, a constant burn at the back of his throat.

It was his fourteenth wedding anniversary. Sophie sat beside him, a bouquet of scarlet roses at her bosom. These Serbs and Croats were a friendly crowd; as the heir apparent of Austria-Hungary, Francis Ferdinand stood to give them an equal voice in his empire. Besides, Sophie was a Slav, the daughter of a noble Czech family. Surely his marriage to a northern Slav had earned him the sympathy of these southern ones.

Yet the Archduke could not divest himself of the notion that there was a menacing edge to the throng. The occasional vivid detail – a sobbing baby, a flower tucked behind the ear of a beautiful woman – was lost before his eyes could fully register it. He glanced at Sophie. In the summer heat he could smell her sweat mingling with the *eau de parfum* she had dabbed on this morning.

She met his gaze and smiled faintly. Beneath her veil, her sweet face shone with perspiration. Back in Vienna, Sophie was snubbed by his court because she had been a lady-in-waiting when she met the Archduke, little better than a servant in their eyes. Francis Ferdinand's uncle, the old Emperor Francis Joseph, forbade the marriage. When the couple married anyway, Sophie was ostracized in a hundred ways. Francis Ferdinand knew it was sometimes a painful life for her, but she remained a steadfast wife, an exemplary mother.

For this reason he had brought her on the trip to Sarajevo. It was a routine army inspection for him, but for her it was a chance to be treated with the royal honours she deserved. On this anniversary of their blessed union, Sophie would endure no subtle slights, no calculated cruelties.

The Archduke had never loved another human being. His parents were hazy memories, his uncle a shambling old man whose time had come and gone. Even his three children brought him more distraction than joy. The first time he laid eyes on Sophie, he discerned in her an empathy such as he had never seen before. Her features, her mannerisms, her soft ample body

– all bespoke a comfort Francis Ferdinand had never formerly craved, but suddenly could not live without.

The four cars approached the Čumuria Bridge. A pall of humidity hung over the water. The Archduke felt his skin steaming inside his heavy uniform, and his uneasiness intensified. He knew how defenceless they must look in the raised carriage, in the Serbian sun, the green feathers on his helmet drooping, Sophie's red roses beginning to wilt.

As they passed over the bridge, he saw an object arc out of the crowd and come hurtling toward him. In an instant his eye marked it as a crude hand bomb.

Francis Ferdinand raised his arm to protect Sophie and felt hot metal graze his flesh.

Gavrilo Princip's pistol left a smell on his palm like greasy coins, metallic and sour. It was a cheap thing from Belgium, as likely to blow his hand off as anything else. Still, it was all Gavrilo had, and he was the only one left to murder the villainous fool whose good intentions would crush Serbia.

He had known the other six would fail him. They were a young and earnest lot, always ready to sing the praises of a Greater Serbia, but reluctant to look a man in the face and kill him. They spoke of the sanctity of human life, a short-sighted sentiment in Gavrilo's opinion. Human life was a fleeting thing, an expendable thing. The glory of a nation could endure through the ages. What his comrades failed to fully comprehend was that it must be oiled with human blood.

He raked his dirty hair back from his face and stared along the motorcade route. It looked as if the cars were finally coming. He took a deep breath. As the wet, sooty air entered his lungs, Gavrilo was seized with a racking cough that lasted a full minute. He had no handkerchief, so he cupped his hand over his mouth. When he pulled it away, his fingers were speckled with fresh blood. He and his six comrades were all tubercular, and none of them expected to live past thirty. The fevers, the lassitude, the night sweats, the constant tickling itch deep in the chest – all these made the cyanide capsules they carried in their pockets a source of comfort rather than of dread.

Now the task was left to him. Mohammed and Nedjelko, the first two along the route, were carrying hand bombs. One of them had heaved his bomb – Gavrilo had seen it go flying – but the motorcade had continued toward City Hall with no apparent damage. His comrades between Čumuria Bridge and City Hall – Vasco, Cvijetko, Danilo, Trifko – had done nothing.

The Archduke's carriage moved slowly through the crowd, then braked and came to a standstill less than five feet from Gavrilo. This struck him as nothing short of a miracle, God telling him to murder the villains for the glory of Serbia.

He fired twice. The pistol did not blow his hand off. He saw Countess Sophie sag against her husband, saw blood on the Archduke's neck. The deed was done as well as he could do it. Gavrilo turned the pistol on himself, but before he could fire, it was knocked out of his hand. The crowd surged over him.

Gavrilo got his hand into his pocket, found the cyanide capsule and brought it to his mouth. Hundreds of hands were rippling at him, pummelling him. His teeth cracked the capsule open. The foul taste of bitter almonds flooded his mouth. He retched, swallowed, vomited, convulsed. The crowd would surely pull him to pieces. He felt his guts unmooring, his bones coming loose from their sockets, and still he could not die.

Sophie stood on the steps of City Hall between her husband and Fehim Effendi Curcić, the burgomaster of Sarajevo. Though Sophie and several of her attendants were bleeding from superficial cuts caused by splinters of the bomb casing, and twelve spectators had been taken to hospital, Curcić obviously had no idea that the motorcade had come close to being blown up. He was surveying the crowd, a pleased look on his fat face. "Our hearts are filled with happiness – " he began.

Francis Ferdinand was white with anger. He grabbed the burgomaster's arm and shouted into his face. "One comes here for a visit and is received with bombs! Mr Mayor, what do you say?"

Curcić still didn't understand. He smiled blandly at the Archduke and launched into his welcome speech again. The Archduke let him continue this time, looking disgusted. Never once did Curcić mention the bombing attempt.

Sophie gripped her husband's hand. She could see Francis Ferdinand gradually pulling himself together. He was a man of inflexible opinions and sudden rages, painfully thin-skinned, capable of holding a grudge for eternity. He was like a spoiled child, bragging that he had shot five thousand stags, darkly hinting that he had brought down as many political enemies. But Sophie loved him. Not even her children fulfilled her vast need to be needed. This man did.

There was a delay while Francis Ferdinand sent a wire to the Emperor, who would have heard about the bomb. The Army wanted to continue with the day's events, but the Archduke insisted upon first visiting the wounded spectators in the hospital.

He turned to Sophie. "You must not come. The risk is too great; there could be another attack."

Fear clutched at her heart: of dying, of losing him. "No, I must go with you," she told him, and Francis Ferdinand did not argue. When they entered their carriage again, Oskar Potiorek, the military governor, climbed in with them. His presence made Sophie feel a little safer.

The motorcade rolled back through the thronged streets. When they turned a corner, Sophie saw a sign marking Francis Joseph Street. Just as she noticed this, Potiorek sat up straighter and cried, "What's this? We've taken the wrong way!"

The driver braked. The motorcade ground to a halt. Sophie felt something graze the top of her head, a sharp stinging sensation. The Archduke's head snapped to one side. At the same time, Sophie felt something like a white-hot fist punch into her belly.

Through a haze of agony she reached for her husband. He leaned toward her, and a torrent of blood gushed from his mouth. She crumpled into his arms. Attendants swarmed around them, asked Francis Ferdinand if he was suffering. The last thing Sophie heard was her husband replying in a wet whisper, "It is nothing . . . it is nothing."

They were both dead before the sun had reached its apex in the blazing sky.

NEW ORLEANS, 1918

New Orleans is commonly thought of as a French and Spanish town. "Creole", a word now used to describe rich food of a certain seasoning and humans of a certain shade, first referred to the inevitable mixture of French and Spanish blood that began appearing several years after the city's founding. The buildings of the *Vieux Carré* were certainly shaped and adorned by the ancestry of their builders: the Spanish courtyards and ironwork, the French cottages with their carved wooden shutters and pastel paint, the wholly European edifice of St Louis Cathedral.

But, block by sagging block, the *Vieux Carré* was abandoned by these upwardly mobile people. By the turn of the century it had become a slum. A wave of Sicilian immigrants moved in. Many of them opened groceries, imported and sold the necessities of life. Some were honest businessmen, some were criminals; most made no such clear distinction. The *onorata società* offered them a certain amount of protection from the hoodlums who roamed the French Quarter. Naturally they required a payment for this service, and if a man found himself in a position to do them a favour – legal or otherwise – he had no choice but to oblige.

The Italians gradually branched out of the Quarter into every part of the city, and New Orleans became as fully an Italian town as a French or Spanish one.

Joseph D'Antonio, formerly Detective of the New Orleans Police Department, had been drinking on the balcony of his second-storey hovel since late this afternoon. Bittersweet red wine, one bottle before the sun went down, another two since. His cells soaked it up like bread.

Two weeks in, this hot and sticky May portended a hellish summer. Even late at night, his balcony was the only place he could catch an occasional breath of air, usually tinged with the fetor of the Basin Canal nearby. Most nights, he had to force himself not to pass out here. These days, few things in his life were worse than waking up with a red-wine hangover and the morning sun in his eyes.

D'Antonio was forty-three. The circumstances of his early retirement had been as randomly cruel as the violence that presaged it. A crazed beat cop named Mullen walked into headquarters one afternoon and gunned down Chief Inspector Jimmy Reynolds. In the confusion that followed, an innocent captain also named Mullen was shot dead. Someone had come charging in and asked what happened, and someone else was heard to yell, "Mullen killed Reynolds!"

The yeller was Joe D'Antonio. Unfortunately, the dead Mullen had been widely known to harbour a strong dislike for Italians in general and D'Antonio in particular. No one accused him directly, but everyone wondered. His life became a hell of suspicious looks and nasty innuendo. Six months later, the new chief persuaded him to take early retirement.

D'Antonio leaned on the rickety railing and stared at the empty street. Until last year he had lived on the fringes of Storyville, the red light district. In the confusion of wartime patriotism, somebody had decided Storyville was a bad influence on Navy boys, and all the whorehouses were shut down. Now the buildings were dark and shabby, broken windows covered with boards or gaping like hungry mouths, lacework balconies sagging, opulent fixtures sold away or crumbling to dust.

D'Antonio could live without the whores, though some of them had been good enough gals. But he missed the music that had drifted up from Storyville every night, often drawing him out to some smoky little dive where he could drink and jazz away the hours till dawn. Players like Jelly Roll Morton, King Oliver, and some new kid named Armstrong kept him sane throughout the bad months just after he left the force. He got to know some of the musicians, smoked reefer with them from time to time, warned them when undercover presence indicated a bust might be imminent.

Now they were gone. There were still jazz clubs in the city, but many of the players D'Antonio knew had moved to Chicago when Storyville closed down. They could record in Chicago, make money. And in Chicago they didn't have to sleep, drink, eat, and piss according to signs posted by white men.

Pissing sounded like a fine idea. He stood, steadied himself on the railing, and walked inside. The place had none of this modern indoor plumbing, and the odour of the slop jar filled the two airless rooms. Still, he'd never stooped so low as to piss off the balcony as some of his neighbours did, at least not that he could remember.

D'Antonio unbuttoned his fly and aimed into the jar. Behind him, the shutters on the French doors slammed shut with a report loud as a double-barrelled shotgun in the airless night. His hand jerked. Urine sprayed the dingy wall.

When he'd finished pissing and cursing the freak wind, he wiped the wall with a dirty sock, then went back to the balcony doors. It was too hot in here with the shutters closed, and too dark. D'Antonio pushed them open again.

There was a man standing on the balcony, and the shutters passed right through him.

Francis Ferdinand scowled in annoyance. The first flesh-and-blood creature he'd met since his inglorious exit from this plane, and of course the fellow had to be stinking drunk.

Perhaps his drunkenness would make Francis Ferdinand's job easier. Who could know? When one had to put himself together from whatever stray wisps of ectoplasm he could snatch out of the ether, it became increasingly difficult to fathom the minds of living men and women.

Joseph D'Antonio had a shock of black hair streaked with silver and a pale complexion that had gone florid from the wine. His dark eyes were comically wide, seeming to start from their sockets. "Hell, man, you're a *ghost*! You're a goddamned *ghost*, ain'tcha?"

English had never been one of his better languages, but Francis Ferdinand was able to understand D'Antonio perfectly. Even the drunken slur and the slight accent did not hinder him. He winced at the term. "A *wraith*, sir, if you please."

D'Antonio waved a dismissive hand. The resulting current of air nearly wafted the Archduke off the balcony. "Wraith, ghost, whatever. S'all the same to me. Means I'll be goin' headfirst off that balcony if I don't get to bed soon. By accident . . . or on purpose? I dunno . . ."

Francis Ferdinand realized he would have to speak his piece at once, before the man slipped into maudlin incoherence. "Mr D'Antonio, I do not come to you entirely by choice. You might say I have been despatched. I died in the service of my country. I saw my beloved wife die, and pass into the Beyond. Yet I remain trapped in a sort of half-life. To follow her, I must do one more thing, and I must request your help."

Francis Ferdinand paused, but D'Antonio remained silent. His eyes were alert, his aspect somewhat more sober than before.

"I must kill a man," the Archduke said at last.

D'Antonio's face twitched. Then he burst into sudden laughter. "That's a good one! You gotta kill somebody, but you can't, 'cause you're a goddamn ghost!"

"Please, sir, I am a *wraith*! There are *class structures* involved here!"

"Sure. Whatever. Well, sorry, Duke. I handed over my gun when I left the force. Can't help you."

"You addressed me as 'Duke' just now, Mr D'Antonio."

"Yeah, so? You're the Archduke, ain'tcha? The one who got shot at the beginning of the war?"

Francis Ferdinand was stunned. He had expected to have to explain everything to the man: his own useless assassination; the ensuing bedlam into which Europe had tumbled, country after country; the dubious relevance of these events to others in New Orleans. He was glad to discover that, at least in one respect, he had underestimated D'Antonio.

"Yeah, I know who you are. I might look like an ignorant wop, but I read the papers. Besides, there's a big old bullet hole in your neck."

Startled, the Archduke quickly patched the wound.

"Then, sir, that is one less thing I must explain to you. You have undoubtedly heard that I was murdered by Serbs. This is the first lie. I was murdered by Sicilians."

"But the men they caught – "

"Were Serbs, yes. They were also dupes. The plot was set in motion by your countrymen; specifically, by a man called Cagliostro. Perhaps you've heard of him."

"Some kind of magician?"

"A mage, yes. Also a doctor, a swindler, a forger, and a murderer. He is more than a century old, yet retains the appearance of a man of thirty. A wicked, dangerous man.

"He was born Giuseppe Balsamo in Palermo, 1743. By the time he began his scourge of Europe, he had dubbed himself Cagliostro, an old family name. He travelled the continent selling charms, potions, elixirs of youth. Some of these may have been genuine, as he himself ceased to age at this time.

"He also became a Freemason. Are you familiar with them as well?"

"Not particularly."

"They are a group of powerful mages hell-bent on controlling the world. They erect heathen temples in which they worship themselves and their accomplishments. Cagliostro formed his own 'Egyptian Order' and claimed to be thousands of years old already, reminiscing about his dalliances with Christ and various Pharaohs. It was power he sought, of course, though he claimed to work only for the 'Brotherhood of Man'.

"At the peak of his European success, he became entangled in the famous scandal of Marie Antoinette's diamond necklace. It nearly brought him down. He was locked in the Bastille, then forced to leave Paris in disgrace. He wandered back through the European cities that had once welcomed him, finding scant comfort. It has been rumoured that he died in a dungeon in Rome, imprisoned for practices offensive to the Christian church.

"This is not so. His Masonic 'brothers' failed him for a time, but ultimately they removed him from the dungeon, whisked him out from under the noses of the French revolutionary armies who wished to make him a hero, and smuggled him off to Egypt.

"The practices he perfected there are unspeakable.

"Fifty years later, still appearing a young and vital man, he returned to Italy. He spent the next half century assembling a new 'Egyptian Order' of the most brilliant men he could find. With a select few, he shared his elixirs.

"Just after the turn of the century, he met a young journalist named Benito Mussolini, who called himself an 'apostle of violence' but had no direction. Cagliostro has guided Mussolini's career since then. In 1915, Mussolini's newspaper helped urge Italy into war."

D'Antonio started violently. "Aw, come on! You're not gonna tell me these Egyptian-Dago-Freemasons started the war."

"Sir, that is exactly what I am going to tell you. They also ordered my wife's death, and my own, and that of my empire."

"Why in hell would they do that?"

"I cannot tell you. They are evil men. My uncle, the Emperor Francis Joseph, discovered all this inadvertently. He was a cowardly old fool who would have been afraid to tell anyone. Nevertheless, they hounded him into virtual retirement, where he died."

"And told you all this?"

"He had no one else to talk to. Nor did I."

"Where's your wife?"

"Sophie was not required to linger here. We were."

"Why?"

"I cannot tell you."

"You keep saying that. Does it mean you don't know, or you aren't *allowed* to tell me?"

Francis Ferdinand paused. After a moment, D'Antonio nodded. "I see how it is. So I'm supposed to dance for you like Mussolini does for Cagliostro?"

The Archduke did not understand the question. He waited

to see if D'Antonio would rephrase it, but the man remained silent. Finally Francis Ferdinand said, "Cagliostro still controls Mussolini, and means to shape him into the most vicious ruler Europe has ever known. But Cagliostro is no longer in Italy. He is here in New Orleans."

"Oh-ho. And you want me to kill him for you, is that it?"

"Yes, but I haven't finished. Cagliostro is in New Orleans – *but we don't know who he is.*"

"*We?* Who's *we?*"

"Myself, my uncle."

"No one else?"

"No one else you would care to know about, sir."

D'Antonio sagged in his chair. "Yeah, well, forget it. I'm not killin' anybody. Find some other poor dupe."

"Are you certain, Mr D'Antonio?"

"Very certain."

"Very well." Francis Ferdinand drifted backward through the balcony railing and vanished in midair.

"Wait!" D'Antonio was halfway out of his chair by the time he realized the wraith was gone. He sank back, his brain seasick in his skull from all the talk of mages and murders, elixirs and dungeons, and the famous scandal of Marie Antoinette's diamond necklace – whatever the hell that was.

"Why me?" he murmured into the hot night. But the night made no reply.

Cagliostro stood behind his counter and waited on the last customer of the day, an old lady buying half a pound of salt cod. When she had gone, he locked the door and had his supper: a small loaf of bread, a thick wedge of *provolone*, a few olives chopped with garlic. He no longer ate the flesh of creatures, though he must sell it to maintain the appearance of a proper Italian grocery.

Above his head hung glossy loops of sausage and salami, rafters of wind-dried ham and *pancetta*, luminous globes of *caciocavallo* cheese. In the glass case were pots of creamy *ricotta*, stuffed artichokes, orbs of *mozzarella* in milk, bowls of shining olives and capers preserved in brine. On the neat wooden shelves were jars of candied fruit, almonds, pine nuts, aniseed, and a rainbow of assorted sweets. There were tall wheels of *parmesan* coated in funereal black wax, cruets of olive oil and vinegar, pickled cucumbers and mushrooms, flat tins containing anchovies, calamari, octopus. Enormous burlap sacks of red beans, fava beans, chickpeas, rice, couscous, and coffee threatened to spill their bounty onto the spotless tile floor. Pastas of every shape, size, and colour were arranged in an elaborate display of bins facing the counter.

The aroma of the place was a balm to Cagliostro's ancient soul. He carried the world's weight on his back every day; he had pledged his very life to the furthering of the Brotherhood of Man; still, that did not mean he could shirk small duties. He fed the families of his neighbourhood. When they could not pay, he fed them on credit, and when there was no hope of recovering the credit, he fed them for free.

He had caused death, to be sure. He had caused the deaths of the Archduke and his wife for several reasons, most importantly the malignant forces that hung over Europe like black clouds heavy with rain. Such a rain could mean the death of millions, hundreds of millions. The longer it was allowed to stagnate, the more virulent it would grow. It had needed some spark to release it, some event whose full significance was hidden at first, then gradually revealed. The assassination in Sarajevo had been that event, easy enough to arrange by providing the dim-witted Serbian anarchists with encouragement and weapons.

His name was synonymous with elaborate deception, and not undeservedly so. But some of his talents were genuine. In his cards and scrying-bowl Cagliostro could read the future, and the future looked very dark.

He, of course, would change all that.

This war was nearly over. It had drained some of the poison from those low-hanging clouds, allowed Europe to shatter and purge itself. But it had not purged enough; there would be another great war inside of two decades. In that one, his boy Benito would send thousands of innocent men to their useless deaths. But that was not as bad as what could be.

Though he had never killed a man with his own hands, Cagliostro bitterly felt the loss of the human beings who died as a result of his machinations. They were his brothers and sisters; he mourned each one as he would a lovely temple he had never seen, upon hearing it had been demolished. He could not accept that their sacrifice was a natural thing, but he had come to understand that it was necessary.

Mussolini was more than a puppet; he was a powerful orator and propagandist who would learn to yank his followers in any direction that pleased him. But he was unbalanced, ultimately no better than a fool, ignorant of the Mysteries, incapable of seeing them when a few of the topmost veils were pulled aside. He would make an excellent pawn, and he would die believing he had engineered his own destiny.

The only reason he could be allowed into power was to prevent something far worse.

Cagliostro had seen another European tyrant in his cards and his bowl, a man who made Mussolini look like a painted tin soldier. Mussolini was motivated exclusively by power, and that was bad enough; but this other creature was a bottomless well of hatred. Given the chance, he would saturate all creation with his vitriol. Millions would die like vermin, and their corpses would choke the world. The scrying-water had shown terrifying factories built especially for disposal of the dead, ovens hot enough to reduce bone to ash, black smokestacks belching greasy smoke into a charred orange sky.

Cagliostro did not yet know this tyrant's precise identity, but he believed that the man would come from Austria and rule Germany. Two more good reasons for the Archduke's death: Francis Ferdinand would have made a powerful ally for such a man.

Cagliostro did not think he could altogether stop this tyrant. He had not foreseen it in time; he had been occupied with other matters. It was always thus when a man wished to save the world: he never knew where to look first, let alone where to begin.

Still, he believed he could stop the tyrant short of global domination, and he believed Mussolini was his key. Members of the Order in Italy were grooming him for Prime Minister. The title would unlock every door in Europe. If they could arrange for Mussolini to become the tyrant's ally, perhaps they could also ensure that Mussolini would in some way cause the tyrant's downfall.

Cagliostro finished his simple supper, collected the day's receipts, and turned off the lights. In the half-darkness he felt his way back to the small living quarters behind the store, where he sat up reading obscure volumes and writing long letters in a florid hand until nearly dawn. Over the past century, he had learned to thrive on very little sleep.

D'Antonio was sitting up in bed, back propped against the wooden headboard, bare legs sprawled atop the sweat-rumpled coverlet, bottle nestled between his thighs. The Archduke appeared near the sink. D'Antonio jumped, slopped wine onto the coverlet, cursed. "You gotta make me stain something every time you show up?"

"You need have no fear of me."

"No, you just want me to murder somebody for you. Why should that scare me?"

"It should not, sir. What should scare you is the prospect of a world ruled by Cagliostro and his Order."

"That guy again. Find him yet?"

"We know he came to New Orleans before 1910. We know he is living as an Italian grocer. But he has covered his tracks so successfully that we cannot determine his precise identity. We have a number of candidates."

"That's good." D'Antonio nodded, pretended to look thoughtful. "So you just gonna kill all of 'em, or what?"

"I cannot kill anyone, sir. I cannot even lift a handkerchief. That is why I require your help."

"I thought I told you last time, Duke. My services are unavailable. Now kindly fuck off."

"I feared you would say that. You will not change your mind?"

"Not a chance."

"Very well."

D'Antonio expected the wraith to vanish as it had last time. Instead, Francis Ferdinand seemed to break apart before his eyes. The face dissolved into a blur, the fingers elongated into smokeswirls; then there was only a man-shaped shimmer of gossamer strands where the Archduke had been.

When D'Antonio breathed in, they all came rushing toward him.

He felt clammy filaments sliding up his nose, into his mouth, into the lubricated crevices of his eyesockets. They filled his lungs, his stomach; he felt exploratory tendrils venturing into his intestines. A profound nausea gripped him. It was like being devoured alive by grave-worms. The wraith's consciousness was saturating his own, blotting him out like ink spilled on a letter.

"*I offered you the chance to act of your own free will,*" Francis

Ferdinand said. The voice was a hideous papery whisper inside his skull now. "*Since you declined, I am given no choice but to help you along.*"

Joseph Maggio awoke to the sound of his wife choking on her own blood. Great hot spurts of it bathed his face. A tall figure stood by the bed, instrument of death in his upraised hand. Maggio recognized it as the axe from his own back yard woodpile, gleaming with fresh gore. It fell again with a sound like a cleaver going into a beef neckbone, and his wife was silent.

Maggio struggled to sit up as the killer circled to his side of the bed. He did not recognize the man. For a moment their eyes locked, and Maggio thought, *That man is already dead.*

"Cagliostro?" It was a raspy whisper, possibly German-accented, though the man looked Italian.

Wildly, Maggio shook his head. "No, no sir, my name's Joseph Maggio, I just run a little grocery and I never heard of no Cagli-whoever . . . oh Jesus-Mary-and-Joseph please don't hit me with that thing – "

The blade glittered in a deadly arc. Maggio sprawled halfway off the bed, blinded by a sudden wash of his own blood. The axe fell again and he heard his own skull crunching, felt blade squeak against bone as the killer wrenched it out. Another searing cut, then another, until a merciful blow severed his jugular and he died in a red haze.

It was found that the killer had gained access to the Maggios' home by chiselling out a panel in the back door. The chisel had belonged to Joseph Maggio, as had the axe, which was found in a pool of blood on the steps. People all over New Orleans searched their yards for axes and chisels, and locked away these potential implements of Hell.

A strange phrase was found chalked on the pavement a block from the Maggios' house: "Mrs Maggio is going to sit up tonight, just like Mrs Tony." Its significance has not been discovered to this day.

Maggio's two brothers were arrested on the grounds that the Maggios were Sicilians, and Sicilians were prone to die in family vendettas. They were released by virtue of public drunkenness – they had been out celebrating the younger one's draft notice on the night of the murders, and had staggered home scarcely able to move, let alone lift an axe.

The detective in charge of the case was shot to death by a burglar one week after the murders. The investigation languished. News of the Romanov family's murder by Bolsheviks in Russia eclipsed the Maggio tragedy. The temperature climbed as June wore on.

"*I detect Cagliostro's influences still at work on this plane,*" the Archduke said. "*We must move on to the next candidate.*"

Deep inside his own ectoplasm-snared brain, which the wraith kept docile with wine except when he needed to use the body, D'Antonio could only manage a feeble moan of protest.

A clear tropical dawn broke over New Orleans as John Zanca parked his wagon of fresh breads and cakes in front of Luigi Donatello's grocery. He could not tell whether the grocer and his wife were awake yet, so he decided to take their order around to the back door. He gathered up a fragrant armful of baked goods still warm from the oven and carried them down the narrow alley that led to the Donatellos' living quarters.

When he saw the back door with its lower left panel neatly chiselled out, his arms went limp. Cakes and loaves rained on the grass at his feet.

After a moment, Zanca stepped forward – careful not to crush any of the baked goods – and knocked softly on the door. He did not want to do so, but there seemed nothing else to do. When it swung open, he nearly screamed.

Before him stood Luigi Donatello, his face crusted with blood, his hair and moustache matted with it. Zanca could see three big gashes in his skull, white edges of bone, wet grey tissue swelling through the cracks. How could the man still be standing?

"My God," moaned Donatello. "My God."

Behind him, Zanca saw Mrs Donatello sprawled on the floor. The top of her head was a gory porridge. The slender stem of her neck was nearly cleaved in two.

"My God. My God. My God."

John Zanca closed his eyes and said a silent prayer for the Donatellos' souls and his own.

The newspapers competed with one another for the wildest theory regarding the Axeman, as the killer came to be known. He was a Mafia executioner, and the victims were fugitives from outlaw justice in Sicily. He was a vigilante patriot, and the victims were German spies masquerading as Italian grocers. He was an evil spirit. He was a voodoo priest. He was a woman. He was a policeman.

The Italian families of New Orleans, particularly those in the grocery business, barricaded their doors and fed their dogs raw meat to make them bloodthirsty. These precautions did not stop them from lying awake in the small hours, clutching a rosary or perhaps a revolver, listening for the scrape of the Axeman's chisel.

In high summer, when the city stank of oyster shells and ancient sewers, the killer returned. Two teenage sisters, Mary and Pauline Romano, saw their uncle butchered in his own bed. They could only describe the man as "dark, tall, wearing a dark suit and a black slouch hat."

Italian families with enemies began finding axes and chisels dropped in their yards, more like cruel taunts than actual threats. Some accused their enemies. Some accused other members of their families. Some said the families had brought it upon themselves. Tempers flared in the sodden August heat, and many killings were done with weapons other than axes. Men with shotguns sat guard over their sleeping families, nodding off, jerking awake at the slightest noise. A grocer shot his own dog; another nearly shot his own wife.

The city simmered in its own prejudice and terror, a piquant gumbo.

But the Axeman would not strike again that year.

D'Antonio came awake with a sensation like rising through cool water into sunlight. He tried to move his hands: they moved. He tried to open his eyes: the ceiling appeared, cracked and water-stained. Was it possible? Was the fucking monster really *gone*?

"Duke?" he whispered aloud into the empty room. His lips were dry, wine-parched. "Hey, Duke? You in there?"

To his own ears he sounded plaintive, as if he missed the parasitic murdering creature. But the silence in his head confirmed it. The wraith was gone.

He stared at his hands, remembering everything he had seen them do. How ordinary they looked, how incapable of swinging a sharp blade and destroying a man's brain, a woman's brain.

For a long time he sat on the edge of the bed studying the beds of his nails and the creases in his palms, vaguely surprised that they were not caked with blood.

Eventually he looked down at himself and found that he was wearing only a filthy pair of trousers. He stripped them off, sponged himself to a semblance of cleanliness with the stale water in the basin, slicked his hair back and dressed in fresh clothes. He left his apartment without locking the door and set off in a random direction.

D'Antonio wandered hatless in the August sun for an hour or more. When he arrived at the *States* newspaper office, his face was streaming with sweat, red as a boiled crawfish. He introduced himself to the editor as a retired police detective, an expert on both Italians and murderers, and gave the following statement:

"The Axeman is a modern Doctor Jekyll and Mr Hyde. A criminal of this type may be a respectable, law-abiding citizen when he is his normal self. Compelled by an impulse to kill, he must obey this urge. Like Jack the Ripper, this sadist may go on with his periodic outbreaks until his death. For months, even for years, he may be normal, then go on another rampage. It is a mistake to blame the Mafia. The Mafia never attacks women as this murderer has done."

He left the *States* office with several people staring bemusedly after him, but they printed the interview in its entirety.

After that, he lived his life much as he had been doing before the wraith's first visit. Armistice Day brought throngs of joyous revellers into the streets, as well as a blessed wave of cool weather; it had stayed sweltering through October. The war was over, and surely the wraith would never come back and make him do those things again.

He could not forget the organic vibration that ran up his arms as blade buried itself in bone.

In fact, he dreamed about it almost every night.

Francis Ferdinand returned in the spring of 1919.

He did not muck about with appearances this time, but simply materialized inside D'Antonio's head. D'Antonio collapsed, clawing at his temples.

"*He deceived me for a time, but now I know he still walks this earth,*" said the wraith. "*We will find him.*"

D'Antonio lay curled on his side, blinded by tears of agony, wishing for the comforts of the womb or the grave.

Giacomo Lastanza was a powerful man, but he had been no match for the fiend in his bedroom. Now he lay on the floor with his head split as cleanly as a melon, and his wife Rosalia cowered in a corner of the room clutching her two-year-old daughter, Mary. Mary was screaming, clutching at her mother's long black hair. As the Axeman turned away from her husband's body, Rosalia began to scream too.

"Not my baby! Please, Holy Mother of God, not my baby!"

The axe fell. Mary's little face seemed to crack open like an egg. Rosalia was unconscious before her skull felt the blade's first kiss.

D'Antonio lay naked on the floor. The apartment was a wasteland of dirty clothes and empty wine bottles. But his body was relatively sober for once – they'd run out of money – and as a result he was sharp enough to be carrying on an argument with the wraith.

"Why in hell do we have to kill the women? You can't be worried one of *them* is Cagliostro."

"He has consorted with a number of dangerous women. When we find him, his wife will bear killing also."

"And until then, you don't mind killing a few innocent ones?"

"It is necessary."

"What about that little baby?"

"If it had been Cagliostro's daughter, he would have raised her to be as wicked as himself."

D'Antonio got control of one fist and weakly pounded the floor with it.

"You goddamn monster – you're just gonna keep wasting people, and sooner or later I'll get caught and rot in prison. Or fry in the chair. And you'll go on your merry way and find some other poor sap to chase down that shadow of yours."

"The next one must be him! He is the last one on the list!"

"Fuck the list."

A bolt of excruciating pain shot through D'Antonio's head, and he decided to drop the argument.

Cagliostro was reading by candlelight when he heard the chisel scraping at his door. He smiled and turned a page.

The creature crept into his room, saw him in his chair with his head bent over a book. When it was ten feet away, Cagliostro looked up. When it was five feet away, it froze in mid-motion, restrained by the protective circle he had drawn.

By looking into its eyes, he knew everything about Joseph D'Antonio and the Archduke Francis Ferdinand. But the creature upon which he gazed now was neither D'Antonio nor the Archduke; this was a twisted amalgamation of the two, and it could only be called the Axeman.

He smiled at the creature, though its eyes blazed with murderous rage. "Yes, poor Archduke, it is I. And you will not harm me. In fact, I fear I must harm you yet again. If only you had accepted the necessity of your death the first time, you would be Beyond with your beloved Sophie now.

"No, don't think you can desert your stolen body as it lies dying. You'll stay in there, my boy. My magic circle will see to that!" Cagliostro beamed; he was enjoying this immensely. "Yes, yes, I know about unfortunate ex-Detective D'Antonio trapped in there. But why do you think it was so easy for the Duke to take hold of your body, Mr D'Antonio, and make it do the terrible things it did? Perhaps because you care not at all for your fellow human beings? 'When they came for the Jews, I did nothing, for I was not a Jew . . .' ah, forgive me. An obscure reference to a future that may never be. And you will both die to help prevent it."

He reached beneath the cushion of his armchair, removed a silver revolver with elaborate engraving on the butt and barrel, aimed it carefully, and put a ball in the Axeman's tortured brain.

Then he put his book aside, went to his desk, and took up his pen.

The letter was published in the *Times-Picayune* the next day.

Hell, March 13, 1919

Editor of the Times-Picayune
New Orleans, La.

Esteemed Mortal:
They have never caught me and they never will. They have never seen me, for I am invisible, even as the ether that

surrounds your earth. I am not a human being, but a spirit and a fell demon from the hottest hell. I am what you Orleanians and your foolish police call the Axeman.

When I see fit, I shall come again and claim other victims. I alone know whom they shall be. I shall leave no clue except my bloody axe, besmeared with the blood and brains of he who I have sent below to keep me company.

If you wish, you may tell the police to be careful not to rile me. Of course, I am a reasonable spirit. I take no offence at the way they have conducted their investigations in the past. In fact, they have been so utterly stupid as to amuse not only me, but His Satanic Majesty, Francis Joseph, etc. But tell them to beware. Let them not try to discover what I am, for it were better that they were never born than to incur the wrath of the Axeman. I don't think there is any need for such a warning, for I feel sure the police will always dodge me, as they have in the past. They are wise and know how to keep away from all harm.

Undoubtedly, you Orleanians think of me as a most horrible murderer, which I am, but I could be much worse if I wanted to. If I wished, I could pay a visit to your city every night. At will I could slay thousands of your best citizens, for I am in close relationship with the Angel of Death.

Now, to be exact, at 12.15 (earthly time) on next Tuesday night, I am going to pass over New Orleans. In my infinite mercy, I am going to make a little proposition to you people. Here it is:

I am very fond of jazz music, and I swear by all the devils in the nether region that every person shall be spared in whose home a jazz band is in full swing at the time I have just mentioned. If everyone has a jazz band going, well, then, so much the better for you people. One thing is certain and that is that some of those people who do not jazz it on Tuesday night (if there be any) will get the axe.

Well, I am cold and crave the warmth of my native Tartarus, and as it is about time that I leave your earthly home, I will cease my discourse. Hoping that thou wilt publish this, that it may go well with thee, I have been, am, and will be the worst spirit that ever existed either in fact or realm of fancy.

THE AXEMAN

Tuesday was Saint Joseph's Night, always a time of great excitement among Italians in New Orleans. This year it reached a fever pitch. The traditional altars made of a hundred or more kinds of food were built, admired, dismantled, and distributed to the poor; lucky fava beans were handed out by the fistful; the saint was petitioned and praised. Still, St Joseph's Night of 1919 would remain indelibly fixed in New Orleans memory as "The Axeman's Jazz Night".

Cafés and mansions on St Charles blazed with the melodies of live jazz bands. Those who could not afford to pay musicians fed pennies into player pianos. A popular composer had written a song called The Mysterious Axeman's Jazz, or, Don't Scare Me, Papa. Banjo, guitar, and mandolin players gathered on the levees to send jazz music into the sky, so the Axeman would be sure to hear it as he passed over. By midnight, New Orleans was a cacophony of sounds, all of them swinging.

Cagliostro walked the streets for most of the night, marvelling (if not actively congratulating himself) at how completely he had brought the city together, and how gay he had made it in the process. No one so much as glanced at him: few people were on the streets, and Cagliostro had a talent for making himself invisible.

He had left the Axeman's corpse locked in the back of the house where it wouldn't spoil the groceries. First, of course, he had bludgeoned the face into unrecognizable mush with the Axeman's own axe. Everything that suggested the murdered man might be someone other than "Mike Pepitone", simple Italian grocer, was in the satchel Cagliostro carried with him.

On the turntable of his phonograph, as a final touch, he had left a recording of Nearer My God to Thee.

When the jazz finally began to die down, he walked to the docks and signed onto a freighter headed for Egypt. There were any number of wonderful things he hadn't gotten around to learning last time.

ITALY, 1945

Toward the end, Mussolini lived in an elaborate fantasy world constructed by the loyal sycophants who still surrounded him.

Whole cities in Italy were sanitized for his inspection, the cheering crowds along his parade routes supplemented by paid extras. When Hitler visited Rome, he too was deceived by the coat of sparkle on the decay, the hand-picked Aryan soldiers, the sheer bravado of *Il Duce*.

He believed he had cost Hitler the war. Germany lost its crucial Russian campaign after stopping to rescue the incompetent Italian army in Albania. Hitler had believed in the power and glory of Italy, and Mussolini had failed him.

Now he had been forced into exile on Lake Garda. He was a failure, his brilliant regime was a failure, and there were no more flunkies to hide these painful truths. He kept voluminous diaries in which he fantasized that his position in history would be comparable to Napoleon or Christ. His mistress Claretta lived nearby in a little villa, his only comfort.

On April 25, Germany caved in to the Allies. The Italian people, the ones he had counted on to save him with their loyalty, turned against him. Mussolini and Claretta fled, making for Switzerland.

A few last fanatical companions attempted to help them escape by subterfuge, but they were arrested by partisans on the north shore of Lake Como, discovered hiding in a German truck, cringing inside German coats and helmets. They were shot against the iron gate of an exquisite villa, and their bodies were taken to Milan and strung up by the heels to demonstrate the evils of Fascism.

All in service of the brotherhood of man.

[AUTHOR'S NOTE: Joseph D'Antonio's statement and the Axeman's letter reprinted from the New Orleans *States* and *Times-Picayune*, 1918–19.]

NORMAN PARTRIDGE

An Eye for An Eye

BRAM STOKER AWARD-WINNING author Norman Partridge writes horror and suspense fiction. His novels include *Saquaro Riptide*, *Slippin' into Darkness* and the forthcoming *Ten Ounce Siesta* (Berkley Prime Crime), a suspense novel which he describes as "*Rocky* meets *The Hills Have Eyes*."

Subterranean Press recently published *Bad Intentions*, a collection featuring some of the best of Partridge's short fiction, while several stories from his DAW anthology *It Came from the Drive-In* (co-edited with Martin Greenberg) were Stoker Award nominees. He is also the author of a graphic novel from Mojo Press, *Gorilla Gunslinger: The Good, the Bad . . . and the Gorilla*, with art by Marc Erickson.

The following story was originally published in *Gahan Wilson's The Ultimate Haunted House*, as the author explains: "When I received an invitation for this anthology, in which each writer would do a story set in a different room of a haunted house designed by cartoonist/author Gahan Wilson, I called editor Nancy A. Collins posthaste and reserved the screening room.

"I knew I'd have fun writing about the ghosts of Hollywood, and I knew exactly what kind of tone I wanted for the story – light, fun, jammed with wisecracks and twists and turns. It's a Gahan Wilson cartoon, only double-spaced . . ."

Wanda's eyesight was bad. She wore these clunky glasses with Catwoman frames and lenses thicker than a Fatburger, but they didn't prevent her from having extended conversations with department store mannequins every once in a while. Anything a foot and a half past her nose might as well have been located on the planet Pluto as far as she was concerned, so it wasn't surprising that it took a dead black cat with a pair of bewitched glass eyes to show us the way to the house where Hollywood died.

The cat belonged to Madame Estrella, a geriatric fortune teller who did readings for the low-rent crowd out by the beach. Ten bucks across her leathery palm and she'd tell you anything you wanted to hear. Not that she was all con and crapola, you understand. She could make some serious connections with the truth when she wanted to. The crone had some power, all right. Power rooted in ages past. Crystal ball kind of stuff.

The old bat sure didn't have much to show for it, though, living as she did in a cramped stucco bungalow which hadn't been painted since the days of Rudolph Valentino. Liked the bottle a little too much, she did. Even so, her mojo could do some serious workin' when she put her mind to it, believe you me.

I mean, I saw well enough with my own two eyes what she did with the dead cat, and I've got 20/20 vision. It breaks down like this – the first time I saw the damn thing, it was *stuffed*, and I don't mean to say our feline friend had pigged out on Friskies. Uh-uh. This little pussy was a taxidermist's dream – gutted and stitched – just like Roy Rogers' famous horse, Trigger.

And that wasn't the only thing the dead cat had in common with Trigger. The kitty had been in the movies, too. Hissed at Karloff and Lugosi in *The Black Cat*, way back in 1934. When the little furball finally turned paws up and headed for that big litter box in the sky in the early forties, its trainer had it stuffed and sold the corpse to a collector – along with a copy of the kitty's contract with Universal Studios as authentication, of course. And then *that* fellow ended up beachside without a pension, at which point he traded the carcass to Estrella for some charms that were supposed to help him put the whammy on a curse.

Whatever she gave him didn't do much good, because a curse straight from the dark heart of Hollywood is a tough nut to crack. At least that's the way I figure it, looking back. But I'll get to that in a minute.

First up, our feline friend. In particular, said kitty's relationship with the powers of one aged fortune teller. Like I said, I saw the cat – stuffed and mounted – the first time Wanda brought me to Madam Estrella's little stucco palace. It's like this – we're sneaking into the house, tripping through shadows because it's way too late and all the lights are out and Wanda's twice as blind in the dark as she is in the light. My eyes are quick to adjust, though, and just when I'm getting the lay of the land I come face to face with the furry terror that once stalked Boris and Bela. Damned thing is crouched on a bookshelf, at eye-level, its lips twisted into an eternal snarl, and the moonlight spilling through the living room window catches its glass eyes just right, and I'm thinking I see dark red pits inside those glowing green orbs, and I gasp just like some stupid ten-year-old, stumbling into Wanda while I'm at it.

Of course, a couple seconds tick off in the direction of eternity and I haven't been clawed to death, at which time I notice that the seemingly ferocious furball is about as mobile as Plymouth Rock. Wanda pokes her nose in the cat's face and realizes what has happened. She starts laughing at me, and I can't really hold that against her, even now. Then she whispers the story in my ear, cluing me in on the dead *gato*'s career in Hollyweird.

"*Damn*," I said (and enthusiastically, because the cash-register in my head was instantly *ding-ding-ding*ing). "If that story of yours checks out, this mangy kitty could bring us some serious *scratch*. Believe it or not, movie nuts will drop some major change for stuff like this. Even weird stuff. In fact, the *weirder*, the *better*."

"I don't know for a fact that the story is true, but it's direct from Madame's lips, and my sixth sense tells me that the old fossil believes it." Wanda winked at me from behind those Coke bottle specs of hers. "Madame also says that her friend knows about a house that's filled with stuff that's way past *mondo* on the weirdness scale. He calls it *the house where Hollywood died*."

"Oh yeah?" I said.

"Yeah." Wanda nodded.

"So where can we find Madame's friend? And how do we know he's on the level?"

"First question – I don't know; the guy hasn't been around in a couple of weeks. Second question – the great Madame swears that the story checks out."

"And what makes her magnificence so sure about that?"

"She's seen the place in her crystal ball, dummy."

"No shit?" says I, and none too quietly, because at that point my enthusiasm had really gone on the boil, crystal ball or no.

"No shit *whatsoever*," says Wanda, putting a finger to my lips. "But quiet down. We don't want to wake Madame. She can get kind of testy, believe me."

Quiet down I did, because I believed the stories Wanda had told me about the old fortune teller's powers. After all, I'd seen Wanda do a spooky thing or two in the month I'd known her, so crystal balls were definitely entering my own personal realm of possibility.

Still, I pretty much forgot about Wanda's warning once we'd made it to the safety of her bedroom. We weren't too quiet then. Wanda didn't help any, of course. She'd purr like a kitten, and then she'd growl, and I'd laugh . . . and finally we got all that purring and growling and laughing out of our systems and fell asleep. But even then the money was never far from my thoughts, or my dreams. Too bad Wanda's warning about Madame didn't stick with me the same way.

Because the next morning when we woke up tangled in Wanda's sheets, the damn cat was right there in the middle of everything. It had traded in the Plymouth Rock act for something a tad more mobile, hissing and clawing for all it was worth while Madame Estrella cackled at us from the bedroom doorway.

It was then that I recalled Wanda's comment about Madame being *testy*. *Testy*, my ass. If a little bedspring symphony could cause the old biddy to raise a cat from the dead and send it scratching and clawing at the bedspring musicians who had offended her, I'd hate to see what she would have done if someone really got on her bad side. I'm gonna have scars, if I live that long. As for Madame –

I certainly didn't put up much resistance – I screamed bloody murder and tried to pull the covers over my head, but the kitty from Hell shredded both blanket and sheet like two-ply toilet paper. Wanda was the one who sprang into action. She fumbled for her glasses and balanced them on her nose. Her eyes went all cold behind those thick lenses, and a couple of words in some weird foreign language boiled over her tongue, and suddenly the cat flew across the room and slammed into the wall.

Wanda blinked and Madame Estrella made like the cat. She jerked straight out of her shoes and shot backward, her bony skull cracking plaster as she hit the wall in the hallway, her dentures rattling.

Such abuse would have chilled me out, mere mortal that I am, but not Madame Estrella. The old bat managed to continue cackling like she had one of those novelty store Bag O' Laughs hidden under her turban, like the whole thing was the best joke in the world. Even from a good ten foot distance I could catch the mingled miasma of vodka and Polident on her breath.

"Good morning, dearies," was all she said.

"Grandma," Wanda said, her voice even and sure. "Sometimes I could just *kill* you."

Wanda didn't mean it, though.

Because when push came to shove, I was the one who ended up killing Madame Estrella.

Wanda wanted it that way, of course. Blood being thicker than water, and all like that. And though the end came pretty *viciously*, it wasn't like the whole thing was particularly *calculated*. Not in a *premeditated* way, anyway. I mean, we wouldn't have killed Wanda's granny unless we really *had* to, and we certainly didn't mean for things to get so *messy*.

Fact is, we tried to be really nice about it. After I was properly introduced, I went out and bought Madame a fifth of vodka. The good stuff – that expensive Russian kind. I bought her a pastrami sandwich, too. And a big bag of Cheetos.

Breakfast of champions was what Madame Estrella called it. She devoured the Cheetos and slammed down half the vodka, posthaste. Then she went to work on the sandwich, and we went to work on her.

"Wanda was telling me about the cat," I began.

Madame nodded, swallowed.

"She says it was a movie star," I said.

"*Ungh*," came Madame's reply as she gobbled another healthy bite of pastrami sandwich.

"Wanda says you got it from a guy who's cursed or something?"

A thin rope of pastrami hung from Madame's mouth; she slurped it down like a raw red worm. "Cursed?" She grinned greasily, sparing me an appraising squint. "Is that what my Wanda told you?"

"Yeah," I said. "She said something about the guy being cursed, and that he traded you the dead cat so you'd work up a charm or something." At that moment the not-so-dead cat brushed up against my leg and my spine went cold, but I pressed on.

"Wanda said that this guy had other stuff, too. Or if he didn't actually *have* it, he knew where to *find* it. Hollywood stuff."

"*Rare* and *valuable* stuff," Wanda said. "Isn't that right, Grandma?"

"Now you two don't go messing with *that*. My friend Mr Arkoff is *cursed*. He *sees* things. The *ghosts* of Hollywood. The ghosts of *monsters*."

The last sentence came to us in a conspiratorial whisper, along with a shower of partially masticated breadcrumbs.

We were quiet for a moment, and then Wanda pushed the crystal ball across the table so that it sat squarely before her grandmother. "Why don't you show us what he sees?" she suggested, her tone completely innocent. "I think Russell needs some convincing."

"Oh no," I put in. "I saw the cat. Anything your grandma says, I'll believe – "

Wanda cut me off with a sharp cough at that point, and I realized that I'd said the wrong thing. I tried to patch it up, saying, "But I'd sure be interested to see how a crystal ball works, Madame Estrella. If you don't mind, that is."

Madame grinned slyly, pushing the ball toward Wanda. "Why don't *you* demonstrate, my dear?"

Wanda tittered like a shy girl at a cotillion, adjusting her glasses. "Oh, Grandma. You know I don't have the sight the way you do."

"Bad genes, I'm afraid." Madame shook her aged head. "That father of yours, he was no good. *Blind as a bat*, to boot."

Wanda moped.

I sighed.

Madame took one last hit of the vodka bottle, then pulled the crystal ball her way, exhaling expansively. "All *right*, if you're both going to be so *childish* about it."

The old woman's hands were little more than arthritic claws, but they proved amazingly supple as they cut strange patterns in the air. For a moment her fingers settled over the glass globe. Smoke seemed to fill the crystal, clearing only when a few words crossed Madame's tongue, words that sounded surprisingly similar to the incantation Wanda had uttered in the bedroom.

A dull halo of light encircled the crystal. The picture which formed in the glass was hazy, like a poorly tuned television, but I could make it out. A shoddy room, similar to the place I rented down by the beach. There was a sagging couch in one corner, and a couple of figures sitting there.

The Frankenstein Monster and Kharis the Mummy.

I didn't say a word, but my jaw literally dropped open. And then the perspective changed, as if a camera were doing a pan of the apartment. I glimpsed an open door ... a bathroom ...

... something big and green in the tub.

"The Creature from the Black Lagoon!" No sooner did the words cross my lips than the perspective changed again. I saw a window. Slivered Venetian blinds. And beyond, in the distance, I could make out a signpost –

It didn't say THE TWILIGHT ZONE.

No. BUD'S GAS was what it said.

"Jesus!" I said, turning to Wanda. "It's the gas station across from my apartment! This guy Arkoff lives in my building!"

If Madame Estrella's eyes had been knives, Wanda would have been slashed to a bloody mess. "You little bitch!" the old woman screeched. "Just forget about it! You're not going to do it! And this dope of a boyfriend of yours isn't going to help you! You don't have the *sight*, Wanda! You weren't meant to have it!" Her arthritic hands floated before her, fingers twisting like rotten twigs. "Don't move an inch, either of you!"

Wanda moved, though. So did I, mostly because I wasn't crazy about being referred to as *this dope of a boyfriend of yours*. Madame kept talking, but her voice had changed, and the words that spilled from her lips were spoken in that strange, unrecognizable tongue.

The old crone's eyes were surprisingly clear and bright, and they burned me to the core. I stumbled backward, but Wanda grabbed me. Held me tight. Whispered that everything would be all right.

It wasn't, though. I blacked out for a second, Wanda's voice a cold river of blood flowing in my head, a cold river that carried words in that strange foreign tongue.

I came to an instant later, and I was scared.

So scared that I was whimpering.

And that wasn't the worst of it. I was down on the floor, on all fours. My mouth was full of fangs. Madame teetered above me, laughing that Bag O' Laughs' laugh of hers, and then she turned her attention to Wanda, saying, "Two legs or four, a coward is still a coward, dearie."

Her words scorched my ears. And suddenly I could feel Wanda there, right inside my head, and just as suddenly I wasn't scared anymore. I was mad – or Wanda was mad – I couldn't decide which, because both of us were in there.

One thing was for certain – a growl rose in my throat, and Madame's laughter died in hers. In an instant her eyes were brimming with fear.

She wasn't afraid for herself, though. No. She whirled surprisingly fast and snatched up the crystal ball. "Mr Arkoff!" she screeched. "Listen to me! They're coming for you! They'll kill you! You've got to run! Hide! You've got to – "

That was when I sprang.

Madame tossed the crystal ball at me.

Missed.

My jaws gaped wide.

A few nasty syllables spilled over Madame's lips.

I tore open the old biddy's throat before the syllables could turn into words, and the words into an incantation that might do me harm.

Her throat was a tender and surprisingly tasty treat. I tasted pastrami marinated with a splash of vodka. I tasted Cheetos, too.

But what really made the meal was the taste of blood.

Wanda stood above me, wiping flecks of blood off her glasses. "You make a pretty good Doberman," she said. "I'd hate to be the one to clean up after you, though."

I was on the kitchen floor, leaning against a cabinet, not quite sure how I'd gotten there. All I knew was that there wasn't much left of Madame, my belly was full, and my muscles felt like they'd been twisted into knots that would defy David Copperfield.

The remnants of the crystal ball covered the floor like so many uncut diamonds. I immediately thought of Mr Arkoff and his Hollywood booty, and I favored Wanda with a worried stare. "Do you think the old codger heard Madame's warning?"

"I don't know." Wanda finished cleaning her glasses and slid them on. She stepped over Madame's corpse, simultaneously treating me to an eager smile.

I got up off the floor, groaning. "So what do we do?"

"Why, we get our avaricious asses in gear, Russell," she said. "That's what we do."

From what we'd seen in the crystal ball, I figured that Mr Arkoff's apartment had to be directly above my own. Checking the name-plates on the mailboxes near the lone staircase confirmed my suspicions. So, with bat-eyed Wanda holding my hand for support and the dead kitty bringing up the rear, I hurriedly climbed the staircase to the third floor, and apartment #305.

Immediately, I knew that we were too late, because Mr Arkoff's front door was unlocked.

Even so it was a little scary entering the place, because I remembered my visions of Frankenstein's Monster, and Kharis the Mummy, and the Creature. But no one was sitting on the couch near the window, and the bathtub was empty. Still, I needed an explanation, so I mentioned it to Wanda, knowing the whole thing sounded crazy.

"It *is* crazy," she said, waving one hand at the apartment walls, which were crowded with movie posters and stills. "Remember, the images we saw in the crystal ball came to us through Arkoff's eyes, and Arkoff believes that he is *cursed*, haunted by Hollywood's past. What we saw were his own private *ghosts*. His *delusions*."

It seemed a reasonable explanation. Wanda seemed sure of it, and at the time it satisfied me. Together, we turned our attention to searching the apartment.

Arkoff had left in a hurry. That much was obvious. A few drawers hung open in the dresser near his bed, and the cramped bedroom closet had been rifled as well.

I dropped heavily onto the bed, suddenly exhausted. The cat followed – pouncing quite gracefully, considering that it was dead – and settled on my belly.

"No telling where the guy has gone," I said. "Too bad the crystal ball got busted."

"The crystal wouldn't do us any good," Wanda corrected, tapping her thick glasses with one finger. "I don't have the sight, remember? And you ate dear old Grandma."

"Don't remind me," I said, my belly suddenly churning under the weight of the undead feline. I gave the cat a little push and suggested it settle elsewhere. "So what do we do now?"

Wanda paced for a couple minutes, thinking it over. "I think we've got to rely on the greed factor," she said finally.

"The greed factor?"

"Yeah." She took a deep breath. "I figure it this way – Mr Arkoff heard Grandma's warning. Now, we know he took that warning seriously, because he's not here. So he's convinced that someone is after him, and he's got to have a pretty good idea why."

"The memorabilia?" I suggested. "The stuff he's got hidden away?"

"Right as rain, Sherlock." Wanda grinned. "Now, our friend Mr Arkoff is scared, but he's also greedy. He's a hoarder. He hasn't sold off his treasure trove. Just look at this apartment – it's packed with stills and posters. The guy would rather live like a pauper than part with his collection. Leaving this stuff behind is probably killing him."

"So . . . what?"

"He *wants* that Hollywood stuff he's got hidden away. He wants it all for himself. That's his *real* curse. And I'm willing to bet that no matter how frightened he is, he's not going to leave town without it."

"Yeah," I said. "I can go along with that. But without Grandma and her crystal ball, how do we figure out where the stuff is hidden?"

Wanda bent down and scooped the cat off the bed. It purred huskily, a sound that made me think of sand and sawdust, and its glass eyes twinkled exactly like two miniature crystal balls.

"Grandma brought our feline friend back to life," Wanda explained, scratching the kitty under its chin.

I smiled, catching on. "And Mr Arkoff brought the little flea-bag to Grandma's, direct from the place where Hollywood died."

Wanda nodded, setting the cat on the floor and ruffling its fur. "Can you show us the way home, puss?" she asked. "You can do that, can't you?"

Just like the door to Mr Arkoff's apartment, the front door of the house where Hollywood died was unlocked. Unfortunately, the door to the particular room we were interested in wasn't.

I've seen some doors in my time, believe me. But I'd never seen a door like this one, not in five years of serious b & e. Three brass knobs on the damned thing. Plus a lock for each knob, every one a burglar's nightmare. Someone's paranoia was running at a fever pitch, all right. But that little info-bite warmed my mercenary heart, because it meant that we'd come to the right place.

"Can you open it?" Wanda asked.

I grinned and reached for my picklock. ASAP, I checked that action, because I was tired, and my powers of concentration were pulsing at near-Neanderthal ebb, and I was just about out of patience. We'd been three hours finding the place, following the cat hither and yon, and as far as I could tell we were directly in the middle of nowhere. Strictly *Borgo Pass* territory, if you remember your *Dracula*.

So I did the dirty with the worn heel of my boot.

The brass plates around the doorknobs buckled when my kick landed.

The molding splintered.

And the door swung open, *open sesame* sweet.

The room was real attractive, if *early conspicuous consumption* happened to be your preferred cup of *decorative motif*.

There was a television in one corner, complete with rabbit ears that a particularly inventive family of spiders was using for a trapeze, judging by the cobwebs. Some weird kind of *objet d'art* TV in the middle of the room, blank screen gleaming like a cyclopean eye. And in the corner, the *pièce de resistance* – stacked high and haphazardly in the Leaning Tower of Pisa manner, gleaming like a J. D.'s ransom of stolen hubcaps – an inviting collection of film canisters. *Frankenstein*, *The Mummy*, *Dracula*, *The Wolf Man*, *Creature from the Black Lagoon* – all the Universal classics.

And everywhere, memorabilia. Posters, stills. Costumes, masks. Stop-motion miniatures. Original screenplays, piled high.

Everything but the mysterious Mr Arkoff.

"You think we missed him?" Wanda asked.

"I don't know. Maybe we got here first."

"Yeah," she said. "Maybe you're right. Let's look around."

Wanda checked out the film canisters. I turned to a projector that sat in one corner of the room. The machine, like the television rabbit ears, was festooned with cobwebs. I slashed through them with one hand, and a black widow tumbled through the air like one of the Flying Walendas on a very bad day.

With grace of which the human machine is incapable, the spider hit the floor and skittered for cover. It disappeared under the *objet d'art* TV, and I took a closer look at the projector. "Check this out," I said to Wanda. "This projector doesn't have a lens."

"You're very observant." It was a man's voice, and it came from the doorway.

I whirled. Mr Arkoff was a small man with a very big gun and a very thick pair of glasses.

The right lens was large and practically square, but the left lens was round, and smaller.

Exactly like the lens of a movie projector.

"They're *my* ghosts," Mr Arkoff said, gun leveled at me as he entered the room. "You're not going to steal them from me. If you take them away, *I'll die*. That's the *curse*."

"Ghosts?" I said, backing off. "I don't know what you're talking about, pal. I came here looking for something I can sell. I admit that. But *ghosts* . . . I don't believe in anything that I can't see."

I didn't really mean that last part, because I'd seen plenty of stuff in the past six hours that pushed the weirdness envelope pretty hard . . . and I believed every bit of it. All I wanted to do was buy some time. I glanced at Wanda, expecting her to do something, the way she had when the dead cat attacked us. But she just stood there, watching.

"My ghosts never actually lived, of course," Mr Arkoff explained, motioning to the menacing figures which graced the movie posters hanging on the walls. "But they were real, in their own way." He tapped the round lens in his glasses. "And they all traveled through this piece of glass, and they all left something behind in it. I don't know why, or how. But when I look through this lens, I can see them . . . and *they* can see me. I wish I'd never put these glasses on . . . but I did, the first time I visited this room so many years ago. And if I ever take them off . . . why, the ghosts of Hollywood will *get* me . . ."

The whole thing was William Castle-weird – *13 Ghosts* to be exact, if you remember your fifties creature features, which I'm sure Mr Arkoff did. Still, I wanted to tell him that I didn't care about his glasses, that I only cared about the masks, the posters, the stuff that sent visions of easy money tangoing through my cerebrum.

But I couldn't say a word. See, that cold river of blood was running in my head again, that cold river that carried words in that strange foreign tongue.

They were Wanda's words. She was in my head again, just as she'd been when she made me attack her grandmother. Any second now, I expected to turn into a Doberman and chow down on Mr Arkoff.

Only that didn't happen. Wanda didn't change me into anything remotely frightening. Instead, she made me take one gigantic but merely mortal step forward. And she made me say, "Give me the glasses, Mr Arkoff."

Arkoff didn't hesitate. Not that he gave me the glasses. The pistol bucked in his hand, and a slug trenched my cheek and tore through my right earlobe. I wanted to scream, but Wanda pushed me forward. I slammed into Arkoff as the gun went off again. The bullet missed me, smashing into the projector with a brittle *clanq*, and then we were fighting over the gun, Arkoff spinning away from me, and as he moved I slapped one hand across his face.

Or, I should say, Wanda made me do it.

Arkoff's glasses slipped over his nose. They dropped, almost gently, to the floor.

Wanda snatched them up before I could make another move. Suddenly she wasn't in my head anymore, and again I went for Arkoff's gun, smashing his hand against the door frame.

The little man grunted. The gun clattered to the floor, and I kicked it into the hallway.

I turned to Wanda. She stared at me, and I saw her eyes clearly, as I'd never seen them before. They were colder than they'd ever been, especially the one framed by the round lens that had come from the movie projector.

Wanda pushed Arkoff's glasses high on her nose. "Grandma was right," she said. "I never had the sight. I always had to rely on other things – like manipulation. Old tricks. Turning men into dogs, and dogs into men." She glanced at me, and I shivered. "But now I'm seeing things pretty clearly. I'm seeing another world. It's beautiful, Russell. Everything is black and white."

"Wanda," I said. "Don't – "

She laughed. "I don't think I'll be needing you anymore, Russell," she said. "I've found some new friends who are a whole lot less squeamish than you."

That was when Mr Arkoff screamed. I whirled just as he was dragged from the room, into the shadowy hallway.

I didn't see a thing, but I could hear well enough. A werewolf howl eclipsed Arkoff's screams, and then came the sound of powerful jaws splitting human bones. Next, as the victim grew quiet, came the whisper of decayed bandages dragging over the stairway, the heavy thump of a Monster's oversized boots in the hallway, and the cold, peculiarly Transylvanian laughter of a vampire.

"No," I said. "They're not *real*. They're only *movies*!"

"Don't worry," Wanda said. "You won't see a thing. Not without the glasses. You'll never see them coming."

I glanced at her, and then at the doorway. An ominous silence lurked in the shadow-choked corridor. Maybe I could make it. The gun was out there somewhere. I doubted that bullets could harm the ghosts of Hollywood, but Wanda was a different story –

"Those are nasty thoughts, Russell."

I glared at her. "Get out of my head!"

Wanda's reply was an amused grin.

And then she wasn't grinning anymore, because – just like she said – she could see things clearly now.

And she saw the dead cat coming, saw clearly the gleam in its eyes as it sprang at her. Maybe she saw her own reflection in those green glass globes, or maybe she saw Madame Estrella. I don't know. I only know that the cat latched onto her head, a fury of scratching claws and ripping fangs, and Wanda went down screaming, and Mr Arkoff's glasses were swatted from her face.

They hit the floor, the lenses covered with blood.

I stepped on them as hard as I could, praying that curses were not simple creations of the imagination.

The lenses shattered under my boot.

And that was when I ran.

It's quiet here, under the boardwalk. Dark, too. If Wanda is alive – which I doubt – I don't think she'll ever come looking for me. Not without those glasses.

The dead cat found me, though. I woke up one morning and there it was, snuggled up next to me, purring its sand and sawdust purr.

We make a good team, down here in the darkness. The cat is pretty good at snaring rats. And when the fog rolls in, covering the beach in a cottony shroud, we hit the dumpsters up on the boardwalk and eat like a couple of kings.

We're careful, though. I'm sure that those ghosts are out there somewhere, even if they can't be seen.

I listen for them, in the dark, in the fog.

I listen for the melancholy wail of a werewolf's howl . . . and the thunder of heavy boots ringing on the boardwalk as a Monster walks the night . . . the unmistakable sound of a mummy's uneven tread, muffled by bandages fashioned near the Nile (or in the wardrobe department at Universal Studios, I'm not sure which).

The sound of a vampire's cape whispering over the sand . . . and the tireless kick of the Creature's webbed feet as he makes his way through cold Pacific tides.

You can hear ghosts, I'm sure, if you listen carefully. I'm not sure if you can ever outrun them, though.

But I plan to try.

DOUGLAS CLEGG

Underworld

DOUGLAS CLEGG WROTE HIS first novel, *Goat Dance*, in 1987. Since then he has published such novels as *Breeder*, *Neverland*, *You Come When I Call You* and *The Dark of the Eye*, while his short fiction has appeared in the magazines *Deathrealm*, *Cemetery Dance* and *The Scream Factory* and such anthologies as *Love in Vein*, *Little Deaths*, *Forbidden Acts*, *Twists of the Tale*, *The Year's Best Fantasy and Horror* and *The Best New Horror*.

A former underwear model, Parisian busker and professional rodeo cowboy, his latest horror novel is *The Children's Hour*, while under his pen name, Andrew Harper, he has recently published *Bad Karma*, a reincarnation thriller. He is currently working on his next horror novel, *The Halloween Man*.

As Clegg reveals, "The first vision I had of this story was when I thought I saw someone I knew who was dead – just for a second, in Manhattan, peering out from the kitchen's round portal window. Of course, it wasn't my dead friend, just someone else. But the image bothered me.

"Also, an incident happened in New York where a person who was a new renter walked into their apartment in the middle of the day and was killed by two strangers (to her) in her living room – seems they always met for their dealings in this woman's living room. Only she walked in at the wrong time.

"And then I also thought: if someone dies and is taken to Hell because of a certain amount of sin, does the unborn child also deserve that after-life fate? I don't believe in Hell as such, but I wondered if the ruler of the Underworld actually had a moral impulse himself . . ."

I

THEY SAY THAT LOVE never dies. Sometimes it goes somewhere else, to a place from which it may return transformed. Jenny, my wife, died in one of those freak occurrences that seem to be getting more common in cities. She was, in fact, murdered.

We were subletting the place on Thirty-Third, just down from Lexington Avenue – it was an eight block walk to my job up at Matthew Bender, across from Penn Station, where I was an ink-stained drudge by day before transforming into a novelist by night. Jenny was getting day work on the soap operas – nothing much, just the walk-on nurses and cocktail waitresses that populate daytime television, never with more than a word or two to say, so it was a long way to her Screen Actor's Guild card. But she made just enough to cover the rent, and I made just enough to cover everything else, plus the feeble beginnings of a savings account which we affectionately named, The Son'll Come Out Tomorrow, because at about the time we opened the account, Jenny discovered that she was pregnant. This worried the heck out of me, not for the usual reasons, such as the mounting bills, and the thought that I might not be able to pursue writing full-time, at least not in this life, but because of a habit Jenny had of sleeping with other men.

It will be hard to understand this, and I don't completely get it myself, but I loved Jenny in a way that I didn't think possible. It wasn't her beauty, although she certainly had that, but it was the fact that in her company I always felt safe and comfortable. I did not want to ever be with another woman as long as I lived; I suppose a good therapist would go on and on about my self-image and self-esteem and self-whatever, but I've got to tell you, it was simply that I loved her and that I wanted her to be happy. I didn't worry if I was inadequate or unsatisfying as a lover; and she never spoke openly about it with me. I was just aware she'd had a few indiscretions early in our marriage, and I assumed that she would gradually, over the years, calm down in that respect. I felt lucky to have Jenny's company when I did, and when I didn't, I did not feel deprived. I suppose that until you have loved someone in that way it is impossible to understand that point of view.

So I wondered about the paternity of our child, and this kept me up several nights to the point that I would slip out of bed quietly (for Jenny often had to be up and out the door by 5 a.m.), and go for long walks down Third Avenue, or down a side street to Second, sometimes until the first light came up over the city. During one of these jaunts, in late January, I noticed a curious sort of building – it was on a block of Kip's Bay that began in an alley, and was enclosed on all sides. Yet, there were apartments, and a street name (Pallan Row, the sign said), and two small restaurants, the kind with only eight or nine tables, one of them a Szechwan place, the other nondescript in its Americanized menu; also, a flower stand, boarded up, and what looked like a bit of a warehouse. The place carried an added layer of humidity, as if it had more of the swamp to it than the city.

I am not normally a wanderer of alleys, but I could not help myself – I had lived in this neighborhood about a year and a half, and in that time had felt I knew every block within about a mile and a half radius. But it was as if I had just found the most wonderful gift in the world, a hidden grotto, a place in New York City that was as yet undiscovered except by, perhaps, the oldest residents. I looked in the windows of the warehouse, but could see nothing through the filthy windows.

All day at work, I asked friends who lived in the general vicinity if they knew about Pallan Row, but only one said that she did. "It used to be where the sweatshops were – highly illegal, too, because when I was a kid, they used to raid them all the time – it was more than bad working conditions, it was white slavery and heroin, all those things. But then," she added, "so much of this city has a history like that. On the outside, carriage rides and Broadway shows, but underneath, kind of slimy."

On Saturday, I convinced Jenny to take a walk with me, but for some reason I couldn't find the Row; we went to lunch. Afterwards, I remembered where I'd led us astray, and we ended up going to have tea at the Chinese restaurant. The menu was ordinary, and the decorations vintage and tacky.

"Amazing," Jenny said. "Look, honey, the ceiling," and I

glanced up and beheld one of those lovely old tin ceilings with the chocolate candy designs.

The waiter, who was an older Asian woman, noticed us and came over with some almond cookies. "We usually are empty on weekends," she said, and then, also looking at the ceiling, "this was part of a speak-easy in the twenties – the cafe next door, too. They say that a mobster ran numbers out of the backroom. Before that, it was just an ice house. My husband began renting it in 1954."

"That long ago?" Jenny said, taking a bite from a cookie. "It seems like most restaurants come and go around here."

"Depends on the rent," the woman nodded, still looking at the ceiling. "The owner hasn't raised it a penny in all those years." She glanced at me, then at Jenny. "You're going to have a baby, aren't you?"

Jenny grinned. "How did you know?"

The woman said, "Young couples like you, in love, eating my almond cookies. Always brings babies. You will have a strong boy, I think."

After she left the table, we laughed, finished the tea, and just sat for a while. The owner's wife occasionally peeped through the round port-hole window of the kitchen door, and we smiled at her but shook our heads to indicate that we weren't in need of service.

"When the baby comes," Jenny said, "Mom said she'd loan us money to get a larger place."

"Ah, family loans," I warned her.

"I know, but we won't have to pay her back for a few years. Can you believe it, me, a mother?"

"And me, a father?" I leaned over and pressed my hand against her stomach. "I wonder what he's thinking?"

"Or she. Probably, 'get me the hell out of here right now!' is what it's thinking."

"Babies aren't 'its'."

"Well, right now it is. It has a will of its own. It probably looks like a little developing tadpole. Something like its father," she gave my hand a squeeze. I kissed her. When I drew my face back from hers, she had tears in her eyes.

"What's the matter?"

"Oh," she wiped at her eyes with her napkin, "I'm going to change."

"Into what?"

"No, you know what I mean. I've been living too recklessly."

"Oh," I said, and felt a little chill. "That's all in the past. I love you like crazy, Jen."

"I know. I am so lucky," she said. "Our baby's lucky to have two screw-ups like us for parents."

Now it could be that I'm just recalling that we said these words because I want her memory to be sweeter for me than perhaps reality will allow. But we walked back up Second Avenue that Saturday feeling stronger as a couple; and I knew the baby was mine, I just knew it, regardless of the chances against it. We caught a movie, went home and made love, sat up and watched *Saturday Night Live*. Sunday we took the train out to her mother's in Stamford, and then as the week was just getting under way, I walked through the doorway of our small sublet, to find blood on the *faux* oriental rug.

Yet the door had been locked. That was my first thought. I didn't see Jenny's body until I got to the bathroom, which is where her murderer had dragged her, apparently while she was still alive, and then had dropped her in the tub, closed the shower curtain around her. It wasn't as gruesome as I expected it to be – there was a bullet in her head, behind her left ear, but she was lying face up so I didn't see the damage to the back of her scalp. She didn't even look like Jenny anymore. She looked like butcher's shop meat with a human shape. She looked like some dead woman with whom I had no acquaintance. I was pretty numb, and was thinking of calling the police, when it occurred to me that the killer might still be in the apartment. So I went next door to Helen Connally's and knocked on the door. Helen, in her sweats, saw my panic, let me in, and made me some tea while we waited for the police. I hated leaving Jenny there, in the tub, for the ten minutes, but if the murderer was still lurking, I had no way of defending myself.

After the police and the neighbors and Jenny's mother had picked my brain about the crime, it hit me.

I had not only lost my partner and lover, but also my child. I cried for days, or perhaps it was weeks – it was like living, for a time, in a dark cave where there was no hour, no minute, no day, only darkness.

When I emerged from my stupor and weeping, the police had

arrested a suspect for my wife's murder, and then the mystery unraveled: we had been subletting an apartment from a man who had several such places around the city, and each one was used, occasionally, by the man's clients, as a place of business on certain weekdays for drug dealing. The dealers' assumption had been that on a given day of the week, no one was home. Best the detectives could tell, Jenny had come home too early on the wrong Tuesday, a drug deal was in progress, and one of the men had killed her as soon as she'd come in the door. I was devastated to think that strangers could be in our apartment; but of course, it wasn't really ours. The renter of the apartment was arrested; he pointed the finger at a few associates; and within a year, the guilty were behind bars, and I was living in a place off Houston and Sullivan Street, over in the SoHo area. I was seeing, on a friendly basis, Helen Connally, my former neighbor – it was almost as if the tragedy of my wife's death had given us a basis on which to form a friendship. Helen was thirty-two to my twenty-eight, and, while I knew I would never love her the way I loved Jenny, she was a good friend to me through a most difficult time. We spent a year being slightly good friends, and then we became lovers.

I was taking some out-of-town friends of ours on an informal sightseeing tour of the Big Apple, and brought them down to little Pallan Row. I thought the Szechwan place would be good for lunch, but when we entered the alley, both it and the cafe were closed; windows were boarded up. "Jesus," I said, "just a year ago, the woman running it told me that they'd had it since the fifties."

Helen took my elbow. "C'mon, we can go get sandwiches up at Tivoli. Or," she turned to the couple we'd brought, "there's a great deli on Third. You guys like pastrami?"

Their voices faded into the background, as I looked through the section of the Chinese restaurant's window that was clear, and thought I saw my dead wife's face back along the wall, through the round glass window of the door to the kitchen.

"Oliver," Helen said, looking over my shoulder, "what's up?"

"Nothing," I said, still looking at Jenny, her dark hair grown longer, obscuring all but her nose and mouth.

"It must be something."

"It's just an old place. It was once a speak-easy, back in the twenties. Think of all that's gone on in here," I said. Jenny's face, in that round window, staring at me.

"Cool," Helen said. She was originally from California, so "cool" and "bummer" had not yet been erased from her vocabulary of irony. She stood back, and her friend Larry whispered something to her.

I watched Jenny's face, and noticed that when her hair fell more to the side of her face, there were no eyes in her sockets.

"Let's go," Helen whispered. "They want to take a ride on the ferry before it gets dark."

"Okay, just a sec," I said.

Jenny moved away from the round window.

My heart was beating fast.

I assumed that I was hallucinating, but the thought of spending the rest of the afternoon escorting this couple around town when I had just seen my dead wife was absurd. I made an excuse about needing to be by myself – Helen always took this well, and I caught an understanding look from Anne, who nodded. I knew they would go on to a late lunch and talk about how I still hadn't quite recovered from Jenny's death; and I knew Helen would act the martyr a bit, because it was so hard to play nurse to me over a woman who had cheated constantly behind my back. I adored Helen for her care and caution around my feelings; I wished them a good afternoon, and stood there, along the Row, watching them, until they had rounded the corner and were out of sight.

After a few minutes, I took off my shoe and broke the windowglass, and tugged at one of the boards until it gave. Within half an hour, I stepped in through the broken window, and walked across the dusty floor to the kitchen.

The kitchen was all long shiny metal shelves and drawers, pots and pans still piled high. But it was dark, and I saw no one. I walked across the floor, back to the walk-in freezer, and looked through its frosty pane of glass. Although I could see nothing in there, I found myself shivering, even my teeth began chattering, and I had the sudden and uncomfortable feeling that if I did not get out of that kitchen, out of that boarded-up restaurant right then, something terrible would happen.

It didn't occur to me until I was on the street again that there should've been no frost on the glass pane of the walk-in freezer, that, in fact, there was no electricity to the entire building, perhaps to the entire block.

II

Helen noticed, over the next few days, that I was becoming nervous. We sat across from each other in our favorite park, me with the *Times*, and her with a paperback; I looked up and she was watching me. Another day, we went to a coffee shop, and she mentioned to me that my knees, under the table, were shaking slightly. She said this with some seriousness, as if shaking knees were an indicator of some deeper problem. But I doubted myself then, and I did not want to talk about seeing my dead wife in the Chinese restaurant kitchen on Pallan Row. Finally, my restlessness turned nocturnal, and I tossed and turned in my sleep. Helen, sleeping over, finally sat up in bed at four in the morning and flicked on the bedside lamp. Her eyes were bloodshot.

"You have not slept a full night for two days," she said. "You tell me what's going on."

I spent about an hour dodging the issue, until finally, as she pushed and pushed, I told her about seeing Jenny.

"She was blind," Helen said, speaking to me like I was a lying twelve-year-old.

"Not blind. She had no eyes. I felt she could see me, anyway. She was staring at me. She just had no eyes."

"And you went in there and no one was there . . ."

"But the freezer. Why would it be going?"

Helen shrugged. "I'm going to make a drink. You want something?"

At 5.30 a.m., she and I had vodka martinis, and went and sat out on the fire escape as all of Manhattan awoke, as the sky turned several shades of violet before becoming the blank light of day.

"I don't believe in ghosts," I said, sipping, and feeling drunk very quickly. "I don't believe that the dead can rise or any of that."

"What do you believe?"

I watched a burly man lift crates out of the back of his truck down in the street. "I believe in what I see. I saw her. I really saw her."

"Assuming," she said, "that it was Jenny. Assuming that the freezer was running on its own energy. Assuming you saw what you saw. Assuming all those things as givens, what does it mean?"

"I have no idea. I thought at first maybe I was just crazy. If I hadn't seen the frost on the freezer window, I don't think I would've believed later on that it had been Jenny at all. Or anything but an hallucination."

Helen was obstinate. "But it's got to mean something."

"Why?" I asked.

I slept through the next day fairly peacefully, and when I awoke, Helen was gone. I watched television, and then called a few friends to set up lunches and dinners for the following week.

Helen walked through the door at 6.30 in the evening, and said, "Well, I found that alley again. I pulled back one of the boards."

When she said this, I felt impulsively defensive – it was my alley, it was my boarded-up restaurant, I felt, it was my hallucination. "You didn't have to," I told her.

She halted my speech with her hands. "Hang on, hang on. Oliver, the windows are bricked up beneath the boards."

"No they're not."

"Yes," she said, "they are. You couldn't have gotten in there."

We argued this point; we were both terrific arguers. It struck me that she hadn't found the right alley, or even the right Pallan Row. Perhaps there were two Pallan Rows in the city, near each other, perhaps even almost identical alleys. Perhaps there was the functional Pallan Row and the dysfunctional Pallan Row.

This idea seemed to clutch at me, as if I had known it to be true even before I thought it consciously.

The idea took hold, and that night, on the pretext of going to see a movie which Helen had already seen twice with friends, I took a cab over to Pallan Row.

III

It was colder on Pallan Row than in the rest of the city. While autumn was well upon us, and the weather had for weeks been fairly chilly, down the alley it was positively freezing. My curiosity and even fear took hold as I peeled back one of the window boards, the very one I had pulled down on my last visit. Helen had been right: the windows were bricked-up beneath the boards. But then, I had to wonder, why the boards at all?

I touched the bricks; had to draw my fingers back quickly, for they seemed like blocks of ice. I remembered the owner of the Chinese restaurant telling Jenny and me that it used to be an ice house. I touched the bricks again, and they were still bitingly cold – it hadn't been my imagination.

I walked around the alley, but saw no way of getting into the buildings again, for all were bricked up.

And then I heard it.

A sound, a human sound, the sound of someone who was trapped inside that old ice house, someone who had heard me pull the board loose and who needed help.

I am no hero, and never will be. For all I knew, there were some punks on the other side of that wall torturing one of their own, and if I walked into the middle of it, I would not see the light of day again.

And yet I could not help myself.

I found that if I kicked at the bricks, they gave a little. The noise from within had ceased, but I battered at the bricks until I managed to knock one of them out. It seemed to be an old brick job, for the cement between the blocks was cracked and powdery. After an hour, I had managed to dislodge several.

To my surprise and amazement, there was light on within the old restaurant. I looked through the sizable hole I'd made, and saw the former proprietress of the Chinese restaurant standing behind the bar, dressed in a jade-colored silk gown, talking with her barman. A few people sat at the tables, eating, laughing. None of them had noticed my activity at the window.

As I put my face to the hole, I breathed in air so cold that it seemed to stop my lungs up.

I moved back, and stood up. I was sure that this was a delusion; perhaps I needed some medication still, for immediately after Jenny's death, I had begun taking tranquilizers to help blot out the memory of finding her dead. Perhaps I still needed some medical help and psychological counseling.

I crouched down again to look through the opening, and noticed that at one of the tables, facing the other way, was a woman who looked from the back very much like Jenny.

I noticed the ice, too. It was a shiny glaze along the walls and tables; icicles formed teat-like off the chocolate-patterned tin ceiling. I watched the people inside there as if this were a television set; I lost my fear entirely, all my shivering came from the arctic breezes that stirred up occasionally from within.

I thought I heard someone out in the alley behind me, and turned to look.

Helen stood there in a sweatshirt and pants, my old windbreaker around her shoulders; she held a sweater in her arms.

"I figured you'd be here. Look, it's getting chilly." She passed the sweater down to where I sat on the pavement. She noticed the bricks beside me, and the light from within the building. "I see you've been doing construction. Or should I say, de-construction."

"Do you see the light?" I asked her.

She squatted down beside me. "What light?"

"I know you see it," I said, but when I glanced again through the hole, the place within had gone dark.

"What is it about this place for you?" she asked. "Even if you did see Jenny here, or her ghost, whatever – why here? You and she only came here once. Why would she come here?"

"I think this is Hell," I said. "I think this is one of those corners of Hell. I think Jenny's in Hell. And she wants something from me. Maybe a favor."

"Do you really believe that?"

I nodded. "Don't ask me why. There is no why. I think this is a corner of Hell that maybe shows through sometimes to some people. I don't even think maybe. I know that's what this is."

"You may be right," Helen said. She stood up, stretched, and offered me her hand to help me get up. I took it. Her hand was warm, and I felt a rush of blood in the palm of my hand as if she had managed to transfer some warmth to me.

And then, the sound again.

A human voice, indistinct, from within the walls.

Helen looked at me.

"You heard it, too," I said.

"It's a cat," she said. "It's a cat inside there."

I shook my head. "You heard it. It's not just me. Maybe Jenny can only show herself to me. Maybe Hell can only show itself to me, but you heard it."

"Wouldn't Jenny's ghost be in your old apartment where she died?" Something like fear trembled in Helen's voice. She was beginning to believe something that might be dreadful. It made me feel less alone.

"No. I don't think it's her ghost. A ghost is spiritual residue or something. I think she is in here, it's really her, in the flesh, and I think there are others in here. I need to go back in and find out what exactly she wants from me."

The noise again, almost sounding like a woman weeping.

"Don't go in there," Helen said. "It may not be anything. It may be something awful. It may be somebody waiting in there the way somebody waited for Jenny."

I took her face in my hands and kissed her eyelids. When I drew back from her face, I whispered, "I love you, Helen. But I have to find out if I'm crazy. I have to find out."

We went and sat in an all-night coffee shop talking about love and belief and insanity. Because I was beginning to convince myself that Pallan Row was a corner of Hell, I waited until the sun came up to investigate further within its walls. Helen returned with me, and between the two of us, we managed to break enough bricks apart and away from the wall so that the hole grew to an almost window-sized entrance.

I asked her to wait outside for me, and if anything happened, to go get help. I went in through the window, scraping my head a bit. The room on the other side was empty and dark, but that unnatural ice breath was still there, and, through the kitchen portal window, there came a feeble and distant light.

Helen asked, every few seconds, "You okay, Oliver? I can't see you."

"I'm fine," I reassured her as often as she asked.

I walked slowly to the kitchen door, looked through the round window pane. The light emanated from the freezer at the other end of the long kitchen. I pushed the door open (informing Helen that this was my direction so that she wouldn't worry if I didn't respond to her queries every few minutes), and moved more swiftly to the walk-in freezer.

The freezer door was unlocked. I opened it, too, and stepped inside.

The light was blue and as cold as the air.

Through the arctic fog, I could make out the shapes of human beings, hanging from meat hooks, their faces indistinct, their bodies slowly turning as if they had but little energy left within them. I did not look directly at any of these bodies, for my terror was becoming stronger – and I knew that if I were to remain sane as I walked through this ice-house of death, I would need to rein in my fear.

Finally, I found her.

Jenny.

Ice across her eyeless face, her hair, strands of thin, pearl-necklace icicles.

She hung naked from a hook, her head, drooping, her arms apparently lifeless at her side.

Her belly had been ripped open as if torn at with pincers, the skin peeled back and frost-burnt.

I stopped breathing for a full minute, and was sure that I was going to die right there.

I was sure the door to that freezer, that butcher-shop of the damned, would slide shut and trap me forever.

But it did not.

Instead, I heard that human sound again, closer, more distinct.

I heard my heart beating; my breathing resumed.

The sound came from beyond the whitest cloth of fog, and I waved my hands across it to dissipate the mist.

There, lying on a metal shelf, wrapped in the clothes which Jenny had been buried in, was our baby, his small fingers reaching for me as he began to wail even louder.

I lifted him, held him in my arms, and wiped the chill from his forehead.

Someone was there, among the hanging bodies, watching me. I couldn't tell who, for the fog had not cleared, neither had the blue light increased in intensity. I could not see to *see*. I felt someone's presence though, and thanked that someone silently. I thanked whoever or whatever had suckled my child, had warmed his blood, had met his needs. The place no longer frightened me. Whatever energy the freezer ran on, whatever power inspired it, had kept my child safe.

I took my son out into the bright and shining morning.

"This was why I was haunted," I told Helen, upon emerging from the open window. "This is what Jenny wanted to give me."

I can only describe Helen's expression, through her eyes, as one approaching dread. She said, "I think you should put it back where it belongs."

"Babies aren't 'its'," I said, and recalled saying this to Jenny once, too, at this very place. I glanced down at my boy, so beautiful, as he watched the sky and his father, breathing the vivid air.

Across his forehead, I saw a marking, a birthmark, a port-wine stain, perhaps, which spread across his skin like fire until he became something other than what might be called flesh.

CHERRY WILDER

The Curse of Kali

CHERRY WILDER IS A New Zealander living in Germany who writes science fiction, fantasy and horror. Her latest SF novel, *Signs of Life*, was published by Tor Books in 1996. Her horror fiction has recently appeared in *Asimov's Ghosts, Interzone, Strange Fruit* and previous volumes of *The Best New Horror*.

A science fiction story, "Dr Tilmann's Consultant", from *Omni* Online for November 1996, has been reprinted in *Year's Best SF 14* edited by Gardner Dozois and in *Year's Best Australian SF and Fantasy* edited by Jonathan Strahan and Jeremy G. Byrne.

"'The Curse of Kali' is about the revenge of the powerless or the weak," explains the author. "Women are often empowered by divine or supernatural means in myths and stories.

"When my friend, New Zealand horror writer Joy Tonks, referred to this story as containing 'an evil cat and an Indian Goddess', I was quick to point out that Ranji the cat is not evil at all – he's just a clever cat, surviving by his wits in the world of the humans . . ."

GWEN BEGAN TO NOTICE the house next door after Miss Pallisser's death. The old lady had been quiet and reclusive, not much given to gardening, and Gwen, in her new flat, was very quiet herself. One day the milkman found the previous day's bottles uncollected and promptly called the police. In no time at all Miss Pallisser's mortal remains had been taken away in a coffin-shaped plastic container: it was as if the world had been waiting for her to die. Some days later there was a knock on the door of Gwen's sitting room; Rose Benton, her landlady, burst in and hurried to the bay window.

"They're clearing out her things," she said. "I knew there would be a good view from this window!"

Gwen got up from her desk, and the two women stared into the next door garden. It was damp and dark, with two old deodar cedars and a high wall of grey stone. Two men in overalls brought out a sofa, a third man wheeled a battered fridge on a trolley. A young fellow in a jeans suit followed, carrying a tall brass vase filled with peacock feathers.

"Who owns the house now?" asked Gwen.

Rose chuckled.

"Not a word to a soul," she said, "but we do. Have for several years. Own the contents too, such as they are. The lawyers saw it our way."

Rose was a driving force in MOR (as in 'MOR for your money') Real Estate. Gwen, who had never owned a scrap of real estate, knew that there was much to admire in the Benton family. They were good-looking and well dressed, none more so than Rose who was tall, fresh-faced, and dark blonde.

Jock Benton was a jolly man, a management consultant who was a drinking companion of her editor. He had had the bright idea of letting Gwen this comfortable flat so that she could finish her book in peace. Gwen had been out of house and home since Polly's death, five months ago.

"What will happen to the old lady's things?" asked Gwen.

The removalists, with straps around their bodies, brought out an upright piano balanced on a small, wheeled platform.

"Most of it goes to the junk yard," said Rose. "A few bits and pieces have been ticketed. Our Arnold down there is seeing to them."

A window had been flung up on the second floor of the house, and a workman began to throw out blue plastic sacks.

"Clothes and oddments," said Rose. "Place was pretty run down."

Gwen moved the window curtain to get a clearer view. She saw for the first time that the house next door was a mirror image of the Bentons' house. The man was dropping sacks of clothing from a bay window identical with her own but on the near side of the house. The Bentons' house was pearl grey, elegant but comfortable, with an inviting front lawn, a rowan tree, and a rack for the children's bicycles. Miss Pallisser's house was dark grey, stained, and dilapidated.

A small boy in a green track suit and bouncy, three-coloured gym shoes was playing under the deodar trees. He got in the way of the workmen. Rose Benton flung up the heavy sash window and called in a threatening but carefully modulated voice:

"Paul! Come out of that garden at once!"

Paul, the youngest Benton, did not share the family good looks. He was a funny looking kid, still a *little* boy at nine years old, with shaggy, dark hair and thick glasses. Now he cocked his head on one side, squinting at the sun, then headed in more or less the right direction.

"Well, I'm off again!" said Rose. "You'll be down for a bit of barbecue, later on . . ."

She went striding out, and Gwen shut the window. There was something very cheerless about the trundling of Miss P's furniture and personal effects through her grey garden. It was as if the weather were cloudy at 26A and sunny at 26. Down on the lawn, under the rowan tree, Amy Benton, aged fifteen, was reading a magazine and looking at her watch.

Gwen went through into her bedroom and looked at the backs of the two houses. The contrast was more strongly marked than ever: Miss Pallisser's yard was dry and wretched, choked with deformed weeds. The Bentons, on the other hand, had a beautiful back garden, Mediterranean style, with espalier fruit trees, bougainvillaea, and a patio with a brightly striped awning. There was an empty rabbit hutch beyond the barbecue; Roger, the middle child, had never replaced his rabbits.

"Bit of a giver-upper, old Rodge," Jock had confided. "Plans things, then mopes when they come to nothing."

"Don't we all?" had been Gwen's comment, and it had shocked her landlord.

"Good God, no!" he said. "What a depressing notion! Better planning, Gwen, old girl . . . that's what's necessary."

He stared at her and diagnosed a fresh attack of grief. He poured her a double scotch and ordered her to perk up the old social life a bit. The point was, Gwen thought now, seated on the bed staring blindly into the dark backyard of 26A, they had never had a social life. She and Polly had lived for each other.

They had kept up the old house in the Cotswolds, cared for old Mr Maitland, Polly's father, cared for the cats and dogs, cared for the garden. Really, it had been no trouble. How she had written in those days, how they had researched, how they had bottled pears and cherries. Then, when the old man had passed on and they were ready to travel, Polly became ill. Now it was over. Who would index her history books now that Poll was gone? Who would love her again?

She blinked; there was a white disc on the weedy brick path to Miss Pallisser's back gate. She deduced a saucer. The old lady had had a cat. Something caught her eye in the sitting-room: a round patch of reflected sunlight was hovering above her desk. When she went to look, the patch flew up to the ceiling and down again. A dazzling star of light was shining from the bay window of Miss Pallisser's house where the workmen were still busy. Down below she saw Roger Benton stride down the front path, purposeful as his mother, carrying a plastic bag. He exchanged a business-like nod with his sister.

Drinks were served by Monika, the au pair girl, at half past six. Jock was late back; he bustled into the back garden shedding jacket and tie.

"We're all coping very nicely," said Rose. "Relax for a moment. When does your plane leave?"

"Some ungodly hour," said Jock. "Come on, Amy, what are you playing at there?"

"Salad," said Amy. "Roger is doing the steak."

"Steak takes some doing," said Jock. "How about it, Gwen? Are you game?"

Gwen accepted a piece of steak and a foil-wrapped potato.

"Where is Paul?" asked Monika. "I am not seeing him all afternoon."

"Give him a call, Amy!" ordered Rose.

Amy brushed back her long, golden hair and drifted into the house. She could be heard calling loudly all the way to the front gate.

"Nuisance!" said Jock. "Did he have bloody wolf cubs or something?"

"Perhaps he's at Nigel's," croaked Roger.

He was still working energetically at the barbecue; now the coals flared up as he turned a steak.

"Go through the house, Roger!" ordered Rose. "Little beast might be watching a video."

"I'm doing the steaks!"

"Cut along!" snapped Jock. "You've done enough damage. Monika can take over."

"We saw Paul at about midday," said Gwen. "Do you remember, Rose? He was in Miss Pallisser's front garden."

Her words were lost; Roger knocked the tray of cutlery to the ground on his way through the garden. When the two elder children came back after searching and calling, it was past eight o'clock.

"I'll half-kill that child!" said Rose. "Monika, I know it's your free weekend. Please go!"

Monika, a slender well-tanned girl in jeans, was proof against the Benton family. She went without a word.

Rose sprang up from her white cane chair and said: "I have exactly forty minutes to change. Shall we drop you at a terminal, Jock?"

"No thanks," said Jock. "Too early."

He settled in her chair with a fresh martini.

"You're both going away again?" asked Gwen.

"Price of success!" said Jock. "Amy, the money for Mrs Chand is on the desk in the den."

"Mmm," said Amy.

She sat with her brother on a garden seat beyond the empty rabbit hutch. Gwen noticed that they were not eating very much.

"So La Pallisser finally dropped off the twig," said Jock. "Must have been every day of seventy-five. Used to work for a firm of importers who went back to the tea clippers."

Gwen was embarrassed. If she ducked her head a little she could see the dark uncurtained windows of 26A.

"Daughter of a chap who spent a lot of time in India," continued Jock. "Language expert. Wrote books about the mysterious east. Don't know what you'd call him, really . . ."

"An orientalist," said Gwen. "Pundit Pallisser."

"Ha-ha! That's the man. Left her with nothing but a few curios and the property hopelessly tied up."

"Surely his library . . . ?"

"Priceless!" said Jock. "He left it to the University of bloody Allahabad or some such place. We saw quite a lot of the old doll up until a few years ago. I don't believe she ever forgave Rose for taking up the option on the house."

"Dad," said Roger, "is it too late to ring Nigel's people about Paul?"

"Not if you're quick about it," said his father. "He may stay the night, if they can put up with him."

Roger went traipsing into the house again, and the phone began to ring. Gwen found herself hoping that it was Nigel, asking if Paul could stay the night. Instead it was a call for Jock from Frankfurt am Main. He spoke briefly in German then could be heard dashing about and climbing the stairs.

"He'll take an earlier plane," observed Amy. "I wonder what has happened to Paul?"

"When did you see him last?" asked Gwen.

"I haven't set eyes on him all day," said Amy.

Roger came back briskly.

"He's not at Nigel's," he announced. "I'll just take a walk round the block and search for him."

"No!" said Amy. "Wait. They're coming down."

"It's a bit early," said Roger. "Not properly dark yet or anything..."

Presently Rose and Jock appeared, perfectly turned out. Rose wore a linen suit, Jock was outfitted by BOSS; they carried identical briefcases.

"All right then," said Rose. "My schedule is on the pinboard in the living room. Don't forget to put out the dustbin."

"Mummy," said Roger, "Paul isn't back. No one has seen him."

"God give me strength!" said Rose. "*You* used to do this, Roger, do you know that?"

"What did I do?"

"Take off just before one of our trips," said Jock. "I missed a conference once when you were five. Time you hid in the gardener's hut in the park."

"Paul is mine," said Amy, "but a bit retarded."

"Is that the car?" asked Rose.

"Personally," said Amy, "I think one of you should stay. Probably Mummy. It really would look better..."

"This opening of the Cherbourg subdivision has been planned down to the last detail," snapped Rose. "What do you mean 'look better'?"

"If Paul doesn't turn up," said Amy.

"I expect kids do it all the time," said Roger. "I mean, stay out all night. In rough neighbourhoods."

"Jock?" said Rose.

"Out of the question!" said Jock fiercely. "Mine is an emergency. Rose, I told you how the situation had deteriorated!"

"In Calcutta and places," said Roger, "children *live* in the streets. No one seems to care . . ."

Jock swung a fist at Roger and half-connected with his midriff. Roger moved out of range behind a stone urn filled with geraniums.

"I will *not* be blackmailed by that little bastard!" said Rose. "There! That really is the car."

"Mind you," said Amy, "I suppose you will be able to say there were other adults in the house."

Gwen, who had been making herself invisible in her chair, was aware that the four Bentons paused in their noisy confrontation and glanced at her.

"I've had about as much of this as I can stand!" said Jock. "What on earth must Gwen – Miss Cross – be thinking of this carry-on!"

"I just want a plan of action," said Roger. "When do we call the police?"

"I'm not staying to listen to this nonsense," said Rose. "He'll be back in ten minutes. Come along, Jock! I'm going!"

"Yes, you really are going," said Amy.

"I'll be at the Plaza Hotel, Frankfurt, by midnight," said Jock. "*Don't* try to reach your mother on that damned auto telephone."

"Okay," mumbled Roger.

He collapsed on to the garden seat and ate potato crisps from a bag. Rose and Jock hurried away through the house just as the driver from MOR Real Estate began to honk the horn of the Bentley. Amy sat beside her brother. They slapped hands like Black Panthers sealing a bargain.

Gwen was suddenly very irritated with the Benton family. She felt no solidarity with the parents, and she had an uneasy feeling that Amy and Roger knew perfectly well where their brother was. She hoped very much that Paul *would* come bouncing in after ten minutes and give the game away with a cry of "Have they gone yet?"

She said warily: "Have you looked next door?"

"I asked old Lever first thing," said Roger. "He was watering his roses."

"No," said Gwen. "I mean the house on this side. Miss Pallisser's house."

"He'd never go there," said Amy.

Gwen, who was thin and agile and not unsuitably dressed, decided to look over the wall. She carried one of the sturdy wrought-iron chairs down the path and chose a good place. The children did not move. She stood on the chair, clutching the gritty top of the wall, and scrambled higher up with the aid of an espalier tree.

"Mummy will be livid," called Roger, "if you break that apple tree."

Gwen looked into the backyard of Miss Pallisser's house, cold and grey in the summer night. The lamp at the corner of the street, beyond the far wall, admitted a few feeble rays of blue light; a leaning dustbin looked like a tombstone, the back gate was ajar. There was the white saucer on the path and there was a shadow sitting hopefully beside it . . . the cat.

Before Gwen could utter a word, the telephone rang inside the Benton house. Amy and Roger charged indoors to answer it, and all the lights in the garden went out. One of them must have tripped over a cord or brushed against a switch. She was marooned up against the wall, feet entangled in the precious apple tree. She waited a moment for someone to notice her plight, but no one did.

"Wait there!" she said to the cat.

It had already gone. Gwen saw circles of light from the Bentons' flourishing garden superimposed upon the dark wasteland of 26A. She clutched the rough wall painfully hard, felt her heart thumping in her chest. It came over her like a gust of warm wind rising unaccountably from Miss Pallisser's backyard. She was engulfed by a wave of terror and revulsion. The feelings came first, and then she saw it. A dark figure at the corner of the house, yes, the edge of a window was hidden, momentarily blotted out. Then the street light flushed again, between the branches of a scrawny plum tree: the yard was empty.

Gwen breathed deeply. She climbed down on to the chair and was making her way to the barbecue when Amy switched on the patio light.

"You were in the dark," she said.

"Never mind," said Gwen. "Any news of Paul?"

"Little beast!" said Amy. "He's at the pictures with Nigel."

Roger came bursting out of the house again.

"At least we think so!" he said loudly. "He's *probably* at the pictures."

Gwen had cut up the remains of the steak into bite-sized pieces on a paper plate.

"Do you know Miss Pallisser's cat?" she asked.

"It's Ranji," said Roger, "the only one left."

"She had other cats?" asked Gwen.

"About six," said Roger. "I'm sure you've seen them. There was a white one with blue eyes."

Gwen did remember the white cat. It sat patiently on the garden wall while Paul and Roger banged saucepans to prove that it was deaf. She even had a brief flash of memory concerning a voice, high and sweet, calling "Puss, Puss" in the mornings. Miss Pallisser herself.

"What became of them all?" she asked with resignation.

The lives of cat-lovers were littered with dead cats. It had to do with the differing life span of the two species and the priority given to human activities.

"They were caught and put to sleep," said Amy. "Mummy and the lawyer thought it was best."

"All except Ranji," said Roger, "big dirty-brown fluffy affair."

"He's too cunning," said Amy. "No one could catch him. He still goes networking for food all down the street."

"I thought of giving him this meat," said Gwen. "The back gate is open."

"I could do that!" said Roger eagerly. "Let me, Miss Cross!"

"Fine," said Gwen. "Shall I help you clear away, Amy?"

"Oh no," said Amy. "We can manage. Truly."

They all said goodnight with some relief, and Gwen went into the house. She stood still for a moment in the passageway to pick an apple leaf off her trousers. The acoustics of the house were strange. She heard Roger say:

"*She knows!*"

"Quiet!" said Amy. "Go on! Take Ranji the meat!"

Gwen went stealthily into the hall and ran upstairs on tiptoe. Once inside the flat she switched on a single lamp in the sitting room and hurried into the unlit bedroom for a perfect view of Miss Pallisser's backyard. Roger did exactly what was expected of him. He came through the back gate and set the paper plate down beside the saucer. But then he wandered out of sight around the far corner of the house.

Gwen hurried into the lighted sitting room and lurked behind the curtains of the bay window staring down at the front garden of 26A this time. Roger was nowhere to be seen; she had missed him. Perhaps he had doubled back and gone out the same way he came in. She waited, went away to put on her electric jug for a cup of tea, but was drawn to various windows again. The lights were out in the Bentons' back garden. She listened at the open door of her flat and heard the familiar sounds of shots, shouts, and screaming brakes from the telly.

She made her tea, changed into her oldest tracksuit, and took one of the tranquilizers she had been persuaded to use soon after Polly's death. "Everything is smoothed out," the doctor had said. "You'll see." She fetched a light blanket and sat shivering in her big armchair, waiting for the smoothing effect. What had upset her so, upset her to the point of hallucination? She could not turn on her own telly or even play a record. What was she afraid of? She sipped her tea and did feel better.

Roger's plan took shape in her head. It was Amy's plan, too: a confrontation with Rose and Jock. Paul was a freakish child, who took dares and got into scrapes. She thought of Paul stuffing leaves from the rowan tree into the letterbox of 26A . . . Paul in the snow under the deodars. The place was an "attractive nuisance" for a small boy. Paul was pretending to be lost; Roger was hiding him in the house next door.

Gwen was becoming much more tranquil by now, but she hated this idea. She pushed it away as she had pushed away her grief. No, she would not go downstairs and ask questions. The Benton children were watching television; Paul had just come back from the cinema. She curled up in her big recliner chair, pulled up the blanket, and slept.

There were hints in her dream of the mysterious east: exotic scents and the noise of temple bells. A veiled woman stood alone in a room with figured carpets on the walls. Blood and fire began to edge into the dream. Picture postcards burned, strips of film went up in a sharp burst of flame, and there was blood spreading thickly over the steps that led down to the river. She put her arms tightly around Polly to shield her from falling debris, and they ran through the pools of blood while at their backs a terrible commotion grew and the world ended in a splintering crash.

Gwen was awake. The lamp on her desk looked pale in the daylight. The crash from her dream still reverberated. Something terrible had happened. She sprang up, went to the bay window and saw that its counterpart in Miss Pallisser's house was unscathed. By some trick of the light she could see her own window, her own reflection, in the emptiness of that upper room.

She saw herself, then she saw a different woman, her face became the face of a stranger. The figure was swathed in odd clothes, drifting veils of grey, black, orange-red, and gold. Miss Pallisser was old and not old, motionless yet pulsing with motion, dead yet un-dead; she seemed to have more than one pair of arms. Then the vision fled away leaving a few drifting wisps of grey smoke and, in the innermost reaches of the house, there was a red glow.

Gwen was split into two people: one of them remained at the window harrowed with fear, groping in some unknown dimension. The other broke away, splashed water on her face, and called the fire brigade. An empty house?

"Unoccupied," she said, "but you must hurry! There is a child in that house . . . playing."

She slipped into her shoes and ran down the stairs shouting. Amy came out of the kitchen in her sleepshirt.

"Where is Paul?" cried Gwen, putting things in the wrong order.

"Staying at Nigel's, Miss Cross," said Amy, game to the last. "Didn't we say? After they came back from the picture it was so late . . ."

"Fire!" said Gwen. "Fire in the house next door. Amy, don't lie to me! Where is Paul? Which room is he in?"

"Upstairs on the far side," said Amy. "Roger is there, too."

"Go out on the street," ordered Gwen. "Show the firemen where to go!"

She ran headlong through the Bentons' back garden. There was a light haze of smoke in the backyard of 26A. She had no idea of the way in – the back door was locked – she turned to the kitchen window, ready to attack it with the dustbin, then veered round the side of the house. A side door was propped open, emitting smoke in thick curls about her ankles.

She plunged into the house and found she was doing the impossible. It was dark, filled with smoke; she did not know where to go. She blundered on and came to a place that vaguely resembled the Bentons' hallway; the door to the cellar was open. The cellar was burning, smoke was pouring up the main staircase; runnels of flame from the burning door of the cellar had attacked the bannisters on one side. Gwen tried to shout and choked, then ran up the stairs crouched against the unburnt bannisters. Covering her mouth she called their names.

"Paul! Roger!"

The landing was filled with smoke; she made blindly for the front room on the far side of the house. The smoke had come in everywhere, it oozed between the uncarpeted floorboards. She tripped over a transistor radio, went crawling to the first sleeping bag. She dragged it towards the front window; it must be Paul, from the weight. She heaved it up, shaking and patting at the boy. He was warm, he was sweating. Gwen fought and heaved at the window, and at last it came up. She sat astride the sill, letting the window rest on her shoulder.

She gulped air and heard the sound of the fire engine. She expelled the precious air again, drew the laden sleeping bag across her knees, and let it down as far as she could. Paul's head was uncovered; she saw his rumpled hair, his flushed cheeks. There was no one to help, but the old sloping lintel of the window below, unchanged on this house, began to take the weight, and at last she let go and saw her burden go slithering safely down on to a pile of earth.

She dived back and crawled and found Roger in his sleeping bag. The boy did not stir at first, but as she heaved and tugged him across the floor she felt sure that his body moved. She knew that she was far beyond the end of her strength. Her breath caught in her chest; she had not the relief of crying out. Inch by inch they came towards the open window. She was gone, unconscious for a few seconds, and she returned, on the instant, to her dream again. *A veiled woman stood alone in the room with figured carpets upon the walls.*

Then with a supreme effort she hung Roger Benton, all fourteen years of him, face downwards out of the window and hung there exhausted herself. She was gasping, loud enough for two. Down below a fireman lifted Paul into his arms. Another fireman, wearing a respirator, strode into the room.

Gwen had slept heavily; she suspected it was early morning. She experienced anxiety as she woke up. It was all a dream. She had done nothing, she was back in her flat, rubbing her eyes, switching off the lamp on her desk, looking at her watch. Then the hospital came over her, the reek of disinfectant, the five o'clock rumble of trolleys and crash of bedpans. No, she really had done it. She felt a glow of relief, she basked in it, she was proud of herself. Her muscles ached keenly, she had torn something in her back, her eyes stung, her throat was raw, her chest was painful. One hand was bandaged, her left ankle too, where she had fallen on the way downstairs. She could still feel the iron grip of the fireman, fingers digging into her upper arm as he heaved her to her feet. But the boys were safe.

She was in an ancient hospital bed with high metal sides like a cot; it stood in a curtained-off section of a busy corridor. Presently a woman pathologist came and took another sample of her blood. A Hindu doctor with a clipboard stood and observed the procedure. He looked at Gwen with a curious expression.

"You were a bit under the weather yesterday," he said. "Couple of things we had better go over again."

"How are the boys?" she croaked. "Roger and Paul Benton."

"That would be children's ward," he said. "Completely different department. Just let's get this over with. Name: Jane Ross."

"Gwen Cross."

"Aha, bit of a difference! Gwen Cross, eh?"

He wrote on his form.

"Now the address. Be a bit careful here."

"26 Durbar Place, St John's Wood," said Gwen carefully.

He sighed and wagged a finger at her. A nurse came in, and Gwen was given an injection. She learned that the doctor's name was Singh. When the nurse had gone he commented on the fresh bruises on her upper arm. Gwen's patience was being tested; she explained about the fireman.

"Treated you rough, did they?"

"It was an emergency," she said. "There was a fire in the cellar of an old house. The two boys were . . . camping out, upstairs."

"Yes," he said, "I have a note of the circumstances. Gwen, I'll give you a good tip. Those premises are unoccupied. No point in giving them as an address. Far better to own up and say 'no fixed abode'."

Gwen could not speak.

"Just tell me," said Dr Singh, "exactly where you were when the fire broke out. Were you in the basement? Doing a bit of cooking, for instance? Did you take a drop of something to keep out the cold?"

"I have a flat at 26 Durbar Place," she said. "The fire was at 26A. The house next door."

Dr Singh clicked his ballpoint pen. He came closer again and examined Gwen's eyes, her teeth, the glands on the side of her neck. He rolled up the sleeves of the horrid hospital nightgown, looked carefully at the inner surfaces of both her arms and at her unbandaged right hand. Then he picked up his clipboard again and removed the particulars of the female vagrant, Jane Ross, found on the premises blackened and abraded in an old tracksuit. He quickly began a new form.

"I think we had better start again, Miss Cross," he said gently. "You have a family named Symes or Grimes for next of kin?"

"Mr and Mrs Matthew Grimes," she said. "Mr Grimes is my editor . . . If I could telephone . . ."

"Of course. I can't think how this mix-up came about."

"I kept fading away . . ." said Gwen. "I had difficulty answering the questions."

Dr Singh took off his glasses and polished them.

"So many cruel misunderstandings," he said. "The bureaucracy is going mad. In fact the whole world. I think sometimes we are under a curse!"

Gwen stared at him in wonder. To have her secret thoughts spoken and by a man of his race.

"That house, 26A, was the home of a Miss Pallisser," she said. "Does that mean anything to you, Dr Singh . . . from your reading?"

"Ha-ha!" he said, echoing Jock Benton. "I know exactly whom you mean! Pundit Pallisser! Author of *The Jade Garden*, *Excursions Through the Hindukush*, *Cults of Kali* . . . How are you feeling now, Miss Cross?"

"The Bentons are both away on business," said Gwen.

She was slipping into a role that she had never played very

well. She was a family friend; she stood *in loco parentis* just a little.

"I do hope the young girl, Amy Benton, is being taken care of."

"I am sure she is with friends," said Dr Singh. "I will see that you are moved to a room upstairs."

The injection had taken effect; her pain was receding. She thought of a room full of flowers, a bed of roses. Dr Singh fixed her with his dark eyes; outside the starched pink curtains an old woman began to utter peals of maniacal laughter.

"Miss Cross," he said, "the boys are dead."

Gwen finished her book in a cottage in Cornwall; it was only six months behind schedule. She accepted a certain amount of psychotherapy but then broke off the treatment and decided to remain mad, if that was what she was.

Matthew Grimes and his nice wife, Hetty, cleared out the flat and continued to see to her welfare. She saw none of the surviving members of the Benton family again and tried not to think of them.

She had been keyed up about the inquest where she would certainly have seen them, but in the end she was too sick to attend, and the coroner accepted her affidavit. It was a brief and unspectacular inquest, sparsely reported in the press. The verdict was one of misadventure; the coroner expounded upon the danger of asphyxia through the inhalation of smoke. He spoke of an unfortunate combination of circumstances and the tragic end of a youthful prank or rag. The cause of the fire was, in the opinion of experts, the explosion of a bottle of cleaning fluid in the cellar. A tenant of number 26, Miss Gwen Cross, had called the fire brigade, but all help for Roger and Paul Benton came too late.

Matt Grimes expressed surprise when the Bentons did not visit Gwen in hospital or in the private clinic where she spent some weeks. She felt she understood. A failure as monstrous as hers was unbearable. There were no rewards for good intentions.

In the second summer after the fire she drove back and perceived what had happened. The Benton house was deserted, its paintwork stained, its windows uncurtained and dark. A storm had uprooted the rowan tree; the lawn had turned brown. Next door there was new turf between the deodars and bright garden beds. The house was a picture; the roof had been retiled; window cleaners were at work.

Arnold, the young man from MOR who was supervising, recognized her from Benton barbecues. Yes, indeed, the steam cleaning had worked wonders. They walked into the backyard, which was transformed, prettier even than the Bentons' back garden had been, with a pergola and grape vines. Of course the insurance, such as it was, had helped to pay for the renovations.

"Now we're saddled with that mess next door!" said Arnold.

Gwen stepped up onto a garden seat for a quick look; the Bentons' yard was ugly and desolate.

"Is Rose still with the company?" she asked.

"Terrible thing . . ." Arnold lowered his voice. "Rose wasn't up to much after that. She's in a sanitarium, actually, on the south coast. Girl in boarding school. Jock battling round the trade fairs."

She glanced up at the bay window of her own flat and almost lost her nerve. There was a rustling in the pergola.

"Isn't that the old lady's cat?" she said faintly.

"Super, isn't he?" said Arnold. "Here Ranji, Ranji . . . He's quite tame. We make a pet of him."

He took some cat nibbles out of his pocket and put them into a plastic dish. Ranji, a long-haired Burmese, came forward boldly, tail erect, his amber eyes wide and unafraid. Gwen stroked him from head to tail. She said goodbye to Arnold and walked back to her car around the far side of the house. The new side door was pearl grey with fancy hinges.

She stood at the front gate and trembled, staring at the upper windows.

"*You did it!*" she silently accused Miss Pallisser.

"*I am dead,*" replied Miss Pallisser, soft as smoke. "*Why would I want to do such a thing?*"

"*They bought your house over your head,*" said Gwen, "*and sent your things to the junkyard and had your cats . . . put to sleep!*"

It seemed to her that she had played no part at all in the Bentons' débâcle. Or perhaps not enough. Her own life was no more than a dead weight that she dragged across the floor of a smoke-filled room. She shut her eyes for a second or two; the woman from her dream lowered her veil to reveal a hideous mask.

RICHARD CHRISTIAN MATHESON

The Film

RICHARD CHRISTIAN MATHESON IS a novelist, short story writer and screenwriter/producer. He has written and executive produced more than five hundred episodes of television for over thirty primetime network series, including *Magnum*, *Hunter*, *Amazing Stories* and *Tales from the Crypt*, and was the youngest writer Universal Studios ever put under contract.

He has also written over twenty pilots for series and had four feature films made. To date, Matheson has written and sold more than fifteen original feature scripts, on spec, each in the million dollar category, which is considered to be a record.

His critically acclaimed short fiction has been published in many anthologies and such magazines as *Penthouse*, *Twilight Zone*, *Gallery*, *Rage* and *Omni*. Thirty stories are collected in *Scars and Other Distinguishing Marks*, and a second collection scheduled for 1998, *Dystopia*, contains fifty more. His debut novel, *Created By*, was a Bram Stoker Award finalist and a Book-of-the-Month selection. It has been translated into six languages, setting a record in Italy for the largest sale of any first novel.

About the following story, Matheson admits, "I have no anecdotes, except to say I began it fifteen years ago and only last year decided to take it seriously enough to finish it. *Rage* bought it immediately and parked it alongside digit insertion and ecological diatribes. I guess that's the perfect home."

THE THEATER LOOMED IN deadness.
It rose like some vast ship, wrecked on ash nowhere; rusted steel clawed by sick wind. Marquee letters rattled in the howl and glowed:

The Film

on endless night. Beneath were six riveted doors; locked, massive. Parking for those who'd made it, in Detroit scrap, was to one side. The rest walked; somehow managed. Two men directed cars when an '89 Taurus junked-in, hammering stomp-chomp.

There were four. Oldest, twenty. Names: Blue, Janey, Ameyl, Marg. Met on the diseased veins of what was left.

Blue and Marg fled the East Section when the Boscos guzzed everything. Escaped slaughterhouse pain, took chewed Interstate, squirting toward poison nowhere.

Picked up Janey and Ameyl, hanging thumbs outside Tulsa: now missing; a mesquite boneyard. On their way to ". . . see the motherfucking *movie*!"

They tongued at Blue and Marg like meth-snakes all about *The Film* – not that they'd *actually* seen it. Had two extra tickets for the theater, 1100 miles west. But they'd swap for a ride. And like that, the four were over charscape, throating blister.

"Behold the fucking fuck palace," Blue yelled, staring at the hulking theater; a fortress in zero.

"We late?" Janey looked to Ameyl, her face still beautiful despite everything.

Ameyl puckered lips like a bullet in skin, gave an obscene kiss. Janey looked away as his laughter raked. Blue turned to look, bloodshot.

"Forty-nine hours, a few secs . . ." his smile was a foul hole. His breath stank; Boscos rooting.

"Sex?" Ameyl eeled fingers into Janey's pants. She said nothing; didn't care.

Blue looked up at the theater, dropped eyes to swelling line. "Us. Now. I want up close."

Nearby, sky vehicles roamed barren hills, dropping anti-bacterial plumes. Faint screams of the diseased could be heard, fleeing yellow mist.

Marg hugged Blue as they joined the line. "I feel sick," she whispered. "Took extra Nummers."

He nodded as Ameyl and Janey came up behind, feet raising ash. Around them, the crowd stirred. Impatient misery uglied faces, wore tempers. Sour arguments started, ended.

Blue watched them all, loathing. "Fuckin' head spiders, man."

Ameyl had fingers down throat, like tweezing guts. "Welcome to the Gargle, baby." He tried to laugh but everything hurt and he couldn't make it stop.

Above the hundreds who waited, the huge red letters clung to the marquee, making faces below look bloody.

"Ameyl . . . ?" Janey sounded weak. "Is it scary as everyone says?"

"It's fuckin' nerve damage," said Marg, rubbing at her belly that vised with pain.

Ameyl licked lips. "Okay . . . met a guy . . . we did needle at this shitpit, East Shore. Said it's like fuckin' Boscos chewin'. Said he'd seen *The Film* hundred times."

"Hundred?" Blue smirked; decay fume. He wiped runny eyes, nose slowly bleeding. Yelled: "*I wish this* fucking *line would fucking* move!!"

Janey needed a Nummer; sickness, worse than the others. She slid capsule down throat, closed eyes, waited for guts to stop begging.

". . . they're late," said Blue, paying no attention to Janey coughing blood. He glanced at her, nudged Ameyl and Marg. They stared away.

". . . fucking Boscos," said Marg, to no one.

Many in line did the same, hacking bad red, downing Nummers. But Janey had last-stage and dropped two more capsules into raw stomach. In seconds, the dose kicked; warm dead. She tried to smile at Marg and trickles of blood ran from mouth corners.

"*Vampire*!!" yelled Ameyl, pointing at her.

Janey wiped her mouth, smearing sick blood.

Overhead, a deep voice spoke from giant speakers welded to wall.

"Doors will open in a moment for the next screening of *The*

Film. Present tickets at the door. Once inside, be seated immediately. The show will start once all are seated. Thank you."

Ameyl's eyes popped. "'Bout fuckin' time!"

As the line moved, rain fell. Acid drops hissed ground and the audience raced to entry doors where two ticket takers waited.

Their black Sealer suits protected them head-to-toe and they stared through ruby slits. Their eyes couldn't be seen and they validated tickets, nodding each audience member in.

As the four stepped to the doorway, Janey had the crawl-bad, reached for another Nummer. One of the ticket takers noticed, stopped her, examined her expression.

"You alright?"

She managed a nod.

"How many you taken?"

She looked trapped. The ticket taker remained silent.

"I'm alright," she said.

The ticket taker exchanged an eyeless glance with the other. The second gave no sign. The crowd behind began to complain and the first taker finally placed Janey's ticket under a validator, gestured the four in.

Inside, the lobby was cold.

Four doors led into the main theater. Marg wondered what was upstairs; there seemed to be an entire other floor.

"Welcome to fucking *amazing*," Ameyl yelped.

The crowd moved into the theater and someone was shoving. Blue turned, knocked an old man behind him to the ground. The man was covered with sores. Stared-up, eyes pleading, hands covering face.

Blue spit on him. "Zombie."

The nervous crowd moved into the theater's seating area; filled with metal seats. They shivered, steel-chill sticking and Janey rubbed arms, staring at the concrete ramps between rows of seats that led to the giant screen/wall.

Silent ushers shone turquoise flashlight beams, indicating for all to sit. The four took seats and Ameyl peered around. Wrung fingers. Marg rested her head on his shoulder.

He stared forward, saying nothing. Wondered how scary *The Film* would be. He'd never felt much in his life; only depression, dread. Endless gnaw.

Nobody left was different. Except the old ones. It's why they all hated them; they'd seen good things. Could close tired eyes, remember trees, oceans. Could forget the vacant, septic ill, at least for a moment.

Maybe *The Film* would grind-off the pain, he thought. Replace disease and death with a good scare. Maybe he could forget, too. Maybe he could finally. . .

"*Start the fucking movie!*," some zombie was yelling.

Marg pointed. "Lookit that fuck."

"Meatcan," Blue sneered; dark, insolent. Vile anger in the eyes.

It was insane to Ameyl how long Blue had made it without Nummers. "Weeks," he'd said during the trip. Had to be a lie. Minus enough Nummers, despair became hate; an animal rush.

"*Fuck him!*" Blue screamed.

Around them, people glanced without interest, lost in sickness, though other fights started; furious, violent.

Huge ushers separated them and as the last of the arguing audience members sat, the ushers left. Closed doors.

Lights began to dim and the audience quieted, staring ahead in icy shadow. A few screamed excitedly and everyone laughed; pumped. They sat impatiently, waiting for the wall to flood with terrifying images. A horrid soundtrack. Jolting edits.

But it remained dark. Silent.

The crowd started to yell.

"*Start the fucking movie!!*"

They stood, wanting to know what was wrong, staring at projection windows that should've been spraying light and, one by one, people began to breathe wrong.

"God . . . the air," Marg said.

Ameyl stared up, again, at the projection windows. Thought he saw faces, watching; look away. Heard vents throughout the theater softly inhaling.

"*Fuckers!*" he screamed. "They're pumping it out!"

The audience was gasping for air and began to scramble up the ramps to the locked doors, beating on the metal. The smell of panic was everywhere in the gigantic theater and bodies struggled, some thrown to the floor; trampled, calling out in disbelief.

"*Don't you get it?!*" Blue screamed. "*It's part of the show! They're trying to scare us! It's part of the fucking show!! It's great!!!*" But he couldn't breathe either.

In the tenth row, Janey sat motionless, watching the wall, dosed into stunned calm.

The crowd struggled to escape the airless theater, clawing walls, pounding doors; an infected herd, trapped.

Ameyl and Blue held Marg but she collapsed, unable to breathe. They fought to get to Janey, shoving aside screaming children who'd fallen. Helpless hands reached. Faces twisted.

"Let us out!" a child begged.

"Please . . ." The convulsing wail of an old woman.

Ameyl slumped to the cement, blood trickling from mouth corners.

Blue screamed at him, struggling for air. "We gotta save Janey!"

But Ameyl was dead, mouth half-open.

In the half-dark, Blue forced through dead bodies between himself and Janey, climbing over seats strewn with dying, who grabbed at him, mouths sucking. He kicked a terrified child in the face, continued toward Janey who sat, board-stiff, staring at the screen.

But he collapsed beside an old woman who'd fallen on a baby. He struggled, then froze; gone.

Janey watched it all, Nummed; slowly dying, feeling her chest empty. Her eyes closed as she imagined a pristine forest.

In another minute, they were all dead.

On the second floor of the theatre, in the sealed room, the timer elapsed with a loud *buzz*.

The one running the control board flipped a switch, stared down into the theater, through sealed windows. Under the metal seats, a metallic groan began and sections of floor and ramps began to part. The seats hinged forward and row after row of tangled corpses were dropped into the acid pit under the theater; faces frozen in shock.

A hiss rose as audience members fell into the acid, folding easily; a gory weave. Thick fumes rose. Skin separated from muscle. Facial features melted away, creating momentary monsters, then vanished. Bodies were stripped to bone. Bone began to soften; would soon liquefy.

In the sealed room, the manager sighed. Entered the number into a computer: two-hundred and six. Good week; nearly three thousand. Buy medicine, food. Military paid decent to destroy the sick ones, lure them from hiding. But tomorrow would be worse. Ash storms were making the theater hard to find. How much longer would it all take . . . ?

An usher watched the men outside with flashlights as they counted cars: more profit. "Good screening," he said.

The manager sipped filtered water. Sighed, stared outside, seeing headlights in the far distance.

"Hey, everybody loves a good movie," he said, emptying the bottle of water.

Below, the seats popped up for the next show.

STORM CONSTANTINE

Of a Cat, But Her Skin

STORM CONSTANTINE WRITES FULL time, manages a rock band, and works as a publicist for other bands. She made her novel debut in the late 1980s with the acclaimed Wraeththu trilogy, *The Enchantments of Flesh and Spirit*, *The Bewitchments of Love and Hate* and *The Fulfilments of Fate and Desire*.

Since then her short fiction has been published in *Interzone*, *New Worlds 1* and *Black Thorn White Rose*, and her books have included *Monstrous Regiment*, *Hermetech*, *Aleph*, *Burying the Shadow*, *Sign for the Sacred*, *Calenture*, and the Grigori dark fantasy trilogy: *Stalking Tender Prey*, *Scenting Hallowed Blood* and *Stealing Sacred Fire* – the latter three centred on one of the author's abiding interests, the myths of fallen angels.

As she explains, "'Of a Cat, But Her Skin' originally appeared in Ellen Datlow's anthology of cat horror stories. It was inspired by a monument at a local stately home – Shugborough Hall – but the family in the story who own the estate are fictional, even though there is some evidence that past owners of Shugborough might have dabbled in some esoteric pursuits..."

SHE RAN INTO THE shadows of the trees, down hill, down the worn paths. He called after her "Nina! Nina!" She ignored it. Her sandalled feet hit the bare earth. Another afternoon ruined, another scene. Am I mad? Am I? Only anger, exasperation, gave her the strength and the freedom to run away. And that too would be brief. Still, the experience while it lasted was exhilarating. He did not run after her, knowing she would return eventually, contrite.

Soon, her chest began to ache and she slowed her pace to a walk, panting heavily. She felt shaky at the exertion, but tingling too. For minutes, maybe an hour, she was free. Free of him, her weakness. This was a deserted part of the garden, far from the restored Victorian tea-rooms, the landscaped formal pleasances, the slowly-moving river. Nina preferred this kind of scenery, with its great old trees, hugged by lush grass, too green to be real, perhaps nurtured by unhealthy secrets buried deep. Woody nightshade tumbled across the path, bearing dark purple velvety flowers, with spears of shocking yellow at their hearts. Amaradulcis; the bittersweet poison. It seemed no one had walked here for years. Sunlight came down through the high canopy of oak and beech, stroking raw perfume from the herbs and grasses. Nina paused and took a deep breath. In such an idyll as this, could the real world with all its terrors, cruelties and abuses ever intrude? She felt protected, tranquil, as if the path had closed behind her. Scott would call this yet another symptom of her "dreaminess", as he referred to it. "You're too dreamy; that's your trouble." Perhaps it was true, but if so, why should that be seen as a flaw?

The trees receded and revealed a small glade, ceilinged by ancient branches. A green room. The path seemed to end here. At the centre of the clearing was a weathered black monument: there were many of them scattered around the grounds of the old house. Some had been defaced over the years, others restored. This one appeared unmarked by human vandalism, but neither had it recently been cleaned. A stone dais of two steps supported a wide, four-sided obelisk. Crouched on the apex, was the statue of a lean cat. It was frozen in a pose of alertness, a hunter's stoop, forever gazing back along the path, as if waiting to pounce. Nina sat down on the steps and put her hot face into her hands. What am I going to do? She had asked herself this question many times. The constant arguments with Scott, the groundless accusations, the pestilent silences that gnawed away at her resolve would never go away; she knew that. And yet she felt so powerless; in a financial and emotional sense. She had some money of her own, but not much. She was an illustrator of children's books, but was neither well-known nor well-paid. Scott, a successful designer, held the reins of her life; she was trapped in the traces. But there were good days, weren't there? And she did love him, despite his jealousies, which were fretful and anxious, and therefore cruel. She knew the problem was his, and that it ran very deep. Sometimes, in dark moments of bare honesty, he would weep like a child in fear and frustration. Because of this, she could never leave him. He was a casualty of his own life.

The argument that afternoon had been senseless, as usual. They were taking a couple of well-earned weeks off work, renting out a cottage in the country only a short distance from the city where they lived. So far, they had spent every day exploring local historical sights. Both of them were interested in the past. Admittedly, things had been fine until today, no arguments at all. But something had ignited his temper: the paintings in the hall of Elwood Grange. Nina had admired them, fading reminders of a past age; lords and ladies of haughty mien, long dead, staring down at the milling masses for eternity, disdainful of those who came to pick over their remains. Without thinking, she had remarked that one of the couples portrayed were very striking for their time. "They have an almost twentieth century look," she'd said. "They look like a couple of rock stars, or perhaps people who run a dodgy religion!" Her light comments were a grave mistake.

Scott said nothing at first and then, outside on the wide, sweeping steps, with the heat of summer baking the arms and bare heads of the tourists, he'd presented his sulk to her. Nina had been confused at first. What had she done? She could think of nothing. Nina was used to living her life by walking on eggshells, and had become very adept at doing so. If the fragile shells broke nowadays, it was rarely because of anything she'd actually said or done, but something generated in the hot, aching nest of Scott's fecund paranoia.

"What is it?" she'd asked, wondering if someone else inside the Grange had upset him.

He'd walked off, between a stand of yews, towards the river. She'd followed. "What is it?"

Eventually, the time came for him to wheel round on her. "You always like men who are nothing like me! I don't know why you're with me! You're just sponging off me!"

Nina was aghast. Weariness was invoked immediately as her body reacted in its accustomed manner to verbal attack. "I don't know what you mean," she said.

Scott made an explosive sound. "That pretty fucker in the painting!" He strode off.

Nina followed. "Scott! Don't be absurd!"

They had argued all the way to the river, along the gravel path, past the gazebo and the folly Grecian temple. Eventually, like a chemical flooding her system, something clicked on in Nina's mind. Enough! She almost felt the physical change.

Uttering a wordless cry, she'd fled, prompting curious stares from other tourists.

What now? Nina leaned back against the cool stone. It was so peaceful here. She wondered at the significance of the place. Why the narrow path through the trees to this glade, why the monument dominated by a cat? Scott had the guidebook in his jacket pocket. She wished she'd kept it in her shoulder bag. There was a definite presence to this place, something brooding, and yet she did not feel discomforted by it. If anything, it echoed her mood. She felt strongly that she would not be pursued here, and even doubted whether any other tourists would appear along the path. This was her time and, for these scant moments, her place. It happened to her sometimes. Just when she needed them, she found sanctuaries. It could be an empty car park, a deserted alley, a wooden bench in a park. But whenever she found them, she experienced an encompassing feeling of security, and apartness. Had this only happened to her since she'd lived with Scott? She couldn't remember.

Nina stood up and jumped off the steps, walked around the clearing, looking up at the monument. She'd always wanted a cat, but Scott didn't like them. She felt unable to persevere, sure that if she acquired a kitten, it would suffer at Scott's hands. He wouldn't be overtly cruel, but she envisaged it would not be allowed in at night, and most of the house would be off-limits to it. There would be complaints about mess and smells and hairs. Might as well not have one. She realized, with bitter regret, that was her answer to everything. Easier to give in, to let him have his way. The tense atmosphere in the house when she defied him seemed to burn her skin. She could not bear it.

Behind the monument, the stone was lichened and damp, and it seemed to be less weathered. Details of carvings could easily be discerned. Nina mounted the steps again, slippery here with moss, and put her fingers against the stone. A legend written there. Message from the past. She traced the word "mau". There was a carving of the sun and moon, and the words, "who shall play with a wounded prey". Perhaps the person who built the monument had not liked cats. Nina examined the other sides of the obelisk, but all the engravings were in Greek or Latin. On the most deteriorated side, that facing the path, she thought she discerned Egyptian hieroglyphics. An eclectic arcarnum. Nina smiled. She had already read in the guide book about how one of the nineteenth-century earls of the estate had dabbled in the dark arts. Who, in the aristocracy, hadn't done so at that time, she wondered. It seemed to have been remarkably prevalent then. Gleeful tourist pamphlets sermonized about the mysterious trips abroad, the exposure to exotic belief systems, the desire to transcend the mundane in lives shorn by wealth of petty worries. Nina and Scott had visited many estates in order to search for the folly clues left by past incumbents who'd not been able to resist leaving proof of their obsessions behind, for those who chose to look for them. Nina had rarely felt anything unusual in these places, and she was sensitive to atmospheres.

Now, she stroked the damp, cool stone of the monument, and wondered. Her imagination supplied a history for it. The obelisk would have been commissioned by the woman in the painting, she of the petrol blue gown, the heavy brows, the modern features. She had been a witch, of course, a co-celebrant with her partner of arcane delights. The guide book spoke of earls and scholarly mysticism; the true sorcery remained secret. Nina smiled. Here, the cat, symbol of woman in her most terrifying aspect. Not she of claw and fang and raised cry, nor of motherhood and nurturing, but she of the night, of treachery sheathed with eloquence, of the ability to torture without compassion, of stealth, hidden beauty and disdain, the allure that could wither men's hearts, destroy them. Nina was sure that these were the things men feared existed unseen in women. Although they could never witness the true witcheries of female kind, which Nina thought were intensely personal and impossible to articulate, men found the potential of their existence all the more fascinating and terrifying. She felt that men were always trying to guess what went on in the secret selves of women. Groping to understand a virtually alien species, they imagined they knew the hearts of women, but they could never actually be sure whether the secrets existed or not. And yet, even as they feared, and struck out in every way at the object of their terror, they yearned for their dark suppositions to be realized. The Goddess beneath the skin. The potent, unspoken strangeness that separated women from men was, Nina believed, the very thing that bound men to them. The cat, the familiar of darkness was perhaps the most enduring symbol of this secret power. Nina wondered if that was why she was so drawn to the animal. She herself felt very much in tune with all that the cat represented. The dark, vengeful sibling of the bright, yielding girl. She Who Must Not Be Unleashed. Nina wondered whether she was alone in feeling the presence of this coiled inner self, an aspect of her being she had to control with a firm hand, or whether all women felt her crouching there inside. Nina had never unleashed the cruel one, and never wanted to, fearful she'd be unable to hide it inside herself again afterwards. But in moments of emotional crisis, she was always conscious of the coiled one's presence, her voice.

She smiled and patted the stone, said, "Mau!" The feline: a symbol of liberty, because no animal is as opposed to restraint as a cat. Let any unwelcome intruder tread the path to her grove with caution.

He was still waiting for her, sitting on the bank of the lazy river, throwing stones into the central current. Nina walked up behind him. She felt excoriated, yet vigorous. Her weariness was not rekindled by the sight of his back, rigid with misery. She experienced, in a moment of blinding clarity, a supreme yet serene pity for the man. He would not, and could not, ever grow up emotionally, and yet the strengths of childhood had died in him. She sat down beside him. He turned to look at her, censure in his face. She could not care about it. "Are you hungry?" she asked. "Let's go eat."

He did not mention the argument, which was unusual. She thought he looked at her with wary puzzlement throughout the rest of the day.

The following morning, they drove back to the city. Nina felt removed from reality; she could not stop day-dreaming. Scott, as if sensing her mood, was temperate. They addressed one another across a tidy boundary. They were supposed to have stayed in the cottage for another day, but rain had come – a downpour – too heavy to walk out in. And the rooms of the cottage were gloomy; too small for people with sensitive skins to occupy together.

Nina was relieved to get home – she always was – but regretted not being able to investigate the cat monument further. That evening, she browsed through the guidebook to Elwood Grange. The house itself was not that remarkable, she thought, and the grounds predictable, but for the hidden place where the monument stood. The obelisk was not listed in the index of follies to be found at Elwood, but a map of the gardens showed that the book was out of date, and that the glade with the monument had not been open to the public when it had been published. Flicking through the pages, Nina noticed a photograph of the painting that had caused her argument with Scott. Lady Sydelle and Rufus, Earl of Thurlow. They had been young when the portrait had been painted. Dark garments, dashing, almost foreign-looking features, glossy black hair. They had to be brother and sister, of course, not husband and wife as she'd first thought. The background, like their clothes, was dark; a dusky landscape. Only their white faces and hands glowed from the picture. Lady Sydelle's fingers were curled over something on her lap. Nina lifted the book to hold the photograph close to her table-lamp. Her heart contracted. There was a cat on the Lady's lap. Nina lowered the book. She had to see the picture again, and the monument. She felt as if she had discovered something marvellous. She glanced across at Scott, who was reading yesterday's paper, a can of beer open by his chair. He was back at work next week. So was Nina, although she didn't have to leave the house for it. She had a children's book to illustrate, and the deadline had almost crept up on her. Still, she could justify a trip out to make sketches. The book was about a witch and her cat.

She mentioned it to Scott in bed. "I'm thinking of going back to Elwood Grange. I'm so behind with my work. Lack of inspiration, I think, and I saw some great places at Elwood to use in my illos."

"It's a long way for you to drive alone," he said, which was a mild complaint for him.

"I'll take a friend with me," Nina lied.

After Scott had left for work, Nina telephoned Elwood Grange and spoke to the tourist office. Would they be open that day? No. On Mondays, the Grange was closed to the public. Nina expressed disappointment, mentioned her work. The woman on the other end of the phone hesitated for only a moment. "Ah, well perhaps we can make an exception, in that case," she said.

Nina told her she could be at the Grange in two hours, perhaps sooner if the traffic wasn't bad. The only companion she took with her was the guide-book to the Grange, which lay on the passenger seat beside her. She wanted to be home before Scott got back from work, as she hadn't mentioned her trip to him again this morning. Seemed best not to.

The woman Nina had spoken to on the phone was called Lydia Hunt, and had apparently appointed herself as Nina's personal guide for the visit. Nina was disappointed. She'd wanted to roam around alone, but perhaps that had been too much to hope for. Before looking round the house, they had a cup of coffee in Lydia's office, and Nina talked about her work. Lydia thought one of her children might own a book that Nina had illustrated. "People have come here before to research material for books," Lydia said.

Nina nodded. "These old places have their histories, don't they. It's fascinating. A wealth of material to be plundered!"

Lydia smiled. "Mmm. A lot of the old stories are exaggerated for publicity purposes, I think."

"So tell me about Lady Sydelle," Nina prompted, smiling in complicity over her coffee cup.

Lydia laughed. "Ah yes! Of course you would be interested in her!" She gestured with one hand; a confident, attractive woman, Nina thought. "Lady Sydelle is my favourite character as well. She never married, even though she was a very beautiful woman, and I imagine local gallants must have thronged her threshold. The money too, would have been attractive to them."

"And what were her secrets? I suppose she had some, or they were invented for her?"

"Her brother, the Earl, was rumoured to be rather a rake-hell. Well, to put it bluntly, he was an occultist." Lydia pulled a sour face. "Misguided boy! It was he who commissioned the zodiac ceiling in the music room, and the two Eleusinian folly shrines in the grounds. Lady Sydelle is not associated with her brother's rather insalubrious pursuits, but she did erect the tantalizingly obscure obelisk in the gardens after his death."

"The cat monument," Nina hurriedly interrupted. She felt breathless, almost faint.

Lydia nodded. "It's actually called the Cat Stane. We only opened up that part of the gardens last season, and there's still work to be done there. Scholars presume the Stane's a bitter joke about Rufus's exploits – the melding of mystical symbols from several ancient cultures, none of them making much sense. It's supposed Sydelle was sceptical about the whole thing. She was very fond of Rufus, naturally, and took his death badly. Still, it's an odd memorial."

"How did he die?" The atmosphere in the room seemed to have become tense. Nina found herself thinking that at one time, the servants of Lady Sydelle had occupied this area of the house, whispers would have been exchanged here in times of crisis. Perhaps they still bled from the walls.

Lydia shrugged. "Accounts vary, I'm afraid. His neck was broken. Some say it was caused by a hunting accident, others that he tumbled headlong down the main stairs in a drunken stupor. Whatever happened, he lived for nearly a week after the incident. Sydelle nursed him herself apparently."

"No other legends?"

Lydia narrowed her eyes. "You're looking for mysteries!"

Nina forced a laugh. "Of course I am!"

"Lady Sydelle never divulged her secrets, I'm afraid! After Rufus died, she lived alone here to an advanced age, and died peacefully in her sleep. There are no diaries, no local legends. Nothing. She was a respectable woman."

"But the Stane . . ."

Lydia stood up. "Would you like to see it again?"

"Yes." Nina put down her coffee cup and followed Lydia to the door. "Could I see Sydelle's rooms?"

"If you wish, although she left little mark on them. The furniture is late Jacobean, and other people lived there after she died. Her bedroom is part of the guided tour – you've undoubtedly already seen it – but I can show you her parlour, if you like. It's only available for view by appointment."

"Why?"

"The wife of the present Earl uses it as an office. But the family are never in residence when the Grange is open to the public."

Nina felt downhearted by the time she and Lydia went out into the gardens. It was a dull day but the lush verdure of high summer was unsuppressed by the louring sky. The green was startling, acidic. The gardens held far more presence than the house itself. Nina had felt nothing in the rooms Lydia had shown her. No shade of Sydelle persisted there.

The two women took a slow stroll down to the obelisk. Nina had collected her sketching pad from the car, intent on making a few quick drawings, even though it seemed her impressions of the monument might have been misguided. Lydia talked about how there was debate whether this untamed area of the gardens should be cleared or not.

"No, it shouldn't be touched!" Nina said.

"I agree," Lydia replied. "It's a pleasant walk."

A cool breeze fretted the leaves of the trees overhead; there was a sense of agitation in the air. Then, the monument became visible around a corner.

It is here! Nina thought. The spirit of the place! I wasn't wrong.

"The monument will be cleaned in the autumn, restored," Lydia said.

Nina mounted the steps, wondering whether her guide would approve of that, and touched the stone. "I like it the way it is."

Lydia peered at the hieroglyphics. "It's a shame some of the inscriptions are damaged. This one was perhaps the most intriguing."

"What did it say? Do you know?"

"It is still readable, just, if you can translate the symbols. I understand it says something like 'what can you own of a cat but her skin'."

"How true," Nina murmured, holding the words in her mind. "How true."

Lydia gave her an odd glance. Perhaps she was beginning to think her visitor was a little too intense. "Well, shall I leave you to your drawing? Call back into the office before you leave and have another drink." She glanced at the sky. "Don't stay out here if it rains!"

"Thank you," Nina said.

Lydia hesitated, as if she was about to say something, and then retreated up the path without speaking. Nina did not move for a few moments, so that the atmosphere could close behind Lydia's departing figure. Then, she moved back from the monument, so that she could look up at the cat. Perhaps she should have brought a camera with her. The animal looked as if it was waiting for something. Nina's hand moved quickly over the pages of her sketch pad. She meant to draw faithful representations of the obelisk, but was continually drawn to depict the sombre figure of a woman standing just behind the stone. Her skin prickled. She felt that soon the figure would manifest before her. Lady Sydelle; her hand against the cold stone of her private statement. What is your secret, what? Nina whispered. Tell me. She felt the answer was relevant to her own life. It was no coincidence she'd found this place.

Nina basked in the atmosphere of the glade; it was like rolling over and over in fur. When the rain came, she covered her sketch pad with her jacket and threw out her arms to the sky, let the fast, heavy drops fall onto her. Rain pattered against the foliage around her. She heard distant thunder. Nina shivered, glanced at her watch. What was she doing? If she didn't leave quickly, Scott would be home before her. Where had the afternoon gone?

There was no time to share another coffee with Lydia Hunt, but Nina briefly put her head round the door of the woman's office and thanked her for her help. "My pleasure," said Lydia. There was no offer of a repeat visit. She seemed affronted by the sight of Nina's soaked clothes and hair.

Nina raced down the country lanes, away from Elwood Grange. She felt excited, as if she was going to meet a new lover, which of course she was not. Sad to be so excited about nothing. She pushed a cassette into the tape player, but the music was intrusive. She turned it off. Lady Sydelle, what happened in your life? Nina felt that she knew. The Lady had never married, and the brother had been a rogue. Women of that time had little freedom, bound by convention, by financial dependence. Even the privileged were subject to such restraints. The closeness of the two figures in the portrait was surely unnatural for brother and sister? Was that it, then? Incest? But how could she murder a man she loved? The thought came into Nina's head so forcefully, she had to slow down.

Oh, my God . . .

Nina pulled into the next passing place, and stopped the

car. She leaned her forehead against the steering wheel. It seemed so obvious to her. Sydelle had both loved and hated her brother Rufus. Her emotions had been complex, beyond simple understanding. Magic. Darkness. A cat upon the stairs. A fall. Nina heard the cry; echoing. The footsteps of servants and a tall, slim figure in the shadows at the top of the stairs; a white face, watchful. The figure turned away from the chaotic scene of yelling servants, of blood upon the marble floor below. Something small ran ahead of her up the dimly-lit corridor. A black shape, a cat. Of course she nursed him. Of course. "Who shall play with a wounded prey." She would have kissed his paralysed body. Her cat would have sat upon his chest, tasted his breath. Her soul was her own; dark and potent, full of repressed power, a power that had been repressed in women for centuries. He could direct her physical body, but her soul, her mind, no! What could he own of her, but her skin?

The sky was so dark, it was like twilight. Nina started the car, switched on the windscreen wipers, resumed her journey. On the motorway, she turned on the cassette tape. Faster cars hissed by her. She felt relaxed, at ease. The story might be the product of her own imagination, or not, but the effect was the same.

Scott was already home by the time Nina let herself into the house. "Hi!" she called, brightly. Scott appeared in the hall, wiping his hands on a towel.

"My God, what happened?" Nina cried. His face was bleeding, scratched.

"Where the hell have you been?" Scott demanded, ignoring her question.

"I told you: Elwood." Nina went to look at his cuts. "You look like you've been attacked!"

Scott pulled away from her. "I have! How many times do I have to tell you to check all doors and windows are locked before you go out? You left the kitchen window wide open. It's lucky we have anything left in the house! Anyone could have got in. As it was, we did have a visitor. I found it making itself at home in my chair. Bloody animal!"

"A cat!" Nina said. She wanted to laugh, but managed to repress the urge.

"I don't know what you're grinning at. Damn thing nearly took my eye out when I tried to get rid of it."

"I'm sorry; you're right. I should have checked the windows. I always forget!" Nina breezed past him into the kitchen, noticing his expression of surprise. Normally, she would have curled in on herself, refused to apologize, cringed away from his angry words, which would, of course, have invoked more of them. "Have you started dinner?"

Scott trailed into the kitchen behind her. "No . . ." He knew Nina sometimes bitterly resented doing all the cooking, but she would never say so. He went out to work; she worked at home. It only seemed fair she should cook the meals. She didn't have an hour's drive home through heavy traffic. "What's wrong?" he asked.

Nina shrugged. "Nothing. I feel fine."

"You seem . . . hyped up about something."

"No. I'm not. Shall we order a pizza?"

"If you like." Scott felt uneasy. Buried anxieties patted at their grilles in the depths of his mind.

Nina went to the phone. "What did you do with the cat?"

"It went out the way it came in. Knocked two plants off. I cleared up the mess."

Nina ordered dinner. She felt as if she was about to burst. As she put down the phone, she said, "Scott, I want a cat."

He looked confused. "What?"

"You heard. I was going to mention it tonight. I've always wanted one."

Scott shook his head. "Nina, don't be ridiculous. Who would look after it when we go away? It's such a responsibility. And what about the smell, the . . ."

"Scott, I want a cat."

"I don't think . . ."

"And I'm going to have one." She wondered why she had ever given in so easily to Scott's wishes. What had she been frightened of? It seemed ridiculous now. Scott's strategies involved attack; he was powerless when she attacked first. She marched into the lounge and threw herself down on the sofa.

"You're in a weird mood," Scott said, following her into the room. "Where have you really been? Who were you with!"

Nina threw up her hands and uttered an inarticulate sound of outrage. "I've been to Elwood Grange, alone!"

"I don't believe you! Someone's been saying something to you! You're not yourself."

"Oh shut up!" Nina's voice was low with contempt. "Do you know, I'm sick of the way things are! I'm sick of your jealousy, and your pompous behaviour. Do you really think if I had a lover, I'd put up with you! Do me a favour! Things have got to change."

Meekly, Scott sat down, staring at her with round, shocked eyes. Nina was staggered by his submissive posture; he was like a dog fearing a slap. She had expected a thunderous row, and had braced herself for it. Scott's reaction was the last thing she'd anticipated.

"You're not going to leave me, are you?" he said. It was a child's fear of abandonment.

Nina didn't answer immediately. Was she? She realized she'd always had the choice of walking out. She didn't have to put up with things she didn't like. Lady Sydelle had perhaps not had that choice. Nina had an income, albeit small, but she was not totally dependent. She had become used to a certain standard of living, that was all. "I hope we can sort things out," she said eventually.

The rain came down all night, but the air was hot. Nina opened the bedroom windows wide, and water came in to puddle on the window-sills. Scott made a complaint. Nina told him she'd wipe the water up in the morning. He said nothing more. She decided to make love to him, and let him cling to her afterwards. "I love you," he said. "I love you so much." She stroked his hair. Began to doze.

Something jolted her awake. In the darkness, with the sound of rain persistent against the night, the scent of it coming into the room, Nina saw a dark shape on the bed. She was frightened for only a moment. The dark shape stretched out, advanced towards her slowly. So long and lean. Then she heard it purring. Nina pulled the cat towards her, hugged its wet fur against her naked breasts, inhaled its musky perfume. The animal continued to purr rapturously, limp in her arms.

Scott woke up, turned on the lamp, looked at her. Her face was buried in the black pelt. It was an enormous cat. I don't know her, he thought, I don't know anything about her. He felt that she, like the cat, could leap away from him, out through the window into the wet darkness, knocking things over, breaking things as she went. She turned her head and smiled at him.

"Here's my cat!"

"It's the same one," Scott said in distaste. "The one that scratched me."

"I know. You threw her out, but she's come back." Nina kissed the cat's brow.

Scott risked a strained grin. "It must belong to someone. It's in such good condition. You can't just . . . keep it."

Nina laughed. "No, I can't. No one can own a cat. But she'll stay with me. I know she will."

Scott looked at the muddy paw-marks on the pale duvet. He said nothing. Something seemed to have come into the house, something more than a cat.

"She'll stay with me because she wants to," Nina said in a low voice. "And that is the only reason why any two creatures should stay together."

Scott experienced a stab of panic. "Are we all right?" he asked. "Are we?"

Nina stared at him for a few moments, stroking the cat's head. Then she nodded. "I think so. Go back to sleep." The cat curled up beside her, and presently she leaned over Scott and turned off the lamp. Rich purrs filled the darkness. Nina thought of the glade at Elwood Grange, the monument, the shadow of a long-dead woman against the stone. Was the obelisk bare of its guardian now? She wondered whether she should go back and see, but perhaps that would be disrespectful towards the power blossoming within her. It was a stupid thought anyway. The stone cat would still be crouched upon the stone, staring back along the lonely path. The statue was still there, but the spirit wasn't. The spirit had moved on to seek another hearth. Had found it.

DONALD R. BURLESON

Hopscotch

DONALD R. BURLESON'S FICTION has appeared in *Twilight Zone Magazine, 2AM, The Magazine of Fantasy & Science Fiction, Deathrealm, Terminal Fright, Lore, Wicked Mystic, The Roswell Literary Review*, and many other magazines, as well as several major anthologies, including *The Best New Horror, Post Mortem, MetaHorror, 100 Ghastly Little Ghost Stories, 100 Creepy Little Creature Stories, 100 Vicious Little Vampire Stories, 100 Tiny Tales of Terror, Made in Goatswood* and *The New Lovecraft Circle*.

He is also the author of the short story collections *Lemon Drops and Other Horrors* (Hobgoblin Press), *Four Shadowings* (Necronomicon Press) and *Beyond the Lamplight: Stories from the Dark* (Jack-O'Lantern Press). His novel *Flute Song* (Black Mesa Press), about the Roswell UFO incident, was nominated for the 1997 Horror Writers Association's Bram Stoker Award. Burleson and his wife Mollie, herself a writer, live in Roswell, New Mexico.

The author's explanation for the story "Hopscotch" is simply that he has always thought there was something creepy about children's sidewalk games, which, he says, shows just how screwed up he really is.

IT WAS A GHOULISH-LOOKING place.

Flaunting its decay in a wash of toadstool-colored moonlight, it was the very picture of urban death, this rotting brickpile at the corner of Jespersen Avenue and Sixteenth Street. Where the warm lights of cosy apartments had once shown through their drawn shades like mellow eyes contemplating the night, the glow that bespoke life had long since departed, and the beetling face of the building had caved in, folding its dark eyes appallingly down and under, like collapsed sockets in a miasma of bone. Above what was left of an ancient doorframe, the number 4022 tottered meaninglessly, and somehow that was the worst of all: that such squalor could have an address. She found it hard to believe, now, that life had once flourished here.

But, she reflected with an involuntary sigh, it had.

This whole part of the city was pretty much in ruins: a vastness of dark jutting shapes, remnants of vacant windows and half-collapsed walls and toothlike shells of buildings stretching away into the night in every direction, a ghost town in a dream, with only a flicker here and there of electric light in the distance, or the muted echo of distant traffic, to suggest that this was any real city at all, and not just a sprawling mass of corruption lying half embalmed under a shroud of sky. Off in the distance an ululation of wind sprang up, whistling, touching gaping rows of windows like the stops of some grotesque flute. Now, as she watched, even the few scattered lights were blinking out as if in despair, yielding to darkness. It was ineffably sad. But this corner was the most dismal, probably because she so especially remembered it the way it used to be.

This was what was left, then, of the old neighborhood.

Maybe it wasn't even safe now to linger on the street at night in such a place as this. Despite the attempts of the wan moon to dispel the darkness, the scene was mostly given over to shadow; the only streetlamps, sputtering yellow excrescences on the ends of scrawny goosenecks, were too far away to be of much use. And didn't many of these old buildings attract derelicts, winos, drug addicts? On her way here she had seen furtive figures crouched in dusky corners. But somehow these decrepit edifices at Jespersen and Sixteenth looked devoid of all forms of life, like cadavers forsaken even by the worms.

She was an anachronism now, standing here, seeing the place again after all these years. It has crumbled and died, she thought, yet here I am, come to see it; I have crumbled somewhat too, but I haven't died – I'm like the oldest family fossil, haunting the funeral home and witnessing, wraithlike, the last rites of others, myself surviving to stand owlish and half apologetic beside their remains.

Strange, that the place made her feel this way. She was only sixty-seven, and sixty-seven wasn't old. It just seemed so very long ago, now, that she had been skinny little Linda Sanchez here, all pigtails and braces and scraped knees and eyes aglow with childhood spirit and love of life. Now she was skinny retired accountant Linda Sanchez, the survivor: mousy hair instead of pigtails, false teeth instead of braces, arthritis instead of scraped knees, thick glasses instead of bright young eyes, and a repository of fading memories instead of love.

Somewhere, as if in choral response to this thought, a crowd of young people laughed faintly in the distance and the sound swirled around some corner and was gone. Here, on the old corner of Jespersen and Sixteenth, though, there was no one but her, and she had never felt so alone. Why, why in God's name had she come? Why had she gotten off the bus over on Ninth Street instead of just riding it home? She had lived across town for decades without ever really wanting to return here, and she should have known that it would be depressing here, where nothing remained of her faraway youth, and only urban blight showed its diseased face to the moon.

But was it true that nothing whatever remained?

She turned to her left and walked slowly away from the corner, past the shapeless wreck that had once been her apartment building – Mom, Dad, Lucy, Carlos, the birthday parties, the Christmas mornings, the joys, the sorrows – and stopped in front of the space between that building and what remained of the building next door, now a heap of slag and unaccountable cables lolling half in, half out of the debris like the entrails of some great fallen beast. Between the buildings, a narrow alleyway (irregular and ragged even in those far-off days and flanked by staggering walls of smoke-grimed brick), an oddly crooked, cheerless alleyway had retreated from the sidewalk into realms of increasing mystery, a fissure from dim light to brooding darkness, dead-ending some thirty feet back at a windowless wall, the rear of a building that faced onto Keating Avenue.

And something remained of the old alley. It was more ragged than ever now, with scatterings of crumbled brick on either side, toward the back. Or as far back as she could see, anyway; at best, the moonlight only put tentative fingers part way down the shattered walls to cast a wan patina of light on the pavement back in there; and now scudding black clouds were obscuring the moon from time to time, leaving the alley sometimes utterly black, sometimes half illumined like some bizarre Victorian lantern show. She thought she could just make out, in the darkness at the end of the alley, a tangle of trash and weeds thicker and wilder-looking than the mess of dirty newspapers and soggy cardboard and broken bottles that she remembered always seeing there as a child. It was as if the detritus had gathered back there like some ancient mass of phlegm at the base of a throat that had never quite succeeded in coughing it all up.

She stood on the deserted sidewalk looking at the spot. It fascinated her that despite the passing of so many years the general contours of the old alley remained, a not terribly changed relic of former times. And a reminder.

Of Marnie Blake.

God, she hadn't thought of her for years.

Little Marnie Blake, with her chalky face incongruously framed in crow-black shoulder-length hair, and with pale blue eyes shining out of that face like the beckoning luminescent eyes of a store-window doll. Little Marnie from upstairs, with her peculiar talk and her odd way of seeming to know a great many arcane things. She was always rather like a gypsy child, with some unplaceable sense of strange heritage about her, as if the exotic flavor of farflung places and nameless caravan nights lingered in her bearing in a way that one couldn't quite fathom.

Little Marnie Blake, who had taught them all about hopscotch.

Pale-faced, ethereal little Marnie, who had died horribly.

Horribly, on the very spot where all of them, all the neighborhood kids, had played the game.

Linda wondered if the hopscotch diagram could possibly still be there – and, adjusting her glasses on her nose and peering into the near-darkness of the alley, she saw to her astonishment that indeed it was.

Mere chalk of course would long since have faded away to nothing over the years, but this hopscotch tableau had been laid down in white paint – Marnie had painted it herself – and there it was, fainter now but discernible, emblazoned on the dirty cement like some ancient inscription over which an archaeologist might pause and nod. Imagine: still there, after all this time, that long, narrow configuration of numbered squares and rectangles that looked, Linda thought now, like a scaly, sickly white tongue lying flat in the bottom of a mouth.

The sight of it disturbed her enough to make her shudder and draw the collar of her coat tighter against the chilly air. Something about the scene was distinctly unsavory in its associations, but when she tried to pin down the source of this impression, she couldn't tell, in the sluiceway of her long-neglected memories, whether it was what she remembered of playing hopscotch here or what she remembered of Marnie herself that bothered her more; the two currents of memory were commingled, neither one completely coherent without reference to the other.

Dark-haired and pasty-faced Little Marnie Blake had at times been solemn in a way that perhaps would have seemed comic to an adult, but only seemed sobering, and at times a little unsettling, to other children. Down on hands and knees, painstakingly outlining the hopscotch pattern on the pavement, starting five or six feet inside the alleyway and extending it back into the gloomy shadows of the canyonlike walls, she might spare you a look over her shoulder while daubing white paint with her brush. "Don't you know hopscotch is a very *old* game?" she would ask. "Roman kids played it thousands of years ago."

Linda remembered a boy from down the hall, Kevin she thought his name was, asking, "You mean the Romans, like feeding the Christians to the lions and all that? How do *you* know what they did millions of years ago?"

"Thousands," Marnie said. "I know 'cause I read it in a book. And even before the Romans, people played hopscotch. A long long long long time ago."

"You're crazy," one of Kevin's brothers said.

"She is not," little Mollie from across the hall retorted. "You're just jealous 'cause a girl knows stuff you don't."

And so it went, the usual badinage of childhood – but it was really more than that. There was something about Marnie and her peculiar talk, and something about the avidity with which she played hopscotch, that made you wonder. It wasn't just avidity – she played the game with a sort of religious fervor, as if she were propitiating some vile god who might come for you in a roiling black cloud one day if you slighted him. When she was hopping her way through the numbered spaces she seemed desperate not to make a mistake, and at times the expression on her face would approach a kind of frenzy, as if she were teetering not near the edges of hopscotch squares but on the edge of some frightful abyss.

But now that she thought about it a little longer, Linda felt that a large part of what was bothering her about these memories was the long-suppressed recollection of her own turns at hopscotch, a recollection all the more disturbing because time had rendered it vague without making it less ominous.

In those childhood days she had been lithe, clever, quick on her feet, and having played hopscotch plenty of times before on the school grounds and elsewhere, she at first approached the numbered spaces in the dim alleyway with a swagger of confidence. But there was something odd about the way it worked, there in the alley.

She couldn't quite think what it was, but she recalled that somehow when she started to hop through the squares, it would seem okay at first, but would be different after she got going, different in some peculiar way that, once moving, she couldn't do anything about. She always ended up feeling trapped, tricked, betrayed. What was it? How had it been different from what she expected? She couldn't remember exactly.

What she did remember was one particular time when she had finished and sat down just inside the alleyway with her back to the wall of her building, and Marnie had sat next to her and leaned close to her face and said, with great solemnity, "You almost slipped, you know." Linda had been so astonished at the earnestness of this remark that she hadn't known what to say. But after a moment's reflection Marnie had added: "But then I guess it doesn't matter that much with you. I'm the one."

Linda had shaken her head in puzzlement. "What do you mean, you're the one?"

Marnie had looked at her almost pityingly, like a much older person trying to explain something inexplicable to a child. "I'm – just the one. The one chosen." And that was all she would say.

Linda couldn't be sure, now, how long it was after that, before – God! she shuddered again, remembering more vividly – before whatever happened happened.

One morning she had heard a lot of crying and shouting upstairs, and in the stairwells and outside. People were milling around in great consternation, and the police came, and someone upstairs was sobbing. In those days adults didn't take children greatly into their confidence, and it was left to Linda's own ingenuity to ferret out and piece together what had happened, mostly from the talk among the kids on the street. She gathered that one of the people in the building, a man who lived down the hall from Linda's folks on the first floor, had found poor little Marnie Blake disemboweled and scattered in the alley.

Or at any rate had found as much of her as hadn't apparently been eaten.

The police would call it a vicious and senseless killing, possibly even an act of cannibalism, perpetrated by some homicidal maniac of whom they could find no trace. So far as Linda knew, no one was ever charged with the crime.

She stepped into the alley now and stood looking at the spot where she had sat, those many years ago, beside doomed little Marnie. There on the cracked and dirty pavement she noticed a bottlecap, not a relic from those early days, surely, but suggestive nonetheless.

On an impulse she picked it up, turned it a moment in her fingers, and tossed it onto the square that was still legibly numbered 1.

Now that she stood a little closer she saw that all of the squares and rectangles still bore their old numbers, touchingly now, in Marnie's childhood scrawl: side-by-side squares 1 and 2 in front, then a rectangular bar numbered 3, then side-by-side squares 4 and 5, then rectangular bar 6, then side-by-side squares 7 and 8. This was one of countless existing variants on the game of hopscotch, but it was the one she knew from her youth on these streets.

But *did* she still know how it worked?

Again on an unreflective impulse she drew a breath, steadied herself as best she could, and hopped with her right foot onto square 2. It hurt a little, bringing her weight down on the ankle, but somehow she had to do this, and ignoring the pain she hopped again, planting the same foot in the long block 3. Could she really still do it? She doubted it; the smart thing would be to give it up, step aside, take one reminiscing look around, and start for home. But now she remembered how the game was supposed to go, and she sprang forward again, onto both feet this time, left foot in square 4, right foot in square 5. It was incredible, how the memories came flooding back! This was the point where you were sort of able to catch your breath and regain your balance because you could land on both feet.

But, she remembered now with great clarity, this was also the point where you felt things start to change.

From squares 4 and 5 you were supposed to hop on your right foot into block 6, then – this had been the tricky part, even for a child – hop and *twist* onto side-by-side squares 7 and 8 so that you landed backwards with your right foot in 7 and your left foot in 8; and then hop back out in reverse: left foot in 6, land on both feet (left in 5, right in 4), left foot in 3 and then next in 2, and you would bend and pick up the bottlecap on the way out.

But in the middle, straddling squares 4 and 5 on the way in, she found it changing again, as always.

Somehow when you were in motion the whole tableau seemed *longer* than it was supposed to be. Even as a child she had thought that it was because of the confusing repetition of patterns in the blocks, the similarity of the wide block 3 followed by 4-and-5 and the wide block 6 followed by 7-and-8. It just seemed difficult to think exactly where you were in the process, and even now it was the same – she should only have one wide block and two side-by-side squares ahead of her, but there appeared to be more than that. It was as if the eye couldn't quite come to terms with what was really there, because it looked as if the alternations of numbered blocks stretched nearly to the back of the alley, where now as always an uncouth clutter of dirty newspaper and pale weeds tangled with themselves just beyond the light, a light which kept fading and revivifying with the whims of the clouds that tried to block out the moon.

The pattern couldn't really be different, of course. But it had seemed so to a child, and maybe even an arthritic adult foolish enough to be doing this in intermittent moonlight in an urban wasteland might be gulled into imagining odd things. It was confusing, too, to have her own wavering and indistinct moonlight-shadow projected out at an angle onto the squares before her. She resolved to prove to herself what nonsense it all was, and took a breath and sprang onto her right foot, into block 6, wincing again as she landed on an ankle that was far, far more brittle than that of the little girl Linda who used to play here.

And now came the hard part: she would have to spring off from her right foot and turn her body around and come down backwards with both feet in 7 and 8. But when she sprang, she had barely enough time to register that she mustn't twist after all – that this was to be another straight side-by-side landing, with the twist-point farther ahead somewhere beyond another long bar. There was only supposed to be one straight landing, though, and she must have been confused, thinking that she had already done it and that this could be a second one. She cancelled the twist and came down still facing into the alley, with her feet covering two numbers. Ahead, with the moonlight failing again, she couldn't quite make out the number in the next long bar or in the small squares beyond. She must still be about to proceed to bar 6, though she could have sworn she'd already done that. She hopped onto her right foot, nearly toppling over but managing to keep her balance. Now the tricky part: the twist onto squares 7 and 8, finally.

But no, that wasn't right. Flailing her arms to keep standing on her foot, which was really beginning to hurt now, she squinted into the receding alley and found still more of the diagram ahead of her than should be there. Beyond, the clutter of weeds and paper at the end of the alley loomed a little closer than before, and some stray breath of wind seemed to be stirring it, making shreds of newspaper look like little tentacles in the pallid light. The end of the diagram had to be coming up next, and she was *not* going to let this get the better of her.

Hopping again, she came down with both feet in the next side-by-side squares, whose numbers she couldn't guess at now, as confused as she was. But yes, now this was right. Or sort of right. The cloud cover lifted, and in the brighter moonglow she could see that the bar ahead was number 6, and the adjacent squares beyond were 7 and 8. The only thing was, she had the feeling that it had taken her too long, had taken too great a toll on her aching right ankle, to get here. Why she was doing this at all she couldn't have explained; somehow she just had to, had to go through it and get it *right* and snatch up the bottlecap at the end.

She sprang once more onto her right foot, crying out a little this time when she landed on it in bar 6, and, without giving herself time to hesitate – or without giving the tableau time to change again? – she jumped, did her best to twist around and, considerably surprised at herself, landed on both feet more or less in blocks 7 and 8, facing back out toward the street. She had caught only a glimpse, while turning in the air, of the confusion of weedy rubble just beyond the end of the diagram, and it could only have been the strain of the whole undertaking that made it seem to her as if some of the shredded and filthy newspaper there was disentangling itself from the encroaching weeds and starting to move. In a way, it was comforting to be facing the alley entrance again.

But now something really was wrong. Dreadfully wrong. Wrong in something like the way it used to be when she had been a child, but even worse.

The sidewalk, the street out there looked too far away, much farther than she could have come to get here. The diagram that stretched back toward the healthier light at the entrance to the alleyway was far, far too long, with too many squares. It had to be a trick of the light. Even when she had imagined, hopping across the tableau to get here, that she had landed too many times, there couldn't have been *that* many squares.

In any sane world she should simply have been able to laugh, step off the diagram altogether, walk back out to the street, and leave. But she understood perfectly well now that this little world that she had re-entered was not a sane world, and that to get back, she had to hop through the diagram, as she had had to when she was a girl.

Added to this reflection was the realization now that something was audibly, unmistakably stirring behind her in the back of the alley.

With a sudden sense of urgency she hopped onto her left foot – thank heaven at least it wasn't her throbbing right foot again – and landed in what could only be bar 6. Filaments of sooty cloud were covering and uncovering the moon, and she couldn't read the numbers clearly. Balancing on her left foot, she sprang again, coming down on both feet in what must be squares 4 and 5; even standing this way, her right foot was still in pain. Logically only one long bar and the final two adjacent squares should remain, but that was what troubled her: that a good many bars and squares, like the segments of some nightmare tapeworm, seemed to stretch themselves into the distance between her and the salvation of the sidewalk beyond the alley entrance. There couldn't be that far to go. But there was, and it needed to be quickly too, because something was coming up close behind her. She could hear it, an odd blend of dry paperlike rustling and a sticky-suction sound; and now she could *smell* it as well, a fetor like something grown mushy and phosphorescent in a cellar.

She hopped onto her left foot again, coming down in the next long bar, but there were many other squares ahead, impossibly many others, and her left foot was already starting to hurt. Choking back a sob, she sprang again and landed on both feet, her legs nearly buckling under her this time. In the act of hopping again, she cast a glance behind her and nearly swooned at what she saw.

Something was coming, all right, something ragged and twitching and leprous-white, something that seemed to be trying to get a shape.

But in front of it was another presence, advancing toward her as well, itself pursued, apparently, by what had risen out of the back of the alley. And this other presence, half-transparent like a gathering of bubbles, had the shape of a child.

A child with feverish blue eyes shining out of a bone-white face limned in wildly tossing locks of raven hair.

The child came on silently, terribly, and motioned to her to go on, go on, go *on*.

Linda, blinking away tears now, completed her spring and came down on both feet, barely managing to remain upright. She didn't dare look around again, but hopped once more onto her left foot, which, throbbing now, came very close this time to snapping under her. Behind, a gurgling kind of sound kept coming nearer, together with a sense of something like altered pressure in the air, a small but insistent pushing behind her. She sucked a breath into her lungs and sprang again, landing on both feet, and immediately jumped off again, coming down hard on her left foot, which raged with pain now. Howling, she sprang forward yet again, and another time, and another and another and another, until the agony was almost unbearable.

But at length, heaven be praised!, only one more long bar – number 3 – and the final adjacent blocks, where the bottlecap glinted dully in the moonlight. She cast one rapid glance behind her, a big mistake, because her mind wouldn't accept whatever was there, and that in a way was worse; maybe she could have endured whatever it was, if she could really have looked at it. But as it was, her mind registered only an appalling mass of white putrefaction lurching along behind the smaller shape that kept coming, the translucent little-girl shape whose face desperately implored her now, wide-mouthed but silent, to keep moving.

Linda hopped once more onto her left foot and screamed outright at the outrage of pain that shot up her leg, but she managed to spring one last time into the final squares, and bent with a groan and tried to pick up the bottlecap but missed it – missed it! – before hurling herself out of the diagram.

In her forward momentum she whirled around then to face the alley again, in time to see a childish shape hopping ahead of the thing that came behind it. Even now, little Marnie was faithful to the demands of the tableau, coming down first on one foot, then two, then one, as the seething near-shapelessness welled up nearly upon her. But if she still moved through the eternal ritual with meticulous care it wasn't to save herself – because Linda understood now that Marnie, who popped like a soap bubble and vanished when she hit the stronger light, had been in no danger at all. Her time for being in danger was long since over, and as the pursuer came on through the vanishing apparition and bulged across the remaining space, it was all too clear that someone else was the chosen one now.

STEVE RASNIC TEM

Ghost in the Machine

STEVE RASNIC TEM'S RECENT fiction appearances include *Dark Terrors 3: The Gollancz Book of Horror, Palace Corbie, 365 Scary Stories* and the young adult anthologies *A Nightmare's Dozen* and *Bruce Coville's Book of Spine Tinglers 2*.

A winner of the British Fantasy Award for his story "Leaks", Tem's numerous other tales have appeared in many major horror anthologies, including *The Best New Horror, The Year's Best Fantasy and Horror, Forbidden Acts* and *MetaHorror*, and he edited the World Fantasy Award-nominated anthology *High Fantastic: Colorado's Fantasy, Dark Fantasy and Science Fiction*.

The author's own books include the novel *Excavation* and such collections as *Fairytales, Beautiful Strangers* (with his wife, Melanie), *Absences: Charlie Goode's Ghosts, Celestial Inventory, Decoded Mirrors: 3 Tales After Lovecraft* and *Ombres sur la Route*.

"As for the genesis of the following piece, I really don't have that much to say this time," reveals the author. "It more or less wrote itself late one night (2.00 a.m.) after a long stretch in front of the TV. I think that's what I did instead of dreaming that night..."

"THIS REALLY, THIS REALLY has to stop," Carter said to no one in particular. He suspected that there was someone listening; he just didn't know who. Things happened for a reason, he'd always believed – and his family had reinforced this – and usually there was some sort of agency, some relationship, involved in this happening. For didn't *reason* imply *agency*? Carter's father had always insisted on this. "*Someone* did this, didn't they?" he'd say upon finding a shattered lamp on the living room floor, Carter and his brothers standing dumbly, feigning ignorance. "*Someone* did this," his father would repeat. "So they must have had their *reasons*!" *Reasons* and *agency*, Carter's life had revolved around these two concepts. When his father died of a hit-and-run, knocked a hundred feet down the street in front of their house, Carter had asked for the reason, for the agency, but there had been no one to tell him.

"I mean really, this must stop," Carter said somewhat plaintively. The blue and green striped walls of his apartment paid him sober attention. He would never have chosen such wallpaper – it had been put up by the previous tenant. Up until now he had not considered that he had the right to change the wallpaper. "I really can't deal with this anymore," he said, but his walls and furnishings appeared to have lost interest.

Off in a corner his television murmured to itself, although he had unplugged it days ago. He'd read briefly of electronics, of units called capacitors designed for storing an electric charge. He wondered if the explanation for his lively television lay in some new development in capacitor technology. And yet he knew this was unlikely – the explanation was surely part of some other science.

The screen remained blank, a greyish-green, but the soft murmur was steady, rhythmical, as if his television were reciting some meditative chant to itself. He had vague recollections of religious movements, especially during the late sixties and early seventies, which had centered around chanting, some phrase or series of sounds which, if repeated enough times, led to enlightenment. Quite appropriate for an appliance's prayer, he supposed.

Carter ran into the john (he should be on a first name basis with all the rooms of his apartment, he thought) and dropped to his knees. He vomited up chips and resistors, half-formed bits of circuit board, then mouthful after mouthful of the varieties of capacitors he had once seen in a Radio Shack catalog (Carter had always been an avid reader of catalogs).

Later, he consumed an entire bottle of mouthwash attempting both to rid himself of the taste of warm plastic and to soothe the cuts that lined his throat and crisscrossed his lips.

His neighbor Mr Williams was quite pleased to get Carter's slightly used television for such a good price.

Carter leaned back in his Lazy Boy recliner and stared contentedly at the empty space which had once been filled by the heavy console TV. The thick rug still bore the rectangular footprint of the set. This depression made him vaguely uncomfortable, but he had no idea how such carpet depressions might be removed, except through the passage of years. His mother could have told him, but his mother was dead. She'd suffered a stroke several years before while sitting in front of a comparably-priced television set. The picture tube had burnt out by the time they discovered her body. He would always wonder what show she had watched during those final minutes of her life.

Carter was tired, and soon fell asleep while staring at the rectangular depression in the carpet. An indeterminate amount of time had passed (indeterminate since all the clocks in his apartment ran either fast or slow) when he awakened to discover his old television set back in its spot. The *Jack Benny Show* flickered black and white abstractions across his retinae, creating nervous pulsations in his eyelids, and causing him to remember a childhood some part of him was sure he had never had.

Carter got unsteadily to his feet, confused by the black and whiteness, the silvery greyness, of his living room. He staggered to the lightswitch by his front door, but flipping it up or down had no effect on the quality of light and darkness in the room. He staggered out to his neighbor's door, his apartment strobing painfully behind him.

Mr Williams was in his green pyjamas. Carter rubbed his eyes and the pyjamas changed color. He decided he wouldn't pay any more attention to his eyes – obviously they'd broken – so he closed them and asked of the warm, close darkness, "Why'd you bring my TV back?"

"Whadayamean? It's right there in the living room." Carter opened his eyes. Williams was all red muscle and layers of fat, his skin evaporated. His jaw worked back and forth grotesquely as he spoke. "You been drinkin', Carter? Your eyes are pretty damn red."

Without speaking, Carter pushed past Williams into the man's living room. His old set sat in the middle of the room, a recliner similar to his, pushed (too close!) to the screen. The television prattled merrily, but normally, to itself. The Home Shopping Channel rattled off a litany of prices and features with the kind of rhythm which promised heaven. "But I just saw it," he said softly.

Williams chuckled behind him. "It's like my dead wife. You get so used to seein' her all the time, you see her even when she ain't there. Like a damn ghost or somethin'. Say, maybe you need another drink?"

Carter didn't watch as Williams went into the kitchen. But he could hear the sound of the refrigerator door opening. It made a noise like a lion roaring, and then there was the instant stench of rotting meat. Carter ran back across the hall into the now-manic black-and-white flicker of his apartment. As he closed the door he could hear Williams barking like a dog in an Alpo commercial (Real Meat Flavor!) then the question, "Is your phone working? I could call the repair guy for you!"

The nonexistent television glowed as if filled with milky electricity. He walked over to the slick black telephone and picked up the receiver. It was rank. He stared at the holes in the round earpiece. It looked and smelled like a sewer grate.

He decided to ignore the phone while using it. After all, it was simply an instrument, an agency, a device for communicating with the manager. The phone stuck a tongue in his ear, but he remained calm as he talked to the building manager, struggling not to be too specific with his complaint for fear the man wouldn't send anyone to his aid.

The repairman sent by the building manager arrived a few hours later with a large metal toolbox and several suitcases. "What seems to be the problem?"

Carter felt suddenly empty of all understanding. He struggled for the right words but nothing seemed to come except a string of broken syllables, a chant, an appeal to God. Finally, with much effort, all that would come out was, "Things just haven't been the same since my mother died." He made a broad gesture to indicate his whole apartment, his entire life.

The repairman stared at him, then made a subtle nod. "We all love our mothers," he said, then set the cases down on the rug and opened his toolbox. He pulled out a stiff, heavy brush and began brushing vigorously at the carpet where the television had once stood, but which was now gone again. "Do this a few times to pull up the fibres, and you'd never guess that the television had ever been there."

Suddenly the lights buzzed, smoked, flickered, and went out. The dark apartment smelled strongly of cooking, greasy meat. Then Carter started seeing sparks in the corners of his eyes, which elongated into ribbons of brilliance leading from one glowing node after another, crossing, joining, splitting, until finally he realized it was a glowing diagram of the electrical wiring within his apartment walls.

"I haven't been able to find your set yet," the repairman said. He smelled of rapid decay – otherwise Carter wouldn't have known where he was. "It's so dark in here."

"I gave my television set to my neighbor," Carter said.

"Yeah, I know what you mean," the repairman replied out of the darkness. "Sometimes you get so used to them being there, you feel more comfortable with them than you do with your wife, or any of your living friends. You see them even after you've given them away."

"It was a good set. I should have kept it."

The television floated up out of the darkness, a ghostly sketch of light, a white outline of electricity. "There. That's better," the repairman said. "It explains a lot. Some of these old sets get so charged up with the years of electricity firing through them, well, it's a little technical, but a kind of residue builds up in the air . . ."

Carter tuned out his voice, intent on watching the ghost of the television, whose screen depicted the pale, electrified face of his mother, who appeared to be sleeping peacefully. "When I was a little boy, I never believed she would die. Mommas and daddies don't die. Mommas and daddies aren't like cats smeared across the highway or beef roasting in a pot or bloody hamburger rotting out in a garbage can."

"These old sets, they last forever," the repairman said. "A damn sight longer than you or me. They don't make them like they used to. Hell, they don't make *us* like they used to, do they?"

"She wasn't made like I dreamed she was made," Carter said. "She wasn't my dream after all."

"Oh, it is a dream machine, all right," the repairman said. "Just look at the quality of that picture!"

Carter stared at the ghost of his television, at the image of his mother whose clarity improved steadily, so that the screen expanded until it had taken into it his mother's entire apartment, and then his apartment, filling his eyes and his world with its brilliant, televised light.

Carter opened his untrustworthy eyes and saw his apartment as if transformed within a dream. The walls glowed with a whiteness he hadn't thought possible. The carpet was as smooth and featureless as a photograph of a carpet. In the background kitchen appliances hummed their distant, distracted tunes. The warm scent of cooking vegetables stirred the hairs in his nose. And before him his old television glowed with a soft, grey light. His mother's soft-focus smile, her pewter eyes.

"You do good work," he complimented the vanished repairman.

The repairman's two suitcases rested by Carter's reclining chair.

He opened the first: clocks and gears, handfuls of capacitors, resistors, integrated chips and miscellaneous wiring, folders full of blueprints and foolproof instructions.

A thick redness had seeped out of the bottom of the second suitcase and was now spreading through the loose, porous fibres of the carpet. He opened this suitcase: mounds of decaying meat fell out, greyed and runny, eventually recognizable as his mother's heart and head, his father's torso, hands, legs.

The instructions were difficult to follow, although highly specific. He spent hours wrapping the gooey meat around the various electronic components, embedding the workings carefully so that no trace of them might be found.

Now the apartment filled with the smells of cooking meat. The brilliant walls splattered with equally brilliant blood and the carpet became a sticky, grey slough as Carter worked through the night, worked through the day and his neighbor's drunken pleading, his neighbor's beating on the door, working to restore his parents to the life he had dreamed for them.

JOEL LANE

The Moon Never Changes

JOEL LANE LIVES IN Birmingham, where he works as a freelance editor and writer. A winner of the 1993 Eric Gregory Award for poetry, his stories have appeared in a wide range of magazines and anthologies, including *The Urbanite* (as the Featured Writer in No. 7), *Peeping Tom, Exuberance, Ambit, The Third Alternative, Darklands* and *Darklands 2, The Science of Sadness, Sugar Sleep, Little Deaths, Twists of the Tale: Cat Horror Stories, The Mammoth Book of Dracula, The Best New Horror* and Karl Edward Wagner's *The Year's Best Horror Stories*.

His British Fantasy Award-winning collection of short fiction, entitled *The Earth Wire and Other Stories*, was published by Egerton Press in 1994, and a collection of poetry, *The Edge of the Screen*, appeared from Arc in 1997.

"'The Moon Never Changes' is one of several stories I've written about the psychology of fascism," explains the author. "It's too comforting to regard fascist beliefs as the result of ignorance, as if they could be overcome by a good newspaper. Fascism is a delusional framework of real tenacity. And what is clearly insanity at an individual level becomes evil at the level of an organization."

THE MORNING AFTER THE power cut, Gareth lost count of the number of broken shop-front windows he passed on the main road going into town. The streets had been swept clean, but only a few of the shops had been boarded up. The damage to some suggested that cars had been driven into them. Elsewhere, stones had been thrown through upper windows with no attempt to break in. Some of the shops probably wouldn't reopen; as though the dereliction spreading through the district had suddenly reached its nerve centre.

At least it gave him something to talk to Lorraine about. They both worked in the sale section of the city centre branch of Video World, upstairs from the busier rental section. Weekday mornings were dead; they spent the time pricing up new stock and putting orders through the computer. Lorraine was nineteen, two years younger than Gareth. She'd read in the local paper about the power cut and what it had led to.

"Were you frightened?" she asked him.

"Not a lot. I stayed in. The street was weird — no light at all, except cars going past." There hadn't even been a moon. "Ten minutes after the lights went out, there was a knock at my door. This woman was going down the street, selling candles." They both laughed. "I knew nothing about the looting until I came into work today. They say it was set up — the fire that caused the blackout. The whole thing was organized."

"I'd like to see where you live," Lorraine said as she passed a label-gun across a stack of cassette boxes.

Gareth wondered how much she meant by that. Her face reminded him of Sarah. He was wondering about the best way to invite her round when a customer appeared, an ill-dressed youth with round glasses who wanted an "uncut" version of *City of the Living Dead*. "Sorry . . ." Gareth began, then did a quick double-take. "Well, I can't help you *officially*, but if you want I can get you a copy of the Dutch version. No subtitles. But that has a sequence missing from every other release — where a mother feeds her baby with her own intestines."

The youth's eyes widened. "Wow. Thanks a lot." Gareth smiled politely. He'd done this a few times with customers whose requests irritated him. Lorraine was struggling to look neutral. Gareth promised to have the "unofficial" video in a fortnight's time. As the customer strode buoyantly down the steps, Lorraine laughed in a silent way that was rather odd.

"You're such a good liar," she said. Gareth tensed, fighting down his reaction. Once he would have hit her for a remark like that. But she hadn't meant anything that mattered. *I'm in control*, he told himself. Nobody could call him paranoid.

At one o'clock, he asked Lorraine if she wanted to go out for lunch. She smiled at him. "Tomorrow? I'm off this afternoon. Have to do some shopping." They agreed tomorrow.

In the afternoon, the shop was full of children looking at the videos of TV programmes. Gareth was glad to be busy. He kept thinking of his flat, how cold it had become now the weather was turning. The darkness there seemed to fill the air with webs. Now he had a job, why didn't he leave? If he did that, he'd lose the memory of Sarah. Which was all he had to hold onto, even now.

It was raining when he left the shop. There was a meeting at seven, so it wasn't worth going home in between. Gareth watched the traders packing up in the Bull Ring. How many of them cheated their customers with short weight or bad produce? And how many of them were moonlighting while on the dole? No wonder there was talk of closing the place down. Immigrants had reduced it to a shambles. As they made a mockery of every British tradition. As night pooled between the layers of concrete, the empty stalls were like a harbour of damaged boats. Canvases flapped out of scaffolding frames, laughing to themselves.

The meeting was in the usual place, at the back of an antique shop in Digbeth. There was a genuine suit of armour just inside the doorway. The Union Jack flags in the upper windows had nothing to do with the Gulf War. They were there to let newcomers know that they'd found the right place. The meeting room was sparsely furnished, but always clean. There were a couple of dozen people tonight. Andrew, the group leader from Wolverhampton, gave a talk titled "Something is rotten in the state of England". Gareth liked that; he'd done *Hamlet* in school, and the character meant a lot to him. Andrew was talking about what it meant to be dedicated to unmasking pretences. To let the truth be incarnated in your own life. "Being a man means always remembering what's inside you, and using it to remind the world." Gareth wished he had the confidence to give a talk like this. There was something about Andrew that made him feel afraid – as though Andrew gave out a kind of heat or light that it was uncomfortable to stay close to. He wasn't much older than Gareth, and both of them were younger than most of the group.

Later, there was some discussion of the previous night's

disturbances. James, the Birmingham leader, was scornful of the local newspapers' coverage. "They always try to obscure the pattern. Make out it was a riot, something spontaneous. Nothing in this world is spontaneous. Last night was the criminal underworld showing what it can do. It was terrorism against the decent population. If the police had arms, they could have taken out a few of the bastards. That shows you where our Council's sympathies really lie – and I mean *lie*." Gareth didn't mention that he lived only a block away from the looted shops. It felt better to listen and let his thoughts tie up with the fabric of explanation he was being given. He felt illuminated.

Near midnight, the bus shelter on Colmore Row was full of silent, empty-faced people. Gareth felt the sense of belonging slip away from him. Could vacancy be transmitted like a disease? Past the concrete stage of the Hockley flyover, the main road was boarded up and deserted. A white police car waited at the crossroads by the bus stop, its red light flashing. As he opened the door to his flat, Gareth thought of what Sarah had said when she left him. "I want to forget about you. Forget you even exist." He went straight to bed and lay there thinking about Lorraine. Her bright eyes, her friendly smile that seemed real. Was he real enough for her? Or for anyone? He drifted into sleep, dust falling like a spider-web across his face in the dark.

The next day was overcast and still, like the background to a silent film. Gareth and Lorraine went to the City Plaza for lunch. They sat in a sandwich café on the top floor, watching people rise and descend in the glass lift. A flock of white plastic pigeons hung from the skylight, quivering. Lorraine was in a thoughtful mood. "You seem very nervous," she said to Gareth. "You try to be funny so people won't notice. Do you live with your parents?"

Gareth shook his head. "Got a flat of my own. My mother's dead. I used to live with my aunt. Don't know where my father is . . . Bastard ran away when I was a baby." Lorraine looked steadily at him. He caught her eyes: a mixture of sympathy and warmth. He wanted to explain how the Front had given him a new family, something to believe in. And she'd know, when the time was right. Just as she'd know about Sarah and the others. "Do you live alone?" he asked.

"No, I'm sharing a house with two other girls. I'm from Stafford, originally. Came here to do a college course – travel and tourism.

But I dropped out and got a job instead. I like it here. Well . . . it's not a bad city but there's something false about it. It keeps trying to change its image, without actually changing the way it is. Just an expensive façade." Her eyes moved around, noting without comment the glass roof, the plastic birds, the mock-Italian decor. From below, the piano player seated underneath the escalator started up a new tune.

Gareth smiled. "Just close your eyes," he said. "You could be gliding along a slightly polluted canal . . . in a vacuum-formed plastic gondola." Lorraine giggled and almost choked on her coffee. Then, serious again, she reached out and touched his hand. Their fingers wove together. Gareth felt a rush of security which, almost at once, dissolved and left him exposed. The two linked hands formed a shape like a huge spider. It was almost as obscene as the linking of genitals. He looked into Lorraine's eyes, blue like tinted glass, and made himself smile. On the way back to the video shop, they made a date for Friday night at his flat. Gareth pushed his way clumsily through the New Street crowd; he felt oddly tired.

It rained that evening, but he didn't want to stay in the house. On the Soho Road, most of the shops had new metal shutters. It was like the row of garage doors on the estate where his aunt lived. Someone had sprayed YOUR DEAD on one of the grey screens. Outside the local pub, an ageing couple in plastic coats were kissing determinedly, propped up by each other and the wall. Rain painted their faces. They held small white bottles in the air like charms against evil. Gareth turned down a side-street, heading for another pub he preferred. Lamplight glistened on boarded windows and a few edges of broken glass. Dereliction was spreading. He imagined it forming a web around his house. That might be better than being surrounded by Asians.

The pub stank of spilled beer; in five minutes he was out again, a cold gin flame burning in his chest. Torn sheets of rain flapped around the streetlamps. Two girls in mini-skirts sheltered in the mouth of an alley just beyond the pub. One of them looked up as Gareth passed, but he kept walking. This time he didn't need to bother. Around the next corner was the school, behind a wire fence; then the railway bridge and the familiar smell of rotting stone. It was all constant, like his memories. As a child, he'd dreamed that the moon would never move or change.

Some time near three, Gareth gave up trying to sleep. Shivering in his dressing-gown, he walked past the bathroom to the spare room at the back of his flat, and unlocked the door. Beneath his feet, the floorboards were spongy with dust. He switched on the light. Cobwebs hung around it like a grey chandelier. The bare plaster of the walls was tattooed with damp; clotted masses of webbing stuck to the corners. Gareth was used to all this. What he'd come to see was spread out on the table in the middle of the room. The photographs. The letters. Some gifts and records. A few items of clothing. A wineglass, its inside furred with dust. But above all, the photographs. A framed print, a strip of passport photos, some blurred snapshots. Sarah and Jan and Catherine. Three peaceful, smiling faces. Through each one, he possessed the others. And through Lorraine, he could possess them all. Unless she was like them. It surprised him that he hadn't been infected by their betrayal. He was a photograph, all the way through. He was unable to change or look away. The thought suddenly made him feel sick, as though he had been force-fed with emptiness. He punched the table, and coughed on the dust that flew up.

On the far side of the room, whorls of cobweb hung on the blank wall like faces. He stared, trying to identify them. As he looked back down into Sarah's unseeing eyes, Catherine's eyes that were lit red by a flashbulb, a sudden taste of vomit stung the back of his throat. The two-faced cunts. They'd called him *obsessive. Jealous.* Didn't they understand that it was perverted to give your body to someone you didn't give your heart to? They didn't have the first idea. He understood why. They lived in a culture of lies and façades, their eyes and ears were poisoned. Show them faith and they'd call it obsession. He tried to pity them, but couldn't. He was too lonely.

The feeling of nausea and loss made him drop to his knees. He couldn't look at the pictures any more. Crying to himself in a dry, mechanical way, he crawled back to his bedroom. Still feeling sick, he masturbated viciously into his pillow. The last thought in his mind as he burrowed his way into sleep was of Andrew's words: "Being a man means remembering what's inside you, and using it to remind the world." And with that, the image of Andrew, James and the rest of the group surrounding him like quiet protectors in a dark room.

Friday morning was bright and chilly. Gareth had the day planned. He was going to take the afternoon off, so as to get everything ready for Lorraine's visit. In the bathroom, he saw there was dirt on his hands and feet from the spare room. He scrubbed himself clean, then washed his hair, which was turning brittle from repeated bleaching. He'd have to let it grow out. He disliked the weakness of his image: papery skin, hairless chest. The stubble on his cheeks was like mud that a razor could scrape off. He'd nearly finished shaving when he noticed the spider on the mirror, directly in his line of sight. Why hadn't he seen it before? He flicked water at it uneasily, and it fell to the floorboards.

In the shop, he kept glimpsing Lorraine from an angle, trying to see if her expression changed when she wasn't facing him. *God hath given you one face and you make yourselves another*. He'd see the truth later on. The thought made him feel entirely separate from the people he sold videos to – black coils of tape, to plug the gaps in themselves where money flowed. How easily an image, a logo, an empty box, could deceive people. At midday, he put on his coat. Lorraine waved goodbye to him from behind the computer, where she was entering stock records. "See you tonight," she said, smiling. "Eight o'clock." All afternoon, he struggled with an inner feeling that she wouldn't turn up.

The town centre was crammed with people. Gareth stood outside a burger restaurant, trying to see where the bus queue started. Then the bus stopped, and people poured into it from all directions, their Walkmans buzzing like trapped flies. He hung back from the crowd, and had to wait for the next bus. Once he had a seat, he kept his eyes shut until the bus neared the Hockley flyover. Advertisement boards and new offices crowded the view; a district of façades. Factory smoke and shattered buildings marked the edge of Handsworth. He stayed on past the Albion football ground, and got off in West Bromwich to buy food and wine for tonight. The air was cold, although the sunlight felt warm. The only thing to do was to go through with this ritual; if he failed, so would Lorraine.

But she did turn up. She'd changed her shirt since the morning, and was clutching a bottle of wine. "The other two at the house were dead curious," she said. "They've both got boyfriends, I feel a bit out of place sometimes. You said you had a flat – does anyone else live downstairs?" They'd passed a locked door in the hallway.

"Used to. It's a social security drop-off. You know. This guy comes and collects some letters every now and then. Doesn't stay. Only reason I got this place was . . . well, I needed somewhere private. Had a girlfriend. It didn't work out, though."

"Never mind," Lorraine said. "You're still young."

"Don't feel it," Gareth said. "I'm old in my head." He carried on preparing the meal, slicing mushrooms and dropping them into the meat sauce. "Do you want a drink?"

"Thanks, yeah." He took some wine from the fridge and poured out two glasses. In half an hour the meal was ready. Wine had the effect of making Gareth fatalistic. Whatever happened, it was all beyond his control. Lorraine drank faster than he did, and went from being lively to being quiet and rather serious. She looked around the living-room, which Gareth had tidied and cleaned a few hours before. "Don't you get lonely on your own?"

"Sometimes. But it's better to have your own place. Then you're in control. At least you can trust yourself."

"Can you? I can't." Lorraine laughed, then looked closely at Gareth's face. Her eyes were very still, even when her face moved. "Don't you trust anyone else?"

There was a silence. "Look at it this way," Gareth said. "You don't work because you trust the employer. It's all part of some system you don't know about. They exploit you so you can live. You can't trust the TV or the newspaper, it's part of the same thing, the same kind of web. They deceive you so you can think. And we all live in this culture. What is there to trust? It's all a betrayal."

"What is? Capitalism?"

"I used to think that. But it's not that simple. Socialism's just another way of manipulating people. Everything is a fucking betrayal." *Calm down*, he told himself. He had to probe, test how much she understood. For her, he'd make himself ignorant. Then they'd find the truth together. Lorraine was staring at him.

"Did someone betray you? Someone you loved?" Gareth felt something cold in his chest. Fuck her teen-mag psychology. Yes, he'd been dumped. Three times. But that had helped him to unmask the world. It hadn't *made* him think this way. He didn't just think, he knew.

"Yes," he said, smiling. "Someone I loved."

"A girl?"

"*Of course*," he said. How dare she suggest otherwise? His fists clenched under the table. Lorraine looked almost scared by the force of his reaction. From somewhere, he retrieved his smile and ran it across his face. "She was called Catherine. She left me, that was all. Nothing to worry about." He refilled their glasses. Two empty plates lay on the table between them; Lorraine had praised his cooking. "Can I ask you something?" he said. Lorraine nodded. "How many boys have you been out with?"

"About eight. It depends . . . Do you mean really been out with, or just been to bed with?" Gareth stared at her. How many more times would she surprise him? "Haven't shocked you, have I?" He shook his head. "It's weird," Lorraine said. "When a boy sleeps around, it's fine, he's a great lad, you know? When a girl sleeps around, she's dirty. You'd think it was only women who ever had VD . . . I left home to live with my third boyfriend. We split up. For a while I didn't care what happened. But you don't stop trusting people, Gareth. You just learn to take it in stages. One date at a time. Then one promise at a time."

Gareth was only half-listening. Inside his mind, a pattern was taking shape. The record scratched into silence; he stood up and crossed to the stereo. On the way back, he put his hand on Lorraine's shoulder, then the back of her neck. He sat down. "Do you want me to stay tonight?" she said.

"If you want to. Yes." It seemed so easy. But the next step made him feel cold — as though a door had opened in the middle of the room. "Lorraine." Blue sparks at the edge of his vision.

Outside the bedroom, he paused and drew her close; she kissed him. They would only have to go inside. Suddenly he was afraid, he didn't know what of. He carried on stepping backwards, until they reached the locked door at the end of the hallway. He reached for his key. Lorraine looked confused. "Why do you lock the door?"

"Security," he said. The spare room was dark, even when he switched the light on; and chilly. Lorraine coughed. He pushed her into the room, and shut the door behind them.

"God, what is this?" Lorraine said. "Smells like dust or mildew or something." It had changed since the previous night. The photos and letters on the table were coated with dust; the cobwebs on the walls were almost a seamless façade. Lorraine stepped closer to the wall. Her shadow might be enough to break the plaster.

Gareth stepped behind her, his hands on her arms. "Eyes and ears," he said. Corrupt eyes, mildewed ears. He was close to making out the faces on the far wall. Beyond the table.

Lorraine picked up a grey photograph; the glass was cracked in a weblike pattern. "Forget that," Gareth said quietly. "I'll show you something worth remembering." She turned, and he put his arms around her and pushed her against the wall. Immediately, it began to disintegrate, showering them both with flakes of plaster and whitewash. Lorraine reached behind her, and her hand passed through the white surface into what was behind it. She cried out, wordlessly, and broke free of Gareth's embrace. Strands of webbing trailed behind her like a silvery dress. More plaster fell; behind it was a soft mass of webs, tinged with rust that dried in the light. Gareth reached out and touched the webbing. It was thick, layered in a complex pattern, like some kind of textile. He could see a dark swelling to one side, where a body was embedded in the web. In a moment, he would see what it was.

"Get away!" Lorraine was shouting; the air seemed to muffle her voice. Gareth looked at her. She was inbetween the dusty table and the silver tapestry that had been the wall. She reached up, and he caught her hand. "For God's sake . . ." She was changing too – becoming Sarah, Jan, Catherine. But he was holding her now, kissing a white flake from her mouth, forcing her to turn and look at the wall. Pale streaks and flecks of plaster still clung to the silver-grey fabric, which tensed in different places as the black shape inside it moved. What Gareth could see was a thin body, about half the size of his own: a long spider with jagged broken legs, like a swastika superimposed on its own mirror image.

Lorraine retched suddenly and folded up, then kicked him on the inside of his ankle. As she pulled away, Gareth tried to grab hold of her shirt; but his left leg was numb, and he fell. Splinters jarred his knees. Lorraine kicked him again, just under the ribs. The web in front of him seemed to vibrate and bleed. Gareth's face was resting on the floorboards; he breathed in dust and the dry stink of rotting wood. Then Lorraine was leaning over him. She lifted his head in her hands and stared miserably, trying to speak. Her face was whitewashed. Gareth reached up a hand that was shaking as it touched her hair. His fist closed, and he pulled as hard as he could. Lorraine tumbled over him and fell through the silvery curtain, into the space between the walls.

There was a scraping sound, and a muffled thud. Gareth started to laugh. That would teach them to betray him. The web was pulsing now, turning red near its centre. The dark shape was pushing through, like a bruise coming to the surface. All at once, the silver-grey membrane was open. Gareth stepped closer. All he felt was a single deep sting, like a knife in his side. Then there was a thick, dreamy sense of relief as the web closed around him, becoming a Ferris wheel in a dead fairground, spinning for him and for him alone.

ROBERTA LANNES

Butcher's Logic

ROBERTA LANNES IS A native of Southern California. She has worked as a commercial artist, was a member of a professional improvizational comedy troupe, and did stand-up comedy in a club on Sunset Boulevard. Since 1971 she has been teaching fine art, English, graphics, journalism, and various literature courses in junior and senior high school.

In 1984 she began taking courses in writing genre fiction at UCLA, where she met Dennis Etchison, one of her first teachers. Two years later he published her first horror story, "Goodbye, Dark Love", in his acclaimed anthology *Cutting Edge*. Since then, her many short stories have been published in *AfterHours*, *Fantasy Tales*, *Iniquities*, *Pulphouse*, *Alien Sex*, *Off Limits*, *Splatterpunks* and *Splatterpunks II*, *The Bradbury Chronicles*, *Dark Voices 5*, *Dark Terrors*, *The Mammoth Books of Werewolves*, *Frankenstein* and *Dracula*, *Golden Tears Ruby Slippers*, *Love in Vein II*, *Lethal Kisses*, *The Year's Best Fantasy and Horror* and *The Best New Horror*, amongst others.

In 1997, Silver Salamander Press published her short story collection *The Mirror of Night* with an introduction by Harlan Ellison. The author lives in Los Angeles with her husband, British journalist, Mark Sealey.

"'Butcher's Logic' is the beginning of a departure for me from my 'extreme horror'," explains Lannes. "Although I've written pieces with a similar ambience, none have been as close to my heart, my experience, as this one.

"In fact, I have to say, the kind of quiet horror I saw, grew up with, serves as the most powerful in the end. The characters are real, the experience autobiographical, altered only by the writer's license to fictionalize. With this, I give the child's voice in me an opportunity to whisper its fears."

I GREW UP IN the 1950s, in a sea of tract houses surrounded by orange groves. Shingled roofs on single storey boxes, pruned hedges, snowy white sidewalks, clean streets and lots of space were things I took for granted. The neighbors were more alike than diverse, as they are now. In each home, for three square miles, were white, middle-class, upwardly mobile men with stay-at-home wives, their two or three generally well-behaved children, and a dog or cat. The eleven Rizzoli kids, and Mrs Coleman with her history of six miscarriages, were rarities.

But, from a child's point of view, the neighborhood was full of drama and curiosity; from why Mrs Stedman dressed up each morning for the milkman to why Mr Wolfe was in a wheelchair and never came out except to chase kids from his lawn. And eerie Mr Melcher, the sneering butcher, and his meat locker. No one was allowed to see inside, not even his wife, and we kids were threatened with banishment into the great frozen void if we were trouble enough. Stories abounded of Mr Melcher cutting people up into steaks, grinding them until they were hamburger, and selling them to their own families. How he never let an ounce of blood touch his floor, so no one, ever, could find any evidence of a crime. Subject of great interest, yet feared by us all, we spoke of him only in hushed conversation.

My best friend was a boy, and because I was a pretty blonde girl this was a persistent source of upset to my jealous father. The fact that my friend was half-Puerto Rican and half-Afro-American, turned my outwardly open-minded mother into a wary one. Jesse was tougher than my psycho younger brother Kirk, a frustrating fact for Kirk, but a real blessing to me. My little sister, Trish, loved Jesse, as did I. He was an island of good will and true heartedness in that ocean of bungalows, narrow minds, and mean spirits.

Jesse lived with his parents in the middle of an orange grove, just outside the perimeter of a new housing tract. His father, Monroe, was the grove caretaker; his mother, Cecilia, made and sold the most beautiful lace, crocheting everything from collars and doilies to tablecloths. They welcomed me into their home with honest smiles and sincere offerings, whether it be for water or an entire meal. Unlike my house where other children were allowed only during certain hours (when Daddy wasn't home), and then we had to play outside, regardless of the weather, the Simmonses only required their guests be alive and well.

My mother feigned liberal ideals as I was growing up, such were the values our upwardly mobile neighbors professed. Along with some of the other local girls, I received a "colored" doll for Christmas (that was before I brought Jesse home). I named the doll Sophie. She disappeared a week after Jesse became part of my life. When I asked Mom where Sophie had gone, she told me she was filthy from my having dragged her everywhere, so she'd put her in the washing machine. At the age of eight, I was not ignorant regarding the physics of putting a doll with a porcelain head through the agitation of an ancient egg-beater of a washing machine.

I searched in vain through the garbage for pieces of Sophie. When I told Cecilia, she shook her pretty head, and clucked her tongue. "I think your mother hid your Sophie from you 'cause she don' want nobody colored in her house anymore. Then she dump her with all that other give-away stuff at the thrift store."

For weeks, I prayed it wasn't so. One day Jesse rode me over to the thrift shop on his bicycle. He'd told me we were riding to Lintner's, the five-and-dime next door. "You gotta know one way or the other. 'Wondering'll kill you', Momma says."

Jesse pulled me inside. The musty smell of odd clothes, yellowing pages of discarded books, and the oily scent of once well-cared-for furniture filled the air. The linoleum flooring curled up at its many seams, so we walked with caution.

"She's not here," I protested, my eyes on the ground.

Jesse snorted. "Over there. Look." Gently, he lifted my chin. She was on the doll shelf, my sweet Sophie, her one eye shutting when her head slanted ever so little. I told Jesse I hated him and ran outside. I turned his bicycle over and hurried into Lintner's to lose myself in the racks of coloring books.

Eight is awfully young to lose faith in your mother.

After I forgave Jess, I decided I would marry him when I was thirteen and have sixteen brown babies and be very poor, but extremely happy, all to show my mother and father how wrong they were about people and the world. If an eight-year-old girl could know true love, then I loved that nut-brown boy. For the next year and a half, he was my best friend.

When I was nine, my parents got us a dog. She was a boxer with the sweetest disposition, suffering us kids with immense grace. Jesse thought we should call her Sophie, after my doll, now long gone, but when I suggested it, Mom gave me "the look". Dad thought we should call her something we'd call a little sister. Kirk suggested "Melon Head". Trish liked the name Angel. No one objected, so Angel's what we called her.

Growing up without much physical affection, hugs and the like, we gave Angel all the tenderness we lacked. She responded with leaping at us and licking us with great abandon. My father, who about this time began his secondary career as an alcoholic, started kicking her when he got home, and Mom, incensed with us for not taking adequate responsibility for the dog's feeding and defecation, grew disapproving of our play. Jesse's folks told me they'd take Angel and make her a good home if my parents didn't want her. I had dreams of going to see Angel in the orange grove, knowing she'd thrive in the open space and the love the Simmonses could give.

One night, when Mom and Dad went out bowling, I was finally appointed babysitter. I'd reached the age (nine and a half) and stature of one mature enough to handle a brother whose sole joy in life was terrorizing his sisters into locking themselves in the bathroom while he looted their secret caches of candy, and a sister so fragile emotionally, that her consoling had become an art for me.

Angel served as an ideal buffer. We chased her, tossed her dog biscuits, hugged and wrestled with her until she grew reluctant, then down-right unwilling. She chose to hide behind the sofa. I had the longest arms, so I reached back there, got a hold of her back leg and pulled. Hard.

She gave one quick, sharp cry, then let me yank her all the way out. We did our best to inspire her back into play, but she limped off, glancing back at me once. Later, I recalled that glance as being full of disappointment and pain, but back then I thought she was just dismissing us.

Jesse woke me the next morning by running a stick over my window screen. I hurried into pants, a shirt and sandals, eager to go outside. As I raced into the den, I saw Angel laying on her side, panting roughly, the entire carpet spattered with vomit, shit, and blood. My heart stopped, my stomach clenched, and my mind wrapped around the thought that Angel was dying. I was afraid to touch her, scared I'd hurt her worse.

"Mom. Dad. Come quick. Something's wrong with Angel!"

Neither parent, at this point in our rearing, moved with any alacrity at our calls, long regarding any summons as "crying wolf". Eventually, my mother came out. Jesse, who was never allowed in the house, stood outside, listening.

"What the hell did you do to that dog?"

Angel's sharp cry and her backward glance came back to me with gut-punching force. Tears bled onto my face.

"Mommy, do something. Don't let her die." I managed through my deep sobs.

By then, Kirk and Trish were up, standing in the doorway. Their eyes belied their fear, but they knew they hadn't been responsible. Even if they had been, they'd long ago figured out it was I, the eldest, whose job it was to be the scapegoat.

Mom turned to them. "Do you know what happened to Angel?"

Trish ran to me, seeking protection and consolation. She was only five. She wouldn't need protection. Kirk, the sadist, chose the path of least resistance. He told the truth, a rare act for him – unless it meant I got in trouble.

I ached to go to Angel, tell her how sorry I was, and make it better. I moved toward her. I'd have walked through crap a foot deep, if my mother hadn't chosen that moment to bark, "Don't you *dare* put a foot in that mess. You're going to be cleaning that carpet for a *week*."

I looked back at Kirk, whose satisfied grin called up a mind-numbing rage in me. Mom grabbed my arm, pulling me to the linen cabinet to get towels for the floor. Once we stood before the cupboard, a few feet from where my father snored peacefully, Mom grit her teeth and snarled under her breath.

"I can't believe we left you in charge for three hours and wake up to this. I don't want your father to see or hear any of it, understand? I'm taking Angel to the vet. And you're going to pay every cent it costs to get her fixed up out of your allowance. Meanwhile, you'll soak rags in soapy water and get every bit of that crap off the carpet before your father wakes up. If he finds one trace . . ."

I nodded, tears streaming. I just wanted Angel put back the way she was.

Jesse came inside after my mother left. He wanted to help me clean up and I knew there was no way to erase the scene alone. Kirk had taken off on his bike somewhere, and Trish went back to bed to cower.

We soaped rags until we were up to our shoulders in bubbles. Holding our breaths, we scooped up faeces, clods of undigested dog biscuit and blood. Jesse never said a word, and all I did was sob quietly. When we had the major offending substances in the sink, then down the In-sink-o-rater, we took to our hands and knees to scrub away the stains. The only time Jesse spoke was to whisper that it was lucky we had tweed carpet.

Evidently Mom had left a note for Dad on the bathroom mirror, because when he walked into the den, he was already steaming. Then he saw Jesse.

"What the hell are you two doing?" He grabbed the rag from Jesse and yanked him up to his feet. "And what's *he* doing here?"

Jesse wrenched away and hurried to my side. I stood, rag dripping down my arms, nearly slipping on the wet broadloom.

"We had an accident this morning and I'm cleaning it up. Mommy said . . ."

"I want that boy out of here . . . now!" He glared at Jesse, menacingly. He scared me, but Jesse was undaunted.

"Hey, Mr. Sandler, don't take it out on her. I made her let me help."

"Who do you think you are, talking to me like that?" Dad stepped onto the wet carpet in his leather slippers, reaching out to grab Jesse. Jesse pitched sideways to protect me, catching my father off guard. Jesse never touched my father, there was a good three feet between them. When Dad's feet went out from under him and he landed on his butt, he shouted, "That tar baby threw me on my ass!" The floor shook at his fall. "Get the hell out of my house!" Trish peeked out from behind the door jamb, eyes wide.

Jesse looked at me, his expression a mixture of anger and hurt, shifting to resolve. I quaked in fear, unable to move.

"If he hurts you, I'll kill him." That was the last thing Jesse said to me before he rushed past my prostrate father, awed sister, and astonished mother, just returning from the vet.

Instinctively, I knew better than to ask about Angel before showing concern for my father, but all my thoughts were for her.

As my mother helped my father up and into his chair, she kept giving me "the look". Dad babbled on about suing the Simmons family, making sure that that nigger never set foot in his house ever again, and grounding me until I was seventeen.

As Mom tended to my father, I gathered up the rags and pail and went into the laundry room. The carpet was far from perfectly clean, my father probably crippled for life, I'd never be able to see my best friend again, and my beloved dog was probably unfixable. The year before, I lost my faith, now I was losing a piece of me. A sadness came to settle within my heart.

My mother found me standing at the sink a half-hour later, my elbows hooked inside to hold me up. I got my footing and turned to face her. She had a strange look, one I would now call spiteful, but back then it was intimidating, like all her "looks". She folded her arms and shook her head.

"Well, now you've really hit an all time low. How stupid could you get? Bringing that boy in this house, after you've been told over and over. Doing such a sloppy job on the rug. God, what did you think you were doing there, painting? It's worse now than before. And your father . . . he's in such pain. What did that boy do to him?"

"I . . . I . . ." Hopelessness robbed me of words.

"Well, serves you right, then. Just what you deserve. You killed that dog. Huh. She's *dead*."

I felt nothing, yet everything was brighter-than-bright, distinct, and bottomless in the small space of the laundry room. My body was as cold as my big play magnet and just as hard. I closed my eyes, becoming stone inside and out. I heard my mother chuckle derisively, then pad carefully through the kitchen to the den.

That night, I dreamt I was in jail. Jesse drifted by the bars of my cell, whispering dirty words and telling me he would kill my father. I also dreamt Angel was alive and well, running across an ice field, catching hula hoops in her teeth. When I woke up, I had to go to school and behave as if I was whole.

Jesse rushed to me the moment I set foot on the tarmac.

"Did he hurt you? You okay?"

I shook my head. "Angel died. Mom told me I killed her."

"Ach." Jesse dismissed it. "My momma'll tell you Angel didn't die cause of you. Your mother probably had her put to sleep. They have to shoot a horse if he breaks his leg, you know."

"I broke her leg." My lip quivered and tears filled my eyes.

"Then she had to be shot. It's better for her. She's out of pain, now."

"I hope so." I dragged myself toward the classroom, overwhelmed with sorrow. It would be many years later that I'd learn I'd merely dislocated her hip. That after the incident, she was too fragile to be around children. That my mother had told the vet to keep her, let someone with grown children have her. And finally, that Angel lived out her life not five miles from our house.

Jesse seemed to know there was more, and waited. When we sat in our chairs, I reached into my desk and found a tissue to blow my nose.

"Jesse, I can't see you anymore."

"Bullshit." Whenever he cussed, I grinned. "I'll see you at school. And you can sneak over through the orange grove when they send you to the store."

I nodded sullenly.

At the time, doing what I wanted seemed a luxury I couldn't afford, nor deserved.

Two weeks later, I cut across the orchard on my way to the market. Cecilia opened her arms to me, kissing my face until it was wet. Monroe sat in his straight-back chair carving something ornate from a block of bass wood. He grinned at me, a mouth full of pearls.

"Jesse went to the market for me. He should be back any second. You wait?"

"I might get into trouble. I'm grounded. I should just go on ahead to the store. Maybe I'll see him on the way."

Cecilia nodded, then reached over to her sewing box to take out a cloud of white lace.

"Here." Cecilia handed me a lace collar she'd made. "Wear it to church on that blue dress of yours."

It was beautiful. But I was afraid to take it, certain that if my mother or father saw it, they'd know I'd been at the Simmons's and beat me silly.

Cecilia cocked her head, reading me. "I think that maybe I oughta keep it here, jus' to keep it safe. For now, okay?"

"Yes, please." I nodded. "I'd better go."

I hugged them again, and hurried back onto the path through the grove. Out of the corner of my eye, up ahead, I saw my father's shiny green Plymouth speeding up the road that ran along the length of the orchard. He had to have seen me. Damn. That was it. I was in for a beating.

I was shaking so badly by the time I reached the main road, I was sure I'd throw up. I searched for the Plymouth, keeping my head down, eyes jittering back and forth, hoping I wouldn't run into Jesse and get caught, again. As I walked across the street to Pete's Market, I saw the front of my father's car peaking out from behind where the delivery truck drops off meat for the butcher.

Pure fear drove me on to continue the errand. I wanted to turn and run, go bury myself in sweet loam under a tree in the park so that in time a new me would grow up through the grass. A whole me.

I stepped into the market, afraid every box and tin would betray my secret, and tell my father where I'd been. I looked for him, but he was nowhere around. Behind the dirty lengths of canvas stripping that hung in the doorway to the storage area in back, I could see Mr Melcher shutting the huge freezer door.

I set the list of things my mother wanted on the counter and Mrs Grant, a woman of few words, simply took it, handed it to her bagger, Chuck, who began gathering the items from around the store. I stood there, frozen, watching Mr Melcher wash his hands while Mrs Grant busied herself with straightening the gum in the candy rack. Mr Melcher kept looking at me, then back at his hands. His face was sweaty, though he'd just come from inside the freezer, as if he'd just cut up a lot of meat.

I jumped at the sound of the metal basket hitting the counter. Chuck had completed the list.

"That's . . ." Mrs Grant tapped at the adding machine keys, each computation making the sound of beans rattling in a tin can. "Three dollars, seventy cents."

I handed her a five and let her put the change in an envelope, as usual. She stared at me, as if sizing me up. When she handed me the envelope, she pinched her lips together, glanced back at Mr Melcher, then at me.

"You take that right home. No stopping."

She lifted the bag of goods and settled it into my arms. I thought to suggest putting it in my father's car, which was right outside, but no one had mentioned him at all.

I went out the front door, then hastily made my way around back to see if the car was there. It was. I hurried behind a wall of thick hedge where I could see if he came out.

Mr Melcher came out after my father, grinning. I couldn't recall ever seeing Mr Melcher smile. While they exchanged words, my father rubbed his arms as if he was standing in snow. Then they shook hands, my father got into the Plymouth and drove off. Mr Melcher looked around the parking lot, warily. He waited another minute, then satisfied, went back inside.

I hurried home, wishing the cold inside me was gone. I knew I couldn't beat my father home, but I thought that if I got there in time, I might see something pass between my mom and dad that would explain his behavior. Perhaps I'd even hear their words. Understand. If I understood, maybe the awful feelings I had would go away.

The driveway and garage were empty except for my mother's two-tone Chevy Bel Air. Kirk was in the yard playing some war game with his awful demented friends. I went in the back door, face flushed, still cold inside, and terrified.

"I saw Dad out driving." I was sorry the moment I blurted the words.

Mom set a clean pot under the counter, then took the groceries from me.

"It's Saturday. He was probably on his way to the office to finish up what he left last night." She began pulling out the items, one by one, ticking them off the list in her head.

"Chuck got everything. I just stood there. So if there's anything missing, you can blame him."

"The envelope, young lady . . ." She held out her hand, which I quickly filled. My mother shot me "the look", then continued emptying the bag. "Fine. It's all here. Now go to your room. No television."

I shrugged. After nine years of being sent to my room, I felt as if it was my world. Once there, I spun waking dreams – I planned my wedding to Jesse, had us dancing on a beach in Hawaii, sang my heart out to the world, becoming famous, everyone loving and admiring me. I'd grow up to find part of the dreams – the sand between my toes as warm and real to me then as it had been in the fantasies of my youth.

Monday at school, Jesse was absent. The teacher waited until we were all seated and quiet, then she sat down in a chair like ours, so she was looking into our eyes. It made everyone nervous. Miss Norman had never done that before.

"Class, I have something very important to tell you. One of your classmates, Jesse Simmons, is lost, or went with a stranger over the weekend, and his parents are worried sick. We don't want this to happen to any of you, so let's go over the rules about walking with a friend, again."

To me, her voice became a metallic rasp far down a long tunnel. I stared out the window, imagining Cecilia and Monroe, holding each other, weeping, afraid their only child would never come home. Jesse's parents loved him, and their hearts were breaking. Wondering was going to kill them.

That night, at the dinner table, I couldn't eat. I was sick with sorrow, fear, and longing. I kept waiting for Mom or Dad to ask what was wrong, but no one bothered with me.

Finally, Trish asked me if she could have my peas. I nodded solemnly.

"Jesse's gone." I sighed so heavily, I feared a sob would seep out.

Trish stopped spooning peas. "Where'd he go?"

I looked at my father. His eyes remained riveted on his martini. My mother squinted at him a second, then reached for the mashed potatoes.

"Nobody knows. He got kidnapped, or something. The police are looking for him."

"Maybe he robbed a bank," Kirk offered, his future in crime suggested.

I managed a frown. "Miss Norman lectured us about walking alone." I stared at my mother. "I guess you can't send me to the store without Kirk, now."

She looked at my father. Kirk whined, "Aw, do I have to? She's older'n me."

Dad pulled his eyes from his glass. They touched on me, then went far away. He grumbled to my mother. "Solve this one. I'm going to finish my drink." Then he got up and left the room.

Mom frowned at me. "Eat or go to your room without supper."

Kirk smirked. Trish shrunk beside me. I shrugged, got up, and left. As I passed my father, he was slumped in his lounger, eyes shut. I imagined him in the electric chair, ready to fry, knowing one day I would make it happen.

But that night, I sat on my bed, lights off, my face against the window screen. The cool night air stroked my cheek, and I breathed in the scents of night-blooming jasmine, hyacinth, and juniper. I wondered, for an instant, if Jesse's face was colder, if he smelled the carrion around him, then closed my eyes. There, in my mind, I saw Jesse on the beach in Hawaii, dancing beside Angel, waiting for me. Yes, I thought then, I'd find a way to be with them. Soon, but not before I told what I saw. My father rubbing his cold fat arms. Mrs Grant never looking me in the eyes. And Mr Melcher's lopsided grin.

D. F. LEWIS

Kites and Kisses

D. F. LEWIS HAS been called "a national treasure" by Graham Joyce, and in his introduction to *The Best of D. F. Lewis* (TAL Publications, 1993), Ramsey Campbell described his work as containing "more sustenance than in many a bestseller." As I've remarked before, Des Lewis is a true original.

He has now published an incredible one thousand stories since 1987, many in magazines that are D. F. Lewis specials. His fiction has appeared in five consecutive editions of Karl Edward Wagner's *The Year's Best Horror Stories*, two previous volumes of *The Best New Horror* and has had more than a dozen "honourable mentions" in *The Year's Best Fantasy and Horror*.

With his phenomenal output, perhaps it is not so surprising that when I asked the author to comment on the following, typically bizarre story, he admitted that he can't remember anything about writing it!

"MUMMY, HE'S THERE AGAIN."
The boy stood at the window, stretching his muscles from the tips of his toes.

Carefully positioning her cup and saucer beside her on the coffee table, his mother tried to make her bones forget how they really did hurt the rest of her. She slowly progressed towards the window which framed the silhouette of her son like a poster advertising a dark kiss.

"Yes, there again."

Through the mist which gave dusk an aura of calm flirtatiousness, the mother saw a child flying a kite. Every afternoon, even when there was no wind, the child was there, tugging at grey sky.

"Can I have a kite, like him?" asked her son, with his piping voice that either irritated her or filled her with unutterable love. This evening, it was irritation's turn.

"I've told you before, Clive, rich children like you don't want for things."

Clive didn't answer. He never knew how to respond to his mother, when she was in such a funny mood. If funny were the right word. Clowns were funny. The knife-sharpener man was often funny as he cracked a joke and his grinding-wheel spun sparks. Clive's mother was never funny, was she? The word itself was funny.

"Rich children need nothing," she added, by adding nothing but a disguised repetition.

"So why haven't I a kite? I want a kite."

Clive had now given up looking at the child outside, so he sat on the window-seat and shook out the strains of his craning. From previous experience, Clive knew that if he looked again, the child would be gone. Perhaps tugged up into the sky.

"You haven't a kite, because, if you really wanted one, Clive, you would most certainly have one. The fact you haven't proves you don't, at heart, want one."

That night she sped him to sleep with a mother's sweetest kiss.

Clive gathered a dream, one in which he left his bedroom and saw a mass of large insects on the landing. Each had legs bunched like darkly blotched bananas together with other wirier appendages. Clive tried to stab their pulpy parts with a weapon which the dream had provided, but there were too many for him to cope with alone. What surprised Clive most, however, was the way the insects sluggishly waited for death. They didn't scatter, as normal insects would when attacked. In fact, the more that appeared the more Clive continued his spate of bug-sticking. Their mix of clucking and twittering sounded neither afraid nor angry. Simply pure sounds of sickness.

"Mummy, he's there again!"

Today, Clive merely enunciated it as if he were lip-reading

someone else who had become him. A game he often played. He was bleary-eyed from an ever-turning night, one where he'd gathered dreams, only to lose them amid forgotten memories.

His mother had a visitor. So Clive watched the child fishing the sky for what was probably the biggest kite of all . . . then turned his attention to his mother and the visitor.

"We really can't let this go on for much longer, Mrs Bede."

The man was the type who tended to drink only half-a-pint all night in the company of a non-descript companion. Clive hated the way his moustache was tweezered and hair smarmed back to accentuate encroaching baldness. And the winkle-picker shoes. Yes, those godawful leathered feet that couldn't kick without stabbing. Clive cringed, since he was old enough to understand things too old for him.

"Just a few more days, Mr Court," said his mother. "I'm expecting a cheque from Clive's father."

She was nearly in tears. So much for her show of being rich. This conversation was a ritual every Wednesday morning. It was funny Clive should have that same dream every Tuesday night. The dream he always forgot having.

Clive's father may as well have been dead, for all the good he'd left behind. At least the Railway Children's poverty had granted them a life full of adventure and countryside pursuits and cosy loyalty *and* the eventual return of their dear dear father as he emerged tearfully through the steam-laden mists of the train station.

Mr Court departed at last. The funniest thing was that he drove a large dumpster, parked outside in the drizzle while the Wednesday morning interviews proceeded within the house. The vehicle burst into life with reluctant snorts and trundled through the blurred perspectives. Clive sensed that it knew the sound of its own engine would be the first nightmarish indication of Mr Court coming back.

The child with the kite was still there. When the day was near to sodden, the kite was heavy, rather than lighter-than-air – and it would drag behind on the ground as its master surrendered all hope of a launch that day.

Clive never questioned why he was not allowed to play outside himself. He'd read *The Secret Garden* and knew the answer. He was ill. Perhaps not in body, but certainly in the mind. At least the sick boy in that book had the archetypal premonition of its happy ending – even at the darkest of moments . . . whilst Clive knew, in his heart, that there was no such garden for *him* to play in. No playmates, either. For some reason, the child with the kite was beyond Clive's wildest hopes. The kite that flew a ghost.

Clive laughed at his own conceit. Thoughts were a comfort, especially thoughts without a source. Such thoughts surprised him more than the autonomous children with whom his imagination peopled his more secret moments of play.

Mrs Bede didn't notice that her son had gone upstairs to the nursery, via the dark landing.

"Money can't bring happiness," she said slowly, debating the various permutations of happiness, riches, sadness, poverty, sickness and health, "If you only want what it is possible to have – that's true happiness." And she smiled, as if someone nice had walked over her grave. But that rat, Mr Court – did he actually live in his damn dumpster? "I bet he's happy, making people like me unhappy." She noticed that Clive's place at the parlour window was vacant and she went over to fill it. "Clive must have gone to play with his toy soldiers." She pretended the child outside with the kite was herself as a small child. Soon she'd go upstairs with Clive's kiss.

Clive had a dream that was somehow associated with a different dream which he had never dreamed. Mr Court's dumpster was chock-a-block with the insects which it was his job to collect from house to house as a matter of pest control – or was it rent collection?

"Mummy, he's there again!"

Mrs Bede caught her breath, thinking, for one moment, that Clive meant Mr Court. Surely not on a Friday afternoon? And, no sound of the dumpster. But, no, of course, it was that kid again. The one with the kite.

"The weather's getting colder this time of the year," she said, in answer, as if that were relevant to the child's umpteenth reappearance. Indeed, the cold should have had a counteractive effect on the child's presence with the trusty kite. Still, when she was a little girl, she was a plucky individual – went out to play in all weathers. It was funny she'd never had a kite. Her parents said that kites cheated on God. She never really understood, but imagined that they referred to kite-flying as an attempt to pray better than the other children who simply placed palm to palm in their schoolrooms and projected minds rather than tassel-tailed surrogates. In those days, superstition and religion went hand in hand. Now, religion was far more up to date. All manner of misbehaviour could be condoned without the threat of Hell.

"If it's so cold, wouldn't it be nice to ask him in for tea?" suggested Clive, still as certain that the child with a kite was a boy as his mother was certain in the opposite direction. "We could both play with my toy soldiers and he might lend me his kite."

Mrs Bede frowned.

"If a kite means so very much, Clive, I'll buy you one at the shop tomorrow."

That night he fell asleep, before the arrival of his mother's kiss.

Clive dreamed of watching his mother dream. The insects smothered her face – crawling in and out. This dream was the most outlandish of them all. Indeed, he knew, from the previous dream – only remembered by being a memory within the new dream – that the insects, scale to scale, were too big to thread her nostrils and also to negotiate the soggy see-through sockets where her eyes were snailed.

Mr Court began to visit Mrs Bede on days other than Wednesday. Clive was consigned upstairs to the windowless nursery with the door locked on the landing side. And the solitary clue was the dumpster's characteristic sound that held just the right note to make the walls shudder. The soft click of the front-door and the pad of feet were followed by the rent's increasingly slow-motion collection. Clive's mind was aware of more than he could ever hope to understand.

The toy soldiers were Borrowers. They had lives they lived to lend – and a worldliness that wars had worried into their worn-out ways. Being thus carried away with alliteration was not necessarily Clive's fault. Any observer standing behind the nursery door would indeed wonder how Clive knew more than was good for him then would hear minuscule men mutter to Clive of this and that, including how toys could speak.

Sometimes something crept into the house to listen to things that went on that only went on because it listened to them. Its kite left outside.

Clive began to dream he was the separate subject of his own dream, whilst dreaming everything that the boy called Clive he dreamed about dreamed. The insects had managed to find their way into the boy's head. Their wirier appendages tickled his ear-drums with tantalizing swishes and they coiled down from a nasal chamber to flick upon the tongue. The larger banana-like parts served as levers for the otherwise unwieldy carapace of scales and pulpy innards; they tested, too, the backs of his eyes for gruel. There must have been scores of the things crunching, clucking, twittering – tweaking their soul-mate the brain, the boy's brain. But the worst point of the dream was the empathy of taste. So rancid, yet sweet, with the redolence of marinated tombfruit and long-incubated excremental produce seeping towards the mouth.

Clive woke to a thought that told him that he'd barely escaped from actually becoming the boy in the dream: trapped forever beyond the silhouette of sleep. Then he promptly forgot all about the dream, except for an echo of eating sick and ear-drums throbbing to a distant dumpster engine.

"Mummy, he's here again!"

The child with the kite wasn't there, for once, but Clive said it, nevertheless. Rituals deserved more respect than realities.

"Is he, dear?"

"Yes." This "yes" was a plea for a change in subject, which he provided for himself. "I keep dreaming, Mummy. Every night. And the dreams are getting worse and worse, each time. Until I forget them."

"Do you, dear?"

"And the dream I had last night was the worst dream possible. So bad I scarcely forgot it."

"Well, let's hope they've finished being dreams, then."

"I think I might have to dream again, Mummy."

"Don't worry your little head about your thoughts."

"Do you ever dream, Mummy?"

"Sometimes, but never nightmares."

"Are my dreams nightmares?"

"They sound as if they might be, Clive."

That last night, Clive heard the dumpster's distant drone, never getting nearer. It spent its undercurrents on shudders that grunted within his ears. He had tried to stay awake all night to deter another dream. He had listened to the silence, expecting the twitter of insects, but silence remained priceless – until the onset of judders betokening Court's chugging climb to the power-house at the end of a tow-rope.

Then, he fell asleep. So silent, Clive yearned for noise. So blank, he yearned for blindness. Ever-tugged by God towards a funny Heaven.

The nursery door swung wide to reveal a pair of clucking fan-tailed kites, black creatures silhouetted against an even blacker landing, lent, leant, lending their spiny feelers entwined with each other's and throbbing an unspent passion – intent on renting a kiss from the landlord of the lips. Black borrowers who wanted Clive's goodnight kiss, no doubt, for their own use. But where the headlease dream? Where the dump of dreams? Where the child? Which the mother?

MARNI GRIFFIN

Last Train to Arnos Grove

MARNI GRIFFIN JUST HAPPENED to move into a South London flat a mile and a half from the pub where her great grandfather, John Alden, sailed from England on *The Mayflower*.

Under her maiden name, M.R. Scofidio, she has published stories and articles in *The Urbanite*, *Scavenger's Newsletter*, *Heliocentric Net*, *Bloodsongs*, *Deathrealm* (where she was also a contributing editor), *The Year's Best Fantasy and Horror*, and a new anthology of contemporary supernatural fiction, *Midnight Never Comes* (Ash-Tree Press). Surprisingly, this volume of *The Best New Horror* marks her first publication in the UK.

"I began this story in 1992," she reveals, "less than a year after I'd come to England from Buffalo, New York. Its first rejection was by an editor who wrote, 'Sorry, but I've been on too many last trains to Arnos Grove.' Of course things have changed since then, and some of my references are dated. Interestingly, I got the acceptance letter for 'Last Train' less than two weeks before the 1997 General Election, at just about the same time the story was written five years before."

A T THE INTERSECTION OF Lordship Lane and Wood Green High Street, on the shortest night of the year, Joanna ran out of gas. Damn. She thought of Los Angeles, with its smoggy air and squat ugly repetitive architecture and four service stations to an intersection. Best not dwell on that now.

Joanna knew and could bet her soul on the fact that the

nearest gas station, on Lordship Lane, shut at 10:00 p.m. The car dashboard light failed when the battery died, but not before she'd registered the glowing green dial, hands pointing to just before midnight. 11:48 was her guess. She'd assured Jamie she'd be home by midnight, when he planned to call her from his parents' house in Yorkshire. Joanna thumped the steering wheel and said the ugliest word she could think of, but it wasn't at all comforting.

She stared around the intersection. The WOOD GREEN STATION sign seemed to flicker in the rain, its purplish tones reflected in the oily pavement beneath the black marquee of the Underground. She could hail a black cab; that is, if she could find one in Wood Green. She didn't trust the mini-cabs with recent news stories of women being kidnapped and raped, she'd rather spend a bit more money for the comfort of knowing she was in the hands of a professional. Well, in no one's hands but Jamie's, really . . . *God* this was frustrating! To cap things off, she'd brought the wrong wallet. One gilt pound coin and a bit of silver were all she had. She clambered out of the car, slamming the door with all the force she could manage, and kicked it with a wet boot. When it rained it bloody wept.

She'd lost much of her American bravado in the time spent married to Geoff; now it would never occur to her to walk towards a lit area, flag down a black cab, tell the driver she was in trouble – that her money was in her flat and she could pay him once he got her home. Instead, sighing, Joanna resigned herself to a midnight trip home on the Underground.

Years of horrible relationships with miserable men, culminating in the mistake of wedlock to a man she'd met through a personal ad in the *L.A. Recycler*, had finally done Joanna in. She abandoned, without reserve, any chance of any man ever returning love the way she lavished it – let alone someone good-looking, generous, tall, and a self-employed landscape gardener, as Jamie was. She would try not to think of the disappointment of missing his call. She would concentrate on positive memories instead.

He had come into her restaurant months ago, half a year after she had relinquished her dreams of a soul-mate. They started out as friends; had vibrant arguments about which political party would win the election; would Paddy Ashdown survive his personal scandal, would Red Ken Livingstone ever be taken seriously? Jamie bought her potted plants instead of dying flowers and she slipped him free cups of tea and, when the owner wasn't in the caff, fried breakfasts or toasties. Her cramped flat had begun to look like the beginnings of a jungle when he finally asked her out; they dated for six weeks before she would consent to sleep with him.

Inside the station some of the ceiling lamps had been shattered, leaving it dim and difficult to find her way. An information board gleamed sickly pale in the half-light at the top of the escalator that led down to passenger platforms. LAST TRAIN TO ARNOS GROVE AT 23:57, someone had written with a felt-tip pen in shaky letters, as though palsied or drunk. She had barely time to catch it.

The clock set in the station wall was broken. Heavy black hands paused, the little hand under the 12, the big hand between the 9 and the 10. The ticket collector sat slumped on a stool in a glass cubicle the size of a phone booth, under a jaundiced fluorescent tube. Feeble yellow letters in a lightbox over his head announced the WAY IN.

"Sound asleep, you old son-of-a-bitch," Joanna said very softly, though why she was afraid she might wake him she hadn't a clue. His capless skull was even paler than the board announcing the times. Well, there wasn't exactly a stampede of passengers at this hour. She'd better hurry if she didn't want to miss the train. She could run from Arnos Grove station and reach her flat in five minutes; perhaps Jamie's call would be late. She even imagined she could hear the double burr of the telephone bell.

The pound coin clanked loudly as it dropped into the ticket machine. Joanna gathered up her change, several large and useless five pence pieces (useless except for annoying shopkeepers with) and the bright yellow ticket stamped with the station name. She held the ticket up for inspection as she hurried past the glass booth. The ticket collector was still slumped over his stool. I'd sure like to have a job like that, she thought, and as the escalator was descending, turned on the step just in time to see the ticket collector suddenly sit up and spin his massive head in her direction. She gripped the rail to keep her balance.

Her footsteps were hollow on concrete and her heels made that sharp angry staccato *clack-clack-clack* that in other people annoyed her so much. She told herself she was hurrying because she didn't want to miss the train, not because she was afraid that if she stopped and turned, the ticket collector, his blue lips stretched around nearly to the back of his head, would be right behind her. A blast of chill air slammed her hair back. She lowered her head like a bull and walked straight into it.

It was cold on the platform. Joanna huddled into herself, repeating a comforting mantra to herself: How happy I am. I have been looking for joy for such a long time and just like my mother always said, I found it when I least expected it. *But how do you know?* asked a small still voice, the little ugly one that always seemed to pop up at the worst possible moments, carried like a speck of dirt on a gust of wind.

"Well, I don't," Joanna said aloud, and the words bounced off the far tiled wall and came back to her to stay. But I am, she told herself again, I am delighted, I have found my happiness. She allowed herself the luxury of imagining herself and Jamie in bed together, a Technicolour memory, and when she thought of him in her arms she almost fainted with wanting him. The best part was that she knew, knew without reserve or doubt, knew deep in her heart that he wanted her, too. Love, at last, was hers, in the agreeable form of Jamie. 1993 was going to be brilliant.

"Last train to Arnos Grove," a flat mechanical voice announced over the loudspeakers, and as Joanna marvelled at one of the only announcements she had ever heard on the Underground that was clear and comprehensible, the lights in the station went out. From far away, from what seemed the centre of the earth, she could hear the booming and crashing of the oncoming train.

It might be the Cockfosters train, hopefully not the Bounds Green, in which case she'd have missed the Arnos Grove train. It was a habit she'd picked up from living in London, this not trusting the tube, the most efficient public transport system she had had the luck to experience. Fancy L.A. ever getting a subway! She heard from old friends who wrote that it was being built; but she could never imagine taking that risk, riding under the freeway enraged motorists sped upon. She would always fear a premature burial under a collapse of earth, metal, and flames.

But two words floated in the darkness, ARNOS GROVE, and she glimpsed pale faces in the front carriage. She saw the driver, grey-faced from twelve hour shifts spent in dark track-stitched tunnels. His mouth hung open as if in surprise or agony. His eyes seemed to start out of their sockets; though his face pointed straight ahead, the eyes turned, nearly all whites, staring back at her. The lights came back on. The brakes moaned as the train, shuddering, ground to a halt at the platform. Joanna was walking as fast as she could – not running, not showing panic – as far away from the front carriage as possible. Silvery doors hissed open. No one got off. Joanna happened to look up at the giant station clock hanging over the platform just as she stepped inside the empty car, and almost stepped off again to get another look. She must be mistaken.

A whistle blew. Some joker; this was the Underground, not British Rail. Her arm and foot were extended prepatory to jumping out, but the doors slammed shut again and she had a brief vision of herself chopped in two, one half falling onto the platform. She put a hand over her shuddering heart as the lights flickered and the train lurched forward, rattling, into the tunnel.

That station clock was broken, too. Ten minutes to midnight, it read, as the clock in her car had read some twenty minutes earlier. She was familiar with stories of the brain causing the eyes to see whatever it liked: she knew about optical illusions. Uh-huh; and time everywhere just happens to stop, Sparky, the moment you run out of gas.

The train stank of spilt beer and too many unwashed bodies and industrial vinegar burning into a twist of paper full of chips left squashed on the wooden floor. Rankness was at odds with the exceptionally clean upholstery. She wondered what genius had invented the colour scheme. Green and blue checks *ad infinitum*. Still, it was slightly more soothing than the orange and yellow checked upholstery on the District Line. Arnos Grove station was a dot on the Piccadilly Line, drawn in blue on the tube map. Hence, blue and green checks; now it made sense, though no comfort for the eyes.

Joanna read ads for Gatwick Airport and Stilton cheese. She goggled at a richly described Poem on the Underground, a paean, framed in dirty chrome, to a five-year-old child drawing limitless sky at the kitchen table. The poem spoke of apples, and she thought: Yes, that is Jamie and me. Our happiness is clear and sharp as the scent and sweet bite of apples. She was feeling optimistic about getting home in reasonable time – perhaps Jamie would wait up, perhaps he would ring her again – when the train shuddered and ground to a halt.

She didn't know how long they sat there like that. (They?) She hadn't seen anybody but the driver and his assistant, but there must be other passengers, she couldn't be alone on a London train. The illusion that she was a solitary rider was not helped by the near-silence, white empierced by the panting and low slow hum of the engine. She looked behind her through, the glass window of the connecting car. She could just see a pair of knees and on the next seat, beige plastic carrier bags. The passenger they belonged to sat rigidly motionless. She sat back again in case it was noticed that she was staring.

Joanna guessed they'd been stopped three, maybe five minutes, when the train shook itself and slowly glided, rattling, down the track. So it is a train after all, she thought, not a couch. She gripped the armrests as the train began to pick up speed.

Bounds Green, she thought again, that's the next station, we'll be stopping soon, and then it's Arnos Grove. Maybe her car clock was wrong. Maybe it had only been twenty to midnight when she ran out of gas, maybe the station clock wasn't forever frozen at ten to, maybe, *maybe* . . . But even as she tried to persuade herself Joanna knew this was wrong. Her car clock had always run on BBC time, never slow or fast. The arabic numbers on its face made mistakes difficult. The last train to Arnos Grove stopped in Wood Green at three minutes to midnight. She was on it.

Tugging on a smeared window to let in some air, Joanna peered out at the moving dark. They were coming to a disused, or ghost station. Joanna had heard about these, too, stations started and left unbuilt due to money constraints. She knew there was one between Hampstead and Golders Green stations, but –

There were people on the platform. Shadowy. Waiting.

"Oh for chris*sake*!" she cried, if only to hear the reassuring sound of her own voice. Disappointment and fatigue were putting images into her head of things that didn't exist. Even if people could get to a platform at a ghost station, who in their right mind would wait for a train in a place where it never stopped? And that was when the train did stop, and she heard the doors a few cars down hiss open on a rush of underground wind.

She fell away from the window. She was imagining, having hallucinations, or – Wait. This train should have stopped at Bounds Green ages ago. Slowly twisting around, she craned to peer back through the window of the connecting door. The rigid knees and the carrier bags hadn't moved. Her car and her home and aboveground seemed very far away.

The connecting door two or three cars down opened and closed and the train began to shake as though it were shaking itself apart. Why hadn't they reached Bounds Green? Why stop inbetween stations? Old machinery groaned as cables like a giant's arteries and nerves hurtled past the window.

"Last train to Arnos Grove," a flat mechanical voice announced over the loudspeaker, a humming through the soft pulse of her brain. The lights in the car went out, and from far away, from what seemed the centre of the earth, she could hear the booming and crashing of the train.

Another crash echoed that of the train, and she knew it was the connecting door of the car behind her, opening and slamming shut again. It was too dark to see who else was in the car, but she could hear oncoming footsteps, heavy and tired. In a sudden rush of panic she flung herself backwards against the connecting door, unable to remember which way it opened, forgetting it wouldn't lock, praying, praying. Something fluttered against the window glass. But she was diverted from that sound by the other, the *clack-clack-clack* of hurried footsteps on the platform. The lights in the car came on.

She saw the overhanging station clock, saw the white round face expand and grow closer, saw clearly the little hand before the 12, the big hand between the 9 and the 10. When Joanna saw herself, head bowed and hurrying along the platform towards the train, she screeched and hobbled down the slatted wooden floor, fumbling with the connecting door to the next compartment. The train doors hissed open. She pushed, twisting the handle, and stumbled through.

Someone stepped into the car behind her. The doors slammed shut and the train shot forward into the open dark of the tunnel.

Joanna closed her eyes, gritted her teeth, and pinched herself, hard. No way was she going on like this, torturing herself. Of course she hadn't seen her own double; only another woman who looked a little bit like her. Now at least somebody else had got on the train that wasn't a nightmare after all. She would look through the connecting door glass, see this woman clearly, see her mistake. But when she turned and peered through the window, she saw only the rigid knees, the orange letters on the beige plastic carrier bags and beyond that, an empty row of seats.

No. Impossible. The knees, the bags – those had been in the

car behind the car behind her. The floor rattled under her feet and she gripped the armrests to steady herself.

They were passing the ghost station. She could see them, nearly distinct now, eyes hollow like prisoners' eyes, leaning towards the train as it hurtled past. She could see long narrow hairless skulls, flabby bodies, overlarge hands with swollen joints raising slowly towards the windows –

Next time they would be clearly defined. Closer.

The connecting door two or three cars down banged open and the train began to shake as though it were shaking itself apart. Where was Bounds Green station? Why stop between platforms? Machinery hummed over the faint smell of burnt brakes; cables like veins and nerves hurtled by, and hurtled by, and hurtled by –

"Last train to Arnos Grove," a flat mechanical voice announced over the loudspeakers. Just as she thought she would scream, the lights in the car went out. From far away, from almost the centre of the earth, came the booming and crashing of the train, and nearer: something scraping and scrabbling on the connecting door glass.

"That's right! I'm dead, I had an accident, and this train is going to Arnos Hell," cried Joanna, very loudly, in the same tone as a child who has just discovered how to say "shit". The train was coming into the station. She strained, grinning to herself in the dark, to read the white letters in the giant blue and red circle of the Underground logo, a metal plaque drilled to the tiled wall. WOOD GREEN WOOD GREEN WOOD GREEN sped past the windows, the wall a fading ghost.

"No," Joanna breathed, and the scraping and scrabbling grew louder. She heard the door handle twist on its shaft. "No, no, don't get on." But it came relentlessly, the other sound, the *clack-clack-clack*, louder and louder but somehow also a soft steady tapping in her ears. The lights came on to show the hands of the giant clock in exactly the same position, she didn't have to look to know that. What she might discover if she saw herself she didn't dare imagine.

Stumbling towards the connecting door she heard the train doors hiss, the *smack*! of a face slammed against the outside window. Her own fingers fell clawing against the glass. The doors opened. She tripped into the next car. Someone stepped into the car behind her. "No," rattled from her throat. "Fool." The doors slammed shut. The train wobbled forward. She hunched herself over in her seat, then forced herself to stand.

If she kept moving, she would be fine. This was some crazy silly situation that she and Jamie would have a laugh over in years to come: The Night She Took The Ghost Train On The Purgatory Line, All Souls Riding Behind Her. Purgatory: Piccadilly! It was too funny! Piccadilly, Purgatory. Joanna paced the car, avoiding looking through the connecting door window at the knees or the carrier bags she knew were there. Soon she would be home. Soon she would be on the phone with Jamie. *Soon I will, soon I will,* and the words wove into the rhythm of the rails, she could hear them in the train wheels, *soon I will, soon I will, soon soon soon I will.*

"Last train to Arnos Grove," said the flat mechanical voice, and the lights in the car went out, and Joanna thought, At least I know what happens next, *I* get on, and from far away, from the centre of the earth, but also inside her head, she could hear the booming and crashing of the train, and still above that, the *clack-clack-clack* of footsteps rushing onto the platform. What's the hurry? she asked herself as the lights went back on, and she saw the clock, saw its bloody great face expand and bloat, saw clearly the little hand before midnight, the big hand between the 9 and 10. When Joanna saw herself, head bowed, hurrying along the platform towards the train, she stepped in front of the doors, waited for herself to look up and stare straight into her own face, so that she might be warned: Don't get on this train.

And then the lights went out.

Doors sighed open. Feet stepped into the train, heels clacking onto the wooden floor. Fingers brushed hers, ran along and up the stiff material of her coat. The silvery doors of the train slammed shut upon silence.

As Joanna waited for the lights to come back on, a spongy hand clamped onto hers in the dark.

The train, rattling, roared forward into the open mouth of the tunnel.

for Will.

MARK CHADBOURN

The King of Rain

MARK CHADBOURN WON *Fear* magazine's Best New Author Award for his first published short story, and he has since been nominated twice for the British Fantasy Award. A former investigative journalist, he often found himself in dangerous situations around the globe – among them being shot at in the desert outside Palm Springs, set on fire in the Arctic Circle and attacked by gangsters in Brighton – before settling in the peaceful countryside of his home county, Leicestershire, with his wife Elizabeth and two children. His books include the horror novels *Underground*, *Nocturne*, *The Eternal* and *Scissorman*, plus the non-fiction study of the paranormal, *Testimony*.

"'The King of Rain' was inspired by a trek across the Derbyshire peaks with some old friends like the one experienced by the characters in the story," recalls the author, "– but with the only vengeful spirits being of the alcoholic variety. Being an avowed 'city person', I wasn't best prepared for wilderness walking – it's cold, bleak, windswept, wet and treacherous. But I wasn't as bad as one of the group, a lawyer, who turned up in his work suit. He made one concession – an old pair of shoes. We only found out later they had holes in the soles and were stuffed with newspaper. He leaked blood all over the tent.

"Thrown together in those kinds of conditions, people's real faces begin to emerge, along with all the dark secrets and uncomfortable character traits they try to hide away. We learned some disturbing things about each other over the course of a weekend. We haven't spoken since."

It was raining like it had been raining forever. Not the pregnant, silky drops of summer rain, nor the icy bullets of winter storm. It was inconsequential rain, nothing rain, ever-present in the background, a sheet of grey that dampened the spirits as much as it soaked through every item of clothing. All the greens and golds and browns were washed out of the landscape as we trudged relentlessly across the sheep-clipped grass through the gorse towards the looming high lands which lay heavy against the steel clouds. It wasn't the best time to be there, in that twilight zone after the dog days of summer when the world turned away from the light, but we'd agreed to do it for John, and although the thought was in all our heads, he made it plain there was no turning back.

"Hang on a minute." Gordon Broxtowe was wheezing like he smoked sixty day while he leaned on the wooden staff he'd bought down in the village. Admittedly the climb had been steep so far, but we were only fifteen minutes out of Edale and the worst part still lay ahead. I'd seen the High Peak walk John had mapped out and it looked treacherous.

"Come on, Gordon," Phil snapped in his usual irritable manner. "We've only got one weekend, for Christ's sake. I'd like to be home by Christmas."

Gordon gave *that* smile. You could tell he thought it was winning but it irritated the hell out of everybody else.

"The first rule of hill walking is to go at the speed of the slowest member, Phil." Gordon took off his silver-framed glasses and wiped the raindrops off them. It seemed pretty futile, but that was Gordon; he had an almost pathological urge to waste time, words, anything, like some circumlocutory barrister who was getting paid by the minute. The rain skidded off the bald dome at the front of his head and slicked the greasy, ginger curls at the back of his scalp before eventually riveting round to soak his beard. In the wan light his skin glowed a sickly white. It was hard to see what his wife had been attracted to – he couldn't even affirm *personality* in his defence.

Phil turned away from him, cursing under his breath, and John flashed him one of his cold, cautionary glares. He couldn't help acting the boss, even out of work. Right then I missed Beth more than I had done since the day we met five years ago at a party in some seedy basement bar in the City. But Clapham and the flat seemed a million miles away and I was stuck with three people who I had more than enough of on weekdays. It's amazing the things you do to keep your job prospects fluid.

We set off again with Gordon still smiling superciliously at anyone who caught his eye and Phil muttering grimly to himself. It was a tribute to John that we were all there; none of us really had much in common.

At thirty-eight, Phil Metcalfe, the company accountant, was thirteen years older than me, but it might as well have been thirty. His suits always seemed aimed at a different generation and he had that timeless haircut – short at the sides and back, but not *too* short – that was still favoured by barbers who remembered the War. His cheeks were a little gaunt and at that moment his complexion seemed to match the sky above; a grey man for a grey job.

Who am I to talk? Maybe I'm just being bitter, but you get to thinking that way when you're treated like some kid out of school for having interests outside of the crazy world of business software. You know, a life. "Still reading the *NME*, Sam? At your age?" "You're not going to see a film again, Jordan? You wait till you start a family!" And here I was, letting myself in for an entire weekend of it. I like to punish myself. It's my hobby.

And then there was John Chaucer. He'd never given me a hard time, which was probably the main reason why I'd finally agreed to come along. He'd never been particularly nice to me either; he's not the type for backslapping or bawdy jokes, but I suppose running a company you've built up from scratch doesn't make you a bundle of laughs. His face was lugubrious and his eyes heavy-lidded. He looked a little like Robert Mitchum, but there was a real stiffness there so I guess he's more like Mitchum would look if he hadn't spent his early years smoking dope.

"Now how did I do that?"

Gordon had stopped again, which irritated Phil even more. He pulled back his dripping shirt cuff to examine his plump, white forearm. A broad purple bruise was bright and clear along the soft underside.

"I don't remember banging it on anything."

John moved towards him with surprising speed for his size and then caught himself. His expression shocked me; a glimmer of fear and then a strange, shaky despair like he'd been told he'd got a terminal illness.

"You're mad. You'll never light a fire in this." Phil was hugging his orange windcheater around him as he stared gloomily at the soggy, mildewed wood piled in the circle of stones between the two tents.

"Have faith, Philip. You always look on the black side." Gordon hunched over the kindling with a box of matches clutched tightly to his chest like he was waiting with a snare for a rabbit to pop out of its hole. "Lighting a fire is a mystical act. Bringing illumination into the darkness. You have to find the mood. Follow a ritual. Wish. Pray. Give promises to the gods of the blaze."

"You talk some bollocks, Gordon." Phil's attitude didn't seem to stop him watching the wood with a feverish hope; he needed a fire as much as all of us. Something to make us forget the incessant drizzle whipped from all directions by the wind that swept across the bleak uplands; something to lift the blanket of claustrophobic greyness.

"Come on now, come on," Gordon muttered under his breath.

"It's all wet, you stupid idiot," Phil cursed.

John and I watched from the opening of the tent we were going to share. There was a strange fascination to the scene, like we were looking on some tableau out of time.

Gordon hovered for a second or two more, then he fumbled for a match, struck it once, twice, three times, and flung it into the dark hole under the wood. There was a ringing moment while the smirk started to creep across Phil's face and then we heard the familiar crackle above the sound of falling rain. Gordon turned and showed us all his irritating smile, now coloured orangey-gold. Thick smoke belched up into the growing gloom.

Dinner was chilli from a can heated over the fire and mopped up with French bread. We followed it with swigs from a bottle of Aberlour single malt John had provided as another inducement to accompany him, and after that we felt we had enough fire in our belly and veins to keep us going through the long night.

The tents were pitched in the shelter of an outcropping as twilight began to fall. The argument about who was going to share with who had raged all day and we finally had to settle it in the time-honoured tradition of drawing straws. Of course, no one was happy with the outcome. Then we perched on some uncomfortable lumps of Derbyshire granite under a makeshift tarpaulin shelter and watched the fire while trying to forget the constant drumming over our heads. Every now and then Gordon would dip into the pile of wood he had been locating in sheltered spots all day long, douse a piece in lighter fuel and fling it into the blaze.

"Bloody horrible weather," Phil muttered redundantly.

"Still, we're out of the house for the weekend," Gordon said. "A break from the wife and kids."

Phil agreed. "Sometimes you need to be on your own with a flew blokes to get back in touch with yourself. It's a real strain burying all that stuff that makes us what we really are, just so we're acceptable to the wenches." He chuckled, which was such an out-of-place sound coming from his dour face I had to double-check it was really him laughing. "They wouldn't touch us if they *really* knew. Here we can be ourselves," he added.

"Listen to Iron John," I said mockingly, but Phil didn't respond. They were both wrong, I thought, but there was no sense arguing with them. The company of men always made me appreciate Beth more, acutely even. You go through your days struggling to slot into a comfortable routine with your girlfriend and wife and you forget all their strengths, because they are subtle strengths that disappear at close inspection. It's like the lines some ancient race drew all over the Plains of Nazca in Peru. When you're standing on the ground you can't tell what they are, but when you're soaring up high with the gods you can see they're wonderful works of art, hummingbirds and monkeys. It takes some hairy-arsed man, grunting, belching and beating his chest before the campfire to recapture your true perspective. That's what I think anyway. Like I said, Phil or Gordon didn't agree. Who knows what John thought? He was a closed book as always.

"How much farther is it to the house?" Phil asked suddenly, stirring us all from our thoughts.

John jumped like someone had stuck a finger in his back. "Oh ... we should get there by lunchtime. Sooner if the rain packs in."

"It's been a few years since you've been there, then?" Gordon asked.

"Twenty years."

"Give or take a day or two," I joked pathetically.

"Exactly twenty years. Tomorrow."

"So it's an anniversary," Gordon said cheerily. "Better save some of this malt."

"Nostalgia gets to us all sooner or later," Phil added morosely.

"Why were you so keen to come back?" I asked.

John's heavy lids closed like he was drifting off into sleep and when they opened a second or two later the flames reflected from them liquidly. "I've thought about it more and more over the last few months. Before that, I hadn't thought about it since the seventies. It's funny how things come back to you, out of the blue."

"All part of growing old. The mind starts playing pick 'n' mix with memories." Phil caught himself and added hastily, "Not that I'm saying you're old, John."

The raindrops thudded relentlessly on the tarpaulin. John didn't seem to recognise Phil had spoken. I wondered if he'd had too much whisky.

"I've never sold it. I suppose I should have, really. God knows what state it's in after all this time. The roof's probably fallen in."

"Happy memories, I suppose," Gordon said obliquely. "That's what draws people back."

"I bought it as a holiday home, somewhere to get away from the Smoke, get some fresh air in my lungs, see some greenery. I was doing pretty well at the time. The company had just taken off, within a couple of years of me leaving Oxford. The early seventies were a good time to be young and well-off in London. I certainly made the most of it."

A smile ghosted his face, but it seemed sad rather than reflective of the time he was describing. I wanted to ask him about it, but I knew it was too personal for John. There was something else on my mind which was more acceptable to ask. "You've got a great head for business, John. You've shown that over the last few years. Why did that company go bust if it was doing so well?"

"I lost interest in it. Too many other things on my mind." He took a deep breath like he was coming up for air and then said, "That house was a labour of love. It was a ruin when I bought it, an old hill farmer's croft that hadn't been lived in for a decade or more. I spent every weekend up here, doing it up, getting the builders and electricians in. Cost me an arm and a leg, but it was worth it. When I'd finished it was like a palace. A great little getaway."

"Nice place to bring the totty too, I shouldn't wonder," Gordon said.

"Yes, it saw its share of women." There was a strange inflection in John's voice that I couldn't quite make out.

Then I noticed something that took my mind off it. "Phil, your nose is bleeding."

"Is it?" He dabbed at it and then carefully examined his fingertips in the firelight. It wasn't just bleeding, it was gushing. There was a red smear across his top lip and around to his chin where it dripped into his lap. "I thought it was rain leaking through the roof."

"Better get a hankie on it, old boy," Gordon said without much sympathy.

Phil leapt to his feet, almost knocking over the shelter. A torrent of water gushed over the side from where his head hit the tarpaulin. "Oh God, oh God, I hate blood. Hate it." He was looking at his fingertips like someone had tried to hack them off.

Some of the blood had splattered on to his shirt collar, already sodden from the rain, which poked above his windcheater. It spread out like a water colour sunset. There seemed too much of it for a simple nosebleed; it was almost like he had taken a punch from a heavyweight.

Phil lurched around like a wounded elephant, under the shelter, out near the fire, and back, constantly dabbing at his nose and checking his fingertips as if he thought the flow would suddenly dry up. There was an edge of panic in his voice as he repeatedly muttered, "Christ, oh Christ."

"Sit down," John snapped with uncharacteristic irritation. "You're only making it worse. Relax. Put your head back." He snatched a long gulp of whisky from the bottle.

Gordon almost had to wrestle Phil down to the ground under the shelter, pinning his arms across the granite boulders with what looked like unnecessary force. "If you panic it just makes the blood rush faster, old chap," he said with a tight smile.

Phil wasn't being comforted. We could all see something was wrong and he knew it. With his head back, the blood flowed over his cheekbones and started to collect in his eye sockets. His eyes rolled wildly and he tried to blink them clear, but it was coming too quickly.

"Here let me." I pulled out my handkerchief and held it tightly against his nose. Instantly I was aware of the odd sensation of the blood almost *pumping* out between my fingers, or like it was being sucked out.

"You're not a haemophiliac, are you, Phil?" I asked nervously. He squirmed and muttered something which I took to be a negative.

And then, as suddenly as it had started, the nosebleed stopped. I felt that powerful pumping disappear in an instant like someone had turned a switch. Cautiously, I pulled away the now-sodden handkerchief to check the flow.

"It's finished," I said. Phil went limp. "I've never seen anything like that before. Do you always get nosebleeds like that?"

He shook his head. Behind the scarlet streaks that were starting to dry on his face, his skin was chalk-white.

"Just one of those things," John mumbled. "He's probably got thin membranes in his nose. All that exertion of walking ..." His voice trailed off and he returned to the whisky bottle once again.

He seemed strangely uneasy, almost anxious, and I had this creeping feeling there was something important he wasn't telling us.

As the others clambered into the tents to prepare for the night, I sat under the shelter and watched the dying fire, listening to the hiss and thud of the rain and wishing I was a million miles away.

I don't know how much later I woke, but the rain was still pelting against the canvas and it was obviously dark outside. There was a diffuse light in the tent and it took a second or two to orient myself and realise where it was coming from. John was buried in his sleeping bag with the top pulled over his head like a hood; I could just see his hands protruding. He had a small torch which he was using to illuminate his wallet. In the perspex window was the photo of a woman.

From my oblique angle, she looked beautiful; huge china doll eyes that were black pools in a white oval face, framed by long, shining, dark hair. The picture had the faded glory of a 1970s snapshot, garish colours turned dull and real by age. Yet it was a recent addition to John's wallet. I'd seen him open it up many times in the pub after work and that perspex window had always been empty.

A dim, strangled noise echoed out from the depths of his sleeping bag and the torch shook slightly.

"Are you okay, John?" I asked quietly.

The torch clicked off and the sleeping bag closed over his head without a word being said.

Dawn came with difficulty, breaking blindly behind the slate clouds so the only sign of its arrival was a barely perceptible improvement in light. John had us up early to maximise our walking time, and as I packed away the tent I suddenly realised I could make out details in the windswept landscape, patches of grey and murky green crawling out of the shadows. After an hour we realised the cold, flat light was the best we were going to get. It was as if the sky was pressing down to suffocate the land, and we were trapped between with the rain and the scrubby grass and the occasional wind-stripped tree.

John seemed to be avoiding my eyes over our breakfast of lukewarm baked beans as if he feared I might ask him about the photo. He seemed different that morning, harder, more aloof, as if some dam had broken in his mind during the night.

"I don't believe you had to go through all this every time you wanted to visit your holiday home," Phil said bitterly when we'd been walking for an hour and a half. "Isn't there a damned road up to it? How did you get the furniture up there?"

"There used to be," John replied, "but it was little more than a cart track. It ran along the edge of a ridge, but most of it's crumbled away now. It's too dangerous to use."

"Good luck selling it," Gordon said with what I could only describe as a chortle. "I can see the estate agent's particulars now: 'Close to no amenities whatsoever.'"

"I'll never sell it," John said flatly.

"If it was such a good place, John, why did you abandon it?" I asked. He gave me a look like I'd stepped over some invisible line. Then I noticed he was favouring his left leg. "Have you hurt yourself?"

"I must have twisted my ankle," he said defensively. "It's nothing."

"You shouldn't keep walking on it, John. It won't do you any good," Gordon said.

"It's nothing."

The conversation dried up for the next half hour or so as we put our heads down and concentrated on the walking. My face was starting to sting from the constant wetness and my nose was filled with the smell of damp vegetation and sodden clothes. I started to pray that the cottage was in good enough shape for us to light a fire and dry off before the journey back. Nor did the weather help the tension that seemed to be growing among us with each mile we progressed; it seemed to hum with a charge like the air around a pylon.

It was Gordon who broke the silence, his voice trilling out with a hint of mockery. "No wedding plans then, young Sam?"

"We've talked about it. Maybe in a few years' time." I always felt a tightening in my stomach when they asked me about my private life, mainly because I think I sensed they were going to stamp all over my feelings if they could find an opening. It was like they were all so disillusioned with their own lives they wanted to wreck any which didn't have the bleakness they faced each evening.

"Stay single, that's what I say," Phil chipped in morosely. "Don't go wasting the best years of your life." John was a way ahead of us so he couldn't hear when Phil added under his breath, "And you won't have to go on nightmares like this just to get away from the family."

"Did you marry young, Phil?" I'd learned how to ask questions which deflected attention away from me, and they always fell for it.

"I've always been married." His voice sounded like it had lead weights attached; he seemed to be saying, "I've always been asthmatic", or "I was born with that disfiguring mark".

"Oh, come on, Phil. You have to play the game right." I couldn't understand how Gordon could be so perky in the drizzle and the wind. "You mustn't let it bulldoze you down. Marriage is a wild horse that you have to break."

His voice carried on like a cold breeze through the peaks. I didn't hear any of them talking about romance or caring, but maybe all that hearts and flowers stuff was nonsense for the immature. Perhaps there was a sharp lesson lying ahead for Beth and me. I hoped not.

John had stopped near a lightning-blasted tree and was examining the ordnance survey map which was rapidly taking on the consistency of used tissue paper. A faint, battered path drove a browning trail through the grass ahead and then swung sharply to the right between two large outcroppings of black rock. Beyond, the land seemed to fall away disconcertingly. I could hear a sound like constant thunder.

"What's the matter, John? You're not lost are you?" Gordon slapped John on the shoulders, which made me catch my breath at the familiarity, but Gordon didn't seem to notice. John stared at the map like Gordon wasn't there.

"Much farther?" I interjected quickly before the tension broke into outright annoyance.

John shook his head. "Not too far, but the terrain's rougher. It'll be hard going. I was just..." He paused to moisten his lips; despite the rain streaming down his face they seemed to be bone dry. "There are some falls just over there." He nodded towards the outcroppings. "Spectacular... beautiful... In the summer, when the weather was good, I used to sit next to them and watch the sun set."

"Bit girly for you, John, isn't it?" Phil said uninterestedly.

"Not if he had company, eh?" Gordon nudged Phil theatrically. It caught Phil off balance and he had to stick his hand into the wet grass to stop himself going flat out. He cursed loudly and put John between him and Gordon.

As we moved towards the falls, John hung back until he was several yards behind. Gordon and Phil didn't seem to notice; they were engaged in some rapidfire return I couldn't hear clearly, Gordon's voice irritatingly sing-song, Phil's leaden and bludgeoning.

All of us grew quiet, though, when we passed between the outcroppings and saw the view; it was breathtaking even in the gunmetal atmosphere beneath the lowering clouds. The land fell away from our feet in a dizzying wall of black granite to the lush Derbyshire countryside far below. White water plumed out from a subterranean stream just beneath us and dashed and glistened in an arctic tumble down the cliff face. I took a few paces back and gripped on to an imaginary wall. I had a head for heights like Bernard Manning had feet for dancing. Those patchwork fields and ribbon roads looked too much like my childhood trainset, an optical illusion that could almost tempt me into believing it was just a small step down.

"Come on. We haven't got time to hang around." John was edging along the path behind me. There was a steeliness in his voice and out of the corner of my eye I could see him slinking by with his head down.

"Now, now, old chap. How can you pass by a view like this? It's marvellous. It's probably the high spot of the whole trip." Gordon stood with his hands on his hips looking out towards the horizon, and then he took a few steps and peered over the edge. My knees buckled slightly.

"Don't do it, Gordon," Phil said hopefully.

"This is damned good," Gordon continued. "That water, it's like milk. Mother's milk. I fancy a bit of that, don't you, Phil?"

"Whatever you say."

Gordon scratched his head for a second or two and then fumbled around for his canteen which hung on a strap from his rucksack. "You know, I'm going to get me some of that mother's milk."

Phil looked at him dumbfoundedly. "You're bloody crazy."

"No, there's a path down over the rocks to just below the falls. You can see it. People must use it all the time."

Phil shook his head, and I didn't feel I could move one way or the other, but Gordon had no qualms about climbing over a large boulder and dropping down almost out of sight. Somehow I found it within myself to shuffle forward. There was, as he said, a small pebble-strewn path which wound down to just below where the falls burst from the rocks. The boulders that lined the route were too big for him to tumble over accidentally, but beyond them the cliff face fell away precipitously.

"Bloody idiot. Holding us up more." Phil dragged his fingertips along the wind-smooth edge of a rock. "They're so black, like those ebony African masks everyone used to have in the sixties."

"I wouldn't know about that, Phil."

"Get him away from there!" John had come running back to the lip of the falls, his eyes blazing, his face scarlet with anger beneath the hood of his windcheater. "Get the bloody fool away from there!" He held back, his arms quivering like he wanted to throw himself forward, but couldn't.

Phil and I looked at him curiously.

"Hey! Look at this!" Gordon was waving and grinning and holding the canteen above his head like a Grand Prix trophy. He was right next to the falls, and the white foam flecked his face and mingled with the grey rain. "Mother's milk! I'll fill it to the brim!" He shouted to be heard above the roar of the water.

"John says come back," I yelled to him.

He might have heard and he might not, but he wasn't doing anything about it. He leaned over precariously and thrust the canteen into the depths of the icy torrent.

It was suspended there for a second or two and then suddenly and inexplicably his left foot skidded on some pebbles and shot into the water. Gordon teetered for an instant until his right arm windmilled and clung on to an overhanging rock. His curses floated up with the spray.

"Be careful, you idiot," Phil yelled. His knuckles were white against the boulder on which he was leaning.

Gordon looked up at us again and unveiled his irritating grin to prove he was all right. But as we watched, his stare became fixed, then curious, and the grin began to break up. After a second or two his expression was one of puzzlement and growing fear.

"What's going on?" John barked. He had backed away from the edge until he was pressed against the outcropping.

"Are you okay?" Phil shouted.

Gordon's left leg was still stretched out into the falls; I couldn't understand why he hadn't withdrawn it. His right leg dragged on the pebbles towards the water, almost imperceptibly, but the reaction on Gordon's face was like he had been shot.

"Good Lord, he's going to fall." Phil was up and moving. I was frozen by the expression on Gordon's face which was growing more terrible by the second.

"What's going on?" The anger had left John's voice now and had been replaced by a wet pitifulness.

Gordon's foot skidded again, almost an inch this time. It was curious. The path wasn't sloping; it was almost like he was dragging it himself. Despite the terror on his face which made me feel sick to see, he looked almost comical with one leg and arm stuck out into the water and his other hand clutching on to rainslick rock for dear life.

"Hang on, Gordon. I'm coming." Phil clambered over the boulder and slid down on to the path. It wouldn't take him long to reach Gordon.

"What's going on?" John repeated weakly.

"Phil will be there in a minute, Gordon. Don't worry," I shouted to reassure him.

It didn't work. His face was now so contorted it was almost unrecognisable.

He raised his head to me, his eyes wide and staring, and croaked, "Something's got hold of my ankle."

As the words died, his body jerked like the crack of a whip and he fell sideways into the water and then down, bouncing off the black granite like a rubber ball, sprays of red mingling with the white.

Phil was rooted in horror. I turned away and covered my mouth in a sudden surge of nausea. Away behind me, I saw John, the blood draining from his face, the awful knowledge even though he hadn't seen.

Phil was shaking like a tree in a gale. I grabbed his arm, but he shook me off.

"We've got to get back. Phone the police, ambulance . . . God, who's going to tell his wife. And his children . . . God." Flecks of saliva flew out of his mouth and splashed John and me.

John looked past him, through the rain and out towards the grey horizon, and then he slowly shook his head.

"No? No, we're not going back?" Phil's voice was a shriek of incredulity.

"No, we're not going back."

"You can't do that, John. For God's sake, the man's dead! He's lying there on the rocks."

"We're not going back."

"How can you say that? How can you even think about going on? We . . ."

John went off like a land mine. He was a big man, but I was still surprised at how easily he hauled Phil off his feet with his meaty hands buried in Phil's windcheater. John shook him furiously for a second like a dog with a bone and then threw him backwards where he sprawled winded on the wet grass and rock.

"He's dead. A day or two more won't make any difference." John's voice was a stone wall with no chinks for disagreement.

"I can't believe you." Phil's voice cracked and there were tears in his eyes. "Why is getting to the cottage so important?"

John turned coldly, like some robot, and started to walk on.

"John," I said tentatively.

He whirled, his fists bunching, ready to counter any resistance forcefully.

I felt a coward, but I knew I couldn't stand up to him, not on my own. Yet there was something I needed to know. "When you came back, shouting for Gordon . . . it was like you knew something was going to happen."

He looked deep into my face, searching, like he was trying to read my mind. I couldn't recognize the man I saw in his eyes. He was an alien, some bug-eyed pod person that had snatched his body. He moved away from me, all emotion locked within, and started to stride out across the uplands.

"Look, I can't go on any more," Phil whined. He dropped his rucksack to the ground with a shrug of his shoulders.

We had been walking for a good hour in silence before he had started to complain. I didn't listen to him at first; I think I was in shock. I was too confused, trying to work out what was happening, what was wrong with John. I felt pathetic and broken and stupid, and I wished Beth was there. And I couldn't shake the expression on Gordon's face when he knew he was going to die, that wide-eyed, stupid, "what have I done to deserve this?" look that turns tragedy into comedy. One other thing, too, rattled through my mind – his words: "Something's got hold of my ankle."

John turned round furiously, but Phil looked like a beaten dog who could no longer respond to punishment. Still, I thought John was going to kick him, just to see if he would move.

"My back's in agony," Phil said pitifully. "Will you take a look at it? It feels raw."

"Come on, Phil," I said wearily. "I want to get through this and back as much as you do. There's nothing that could have hurt your back. It's probably just a sore muscle."

"Just have a look, will you?"

He pulled off his windcheater and sat on his rucksack, the rain flattening his thin hair to his head, turning his pink nylon shirt transparent.

"All right. Pull up your shirt. I'm not touching it."

He peeled the material tenderly off his back and bunched it up under his armpits. When I saw his skin between his shoulders and his waist I think I must have caught my breath because he instantly cried out, "What is it? What is it?"

"Jesus, Phil, it looks like someone's been using your back for a butcher's block."

It was a mass of purple bruises and livid, red cuts, some of them oozing blood. I rethought my initial metaphor and decided it looked more like he'd been mauled by a big cat. Some of the cuts went in broad parallel sweeps of four, like he'd been swiped by talons.

"When did this happen?" I asked incredulously and a little

sickened. "How have you been able to walk from Edale in this condition?"

"In what condition? Just tell me what's wrong, for Christ's sake."

I described what I saw and his face took on that same dumbfounded expression Gordon wore at the end. He reached out behind him to feel it and winced when his fingers brushed a raw patch.

"There was nothing wrong with me when I left the car," he said pathetically. "It seemed to be happening while I was walking. My back felt sore. It was like someone was scratching me."

John walked over to us, examined Phil's back and shook his head. Then he said to me as if Phil wasn't there, "There's nothing we can do for him. She's marked him."

"Who's marked me?" Phil looked from John to me and back like he was watching a tennis match.

"What is it, John? What aren't you telling us?" He wouldn't meet my eye.

"She's marked him," he said again.

I started to walk after him to repeat my question when I heard a sound like breaking dry wood behind me and a howl of pain from Phil. I spun round and he was rolling on his back on the grass clutching his left leg. I rushed over and tried to help him, but his face was twisted in pain so I turned to his leg where he was trying to hold it, then whipping his hands away like they had been burnt.

Gingerly, I pulled up his sodden trousers. He howled again and thrashed from side-to-side, but I managed to get them over his knee.

His shin was broken. Not just broken, snapped in two. The bone jutted out, white and red-smeared through the skin. My stomach churned.

"What happened, Phil?" I asked weakly.

He levered himself up to look and then passed out.

John was standing away, watching us obliquely like we were two lovers in the park. He didn't seem at all concerned at Phil's injury.

"Put up the tent. We'll leave him here," he said coldly.

"We can't."

"Put up the tent."

"You can't leave him in this condition, for God's sake! He could go into shock. He might die."

John strode over and punched me so hard on the side of my head I thought my skull was coming off my spine. When I picked myself up off the grass a moment or two later, Phil and Gordon's tent was out of its bag and John was assembling the poles.

"John..." I pleaded.

He shook his head repeatedly. "She's marked him. That's it. At least he'll have the tent to keep him dry."

"If we're quick we can pick him up on the way back," I said hopefully.

John shook his head again. "He'll be dead when we come back."

"You've got to tell me what's happening, John." I felt a growing sense of dread that lay heavy on my disorientation. Most of all I feared for John's sanity. He wasn't my boss any more, that calm, tersely-spoken hard worker who was dedicated to his programs and his marketing schemes and his "end of year" accounts. I couldn't tell what he was going to say or do from moment to moment any more. Violence seemed to be bubbling just beneath the surface, visible in a repressed movement or a flicker of an eyelid. I wondered what terrible thing could have happened in his head to change him.

He didn't answer me at first, although I hadn't really expected a reply. Not a word had passed between us in the twenty minutes since we had left Phil in dazed agony in the tent. I tried to convince myself he really would be okay until we returned, but I didn't fool myself. I was more concerned with my own well-being and trying to prevent John going any further over the edge. That didn't make me feel too good about myself. I tried to pretend you have no say when self-preservation comes into play.

When John did finally speak, it was like he was continuing a conversation which I hadn't been party to. "I'm really not a bad guy, Sam."

"I know you're not, John." I tried to make my answer as bland as possible; I didn't want to say anything he could possibly take the wrong way.

"Sometimes you can hurt people without realising. That's not bad, surely, if it's not conscious. Can you be held responsible for your own blindness? Or stupidity?"

My legs were aching and I felt a blister working its way into raw life on my right sole. Peering through the rain, I tried to see some sign of the cottage, anything that might give me hope of an ending, but there was nothing apart from the sky and the land and the downpour. Yet when I glanced to one side over the rolling scrubland, I had the faintest sensation of movement in the misty distance, a dark smudge, like someone was shadowing our progress. I looked at John and saw that he had noticed it too. His face was like the granite around us, holding the fossils of his emotions.

"Tell me, Sam. Do you think you have to commit a real murder to be haunted? Or is psychological murder enough?"

"I wouldn't know, John."

I prayed it would be over soon.

There was grass and rain and muddy sky and then there was the cottage. It seemed to appear suddenly, like it had been thrust out of the protective folds of the land where it had been brooding silently for years.

I called it a cottage, but it wasn't, not any more. It looked like it had been blasted apart by a bomb. Rubble was everywhere, lumps of stone returning to the land from where it had been claimed. There was no sign of the roof. A third of one end wall stood with one gaping window, and enough of the remaining walls to show its outline around the flagged floor.

I wanted to say: "We've come all this way . . . through all that suffering . . . for *this*." I left John to wander among the broken stones and stand alone with his thoughts in the skeleton of the building. I hoped it was enough to put to rest whatever had been tormenting him so we could return to the warmth and dryness and light.

When he walked back over to me after ten minutes I realized there was little hope of that. "We'll pitch the tent there," he said, pointing to a spot amid piles of stone next to the front of the house. I shook my head and wearily started to unpack the metal poles.

Some semblance of the old John returned when it was finally up and we had kicked off our soaking boots to sit inside and look out at what must have been the view from his front door.

"Nice spot, John."

He nodded. "I used to love it here."

"Pity about the house."

"The weather up here is terrible. You have to constantly keep making repairs or everything gets torn down."

"I suppose the locals must have made off with the furniture."

"I suppose."

"Still, it must have been one hell of a storm."

There it was again, in the dim middle distance, almost lost against the dark peaks at the point where they rose steeply from the uplands. Even squinting I couldn't make out if it was a black, leafless tree or just an optical illusion in the shifting light and shade of the landscape, but it looked like a solitary figure, standing still, watching us. I had a sudden sensation of abject loneliness and despair.

I must have shivered, for John said, "We can light a fire soon. That will get the cold out of our bones."

By the time we had found enough dry wood to get the fire blazing, it was mid-afternoon. Night was never far away at that time of year and already it seemed the gloom was growing deeper, although it was probably just my mood. John kicked around the ruins for a while, and then we heated up cans of stewing steak and new potatoes. I couldn't eat much. I kept thinking about Phil and Gordon.

At just after 5:00 pm, we set up the shelter in front of the fire and sat under it on the front step, with the remains of the whisky. The familiar staccato sound of the rain above my head made me feel strangely nauseous.

"It never used to rain this much when I was coming up here," John said. "All I can remember is the sun behind the peaks and warm nights walking back from the falls."

"It probably did rain a lot, John. The mind plays strange tricks with memories. It only selects the good."

"Oh, I remember the bad, Sam." He took a long swig of whisky. "It's probably hard to tell now, but I was a real lad when I was younger. I liked women. I loved women. Chatting them up, getting off with them. It wasn't a game. It just gave me a thrill to have them, to know that they'd fallen for me. I used to lose interest as soon as I knew that. I still don't really know why."

"The thrill of the hunt."

"Too simple. It was more to do with proving to myself I was a good enough person to be liked, I reckon. Anyway, I seemed to be very good at it. I know I'm no oil painting, but women used to go for me. There was one girl though . . ." His voice trailed off into the drizzling rain. I watched the dark creep up behind the peaks while I waited for him to continue.

"Angela Callis. She joined the company as a secretary. I knew I was going to hire her the minute she stepped through the door. Big eyes, long, dark hair . . ."

"Is she the photo in your wallet?"

He nodded, and almost as an afterthought he pulled his wallet from his pocket, took out the picture and handed it to me. I stared into her pale, beautiful face as he spoke.

"I began making moves on her the moment she started, but she wasn't having any of it. I was baffled. I'd never experienced it before. I'd sit for minutes watching her at her typewriter, wondering what was going through her head. She wasn't frosty or anything like that. She was like a closed book, like whichever part of her controlled her emotions had been switched off. I don't know . . . it was like a red rag to a bull. She became an obsession. I had to get her to go out with me. I tried everything – flowers, chocolates, flattery, innuendo – it all washed over her. Then, just as I was about to give up, she relented. She agreed to go out to dinner with me, and that was when I knew I had her."

"You sound very . . . predatory."

He looked guilty. "I suppose that was how I was . . . back then. After that dinner she agreed to another one, and then another, and then the cinema, and then the theatre. It was like she was desperate to give herself to me, but she was holding back all the time. It was the sex that changed it. That night, about a month after the dinner, it was like a dam broke."

"I know the type."

"No, you don't. Not like her. She put her trust in me, in a way that's almost too big to describe. She took her character, her mind, her hopes, her dreams, her psyche, wrapped it all up and handed it to me. We had a great time, lots of wild dates. I fell in love with her, I think, but I never gave her anywhere near what she gave me. I had never experienced anyone who could give so freely. And I caused it. I gave her the key and convinced her to unlock the door."

Night had fallen. The darkness that covered the uplands was impenetrable. No comforting headlamps flared then disappeared. No street and house lights twinkled. There weren't even any stars. There was just the dark and the rain.

"It was just like playing one of those computer games you like," John continued. "I passed through different levels of her, each time getting closer to the heart. In the end, she gave up everything. Every last drop."

"That must have been quite a responsibility." I held my hands up to the fire, trying to leech some warmth across the wet space between us.

"I didn't realise that at the time. You know what men are like – they only learn their responsibilities to women through maturity. Angie was just another girl to me. And I was already starting to get bored with her. That sounds too callous. I liked her a lot, but once the chase was over she didn't excite me any more, and that was what I wanted – excitement."

"You dumped her?"

"Angie was a very troubled girl. Very troubled. She had been terribly abused by her mother, physically. Beaten so badly she had been hospitalized several times. Her mother's favourite torment was to tie Angie's wrists and ankles together behind her back and lock her in a wardrobe, sometimes for a whole weekend. There was more, so many terrible things I can't even bring myself to talk about them, and it went on from when she was a toddler until she found the strength to run away from home."

"Jesus." I stared at the face in the photograph, at the cold eyes that locked everything inside, and I tried to imagine what it must have been like for her.

"Her entire childhood was a catalogue of the most awful kinds of physical and psychological violence. The only way she had been able to cope with it and go out into the world was to lock it away, become emotionally numb. Those walls she had built were only weak and I'd helped knock them away. You see, I realize now what must have gone through her head when I kept making my advances. She thought my profession of love meant something . . . I don't know . . . deep."

"True love?" I stared into the heart of the fire. "That's the only kind, isn't it?"

"Not when you're that age, Sam. She thought my love meant I was going to help her with her burdens. She wanted me to save her . . . from her memories . . . from a view of the world that was dark and despairing. She trusted me implicitly to do that."

"And you dumped her."

"I brought her up here for one last weekend together. I thought we'd have a good time, give her some great memories before I ended it."

John had been rubbing his leg for some time. Gradually, he rolled up his trousers to inspect the skin in the firelight. There was a large yellowy-green bruise across his calf like it had been lashed with a belt. He pulled his trouser leg down without seeming to give it a second thought.

"How did she take it?" I asked, not really wanting to know the answer.

"She killed herself." The words were like lead weights dropped into a pond. After a second or two, there seemed to be echoes deep in the night. "She hung herself in the kitchen while I slept. She left a note. She couldn't face living now she'd brought down her defences. It was impossible to rebuild them."

He pulled out his wallet again and handed over a cracked, old piece of paper. I unfolded it carefully and read it by the firelight. It said in strained, upright script: 'I wanted to live with you and sleep with you and die with you. You gave me a kingdom of sunshine and hope, and now all there is is rain. Love, Angie.'

"How did you feel?" I asked, hating him a little, knowing I wasn't being fair.

"How do you think I felt?" There was a whiplash in his voice. "Finding her body was the worst moment of my life. Cutting it down . . . awful, just awful."

I suppose I could understand his increasingly bizarre actions during the day. He was looking for some kind of absolution from an act that haunted him down the years and the strain of it must have unbalanced him a little.

"And you came back here to deal with your guilt. Why did you leave it so long?"

"Because two months ago, she came to me."

I turned to look at his face, reddened by the light of the fire. His bald statement chilled me. "What do you mean?"

"I woke in the middle of the night, sweating. She was standing at the end of the bed, staring at me with terrible eyes. Her face was as white as a skull."

"A ghost?"

"I've seen her several times since then. Always so accusing . . . And I started to get injuries – bruises, cuts – like the injuries she told me her mother had inflicted on her. That's what happened to Gordon and Phil. She caused it."

"John, I can understand how you feel," I began, trying to mask my disbelief, "but you've got to realise this was probably all in your mind. Your guilt as the anniversary of her death approached..."

He shook his head. "I know what I saw. And I knew what I had to do. Come back here and make my peace if that was possible. I couldn't do it alone. That's why I had to bring you all with me."

And Gordon and Phil paid the price, I thought bitterly.

"Still, John, I can't believe in ghosts."

He looked away from me gloomily.

We sat in silence like that for what must have been half an hour. I didn't feel like talking any more and John was lost to his brooding, the two of us, poor, pathetic, lost boys out in the cold. After a while, I began to be aware of a change in the atmosphere. Nothing I could put my finger on, but it made my spine tingle. The first tangible signal came out of nowhere, a distant rumble of wind. It seemed to be blasting towards us across the uplands, getting louder and louder, hurricane force. My breath caught anxiously in my throat as I listened to it and then a second later it ripped the shelter up into the air, and roared the fire into a tower of sparks before extinguishing it.

John and I were frozen to the stone step in the rain and the all-encompassing dark; my heart was thumping double-time, my breath caught in my throat. Gradually, as my eyes grew accustomed to the gloom, I thought I saw a movement on the other side of the smouldering ashes of the campfire.

I felt John groping for my arm. "She's here," he said hoarsely.

"I can't see anything," I whispered, peering into the night.

"Her face. Oh God, her face! So terrible. Like a skull."

"John, I can't see anything."

"She wants me, Sam. She's beckoning. Don't let her get me. I'll do anything."

"John." I fumbled for his arm, but suddenly I realised he was no longer next to me. "John?"

I thought I sensed frantic movement in the dark around me. It could have been John alone, stumbling around in the grip of his psychosis, but I had the awful feeling there was more than one person.

Run, I told myself, but I knew that was a mistake, on the uplands, in the dark, and I had been a coward for too much that day. I hurried around the area in the rain, calling out John's name, stumbling over rocks and cracking my bones. And all the time I could hear noises off in the night, awful sounds punctuated by John's agonised cry, but when I ran in their direction there was never anyone there.

After a couple of minutes I crashed madly into the tent and tore it down. While I was floundering around in the folds of plastic, I remembered the torch in John's rucksack. Scrambling around through the puddles that were building on the flattened tent, I eventually found it and clicked it on.

The light played wildly across the grass and stones, images flashing then disappearing like a lunatic strobe, and then I got my bearings and turned and shone it into the depths of what had been the house.

Frozen in the beam like an animal in torment was John. His eyes bulged and his face was hellish red with the blood from a hundred cuts. His mouth was wide in an "O" of horror and mortal dread. And there was something else, behind him and around him, a cloud of black, something ... something ... a hand, bone-white. I held the light on the scene for a moment too long. A face, turning towards me, white like the moon, hideous, so hideous, eyes black pools of malice. Looking at me, mouth opening ...

I dropped the torch and ran. My mind was a mass of fizzing sparks without any conscious thought. I sprinted, fell and winded myself, got up and ran in a different direction, did the same. And then I was running and running, not knowing where I was going, desperate to get away, out into the night. When the cottage was far behind me and I was lost in the dark, I heard John's screaming, like the cry of a curlew, like the life was being sucked out of him, rising up and up and up before it was suddenly cut off.

That should have been an end to it. I slowed to a walk, thoughts starting to appear in my head like bubbles on a pond. John, Gordon and Phil had been punished, but I had been spared. Why? Because I loved Beth so much, and would do nothing to harm her? With relief, I thought that was probably it.

But then I happened to glance behind me and I saw it sweeping across the uplands towards me like a thunderstorm, that white, hideous face shrieking silently.

The fear filled me so much I thought my heart was going to give out. Driven by the terror, I ran as fast as I could, looking back every now and then, only to see it behind me, always at the same distance, however fast I was going.

Her eyes bored into my mind, accusing me, accusing all of us, promising damnation.

And I ran on and on, and then I could no longer feel the ground beneath me, and I was falling like the rain, and the last thing I saw was that cold white face in the night.

I woke with the dawn. My whole body was in agony from an intricate network of cuts. I was suspended in a gorse bush halfway down a sharp incline that ended in a nasty mess of granite boulders. The only reason I was there to see the rain had stopped was blind luck. It took me a good hour to extricate myself from the bush and climb down, and the better part of a day to make it back to civilization. But I would never, ever escape what I saw that night.

This morning I had a nasty purple bruise on my forearm. I noticed it after breakfast. It could have been an accident, of course, but I don't remember banging myself. Last night, I had an argument with Beth, a stupid one brought on by the stress of what I'd been through, but some harsh words were said. And this morning I had the bruise.

Sometimes I even think I see her, in the mirror or out of the corner of my eye. I want to scream out: *I'm not like them. I've done nothing wrong*, but at the last minute I manage to convince myself it's all a trick of my mind.

It doesn't seem fair. John went back for absolution, but he had really been summoned back for punishment. Did he really deserve what happened to him? How can you be expected to cope when you don't know the rules? When you're just trying to do the best you can, but you're hamstrung by immaturity or your own nature? Wouldn't it be terrible if that didn't count for anything. No mitigating circumstances anywhere in life. We're responsible for everything we do, even when we're blind to the repercussions. All of us, guilty and damned.

I look at the bruise and I wonder if she's here watching me, waiting to mete out her terrible vengeance. The awful thing is, I'll never know, for the rest of my life, until I suddenly glimpse that white face again.

IAIN SINCLAIR

Hardball

IAIN SINCLAIR LIVES, WORKS and walks in London. His latest book, *Lights Out for the Territory*, exploits these unfortunate proclivities. Described as "one of the most copiously inventive authors writing", his other books include such acclaimed novels as *White Chappell, Scarlet Tracings, Downriver* (winner of the Encore Award for the year's best second novel and the James Tait Black Memorial Prize), and *Radon Daughters*. He has also published several volumes of poetry and speculative essays, and he recently collaborated with artist Dave McKean on a series of interconnected tales entitled *Slow Chocolate Autopsy*.

Having worked as a rare book dealer, parks gardener, all-purpose labourer and publisher, one of the best jobs he ever landed was painting white lines on more than two hundred football pitches on Hackney Marshes. Those skyscapes were the inspiration for the following story, as he remembers:

"My life would have been healthier (and no doubt richer) if I'd stayed on the marshes and not listened to the spieler who arrived at my door in a dark blue Rolls Royce *Corniche*. 'Hardball' is a hymn of regret and a fragment of alternate biography."

certain measurements of breath were evident
                                             Alan Moore

THE HARDER I GUNNED the engine, the worse the wheels spun. I could hear them coming, thrashing through the reeds, calling to me, my name. I couldn't see a thing. The screen was fogged with my panicking breath. I had no idea how to start the windscreen wipers. I was a walker, not a driver. I'd watched the Pole from the passenger's seat, that's all I had to go on. His eccentricity. The way he swore in Polish, spat out of the window. "Shit on your Arsenal. Shit on beards, Communist wanking bastards. Curly boys, arse-fuckers." That's what it sounded like. Then he would cross himself.

I put my heel to the pedal. Useless. There was smoke coming from the wheels. I was more likely to end up in the river than to find the track across the marshes. What did the Pole do when we were caught on black ice? He fetched out a sack of ashes that he kept among all the other rubbish in the back. He spread grit and clinker around the wheels. He kicked at the thick tread. "Lazy wanking bastards." And it always worked.

I listened. The fog had closed everything down. I couldn't hear them anymore. I chanced it, opened the door. Crept around to the rear of the van. Night sounds were distorted. A weasel crunching a mouse's skull was amplified into a collision of icebergs. My heart was an animal trying to claw its way out of my chest. Any movement, any sigh in the reeds, was a forest fire.

There were two sacks. I had to make my choice by touch. One was tied at the neck with string. It was lumpy with hard round shapes – footballs? The other was slippery, a bin bag. I tore at it with my nails. Ripped it, as if it were the Pole's cheek. I felt the stuff trickle out into my hands. I tasted it. Ash. I dragged the split sack from the van and heaped what I could around the wheels. All of it, all of the sharp bits, the coal splinters, the powder that was as soft as icing sugar. As dream cocaine.

Now they were calling again. It was the kid's voice, turning my name into a joke. He was caught in the undergrowth, blaspheming and yelping like a bitch, then breaking into song. A maniac. I liked him. I'd probably regret it afterwards if I had to stave in his head.

A spade, I'd definitely need a spade. To hold them off or to dig myself out. I fumbled once more through the junk the Pole kept in his van. What the hell did he want with bundles of umbrellas, women's shoes, paperback books he couldn't read, tyres he'd never fit on to a pram? A pickaxe, a broom, a rake. I got my hand on the spade. Left the doors open, rushed back, while there was still time. One last try. The kid was out there, further off. It sounded like he'd blundered into one of the ponds. He was cursing a blue streak. Out of it for the moment, problems of his own.

I heaved myself back into the driver's seat. Gripped the wheel. Deep breaths. Took the clammy grey air down into my lungs, held it like a draw. The pitch of terror was easing. It was going to be all right. I visualized the wheels biting, the van moving off: no lights, pushing a new track through the reeds. Hurtling recklessly towards the sodium necklace marking the road that skirted the industrial estate. That's why none of the street names had been in my tattered *A–Z*. They were new, optimistic, part of the redevelopment, the low buildings, the units that would all, one day, be occupied and busy. I saw the future, prosperity. I'd get a real job, a wife. I might even learn to drive.

The Pole, who was waiting quietly in the passenger seat, reached across for the keys; switched the engine off, took the keys from the ignition. He wound down his window, spat. "Fucking Georgi Greyhead Graham, Communist wanking bastard, thief." Then he patted my knee.

The Pole had never been one for conversation. I worked with him, on the marshes, for three years and got nothing more than grunted orders – recipes for white lime, the number of goalposts required, ritual anathemas on Arsenal, leftists, homosexuals. We didn't see many Afro-Caribbeans among the dog fanciers and coarse-range golfers who patronised the grasslands on weekdays. Which was just as well. Bouncing along in the trailer, behind his tractor, we got used to the way he would come to an unexpected halt. "Shvartzer!" The cursing would continue until he'd worked up enough of a thirst to dig the vodka bottle out from the inside pouch of the mildewed greatcoat he wore, winter and summer, over a leather waistcoat and a couple of rancid sweaters. Cap, muffler, fingerless gloves.

We always operated three-handed. There were over two hundred pitches to be marked out, a task that was as eternal as the painting of the Forth Bridge. Get to the finish and then start again. I loved the pure geometry of it. I pictured the patterns as they might be seen from the air. White mandalas decorating the green. I loved the width of the skies. Once we'd begun for the day, there was plenty of space to avoid each other. I would see the Pole on the horizon, sitting in the tractor cab, arms folded.

Unless I needed to refill my roller, I kept clear of the man, his aura of unquenchable spite.

The casuals who made up the team never stayed long. Two or three weeks was average. The Pole ignored them. Wouldn't answer if they spoke to him, took out a copy of the *Radio Times* and covered his face with it. He didn't have a radio or a television set, I knew that much. "Television whore bastard, no good. Eyes, head." He gestured with two fingers pressed against his eyeballs. He had found the magazine in the tractor when he inherited the job, after one of the wars. Most of the casuals learnt to respect his whims – before they found themselves trying to paint white lines that had the consistency of bone porridge. Before he rolled a crossbar out of the trailer onto an unprotected foot. Some of these gypos and vagrants were crazier than he was: snackers on dog turds, skeletal naturists, baby faces who licked pus from freshly-squeezed blackheads while boasting of the hits they'd got away with, sheep rapists, grass bulimics, hairtrigger millennialists. White trash too weird to be housed in prisons or asylums.

The worst we ever had was a skull called Norton. He was involved, so they said, in some deal with the Twins that went sour. He was a dead man, waiting for it. Wouldn't get his hands dirty, didn't know how. Lived in the shithouse, book on his lap – until the Pole shopped him. Amen, baby, and good-night.

Aliens couldn't take the marshes. The first teabreak and they were gone. They'd trot into the bushes to enjoy a crap, the more sensitive of them, and never be seen again.

But the kid was a sticker. As well as a speed freak. You could hear him rabbiting from the other side of Epping Forest. Football mad. Chased the Hammers up and down the length of the country. Which was why, like me, it pissed him off to have to work on Saturdays and Sundays. Opening up the changing rooms, cleaning the filth that the amateurs left behind: mud, plasters, shampoo sachets, embrocation, even condoms floating in the trough. What did they get up to? Had they saved the knotted rubbers as a macho boast? Or did a win excite them so much they shot off in an orgy of mutual congratulation? The Pole wouldn't have anything to do with it. Too many black athletes. Too much backchat. He drank fiercely in his tractor, waiting until we were ready to take down the goalposts.

My grouse was that I coudn't play myself. I was a loner,

never part of a team, never in thrall to the whistle. Night football was just my way of coming to an understanding with the magnitude of London, seeing it as an anthology of green scraps, fragmented meadows, wastelots, school yards. I cruised as a serial five-a-sider. I'd go anywhere. Set off at random, hop a bus, or simply walk until I was exhausted in a direction that I'd never before attempted. Scuffed trainers, baggy jeans, ready for it. I was a three-and-in, headers and volleys freelancer. I pocketed change (lost it frequently) on park challenges. I'd grown up learning to control a wet tennis ball, shooting at a chalked goal, never losing possession – even to another member of my own team. Elbows out, eyes down, no headers, no percentage play, no long punts into space. A Sunday league kickabout or a pub challenge on proper turf gave me agoraphobia. I could do anything with the ball except pass it.

I scored games against black kids turned off the astroturf in Caledonian Park. We dodged traffic for a Brewery Road shoot-out. I cardiac-arrested a trio of retired Scottish postmen on London Fields, clattered their superior skills. I played as a mercenary for a Kurdish mob in an afterhours playground at the back of Ridley Road Market. I kicked lumps out of middle-class pretenders in Regent's Park. I made up the numbers on Tooting Common. I took a few quid off a heritage film-crew in Charlton Park. Through these contacts, nameless encounters, I mapped the city, the shape of its energy patterns.

When the weather turned, and the speed freak was still with us – Julian Dicks crop, mouthy, sweat-ringed blackcurrent shirt – the Pole started to take the tractor, in the lunchbreak, down to a strip of grass between the canal and the Hackney Stadium, the dog track. He'd open his *Radio Times* and leave us to it. But it just so happened he had a sack of footballs in the trailer. He let us find them, and, in boredom, use them. Three and in (except that the kid refused ever to come out) against a roughcast wall. An ugly place. The wall in slabs, razorwire above it, on which flapping kites of plastic, wingless birds, signalled the breeze. Earth mounds from the stadium's renovation backed up to the wall, and, beyond the mounds, rows of seven-lamped light towers. It was obviously a favoured site for the Pole. And you could see why. Even the Alsatians that various sullen members of the underclass exercised along the perimeter made him feel at home.

The kid fancied himself as a goalie. Dog shit didn't deter him. He flung himself about in wild abandon, climbed reeking on to the trailer. Indoors, he'd have been unbearable. If I got five shots in succession past him, I won a slug of vodka. If he saved three on the trot, it was his turn at the bottle. Half-pissed, we returned to our white lines. Mine meandered into crazed calligraphy, oval pitches, no corners. I got slower and slower and finally bunked off to doze under the poplars. The kid did his wiz and, pin-eyed, scorched the grass like an Exocet. Tramlines that ran for half a mile. Pitches divided up like chessboards. You could hear him rabbiting on. He swore, against all evidence, against the yelping of hounds, that Orient played in the Hackney Stadium. He'd been there, seen them. Had a trial, been offered terms. He could have been a five grand a week man, trading wisecracks with Barry Hearn. He could have followed the former manager to Forest. He was like every politician you've ever heard off, like David Frost. They could all have been pros. Orient were bollocks. It was the Hammers or nothing.

At the end of the afternoon, when the Pole picked us up, he surprised me. He gestured that he had something he wanted us to see. He fumbled beneath the leather waistcoat and retrieved a yellow packet. Photographs, murky, taken at night, football stadia. Highbury, Loftus Road, the Den, the Valley, Upton Park – even Craven Cottage seen from across the river, as well as from Bishop's Park. They weren't bad. They looked gaunt and sinister, floodlights fogging. Broken-down people's palaces. Tarted up leisure and entertainment facilities. Symbols of exclusion. The Pole's album was like the proposal for a Channel 4 documentary. He lacked White Hart Lane to hook the desktop fantasists.

Apparently, and this was the biggest shock of all, the kid had been helping him, taking him around. The speed freak wasn't bothered about getting into the game, if it didn't involve the Hammers. He'd happily play one-on-one, against the car park wall, with some local urchin, uphold the honour of Plaistow and Forest Gate. There was always a wager which the Pole supervised. He didn't explain, not then, what the stake would be.

"Who do you support?" I asked.

"Football shit. Arsenal wankers." Only the grounds interested him, the architecture of enclosure, the baying mob. The dogs, the security cameras. The columns of floodlights. Not for nothing had the partisans of Allende been massacred inside a football stadium. Hadn't the Parisian Jews been rounded up in such a place to wait for transport? The Pole wanted to feed on bad karma, the malign passion of the crowd. He would lurk in the shadows and concentrate all that latent mayhem into his camera. Unwatched football was his metaphor of chaos. He didn't need to see the Christians torn apart by lions. It was much more subtle to listen in the deserted street outside, to interpret every nuance that emanated from the trapped punters. Foiled orgasms of sound. Then pick some ragamuffin nobody would miss to play against his feral gladiator.

I agreed to meet them outside White Hart Lane, at the back of the East Stand. The next evening game, an eight o'clock kick-off, happened to be against Manchester United. Insanity. The way the purity of proletarian Saturday afternoons, one time for all, has been shafted by market forces. The crowd reduced to a rabble of high-profile extras. Extras who pay royally for the privilege of dubbing background noise onto a TV special.

A bleak, damp evening in the post-Christmas lull. I walked there, up the Lea Valley, past the marshes, Springfield Park and the old sewage farm. Nowhere open, nowhere to get a drink to lift the choking poultice of oily air. A Scotch egg and a black coffee from a petrol station was the best I could do. I was in an evil mood by the time I found them, parked up in a dirty blue van.

The Pole was eating cold cabbage from a chipped mug, washing it down with the usual drafts of vodka. The kid was chewing on a pig's foot, wiping the grease into his lank hair. A consumptive Eddie Cochran imitator. The foot was a gesture at grossness. He couldn't hack it. No appetite. Dry lips. Curd at the corners of his mouth. Thirsty for a hit of Cola sugar, a tooth-rotting suck at a sticky can. He dropped the nibbled hoof out of the window. Even the rats refused to take the bait. The mindless vandalism was a provocation aimed at the supposed cultural bias of the Tottenham supporters, a fatty compass tossed derisively in the direction of Stamford Hill. Spurs, as far as he was concerned, were the pits. The acceptable face of football, football for tourists from Hampstead, broadsheet dickheads, flabby essayists hymning Gazza as a cock on legs. Football as a cash cow, a way of laundering sweatshop slush funds, insurance barbecues. Sugar by name, salt by nature. The kid ranted like a decommissioned poet.

The game had been in progress for about half an hour when I found them. Even the technicians hanging about in their caravans seemed to think they'd got it right for once. The crowd were going mad, wave after wave of ecstatic roars, an opera of the masses. Thick vine clusters of electric cable ran from the TV vans, over the wall, into the stadium. The electrification of the unwashed. Not a star in the sky, warm air pushing in from the south, hurting the indignant gloom of the Lea Valley, the trading estates, the night-flashing railway, the dead streets with their boarded-up shops. Football turned Tottenham into Belfast. And the entire country, and probably most of Europe and Asia (bets down), were hooked on this, plugged into this unlikely confrontation. Tottenham were stuffing United. Chris Armstrong, the former Crystal Palace charger, the recreational puffer, had glanced in a header that was worthy of Klinsmann. Hallucinatory madness. Kids were ghosting out of the gloom to peek at the monitors. It was easy to use their excitement to set up a game, a challenge.

There's a carpet pitch behind a fence in the lee of the stadium, lights of its own, a parasitical facility. The lights weren't enough to turn night into day, they spilled a sort of laboratory glow at the corners of the field. The illumination enjoyed by brain-wired beagles. We would be in our element. The flash of the Pole's camera would fuse our spastic actions with the larger drama on the other side of the great white cliff.

Most of the glue-sniffers and night casuals had drifted away from the pitch towards the circle of OB vans. They were hooked on the big match. They wanted to see the plutocrats of Man U come unstuck. Our yids and wops and darkies can stuff yours: that was the message. The two that were left, supposed brothers, were unreconstructed dysfunks, ambulant basket cases. A safe bet for the Pole. He wandered over with his bottle and a shuffle of paper to set up the challenge. A penalty shoot out. First to reach five goals. One player as the nominated goalkeeper and the other as the shooter.

The speed freak pulled on the gloves (motorcycle gauntlets) and jumped up and down, leaking gusts of white smoke. "Yes yes yes." He clapped his hands together. He couldn't wait to showcase his ineptitude. I couldn't afford to miss. I knew that something more than a couple of quid, and a free hit at the vodka bottle, was involved. The Pole had his arm around the kid's shoulder. The kid was mouthing his usual stream-of-consciousness rubbish. Mexicans, Indians, Mayans, sun-worshippers, snake god cannibals. Jungle bunnies with chipped profiles and a winner takes all attitude to life. These Mayans, apparently, saw football as a fate game. They played with their victims' skulls. The geometry of the court reflected a demonic cosmology. I had a bad feeling about this. Every touch of the ball was prophetic. If I hit the back of the net, so would Spurs, so would England, so would the white races, so would the order of angels. If I failed... Heads would surely roll.

I failed. For my first shot I concentrated on placement, not pace. I feinted left, then hit it low towards the righthand corner. The goalkeeper bluffed me. He wasn't a mover. Stood like a funeral mute, arms hanging awkwardly, until I put toe to leather. Then he sprang, anticipated me, read the flight. Tipped it, effortlessly, around the corner. Their penalty taker, a rickety beanpole who could barely stand erect without his calipers, didn't bother with a run up; smashed the ball, with no backlift, straight through the kid's arms. There was no way back. But we had to carry on to the death.

I blasted shots two and three safely into the top left corner. The same way twice, fooling nobody. The spider-monkey guessed right both times, but couldn't hold them. Their second attempt rocketed down off the post and in. The third, by some miracle, was saved. Keep diving the wrong way and sooner or later, by accident, you'll get it right.

The Pole went back to the van, fetching a black bag that, he said, contained a couple of bottles for the winners. Spurs must have tucked away their third goal, Armstrong's kneeling header, as I scored ours: top left corner again. I felt like praying. I would have been down there crawling if I could, duplicating the position of the Tottenham striker.

Could the speed freak take it to the wire? Not on his own. But the Pole had moved around directly behind the posts and his unblinking glare, red eye in the sodium-puddled darkness, threw the thin streak's concentration. He ballooned it gently into the kid's grateful grasp. See him dance and cavort. "Come on you Irons." He jigged and punched the air. He tried to embrace the Pole. Shove his tongue down his throat.

I pushed my luck with the final shot, tried for my lucky corner, and had the keeper fingertip it on to the bar. Their last effort was a formality, depositing kid and ball, together, in a tangle in the corner of the net.

I was all for shaking hands, calling it an honourable draw, three apiece, and home – when the roar of the fourth Spurs goal overwhelmed us. News of madness. An andrenalin hit that was not to be denied. All or nothing. The Pole was playing with the neck of his bag. His big fists clenching and unclenching. Now the problem was the quantity of electronic interference in the air. Commentators blathering about upsets. Action replays. Slo-mo distortions. Real time fractured and tormented. World Cups recalled. I kept seeing Waddle punting it high, wide and handsome. We were wired. In a mind game, we were bound to be losers: the kid with his free associating meltdown of West Ham mythology and misunderstood Mayan blood rituals, his arcane pulp images of terror, and my own crippling sense of psychogeography. His racist bile, my singular attitude towards landscape. Too much memory. We were too easily accessed. The other pair existed only in the present. Autistic innocents. Drooling but functional.

We tossed for first kick. They took it. A mishit trickled through the kid's legs. He was frozen in a drama of self-sacrifice. It was more dramatic, at this juncture, to lose heroically. Who remembers the man who hits the winning goal? But who can forget the goalkeeper's fantastic error? Gary Sprake fumbling it or the backpedalling Seaman looped from the touchline?

I travelled behind the picture of my failure. I saw the ball sailing over the bar and into the road. I heard it thump against the roof of the van. That was what the story needed and that was what I did. The full Waddle impersonation. The bandy-legged slouch. The loser's sleepwalking approach. The Marseilles scoop.

The Pole handed over cash and bottles and we walked in silence to the van. We had to get away before the real match terminated and celebrating thousands rushed out into the streets to get home to have their triumph confirmed on *Match of the Day*. To have Alan Hansen put the damper on it.

I was never much good at directions, but when the van went off the road – to avoid the worst of the traffic – and took the track through the reed beds, across the marshes, I knew we weren't heading for Hackney. The kid was in the back, blowing his bubbles, and swilling firewater. The Pole drove in silence. I couldn't see much. The fog mixed with smoke and the damp night to seal us off. When we stopped, I couldn't have guessed where we were. On the edge of the river or at the centre of a swamp. The Pole told the kid to get out and start a fire. Sat beside me, the windows wound up, headlights off, listening to the kid stumble about, whimpering that he was cold and wet and couldn't find any dry wood. The Pole left the keys in the car and swung himself out to take control.

That's when I decided to make my run for it. When I started the engine and juddered off, blind, in the direction the van was already facing. I didn't know anything about gears, but it worked. I was moving, reeds thrashing across the windscreen. Voices behind me. It went well until the wheels stuck in the mud at the edge of the black river. Until they spun and screamed and the Pole caught up with me, claimed his forfeit.

Icy cold. Turning slowly through the water, the tangle of weeds, a taste of iron and powdered asprin. Blood clogging to silt. Spinning over and over. Tunnels of light splintering ahead of me. I hadn't thought the Lea was so deep. But I knew everything now, knew that the ashes I had been spreading so cavalierly around the wheels of the van were the ashes of men. Victims. Sacrifices. I could feel the light but not see it. I tried to scrape off the lily pads that were covering my eyes. Scratch the caul from my face. I had no face. Those were not footballs in the Pole's sack. They went with the rest of his collection. One hard thing hidden away for each night stadium photographed. I could hear the kid chanting "come on you Irons" as he rolled my head through the fire, as he prepared it for the place it would always occupy.

THOMAS LIGOTTI

Gas Station Carnivals

THOMAS LIGOTTI HAS BEEN described by the *Washington Post* as "The most startling and unexpected literary discovery since Clive Barker", while Ramsey Campbell called the author's first volume of stories, *Songs of a Dead Dreamer*, "one of the most important horror books of the decade."

Since then, Ligotti has published such further collections as *Grimscribe* and *Noctuary*, as well as a volume of short stories entitled *The Agonizing Resurrection of Victor Frankenstein and Other Gothic Tales*. His most recent book is the Bram Stoker Award-winning *The Nightmare Factory*, a bumper compilation of previously collected and new stories.

According to the author, "One morning I woke up and, in a normal tone of voice, spoke the words 'Gas Station Carnivals'."

O UTSIDE THE CRIMSON CABARET was rain and darkness. At intervals, whenever someone entered or exited through the front door of the club, one could clearly hear the rain and got a brief glimpse of the darkness. Inside it was all amber light, tobacco smoke, and the sound of the rain hitting the windows, which were all painted black. Sitting at one of the tables in that small room on a rainy night often filled me with an infernal merriment, as if these were the last moments just before the end of everything and I could not care less about it. I liked to imagine that I was in the cabin of an old ship during a really vicious storm at sea, or in the club car of a luxury passenger train that was being rocked on its rails by ferocious winds and hammered by a demonic rain. Sometimes, when I was sitting there on a rainy night, I thought of myself as occupying a waiting room for the abyss (which of course was exactly what I was doing) and, between sips from my glass of wine or cup of coffee, I smiled sadly and touched the front pocket of my coat where I kept my imaginary ticket to oblivion.

However, on that particular rainy November night I was not feeling very well. My stomach was slightly queasy, as if signalling the onset of a virus or even food poisoning. Another source for my malaise, I thought to myself, might well have been my longstanding nervous condition, which fluctuated from day to day but was always with me in some form and manifested itself in a variety of symptoms both physical and psychic. I was in fact experiencing a faint sensation of panic, although this in no way ruled out the possibility that the queasiness of stomach was due to a strictly physical cause, either viral or toxic. Neither did it rule out a *third* possibility which I was trying to ignore at that point in the evening. What ever the aetiology of my stomach disorder, I felt the need to be in a public place that night, so that if I should collapse – an eventuality I often feared – there would be people around who might attend to me, or at least shuttle my body off to the hospital. At the same time I was not seeking close contact with any of these people, and I would have been bad company in any case, sitting there in the corner of the club drinking mint tea and smoking mild cigarettes out of respect for my ailing stomach. For all these reasons I brought my notebook with me that night and had it lying open on the table before me, as if to say that I wanted to be left alone to mull over some literary matters. But when Stuart Quisser entered the club at approximately ten o'clock, the sight of me sitting at a corner table with my open notebook, drinking mint tea and smoking mild cigarettes so that I might stay on top of the situation with my queasy stomach, did not in the least discourage him from walking directly to my table and taking the seat across from me. A waitress came over to us. Quisser ordered some kind of white wine, while I asked for another cup of mint tea.

"Mint tea, now," Quisser said as the girl left us.

"I'm surprised you're showing your face around here," I said by way of reply.

"Oh, I thought I might try to make up with the proprietress."

"Make up? That doesn't sound like you."

"Nevertheless, have you seen her tonight?"

"No, I haven't. You humiliated her at that party. I haven't seen her since, not even in her own club. I don't know if you're aware of this, but she's not someone you want to have as an enemy."

"Meaning what?" he asked.

"Meaning that she has connections you know absolutely nothing about."

"And of course you know all that stuff inside out. I've read your stories. You're a confessed paranoid, so what's your point?"

"My point," I said, "is that there's hell in every handshake, nevermind an outright and humiliating insult."

"I had too much to drink, that's all."

"You called her a *deluded no-talent*."

Quisser looked up at the girl as she approached with our drinks, and he made a hasty hand-signal for silence. When she was gone he said, "I happen to know that our waitress is very loyal to her boss, the crimson woman. She will very probably inform her about my visiting the club tonight. Do you think she'll be receptive to a sincere apology?"

"Look around at the walls," I said.

Quisser set down his glass of wine and scanned the room. "This is serious," he said when finished looking. "She's taken down all her old paintings. The new ones don't look like her work at all."

"They're not. You *humiliated* her."

"And yet she seems to have done something with the stage. New decor or something."

The so-called stage to which Quisser referred was a small platform in the opposite corner of the club. This area was entirely framed by four long panels, each of them painted with black and gold sigils against a glossy red background. Various events occurred on this stage: poetry readings, tableaux vivants, playlets of sundry types, puppet shows, artistic slideshows, musical performances, and so on. That night, which was a Tuesday, the stage was dark. I observed nothing different about it and asked Quisser what he imagined he saw that was new.

"I can't say exactly, but something seems to have been done.

Maybe it's those black and gold ideographs or whatever they're supposed to be. The whole thing looks like the cover of a menu in a Chinese restaurant."

"You're quoting yourself," I said.

"What do you mean?"

"The Chinese menu remark. You used that in your review of the Marsha Corker show last month."

"Did I? I don't remember."

"Are you just saying you don't remember, or do you really *not* remember?" I asked this question in the spirit of trivial curiosity, my queasy stomach discouraging the strain of any real antagonism on my part.

"I *remember*, all right? Which reminds me, there's something I wanted to talk to you about. It came to me the other day, and I immediately thought of you and your . . . stuff," he said, gesturing toward my notebook of writings open on the table between us. "I can't believe it's never come up before. You of all people should know about them. No one else seems to. It was years ago, but you're old enough to remember them, you've *got* to remember them."

"Remember what?" I asked, and after the briefest pause he replied:

"The gas station carnivals."

And he said these words as if he were someone delivering a punch line to a joke, the proud bringer of a surprising and profound hilarity. I was supposed to express an astonished recognition, that much I knew. It was not a phenomenon of which I was *entirely ignorant*, and memory is such a tricky thing. This, at least, is what I told Quisser. But as Quisser told me *his* memories, trying to arouse mine, I gradually realized the true nature and purpose of the so-called gas station carnivals. During this time it was all I could do to conceal how badly my stomach was acting up on me, queasy and burning. I kept telling myself, as Quisser was talking about his memories of the gas station carnivals, that I was certainly experiencing the onset of a virus, if, in fact, I had not been the victim of food poisoning. Quisser, nevertheless, was so caught up in his story that he seemed not to notice my agony.

Quisser said that his recollections of the gas station carnivals derived from his early childhood. His family, meaning his parents and himself, would go on long vacations by car, often driving great distances to a variety of destinations. Along the way, naturally, they would need to stop at any number of gas stations that were located in towns and cities, as well as those that they came upon in more isolated, rural locales, which were usually not far from a particular small town. These were the places, Quisser said, where one was most likely to discover those hybrid enterprises which he called gas station carnivals.

Quisser did not claim to know when or how these specialized *carnivals*, or perhaps specialized *gas stations*, came into existence, nor how widespread they might have been. His father, whom Quisser believed would be able to answer such questions, had died some years ago, while his mother was no longer mentally competent, having suffered a series of psychic catastrophes not long after the death of Quisser's father. Thus, all that remained to Quisser was the memory of these childhood excursions with his parents, during which they would find themselves in some rural area, perhaps at the crossroads of two highways (and often, he seemed to recall, around sunset), and discover in this isolated location one of those places which he described to me.

They were invariably small *filling stations*, Quisser emphasized, and not *service stations*, which might have facilities for doing extensive repairs on cars and other vehicles. There would be, in those days, four gas pumps at most, often only two, and some kind of modest building which usually had so many signs and advertisements applied to its exterior that no one could say if anything actually stood beneath them. Quisser said that as a child he always took notice of the signs that advertised chewing tobacco, and that as an adult (who was also an art critic), he still found the sight of chewing tobacco packages very appealing, and he could not understand why some artist had not successfully exploited their visual and imaginative qualities. It seemed to me, as we sat that night in the Crimson Cabaret, that this chewing tobacco material was intended to lend greater credence to Quisser's story. This detail was so vivid to him. But when I asked Quisser if he recalled any particular brands of gasoline being sold by these particular filling stations which had carnivals attached to them, he became slightly defensive, as if my question was intended to challenge the accuracy of his childhood recollection. He then shifted the focus of the issue I had raised by asserting that the carnival aspect of these places was not exactly *attached* to the gas station aspect, but that they were never very far away from each other and there was definitely a commercial liaison between them. His impression, which had been instilled in him like some founding principle of a dream, was that a substantial purchase of gasoline allowed the driver and passengers of a given vehicle free access to the nearby carnival.

At this point in his story, Quisser became anxious to explain that these gas station carnivals were by no means elaborate – quite the opposite, in fact. Situated in the ample empty landscape alongside, or sometimes behind, a rural filling station, they consisted of only the remnants of fully fledged carnivals, the *bare bones* of much larger and grander entertainments. There was usually a tall, arched entranceway with colored lightbulbs that provided an eerie contrast to the vast and barren land stretching on all sides of it. Especially around sunset, which was usually or always when Quisser and his parents found themselves in one of these remote locales, the colorful illumination of a carnival entranceway created an effect that was both festive and sinister. But once a visitor had gained admittance to the actual grounds of the carnival, there came a moment of let-down at the thing itself – that spare assemblage of equipment that appeared to have been left behind by a travelling amusement park in the distant past.

There were always only a few carnival rides, Quisser said, and these were very seldom in actual operation. He supposed that at some time they were in functioning order, probably when they were first installed as an annex to the gas stations. But this period, he speculated, could not have lasted long. And, no doubt, at the earliest sign of malfunction each of the rides was shut down. Quisser said that he himself had never been on a single ride at a gas station carnival, though he once insisted that his father allow him to sit atop one of the wooden horses on a defunct merry-go-round. "It was a *miniature* merry-go-round," Quisser told me, as if that gave his recollected experience an aura of meaning or substance. All the rides, it seemed, were miniature – small-scale versions of carnival rides he had elsewhere known and actually had ridden upon. Beside the miniature merry-go-round, which never moved an inch and always stood dark and silent in a remote rural landscape, there would be a miniature ferris wheel (no taller than a bungalow house, Quisser said), and sometimes a miniature tilt-a-whirl or a miniature roller coaster. And they were always closed down because once they had malfunctioned, if in fact any of them was ever in operation, they were never subsequently repaired. Possibly they never could be repaired, Quisser thought, given the antiquated parts and mechanisms of these miniature carnival rides.

Yet there was a single, quite crucial, amusement that one could almost always expect to see open to the public, or at least to those whose car had been filled with the requisite amount of gasoline and who were therefore free to pass through the brightly lit entranceway upon which the word CARNIVAL was emblazoned in colored lights against a vast and haunting sky at sundown somewhere out in the sticks. Quisser posed to me a question: how could a place advertise itself as a carnival, even a gas station carnival, if it did not include that most vital element – a sideshow? Perhaps there was some special law or ordinance regulating such matters, Quisser imagined out loud, an old statute of some kind that would have particular force in remote areas where certain traditions have an endurance unknown to urban centers. This would account for the fact that, except under extraordinary circumstances (such as dangerously bad weather), there was always a type of sideshow performance at these gas station carnivals, even though everything else on the grounds stood dark and damaged.

Of course these sideshows, as Quisser described them, were not terribly sophisticated even by the standards of the average carnival, let alone those that served as commercial enticements for some out-of-the-way gas station. There would be only a single sideshow attraction at a given site, and outwardly they each presented the same image to the carnival patrons: a small tent of torn and filthy canvas. At some point along the perimeter of the tent would be a loose flap of material through which Quisser and his parents, though sometimes only Quisser himself, would gain entrance to the sideshow. Inside the tent were a few wooden benches that had sunk a little bit into the hard dirt beneath them and, some distance away, a small stage area that was raised perhaps just a foot or so above ground level. Illumination was provided by two ordinary floor lamps – one on either side of the stage – that were without lampshades or any other kind of covering, so that their bare lightbulbs burned harshly and cast dramatic shadows throughout the interior of the tent. Quisser said that he always noticed the frayed electrical cords that trailed off from the base of each lamp and, by means of several extension cords, ultimately found a source of power at the gas station, that is, from within the small brick building which was obscured by so many signs advertising chewing tobacco and other products.

When visitors to a gas station carnival entered the sideshow tent and took their places on one of the benches in front of the stage, they were not usually alerted to the particular nature of the performance or spectacle that they would witness. Quisser remarked that there was no marquee or billboard of any type that might give such a notice to the carnival-goers either before they entered the sideshow tent or after they were inside and seated on one of the old wooden benches. However, with one important exception, each of the performances, or spectacles, was much the same rigmarole. The audience would settle itself on the wooden benches, most of which were about to collapse or (as Quisser observed) were so unevenly sunken into the ground that it was impossible to sit on them, and the show would begin.

The attractions varied from sideshow to sideshow, and Quisser said he was unable to remember all of the ones he had seen. He did recall what he described as the Human Spider. This was a very brief spectacle during which someone in a clumsy costume scuttled from one side of the stage to the other and back again, exiting through a slit at the back of the tent. The person wearing the costume, Quisser added, was presumably the attendant who pumped gas, washed windows, and performed various services around the filling station. In many sideshow performances, such as that of the Hypnotist, Quisser remembered that a gas station attendant's uniform (greasy gray or blue coveralls) was quite visible beneath the performer's stage clothes. Quisser did admit that he was unsure why he designated this particular sideshow act as the "Hypnotist," since there was no hypnotism involved in the performance and, of course, no marquee or billboard existed either outside the tent or within it that might lead the public to expect any kind of mesmeric routines. The performer was simply clothed in a long, loose overcoat and a plastic mask which was a plain, very pale replica of a human face, with the exception that instead of eyes or eyeholes there were two large discs with spiral designs painted upon them. The Hypnotist would gesticulate chaotically in front of the audience for some moments, no doubt because his vision was obscured by the spiral-patterned discs over the eyes of his mask, and then stumble off stage.

There were numerous other sideshow acts that Quisser claimed to have seen including the Dancing Puppet, the Worm, the Hunchback, and Dr Fingers. With one important exception, the routine was always the same: Quisser and his parents would enter the sideshow tent and sit upon one of the rotted benches, soon after which some performer would appear briefly on the small stage that was lit up by two ordinary floor lamps. The single deviation from this routine was an attraction that Quisser called the Showman.

Whereas every other sideshow act began and ended *after* Quisser and his parents had entered the special tent and seated themselves, the one called the Showman always seemed to be *in progress*. As soon as Quisser stepped inside the tent – invariably preceding his parents he claimed – he saw the figure standing perfectly still upon the small stage *with his back to the audience*. Of course there were never any other persons in the audience when Quisser and his parents stopped at twilight and visited one of these gas station carnivals – with their second-hand, defective amusements – there was only the figure of the Showman standing with his back to a few rows of empty benches that might break up while you were trying to sit on them. And whenever Quisser entered the sideshow tent and saw that it was the Showman onstage, he wanted to immediately turn around and leave that place. But then his parents would come pushing into the tent behind him, he said, and before he knew it they would all be sitting on one of the benches in the very first row looking at the Showman. His parents never knew how terrified he was of the peculiar sideshow figure, Quisser repeated several times. Furthermore, visiting these gas station carnivals and especially taking in the sideshows, was all done for Quisser's benefit, since his father and mother would have preferred simply filling up the family car with gasoline and moving on toward whatever vacation spot was next on their itinerary.

Quisser contended that his parents actually enjoyed watching him sit in terror before the Showman, until he could not stand it any longer and asked to go back to the car. At the same time he was quite transfixed by the sight of this sideshow character who was unlike any other that he could remember. There he was, Quisser said, standing with his back to the audience and wearing an old top hat and a long cape that touched the dirty floor of the small stage on which he stood. Sticking out from beneath the top hat were the dense and lengthy shocks of the

Showman's stiff red hair, Quisser said, which looked like some kind of sickening vermin's nest. When I asked Quisser if this hair might actually have been a wig, deliberately testing his memory and imagination, he only gave me a contemptuous look that seemed to reply that *I* had not seen the stiff red hair and *he* had seen it sticking out from beneath the Showman's old top hat. The only other feature that was visible to the audience, Quisser continued, were the fingers of the Showman, which grasped the edges of his long cape. They appeared to be deformed, curling together in little claws, and were a pale greenish color, Quisser said. Apparently, as Quisser viewed it, the entire stance of the figure was calculated to suggest that at any moment he might twirl about and confront the audience full-face, his moldy fingers lifting up the edges of his cape, reaching to the height of his stiff red hair. Yet the figure never budged. Sometimes it did seem to Quisser that the Showman was moving his head a little to the left or a little to the right, threatening to reveal one side of his face or the other, playing a horrible game of peek-a-boo. But ultimately Quisser concluded that these perceived movements were illusory and that the Showman was always posed in perfect stillness, a nightmarish mannikin that invited all kinds of imaginings by its very forbearance of any gesture.

"It was all a nasty pretense," Quisser said to me and then paused to finish off his glass of wine.

"But what if he had turned around to face the audience?" I asked. While awaiting his response I sipped some of my mint tea, which did not seem to be doing much good for my queasy stomach, yet at the same time was causing no harm either. I lit one of the mild cigarettes that I was smoking on that occasion. "Did you hear what I said?" I said to Quisser, who had been looking away from and toward the stage located in the opposite corner of the Crimson Cabaret. "The stage is the same," I said to Quisser quite sternly, attracting some glances from persons sitting at the other tables in the club. "The panels are the same and the designs on them are also the same."

Quisser played nervously with his empty wine glass. "When I was very young," he said, "there were certain occasions on which I would see the Showman, but he wasn't in his natural habitat, so to speak, of the sideshow tent."

"I think I've heard enough tonight," I interjected, my hand pressing against my queasy stomach.

"What are you saying?" asked Quisser. "You remember them, don't you? The gas station carnivals. Maybe just a *faint* memory. You would be the one to know about them, I was sure."

"No, that's not what I'm saying. I'm saying that I've heard enough of your gas station carnival story to know what it's all about."

"What do you mean, 'what it's all about'?" asked Quisser, who was still looking over at the small stage across the room.

"Well, for one thing, your later memories, your *purported* memories, of that Showman character. You were about to tell me that throughout your childhood you repeatedly saw this figure at various times and in various places. Perhaps you saw him in the distance of a schoolyard, standing with his back to you. Or you saw him on the other side of a busy street, but when you crossed the street he wasn't there any longer."

"Something like that, yes."

"And you were then going to tell me that lately you've been seeing this figure, or faint suggestions of this figure – sketchy reflections in store windows along the sidewalk, flashing glimpses in the rear-view mirror of your car."

"It's much like one of your stories."

"In some ways it is," I said, "and in some ways it isn't. You feel that if you ever see the Showman figure turn his head around to look at you that something terrible will happen, most likely that you'll die from some kind of monumental shock."

"Yes," agreed Quisser. "An unsustainable horror. But I haven't told you the strangest part. You're right that lately I have had glimpses of . . . that figure, and I did see him during my childhood, outside of the sideshow tent, I mean. But the strangest part is that I remember seeing him in other places even *before* I first saw him at the gas station carnivals."

"This is just my point," I said.

"What is?"

"That there *are no gas station carnivals*. There never were any gas station carnivals. Nobody remembers them because they never existed. The whole idea is preposterous."

"But my parents were there with me."

"Exactly – your dead father and your mentally incompetent mother. Do you remember ever discussing with them your vacation experiences at these special gas stations with the carnivals supposedly annexed to them?"

"No, I don't."

"That's because you never went to any such places with them. Think about how ludicrous it all sounds. That there should be filling stations out in the sticks that entice customers with free admission to broken-down carnivals – it's all so ridiculous. *Miniature* carnival rides? Gas station attendants doubling as sideshow performers?"

"Not the Showman," interrupted Quisser. "He was never a gas station attendant."

"No, of course he wasn't a gas station attendant, because he was a delusion. The whole thing is an outrageous delusion, but it's also a very particular type of delusion. Should I tell you what type that is?"

"I suppose," said Quisser, who was still sneaking glances at the stage area across the room of the Crimson Cabaret.

"It's not some type of psychological delusion, if that's what you were thinking I was about to say. As you, I'm without any qualifications in that area. But I am qualified to diagnose you as suffering from a *magical* delusion. Even more precisely, you are suffering from a delusion of *art-magic*. And do you know how long you've been under the influence of this art-magic delusion?"

"You've lost me," said Quisser.

"It's simple," I said. "How long have you imagined all this nonsense about the gas station carnivals, and specifically about this character you describe as the Showman?"

"I guess it would be more or less absurd at this point to insist to you that I've seen this . . . figure since childhood, even if that's exactly how it seems and that's exactly what I remember."

"Of course it would be absurd, because you're definitely delusional."

"So I'm delusional about the Showman, but you're not delusional about . . . what do you call it?"

"Art-magic. For as long as you've been a victim of this particular art-magic, this is how long you've been delusional about the gas station carnivals and all related phenomena."

"And how long is that?" asked Quisser, not quite sincerely.

"Since you humiliated the Crimson woman by calling her a *deluded no-talent*. I told you that she had connections you knew absolutely nothing about."

"I'm talking about something from my childhood, something

I've remembered my entire life. You're talking about a matter of weeks."

"That's because a matter of weeks is exactly the term that you've been delusional. Don't you see that through her art-magic she has caused you to suffer from the worst kind of delusion, which might be called a *retroactive* delusion. And it's not only you who has been afflicted in the past weeks and months. Everyone around here has sensed the threat of this art-magic for some time now. I'm beginning to think that I've found out about it too late myself, much too late. You know what it is to suffer from a delusion of the retroactive type, but do you know what it's like to be the victim of a severe stomach disorder? I've been sitting here in the Crimson woman's club drinking mint tea served by a waitress who is the Crimson woman's friend, thinking that mint tea is just the thing for my stomach when it very well may be aggravating my condition or even causing it to transform, in accordance with the principles of art-magic, into something more serious and more strange. But the Crimson woman is not the only one practicing this art-magic. It's happening everywhere around here. It drifted in unexpectedly like a fog at sea, and so many of us are becoming lost in it. Look at the faces in this room and then tell me that you alone are the victim of a horrible art-magic. The Crimson woman has quite a few adversaries just as she is connected with powerful allies. How can I say exactly who they are – some group specializing in art-magic, no doubt, but I can't say with a fatuous certainty, yes, it must be some particular gang of illuminati, or *esoteric scientists*, as so many have begun styling themselves these days."

"But it all sounds like one of you stories," Quisser protested.

"Of course it does, don't you think *she* knows that? But I'm not the one with that grotesque yarn about the gas station carnivals and the sideshow tent with a small stage not unlike the stage on the opposite side of this room. You can't keep your eyes off it, I see that and so can the other people around the room. And I know what you think you're seeing over there."

"Assuming *you* know what you're talking about," said Quisser, who was now forcing himself look *away* from the stage area across the room, "what am I supposed to do about it?"

"You can start by keeping your eyes off that stage across the room. There's nothing you can see over there except an art-magic delusion. There is nothing necessarily fatal or permanent about the affliction. Just as when you have a non-fatal physical disease, you must believe that you will recover, or you have a non-fatal psychic disease, from which you still must believe you will recover. Otherwise these diseases may turn into something far more deadly, because ultimately all diseases are magical diseases, especially your art-magic delusion."

I could now see that the intense conviction carried by my words had finally had its affect on Quisser. His gaze was no longer drawn toward the small stage on the opposite side of the room but was directed full upon me, distraught and quizzical in the face of the truth about his delusion. Yet he seemed to have settled down considerably.

I lit another of my mild cigarettes and glanced around the room, not looking for anything or anyone in particular but merely gauging the atmosphere. The tobacco smoke drifting through the club was so much thicker and the amber light was several shades darker, it seemed. The drone of exotic background music still mingled with the sound of raindrops against the black painted windows of the Crimson Cabaret. I was now back in the cabin of that old ship as it was being cast about in a vicious storm at sea, utterly insecure in its bearings and profoundly threatened by uncontrollable forces. Quisser excused himself to go to the rest room, and his form passed across my field of vision like a shadow through dense fog.

I have no idea how long Quisser was gone from the table. My attention became fully absorbed by the other faces in the club and the deep anxiety they betrayed to me, an anxiety that no doubt had a natural, existential source but also one that was caused by peculiar concerns of an uncanny sort. What a season is upon us, these faces seemed to say. And no doubt their voices would have spoken directly of certain peculiar concerns had they not been intimidated into weird equivocations and *double entendres* by the fear of falling victim to some kind of unnatural affliction that had made so much trouble in the mind of the art critic Stuart Quisser. Who would be next? What could a person say these days, or even think, without feeling the dread of repercussion from powerfully connected groups and individuals? I could almost hear their voices asking, "Why here, why now?" But of course they could have just as easily been asking, "Why not here, why not now?" It would not occur to this crowd that there were no special rules involved; it would not occur to them, even though they were a crowd of imaginative artists, that the whole thing was simply a matter of random, purposeless terror that converged upon a particular place at a particular time for no particular reason. On the other hand, it would also not have occurred to them that they might have wished it all upon themselves, that they might have had a hand in bringing certain powerful forces and connections into our district simply by wishing them to come. They might have wished and wished for an unnatural evil to fall upon them but, for a while at least, nothing happened. Then the wishing stopped, the old wishes were forgotten yet at the same time gathered in strength, distilling themselves into a potent formula (who can say!), until one day the terrible season began. Because had they really told the truth, this artistic crowd might also have expressed what a sense of meaning (although of a negative sort), not to mention the vigorous thrill (although of an excruciating type), this season of unnatural evil had brought to their intolerable lives.

It was during the moments that I was looking at all the faces in the Crimson Cabaret, and thinking my own thoughts about those faces, that a shadow again passed across my foggy field of vision. While I expected to find that this shadow was Quisser, my table-companion for that evening, on his way back from his trip to the rest room, I instead found myself confronted by the waitress whom Quisser had claimed was so loyal to the Crimson woman. She asked if I wanted to order yet another cup of mint tea, in saying it in exactly these words, *yet another cup of mint tea*. Trying not to become irritated by her queerly sarcastic tone of voice, which would only have further aggravated my already queasy stomach, I answered that I was just about to leave for the night. Then I added that perhaps my friend wanted to drink yet another glass of wine, pointing across the table to indicate the empty glass Quisser had left behind when he excused himself to use the rest room. But there was no empty wine glass across the table; there was only my empty cup of mint tea. I immediately accused the waitress of taking away the empty wine glass while I was distracted by my reverie upon the faces in the Crimson Cabaret. But she denied ever serving any glass of wine to anyone at my table, insisting that I had been alone from the moment I arrived at the club and sat down at the table across the room from the small stage area. After a thorough search of the rest room, I returned and tried to find someone else in the club who had seen the art critic Quisser talking to me at great length about his gas station carnivals. But all of them said they had seen no one of the kind.

Even Quisser himself, when I tracked him down the next day to a hole-in-the-wall art gallery, maintained that he had not seen me the night before. He said that he had spent the entire evening at home by himself, claiming that he had suffered some indisposition – some *bug*, he said – from which he had since fully recovered. When I called him a liar, he stepped right up to me as we stood in the middle of that hole-in-the-wall art gallery, and in a tense whisper he said that I should "watch my words". I was always shooting off my mouth, he said, and that in the future I should use more discretion in what I said and to whom I said it. He then asked me if I really thought it was wise to open my mouth at a party and call someone a *deluded no-talent*. There were certain persons, he said, that had powerful connections, and I, of all people, he said, should know better, considering my awareness of such things and the way I displayed this awareness in the stories I wrote. "Not that I disagreed with what you said about you-know-who," he said. "But I would not have made such an open declaration. You *humiliated* her. And these days such a thing can be very perilous, if you know what I mean."

Of course I did know what he meant, though I did not yet understand why he was now saying these words to me, rather than I to him. Was it not enough, I later thought, that I was still suffering a terrible stomach disorder? Did I also have to bear the burden of another's delusion? But even this explanation eventually fell to pieces upon further inquiry. The stories multiplied about the night of that party, accounts proliferated among my acquaintances and peers concerning exactly who had committed the humiliating offense and even who had been the offended party. "Why are you telling me these things?" the Crimson woman said to me when I proffered my deepest apologies. "I barely know who you are. And besides, I've got enough problems of my own. That bitch of a waitress here at the club has taken down all my paintings and replaced them with her own."

All of us had problems, it seemed, whose sources were untraceable, crossing over one another like the trajectories of countless raindrops in a storm, blending to create a fog of delusion and counter-delusion. Powerful forces and connections were undoubtedly at play, yet they seemed to have no faces and no names, and it was anybody's guess what we – a crowd of deluded no-talents – could have possibly done to offend them. We had been caught up in a season of hideous magic from which nothing could offer us deliverance.

More and more I found myself returning to those memories of gas station carnivals, seeking an answer in the twilight of remote rural areas where miniature merry-go-rounds and ferris wheels lay broken in a desolate landscape. But there is no one here who will listen even to my most abject apologies, least of all the Showman, who may be waiting behind any door (even the rest room of the Crimson Cabaret). And any room that I enter may become a sideshow tent where I must take my place upon a rickety old bench on the verge of collapse. Even now the Showman stands before my eyes. His stiff red hair moves a little toward one shoulder, as if he is going to turn his gaze upon me, and moves back again; then his head moves a little toward the other shoulder in this neverending game of horrible peek-a-boo. I can only sit and wait, knowing that one day he will turn full around, step down from his stage, and claim me for the abyss I have always feared. Perhaps then I will discover what it was I did – what any of us did – to deserve this fate.

THOMAS TESSIER

Ghost Music
A Memoir
by George Beaune

THOMAS TESSIER IS A playwright and poet and the author of several acclaimed novels of terror and suspense. These include *The Fates*, *The Nightwalker*, *Shockwaves*, the World Fantasy Award-nominated *Phantom*, *Finishing Touches*, *Rapture*, *Secret Strangers* and his latest, *Fog Heart*. His short stories have appeared in numerous anthologies, including *Lethal Kisses*, *Dark Terrors 2*, *The Year's Best Fantasy and Horror* and *The Best New Horror*.

Educated at University College, Dublin, he spent seven years in London, where he was a regular contributor to *Vogue* and involved with the publishers Millington. He now lives in his native Connecticut, where he is at work on a new novel.

"I first heard Peter Warlock's music around four o'clock on the FM, an eerie, haunting song called 'Balulalow'," recalls the author. "It made me an instant fan, and I found that Warlock's life was almost as extraordinary as his compositions, which drew on and were heavily influenced by old English music.

"Ghosts are at least as much about *us* as they are about themselves. The whole question of influences in both art and life is endlessly fascinating, and 'Ghost Music' is another little take on it."

I NEVER WANTED TO tell this story, but there's no longer any point in sitting on it. I'd like to think that it might serve as a very small footnote to a very small entry in music history, but that seems rather unlikely.

Does anyone still remember Eric Springer?

Do you know who Mandy Robbins was?

A couple of months ago I was skimming *The Times* and saw the brief news item about the train wreck south of Cairo. The usual disaster in an under-developed country, dozens of people dead. I took it in and quickly passed on without a second thought, but a short while later I received a telephone call from an old friend in London. Did I know that Mandy Robbins was on that train, and had died in the crash? I was stunned. No one had heard from her in ages, though at various times rumour had it that she was living in a dark apartment in Buenos Aires, or a tiny cabin in a remote Norwegian fishing village, or a villa on a resort island in the Adriatic. But no one really knew, and after a while the stories dried up. We all more or less forgot about her, or we filed her away among our less happy memories – with Eric.

Mandy Robbins was *en route* to Luxor when the train accident occurred. Twenty years later, she was still running.

I live in Dutchess County now, about seventy miles north of Manhattan. I edit (and write most of) *Tonal/Atonal*, a monthly newsletter. My articles and reviews also appear in several other publications that cover twentieth century music, and my monographs on Hartmann and Lutoslawski have sold well to libraries throughout the world. I'm working on Arvo Part now, and I teach a course at the local high school. It all adds up to a reasonable income and I suppose I'm happy enough in my A-frame. I own about 5,000 CDs, records and tapes, as many books, a superb stereo system, and I occasionally have an affair with a divorcee.

You know, it *is* life.

But in 1976 I was living in London and I sincerely believed in the importance of great art, literary and musical. There were classics, old and modern, and they truly mattered – perhaps more than anything else. A new composition by Berio was greeted as an event of quasi-religious significance. Art was in some ways more real than life itself, I thought. Back then, I hadn't yet given up on myself, though I was already beginning to cobble together a sideline career as a commentator rather than a composer.

Eric Springer was an old friend with more talent and better luck. I was thrilled when he wrote to say he'd be coming to stay in London for several months. We hadn't seen each other in a while, though we kept in touch with postcards. Eric's "Variations for Piano and Oboe" had been heard on a late-night FM station in California by a young producer who decided to use it in his next film. *No-Hopers* was a cult success and the soundtrack sold quite well. Eric had already earned a measure of critical praise as a promising young composer, but now he had the added pleasure of an unexpected payoff from the world of popular entertainment.

He was coming to London to write a quartet, commissioned by the Claymore Foundation, and to be with the new love of his life. Mandy Robbins was then twenty-three, attempting a comeback in a career that had never quite happened. She'd been a bright young prospect as a violinist at the age of fourteen, but the assorted stresses of high expectations, touring, and family problems had combined to derail her. At eighteen, she packed it all in and took a couple of years off to put her life in order. Then she began slowly and carefully to make her way back as a performer.

By the spring of 1976 she had done well enough to have a new agent and a challenging but very sweet job: she would perform the Berg Violin Concerto at the upcoming Proms. A friend and wealthy patron offered her the free use of his house in London, and she intended to spend four months mastering the technically difficult and emotionally taxing composition. It would be her breakthrough concert. There was talk of a live recording, and a contract for studio albums later. Mandy would also be the star soloist at the début of Eric's quartet, sometime in the future.

Eric and Mandy, Mandy and Eric. When I met them at Heathrow in late April of 1976, the air seemed charged with the excitement of their romance and the dazzling music they were setting out to create. It all seemed to be coming together for both of them and I was swept up in it as well – happily so. I felt privileged to be the friend at hand.

They quickly settled into their new home, a Georgian brick house in one of the narrow streets behind Edwardes Square, on the edge of Kensington and Earl's Court. The owner had spent a small fortune renovating and redecorating, and it featured a music room with a Bosendorfer grand on which Eric could help Mandy rehearse, using a piano reduction of Berg's orchestral score. There was a separate den with a spinet in the converted basement, where Eric could work on his own composition.

It was ideal for them, and by happy coincidence I was living in a tiny flat behind Olympia, a short walk from their place. We spent a lot of time together in the early days, as I showed them around London, took them on pub outings, introduced them to Indian food, and helped them find some of the less obvious sites that they were interested in seeing – like the modest house in Chelsea where Peter Warlock came to his sad and lonely end, and the rather dreary old pile that Edward Elgar had lived in near the North End Road.

Eric and Mandy both took to London at once; they loved going for long walks around the city and soon began to talk about the possibility of finding an affordable place of their own after the Proms and staying on indefinitely.

I liked Mandy from day one. She was obviously intelligent, especially about music, though she wasn't nearly the compulsive talker on the subject that Eric and I were. She was petite, and still had a look of girlish prettiness about her, but you would occasionally catch a brief glimpse of adult sadness in her eyes when something was said that brought an unhappy memory to mind. I knew that she had struggled to escape a possessive father who'd attempted to control every aspect of her life and career; she was eventually successful in breaking away, but she still carried the emotional scars.

Most of the time, however, Mandy was buoyant and energetic, fun to talk to and be with, and it was very clear to me that she cared deeply for Eric – and that he felt the same about her. He had found her at exactly the right time in his life.

Eric was fast approaching thirty. He'd been something of a playboy for rather too long, and was in danger of being written off as an underachiever. He had never produced as much new music as some people felt he should. Now he was apparently making real progress at last. The movie success and the Claymore commission both helped enormously, but Mandy was the vital factor. She gave him love and a sense of stability, for what was perhaps the first time in his life. The two of them shared an ambitious vision — they wanted both greatness for each other in music, and to have a great love affair together forever.

Well, why not? At that age we all want everything, and we can't imagine why we shouldn't get it. I was beginning to sense my own limitations, but I still believed in Eric. And the first time I saw Mandy strike the violin strings with the edge of her hand in the famous "warm-up" of the Berg piece — a kind of firm but very delicate chopping motion, an incredibly difficult thing to do properly — I believed in her as well.

Eric and I were sitting on the small patio outside the *Lord Edwarde* one balmy evening a few weeks into their stay when I got the first indication that there were problems. Eric seemed to be distracted and had little to say. Mandy, who was not one for drinking, had stayed home to take a hot bath; lately, she was being bothered by aching muscles in her shoulders and legs. Eric said she was rehearsing too much, and there may have been a minor disagreement between them.

I was sympathetic, but I sensed there was something else on Eric's mind. He was a tall, sturdy guy, but that evening he sat hunched over his pint in a way that suggested defeat. He looked like one of the dazed old-timers at Ward's. He had even gone for three or four days without shaving, which was not his style. We chatted fitfully for a while, and then I asked about his quartet. If there was trouble, it had to be with the music.

"Want to read some of it?"

"Of course, I'd love to."

I'd been looking forward to the moment when Eric would show me some of his new work. He reached down and unzipped the slim briefcase he always carried with him, fished out a few sheets of music paper and handed them to me. He had a smile on his face, but there was something sour in it.

The first page bore the hand-printed title "Quartet" and the dedication "for Mandy". My eyes scanned down the page and across the staves. I was amazed. It was pre-Serial, in fact it seemed to be pre-Romantic — an altogether astonishing turn back to the past for a composer like Eric. Another shock: the quartet opened with a *basse danse*. It was incredible. Nothing in his previous work had ever looked in this direction. But I was going too fast to hear it in my mind. I started over again, caught it — and a tremendous sense of confusion washed through me.

"You're quoting Warlock," I said without looking up.

"Am I," Eric said with a hollow laugh.

"This is his Capriol Suite."

"I know."

It continued for the next five pages, what was then the only fairly well-known piece of music composed by Peter Warlock, circa 1926. The restless flurry of notes ended abruptly in the middle of the seventh page, with a large "X" scrawled across it, and the words SHIT SHIT SHIT.

"I don't understand," I said.

"Neither do I."

"Surely you don't mean to quote at this length, and here at the very beginning of your own work."

"No, of course not."

"Well . . . ?"

"I'll tell you what's really kind of scary about it," Eric said, staring at his pint. "I've worked on that for weeks, ever since we got here, but it was only the other day when I realized what it was. Until then I had no idea." He looked up at me. "I honestly thought it was all mine."

I let that pass for the moment because I couldn't think of a thing to say. All composers and writers are influenced by those who came before; as they mature they outgrow their influences and find their own voices, or else they come to a dead end. But this was not a case of excessive influence. Eric had Peter Warlock's music note for note, as far as I could tell.

"That's not scary. Embarrassing, maybe."

"Yes." He smiled sheepishly. "It is embarrassing."

What *was* scary, I thought but did not say, was that this was all he had to show for a month of steady work.

I told him not to listen to any other music (except the Berg that Mandy was practising) and to begin again on his quartet. We both knew that the history of great works of art is littered with false starts. Or as Edward Albee said, you nose around and nose around like a dog, until you find the right place to squat. Eric was clearly relieved when I brushed aside the incident.

Privately, I was disturbed, and I knew he was too. Why else would he even show me those self-damning pages? And how could it be explained? Eric had been living quietly with Mandy for all of that month, up to nothing worse than a few pints at night after a long day's work – and who could begrudge him that? I understood influence, but how anybody could virtually transcribe the work of another person and not know that they were doing it is beyond me. Yet I had no doubt Eric was being truthful.

A few days later, on the weekend, the three of us went up to Portobello Road and poked around among the flea market stalls. I didn't find anything, but Eric bought Mandy a lovely silver charm of a cat, sleek and vaguely Egyptian, with a fleck of amber inset as an eye. It came on a thin chain, and Mandy immediately put it around her neck. Mandy was very fond of cats, and if she and Eric stayed on in London they intended to get one.

We had a pleasant pub lunch on Church Street, and while Eric was at the bar buying another round I asked Mandy how her work on the Berg concerto was coming along.

"The music's fine, and I love it, but it's so demanding, and my body is behind schedule." She sipped her spritzer (as usual, the only one that she would have). "My legs get very sore after I've been standing for a while, and I seem to get tired quickly." I nodded. For the concert soloist, physical training and stamina are every bit as important as they are for the athlete. "But I'm following an excellent programme of exercises, so hopefully I'll be in peak condition by the end of August."

"Good. I'm sure you'll be fine," I told her. "And how is Eric's work? He seems cheerful enough, but he hasn't said very much to me about it."

Mandy's face brightened. "I heard some of it last night and it was gorgeous. And I'm not just saying that, it really was the most beautiful music I've heard in ages."

"What was?" Eric asked before I could speak. He was back at the table with two fresh pints.

"The theme you were working on last night," Mandy said.

"Oh, yes." Eric smiled at me, looking pleased with himself. "She's right, too. It's the best thing I've ever done."

"Great," I responded. "I can't wait to hear it."

By the time we got back to their place, Eric and I were quite jolly with beer and Mandy was tolerantly amused. I insisted that they both give me at least a brief preview of their work before I tottered off home. Mandy took out her violin while Eric poured a very ordinary scotch for the two of us.

Some people don't like Alban Berg. They just don't get that whole second Viennese school. But I find his music heartbreaking, especially the Violin Concerto, his own farewell to life. Mandy nearly had me in tears within a few moments. She only played the final part, the adagio, but that was enough. She sat down with a wince and a groan, and put her feet up on a hassock. I told her how good she was, several times. Then Mandy and I badgered Eric to play a bit of his new music. It didn't take much. He seemed genuinely eager and he stepped briskly to the piano.

"Remember, it's just an idea I'm fooling around with," Eric told us. "And you must hear it in strings."

He began to play, taking up his theme and exploring it, much as a jazz musician will improvise around a song line. It was far from developed, still spare and skeletal – but Mandy was right, it was a gorgeous idea that just hinted teasingly at rich colours and deeply moving harmonies.

Eric played for about ten minutes. Mandy and I clapped, and he grinned as he flopped down in the armchair and reached for his whisky glass. I came up with some encouraging words and somehow managed to hide the huge distress I felt.

I still wasn't quite sure what he'd been playing, but I knew that I knew it – and it wasn't Eric Springer's music.

My knowledge of twentieth-century music is far from encyclopedic. I'm patchy on the Americans, Scandinavians, Russians, the Spanish and much of the rest of the world. But in 1976 I was really into British composers, particularly the more obscure ones lost in the enormous shadows cast by Vaughan Williams and Britten (since then I've concentrated on the Germans and East Europeans).

The next day I could still hear the theme in my head, and I began to work out what it might be. By late that afternoon, I at least had a pretty good idea of who the composer was. I dreaded speaking to Eric about it, but there was no choice in the matter. I rang and asked if I could stop by, knowing that was the time of day he usually finished working.

When I got there, Mandy was out and Eric was ready to go for a walk and a pre-dinner pint. That was fine with me, but first I had him play the theme for me again. He had developed it quite a bit in only twenty-four hours, but hearing it again merely served to confirm my suspicions. While we were out walking I spoke in a general way about the music and how it was so different from his previous work. We went to the *Britannia* in Warwick Road.

"Now," I said after we'd taken our first sip of Young's, "I have to tell you what I don't like about it."

"Okay, fire ahead."

"It's by Ernest Moeran," I said. Eric stared at me as if he couldn't believe what I'd just said. "I'm pretty sure it's from his String Trio, composed in 1931. That, or his Violin Sonata of 1923. Anyhow, I'm certain it's E.J. Moeran."

"I've never even heard of him," Eric insisted anxiously, his face flushed and agitated. "And I'm damn sure I've never heard a note of his music."

"I believe you, but . . ."

"You must be wrong, you've got to be."

"Check it out yourself," I said. "And do it before you play or show that music to anyone else, because you'll be embarrassed, and you might even find yourself with legal problems."

"Jesus." Eric sat back, worried and subdued. "What's going on here?"

"I don't know."

"Who the hell is Ernest Moeran?"

"A minor English composer," I explained. "Born 1894, died 1950. A few of his works are of real, lasting quality. He's the kind of composer I love to find, overlooked by most people." At that point, I hesitated. But I had to go on. "When I first got into Peter Warlock seriously a couple of years ago, I came across Moeran. He and Warlock were very close friends."

Eric stared at me.

I did not tell him the saddest details of all about Ernest Moeran. We never got around to them, or maybe I just didn't want to risk making matters worse for Eric. In 1950, at the age of fifty-five, on one of his many trips to Ireland, Moeran was found dead in a river, apparently the victim of a heart attack. In 1926, Moeran had a colossal failure – he could not complete work on a symphony that had been commissioned by the Halle Orchestra.

His friendship with the remarkable, but very strange, Peter Warlock had nearly destroyed Moeran's life while he was still a young man. In fact, there were people who knew them both and who believed that the best thing that ever happened to Moeran was the mysterious death of Warlock himself in 1930.

I didn't see Eric again until the end of the following week. I knew he would need some time to sort himself out, and I had to put my own thoughts in order – or at least try. I used the time to do a bit of research on Peter Warlock, but that didn't help me understand what was happening with Eric. The only explanation I could come up with was that he had to be going through some kind of mental breakdown. That he did know the Moeran piece, as he'd admitted he knew the Warlock, and he had begun to re-compose them both in the mistaken belief that they were his own – as a result of some deep confusion or psychological crisis.

But, aside from the music itself, I had seen nothing in his habits or behaviour that would support such a theory. He appeared to be fine in all other respects, and Mandy had given no hint of troubles with him. All I could think was that something bizarre happened whenever he sat down at the piano to compose – perhaps the pressure to justify such an important commission became too great to handle and his mind lurched off on its own, dredging up music he knew but dissociating it from its source.

Every Friday I spent a couple of hours at Bush House editing and polishing the English translations of *émigré* texts broadcast on the BBC World Service. It was a handy job, and it eventually led to my interest in the so-called dissident composers from the Eastern Bloc, like Gorecki.

Eric phoned, knowing I'd probably be there. He asked me to meet him at a place called the *New Ambassador Club*, which turned out to be a humble drinking den up one flight of stairs on Orange Street. I have no idea how Eric found such a place, or became a member, but he was at the last table at the back.

I almost didn't recognize him. The four-day stubble was now about two weeks old and had been shaved down to form an emerging goatee and a disconnected moustache. That was startling enough in itself, because Eric had never sported facial hair. But he also looked thin and gaunt, his skin was grey and his eyes were tired. Obviously he wasn't eating or sleeping properly.

"All right," he said, after fetching some ale. "I've got a problem. I know I heard Warlock last summer at the Hartt School. Maybe it was the music, or his odd name, but I was curious to see the place where he died shortly after we got here."

"Yes."

"And maybe Moeran was on the same concert programme. I don't remember it, but maybe he was. That has to be what happened – how else would I pick up their music?"

"I'm inclined to agree."

"But that kind of music doesn't even interest me," Eric said with exasperation. "It never has. Tone-colour, lyrical harmonies and the old modes. It's an *old* language."

"I know," I said. "That's never been your style."

"So why is that all I can do now? When I sit down and write or when I fool around on the piano, the only thing that comes out is that kind of music. And then I realize what it is, and I have to throw it out and start all over again."

"Do some exercises in dissonance," I suggested.

"I've tried," Eric told me. "But whenever I consciously try to set off in a particular direction I immediately come to a dead end. I get nowhere." He leaned across the table and spoke in an urgent voice. "I've been here going on two months now, and I've written nothing of my own. Not one note."

"It sounds like writer's block," I said sympathetically. "I guess the only thing you can do is to keep working until you work your way out of it. And you will, sooner or later."

Eric looked as if he didn't entirely believe me. In fact, I wasn't sure I believed it myself. Eric had another theory. The success of the movie soundtrack had somehow leached away at his self-confidence. He was afraid of not being taken seriously, of being dismissed as a popular hack. His quartet would be an easy target for that charge from people who resented his windfall, and fear of this was now blocking him creatively.

There may have been a small grain of truth in what he said, but there was also a large blob of paranoia. The music community didn't follow him that closely. Eric was just one of many young composers with true potential but a tenuous hold on the art, and he was not yet the focus of widespread interest.

"That's a stretch," I told him. "The movie money started to come in a couple of years ago. It's in the past now, so you can forget about it. And there's no point in worrying about what the critics will say about the quartet until you finish it. You have a massive case of self-consciousness, that's all, and the way out of it is to keep working. You'll break through."

Eric thought about that for a few moments and then he said, "Tell me more about Peter Warlock."

"This is not really about Peter Warlock," I said. "This is all about you, and your music."

"I know," Eric replied. "Still . . ."

"Well, he was a brilliant scholar and a very good composer," I said. "Some of his songs are among the best in English music. He was born in 1894, and his real name was Philip Heseltine. But his music criticism offended so many people that when he came to publish his own music, he decided it would be best to use a pseudonym. No one – "

"Look at that," Eric interrupted. "He was so worried about what people would say that he took another name."

"Yes, but it didn't work. People soon knew that Warlock was Heseltine. By the way, nobody seems to know how he came up with that name, but he had a strong interest in the occult and there were stories about experiments with Satanism and drugs. Warlock certainly had his darker side. Some people remember him as being distinctly sinister and he was prone to extended drinking binges. E.J. Moeran was so much under Warlock's influence that he shared a place with him for a while, but eventually he realized that the lifestyle was destroying his work and ruining his health, and he had to get out. But there were other people who said that Peter Warlock was essentially warm and caring, a very good friend, and that his occasional outbursts of wildness were merely a release from the intense pressure of work. When it came to his music, it seems he was a hard taskmaster on himself."

"Why did he kill himself?" Eric asked.

"We can't be sure he did. The gas valve was very loose, and it may be that he stretched out for a nap and a leak did him in. On the other hand, his personal life was troubled, his finances were always in bad shape, he suffered bouts of depression, and he thought he was a failure. His music bucked the trends of the day – this was 1930 – and he thought he was going nowhere. He did mention suicide to a few friends and later they regretted not taking him seriously. The inquest returned an open verdict, but that was probably an act of kindness. From all the evidence, it certainly does look like suicide."

"He was what, thirty-six?"

"Right, and it's only just in the last few years that people have started listening to him again and liking what they hear. He had an intense, charismatic personality, there's no doubt about that. Most people who met him either hated and feared him, or else they simply adored him."

"Hmmm." Eric shrugged. "Sometimes I think there's a weird story behind every composer who ever lived – except Sibelius, of course." I laughed. "Warlock sounds as peculiar as they come, but what he has to do with me, I have no idea."

"I'll tell you one more thing about him."

"What?"

"He was tall, like you," I said. "Some people described him as Mephistophelean in appearance. I've seen a photograph of him, and they're right about that. He had a moustache and goatee, just like the ones you've sprouted."

Events got in the way and I wasn't able to see Eric or Mandy for another two or three weeks after that. I did speak to him on the phone once and he assured me that he was at last beginning to make a little headway with his work. He sounded distracted and I took that to mean that his mind was entirely on his music. The next time I called I spoke to Mandy. Eric was out. He went out every day late in the afternoon and came back late at night, usually in a boozy state. When he worked, the music she heard was not music at all, just doodling at the keyboard. She was worried.

A few days later she rang and asked if I knew where he might be. She was in a state, and I got the impression that he had not been home at all the night before – or if he had, he'd gone out again. It was early evening and she couldn't stand waiting there alone, not knowing where he was or when he might return. I tried to calm her down and promised to look for him.

I didn't think there were very many places Eric might wander to, since he still wasn't terribly familiar with London. I tried his little drinking club in Orange Street first. He wasn't there but the large woman behind the bar told me that he had left about an hour ago, with a lady friend.

I tried the *French* and a couple of other pubs in Soho before I found him at the *Colony Club*. It was even drabber than the *New Ambassador*, but it had a better clientele – literary publishers, freelancers, the art crowd arrayed lovingly around Francis Bacon and Lucien Freud.

Eric was off in a corner at a typically rickety table with a woman dressed entirely in black. She had a long, horsey face, and long, straight blonde hair. Her name was Gillian, or Francesca. They were both moderately pissed and they each thought the other was wonderfully amusing, I most amusing of all. It took me one round of drinks and not much effort to detach Eric, and I got him into a taxi. He was humming like a tractor, but unfortunately it was nothing more exalted than the refrain from "Lola".

"What the hell are you doing?"

"I'm turning into Peter Warlock." He laughed.

"No you're not," I told him. "You're just acting like a big child – dodging your work, leaving Mandy alone for hours on end. It's stupid, Eric, stupid and uncalled for."

"Maybe he's taking me over." Another laugh.

"Why would he bother?" I snapped. "Peter Warlock is resting happily in his grave, his reputation is secure."

It turned out to be a vicious remark and I was immediately sorry I'd made it. We were miserably silent the rest of the way. I went in with him to say hello to Mandy. Eric smiled and gave her a kiss on the cheek, and then sloped off down to his study in the basement. Mandy was in tears, obviously not in the mood for much talk. The front room was a bit messy and I noticed that she was still moving very stiffly.

"Where was he?"

"Having a drink at a club with Francis Bacon." It's amazing how you can find the gloss when you need it. "Wait till tomorrow to have a chat with him. I'll do the same in a day or two. He's just having a hard time getting going with the quartet, but he'll snap out of it soon enough."

"I hope so."

"You'll see."

"George, thank you so much."

"Not at all. How're you feeling, love?"

"Otherwise?" A faint sardonic smile. "Still sore and achy, but I'll be okay. As soon as Eric gets back to normal."

I went straight round to the *Black Hart* in Earl's Court Road and had two quick shorts. There is a natural instinct to assume the best about our friends, and a concern about how much you can interfere in their lives before you go a little too far and they shut you out. I feared greatly for Eric – that he was using his music troubles as an excuse to fritter away his time on clubbing, boozing and chatting up the girls. He could easily wake up one morning soon and find that he'd blown the Claymore commission and lost Mandy, and I couldn't imagine how he would recover from two such devastating, self-inflicted failures.

I walked home that night trying to figure out how I might be able to get through to Eric, to shake him out of his funk without alienating him. I had no idea that it was already far beyond me. Even now, looking back twenty years later, I wonder. Weren't the signs all there, waiting to be seen? Shouldn't I have known what was really going on? But I didn't see, I didn't know – or if I did, some part of me must have been unwilling to face it.

Eric seemed subdued when I met him two days later. He had a slightly dishevelled look about him, his clothes were rumpled and his hair was brushed back in slick clumps that tended to separate and dangle down on the side of his face until he shoved them back again. Eric wanted to go for a pint but I wouldn't, so we sat in the sun at Holland Park, which only made him look more bedraggled and forlorn.

I can't remember much of what we said, but it wasn't of any special importance. I was going to Italy for a few days to do an interview with Luigi Nono. Eric gave me some very good questions to ask, which showed that his critical thinking was still in fine form, and that cheered me somewhat.

He didn't attempt to explain or apologize for the evening I brought him home from the *Colony*. He didn't refer to it at all, and neither did I: I've never seen any point in rehashing boorish or childish behaviour. Since then, of course, I've often wondered about everything we left unsaid.

I wish I'd given in a little and gone along to the *Britannia* or the *Black Hart* with him for a pint. But I wasn't in the mood, I was trying to discourage him from the beer, and we always want to believe there will be time for another pint, another day. But when we parted on the High Street a short while later, it was the last time I saw Eric Springer alive.

I rang them two or three times after I returned from Italy, but no one answered the phone. I meant to go around, but I had a number of assignments to catch up with, and so the days stretched into a week. It was about eleven o'clock one morning when I got the call. At first the voice was so faint that I almost hung up, thinking no one was there. But then I caught it – not much more than an exhalation.

"Mandy? Is that you?"

"Can you . . . help me."

"I'll be right there."

I'd never heard a human voice sound so weak and helpless. I think I ran all the way from my flat to their house. I tried the door at once and found it unlocked. I shouted for both of them as I went into the front hallway, but got no response.

The front sitting-room was empty, and the main music room as well – I hesitated there just long enough to glance at the loose pages of sheet music scattered around the place, hoping that some of it might be Eric's quartet, but it was the Berg score. Plates of half-eaten fast food had been left on the floor and perched on the arms of chairs, looking as dry and hard as wax imitations.

I hurried downstairs to the room where Eric worked. It was dark, and there was a damp chill in the air. It reeked of stale tobacco. I turned on a table lamp and saw some ashtrays full of cigarette butts. There were a couple of virtually new pipes on a side table. Eric had never smoked, and I was sure I'd never told him that Peter Warlock did, both cigarettes and a pipe.

There were no books, tapes or records in the room, it was as simple and austere as a monk's cell. A chaise – for one frantic second I thought I saw Eric stretched out on it, the thin blanket tucked up under his chin, just as they found Peter Warlock. Eric wasn't there, but there were more loose sheets of music scattered all over the place. Each page was clean and unmarked, lined with blank staves that lanced my heart.

Just as I got back to the ground floor, I heard a noise from upstairs. I found Mandy in the main bedroom. She was curled up beneath a sheet, barely conscious. Her face was desperately pale and her hair clung to her face in sweaty snarls. She saw me, but she didn't seem to register who I was.

"Help . . . Eric . . ."

"It's all right, love," I told her. "Eric's not here at the moment. He must have gone out."

"Eric . . ."

"No, it's George," I said with a grin. I sat on the edge of the bed and stroked her face lightly. "You're not well, are you? Have you seen a doctor?"

"George." Her eyes found me then. "I can't move."

"Why – "

At that moment I noticed Mandy's legs poking out from under the sheet, and I was horrified. Her toes were curled tightly and her calves appeared to have shrivelled. I pushed the sheet up and saw the same slack and wasting flesh all along the lower part of her thighs. I could barely find words to speak.

"Mandy, what – "

It was absurd, but thoughts of Berg and his "Violin Concerto" suddenly swarmed in my mind. The piece Mandy had been preparing to play in the last week of the Proms. I've always thought of it as Berg's farewell to life, since it was all about both life and death, and Berg died (his own bizarre, absurd death) within a few months of completing it.

But there was another person involved. Manon Gropius, the lovely young daughter of close friends and a special favorite of Berg's. At the age of eighteen, just before Berg was commissioned to write the Concerto, Manon lost her long and heroic battle against the ravages of polio. Berg was deeply moved, and dedicated the Concerto to her – "to the memory of an angel".

Now, staring at Mandy's legs, I felt a confusion that seemed to boil up out of my bones and surge through me, leaving me dazed and paralyzed. Finally I heard Mandy's faint voice again.

"Save Eric."

"He's not – "

"The kitchen."

I seemed to come back into my own body then and I raced down the stairs. I hadn't even thought of checking the kitchen at the rear of the ground floor. It had a gas stove. The door wouldn't budge. I was sure I could smell gas. As I rattled the doorknob uselessly, I noticed something hanging from it. The thin silver chain with the charm that Eric had bought for Mandy at Portobello Road, the Egyptian cat with the amber eye.

In a moment of awful certainty, I knew I'd never told Eric the single most revealing detail about Peter Warlock's death, the sign that strongly pointed to suicide rather than an accident. A few minutes before he stretched out on the chaise and tucked the blanket up beneath his chin, Warlock had taken his cat and put it safely outside the room. It was the cat's frightful wailing and mewing that eventually drew the landlady's attention.

I got Mandy out first. While the neighbours looked after her and alerted the police and fire brigade, I went back for Eric. I expected the house to blow up at any moment. I took a chair and smashed the kitchen window, unlocked the outside door, got in and turned off the gas. I waved a towel around, trying to clear the air. I had to step outside twice to overcome dizziness, but then I was finally able to go to Eric.

He was slumped back in a chair, his head pointing north, his feet crossed at the ankles and propped on the edge of the wooden table. He looked for all the world like someone who'd just dozed off while waiting for the kettle to boil.

But his lips and cheeks were as red as a tanager, and there was about his mouth the slightly bemused smile of the dead.

I visited Mandy at St Mary Abbot's Hospital, and I saw her again shortly before she left London. She recovered quickly from what the doctors said was probably a psychosomatic illness. She wasn't having any of that and neither was I, but there seemed no point in trying to argue otherwise – with anyone.

Mandy and I, sadly, found that we had little to say to each other. It was as if we both wanted, or needed, to retreat from a terrible experience we had shared unwillingly. I felt more than a little guilty for not paying serious attention to what had been happening to her, so preoccupied was I by Eric's situation. She scratched the Proms, of course, and disappeared. I have no idea whether any of the rumours I occasionally heard about her over the years were true, but she never performed in public again.

If Eric Springer is remembered at all today – by people who never knew him – it is probably not as the promising composer of the plaintive and Webernist "Variations for Piano and Oboe", but as the composer of a sweetened-up movie theme based on it.

Notes

"(his own bizarre, absurd death)"
Not long after he completed his great "Violin Concerto", Alban Berg (1885–1935) suffered an insect bite on the back. From neglect or mistreatment, it formed an abscess. Berg was so poor

at the time that he and his wife attempted to lance it themselves. They used toenail scissors. Berg's condition worsened steadily and he died soon after he finally entered a hospital. No effort was made to determine the exact cause of his death but it was most likely due to blood poisoning.

"To those whom God has forsaken is given a gas-fire in Earl's Court." – Patrick Hamilton, *Hangover Square*

I came across this line several years after Eric's death, and for obvious reasons it made a deep impression on me.

Hamilton is probably best-known as the author of the plays *Rope* and *Gaslight*. He hated the movies that were based on them. His novel *Hangover Square* is set in Earl's Court on the eve of World War II. It ends with the hero killing two people and then taking his own life – by gas – after leaving a note asking the police to look after his cat. Oddly enough, when the novel was filmed, this character, who had nothing whatsoever to do with music, was transformed into a homicidal composer.

Years earlier, Hamilton had been struck by a car and seriously injured. He recovered but his face was disfigured. He took to wearing a grotesque artificial nose for a while. This accident contributed enormously to the alcoholism that eventually killed him. It occurred in the narrow side street directly behind the house in which Eric Springer died, years later.

G.B.

GREGORY FROST

That Blissful Height

GREGORY FROST IS THE author of four published novels. Three – *Lyrec*, *Táin* and *Remscela* – are fantasies, and have been compared favourably with the works of T.H. White and Evangeline Walton. The fourth novel, *The Pure Cold Light*, is a work of science fiction, and was a semi-finalist for the 1994 Nebula Award.

His shorter work has appeared in many of the major fantasy and SF magazines as well as various anthologies, most recently in *White Swan, Black Raven*, edited by Ellen Datlow and Terri Windling. In 1996 he was principal researcher on an episode of Discovery Global Network's series, *Science Frontiers*, entitled, "Wolf Man: The Myth & the Science". At present, he's writing a non-fiction book and undertaking a large fantasy project, "Shadowbridge", the first story of which recently appeared in *Asimov's Science Fiction Magazine*.

Regarding "That Blissful Height", the author explains: "This story evolved as a result of my wife's wish to take the historical tour of Independence Park in Philadelphia, where I encountered a portrait of Robert Hare. The plate identifying him mentioned that he had invented "the spiritoscope". I wrote this down, and later found most of his books and articles in the special collections section of the University of Pennsylvania, where he chaired the Chemistry Department in the 1830s. I sat on the data for over a year while I finished an SF novel. I had to write a story for John Kessel's Sycamore Hill workshop, and decided to use the material to fashion a tale that paralleled my own experience reading Hare's 1855 book, *Experimental Investigation of the Spirit Manifestations*. I revised it from comments received in the workshop, in which related anthology it appeared.

"However, as it happens, that turns out not to be the end of the story. The material on Hare has gotten under my skin to such an extent that I'm writing a non-fiction book called *Spirits of the Dead* about American Spiritualism in general and Hare in particular, which in itself is already producing weird potential shoots – a collaborative short story with Michael Swanwick, and a steampunk novel in progress. God knows where it will end."

Populus vult decipi . . . decipiatur!

I Post Trance

"THINK OF ME," THE child's voice fades, "as you do a gentle moonbeam . . ." The medium's arms spread as wide as her dark hoop skirt and she sinks down until her head presses against the rosewood breakfast table. Its tip-up top wobbles slightly from palm to palm as if the securing bolt has loosened and is about to flip it vertically. Mercifully – not for the woman, but for the couple who hang upon her every gesture – it does not.

They are young, in their early twenties, still struggling to make their way in the world of 1850. The loss of their six-year-old daughter has been as cruel as anything can be; as cruel, thinks Robert Hare, as the loss of his own sister so long ago. Their misery has driven the poor couple, named Howitt, out of the objective sphere: their need to believe has become their universe. Is it truly the voice of their daughter that has emerged from the seemingly unconscious medium? How can anyone be certain when the girl has been dead so many months?

Hare recalls the words of the great Scottish philosopher Sir William Hamilton: "Is it unreasonable to confess that we believe in God, not by reason of Nature which conceals Him, but by reason of the supernatural in Man which alone reveals and proves Him to exist?"

If that question needs proving, here the proof lies. The weeping wife supplicating the Deity while her husband, pale and teary-eyed but determined to be the rock against which she can lean, gathers her up. The shoulder seam of his coat has begun to unthread.

At the sound of rustling skirts, the medium stirs. Her hands slide together and she pushes herself upright, disheveled hair wisping her forehead, her eyes shifting as if to re-establish her surroundings. Hare watches her with a skeptical eye. She composes herself in time to collect her fee from the dazed Mr Howitt before he can maneouver his wife through the door.

Once she has led the couple from the room, Hare glances at his friend, Joseph Hazard, positioned opposite him on the far side of the table in order to have a clearer view of the medium during the performance. Hazard cocks an eyebrow and shakes his head sadly as if to say, "Those pitiable people."

Hare rises from the mahogany side chair, what they call a wheelback chair, although the design it has pressed into his frock coat looks more like a spider's web than a wheel. All the chairs in the room bear this design.

The medium, Margaret Fox, returns from the foyer. She's a small woman, of shy and genteel character – not a low-class trickster as many of her peers seem to be. Because of this alone he finds it hard to dismiss her. Her color has lost its flush. She is composed as she takes her seat at the table, and smiles to both men with a sympathetic serenity. "They know now," she says, "that their girl is well and they need not be concerned." She clasps her hands. "Praise God, and it's as much as I ever hope for."

"You've helped them, you mean," says Hare.

"Can I do less, Professor Hare?" Her blue eyes sparkle.

"Retired, ma'am, near six years," he corrects her, although it's nice to hear the title now and again.

"I think it a good thing that such as yourself – a scientist, one who seeks for great truths – should open yourself to our small society."

"The society of spirits? Well, and I wish to believe, Miss Fox, that all this which Mr Hazard and I have witnessed *is* real."

Her brow creases for a moment, no more. "You entertain doubts even now?"

He bows slightly, his knees stiff from so long being seated. He is over seventy. "As you say, Miss Fox, I'm a scientist. For me there can be no absolutes."

"What about death, sir? Is that not an absolute – the certainty of death?"

"Yet," interjects Hazard, "while he must play the skeptic, I know he was moved, as was I, Miss Fox, and I'm certain he will return for another session with you."

"As will you?" she asks, a hint of coquetry beneath the words, so slight as to be disregarded given the absolute decorum she has maintained. She is so young, her gentle tease is but a trick played upon old men's vanities.

"Mayhaps, ma'am, another day." He adds, "Alas, *I* am not retired, and still must perform."

For an instant Hare stands apart from these two, and seems to hear them speaking some cloaked language, full of amatory import; but he knows better than to act on such indistinct supposition. He wouldn't even ask. Hazard would be shocked, and what can Hare know but that what he has inferred comes from within himself and not without? No, he can say nothing.

"Robert, come, I've my afternoon appointments yet to keep." Hazard turns.

The two men are shown out onto Arch Street. It's warm in the sun, positively an August heat on this late April day in Philadelphia. The door closes behind them and they climb down the five steps to the walk, as a carriage passes. Hazard signals to one further up the street and its reins flash. He won't allow Hare to walk anywhere, so concerned is he over his friend's condition. He is, Hare thinks, more like a mother hen than a lawyer.

Hazard turns to him. "Now you must tell me, you suspect what of Miss Fox?"

"Everything. The spiritualist is artful, perhaps by nature. Whether or not deceitful has yet to be established, but when I witness such a performance, when I see her come to her senses before her clients can elude her in their misery, what am I to make of it? I cannot *help* but suspect. There's not enough here to trust."

Hazard nods. "I tell you, Robert, I have seen tables caper, and ghosts display impossible knowledge through the use of alphabetic cards such as she manipulates, but in the face of it all remains the niggling doubt that some cunning is at work. I can prove nothing. Nothing in Margaret Fox's actions evinced deception. How, other than by supernatural means, *did* she know so much about the daughter, when I could find nothing near as much about the child through the legal process? Yet I began to wonder in the midst of the child's appearance if those people would have confirmed anything she said, however far it might be from true. Out of their suffering. And so –"

Hare takes hold of his arm. "Precisely, Joseph. What can you know from a woman pointing her fingers at a card full of letters?" He smiles conspiratorially. "To which end I have ordered materials for construction."

The carriage rolls to a stop before them. Hazard turns to help his friend, but Hare grabs hold of the splashboard rail and pulls himself up. "Materials? What would you do, Robert – box in your spirits?"

Hare takes his seat. "What would I do? Know absolutely the fate of –" his smile falls slack "– of them all." The carriage jerks forward and Hazard drops into the seat beside him.

It's the age of the supernatural. Ever since Walpole's *Otranto* ninety years earlier, Gothic subjects have freighted the literature, and matters wholly fantastic have been embraced by the greatest minds. Hare knows well that he's in good company.

As man is enveloped in systems of weather, he may also be surrounded by invisible and wondrous forces, most as yet undetermined save that their presence is detected. Mesmer's magnetic fluid, Franklin and Kinnersley's electricities; somnambulism, clairvoyance, mediumship – all are squintings into the inexpressible. Hare's own concentration – chemistry – promises similar revelations one day, and perhaps will tie the disparate elements of mind, body and energies together. Not simple-minded alchemical transubstantiation, no. More remarkable discoveries, which a generation other than his will behold – energies he can but imagine. And who knows but that a doorway will open between the corporeal and spirit realms? Are they alive who have gone before? Is his sister there, waiting for him? Dear, dear Anna – he must know.

He thinks: *As Mrs Crowe argued in her wonderful book,* The Night Side of Nature – *all phenomena must be open to the proofs of science, even if the means to prove do not yet exist. Not yet. But I have within me the capacity to change that. When I return to the world of the spiritualists, I will shake that world till the truth falls out. One way or the other, I will know.*

Enquiries thus far have already estranged former colleagues from the University of Pennsylvania, where he once chaired the School of Chemistry. What he proposes to investigate is deemed unworthy of serious contemplation. Not, mind you, blind acceptance; on the contrary, the mere contemplation of *possibility*.

When he plunged concentric coils of copper and zinc into troughs of muriatic acid, producing not only electricity but a heat intense enough to consume charcoal, they were not shocked, although the specifics of what was happening and why were not immediately known. Yet, when he turns to something that may be no less explicable, they turn their backs. Well, he's old, and has pried at one time or other into everything from chemistry to meteorology to banking, and don't forget the brewing of porter. He'll address former colleagues as he does the Christians, who have no trouble swallowing the camels of Scripture, yet dismiss Spiritualism, about which they know nothing. In the end, in print he'll declare his findings and let the findings speak. Proof he will offer, the requirement of science.

Of those scientists who once called him friend, only Seybert and Silliman remain allies. Seybert inadvertently pushed him in this direction years ago with questions regarding the afterlife. To the extent that Hare refuses to countenance divine revelation, he has regrettably alienated Silliman: how can anyone – Silliman in particular – accept on blind faith the validity of his religious inclinations while demanding absolute proofs about everything else? There can be no dichotomy of thought. *Everything* must submit to testing. Still, for all that they differ and will neither yield, he loves and respects Silliman. Though they don't speak any longer, it's to Silliman that his proof will be, however obliquely, proffered. Whatever the outcome, he must sway *someone*.

In the carriage, he surprises Joseph Hazard as he suddenly blurts out, "It's precisely as you say: the cards by which these guides communicate with their audience are unreliable under the best of conditions. Pushing a finger from letter to letter to spell out any word one chooses – how can rational men such as we countenance that? It requires a leap of faith across too vast a chasm. No more defensible than Bechworth's absurd argument that six to eight people gathered around a table produce an electric current capable of causing everything that's attributable to spirit phenomena." He laughs. "Do you think Bechworth ever in his life *beheld* an electric current? 'A dry wooden table,' I responded in my letter in the *Inquirer*, 'is very nearly a perfect non-conductor.' That fool."

Hazard agrees, somewhat edgily.

"You mention table motion – I'll tell you the substance of table motion: accumulated muscular force. It's as Faraday suggests: the hands upon the table do the actual moving. So long as there are hands upon the table, you and I and the rest will harbor doubts. I say: no hands upon the table then, no fingers upon a card." He waggles his own finger to emphasize.

Hazard ponders, lulled by the clopping of the horse's hooves. He remarks, "You would think, on the face of it, that Christians would *wish* the afterlife legitimized, wouldn't you?"

"Fah. The truth is they only want it to conform to what, without a shred of evidence, they already hold that it is. If anything, the Christians are worse than Bechworth. *They* ascribe all these goings on to Old Nick. If there is anything imaginary in the whole of these proceedings, it is the supposition that the phenomena are brought on by the interference of the devil. That – *that* is the sage opinion of a church that extirpated the Canaanites, the Albigenses, that created the *auto da fé*, the inquisition, the massacre of St Bartholemew, set the fires of Smithfield, roasted Servetus, and have persecuted even here Quakers and witches!" He could list many more examples, but speaks to the point: what could be more devilish than for God the creator to have created the Devil? The Devil is nothing more than a means for small men to disavow their own evil passions and disguise their own villainous handiwork."

Jumping from thought to thought like a child leaping stones to ford a stream, he then abruptly announces, "Comté is a fool to think that reliance upon scripture will magically shrink as science grows. Science would have developed already on this ghostly front and resolved it had not the entanglements of Biblical intolerance confounded every effort." He falls then into silence, his features apoplectic.

Hazard keeps still, but gives his friend a sidelong glance.

Hare's keen dark eyes smolder with the inner fire of his contemplation. His chin juts, the jaw clenches. It's a formidable profile – one befitting a Roman statue – and that has kept more than a few men from voicing unworthy opinions. Hazard knows him well enough to know such fear is groundless.

He has been friends with Robert Hare for many years. No

less hostile or arrogant man exists. Hare has always been so vivacious and agreeable in his conversation that he willingly gives opponents any opportunity for rebuttal while he soundly defeats their every objection as though he had run through it all before them. After which the opponent is respected for his attempt to scale the heights. There seems to be no subject with which he is unacquainted; but this one is different. This dark investigation stirs the old man's blood in ways that voltaic chemistry does not.

Hare has had his enemies – the early ones, like the Englishmen Clarke and Maugham, who tried to appropriate credit for his oxyhydrogen blowpipe, were thieves and ultimately revealed as such. Hare had only to hold his ground and let others vindicate him. That won't work here, Hazard knows.

This time, the people on his side are the ones about whom there are questions.

II The First Device

On a hot June morning, two men unload from the back of their wagon a canvas-draped object that ends in four beautifully turned table legs. Unlike a table, it bulges on one side, where the canvas is pushed up in an off-center hump. A woman holds open the door at 178 North Tenth Street to let them carry it up the steps and into the rowhouse.

Mrs Margaret B. Gourlay is of medium height, with dark hair pulled back into a large bun. She has a broad, handsome face just beginning to lose its definition. Her eyes are brown and warm: gentle and honest eyes. She is dressed very plainly in dark green, although the fullness of her brown skirt over cage-crinoline requires her to retreat from the door far enough to let the freightmen inside. They carry their burden into the parlor where her clients come.

Her husband, Dr Gourlay, stands in the doorway from the dining room and looks on in some bewilderment as the twine is untied and the canvas lifted, revealing an arcanely cobbled device. He watches the men tie a sinker weight to a vertical cord so that it hangs a few inches above the floor. A second, larger weight is tied to the end of a second line and set forward of the table like a small iron doorstop, the line stretched taut.

Finished, the men gather up the canvas and ropes, then wait

for money, although Hare has paid them at the loading. Dr Gourlay reluctantly tips them, not generously by any means, and, feigning indignation, they depart. His wife's voice echoes from the foyer.

He approaches the device with grave caution.

It is a lovely satinwood needlework table – or once was. Now, attached to the top, marring more than half of the veneer, sits a tall metal box with a steeply angled lid, a kind of enormous bread box. From the back of this emerges the cord on which the sinker weight ultimately dangles, but first the cord wraps around the spindle of a large wheel. The wheel hangs off the side of the table. It has letters inscribed around its rim: ZJWKERUCFH&ALUSMOP around the top half, GTNXOBIVD around the bottom. Where the spindle protrudes through the center of the wheel, the line from the iron counterweight attaches. There is also a thin metal rod that sticks up to mark which letter is to be read. At the moment it rests upon the letter "F".

The doctor circles the table. Around behind the wheel, the metal box is open. Inside it is some sort of lever. Gourlay leans on the table, bending slightly, and reaches to put his hand in the box and press the lever.

From the doorway, his wife says, "Don't."

The doctor straightens. "I was going to –" He stops, for he does not know what he intended. "Did you know of this ... this contraption of his? How it works?"

"No," she replies. "I've put my trust in Professor Hare as he has in me."

Her husband brushes his hand across the table as if in defiance of her. He turns smartly on his heel, sweeps up his gray stovepipe hat from the chairback settee where his wife's clients usually sit, and marches out of the parlor. "I shall refrain from interfering, of course, in *spiritual* matters," he tells her, then leaves the house. Mrs Gourlay waits until the vibrations of the front door have ceased reverberating before she sets foot in the parlor.

When Hare arrives some hours later, Mrs Gourlay meets him at the door in an excited state. "She's spoken to me," she tells him. "Come see, come see." And she leads him by the hand into the parlor. She has drawn a dining room chair to the table, on which she settles, her skirts billowing around her. "Look," she says. Hare takes a seat where he can read the wheel and watch the medium.

For a time she sits in seeming contemplation, her gaze unfixed. Then her eyelids flutter and close. She leans forward as her hands, within the box, begin to press upon the lever. The wheel answers her pressure, rolling clockwise in sluggish rotation. Around and around on its axle the wheel spins, stopping briefly, sometimes with difficulty, upon each letter in sequence, having to rotate around a full turn to spell the same letter twice. By then he knows; a cold apprehension suffuses him like a chemical reaction overflowing a flask. The medium doesn't seem to be aware. Her head is down. He can't see her eyes at all. She cannot be watching the wheel, and couldn't see the letters on its face in any instance.

The wheel spells out the fourth letter, the name ANNA. His sister's name. Mrs Gourlay's head remains lowered.

The wheel continues to spin another quarter hour, until he has recorded the message: ROBERT WELCOME. At that point, Mrs Gourlay exhales sharply and draws back from the device. Her head circles, coming upright. She opens her eyes and looks at him. "It is so difficult, so draining, to use this machine. But she came, did she not?"

"Who?"

"Your sister, Professor Hare."

"My sister?" He tries to seem unenthusiastic.

"Yes, that was her relation to you, I'm sure of it. A sister." She glances at the wheel. "You hadn't told me of your sister."

Had he though? No, he's quite certain he withheld everything. He replies, "I hadn't thought –" He had not dared hope.

"Your device is a most cumbersome thing to use. Levers and wheels."

Here's something he can speak to. "Cumbersome, yes. And yet you succeed in demonstrating its merit, Mrs Gourlay. More than that, I believe you've made a case here for the truth of your claims and those of other mediums. This is a great stride forward, do you have any idea? The first scientific validation of your craft, Mrs Gourlay. Exhausting or not, please apply yourself again to the spiritoscope, if you would be so kind."

"Spiritoscope." She stares apprehensively at the thing before replying. "I must tell you, sir, that it takes *all* my energy to maneouver it."

"*Your* energy?"

"Indeed, sir. 'Tis after all mine that the spirits utilize. Look how quickly I was drained. How quickly she withdrew from me – one message and no more. A card is very easy for them, as you can imagine. It takes but a finger." As she says this, she raises her index finger.

Precisely. That was the point. But now the point impedes. He wants only to hear from Anna again. He contemplates the machine awhile in silence.

Mrs Gourlay doesn't begin, and instead pushes her chair back from the table. "Might I offer you some tea, Doctor? I'm, myself, quite thirsty just now."

"Please," is all he says. His gaze does not shift from the table, even after she has risen and gone away.

He reconsiders the design of his spiritoscope. He has re-engineered everything he ever constructed – he modified the oxyhydrogen blowpipe a dozen times in twenty years to make it more efficient, even though the original was already the hottest heat source in the world. Nothing that is humanly engineered cannot be improved upon.

His father, the senior Robert Hare, was a brewer. *Hare's American Porter* was a superb ale, the most popular in Philadelphia at the turn of the century; yet he was forever working with the formula, experimenting with different roasts of malt the further to enhance the flavor. His son, apprenticed to him, assisted in much of the experimentation, from whence came his fascination with chemistry but also with sources of heat, with all that heat could do. The slightest increase or decrease in the temperature or duration of roasting of the malt changed the characteristics of the finished porter significantly – in many instances, beyond drinking. The younger Hare's mind raced along as it contemplated variables and cobbled a device to roast the malt faster, thus enabling his father to increase his output. The process existed; he refined it. As he will do here.

The problem served up by Mrs Gourlay is how to make working the spiritoscope easier without sacrificing the safeguards built into it. He can't communicate in two-word dribs and drabs like this. He dwells upon it to such an extent that he barely notices her return, doesn't see the china cup and saucer set before him, hardly recollects the tea, and only returns to his senses when she says to him, "You know, Professor Hare, I must tell you a thing I've sensed about you since first Miss Fox introduced us."

He finds he's perched on the edge of his chair. Tea steams

out of his cup. "What you sense about me," he repeats, as if the repetition will explain what she has said.

"Yes, sir."

He regards the tea as a fortune teller might before sipping it, as if it might yield a secret, and compresses his lips as he swallows the bitterness. "What would that be, ma'am?"

"Why, that you share the spiritualist's gift."

Whatever he thought she might say, this isn't it. "I'm sorry, I don't know that I understand you. Do you mean to imply I should be able to speak to them?"

"And they to you."

"How, then, do you explain that I have never in my life received any communication whatsoever from the spirit world? Even as I would have hoped and prayed to hear of the continuance of my sister, there was no rapping on walls, no shifting of furnishings." He abhors the suggestion. Hands trembling, he sets aside the cup. "Indeed, it is outrageous, madam."

"Oh, but, *sir*, you would not be aware. You have no training in the spiritualist's art. Your faculties lie dormant, untapped and untried. I and my spirit guide do both sense about you such powers, restrained, awaiting release, that with training –"

"Please, Mrs Gourlay, *no more!*" He waves her to silence. "I have in my time been a brewer, a chemist, a professor, an economist, and an inventor in all of these rôles." The thought slides in below his words: *and neglectful of her in all of them*. "I believe I have quite enough talents for a lifetime without adding spiritualism to the list. Especially –" he hesitates, wrestling his ire under control "– especially as the city is quite well populated with such like already. Inventors seem far less procurable." He stands, leaning upon the table for support. "And now, as the demonstration has exhausted you, Mrs Gourlay, I will be on my way. You've set me a fine challenge, to improve upon my invention. I'll consider it. But, I would like you to utilize the spiritoscope as much as possible. You may find it easier to maneouver as time goes on. Also, as I intend to publish my findings, you will likely find yourself with a clientele desirous to witness its demonstration."

Her smile as she sees him off is stiff – no doubt, he thinks, as a result of what he has said of her spiritualist compeers. But it's true: Philadelphia is a haven for spiritualists. There must be one for every street in the city. Mrs Gourlay has a reputation as one of the more upright of her kind ... which is to say that no one has ever caught her in a deception. That's why he chose her to receive the first machine. It was to be Margaret Fox, whom he no longer entirely trusts. But to suggest that he ought to practice spiritualism himself is —

"Is what?" he asks himself.

By the time he has been coached safely home, he has the answer.

"Terrifying. It is terrifying."

III Expansionism

He has dreams after his meeting with Mrs Gourlay in which his sister visits him. In one, she divides like a cell, becoming three of herself, in wide-striped skirts and puff-sleeved blouses, her long chestnut hair crimped and coiffured into chains encircling each of her heads. The nineteen-year-old sisters knock wooden balls across the lawn of the chemistry building with croquet mallets. He has a mallet, too, but the multiplicity of sisters play their game around him, never offering him a turn, as though they don't notice him in their midst. Annas enclose him; the wickets trip him up and like bear traps catch his ankles. The mallets clack familiarly as they strike. The croquet balls roll up against the posts and stop; there are three posts, and he thinks that this is wrong, there should be only two. The sisters pause over the balls, leaning on their mallets as they stare straight through him to one another in silent communion. If he could only move, if he could reach one and warn her, protect her. The wickets are driven through his legs, and when he tries for her, he totters and falls.

The instant he hits the ground he opens his eyes. His heartbeat hammers, his nightshirt is stuck, twisted, to him. He wipes spittle from his cheek and sits up in the darkness.

She was so close that he heard her skirt swishing as she strode about. What if she is always as near as that? He has no way to know.

For days and weeks afterward, intense dreams interrupt his cerebration and render him incapable of invention. He broods upon her, turns her over like a coin, each turn a painful remembrance.

She grew up a tomboy, fearlessly investigating what she was

not supposed to see, what girls were supposed to stay out of. She made him teach her conkers, a game that only boys ever played. They picked out chestnuts together, he advising her on the quality of each one she brought to him. He took the acceptable chestnuts, soaked them in vinegar awhile, and then nailed a hole through the light caps of six of them. After tying a bootlace through each, he left them dangling from a clothes peg beside her bed. Then he waited. The thrill of her squeal as she discovered what he had made for her still sped his heart. She came out of her room, the conkers clacking together, and she kissed him. With that kiss she transformed from the tomboy sister into Anna. Anna, the perfect jewel. Who married late and died young; who survived the yellow fever plague of 1793, only to surrender to consumption before she had even borne a child of her own. When he thinks of her, he thinks of those clacking chestnuts swinging like simple pendulums on their laces – a moment suspended in time to which all other memories lead ... because he, from the moment he began to help their father at the brewery, became so bound up in his researches that he barely noticed her, eventually losing sight of her. He thought she would always be there. As if, had he paid her more attention, she would have lived. His guilt coils into a wall of thorns around the spiritoscope.

He turns to other, less cumbered fronts.

There are some improvements he has wanted to make to his deflagrator, and another paper to deliver upon the caloric properties of weather systems: for some years he has studied the possibility that warm water from the Gulf of Mexico charges the air above it with such heat that, as the heat meets the cooler inland air above the mountains, it produces violent weather such as tornados, which are themselves – so he has determined – comprised of electrical currents of air. That study returns him to his calorimotor, and its production of heat in tandem with electricity. The circle of phenomena with which he's familiar ever expands, ever merges.

Through the sciences he finds he can approach the subject of spirits again. Might the realm of the spirits incorporate such things as electricity and heat? Are spirits cold? Mediums often describe a chill that settles upon them, and he once gripped a medium's hand that had gone ice cold in an instant, but that is hardly the sort of proof he can use. Are they electrical in nature, the souls that guide Mrs Gourlay's hands? It seems fitting that they should be – they would add another layer to what he already knows of electricity. Why shouldn't it be the unifying principle? All the world and all the energies, driven by electrical forces.

Hare recalls when he was twenty-two and fused strontianite for the first time with his oxyhydrogen blowpipe. Silliman assisted. Woodhouse and Seybert were practically beside themselves with excitement and wasted no time pushing through his election to the Chemical Society. He remembers thinking that his future would be like this. He would continue to invent, continue to win praise. Nothing could stop him. He had no inkling then of spiritualism – Seybert's fascination was not expressed until so much later – or that he would run up against such ignorance and prejudice within his own society. They forget that it was he who first fused heavy spar and threw platinum, gold and silver into a state of ebullition. He whose process, under names such as Drummond light and Calcium light, illuminate lighthouses the world over. He whose Compendium of Chemical Instruction is the standard text to which all chemistry students are referred. He who possesses the Rumford Medal for his discoveries. He who is a life member of the Academy of Natural Sciences. It isn't arrogance. He *has* accomplished all these things. And he's not done yet.

With renewed purpose, he completely redesigns his spiritoscope.

Invited to speak in New York, he loads the new version onto a wagon and has it carted there.

He's allowed to choose the nature of his talk in New York – they know how broad his range is; nevertheless, the audience of professional and amateur scientists gathers in anticipation of a discourse related to chemistry.

Instead, Hare pounces upon the infinite chimeras of scripture, blasting the Bible, and then describes the possibilities of spirit communication. Finally, like a stage magician who has saved his best trick for last, he offers a brief demonstration of the new, improved spiritoscope. He wants them to appreciate the mechanics of the machine.

It's a rectangular dining table now. The same revolving wheel hangs off one of the long sides of the table, facing the audience. He, as acting operator, sits across from them. On his left the two table legs end in small truckles, whereas on the right they're fitted with larger wheels connected by an axle. Rolling the table back and forth turns the axle, which drives the lettered wheel. His maxim remaining "no hands upon the table," he has placed a small wooden tray on casters of its own. The operator moves the table by rolling the tray back and forth upon it. Cumbersome once again, but less so, he feels, than the earlier version Mrs Gourlay is mastering; and if it works it removes the medium even further from direct contact with the wheel.

But when Hare attempts to demonstrate it for the audience, he can't move the table at all. Discouraged, he finally sets the tray aside and pushes the table back and forth manually. The wheel turns, but spins without any inclination to stop. He can spell out nothing. So much, he thinks, for his latent powers. So much for the proof of his claims. Even though the presence of a medium would have given his audience an easy excuse to dismiss him, he sees he has been stupid not to bring one. Something remarkable might have happened. He can see that the people don't care what he's doing. They can't wait to get out of the hall.

His reputation saves him from direct humiliation. So exhausted is he from trying to wrestle the table back and forth that he disregards the disappointment in the voice of the professor who arranged the talk – "that was a most singular performance, Doctor Hare" – and falls asleep in the carriage that takes him to his hotel.

Within the month of his appearance, a letter arrives from a man named Isaac T. Pease of Thompsonville, Connecticut. Pease has learned of the spiritoscope. Perhaps he attended the New York lecture or knew someone who did. In ingratiating language he explains that he has experimented with a similar device at the urgings of local spiritualists and redesigned it on a much smaller scale than Hare's grand spiritoscope. He includes schematics of his devices, which he has dubbed "Pease's Dials". Looking them over, Hare doesn't know whether to be pleased or furious, remembering how the British attempted to steal his credit for the blowpipe.

He admits that Pease has made one or two improvements: rather than the wheel, he has the index needle spin, which seems much easier to accomplish once considered; the activator operates by a spring rather than a system of cables and weights and axles, and directly affects the index. The smaller disks, which can be adjusted for the medium to see, incorporate phrases as well as letters. The needle can point to "Think So" or "Must Go", "Yes" or "Doubtful", "I'll Spell it Over", "Done", "I'll Come

Again", and even "Good-bye" – all spread around the wheel, written as if along the spokes. Ultimately, Hare is too impressed at the ingenuity to be angry. He admires invention too much to discount it even when accompanied by apparent hubris: "Pease's Dials" indeed. He'll catalogue them in his book, but otherwise, with their simple mechanisms, they return too much control to the medium for his necessary proof.

For the summer, Robert Hare departs Philadelphia and travels with his household staff to the Atlantic Hotel on Cape May Island. The New York spiritoscope makes the journey with him, to be set up in the salon of his suite where he essays it from time to time in solitude. For all that he denies it, Mrs Gourlay's pronouncement on his powers has burrowed into him. Silently, he turns over and over the question: where does the supernatural mechanism dwell? And is it likely we all possess it?

Throughout the month of June he sits before the table at night, often with a cellar-chilled pint of Hare's American Porter – his private stock – and rests his fingers upon the sliding tray. Night after night, when he lets his thoughts drift, the back and forth pushing of the small board on casters begins to move the table and the wheel. He can't see the face, but what the wheel is spelling doesn't matter. It's moving now under his impetus, if not control.

Finally, he watches in awe as the table rolls from side to side as if loose upon the deck of a rocking ship and the wheel stops, moves, stops, reverses. The back of his neck prickles with the electricity of terror.

"I cannot be doing this," he says to the empty room. Therefore he is not. Something else – unseen – is there with him. The table stops.

He retracts his hands from the tray and retreats to his bed, where he lies for hours, alone, nervous and awake. Night surf on the cape roars in the distance and salty ocean breezes swirl through the stuffy room. Trees outside the windows hiss. The moonlit shadows of their dancing branches anthropomorphize the wallpaper and furnishings. The branches slap together: "clack, clack, clack." Dark ghosts whirl about him. The whole room tilts and spins. "Anna," he sobs, and drifts into a fitful sleep.

He meets a number of people at the hotel, including a Dr Thomas

Bell from Somerville, Massachusetts, who will later contribute much information to his book. Bell, a thin, dark man, is a head taller than everyone around him and speaks with a twisted curve to his words somewhere between Cockney and Bostonian English. He asks, then wheedles, and finally demands to see the spiritoscope and, when Hare takes him to the salon, insists on a demonstration. Other men and women present in the public dining room drift after Bell, coming to see, spilling in through the foyer past Hare's surprised servant, Gilhay. They hang in the doorway. Some have snifters in their hands, and cigars, and whisper to one another. This is so casual for them, a lark to pass the evening.

He determinedly takes his place, ponders for a moment, then closes his eyes. His fingers begin to push the tray on casters back and forth, and even forward. Sluggishly, the table begins to roll, the wheel to rotate.

"It's spellin' out something," whispers a woman, and he opens his eyes. She's a large, fish-faced creature, but he tries not to see, not to think.

Bell has his note pad out and a stub of a pencil. It takes ages for each roll of the table, for the wheel to stop on each letter. The crowd stands silent, motionless, until the sixth letter, and the table comes to a stop. "W-A-R," says Bell, "U-E-N. What's that, then, Dr Hare? Waruen?"

Hare settles his hands palm up in his lap. He stares at them uncomfortably. "Warren," he replies, "the U and R are side by side, it was supposed to be another R, I'm sure."

"Who might 'e be?"

Hare's eyes glitter bright. "Mr Warren was my father's partner in business before I was born. He left Philadelphia and sided with the British in the war – that's who he is."

Bell and the others seem unable to put this together with anything – their expressions betray what's missing from his answer.

He explains, "I was asking, don't you see. Asking the spirits to give me some information only I knew. And they spelled out his name, didn't they?"

"I suppose," says the fish-faced woman, and she glances sidelong at others. Gilhay, his manservant standing beside the door, looks no less troubled by this revelation.

Hare wants them all gone now. "Well, thank you. I didn't

know what was being spelled out, if it was an answer to anything. I've no idea when it works, if it works. That's the way I've designed it."

"Oh, continue, please, sir," Bell insists. "Let *us* ask something."

Hare dismissively waves his hand and falls back on Mrs Gourlay's excuse. "It's too enervating. One answer – a single word – exhausts me. I'm not a skilled practitioner." He can see it in their faces – the same look he has given to spiritualists, to Margaret Fox – skeptical smiles, the identical doubts expressed by the look of the audience in New York and by the look in Gilhay's eyes, embarrassed on his behalf. Oddly, the doubt is harder to take from strangers. But there's nothing like doubt on Bell's face. Bell is thrilled.

Seeing that the performance is truly over, people begin to withdraw, all save Dr Bell.

Gilhay lingers uncertainly behind him. He's an Irishman. His people know about spirits and demons, ghosts and *ban sidhes*, know the treacheries they can perform. Even dead friends will play tricks upon the living now and again – Hare's heard countless supernatural tales from him since undertaking this project. Also, it might be that Gilhay despises Bell as an Englishman. That would be enough to set him scowling at the intruder's back. He looks to Hare for a signal to eject Bell, but Hare shakes his head and Gilhay finally abandons the open door and retreats to his own small quarters.

Bell says, "Doctor, I'd like to contribute to your investigations. Already, I've looked into the matter substantially on me own. In Boston there are practitioners of remarkable skill who I've met. Once I stood at the end of a ten-foot table and watched a small woman sitting beside it put out her hands above without touching it, like someone working a puppet, and make it move, glide a foot or two at a time, this way and that. We set an iron rod in between folding doors at the bottom, and the table clambered over the rod into another room. Then it come back, right over the rod again. I noted in me journal that if the medium raised her hands above two foot from the table, all movement ceased. Whatever it was driving that thing, it was coming through her. I'm a tall man, you'll mark, and I could see down the whole length of the table that nobody was touching it. Not a soul – well, not a corporal one." He smiles. "There's much more that I could describe for you if you'd let me further my investigations and add them to the weight of your own."

Hare sits dumbfounded. A colleague in this business? "Dr Bell, I should be most honored," he hears himself say, as if listening to the conversation from another room. "I'm compiling proofs to present to the scientific community. I would well appreciate yours, if they're objective."

Bell smiles once more. His teeth aren't very good. "I understand too well the rejection of traditionalists. No imagination in 'em. Have you read Poe, sir? *There's* a soul who understood the nature of life beyond death."

"Poe, yes." He recalls that name vaguely: he doesn't follow the careers of sensationalist writers. "Very good, Dr Bell," he says, and moves forward, effectively urging Bell out the door. "Compile all you like. I'll certainly consider whatever you have to show. And of course we'll talk again here at the hotel."

"Of course, sir." He steps back into the hallway, bows formally. "I bid you good night then."

"Good night." Hare shuts the door. He turns, leans against it and stares at the spiritoscope, expecting almost to see it rear up on its hind legs and caper through the salon. The table remains at rest.

Thereafter Hare takes his meals in his rooms or at off-hours to avoid Bell's company. He can't say why exactly, but he doesn't want to share his work with Bell. Maybe not with anyone else. Having accepted the role of iconoclast he's unwilling to part with it. He is his own hair shirt, he thinks, and chuffs at the inadvertent pun.

By the end of June, he has improved his skill upon the spiritoscope. His mind drifts, the wheel spins freely.

He has established communication with Anna. It's as if she sits out of sight in another room, listening to his questions and writing him notes in response. If only it were true and he could look round the corner and find her.

Gilhay transcribes what the wheel dictates. One time he writes down a slightly misspelled "pulsatque versatque", and Hare snatches his hands off the tray in amazement. "My *father* is with us! That was one of his favorite phrases. It referred to the beating Entellus gave Dares in the *Aeneid*, beating him so that he spun. My father used to recite it to me to warn me what I was about to get if I didn't behave. It can't be anyone else! Who else would know?" Gilhay glances around the room uncomfortably.

Although the manifestations of Anna and his father delight him, Hare comes to realize that he must produce something more by way of proof for others, else he is no different than any performing medium. The truth of what passes through him to operate the wheel can't be determined by this exercise. It has meaning for him alone. Spirits come and talk to him, but who else would recognize them?

He would dearly like to speak with Franklin and Washington, both of whom he admires so, if only he could draw them about himself like some great incorporeal cloak.

A few weeks later he's taking a late supper of cold chicken and leeks in the dining room when Dr Bell appears, towing behind him a severe blond woman named Miss Julia Hayden. She's from New York, and wears a dull black dress as if in mourning. Bell says, "She was 'ere on holiday. A remarkable medium, you must let her try your device." And so, pressed to it, he has to yield. They let him finish his meal, then he leads them up to the salon and the spiritoscope.

To his surprise (and delight), Julia Hayden is incapable of using the thing. The wood tray rolls back and forth on its casters. The table budges not an inch.

Eyes closed, she grimaces, twists her features, contorts her lips in a gruesome spectacle. Her face fades to the color of a winding sheet. Her hands tremble on the tray, slide off and lie slack upon the table surface. Her head lolls, her expression gone loose. With a sharp breath, she opens her lips and the words commence: "Brother beloved, I am here."

It is not Miss Hayden's normal voice, but creaky and burbling. His sister died with her lungs full of liquid. The sound puts him back beside her as she failed, his hands wrapped tightly around hers as he desperately, uselessly, willed his life into her weak body. He doesn't want to hear this.

"Please," he indicates the table. "That's how she's supposed to communicate."

The medium's head shakes as if someone is clutching the back of her neck and twisting. "Not physical . . . vocal. She has no skill here," she says, nodding at the wheel.

"Who are you?"

"You have to ask?" The words come slow as molasses dripping from a jar. A small bright drop of blood appears on her lip.

A sudden frost coats his lungs.

"Robert. You seek a proof you cannot receive from the table. I'm present to deliver it."

"Deliver? How do you intend?"

"Give me a message."

"A message for whom? I don't –"

"To Gourlay."

His jaw stiffens. He peers at Bell, at the medium, as if betrayed. How could her name be known to them? He hasn't mentioned it. She never came up in his brief conversations with Bell. No, this must be real.

What sort of message will do then? Something involving other people, not Mrs Gourlay alone. Proof beyond the medium and the devices, that's what he requires, his spirit sister is right about that. He must involve someone who doesn't believe. He casts about and the answer comes of its own free will.

"Go to her, then, and tell her to instruct her husband to proceed to the bank at 1.00 p.m. tomorrow, find out when the note is due on the brewery property and report what he has found to me at home at 3.30." This will prove everything. There's no telegraph between Cape Island and Philadelphia, no way for the message to make the journey any quicker than he can.

There comes no reply, no confirmation. The medium suddenly draws a breath, sits stiffly upright, then sags. Within a minute, color floods her cheeks as if she has just performed something strenuous. She raises her head. He is amazed at this transformation. It isn't something she could induce – the suffusion of blood into her cheeks. Eyes enclosed in sickly darkness, she glances from Bell to Hare, blankly. Then at the spiritoscope. "Did I . . ." she begins, removes her fingers from the tabletop, folding her hands before her throat.

She glances at Bell for confirmation. He leans solemnly forward. "You were directed, ma'am, by someone else."

Hare remains silent, looking for any hidden messages passing between these two. He finds himself asking how he can continue to suspect them when he has been operated by the same unseen forces in that very chair and endured the same suspicions from others.

He thinks, *we are all of us in uncharted waters.*

When no one speaks or moves for an interminable moment, Hare asks, "Do you know if she received my message, Miss Hayden?"

The woman – strange how severe she first appeared and how timid, helpless and confused she now seems – replies with her own question: "Message? For whom?"

Hare asks nothing more. The medium wishes to retire and Bell escorts her out of the apartments. He turns back at the door to offer an apologetic, "I hope this hasn't proved an intrusion, Dr Hare. I sensed immediately you'd want to meet her. We strive to maintain open minds about all forms of spirit communication, do we not, sir? We must consider the non-physical a legitimate expression, too, and this clever proof you've devised will establish her defense as well as yours. Please do contact me at your earliest convenience as to its outcome."

"Of course. Another time, Dr Bell. I will have to leave early on the morrow." Hare nods to Miss Hayden beyond Bell, who rewards him with a weary smile. "Rest, ma'am."

Bell gives him a final, troubled glance, as if sure he's going to miss a critical event here.

As he closes the door, Hare hears behind him Gilhay's door bump closed. Hare smiles to himself. The ever-protective retainer.

Although he will eventually use much material uncovered by Bell in his book, he never meets with him again. They communicate thereafter through the mail.

IV Proofs

Upon his return to Philadelphia, Robert Hare sits through an edgy, sweltering hour and a half of waiting until the appointed time. 3.30 arrives. His appointment does not. He has failed, his communication was not received. He rises from the French settee. The clothing that he has worn for the hasty journey from Cape May sticks to him everywhere like a wet sausage skin and is discolored by large patches of perspiration. Sweat from his brow stings his eyes. He looks out upon the tree-lined street where no breeze blows. Below him, roses stand, dappled with sunlight through the maple tree across the way. He hears the hooves of horses on the stones of nearby Chestnut Street. The carriages rarely come past the front of the house, situated as it is on a close.

A woman's figure passes by. It looks – but she has turned into his yard, and he leaves the window, nearly runs out of the room as the knocker raps like a musket shot through the front hall. He opens the door upon Mrs Gourlay.

The look on his face must perplex her. She says, "But surely you were expecting me."

"I did so, but – well, please come in. I despaired as the time passed."

"Oh, it has? Our mantle clock is not reliable. It runs both fast and slow and the doctor takes his continental watch with him."

He seats her on the red Empire sofa there in the entrance hall below the stairs. "Tell me," he says.

She does. She had been working with his device when her contact was interrupted by an errant spirit, his sister, with an urgent message. Receiving it, she sent her brother to find her husband, and the two men went to the bank together. They determined that the note was not due for more than a year – which Hare knew already but anticipated no one else would, as it was so far outside the range of what anyone – even someone who had researched his family – would investigate. But there is more. She unfurls a piece of paper on which she has scrawled a poem in stiff handwriting.

"Brother beloved," it begins, "of ardent soul,
Striving to reach a heavenly goal;
Wouldst thou attain the blissful height.
Where wisdom purifies the light . . ."

He folds the sheet of foolscap and lowers his moist gaze. He has never seen the poem before, but its authorship is clear; nor can he can read further just now. His joy is inexpressible. "Thank you, Mrs Gourlay. More than you realize, you've sped away the clouds of my doubt. I must now endeavour to show the world what you and I recognize in our hearts."

"Let me help," the medium says.

"I shall. Believe me, I'll require all your assistance. We've much to undertake now."

He begins work on his book in earnest as accounts come trickling in. Bell reports that entities who've spoken to him through verbal mediums are able to read his thoughts and see what he can see, yet lose their knowledge when answering what he and the medium do not know, a supposition he tests by asking them to duplicate a signature in a folded letter that he hasn't seen. They can't. But the moment he opens the letter and looks upon it, the medium's hand begins to write in imitation of what he beholds. Bell proposes that what he has uncovered is more than mere spirit communication, but a form of clairvoyance. He writes: "What the questioner knows, the spirit knows; what the questioner does not know, the spirits are entirely ignorant of." It's a provocative observation, one for which Hare has no answer.

Inquiries made earlier to acquaintances on the continent have also begun to bear fruit.

He receives a report that the Archbishop of Paris attended a seance and witnessed communication via rappings on a table. The spirit identified itself as Soeur Francoise, deceased the week before in a Paris convent. And when an abbot present demanded in the name of Christ the woman manifest, she did appear to them and answered questions. All the participants were afterward several days indisposed, as if the spirit had drawn upon them for her energy.

From Germany, a Dr Geib communicates to him about table-moving phenomena, giving a name to the spirits responsible: *klopferle*, for "rapping specter".

It's generally believed, says another correspondent, that this phenomenon has arrived, like some plague, off a ship from America. One day there's nothing, the next, with an American medium present, tables turn, hats swivel on heads, and chairs spin on one leg. The news agencies, fearing for their reputations, refuse to report on these initial events. Even Hare has to wonder at what sounds, on the face of it, like a great fraud.

To his amusement, French scientists attempt to explain it with no more logic than Bechworth applied. They claim electricity is the culprit, or imperceptible muscular action, moving the tables. "Humidity of the palms" is responsible, asserts another expert, an explanation that takes its place beside magnetisms and polarities, and even "two interacting nervous atmospheres." However perversely, the press now turn their sights not on the phenomena but on the accepted theorists. In response to the comment about nervous atmospheres, one French journal suggests that, given the dullness of the theoretician, "the nervous system of the table (disgueridon) must be *very* sensitive." The journal later describes an episode where French scientists attempted to move a table by use of those proposed magnetisms while a spiritualist sat aside and watched in bewilderment. When they failed utterly and retreated outside, the table, left alone, began to buck.

From England, a Mr Robert Owen writes to him of an apron untied from a woman and passed around a group at a seance, and which was then ripped away from them by invisible hands. These same hands passed Owen a flower. His handkerchief was snatched from his pocket and formed into a hat. One spirit shook his hand, "and, sir, I could feel the individual fingers." In a passing remark, Owen's report mentions a spirit stating what Owen believes to be true but which later proves to be false – information which seems to have come from his own thoughts, much as Bell has suggested. Both observations he will include in the book. Let readers draw their own conclusions.

Hare has become a magnet for spiritualist data. Every day brings more letters, many impossible to use, some impossible to comprehend. Meanwhile, he routinely visits a coterie of spiritualists to whom he has been introduced by Mrs Gourlay.

In the presence of local medium Henry Gordon, he watches a table float into the air.

When he takes his seat in the salon of Mrs Ann Leah Brown, he finds his name written on a scrap of paper lying beside him on the carpet. Mrs Brown denies all knowledge of it and, when she applies herself to one of "Pease's Dials", through her a spirit explains that an old friend, William Blodget, has written it. Blodget is some six years deceased.

While Mrs Brown communicates, a table against the wainscoted wall over a foot away from her begins to slide back and forth on the floor like one of his trays on casters. Both he and the medium sit in stupefaction.

"I've never seen the like," she confesses to him when the activity has stopped. "It is you, sir, causing this." And though he doesn't express it to her, he does feel uncanny energy pervading the air, like a huge bubble filling the room.

Phenomena spring up on all sides, as if casting him headlong toward some explosive event. Darkness is at his back. Friends have fallen away. In his absence he's either pitied or scorned, but he notices none of it. His whole world has become the spirit one.

In January, Joseph Hazard returns from Rhode Island. His reason for visiting: "I have to check up on my old friend now and again, and business at present is sluggish." Hare refrains from admitting that just now he finds Hazard's appearance intrusive, like a distraction concocted by his enemies to slow him down, just as Hazard refrains from confessing that mutual friends whom Hare might currently consider enemies have urged him to come.

Hazard intrudes further when he insists on accompanying Robert Hare to spirit meetings, two or three times a week.

In various parlors they sit apart as they did with Margaret Fox. With Hazard present, tables don't dance and caper but rattle only mildly in corners or shift under the spiritualist's hands. If Hazard spots trickery or harbors doubts, he says nothing, only watches. His presence acts as a damper to Hare's elation as well as to the proceedings themselves, wherever they go. Yet Hare can't bring himself to ask his old friend to leave. Silliman's an abstraction, Hazard concrete; and if he can convert Hazard, the exemplar of a rational mind, that may silence the naysayers once and for all.

The first week of February in 1855, Hare goes to a sitting alone, returning late in the evening. Gilhay lets him in.

Hazard awaits in the dining room, and pours a mug of hot buttery cider to warm him. Two other mugs on the table indicate that Gilhay and Hazard have been sitting together awhile.

Still wrapped in his heavy coat, Hare sits heavily and sips the steaming cider. A few minutes pass in uncomfortable silence. Then he says, "There is to be a convocation of spirits at the home of Mrs Gourlay. This is what I've been flung toward, Joseph, and could not see in advance – all the strange events that have led me this far – *this* is where they were leading."

"To a gathering of the tribes," Hazard comments, then apologizes. "I don't mean to make it sound trivial. But how else does one describe it?"

Hare waves at the air. "Describe it however you choose. But this event *you* must attend. Many from her group will be there, adding the strength of their energies to Mrs Gourlay's, calling upon the spirit world to come and speak and inform. They're about to reveal everything of the afterlife to us. Everything, Joseph! Say you'll accompany me. I need you to transcribe for me. My hands shake too much in the presence of the spirits.

And there must be more than one witness to so incomparable an event. It might never happen again."

"Of course, of course I will," Hazard assures him. He would have it no other way.

After finishing his cider, Hare retires to his study and writes furiously for two hours as he does each day, compiling his notes, his arguments, his proofs, his rebuttals into what he has now titled *Experimental Investigation of the Spirit Manifestations*. The gathering of the tribes, as Joseph put it, will be the climax.

V The Convocation of Spirits

At 9.00 a.m. on February 18, Hare and Hazard sit in Mrs Gourlay's parlor, surrounded by mediums and believers. Word has gotten out. There is Miss Fox, who breaks into a demure smile each time Hazard glances her way; Mrs Brown, solemn and nervous; Henry Gordon, who looks to have steadied himself with drink for the event; Julia Hayden, sent by Dr Bell. There are even people such as the Howitts.

As Mrs Gourlay lowers her head and rolls the tray upon the table, the dial spins and spins, and Hazard writes down each name as it is spelled out. More spirits than corporeal forms surround the two men at the center. The spirits sign in: George Washington, John Quincy Adams, William H. Harrison, W.E. Channing, H.K. White, Isaac Newton, Andrew Jackson, Henry Clay, Benjamin Franklin, Lord Byron, Martha Washington – the list goes on and on, like the signatories of the Declaration of Independence coming forward one by one to take up the quill. The cataloguing seems to last for hours. Hazard fills two entire pages with names, having written too large at first. He couldn't have known.

When the wheel does finally come to rest, the entire room seems to sigh as one. Hazard sits back from his writing board and flexes his hand awhile before taking up the steel-point pen again.

After first offering a welcome to the invisible guests, Hare begins the questioning. "How do we arrive where you are?" he asks.

The wheel spins, and with it the story.

"After death, the soul awakens from a profound sleep into a state of consciousness very like dreaming. Bright and shadowy forms appear to it, as does the body it has left. These forms soon solidify into spirits, usually those of departed friends. They greet the nascent spirit with affection and conduct it to a celestial abode in accordance with its moral state at the time of death."

He ponders briefly, then asks, "How is the spirit world composed?"

The answer comes: "Between Earth and moon lie seven concentric rings, the regions of the spirit world. These have terrestrial scenery – mountains, streams, plains, rivers, birds, beasts, but all of greater beauty, and at each successive, ascending level, more lovely. The last is so glorious, it cannot be described."

Then, as if someone else of a slightly different opinion has wrested control, the answer is revised. "Earth is the first level. The remaining six spheres compose the spirit plane. They commence about sixty miles up, rising out into space."

"The sun, then, illuminates your world as it does ours."

"No", comes the answer. "A black sun shines upon the spirit world, although its nature cannot be satisfactorily explained to mortals. Its rays consist of an all-pervading ethereal fluid. *We live in a realm of perpetual day, full of aromatic flowers, herbs, fountains and rushing water underfoot. And singing floats through the air.*"

"Then how do you see yourselves? What are you like? How do you appear differently that you make a distinction from the body cast off?" he asks. Hazard nods encouragingly as he writes. He was wondering the same thing.

The reply: "*We are luminiferous. Like lightning bugs we glow.* Each spirit has a circumambient halo passing from dimness to effulgence as the spirit moves to higher planes."

"These spheres. How do you move to higher ones?" he asks, trying to grasp this. Is it fair? Does it seem reasonable? It sounds, upon the face of it, like a caste system, which is not how he wants heaven to be. Underneath his questions, he wonders too, which of the great and famous men is speaking to him.

"Each ascends as he or she improves in purity. Purity, which can take two forms: love, and love/wisdom."

George Washington resides already in the seventh sphere, as Hare anticipated. Infants – which are considered blessed in their untimely death – ascend directly to that sphere, where they're instructed and grow up. They then return to earth to watch events unfold. He recalls the Howitt child whose spirit told its parents to think of it as a "gentle moonbeam," and glances over his shoulder at them. The husband nods to him, a painful joy inscribing his features.

"Angels," remarks Hazard as he writes this down.

Hare turns around. "Just so, Joseph, angels."

Hazard looks at Mrs Gourlay with her head bowed. "But I'm troubled," he says before Hare can think of another question. "What of those who aren't in the seventh level?"

"*Degradation*," the wheel spells out, "*is an inevitable consequence of vice*. Not punishment – there's no punishment necessary, for God is all-love. The afterlife follows the apostles' injunction: Hold fast that which is good. They exist in what can only be called a republican order. Too, some crimes occur in the lower spheres, and punishments are meted out in accord with these."

Hazard's brow knits as he writes this seeming contradiction down.

Hare, too, tries to understand. "How can one expect to rise in such a place?"

"Love is the simplest way. Those who know unfettered love rise immediately. For the rest, there are teachers on each level who impart wisdom to those who seek it – wisdom that, conjoined with love, advances them."

"Can we not see anything of your world?" Hare asks. "We're here to establish proof that we can show to anyone, so that they'll understand without having to come as far as I've done to arrive at enlightenment."

The wheel falls silent for so long that Hare fears contact has been broken. When it moves again, he leans forward as if to hear more clearly that which is said in silence.

The wheel spells out "J-U-P-I-T-E-R."

The spectators exchange confounded glances. Hare, who has seen the night sky through a reflecting telescope, suspects he's hearing now from Isaac Newton. He says, "Please explain further, sir."

The wheel tells him: "*The bands that can be seen around Jupiter are the spirit spheres of that world. Look upon Jupiter for evidence of our realm.*"

Hare nods, slowly at first but with increasing effusiveness. Hazard, who also has astronomical knowledge and has many times looked upon the Jovian sphere, raises his head sharply from the page and asks, "How then do you account for the changes in the appearance of those bands? For they do change. I know."

The wheel hangs, then spells out simply: "*optical delusions.*"

Hazard sits grim-faced for a moment before he dips the pen and writes down these two words. He is unaware of shaking his head as he does so.

Late that same night, in the dining room of Hare's home, the two men sit divided by the dark table. Steam from a bowl of hot cider and their individual mugs floats between them. They're bundled up, though they returned nearly an hour earlier. The fire in the hearth softens the edge of the cold but not its heart.

Hazard has done little more than murmur since the convocation ended. He took copious notes – Hare rejoices at the precision of the transcription. But a chasm has opened between them that was not apparent even as the event began – broader than the chasm between the living and the dead.

Hare takes the transcript between his hands and straightens it, tapping the sheaf against the table. "It's marvelous, Joseph, it truly is. I need add nothing to your words."

"Not mine," mutters Hazard, not looking at him.

Hare hesitates, almost asks what he means, but thinks better of it. Hazard won't meet his gaze however hard he stares. "Mmm," he adds finally, a non-committal assent, but he must say something more than that. They ought to be celebrating. "Still marvelous, whoever's words –"

"Good Christ, Robert! Whose do you think they were? Monsieur Valdemar's?"

Hare doesn't know the name, but it doesn't matter. The doubt he's cast off threatens to ignite and consume everything.

Hazard continues to stare at the surface of the table, where his hands lie flat. "You genuinely believe you sat in the presence of Washington and Franklin and Newton," he says, and glances up finally, his eyes squinched with the pain of awareness. "You know what you've done? You've become the Howitts. You're as possessed as any medium ever claimed."

"Joseph, stop this."

"Because you'll lose Anna if you admit it? Robert, you lost her decades ago."

Hare's jaw sets and his brown eyes catch fire. "And I found her again."

"Where, in the bands of Jupiter?"

"And I am to gather you know for a fact what those bands are?"

"No, of course I don't know. No one knows. That's beside the point."

"I thought, Joseph, you weren't like the others, that you were capable of contemplating things considered unnatural, that you could see through their fog of superstition and religious eyewash. I hoped . . ." He breaks off.

Hazard leans closer. "Old friend, you say yourself that I copied the details of the dialogue perfectly. That being the case, look at the descriptions both of the spirit realm here and there. Seven concentric rings or spheres rising into space with the Earth at their core – the physical realm at the bottom. That's how the spirit world was described. Not as latitudinal bands, do you understand? The two explanations are contradictory. They look nothing alike at all." Hare seems puzzled, doubtful. "Oh, think, Robert. Look at it, read it."

"No." He slaps down the pages. "I've thought everything through, eliminated all possibility of treachery. The spirits are confused, nothing more. Or we are. I've spoken to Anna, I've used the spiritoscope, I know. Who's to say that the spirit world here wouldn't look the same to someone on Jupiter as theirs does to us. We can't be sure."

Hazard stops arguing. Anna occupies the heart of him; he can't win against her. Robert Hare created the perfect device to defeat spiritualist trickery, and so of course what comes pouring out of it must be true. Confused, misunderstood perhaps by the very audience of experts gathered round, but not an outright lie. Anna could never lie.

He might have thought as much himself had they not hauled in the planet and violated their own definitions. Optical delusions, indeed. The bands of Jupiter do change form. It's well enough documented, and a scientist would know that. Hazard can no longer pretend to believe, as he can do nothing for his old friend. He climbs to his feet and says, "Good night."

Hare sits awhile longer, wounded, confused, and angry. Then he gets up and retires to his study to write up the convocation while it's still fresh in his mind. The work is what matters.

When Hazard departs the following morning, Hare is lying asleep at his desk upon the document.

Five months later, Hare has assembled all his notes into a coherent volume and threaded throughout it his opinions on the unreliability of scripture.

He points out for instance that we have only Moses' testimony of his communication with God – a report that has God slaying three thousand who were led astray but sparing Moses' brother, who *made* the golden calf. Hare calls the Old Testament a "pernicious idol" that patronizes men of a chosen seed, though they are guilty of robbery, fraud and murder, and quotes St Jerome's preface to the gospels wherein the saint complained that no one copy resembled another, the translations were so poor.

His final act is to attach a preface, including a letter from his spirit father that he receives only days before he turns in the manuscript. The spirit says: "Ask yourself how much happiness you have found in the contemplation of the fact which has been demonstrated, not only to your wishes but to your senses, that the thinking mind *never dies* . . . that it lives on, lives ever, and must throughout the ceaseless ages of eternity continue to unfold its power."

With the book at the publishers, he offers to exhibit his spiritoscope to a convention of his own clergymen and is rebuffed. In November, invited again to New York, he gives a lecture on the evidence he has compiled. It's well attended, if only by those already converted.

After the book comes out, there follows no upheaval, no slanderous assault, no clear enemy at which to take aim. He's not vilified, he's disavowed.

Not one to sit idle even then, he turns his attentions to other subjects. Spirits continue to warn him to prepare himself, and he continues secretly to await the attack, but it never comes.

In 1857, not long before his death, he exhibits, at the Franklin Institute, an apparatus for determining whether phenomena attending the attrition of pieces of quartz, when rubbed briskly together, have anything to do with the new substance described by Schönbein as "ozone". His reception is cool. Some noise is made about the apparatus, but most of the dialogue is traded as if he were not in the room among them, or they cannot see him. Forlorn, he goes home.

Maple leaves blow in through the door before he can close it. He drops his cloak upon the Empire sofa in the entrance hall, and drifts to his study through the silent house. He stokes red embers in the hearth and adds new wood to the fire, then takes his seat before one of "Pease's Dials" he has set upon his desk.

He opens his glass inkwell and places beside it a steel-nibbed pen, inadvertently bumping a large anomalous chestnut he uses as a paperweight – actually two grown together into a single mass – hard enough that it tumbles off the side of the desk and rolls beneath his feet, where he can't reach it.

With a resigned sigh he lets it go and turns to the device. He adjusts the wheel so that he can see clearly anything spelled out there.

He presses his fingertips to the sprung plate that operates the machine and, thus poised, awaits his Anna.

VI. Epilogue: The Seybert Commission

In 1883, Henry Seybert, a descendent of the same Seybert who once urged a young Robert Hare to consider the afterlife, endows a chair of Philosophy upon the University of Pennsylvania, conditional on the university investigating the truth of modern spiritualism. A commission is assembled, including William Pepper, Provost of the University, and Joseph Leidy, the anatomist. Horace Howard Furness chairs the committee and writes up its findings. His wife died relatively young and he has good reason to want the continuance of the soul proved true.

Seybert himself dies before the commission can even begin its investigation, but the money is set aside and the work goes forward. The commission examines the subject for three years, inviting the most prominent mediums to conduct seances before it. Those who accept include one Mrs Margaret Fox Kane, who is truly celebrated within her ranks. Furness finds her small and genteel, and so unassertive that she immediately wins him over. Yet, as the evening progresses, he slides into doubt.

She communicates with spirits through raps on the table. The spirits, while appearing to have intimate acquaintance with family affairs of some of those present, send Furness's brother a message from his spirit father. Except that his father is still alive. Later, the rapping is determined to be the product of Mrs Kane's ankle striking the table while she seems to sit away from it, her hands in plain sight. She is, it would appear, usefully double-jointed.

The devices of Robert Hare are neither used nor mentioned, nor is his work cited. His work, in this arena, is forgotten.

The commission's report, published in 1887, causes a great stir in that it finds not a single fact upon which to base any belief in spiritualism. In summing up, Furness reports that no truth could be established because the whole business is so clouded with trickery that no phenomenon can be trusted. Filled with regret, for now he can know nothing of his wife's continuance, he confesses how desperately he wished to be converted by "these shabby charlatans."

NICHOLAS ROYLE

Skin Deep

NICHOLAS ROYLE WAS BORN in Sale, Cheshire. He is the author of three novels – *Counterparts* (Penguin), *Saxophone Dreams* (Penguin), and *The Matter of the Heart* (Abacus) – in addition to more than one hundred short stories which have appeared in a variety of anthologies and magazines, most recently *Dark Terrors 2*, *Twists of the Tale*, *Phantoms*, *Love in Vein II*, *The Mammoth Book of Dracula*, *Dark of the Night* and *The Third Alternative*.

He has edited five anthologies, including *A Book of Two Halves*, *The Tiger Garden: A Book of Writers' Dreams* and *The Time Out Book of New York Short Stories*. The winner of three British Fantasy Awards, his book reviews and other journalism have appeared in *Time Out*, the *Guardian*, the *Observer*, the *Independent*, the *Literary Review*, the *New Statesman* and elsewhere. He is married and lives in west London, where he is working on a new novel and, as always, new stories.

"I've been fascinated by taxidermy since my first confrontations with stuffed animals as a small boy being taken around museums," the author recalls. "These days, still exhibits are considered old hat – everything has to be animatronic and interactive – but give me dusty old glass cases full of glass-eyed beasts any day. As part of the research for this story, I attended a practical demonstration by a taxidermist who stuffed a pheasant. Feathers *everywhere*."

Henderson only agreed to go on the expedition because he thought Elizabeth was going along, so when he turned up at the Washington services on the A1(M) and found only Bloor waiting to meet him, he felt like a child with an empty Christmas box. It was important, however, not to show too much disappointment, given that Elizabeth was Graham Bloor's wife. Bloor waited for Henderson to ask, then explained.

"Elizabeth wasn't feeling up to it at the last minute," he said, flicking ash from his cigarette into the little foil tray that sat on the plastic tabletop between the two men. "Women's things, you know." He placed the cigarette between his lips with his forefinger and thumb. Henderson wasn't sure if he mistrusted *all* men who held their cigarettes in this particular way, or if it was just Bloor. Certainly the man wouldn't win any charm contests, and Henderson *was* screwing his wife.

"So it's just the two of us then," Henderson said, eyes sliding across Bloor's heavy, jowly features to the other tables in the cafeteria. Apart from a couple of thickset lorry drivers sipping scalding tea from greasy mugs and a rep in a grey double-breasted suit taking dainty bites round the edge of a white bread sandwich, they were the only customers. It was still early, not long after eight. The only two kitchen staff – women in their forties with tight curly perms and pink house coats – were leaning against opposite sides of a doorway chattering in low voices.

"Looks like it, doesn't it?" Bloor said, picking his cigarette out from between his lips for the last time before grinding it out in the ashtray.

The plan was for Henderson to leave his car in the carpark and go with Bloor. The idea had appealed to him when it had included Elizabeth sitting in the passenger seat. He had imagined sitting in the back and watching the soft spring of hairs on the back of her neck. She would have put her hair up in a grip especially, because she was no slouch when it came to understanding her own appeal. But with Elizabeth left at home – she and Bloor shared a sizeable detached house in Gosforth – it was sadly inevitable that Henderson should take the seat alongside Bloor. He drove the Mercedes the way Elizabeth said he made love – fast, undeviating and without a backward glance. The way he dangled his arm out of the window was telling.

As Bloor put more miles between them and the services carpark, Henderson became increasingly miserable. Not even the bleak splendour of the Borders cheered him up, unable as he was to think of anything other than Elizabeth arching her back catlike in bed.

She complained unceasingly about Bloor, his habits and the way he treated her; the oily manner he adopted with female shop assistants and waitresses, the unshakable confidence that she was his and would never leave him. And in that, at least, he appeared to be right, not that Henderson felt able to criticize her for staying: Bloor's success in various businesses had provided comforts aplenty; they wanted for nothing on the material side, and Elizabeth was a material girl. Henderson knew this – she would pick at the cloth of his lapel disdainfully and frown at his chainstore shoes – but it in no way coloured his feelings for her. She was a deeply attractive woman and Henderson knew he had to be doing a lot better than he was as a business studies lecturer to lure her away from her Gosforth lair for more than a night at a time. He didn't blame her, because he would have done the same in her position.

"So where are we heading?" Henderson asked to break the silence.

"The Highlands, of course." Bloor pressed the cigarette lighter home.

"I know, but whereabouts?"

"Oh I forget the name. Some place. We'll leave the car and go on foot. Find somewhere to pitch the tent when it gets dark. And hopefully get lucky either tonight or tomorrow."

"But there's no guarantee, is there? That we'll find one." Henderson's heart was sinking still further at the prospect of more than a single night spent with Bloor.

"No guarantee, that's right, but plenty of incentive. Curtin's offering two grand. His client must be offering double that."

"Christ," said Henderson. "Why would anybody pay four grand for a stuffed cat?" He looked out of the window at the passing outposts of Scots pine, wondering again about the ethics of the job.

"It's not just any old cat. The wild cat's as rare as rocking horse droppings. Two grand though, eh? Not bad for a couple of days' work. And it's like I said: fifty fifty."

"What about Elizabeth's share?" Henderson asked.

"What share? Would you expect to get paid if you'd stayed at home?"

Henderson bristled with righteous anger. Elizabeth was entitled to her share, and he'd no doubt she'd still be expecting it. She'd helped with the research after all, picked the most likely spot to yield a wild cat. He'd offer her part of his share when they got back, assuming of course they found one of the damn things and managed to catch it and kill it without damaging the pelt. Curtin had made it quite clear to Bloor that if the cat was disfigured he wouldn't pay them a penny. Quite why he was being so fussy was a mystery to Henderson who never would have expected taxidermists to adhere so strictly to whatever moral code prevented the man substituting a swatch of tabby fur. Maybe his client was enough of an expert to be able to tell the difference: why else would he offer such silly money? The wild cat's basic colour was yellowish grey and while five out of ten domestic strays could match that, they wouldn't have the wild cat's strong black vertical bars and dorsal stripe, nor its broad, bushy tail which the textbooks – and Elizabeth – had taught them was the surest means of identification. The last thing they wanted to do was turn up at Curtin's with a feral moggy.

Henderson, though, had had grave doubts about the expedition's viability since it had been mooted. Indeed, he had needed to be convinced the wild cat actually existed, having grown up with the idea that the British Isles were devoid of any genuine wildlife. And then the books Elizabeth had trucked back from Newcastle Library all said how elusive the wild cat was and how the closest encounter you could reasonably hope for was a set of paw prints in fresh snow, or twin mirrors startled in car headlamps. Systematic tracking, the naturalists wrote, would very rarely produce a result.

So when Bloor swung the wheel of the Merc in a wide arc and scrunched to a halt in pine cones and dirt at the edge of the unmetalled road in the Middle of Nowhere, Highland region, Henderson felt their chances were minimal.

"Got everything?" Bloor asked before centrally locking the boot and doors.

Henderson nodded, hefting his rucksack and peering up the track. Bloor bent down and tucked the keys under a rear wheel arch.

"No point carrying anything we don't have to," he said, "and who's going to nick it out here? Let's go. We have to go as quietly as we can. They're very shy."

"Do you really think we'll find one?" Henderson asked.

"I'm not going home without one." And with that he immediately got into his stride. Henderson followed him into the semi-gloom of the forest. Once he'd got used to the sound of their passage, Henderson listened out for other noises but the forest remained silent: no clouds of flies buzzing in stray patches of sunlight, no tiny creatures scratching through the undergrowth, and, most surprising of all, no birds clattering through the tops of the trees. He didn't get too close to Bloor but was careful not to lose sight of his broad shoulders rising and falling twenty yards in front.

"It's getting dark," he shouted forward when he realized the trees had started to close in around them.

"Ssh." Bloor flapped a hand in the air. "Wild cats are nocturnal," he said, catching his breath when Henderson had drawn level. "The darker it gets the better our chances, but we've got to be quiet."

They set off again, Henderson bringing up the rear, thinking about Elizabeth. They'd met two years previously holidaying on Paxos. Henderson had been struck by the unmistakable look of a bored wife when he'd happened to take breakfast on a couple of occasions at the same time as she and Bloor. He followed them one evening to a taverna that was well off the tourist trail and sat in a dim corner with a bowl of olives and a bottle of white wine. Bloor tucked into course after course while Elizabeth looked over his shoulder and once or twice crossed sightlines with Henderson. Walking back to the hotel, she looked back a couple of times and he was there at the edge of the surf, trousers rolled up, jacket slung over his shoulder with calculated nonchalance. So when she came downstairs half an hour after going up with Bloor to find Henderson drinking alone in the bar, neither of them was really surprised.

Henderson ordered another bottle of wine and they shared it with a round of conversational hide and seek.

"You do the shopping together every Thursday evening," Henderson guessed. "You push the trolly and load in all the basic stuff while he marches in front picking up vacuum packs of continental sausages and firelighters for the barbecues you never get round to having."

"You ring programmes in the *Radio Times*," she said, raising her glass to her painted lips, "then forget to watch them, sitting there listening to music instead and nursing a bottle of beer. Old jazz stuff probably or movie soundtracks. Comfort music."

"And then when I do remember to set the video for something," he continued, "I never watch it but record the next thing over the top of it instead. I have tapes filled with the ends of shows I wanted to watch."

"You don't go to singles bars," she crossed her legs, dress riding up, "but you do watch women in pubs, always married women. You try to catch their eye when their husband goes to the toilet."

"You take long, long showers after he's gone to work, loving the feel of the water on your body. Then you might stretch out on that extravagant sheepskin rug in the living room."

"Like a cat," she added, draining her glass. And so they wandered down to the sea, talked some nonsense about the stars and returned to the hotel, to Henderson's single room. She showered and slipped back to her own room before dawn, with Bloor none the wiser.

In the week that remained it was inevitable that Henderson should get drawn into the group; it was the only way to escape suspicion. Henderson cultivated the other man's friendship at the same time as screwing his wife, who suddenly developed a taste for long solitary walks, usually to deserted stretches of coastline but occasionally just up to Henderson's room on the top floor. Bloor, though already a successful businessman, was attracted to the older, unflashy lecturer, and would sit for hours fascinated by his theories, the names he dropped so casually: dinner with the head of the CBI, invitations to the wedding of the ICI chief executive's daughter.

"How much of it is true?" Elizabeth asked on one of their walks.

"Enough," he said. "The rest is just confidence."

Henderson played him like a fish, paying out line when he praised Bloor's acumen, comparing his strategies to those of topflight Germans and Japanese, tactfully offering advice like a speechwriter deferring to a senior minister. Bloor glowed and bubbled for the remainder of the Greek holiday, persistently cracking terrible jokes about the name of the island: "Do you know this is where they make the stuffing?" he would grin and splutter from the dregs of yet another bottle of ouzo. "Paxos," he'd repeat time after time, "Paxos, Paxos," and trail off in incomprehensible mutterings, Elizabeth's hand on his arm (her other under the table on Henderson's linen trousers) and a smile on Henderson's lips.

They were booked back on the same charter and Bloor actually suggested to Elizabeth that she sit with Henderson rather than suffer the smoking section. At Gatwick, they made plans for Henderson to come up to Newcastle as soon as his teaching schedule would allow. In fact, he was to make many more trips up the A1 than the ones Bloor would know about. After a weekend as their guest in Gosforth he'd come up again on the Wednesday night, every other week his Thursday being completely free, and get a room at the St Mary's in Whitley Bay where Elizabeth would join him once Bloor was out of the way at work. They'd walk along the windswept beach as far as Cullercoats and make jokes about how it compared to Paxos. Neither of them spoke of love – except Elizabeth when talking about Bloor ("He does love me, you know") – and yet there was clearly a need of some kind on both sides. She would get on the phone to Henderson when Bloor was called away at short notice, as he was with increasing frequency, to Copenhagen and Brussels, and Henderson's car would find itself pressed into more and more demanding service.

They snatched a weekend together in Alnwick when Bloor was in London. He left long, whining messages on the answerphone which they heard when Henderson accompanied Elizabeth back to the house before driving back down to Leicester. Where was she? Why hadn't she called him back? Then he'd wheedle: "Don't worry, darling. I just hope you're having a nice time. I'll see you when I get back." It gave Henderson no little grim pleasure as he motored south to think that at some point Bloor would pass him going north on the opposite carriageway. He had begun to feel jealous of the man and started inventing excuses to avoid coming up for weekends at their house, no longer could he easily bear seeing them together. He didn't know if Bloor had put on weight or if he just *saw* him as fatter, slower and more complacent. After all, for all her abandon in bed at Whitley Bay, Elizabeth was still married to the man.

The expedition had been on the cards for a few weeks, ever since Bloor had bumped into his old friend Curtin at a Rotarians dinner and the taxidermist had raised the subject of wild cats. Elizabeth did her research and suddenly the trip was on, but minus one person.

Bloor had come to a halt and Henderson caught up with him.

"Isn't it getting too dark to see one now even if there are any?" Henderson asked, wiping sweat from his forehead.

"Not if you're looking." Bloor hitched his rucksack up his back. Heavier than Henderson's, it contained the tent, a primus stove and some provisions. "We're more likely to see evidence of a cat before we see the cat itself. The carcass of a hare or a buzzard. Try and keep an eye out."

There was a note of sarcasm in his voice that Henderson had not heard before and didn't much care for. It occurred to him that apart from moments when she'd slipped to the loo, it was the first time he'd been in the company of Bloor without Elizabeth.

Around 11.30 p.m., still having seen no trace of their quarry, they found a tiny clearing and set up camp, Bloor pitching the tent while Henderson got the primus going. The sky above the pines was an indigo velvet pin cushion.

"I envy you sometimes," Bloor said as they sat back after a fairly basic meal of beans with mini-frankfurters, followed by an apple each, "being single."

"Oh?" Henderson said neutrally.

"Well, you know, the freedom. You can do what you like." Bloor leered, waggling his eyebrows.

Henderson thought about his response. "I suppose so, although I don't really have much time for any of that."

Bloor said, "Is that right?" and for the first time Henderson wondered whether he might possibly suspect. "I thought with your job there would be a lot of free time and what with all those nubile young students hanging around you could be, you know, making the most of it while you still can." He tapped a cigarette out of his Camel softpack and continued: "Only I'm beginning to wonder if I'm past it. You know. I'm forty-six, not as fit as I was. I don't know if I still satisfy Elizabeth." He stared at Henderson, then placed the cigarette between his lips and spun the wheel on his Bic lighter. "She's still a young woman."

"I don't think age comes into it," Henderson said.

"No, I don't suppose it does." Bloor flicked ash over the primus. "I mean, look at you. You're older than both of us."

"Put together," Henderson laughed, but it was a nervous laugh and he couldn't imagine that Bloor wouldn't spot it and start working things out, if he hadn't already.

For a few minutes the only sound in the night, apart from

the occasional hoot of an owl, was the hiss of Bloor dragging on his cigarette. Then he spoke again. "I've got something I want to ask you," he said, and Henderson's stomach muscles clenched. "Would you . . . and tell me if you think I shouldn't even have asked . . . but would you sleep with Elizabeth, if she wanted you to?"

Henderson was speechless.

Bloor stubbed out his cigarette.

"OK, look, I shouldn't have asked. Forget I said anything, OK?"

Henderson still couldn't find the right words.

"It's been a long day," Bloor was saying. "I think we both need some sleep. We've got to find that damn cat tomorrow and the earlier we get up the more chance we'll have." So saying he crawled into the tiny two-man tent.

"I'm going to sit up for a while," Henderson said because he couldn't face climbing into the tent while Bloor was still awake. "I won't be long."

Henderson woke at dawn, shivering and hungry, to discover that Bloor was already up. His sleeping bag had been rolled and folded into a tiny pouch and his rucksack stood ready to go. Henderson dragged himself out of his own sleeping bag and took a swig from a bottle of mineral water he kept tucked away. He pulled on some clothes and half-heartedly performed a couple of press-ups. Bloor appeared while he was taking a leak at the edge of the clearing and they set off soon after without either of them having ventured more than a "good morning".

Mid-morning they came across a rabbit, or more precisely, its skin. Something had eaten all the meat – odd bones lay scattered around – and tossed the skin aside, expertly turned inside out. Bloor took it in his hand and held it up so that the skin fell back over itself like a glove puppet.

"Wild cat," he said.

"Really?"

"They can be vicious," he added, turning the rabbit skin so that the head, which was still intact, flopped this way and that. "Mind you, a domestic cat can do this just as easily."

They pressed on deeper into the forest. Bloor stayed in front and Henderson stared as hard as he could into the soft light between the boles of tall pines, because the sooner they found the cat the sooner they could get back home. Surprisingly, it bothered him that he couldn't get to a phone to ask her how she was feeling. Her periods were generally over fairly quickly, two or three days at most, and although she suffered a little, she, and Henderson, always celebrated their arrival as proof that they'd got away with it for another month. They took precautions but, because of the circumstances, they worried a little when it got to three weeks.

It was just before they were going to stop for food, around 6.00 p.m., that they came across the weasel. It had been skinned as cleanly as the rabbit. Bloor held it up triumphantly, appearing to scent success and money.

"Curtin couldn't have done a better job himself," he said as he turned the skin over in his hands.

"What do you mean?"

"This is what he does. He skins the animal – dead, obviously – and then uses the carcass to make a mould, usually in fibreglass, unless it's something this small."

During their reconstituted meal Bloor continued.

"He invited me to spend a day at his workshop when he was mounting a puma he got from the zoo. The puma died of old age and he was commissioned to mount it for a museum somewhere in Wales. It takes weeks to do a big cat apparently, but I was there on the day he skinned it."

Bloor pushed his paper plate away and lit a cigarette. The shadows around the clearing were thickening as the sky was gradually leached of daylight.

"He hung the carcass upside down from a chain fixed to a beam and it's amazing how easily the skin comes away. He'd pull a bit and it would unravel a further inch or so, then he'd take the scalpel and delicately free it from the fat and gristle. It's bizarre when you see the skinned carcass with its bug eyes and exposed muscle and tendons. It's beautiful in a way."

Henderson rigged up the little kettle on the primus to have an excuse to look away from Bloor, whose face had taken on a look of mixed revulsion and fascination.

"What does he do with the carcass?" Henderson asked.

"Takes a mould in fibreglass then calls up the knackers yard who come along and take it away. Unless it's something small like a bird, or that weasel, in which case he slings it into the field. Apparently there's a lot of fat foxes round where he has his workshop."

"So the stuffed animal you see in a museum isn't an animal at all. It's just the skin with some kind of cast inside?"

"Exactly. He generally uses expanding foam. You could pick up a tiger with one hand, they're so light."

"It's a bit disappointing, isn't it?"

"Not really. It depends where you think the essence of the animal really is: in the carcass or in the skin. Because once you've skinned an animal all you've got on the one hand is a lump of meat, and on the other you've got the skin, which was all you saw while it was alive, after all."

"But it's only skin deep."

"Aren't we all though?" Bloor said with a grimace, plucking his cigarette from between his lips. "What would you rather see in a museum, or in your front room for that matter, a bloody carcass or a stuffed skin? I know which I find more attractive."

Henderson wasn't entirely convinced by Bloor's logic. Obviously, the carefully prepared, titivated thing in the glass case was more attractive, but if you'd slung the beast's beating heart in the bin and scraped all trace of its brains from its skull, how could you still call it an animal, albeit a stuffed one?

"What about my wife?" Bloor asked suddenly from out of the darkness. "Don't you find her attractive?"

Henderson cast around for a way to answer but ended up spluttering: "I don't know. I haven't, you know, I don't see her in that light. She's your wife."

"But she's a beautiful woman. Surely you find her attractive?"

"Well, yes, she's attractive, of course. But I don't see how it's relevant."

"Just making a point," Bloor said, sucking on his cigarette and causing the end to glow as it crept further towards his lips. "We only see the surface of things, you see."

The blue flame on the primus sputtered and died.

"Shit," said Henderson. The water hadn't yet boiled. "Have you got another gas canister?"

"Over there." Bloor pointed towards his rucksack. "Side pocket."

Henderson got the wrong side, fiddled around in one of the pockets and found nothing.

"Chuck me a torch, will you."

Bloor lobbed him the thin pencil torch he kept in his jacket and Henderson peered into the rucksack.

The redness was shocking.

Stuffed into a zip-up compartment that had not been fastened were several screwed-up tissues, all spotted and streaked with dried blood. Some instinct told him to conceal his discovery from Bloor, but the sight of blood had set his heart thumping and he had to remain bent over the rucksack even after he'd located the new canister.

Bloor's disembodied voice brought him back to his senses: "Can't you find it?"

"Got it," he said, twisting round to the little stove and fixing the new canister in place as Bloor dampened his cigarette butt and flicked it into the darkness. "Call of nature," Henderson said, getting up and disappearing into the trees.

He needed to get away from Bloor for a moment to take in what he'd just seen. Clearly, the most likely explanation was that Bloor had had a nose bleed and had kept the tissues in his rucksack rather than litter the countryside (despite his tendency to drop cigarette ends). But something was nagging at Henderson, plucking at his brain: hadn't Bloor seemed just a little bit too knowledgeable in the business of skinning animals, and where for that matter had he been to so early in the morning?

"Something wrong?"

Henderson jumped. Bloor was a few feet behind him and would have seen that Henderson was just standing there, no trickle of water between his legs.

"Can't seem to go," he said, miming zipping up his fly. Bloor grunted, lit a cigarette and turned to look into the forest. It was very dark by now, like an old house, the tree trunks like table legs. The whole place was deathly silent apart from the occasional floorboard creak as an owl alighted on a high branch.

"It's out there somewhere," Bloor said.

Something is, certainly, thought Henderson. Even if it was only the hidden animal in Bloor, the dark side of his character that enjoyed tearing small creatures apart. Though, presumably, if he was responsible, he was doing it either to frighten Henderson or convince him that the wild cat was within their grasp and thereby persuade him to go deeper with him into the forest, and into the night.

Henderson was suddenly convinced that Bloor knew exactly what was going on with Elizabeth.

The two men stood there staring into the gloom. Bloor spat

on his spent cigarette and flicked it into the forest where it was accepted silently by the carpet of needles.

When they'd packed up and were heading off again Henderson followed close behind Bloor, extremely tense, wondering what he would say next. He felt like a small boy with an angry, unpredictable father, and, like a child, he didn't seem to possess the courage either to run away or talk straight. As they walked, Henderson even started thinking that the whole premise for the jaunt could have been made up: there was no deal with Curtin and they were as likely to find a tiger as a wild cat in this godforsaken corner of the Highlands. He felt a strong urge to call off the search and return home: Bloor was no more the country boy than he was, but the other man at least had the advantage of knowing where they were going. Henderson started watching his surroundings with greater interest – the way the hills on his left seemed to rise to three distinct peaks; the change from pure pine forest to a mixture of larch and Scots pine – so that he felt a little less dependent on Bloor.

"What's next then, Graham?" he heard himself asking, to make it seem as if he still believed they were actually hunting wild cat and everything was normal.

"Black panthers," Bloor replied without a moment's hesitation. "They've been seen just outside Worcester."

"That's ridiculous. There are no big cats in England."

"What do you know about it?" Bloor spun round and glared at Henderson. "Hmm?" His dimpled chin jutted forward. "What do you know?"

Henderson watched Bloor's eyes but it was too dark to distinguish pupil from iris, so they were just black holes.

"Curtin knows a woman called Meech, a photographer, who lives down there and she saw one. OK?"

Bloor's sarcastic tone tipped the scales a fraction and Henderson felt some power flow his way; just a drop but he lapped it up. "A black panther?" he said.

"Well, it was black, it was a cat and it was the size of an Alsatian, so what do you suggest?" Bloor took out a cigarette and bathed his face in a cup of orange fire to light it.

"She could have been mistaken."

"She's a wildlife photographer."

"Did she get a picture of it?"

Bloor dragged on his cigarette and blew a column of smoke directly into Henderson's face. "She wasn't quick enough."

"Shame," said Henderson, stepping around Bloor and taking the lead for the first time. There was no path but he marched off in what had been a straight line for the last twenty minutes. After a moment he heard Bloor mutter something and start following. Henderson hid his growing unease with a confident stride but he knew he didn't possess the bluff to carry it off for very long. If Bloor was lying about the black panther he'd done so convincingly.

They marched for another half-hour. There could have been dozens of wild cats watching them from the trees for all Henderson was aware. His mind was focused exclusively on Bloor and he didn't slow his pace until the shout came: "We'll stop here." In the renewed quiet, Bloor's breath chugged like an idling locomotive. "We need some rest," he added as if he now needed to justify his orders. "It's mental as well as physical. If we're not alert we don't stand a chance."

He had echoed Henderson's own conviction but the older man was unable to prevent himself falling asleep next to Bloor in the two-man tent, and when he awoke Bloor was gone. The power shift, if it had happened at all, had been reversed. Bloor was out there somewhere either tracking rabbits and mice and gutting them with his bare hands, or he was watching Henderson from behind a tree. Maybe he was genuinely searching for the wild cat, but there were too many maybes: Henderson had had enough. If he was right and Bloor knew about them, then Elizabeth needed to know, otherwise she'd be at a disadvantage when Bloor got back to Gosforth.

There wouldn't be a phone for miles. The only thing for it was for Henderson to retrace their steps to the car and get the hell out. It wouldn't take more than a couple of hours to bomb it down to Newcastle. He could be with her – quick glance at his watch – by 7.00 am. He was sure enough of Bloor's knowledge now to take the not inconsiderable risk of stealing his car.

Henderson started packing his rucksack, suddenly terrified that Bloor would return and catch him in the act, but he had a thought and scribbled a quick note telling Bloor he'd woken up early and gone looking for him. He took from his own bag only the essentials and slipped out of the tent. The note could buy him an extra hour or two, enough time for Elizabeth to pack a bag and leave with him if she wanted to. It wouldn't be ideal, but at least she'd have a choice.

He crept through the trees for the first hundred yards in case Bloor was close by, then broke into a steady run, ducking and darting between the trunks. It was still dark, but he was surprised by the clear tracks they'd left the day before: the path was easy to follow. Cresting a rise he stopped dead, blood hammering in his chest, sweat trickling down from his scalp. Twenty yards away, crouched down between the lines of trees, ears flattened against its skull and broad tail beating on the soft forest floor was a cat. A wild cat. It bared its bone-white teeth in Henderson's direction, then, with a twitch, was gone, swallowed up by the darkness. Henderson started breathing again, exhilarated and privileged to have been allowed those two seconds' intimacy. He suddenly felt overwhelmingly grateful they had not found a wild cat: he couldn't have killed it and he would have been unable to prevent himself staying Bloor's arm.

The wild cat had gone and Henderson was free to do the same. He slipped between the thin trunks like a wraith, glancing up at the three hills on his right, the sky beginning to glow with the soft breath of dawn. He ran, just ran, and whether he possessed a keener sense of direction than he realised, or did it simply because he had to, he covered the distance and tumbled out of the forest which seemed to snap shut behind him. The Mercedes gleamed in the early light. Henderson bent down and reached under the wheel arch for the keys, found them, almost dropped them, flung the door open, started the engine and spat gravel at the dark line of trees already receding in the rearview mirror. Somewhere in that lot was Bloor, hopefully now sitting by the tent waiting for Henderson to come back.

The house was quiet. Set back from the road and protected by high hedges – you couldn't even hear the traffic unless you made an effort. Getting no response ringing the bell, Henderson went around to the back – vaulting a high white wooden gate – and found the kitchen door open. He called Elizabeth's name but could only hear the blood rushing in his ears. The kitchen was clean, devoid of signs of breakfast, and the wall clock read 9.25. The return trip had taken only a little longer than expected. She would normally be up and have had breakfast, although Bloor's absence would obviously allow for a change in routine should she wish it.

Henderson made his way into the hallway, fingering the banister rail as if it were made of china.

"Elizabeth," he called once more and was disturbed to hear his voice break. He felt his face burning red and a little knot in his stomach tightening.

He stood silently on the landing for a couple of beats. The house was still. An impossible draught brushed the back of his neck and a ripple ran over his scalp, pulling the smallest hairs erect. He took another step towards Elizabeth's bedroom, pushed open the door and stood on the threshold.

Amid a jumble of mad thoughts and a nauseous sinking sensation, he wondered how long he'd known at the back of his mind that this was what he would find. He approached the bed, determined to retain enough strength in his legs to stay standing.

He took her in his arms and was careful not to hold her too tight in case the stitching broke. As he sat on the bed rocking gently forward and back, forward and back, he thought with infinite sadness that here was a woman he could have loved, if he didn't already. Flooding through came the realization that subconsciously he had strongly desired her separation from Bloor. Each time he looked at her – the puckered skin around the eyes, the lopsided mouth – he pictured Bloor at work. He relaxed his hold.

Later, outside by the white gate he'd vaulted to gain entrance to the grounds, he found a large bundle of sacking material. It was damp and sticky to the touch but gently he peeled the layers away to get at what lay inside, which he then lifted out and cradled in his arms, unmoved by the powerful smell and seeping fluids.

The sun crossed the sky slowly, passing overhead, burning only dully through the gathering scraps of cloud. The house remained silent apart from the creak of Henderson, upstairs once more, rocking to and fro on the bed, sheets sliding, slats groaning.

"Curtin told me that's how he started," said Bloor.

Henderson tensed but didn't let go. He turned his head enough to see Bloor in the doorway hugging the slippery carcass to his chest, tears tumbling from his ravaged, poisoned eyes.

"Mounting the things he loved – his dog and his cats – because he couldn't bear it when they went away. It must be different with pets," he added blankly. "Which one of us has got her now, do you think?"

Henderson traced his finger over her skin, stretched tight across the mere shape of her shoulder. He didn't know what to say.

MICHAEL MARSHALL SMITH

Hell Hath Enlarged Herself

MICHAEL MARSHALL SMITH WAS BORN in Cheshire, England, but spent most of his childhood in America, South Africa and Australia. After attending Cambridge University, he earned a living as a graphic designer for several years, but now works full-time as a novelist and film screenwriter.

His short stories have been published in a variety of anthologies and magazines on both sides of the Atlantic, including several volumes of the *Darklands*, *Dark Voices*, *Dark Terrors*, *Mammoth Book of*, *The Year's Best Fantasy and Horror* and *The Best New Horror* series. His first novel, *Only Forward*, won the August Derleth Fantasy Award; his second novel, *Spares*, has been optioned by Steven Spielberg's company DreamWorks SKG. He is currently working on his third novel, *One of Us*, a movie adaptation of Robert Faulcon's "Nighthunter" series, and a number of film and television projects as a partner in Smith & Jones Productions.

"'Hell Hath Enlarged Herself' was inspired by two basic ideas," reveals Smith. "The first came after meeting a friend of a friend who is a medium – and who genuinely appeared to have something odd about them. I wondered what it would be like if one had such an ability, but could only speak with spirits who would be hurtful to your clients.

"The second was a desire to write a story set in places that had childhood resonance. I grew up in Gainesville, Florida, my father was indeed in the Geography faculty at the University there, and

Sarasota was one of the two places we always holidayed. It was oddly comforting to write about these places twenty years later, sitting in north London."

I ALWAYS ASSUMED I was going to get old. That there would come a time when just getting dressed left me breathless, when I would count a day without a nap as a victory; when I would go into a barber's and some young girl would lift up the remaining grey stragglers on my pate and look dubious if I asked her for anything more than a trim. I would have been polite to her, and tried to be charming, and she would have thought to herself how game the old bird was, while cutting off rather less than I'd asked her to. I thought all that was going to come, some day, and in a perverse sort of way I had even looked forward to it. A quiet end, a slowing down, an ellipsis to some other place.

But now I know it will not happen, that I will remain unresolved, like some fugue which didn't work out. Or perhaps more like a voice in a symphony, because I won't be the only one. I regret that. I'm going to miss having been old.

I left the facility at 6.30 yesterday evening, on the dot, as had been my practice. I took care to do everything as I always had, carefully collating my notes, tidying my desk, and making a list of things to do tomorrow. I hung my white coat on the back of my office door as always, and said goodbye to Johnny on the gate with a wink. For six months we have been engaged in a game which involves making some comment on the weather every time I enter or leave the facility, without either of us recoursing to speech. Yesterday Johnny raised his eyebrows at the dark and heavy clouds overhead, and rolled his eyes – a standard gambit. I turned one corner of my mouth down and shrugged with the other shoulder, a more adventurous riposte, in recognition of that fact this was the last time the game would ever be played. For a moment I wanted to do more, to say something, reach and out and shake his hand; but that would have been too obvious a goodbye. Perhaps no one would have stopped me anyway, as it has become abundantly clear that I am as powerless as everyone else – but I didn't want to take the risk.

Then I found my car amongst the diminishing number which still park there, and left the compound for good.

The worst part, for me, is that I knew David Ely, and understand how it all started. I was sent to work at the facility because I am partly to blame for what has happened. The original work was done together, but I was the one who had always given creed to the paranormal. David had never paid much heed to such things, not until they became an obsession. There may have been some chance remark of mine which made him open to the idea. Just having known me for so long may have been enough. If it was, then I'm sorry. There's not a great deal more I can say.

David and I met each other at the age of six, both of our fathers having taken up new positions at the same college – the University of Florida, in Gainesville. My father was in the Geography Faculty, his in Sociology, but at that time – the late eighties – the departments were drawing closer together and the two men became friends. Our families mingled closely, in countless back-yard barbecues and summer clam-bakes on the coast, and David and I grew up more like brothers than friends. We read the same clever books and hacked the same stupid computers, and even ended up losing our virginity on the same evening. One Spring, when we were both sixteen, I borrowed my mother's car and the two of us loaded it up with books, a modem and a laptop and headed off to Sarasota in search of sun and beer. We found both, in quantity, and also two young English girls on holiday. We spent a week in courting spirals of increasing tightness, playing pool and talking fizzy nonsense over cheap and exotic pizzas, and on the last night two couples walked up the beach in different directions.

Her name was Karen, and for a while I thought I was in love. I wrote a letter to her twice a week, and to this day she's probably received more mail from me than everyone else put together. Each morning I went running down to the mailbox, and ten years later the sight of an English postage stamp would still bring a faint rush of blood to my ears. But we were too far apart and too young. Maybe she had to wait a day too long for a letter once, or perhaps it was me who, without realizing it, came back empty-handed from the mailbox one too many times. Either way the letters started to slacken in pace after six months and then, without either of us ever saying anything directly, they simply stopped altogether.

A little while later I was with David in a bar and, in between shots, he looked up at me.

"You ever hear from Karen any more?" he asked.

I shook my head, only at that moment realizing that it had finally died. "Not in a while."

He nodded, and then took his shot, and missed, and as I lined up for the black I realized that he'd probably been through a similar thing. For the first time in our lives we'd lost something. It didn't break our hearts. It had only lasted a week, after all, and we were old enough to begin to realize that the world was full of girls, and that if we didn't get a move on we'd hardly have got through any of them before it was time to get married.

But does anyone ever replace that first person? That first smile, first kiss, first fierce hug hidden in the sand amidst darkness, dunes and grass? Sometimes, I guess. I kept the letters from Karen for twenty years. Never read them, just kept them. Last week I threw them all away.

What I'm saying is this. I knew David for a long, long time, and I understood what we were trying to do. He was just trying to salve his own pain, and I was trying to help him.

What happened wasn't our fault.

I spent the evening driving slowly down 75, letting the freeway take me down towards the Gulf coast of the panhandle. There were a few patches of rain, but for the most part the clouds just scudded overhead, running to some other place. I didn't see many other cars. Either people have given up fleeing, or all those capable of it had already fled. I got off just after Jocca, and headed down minor roads, trying to cut round Tampa and St Petersburg. I managed it, but it wasn't easy, and I ended up getting lost more than a few times. I would have brought a map but I'd thought I could remember the back way. I couldn't. It had been too long.

We'd heard on the radio in the afternoon that things weren't going so hot around Tampa. It was the last thing we heard, just before the signal cut out. The six of us remaining in the facility just sat around for a while, as if we believed the radio would come back on again real soon now. When it didn't, we got up one by one and drifted back to work.

As I passed the city I could see it burning in the distance, and I was glad I had taken the back way, no matter how long it took.

If you've seen what it's like when a large number of people go together, you'll understand what I mean.

Eventually I found 301 and headed down it towards 41, towards the old Coast Road.

Summer of 2005. For David and I it was time to make a decision. There was no question but that we would go to college – our families were both book-bashers from way back. The money was already in place, some from our parents but most from holiday jobs we'd played at. The question was what we were going to study.

I thought long and hard, but in the end still couldn't come to a decision. I postponed for a year, and decided to take off around the world. My parents shrugged, said "Okay, keep in touch, try not to get killed, and stop by at your Aunt Kate's in Sydney." They were that kind of people. I remember my sister bringing a friend of hers back to the house one time; the girl called herself Yax and her hair had been carefully dyed and sculpted to resemble an orange explosion. My mother just asked her where she had it done, and kept looking at it in a thoughtful way. I guess my dad must have talked her out of it.

David went for computers. Full-on systems design. He got a place at Jacksonville's new Center for Advanced Computing, which was a coup but no real surprise. David was always a hell of a bright guy. That was part of his problem.

It was strange saying goodbye to each other after so many years in each other's pockets, but I suppose we knew it was going to happen sooner or later. The plan was that he'd come out and hook up with me for a couple of months during the year. It didn't happen, for the same reason that pacts between old friends usually get forgotten. Someone else entered the picture.

I did my grand tour. I saw Europe, started to head through the Middle East and then thought better of it and flew down to Australia instead. I stopped by and saw Aunt Kate, which earned me big brownie points back home and wasn't in any way arduous. She and her family were a lot of fun, and there was a long drunken evening when she seemed to be taking messages from beyond, which was kind of interesting. My mother's side of the family was always reputed to have a touch of the medium about them, and Aunt Kate certainly did. There was an even more entertaining evening when my cousin Jenny and I probably overstepped the bounds of conventional morality in the back seat of her Jeep – but I plead the Fifth on that. After Australia, I hacked up through the Far East for a while until time and money ran out, and then I went home.

I came back with a major tan, an empty wallet, and still no real idea of what I was going to do with my life. With a couple of months to go before I had to make a decision, I decided to go visit David. I hopped on a bus and made my way up to Jacksonville on a day which was warm and full of promise. Anything could happen, I believed, and everything was there for the taking. Perhaps that was adolescent naiveté, but I was an adolescent. How was I supposed to know otherwise? I'd lead a pretty charmed life up until then, and I didn't see any real reason why it shouldn't continue. I sat in the bus and stared out the window, watching the world go by and wishing it the very best. It was a good day, and I'm glad it was. Because though I didn't know it then, the new history of the world probably started at the end of it.

I got there late afternoon, and asked around for David. Eventually someone pointed me in the right direction, to a house just off campus. I found the building and tramped up the stairs, wondering whether I shouldn't maybe have called ahead.

Eventually I found his door. I knocked, and some man I didn't recognize opened it. It took me a couple of long seconds to work out it was David. He'd grown a beard. I decided not to hold it against him just yet, and we hugged like, well, like what we were. Two best friends, seeing each other after what suddenly seemed like far too long.

"Wow, big bonding," drawled a female voice. A head slipped into view from a round the door, with wild brown hair and big green eyes. That was the first time I saw Rebecca.

Four hours later we were in a bar somewhere. I'd met Rebecca properly, and realized she was special. In fact, it's probably a good thing that they'd met six months before and that she was so evidently in love with David. Had we met her at the same time, she could have been the first thing we'd ever fallen out over. She was beautiful, in a strange and quirky way that always made me think of forests; and she was clever, in that particularly appealing fashion which meant she didn't always have to prove it. She moved like a cat on a sleepy afternoon, but her eyes were always alive – even when they couldn't co-operate with each other enough to allow her to accurately judge the distance to her glass. She was my best friend's girl, she was a good one, and I was very happy for him.

Rebecca was at the School of Medical Science, designing little machines, not much bigger than molecules, which could float around the body doing maintenance work. Nanotech was just coming off big around then, and it looked like she was going to catch the wave and go with it. In fact, when the two of them talked about their work, it made me wish I hadn't taken the year off. Things were happening for them. They had a direction. All I had was goodwill towards the world, and the belief that it loved me too. For the first time I had that terrible sensation that life is leaving you behind and you'll never catch up again.

Around 1.00 a.m. we were still going strong. David lurched in the general direction of the bar to get us some more beer, navigating the treacherously level floor like a man on stilts for the first time.

"Why don't you come here?" Rebecca said suddenly. I turned to her, and she shrugged. "David misses you, I don't think you're too much of an asshole, and what else are you going to do?"

I looked down at the table for a moment, thinking it over. Immediately it sounded like a good idea. But on the other hand, what would I do? And could I handle being a third wheel, instead of half a bicycle? I asked the first question first.

"We've got plans," Rebecca replied. "Stuff we want to do. You could come in with us. I know David would want you to. He always says you're the cleverest guy he's ever met."

I glanced across at David, who was conversing affably with the barman. We'd decided that to save energy we should start buying them two at a time, and David appeared to be explaining this plan. As I watched, the barman laughed. David was like that. He could get on with absolutely anyone.

"And you're sure I'm not too much of an asshole?"

Deadpan: "Nothing that I won't be able to kick out of you."

And that's how I ended up applying for, and getting, a place on Jacksonville's nanotech program. When David got back to the table I wondered aloud whether I should come up to college, and his reaction was big enough to seal the decision there and then. It was him who suggested I go nanotech, and him who explained their plan.

For years people had been trying to crack the nanotech nut.

Building tiny biological "machines", some of them little bigger than large molecules, designed to be introduced into the human body to perform some function or other: promoting the secretion of certain hormones; eroding calcium build-ups in arteries; destroying cells which looked like they were going cancerous. In the way that these things do, it had taken a long time before the first proper results started coming through – but in the last three years it had really been gathering pace. When David had met Rebecca, a couple of weeks into the first semester, they'd talked about their two subjects, and David had immediately realized that sooner or later there would be a second wave, and that they could be the first to realize it.

Lots of independent little machines was one thing. How about lots of little machines which worked together? All designed for particular functions, but co-ordinated by a neural relationship with each other, possessed of a power and intelligence that was greater than the sum of its parts. Imagine what *that* could do.

When I heard the idea I whistled. I tried to, anyway. My lips had gone all rubbery from too much beer and instead the sound came out as a sort of parping noise. But they understood what I meant.

"And no one else is working on this?"

"Not yet," David said, and I had to smile. We'd always nurtured plans for world domination. "With the three of us together, no one else stands a chance."

And so it was decided, and ratified, and discussed, over just about all the beer the bar had left. At the end of the evening we crawled back to David and Rebecca's room on our hands and knees, and I passed out on the sofa. The next day, trembling under the weight of a hangover which passed all understanding, I found a place to stay in town and went to talk to someone in the faculty of Medical Science. By the end of the week it was confirmed.

On the day I was officially enrolled in the next year's intake, the three of us went out to dinner. We went to a nice restaurant, and we ate and drank, and then at the end of the meal we placed our hands on top of each other's in the centre of the table. David's went down first, then Rebecca's, and then mine on top. With our other hands we raised our glasses.

"To us," I said. It wasn't very original, I know, but it's what

I meant. We drank, and then the three of us clasped each other's hands until our knuckles were white.

Ten years later Rebecca was dead.

The coast road was deserted, as I had expected. The one thing nobody is doing these days is heading off down to the beach to hang out. I passed a few vehicles abandoned by the side of the road, but took care not to drive too close. Often people will hide inside or behind and then leap out at anyone who passes, regardless of whether that person is in a moving vehicle or not.

I kept my eyes on the sea for the most part, concentrating on what was the same, rather than what was different. The ocean looked exactly as it always had, though I suppose usually there would have been ships to see, out on the horizon. There probably still are a few, floating aimlessly wherever the tide takes them, their decks echoing and empty or awash with blood. But I didn't see any.

When I reached Sarasota I slowed still further, until I pulled to a halt in the centre of the square. It's not a big town, Sarasota. Many, many years ago I suspect it had class, before the tide of its fashionability drew out. For the last forty years or so it has only had the ocean, but that was enough. Though the stores around the square were more than full of the usual kind of junk, the restaurants were good, and some of the old, small hotels were attractive, in a dated kind of way. Not as flashy as the deco strips on Old Miami Beach, but nice enough.

Last night the square was littered with burnt-out cars, and the pizzeria where we used to eat was still smouldering, the embers glowing in the fading light.

We worked through our degrees and out into postgraduate years. At first I had a lot to catch up on. Sometimes Rebecca snuck me into classes, but most of the time I just pored over their notes and books, and we talked long into the night. Catching up wasn't so hard, but keeping up with both of them was a struggle. I never understood the nanotech side as well as Rebecca, or the computing as deeply as David, but that was probably an advantage. I stood between the two of them, and it was in my mind where the two disciplines met most equally. Without me there, it's probable none of it would ever have come to fruition.

So maybe if you come right down to it, and it's anyone's fault, it's mine.

David's goal was designing a system which would take the input and imperatives of a number of small component parts, and synthesize them into a greater whole – catering for the fact that the concerns of biological organisms are seldom clear cut. The fuzzy logic wasn't difficult – God knows we were familiar enough with it, most noticeably in our ability to reason that we needed another beer when we couldn't even remember where the fridge was. More difficult was designing and implementing the means by which the different machines, or "beckies", as we elected to call them, interfaced with each other.

Rebecca concentrated on the physical side of the problem, synthesizing beckies with intelligence coded into artificial DNA in a manner which enabled the "brain" of each type to link up with, and transfer, information to the others. And remember, when I say "machines" I'm not talking about large metal objects which sit in the corner of the room making unattractive noises and drinking a lot of oil. I'm talking about strings of molecules hardwired together, invisible to the naked eye.

I helped them both with their specific areas, and did most of the development work in the middle, designing the overall system. It was me who came up with the first product to aim for, "ImmunityWorks".

The problem of diagnosing malfunction in the human body has always been the number of variables, many of which are difficult to monitor effectively from the outside. If someone sneezes, they could just have a cold. On the other hand, they could have flu, or the bubonic plague – or even just some dust up their nose. Unless you can test all the relevant parameters, you're not going to know what the real problem is – or the best way of treating it. We were aiming for an integrated set of beckies which could test all the relevant conditions, share their findings, and determine the best way of tackling the problem – all at the molecular level, without human intervention of any kind. The system had to be robust – to withstand interaction with the body's own immune system – and intelligent. We weren't intending to just tackle things which made you sneeze, either: we were never knowingly under-ambitious. Even for ImmunityWorks 1.0 we were aiming for a system which could cope with a wide range of viruses, bacteria and general senescence: a first aid kit which lived in the body, anticipating problems and solving them before they even got started. A kind of guardian angel, which would co-exist with the human system and protect it from harm.

We were right on the edge of knowledge, and we knew it. The roots of disease in the human body weren't properly understood, never mind the best ways to deal with them. An individual trying to do what we were doing would have needed about 300 years and a research grant bigger than God's. But we weren't just one person. We weren't even just three. Like the system we were trying to design, we were a perfect symbiosis, three minds whose joint product was incomparably greater than the sum of its parts. Also, we worked like maniacs. After we'd received our Doctorates we rented an old house together away from the campus, and turned the top floor into a private lab. Obviously there were arguments for putting it in the basement, historical precedents for example, but the top floor had a better view and, as that's where we spent most of our time, that kind of thing was an issue. We got up, we did enough to maintain our tenure at the University, and we worked on our own project in secret.

David and Rebecca had each other. I had an intermittent string of short liaisons, each of which felt I was being unfaithful to something or to someone. It wasn't Rebecca I was thinking of. God knows she was beautiful enough, and lovely enough, to pine after, but I didn't. Lusting after Rebecca would have felt like one of our beckies deciding only to work with some, not all, of the others in its system. The whole thing would have ground to a halt.

Unfaithful to us, I suppose is what I felt. To the three of us.

It took us four years to fully appreciate what we were getting into, and to establish just how much work was involved. The years after that were a process of slow, grinding progress. David and I modelled an artificial body on the computer, creating an environment in which we could test virtual versions of the beckies Rebecca and I were busy trying to synthesize. Occasionally we'd enlist the assistance of someone from the medical faculty, when we needed more of an insight into a particular disease; but this was always done covertly, and without letting on what we were doing. This was our project, and we weren't going to share it with anyone.

By July of 2016 the software side of ImmunityWorks was in beta and holding up well. We'd created code equivalents of all of the major viruses and bacteria, and built creeping failures into the code of the virtual body itself – to represent the random processes of physical malfunction. An initial set of 137 different virtual beckies was doing a sterling job of keeping an eye out for problems, then charging in and sorting them out whenever they occurred.

The physical side was proceeding a little more slowly. Creating miniature biomachines is a difficult process, and when they didn't do what they were supposed to, you couldn't exactly lift up the hood and poke around inside. The key problem, and the one which took the most time to solve, was that of imparting a sufficient degree of consciousness to the system as a whole – the aptitude for the component parts to work together, exchanging information and determining the most profitable course of action in any given circumstance. We probably built in a lot more intelligence than was necessary in the end, in fact I know we did; but it was simpler than trying to hone down the necessary conditions right away. We could always streamline in ImmunityWorks 1.1, we felt, when the system had proved itself and we had patents nobody could crack. We also gave the beckies the ability to perform simple manipulations of the matter around them. It was an essential part of their role that they be able to take action on affected tissue once they'd determined what the problem was. Otherwise it would only have been a diagnostic tool, and we were aiming higher than that.

By October we were closing in, and were ready to run a test on a monkey which we'd infected with a copy of the Marburg strain of the Ebola virus. We'd pumped a whole lot of other shit into it as well, but it was the filovirus we were most interested in. If ImmunityWorks would handle that, we reckoned, we were really getting somewhere.

Yes of course it was a stupid thing to do. We had a monkey jacked full of the most communicable virus known to man *in our house*. The lab was heavily secured by then, but it was still an insane risk. I think, in retrospect, that we were so caught up in what we were doing, in our own joint mind, that normal considerations had ceased to really register. We didn't even need to do the Ebola test. That's the really tragic thing. It was unnecessary. It was pure arrogance, and also fantastically illegal. We could have just tested BodyWorks on plain vanilla viruses, or artificially-induced cancers. If it had worked we could have contacted the media and owned our own islands within two years.

But no. We had to go the whole way.

The monkey sat in its cage, looking really very ill, with any number of sensors and electrodes taped and wired on and into its skull and body. Drips connected to bioanalysers gave a second-by-second readout of the muck that was floating around in the poor animal's bloodstream. About two hours before the animal was due to start throwing clots, David threw the switch which would inject a solution of ImmunityWorks 0.9b7 into its body.

The time was 16.23, 14 October 2016, and for the next twenty-four hours we watched.

At first the monkey continued to get worse. Arteries started clotting, and the heartbeat grew ragged and fitful. The artificial cancer which we'd induced in the animal's pancreas also appeared to be holding strong. We sat, and smoked, and drank coffee, our hearts sinking. Maybe, we began to think, we weren't so damned clever after all.

Then . . . that moment. Even now, as I sit here in this abandoned hotel and listen for sounds of movement outside, I can remember the moment when the read-outs started to turn around.

The clots started to break up. The cancerous cells started to lose vitality. The breed of simian flu which we'd acquired illicitly from the University's labs went into remission.

The monkey started getting better.

And we felt like gods, and stayed that way even when the monkey suddenly died of shock a day later. We knew by then that there was more work to do in buffering the effects the beckies had on the body. That wasn't important. It was just a detail. We had screeds of data from the experiment, and David's AI systems were already integrating it into the next version of the ImmunityWorks software. Becky and I made the tweaks to the beckies, stamping the revised software into the biomachines and refining the way they interfaced with the body's own immune system.

We only really came down to earth the next day, when we realized that Rebecca had contracted Marburg.

Eventually the sight of Sarasota's dying heart palled and I started the car up again. I drove a little further along the coast to the Lido Beach Inn, which stands just where the town starts to settle into a line of beach motels. I turned into the driveway and cruised slowly up to the entrance arch, peering into the lobby. There was nobody inside, or if there was, they were crouching in the darkness. I let the car roll down the slope until I was inside the hotel court proper, and then pulled into a space.

I climbed out, pulled my bag from the passenger seat, and locked the car up. Then I went to the trunk and took out the bag of groceries which I'd carefully culled from the stock back at the facility. I stood by the car for a moment, hearing nothing but the sound of waves over the wall at the end, and looked around. I saw no one, and no signs of violence, so I headed for the stairs to go up to the second floor and towards Room 211. I had an old copy of the key, "accidentally" not returned many years ago, which was just as well. The lobby was a pool of utter blackness in an evening which was already dark, and I had no intention of going anywhere near it.

For a moment, as I stood outside the door to the room, I thought I heard a girl's laughter, quiet and far away. I stood still for a moment, mouth slightly open to aid hearing, but heard nothing else.

Probably it was no more than a memory.

Rebecca died two days later in an isolation chamber. She bled and crashed out in the small hours of the morning, as David and I watched through glass. My head hurt so much from crying that I thought it was going to split, and David's throat was so hoarse he could barely speak. David wanted to be in there with her, but I dissuaded him. To be frank, I punched him out until he was too groggy to fight any more. There was nothing he could do, and Rebecca didn't want him to die. She told me so through the intercom, and as that was her last comprehensible wish, I decided it would be so.

We knew enough about Marburg that we could almost feel her body cavities filling up with blood, smell the blackness as it coagulated in her. When she started bleeding from her eyes I turned away, but David watched every moment. We talked to her until there was nothing left to speak to, and then watched powerless as she drifted away, retreating into some upper and hidden hall while her body collapsed around her.

Of course we tried ImmunityWorks. Again, it nearly worked. Nearly, but not quite. When Rebecca's vital signs finally stopped, her body was as clean as a whistle. But it was still dead.

David and I stayed in the lab for three days, waiting. Neither of us contracted the disease. Lucky old us.

We dressed in biohazard suits and sprayed the entire house with a solution of ImmunityWorks, top to bottom. Then we put the remains of Rebecca's body into a sealed casket, drove upstate, and buried it in a forest she would have liked. Her parents were dead, and she had no family to miss her, except us.

David left the day after the burial. We had barely spoken in the intervening period. I was sitting numbly in the kitchen on that morning and he walked in with an overnight bag. He looked at me, nodded, and left. I didn't see him again for two years.

I stayed in the house, and once I'd determined that the lab was clean, I carried on. What else was there to do?

Working on the project by myself was like trying to play chess with two-thirds of my mind burned out: the intuitive leaps which had been commonplace when the three of us were together simply didn't come, and were replaced by hours of painstaking, agonizingly slow experiment. On the other hand, I didn't kill anyone. I worked. I ate. I drove most weekends to the forest where Rebecca lay, and became familiar with the paths and light beneath the trees which sheltered her.

I refined the beckies, eventually understanding the precise nature of the shock reaction which had killed our two subjects. I pumped more and more intelligence into the system, amping the ability of the component parts to interact with each other and make their own decisions. In a year, I had the system to a point where it was faultless on common viruses, like flu. Little did the world know it, but while they were out there sniffing and coughing I had stuff sitting in ampoules which could have sorted them out forever. But that wasn't the point. "ImmunityWorks" had to work on everything. That had always been our goal, and if I was going to carry on, I was going to do it our way. I was doing it for us, or for the memory of how we'd been. The two best friends I'd ever had were gone, and if the only way I could hang onto some memory of them was through working on the project, that was what I would do.

Then one day one of them reappeared.

I was in the lab, tinkering with the subset of the beckies whose job it was to synthesize new materials out of damaged body cells. The newest strain of biomachines were capable of far, far more than the originals had been. Not only could they fight the organisms and processes which caused disease in the first place, but they could then directly repair essential cells and organs within the body to ensure that it made a healthy recovery.

"Can you do anything about colds yet?" asked a voice, and I turned to see David, standing in the doorway to the lab. He'd lost about twenty-eight pounds in weight, and looked exhausted beyond words. There were lines around his eyes, and he looked older in other ways too. As I stared at him he coughed raggedly.

"Yes," I said, struggling to keep my voice calm. David held his arm out and pulled his sleeve up. I found an ampoule of my most recent brew and spiked it with a hypo. "Where did you pick it up?"

"England."

"Is that where you've been?" I asked, as I slipped the needle into his arm and sent the beckies scurrying into his system.

"Some of the time."

"Why?"

"Why not?" he shrugged, and rolled his sleeve back up.

I waited in the kitchen while he showered and changed, sipping a beer and feeling obscurely nervous. Eventually he reappeared, looking better but still very tired. I suggested going out to a bar, and we did, carefully but unspokenly avoiding those we used to go to as a threesome. Neither of us had mentioned Rebecca yet, but she was there between us in everything we said and didn't say. We walked down winter streets to a place I knew had opened recently, and it was almost as if for the first time I felt I was grieving for her properly. While David had been away, it had been as if they'd just gone away somewhere together. Now he was here, I could no longer deny that she was dead.

We didn't say much for a while, and all I learned was that David had spent much of the last two years in Eastern Europe. I didn't push him, but simply let the conversation take its own course. It had always been David's way that he would get round to things in his own good time.

"I want to come back," he said eventually.

"David, as far as I'm concerned you never went away."

"That's not what I mean. I want to start the project up again, but different."

"Different in what way?"

He told me. It took me a while to understand what he was talking about, and when I did I began to feel tired, and cold, and sad. David didn't want to refine ImmunityWorks. He had lost all interest in the body, except in the ways in which it supported the mind. He had spent his time in Europe visiting people of a certain kind, trying to establish what it was about them that made them different. Had I known, I could have recommended my Aunt Kate to him – not, I felt, that it would have made any difference. I watched him covertly as he talked, as he became more and more animated, and all I could feel was a sense of dread, that for the rest of his life my friend would be lost to me.

What he believed was this. He believed that mediums – people who can communicate with the spirits of the dead – do not possess some special spiritual power, but instead a difference in the physical make-up of their mind. He believed that it was some fundamental but minor difference in the wiring of their senses which enabled them to bridge a gap between this world and the next, to hear voices which had stopped speaking, see faces which had faded away. What he wanted to do was determine where this difference lay, pin-point it and learn to replicate it. He wanted to develop a species of "becky" which anyone could take, which would rewire their soul and enable them to become a medium.

More specifically, he wanted to take it himself, and I understood why, and as I realized what he was hoping for I felt like crying for the first time in two years.

He wanted to be able to talk with Rebecca again, and I knew both that he was not insane and that there was nothing I could do except help him.

He put his hand down on the table and I placed mine on top of it.

Room 211 was as I remembered it. Nondescript. A decent-sized room in a mid-range motel. I put my bags on one of the twin beds and checked out the bathroom. It was clean and the shower still gave a thin trickle of luke-warm water. I washed and changed into one of the two sets of casual clothes I had brought with me, and then I made a sandwich out of cold cuts and processed cheese, storing the remainder in the small fridge in the corner by the television. I turned the latter on briefly and got snow across the board, though I heard the occasional half-word which suggested that someone was still trying somewhere.

I propped the door to the room open with a Bible and dragged a chair out onto the walkway, and then I sat and ate my food and drank a beer looking down across the court. The pool was half full, and a deck chair floated in one end of it.

Our approach was very simple. Using some savings of mine we flew to Australia, where I talked Aunt Kate into letting us take minute samples of tissue from different areas of her brain, using a battery of lymph-based beckies. We didn't tell her what the samples were for, simply that we were researching genetic traits. Jenny was now married to an accountant, it transpired, and they, Aunt Kate and David and I sat out that night on the porch and watched the sun turn red.

The next day we flew home again and went straight on to Gainesville, where I had a much harder time persuading my mother to let us do the same thing. In the end she relented, and despite claiming that the beckies had "tickled", had to admit it hadn't hurt. She seemed fit and well, as did my father when he returned from work. I saw them once again, briefly, about two months ago. I've tried calling them since but the line is dead.

Back at Jacksonville, David and I did the same thing with our own brains, and then the real work began. If, we reasoned, there really was some kind of physiological basis to the phenomena we were searching for, then it ought to show up to varying degrees in my family line, and less so – or not at all – in David. We had no idea whether it would be down to some chemical balance, a difference in synaptic function, or a virtual "sixth sense" which some subsection of the brain was sensitive to – and so, in the beginning, we just used part of the samples to find out exactly what we'd got to work with.

We drew the blinds and stayed inside, and worked eighteen hours a day. David said little, and for much of the time seemed only half the person he used to be. I realized that until we succeeded in letting him talk with his love again, I would not see the friend I knew. We both had our reasons for doing what we did.

It took a little longer than we'd hoped, but we threw a lot of computing power at it and in the end began to see results.

They were complex, and not absolutely conclusive, but appeared to suggest that all three possibilities were partly true. My aunt showed a minute difference in synaptic function in certain areas of her brain, which I shared, but not the fractional chemical imbalances which were present in both my mother and I. On the other hand, there was evidence of a loose meta-structure of apparently unrelated areas of her brain which was only present in trace degrees in my mother, and not at all in me. We took these results and correlated them against the findings from the samples of David's brain, and finally came to a tentative conclusion.

The ability, if it truly was related to physiological morphology, seemed most directly related to an apparently insignificant variation in general synaptic function which created an almost intangible additional structure within certain areas of the brain.

Not, perhaps, one of the most memorable slogans of scientific discovery, but that night David and I went out and got more drunk than we had in five years. We clasped hands on the table once more, and this time we believed that the hand that should have been between ours was nearly within reach. The next day we split into two overlapping teams, dividing our time and minds as always between the software and the beckies. The beckies needed redesigning to cope with the new environment, and the software required yet another quantum leap to deal with the complexity of the tasks of synaptic manipulation. As we worked we joked that if the beckies got much more intelligent we'd have to give them the vote. It seemed funny back then.

November 12, 2017, ought to have a significant place in the history of science, despite everything that happened afterwards. It was the day on which we tested MindWorks 1.0, a combination of computer and corporeal which was probably more subtle than anything man has ever produced. David insisted on being the first subject, despite the fact that he had another cold, and in the early afternoon of that day I injected him with a tiny dose of the beckies. Then, in a flash of solidarity, I injected myself. Together till the end, we said – though, at the end, we weren't.

We sat there for five minutes and then got on with some work. We knew that the effects, if there were any, wouldn't be immediate. To be absolutely honest, we weren't expecting much at all from the first batch. As everyone knows, anything with the version number "1" will have teething problems, and if it has a ".0" after it, then it's going to crash and burn. We sat and tinkered with the plans for a "1.1" version, which was only different in that some of the algorithms were more elegant, but couldn't seem to concentrate. Excitement, we assumed.

Then in the late afternoon David staggered, and dropped a flask of the solution he was working on. It was full of MindWorks, but that didn't matter – we had a whole vat of it in storage. I made David sit down and ran a series of tests on him. Physically he was okay, and protested that he felt fine. We shrugged and went back to work. I printed out ten copies of the code and becky specifications, and posted them to ten different places around the world. If this worked it was going to be ours, and no one else was taking credit for it. Such considerations were actually less important to us by then, because there was only one thing we wanted from the experiment – but old habits die hard. Ten minutes later I had a dizzy spell myself, but apart from that nothing seemed to be happening at all.

We only realized that we might have succeeded when I woke to hear David screaming in the night.

I ran into his room and found him crouched up against the wall, eyes wide, teeth chattering uncontrollably. He was staring at the opposite corner of the room. He didn't seem to be able to hear anything I said to him. As I stood there numbly, wondering what to do, I heard a voice from behind me – a voice I half-thought I recognized. I turned, but there was no one there. Suddenly David looked at me, his eyes wide and terrified.

"Fuck," he said. "I think it's working."

We spent the rest of the night in the kitchen, sitting around the table and drinking coffee in harsh light. David didn't seem to be able to remember exactly what it was he'd seen, and I couldn't recapture the sound of the voice I'd heard, or what it might have said. Clearly we'd achieved something, but it wasn't clear what it might be. When nothing further happened by daybreak, we decided to get out of the house for a while. We were both too keyed up to sit around any longer or try to work, but felt we should stay together. Something was happening, we knew: we could both feel it. We walked around campus for the morning, had lunch in the cafeteria, then spent the afternoon downtown. The streets seemed very crowded, but apart from that nothing else weird happened.

In the evening we went out. We had been invited to a dinner party at the house of a couple on the medical staff, and thought we may as well attend. David and I were a little distracted at first, but once everyone had enough wine inside them we started to have a good time. The hosts got out their store of somewhat elderly dope, and by midnight we were all a little high, comfortably sprawled around the living room.

And of course, eventually, David started talking about the work we'd been doing. At first people just laughed hysterically, and that made me realize belatedly just how far outside the scope of normal scientific endeavor we had moved. It also made me determined that we should be taken seriously, and so I started to back David up. It was stupid, and we should never have mentioned it. It was one of the people at that party who eventually gave our names to the police.

"So prove it," this man said at one stage. "Hey, is there a ouija board in the house?"

The general laughter which greeted this sally was enough to tip the balance. David rose unsteadily to his feet, and stood in the centre of the room. He sneezed twice, to general amusement, but then his head seemed to clear. Though he was swaying gently, the seriousness of his face was enough to quieten most people, although there was a certain amount of giggling. He looked gaunt and tired, and everybody stopped talking, and the room went very quiet as they watched him.

"Hello?" he said quietly. He didn't use a name, for obvious reasons, but I knew who he was asking for. "Are you there?"

"And if so, did you bring any grass?" the hostess added, getting a big laugh. I shook my head, partly at how foolish we were seeming, partly because there seemed to be a faint glow in one corner of the room, as if some of the receptors in my eyes were firing strangely. I made a note to check the "beckies" when we got back, to make sure none of them could have had an effect on the optic nerve.

I was about to say something, to help David out of an embarrassing position, when he suddenly turned to the hostess.

"Jackie, how many people did you invite tonight?"

"Eight," she said. "We always have eight. We've only got eight complete sets of table ware."

David looked at me. "How many people do you see?" he asked.

I looked round the room, counting.

"Eleven," I said. One of the guests laughed nervously. I counted them again. There were eleven people in the room. In addition to the eight of us who were slouched over the settees and floor, three people stood around the sides. A tall man, with long and not especially clean brown hair. A woman in her forties, with blank eyes. A young girl, maybe eight years old.

Mouth hanging open, I stood up to join David. We looked from each of the extra figures to the other. They looked entirely real, as if they'd been there all along. They stared back at us, silently.

"Come on guys," said the host nervously. "Okay, great gag – you had us fooled for a moment there. Now let's have another smoke."

David ignored him, turning to the man with the long hair.

"What's your name?" he asked him. There was a long pause, as if the man was having difficulty remembering. When he spoke, his voice sounded dry and cold.

"Nat," he said. "Nat Simon."

"David," I said. "Be careful."

David ignored me, and turned back to face the real guests. "Does the name 'Nat Simon' mean anything to anyone here?" he asked.

For a moment I thought it hadn't and then we noticed the hostess. The smile had slipped from her face and her skin had gone white, and she was staring at David. With a sudden, ragged beat of my heart I knew we had succeeded.

"Who was he?" I asked quickly. I wish I hadn't. In a room that was now utterly silent she told us.

Nat Simon had been a friend of one of her uncles. One summer, when she was five-years-old, he had raped her every day for two weeks. He was killed in a car accident when she was fourteen, and since then she'd thought she'd been free.

"Tell Jackie I've come back to see her," Nat said proudly, "And I'm all fired up and ready to go." He had taken his penis out of his trousers and was stroking it towards erection.

"Go away," I said. "Fuck off back where you came from."

Nat just smiled. "Ain't ever been anywhere else," he said. "Like to stay as close to little Jackie as I can."

David quickly asked the other two figures who they were. I tried to stop him, but the other guests encouraged him, at least until they heard the answers. Then the party ended abruptly.

Voyeurism becomes a lot less amusing when it's you people are staring at.

The blank-eyed woman was the first wife of the man who had joked about ouija boards. After discovering his affair with one of his students, she had committed suicide in their living room.

The little girl was the host's sister. She died in childhood, hit by a car while running across the road as part of a dare devised by her brother.

By the time David and I ran out of the house, two of the other guests had already started being able to see for themselves, and the number of people at the party had risen to fifteen.

After four beers my mind was a little fuzzy, and for a while I was almost able to forget. Then I heard a soft splashing sound from below, and looked to see a young boy climbing out of the stagnant water in the pool. He didn't look up, but just walked over the flagstones to the gate, and then padded out through the entrance to the motel. I could still hear the soft sound of his wet feet long after he'd disappeared into the darkness. The brother who'd held his head under a moment too long; the father who'd been too busy watching someone else's wife putting lotion on her thighs; or the mother who'd fallen asleep. Someone would be having a visitor tonight.

When we got back to the house after the party and tried to get back into the lab, we found that we couldn't open the door. The lock had fused. Something had attacked the tumblers, turning the mechanism into a solid lump of metal. We stared at each other, by now feeling very sober, and then turned to look through the glass upper portion of the door. Everything inside looked the way it always had, but I believe even that early, before we knew what was happening, everything had already been set in motion. The "beckies" work like God, it would appear, in strange and invisible ways.

David got the axe from the garage and we broke through the door to the laboratory. We found the vat of MindWorks empty. A small hole had appeared in the bottom of the glass, and there was a faint trail where the contents had flowed across the floor, making small holes at several points. It had doubled back on itself, and at several points it had also flowed against gravity. It ended in a larger hole which, it transpired, dripped through into a pipe. A pipe which went out back into the municipal water system.

The first reports were on CNN at 7.00 the next morning. Eight murders in downtown Jacksonville, and three on the University campus. Reports of people suddenly going crazy, screaming at people who weren't there, running in terror from voices in their head and acting on impulses that they claimed weren't theirs. By lunchtime the problem wasn't just confined to people we might have come into contact with: it had started to spread on its own.

I don't know why it happened like this. Maybe we just made a mistake somewhere. Perhaps it was something as small and simple as a chiral isomer, some chemical which the "beckies" created in a mirror image of the way it should be. That's what happened with Thalidomide, and that's what we had created. A Thalidomide of the soul.

Or maybe there was no mistake. Perhaps that's just the way it is. Maybe the only people who stick around are the ones you don't want to see. The ones who can turn people into psychotics who riot, murder, or end their lives, through the hatred or guilt they bring with them. These people have always been here, all the time, staying close to the people who remember them. Only now they are no longer silent.

A day later there were reports in European cities, at first just the ones where I'd sent my letters, then spreading rapidly across the entire land mass. By the time my letters reached their recipients, the "beckies" I'd breathed over them had multiplied a thousandfold, breaking the paper down and reconstituting the molecules to create more of themselves. They were so clever, our children, and they shared the ambitions of their creators. If they'd needed to, they could probably have formed themselves into new letters and lay around until someone posted them all over the world. But they didn't, because coughing, or sneezing, or just breathing, is enough to spread the infection. By the following week, a state of emergency was in force in every country in the world.

A mob killed David before the police got to him. He never got to see Rebecca. I don't know why. She just didn't come. I was placed under house arrest, and then taken to the facility to help with the feverish attempts to come up with a cure. There is none and there never will be. The "beckies" are too smart, too aggressive, and too powerful. They just take any antidote, break it down, and use it to make more of themselves.

They don't need the vote any more. They're already in control.

The moon is out over the ocean, casting glints over the tides as they rustle back and forth with a sound like someone slowly running their finger across a piece of paper. A little while ago, I heard a siren in the far distance. Apart from that all is quiet.

I think it's unlikely I shall riot, or go on a killing spree. In the end, I will simply go.

The times when Karen comes to see me are bad. She didn't stop writing to me because she lost interest, it turns out. She stopped writing because she had been pregnant by me, and died through complications in childbirth. When David and I talked of her over that game of pool she was already dead. She will come again tonight, as she always does, and maybe tonight will be the night when I decide I cannot bear it any longer. Perhaps seeing her here, at the motel where David and I stayed that summer, will be enough to make me do what I have to do.

If it isn't her who gives me the strength, then someone else will, because I've started seeing other people now too. It's surprising quite how many – or maybe it isn't, when you consider that all of this is partly my fault. So many people have died, and will die, all of them with something to say to me. Every night there are more, as the world slowly winds down. There are two of them here now, standing in the court and looking up at me. Perhaps in the end I shall be the last one alive, surrounded by silent figures in ranks that reach out to the horizon.

Or maybe, as I hope, some night David and Rebecca will come for me and I will go with them.

CHRISTOPHER FOWLER

Unforgotten

CHRISTOPHER FOWLER HAS RECENTLY written the screenplays for two of his novels, *Spanky* and *Psychoville*, the latter as a vehicle for the new "Britpack" stars, at their request. His other novels include *Roofworld*, *Rune*, *Red Bride* and *Disturbia*. His latest collection of stories is titled *Personal Demons*, he is also the author of a graphic novel from DC Comics, *Menz Insanza*, illustrated by John Bolton, and he is currently working on his next novel, entitled *Sohodevil*.

"'Unforgotten' was inspired by the interior life of certain central London city blocks," explains Fowler. "Behind the street façades of smart new shops and trendy bars, one very often finds sections of ancient buildings: rear walls, courtyards, forgotten rooms, boarded-up doors, and these remain the same through the decades. I first discovered this climbing onto the roof of 13 Bateman Street, Soho, from which one can see pieces of the old city, and a Dickensian view of London no tourist ever gets to see.

"Notably among these are the alleyways behind Bond Street, the areas surrounding Columbia Road and Petticoat Lane, behind St Peter's Church, Clerkenwell, and behind Spitalfields. Until very recently, Becky's Dive Bar in the basement of the Corn Exchange had a men's toilet that one could only reach by crossing a section of the underground River Fleet. It occurred to me that the ancient city could still have a few tricks up its sleeve, and that an unsympathetic developer could still be dealt a nasty surprise."

* * *

IT CANNOT THINK, fanciful to imagine it could, for how would so many millions of lives make themselves heard, distilled into a single voice? But if – just if – there was such a thing as a collective intelligence, what would it be saying now, the voice of London?

During the trial of Captain Clarke at the Old Bailey in 1750, the court became so hot that the windows had to be opened, and the foul germ-laden stench from nearby Newgate Prison that blew in killed everyone sitting on the window-side of the court – all forty-four people.

"How much do they want for the sale?"

"Three hundred and seventy grand. That's what they figure it's worth at today's prices."

"I'm in this business to make a living, not to be bent over a table and fucked stupid."

"I'm sorry, that's what their man told me to tell you."

"Well, you can tell them – " The door opened behind Marrick and his exhausted secretary stuck her head into the room. Marrick nearly fell off his chair trying to see who it was.

"For fuck's sake, Doris," he exploded, "will you stop creeping around like Marley's fucking ghost?"

"I'm sorry, Mr Marrick, I'm about to vanish for the night, and your wife is here."

Doris tossed the information into the room like a lit firecracker and beat a hasty retreat.

Marrick banged his chair upright. "Harrods must have declined her credit cards again. This is all I fucking need. Excuse me, gentlemen. Jonathan, see if you can talk some fucking sense into the sales agent. Try to make him see that I'm not a completely heartless bastard. You know – lie." The door slammed and he was gone in a cloud of acrid cigar smoke.

Jonathan Laine didn't much like his boss; the man had no respect for anything or anyone. Adrian Marrick trampled a path through life in a cheap suit, shouting and shoving all the way. The technique worked, up to a point, but Jonathan could not see the company expanding beyond this dingy Holborn office. There were barriers of class in the city, invisible lines that could not be crossed by a marauding loudmouthed oik from south London.

Jonathan was not complaining; at the age of fifty-seven he

was at least still employed and making a subsistence wage. His boss was just past his twenty-fourth birthday, and although it sometimes seemed strange to be working for a such a young man, Marrick possessed a cunning far beyond his years. He could even be fun in an appalling way – chain-smoking, swearing, drinking, and dealing through the property market, and he was a good teacher so long as you remembered to isolate the immoral and illegal elements of his advice. His observations about his fellow man could be jaw-droppingly crass, and yet there was often a horrible accuracy to them. He was part of a new generation whose tastes were decided by price. "You owe us, old sport," he would say in one of his magnanimous after-dinner moods. "We're burying the past, chucking away the old rules. Giving commerce a chance to breathe."

Jonathan considered himself to be a reasonably moral man. He had never meant to end up working in a place like this. The pleasures of his life stemmed from peaceful pursuits, his interests inclined to classical studies. He had always held an unformulated plan in his head, to succeed as some kind of architectural historian. Instead he had married young, looked after his parents, raised a child, suffered a nervous breakdown. He had been sidetracked by his need to make money, distracted by the fuss of living, misrouted from his original goal. And now, here he was in the centre of one of the most historically important cities in the world, and the only work he had found since the death of Connie was in property speculation, helping to asset-strip and destroy the very thing he cared about most dearly. A typical Gemini trait, he thought, to be both destroyer and creator. Well, one day he would find a way to repay the debt, redress the balance. Until then . . .

He turned back to a desk smothered in unprocessed documents. Darren, the office junior, was laboriously clipping surveyor's reports together and arranging them in files. Today's problem had been growing for a while now. The building in question was a run-down Victorian house presently occupied by an electrical appliance contractor. The freehold was owned by the Japanese property conglomerate Dasako, and the lease had been granted on a short-term basis that was now reaching an end. Jonathan's case notes ran to dozens of pages. Marrick was desperate to purchase the building outright because it stood between two other properties he owned under different company titles. Individually, neither was worth much above land value, but collectively they represented a highly attractive proposition. Jonathan assumed that ownership of the third property would increase access to the other two, but Marrick had never explained why he wanted to own such a large chunk of property. He never explained anything. He was guided by an unerring instinct for making money.

Jonathan was sure that Dasako had no knowledge of Marrick's involvement in the surrounding offices; the names on the company records would mean nothing to them. Even so, their asking price for the soon-to-be vacant property was way too high. The area would not support such a valuation. There had to be a reason for pricing themselves out of the market, but what could it be?

"Tell you what," said Marrick in the pub later that evening, "I've got an idea," and he threw Jonathan a crooked grin which normally meant something dishonest was coming. He made a meaty fist around the handle of his pint, his rings glittering like gold knuckle-dusters. "Get me the plans for the city block, would you?"

"The whole block?"

"Yeah. There's something I remember seeing the last time I went over the place. I've got a feeling we can stitch up these tossers without moving a fucking muscle." He drained his glass and banged it down, then felt his jacket for his cigars. "Three hundred and seventy K for an almost derelict building, bollocks! I know their fucking game."

"You think they're going to find a new tenant?"

"Nope," said Marrick, lighting up an absurdly large cigar. "Of course not. Crafty bastards have other plans. They're gonna get it listed and restore all the original features." He sucked noisily at the stogie.

"How can you be so sure?" asked Jonathan, shifting beyond his boss's smoke-ring range.

"Ah, well you see, while you're still snuggled up in bed in your pyjamas dreaming about retirement, I'm up with the fucking larks collecting information, and I hear that Dasako are currently employing the services of a design company that specializes in restaurants. Fucking great big Conran-style eateries that seat 700 diners at a time. If they get a restaurant in that space and it's a success, we'll never fucking get them out."

"So what do you propose to do?" asked Jonathan. He ran a hand through his straggling grey hair and waited while his employer picked flakes of tobacco from his lip.

"I'm gonna buy 'em out, pull the whole lot down and resell. It's worth fuck-all as it is. The upper floors are falling apart. Just get me the plans of the block."

The teeming humanity that passes through London as the centuries rise and fall! The sheer weight of life borne by such a small area of land! The city transforms itself from a Roman capital with an amphitheatre, forum and basilica, its Temples of Mithras and Diana giving way to the spired cathedrals of Christianity. Walls, gates and defences rise, parish churches are built over Saxon villages, medieval commerce packs the streets with wood-beamed houses, and the kaleidoscope of history spins wildly on through coronations, insurrections and disharmonies, mutiny and jubilation eliding past, present and future. And through these pullulating voices one word is heard most clearly; Charles I, stepping up to his execution before jeering crowds in Whitehall, turns to his bishop-confessor and cries "Remember!"

When old London Bridge was widened in the 1760s, it was realized that the new footpath would have to cut through the hundred-year-old tower of St Magnus the Martyr on the eastern side of the bridge. Incredibly, Sir Christopher Wren had built the church in anticipation that this problem would occur a century later, and had already provided the tower's arches with removable sections to create such a passageway.

London's building plans are a mess. The Second World War saw to that. In some parts of the capital, virtually every other building was destroyed in the firestorm of the Blitz, and the once elegant streets gaped like the rotten teeth of a corpse. Between 6.00 p.m. and 9.30 p.m. on Sunday, 29 December 1940, the second great fire of London occurred when the German Luftwaffe dropped 127 tons of high explosive and more than 10,000 incendiary bombs on the city. A famous photograph of that night shows St Pauls rising unharmed through a raging sea of flame.

Jonathan looked up at the squat brown building standing between two fifties office blocks and tried to imagine how it had been that terrible night: the din of tumbling masonry, the blasts of the firefighters' hoses. He had been two-years-old and living far away, in north Yorkshire. *London Can Take It* – some motto. But the city had managed it in the past, so many times, surviving the plagues and the fires only to be brought to its knees at the end of the twentieth century by traffic and developers. A city as old as Christianity itself was fighting for its life. Jonathan pulled the camera from his jacket and snapped a few shots; the grimy storefront with the yellow plastic sign reading AIKO ELECTRICS, the four floors of crumbling Victorian redbrick, (third and fourth clearly on the verge of collapse), the ill-fitting modern roof, what an invisible, unimpressive – and unlisted – building it was. Perhaps it deserved to be pulled down. It wasn't always a good idea to cling to the past. Marrick would have no qualms about demolishing the Albert Hall if it suited his plans.

But then he looked up at the building again and tried to imagine it restored and filled with people. That was when he noticed the details; the dusty turquoise glazing bars on the tops of the third floor windows, the swagged ornamentation on the broken rainwater head at the top of the drainpipe, the rusticated keystone above the archway leading to the building's side-alley, and he realized then that a magnificent building was hiding behind its wounds and beneath a caul of dirt, that it could all be restored, because it had been a restaurant once before, long ago, and Dasako had spotted it even if Marrick hadn't. On the pavement was another telltale sign; a shattered section of black and white mosaic in which the name of the establishment would have been set in curlicues of brass. And most miraculous of all, there on the wall beside the door, a battered cone of blackened metal, a snuffer! These rarely-spotted pieces of street furniture were used to extinguish the tar-covered brands of the link-boys who escorted the restaurant's visitors through the unlit streets. Dasako's architects had seen all this. The Japanese respected the traditions of the past. With patience and planning, they would allow this building to spring to full-blooded life once more, filled with gaiety and beauty. Its restaurant would stand as a magnificent testament to the pleasures of the past, and the possibilities of the future.

But there was something else here as well, something that could only be seen away from the light, something less wholesome and only just hidden from view. Jonathan could feel the strange sensation creeping across him like a stormcloud obscuring the sun. There was something here that hid within the bricks. The weight of history was giddying and he felt suddenly sick. He ceased pacing in order to catch his breath, then walked on past the central building, turning the corner at the end of the block. Three buildings constituted its longest side; the other three sides were shorter, comprising two buildings each. The one in the centre of the long side, the building owned by Dasako, grew narrower toward the rear and was truncated to allow a central courtyard within the block, although according to Marrick little evidence of this could be seen from its windows, the courtyard having been largely built over.

Jonathan looked up at the rapidly darkening sky and felt a speck of rain. At his back, traffic thrummed endlessly around a one-way system toward Hackney Town Hall. He realized with a start that he was standing near the spot where he and Connie were married. The little church had been demolished in the seventies to make way for wider traffic lanes. In his mind's eye, he saw Connie turning on the steps and crying delightedly, confetti drifting from her shoulders as a passing car sounded its horn in celebration. Harder to see her now, of course; harder each day to capture each retreating memory.

He pocketed the camera and turned his collar up, preparing for his next stop – the building registry office just behind Lombard Street. Why did Marrick want plans for the entire block? What was going through his mind? Sometimes his cunning displayed the most surprising lateral thinking. As he headed for the Old Street tube station, the only certainty Jonathan had was that money would once more change hands in deceitful circumstances.

London is an old, old woman, heartsick and tired. Her aches have now grown into a solid constant pain, nagging and unrelieved. To have survived the poverty, the misery, the riots, the ravages of sickness and disaster, to have outlived the numbing terrors of the bombs – and for what? To see the city's heart torn out and cast aside, to see her body desecrated and her soul destroyed. She has always fought back, but now her fighting days are at an end, and the battle is all but lost.

There is little that is truly Christian about London. Hawksmoor's churches have long been noted for the strange profanity of their design, but there are many acknowledgements of other gods. The building of Bush House will never be completed. If you walk through the western colonnade which connects the Strand to the Aldwych, you'll see that one of the building's columns has an incomplete capital in order to comply to an old adage; "Perfection is an attribute of Allah; Impiety to achieve perfection."

Jonathan had to support the drawer of the plans chest on his bent knee in order to remove the architectural layouts without damaging them. They appeared to have been drawn in the 1930s and poorly updated in the late fifties. Presumably there were earlier versions stored somewhere, but nobody seemed to know where. The paper was fine and brittle, carelessly stored beside a radiator for too many years. He gently laid the plan to one side for photocopying, and noticed the scrap of map wedged beneath it. It was old, certainly early-nineteenth century. His finger traced a path across botanical gardens in faded emerald ink, through the fields of Kensington, over meadows and market gardens to the straggling canalways and riverbanks of north London. He loved maps. To be perched dizzyingly high in the clouds from the cartographer's viewpoint, peering down across a metropolis that is trapped forever in a single moment.

"Are you going to be much longer with that?" A listless secretary clumped past. There was a vague, unfocussed hatred in her eyes, a suspicion of age, of gender, of everyone and everything. Jonathan so often saw it in the eyes of the young. He reluctantly closed the drawer and rose. He could spend all day here, sifting through the blueprints of the past, but Marrick would have a heart attack. As soon as his copies were ready he folded them into his case and stepped back into the penetrating rain.

* * *

He found the drawing at his local library, in a book on Edwardian London. An attenuated young lady in a peach-coloured gown with a fur collar was alighting from a carriage on the arm of her evening-suited beau. In his free hand, the man held a top hat and a pair of white gloves. Rain glossed the street. The restaurant before them was a shimmering wall of light. Great chandeliers sparkled above the elegant dining lounge. The maitre d' stood beneath a silvered canopy awaiting the new arrivals. A copperplate sign was illuminated by rows of dazzling bulbs: *La Belle Epoque*. Of course. The place was world-renowned. Jonathan pored over every detail. You could even see the snuffer beside the entrance. It all looked so – what was the word? *Swanky*. An Americanism, of course, but quite old and entirely appropriate. He savoured the picture, longed to tear it out and hide it inside his overcoat. Instead he rose and returned to his cold flat above the fishmongers in the high street, to pass the evening in his books and his dreams.

"Piece of piss" said Marrick, wiping a chunk of bread around his plate and popping it in his mouth. "Between the end of Aiko's lease and Dasako's application for listed building status, I bunged an offer in to them – 260 K."

They were having lunch, several weeks later, in a vast and deafening Wardour Street restaurant. Marrick hated the food but ate here because it was fashionable. The hard wooden seats were designed to discourage lingerers and Jonathan had to shift awkwardly about to stop his legs from going numb. "I don't understand," he said as the appalling truth sank in. "Why would they have accepted such a bid?"

"Because they can't build a restaurant there any more. No fucking planning permission. Modern laws require safety exits, and they ain't got any."

"I'm sure I saw an alleyway at the side of the building. Couldn't they have applied to make use of that?"

"Could have done if it was theirs, old fruit, but it's not. It belongs to the building next door, my little auction-purchase. Their bloke contacted me and tried to get the right-of-way signed over."

"And what happened?" asked Jonathan, dreading the answer.
"I told him to fuck off, obviously."
"But surely they can appeal?"
Marrick looked at him suspiciously and seemed about to speak,

then changed his mind. "No," he said finally, raising his glass and draining it. "They can't appeal. How can they build exits when the only other properties bordering theirs are mine? Anyway, the deal's already going through. Their hands are tied good and proper. They'll find some other dump to tart up. I'll have all three buildings down within a month, crash, bang, bosh, clear the space and flog it off as office units. I feel like celebrating. Let's get another bottle of this, if we can find a fucking waiter."

It made perfect sense, of course. He'd seen it on the map, but had chosen to ignore an obvious truth; the three properties were worth more knocked flat and sold in newly-arranged packages of landspace. The packages could be tailored to suit modern business requirements. London's existing old buildings found it difficult to incorporate the conduits that were required to carry computer cables.

In Jonathan's mind the golden windows of *La Belle Epoque* dimmed, the glittering crystalline structure dismantled itself and disappeared into the night, leaving behind a deep, dirty pool of shadow. He could not bring himself to hate Marrick; he was merely disappointed that the past had been cheated out of a chance to return.

The spirit of London sinks from a powerful roar of flame to a single glowing ember, and soon that too will be extinguished. For cities, like people, must eventually grow old and die. Even a city as ancient as this.

Scotland Yard, named after the palace where the kings of Scotland lodged when visiting London, is founded on the site of an unsolved murder. Mutilated portions of a woman's body were secreted on the building site in the 1880s, and the officers of the C.I.D. were never able to discover the identity of the murderer or his victim.

Jonathan turned on the desk light and tilted back the green glass shade, then unfolded the photostat across the cleared surface of his desk. Marrick was planning to inspect the vacated premises with him tomorrow. After that, it was simply a matter of sorting out the paperwork and waiting for the demolition order to be cleared. He withdrew a magnifying glass and checked each of the rooms and staircases in turn. Something about the map bothered him. Or rather, something about the way it matched the experience of actually visiting the property. He checked the specifications of each of the buildings against the photographs he had taken, but the anomaly eluded him. Why couldn't he see it? Something was wrong, something at the heart of the land itself. He removed his reading glasses and massaged the bridge of his nose. Perhaps the answer would come to him tomorrow. He refolded the map, switched off the desk-lamp and wearily headed for bed.

"I don't know why they had to turn the fucking lights off," moaned Marrick as he and Jonathan passed beneath the cracked AIKO sign and entered the ground floor of the building. "Look at it out there, ten in the morning and you'd think it was fucking midnight. Did you bring a torch?"

"Yes. The main staircase is to the rear of this room." Jonathan clicked on the flashlight and raised its beam. The showroom had been stripped to a few piles of mildewed carpet tiles and some battered old shelf units. It smelled bad – damp and sickly. From far above them came the drone of heavy rain and the warble of sheltering pigeons. They reached the foot of the stairs and started up.

"I wanna make sure they cleared everything out. Barney couldn't get here this morning, his wife's sick or something." Barney was an ex-bouncer and former prison warden whose aggressive temperament perfectly qualified him for his position as Marrick's site manager. Unpleasant things happened in Marrick's company that Jonathan did not know about, that he could not allow himself to discover. Not if he wanted to keep his job and his sanity.

Although Marrick was young, he was considerably overweight; the stairs were already defeating him. He reached the second floor landing and looked up through the centre of the well, catching his breath. "You can check out the top two floors, Jon, make sure we ain't got any squatters in. Fucking hell, it stinks in here."

Jonathan stopped on the staircase and stared out of the rain-streaked window into the centre of the block, where the backs of the buildings met.

Rooms. Something odd about the rooms. He studied the brick walls of the courtyard formed by the other properties. He felt as if he had a cold coming on. Getting his jacket so wet hadn't helped matters. He should have bought himself a new umbrella. He sneezed hard, wiped his nose on a tissue. Spots of dark blood, a crimson constellation. He looked from the window again. The bricks. That's what it was. The bricks to the right of the window. They were in the wrong place. There should have been an empty space there. It was marked on the map, but not there from the window.

There was one room too many.

"Adrian, come and look at this a minute." He beckoned Marrick down and pointed from the glass. "There shouldn't be another room in the centre-well. The old wall to the right, do you see?"

"Yeah, so?"

"It's not on the plans."

"Why would that be?"

The brickwork was ancient, and the spaces between the blackened bricks were filled with bedraggled weeds. Near the top of the wall was a tiny window less than a foot long. There was no glass in it, just a single iron bar running across the gap. Jonathan frowned, trying to understand. "The 1933 plans were drawn over much older ones, but when they traced the new buildings in, they didn't add the existing layout."

"So what was there before?"

"I don't know. The originals drawings have been lost, misfiled somewhere."

Marrick looked at him as if he was going senile. "I'm not following you, Jon."

"There was another building already here at the centre of the site, or at least part of one. A very old one. Look at the bricks. There must be an entrance to it."

"Wait, before you go off on a fucking treasure hunt, how about we finish what we came here to do?"

"This building has been cleared." Jonathan scrubbed his fist across the filthy pane. "We have to find a way into that room."

"Why?" It was useless to assume that Marrick had a natural sense of curiosity, so Jonathan appealed to his greed. "It could have been sealed off for years. There might be something of value in there."

"If there was, it was probably nicked years ago. Someone's bound to have been in there already."

"I think that's unlikely. There's no immediate access, and it looks like it belongs to part of another building. It's hard to even see."

"Hmm. You have a point there." They both started looking for a doorway. There was nothing on any of the landings, or on the second floor. At the bottom of the stairs they found a door leading to a basement, but it was locked and there was no key. Marrick picked up a chunk of discarded pipe and smashed at the lock until the damp wood around it splintered and fell away.

"Fucking hell! What died?" Marrick waved a hand in front of his nose. "Shine your torch down there. These steps look rotten." The beam rippled back at them. The whole of the basement was under an inch of filthy water. On the far side was an arched passage. Jonathan instinctly knew that this was the way to the room at the centre of the building. He'd seen this type of layout in old architectural books.

"We have to go over there." He pointed at the arch.

"You're joking. These shoes cost a fucking fortune. I'm not going down there."

Jonathan's torch caught a stack of planks piled under the stairs. It was a simple matter to lay them like duckboards across the basement. The ceiling was low, and Marrick swore spectacularly as he banged his head. They arrived at the far side of the room, and Jonathan reached out to touch the heavy oak door set before them. He could hear running water. The torch illuminated the source through a crack in the wood; a brick channel filled with sluggishly moving liquid, cut through an arched tunnel that led off to an iron grate in the wall. "The Fleet," said Jonathan excitedly, "it's a tributary of the Fleet."

"What the fuck is that, a river?"

"Certainly a river. It was used as a rubbish dump for centuries. Runs from Hampstead down to Holborn and right across London."

"What do you mean 'runs'? It's still there?"

"It was finally channelled underground at the end of the eighteenth century, but the main part is still used as a sewer. There's a whole network of tributaries attached to it, and this looks like one of them. A lot of basements used to have access to the city's sewer system." Marrick had lost interest. He pulled at the edge of the door, and it shifted inwards.

"Doesn't look like it's being used anymore," said Jonathan. "The water's clean." He shone his torch further along the channel and found another, much smaller door. This one was painted black and studded with iron bolts. "That has to be the way to the centre-well."

They carefully stepped across the open water-pipe and examined the door. It was set two feet from the ground, presumably to keep the area behind it dry and avoid the danger of flooding.

"It's locked. I wonder who has the key."

Marrick dug about in his pocket and produced a handful of loose Yales. "Take your pick, there's these and dozens more of the bastards back in the office." But all of them proved too small to fit the lock.

"The mechanism will probably need oiling, anyway," said Jonathan. "We wouldn't be able to shift it by ourselves, not if it's been shut for years." They resolved to come back down on Monday morning.

London was once settled much lower in the ground. Layers were added; strata of gravel and stone and tarmacadam, layers of bones, the residue of corpses stricken by pestilence and firestorm, three decades of cholera victims, the sickly paupers from debtors' jails and workhouses, the silent majority of the city. Denied a voice in life, how they longed to speak and be heard.

The first tunnel under the Thames was a private enterprise built by Marc Brunel and opened, after considerable loss of life, in 1843. Within 15 weeks, a million pedestrians had paid a penny each to walk through it, but the novelty wore off fast, and for the next decade the gloomy arched passageways underneath the river became the favoured haunt of thieves and prostitutes.

Jonathan was unable to find a key which would fit, so Marrick asked his foreman Barney to take the door off its hinges. Barney did so that Friday morning, following Marrick's instructions not to go inside. Marrick, who now fancied himself as a bit of an Indiana Jones, was determined to retain that privilege for himself. Later on in the afternoon, as the biggest storm of the autumn broke over their heads, Jonathan accompanied his employer back to the cellar, and they crossed the sewage channel to the door in the wall.

Barney had set the square iron panel to one side. Marrick assumed proprietorial charge of the flashlight, and now wielding a crowbar in his other fist, shone his beam ahead into a rubble-filled corridor. Jonathan followed him through, pausing beside a crumpled sheet of newspaper, *The Daily Sketch*, 18 May 1949. He rose, disappointed, hoping to find something older. At least it was dry in here. They had to be under the centre-well of the buildings now. The room he had seen would be above them at the end of the passage and to the right.

"I don't know why I'm fucking wasting my time down here. I should never have let you talk me into this." Marrick picked his way across the littered floor, leaving Jonathan to fend for himself in the dark. From far above them came the distant rumble of thunder, like masonry being emptied into a skip. Jonathan listened to his boss's muttered complaints, knowing that the merest sliver of hope would drive him forward. "You never know what we might find," he said. "There, at the end, where you just pointed the torch. What is that?"

Twisted curlicues of iron hung from the ceiling. A number of sections had rusted through, and lay on the floor like giant fruit-rinds. Marrick cast the beam upwards. "Looks like part of a staircase," said Jonathan.

"Not like any fucking staircase I've ever seen. You reckon this room of yours is above here?"

"There's nowhere else it could be." He raised his eyes to the stained plaster ceiling and saw the slightly protuberant square of plaster in the corner of the passage. It was half the size of the first door, but large enough for a man to climb through. "There's your door," he said excitedly. "There should be an iron ring set flat in the front section, buried under the plaster."

"How could you know that?" Marrick stopped and stared back at him through the glare of the torch beam. "You haven't been down here before."

"I've read about these things. It's a relic room. Lots of wealthy old houses used to have them. You built a special room, just a small one, and sealed a treasured possession inside, and built the rest of the house around it."

"Then what?"

"Then nothing. You sealed the room up from the outside and forgot all about it, and the building would have good luck all of its life. It was a pagan thing. By giving up something precious you appeased the household gods. The old Roman habits died hard. Not all Londoners were Christians, you know."

Marrick's eyes glittered in the gloom. "So you reckon there's something really valuable in there?"

"There could be, I don't know. They tucked away all sorts of belongings. Gold candlesticks, silver and pewter plate, chalices, they were all popular sacrifices."

"Reading all them books of yours finally paid off, eh?" Marrick thumped the ceiling square with the end of his crowbar. The plaster coating that covered it sounded thin. A few more thumps rained wafer-fine pieces onto his shoulders. It only took a few minutes to reveal the edges of the door. When he shone the torch back up, they could both see it; a dirty iron ring, recessed into the square.

"Give me a hand here," said Marrick, thrusting the torch at him. "Hold that steady." His fingers followed the outline of the ring and dug around it, pulling it down toward him. As he brought his weight to bear on it, the door grudgingly opened downwards in a shower of plaster fragments.

"Christ, this thing must be on a fucking spring," Marrick cried, "I can barely hold it."

"Do you want me to help?"

"You'd give yourself a hernia. Just grab the bottom corners as soon as you can reach them." He was right. Jonathan could feel the power of the door as it tried to close itself. Marrick moved the torch to the inside of the hole. Pinpoints of reflected light glittered back. "There's definitely something in there all right. Keep a hold on the door."

Marrick braced his feet against the walls and raised his arms into the open hole, pulling himself up. "Used to – ugh – do this sort of thing in gym," he gasped through gritted teeth. As his torso, his legs and finally his expensive Italian shoes disappeared into the hole, Jonathan shoved against the door with all his might to keep the heavy spring from slamming it shut.

"What can you see?" he called.

"Hang on a minute, let me get my breath – " Marrick shone the torch around the room, which was less than five feet square. The air was thick and old, but breathable. His head brushed against the brick ceiling. Beside him at head-height was the tiny window he had seen from outside.

"Plate," he called down finally. "Silver plate by the look of it." He shifted his feet either side of the trapdoor hole. A great mound of the stuff was stacked in a corner. Each piece was twice the size of the average dinner plate. It looked like the municipal tableware they used for mayoral banquets. He bent down and pulled the largest one free in a cloud of straw-dust. It was badly tarnished, but he could still make out the leaping stags, the coat of arms, the portrait of some ugly bird in a pointy headdress. His heart was beating faster. Even an idiot could see that this lot was worth a fucking fortune. He turned it over, and there on the reverse was an inscription, hard to read because the "S"s were substituted with "F"s, but the date was clear; 1503. Dear God in Heaven, he was rich.

"Here, cop hold of this." He passed the plate down to Jonathan, who was propped against the trapdoor and had trouble accepting the heavy metal dish. Marrick switched the torch into the opposite corner, no more than two feet behind him. His mouth fell open.

Jonathan's arms were tiring. He was not sure how much longer he could manage to keep the door down. Beyond in the darkness he could hear the steadily-augmenting sound of rushing water. The deluge above them was filtering through the pipes of the building and swelling the sewer channel. "Hurry up," he called anxiously. "The storm's bringing a lot of water down."

Marrick did not hear. He was staring back at a dead body. It was centuries-dead and dried out, so that it appeared as little more than a skeleton with yellow skin vacuum-formed across its bones. It was small, just over four feet high, its head tilted back and its jaw wide open so that it appeared to be laughing, or screaming. There were iron rings around its wrists, manacling it to the wall. They seemed unnecessarily heavy on such a small frame. A chill crept over Marrick as it occurred to him that the poor creature had been chained up alive and left to die here, and that it was most probably a child.

"Oh, Christ – "

"What's the matter?"

"They walled up something precious to bring themselves luck – "

Several things happened at once just then. An enormous roll of thunder made itself heard all the way to the basement, there was a sudden renewed rush of water through the sewer duct, and Jonathan started in surprise, moving his shoulder from the trapdoor. The spring tightened, the lid swung unstoppably up and slammed shut with a deafening bang. For a moment both men were shocked into silence. Then Marrick began shouting and thumping about in his tiny cell, but the sound of his rage was not enough to carry clearly through the heavy sealed door.

Marrick stood up sharply and cracked his head on the ceiling. His heart was pounding in the darkness. The walls pressed forward. He was unable to catch his breath. Claustrophobia hemmed him in. The dead air in his throat stifled him. He gasped and bellowed at Jonathan, every filthy insult he could conjure, and threw himself to the floor in an attempt to dislodge the trapdoor. But it was somehow arranged so that it could only be opened from the iron ring outside – and only he had had the strength to pull it down. Jonathan would never be able to manage it alone. He forced himself to calm down for a moment. Barney. Jonathan would have to go and get Barney. He might still be at the office. He wished he had not left his mobile phone in his briefcase on the ground floor.

"Jon," he shouted at the floor, "go and get Barney to help you! Call him! Get Barney!" He held his breath and listened, but all he could hear was the rain outside and the distant rushing water below. "Jon, for fuck's sake what are you doing?" His voice rose in fright as the beam from the torch grew yellow and died. He dropped to his knees and scrabbled at the seams of the unmoving door until he could no longer feel his fingers.

Jonathan made his way back along the passageway in total darkness. He soaked his legs crossing the sewer duct, which was now overflowing the sides of the brick channel. A faint light showed from the distant cellar entrance. When he reached the top of the stairs, he collected Marrick's briefcase. Then he went back to the rumbling river.

Positioning himself by the water that boiled and rushed through the iron grating, he emptied the contents of the case, Marrick's pens, his mobile phone, his cocaine, his lunch receipts, and all the contracts he had drawn up for the purchase and eventual demolition of the building. Jonathan watched as they passed through the wide iron mesh on their underground journey to the city's dark heart.

"There are no kind gods," he said aloud. "The price of true belief will always be terrible."

Back on the ground floor he studied the huge plate Marrick had passed to him, the lauded ceremonial plate commemorating the death of Elizabeth Of York, daughter of Edward IV, sister to the murdered princes in the Tower, beloved mother of Henry

VIII. On the back was engraved an elegy, written for her by Sir Thomas More. He was holding a cornerstone of history, long thought lost, finally restored to safe hands. He would never know what else the *oubliette* contained – apart from the large useless article that would now serve the birth of a new urban deity.

Several days later, Jonathan returned to the stairwell window and looked out into the centre of the building. It was a still, sunny day, and a sparrow perched on one of the sturdy weed-stems that sprouted from the wall of the hidden room.

Jonathan stared at the tiny window with the thick iron bar across it, and occasionally – as if it could sense that someone was watching – a pale face, despairing and nightmarish, passed before the gap like the moon fleetingly glimpsed through clouds. It was a sight that he would never forget, an eternal penance. His skin prickling, he hastily returned to the warm city streets and the choking traffic beyond.

There is a brief respite in the sobbing, crying maelstrom. The city's agonies are temporarily assuaged. A sacrifice accepted; a building restored. For the most fleeting of moments, the tough old woman raises her crumpled face to the sun and smiles.

A century and a half ago, within the thick Wren walls of the Theatre Royal, Drury Lane, a body was discovered with a dagger in its ribs. Somebody was murdered in the theatre and quietly bricked in. Nobody knows why or whether the victim was still alive when the last brick was cemented into place.

SCOTT EDELMAN

A Plague on Both Your Houses

SCOTT EDELMAN WORKED AS an assistant editor for Marvel Comics in the early 1970s, writing everything from display copy for superhero "Slurpee cups" to the famous Bullpen Bulletins Pages. He subsequently went freelance, and worked for both Marvel and DC Comics. In 1979 he attended the invitational Clarion Science Fiction Workshop.

His first novel, *The Gift*, published by Space & Time, was a finalist for a Lambda Literary Award in the category Best Gay SF/Fantasy Novel. His short stories have been published in such magazines as *Twilight Zone*, *Science Fiction Review*, *Pulphouse*, *Nexus*, *Fantasy Book*, *Eldritch Tales*, *Weirdbook* and many others. A chapbook of his fiction, *Suicide Art*, appeared from Necronomicon Press, and his anthology appearances include *Tales of the Wandering Jew*, *MetaHorror*, *Quick Chills II: Best of the Small Press* and *Best New Horror 4*.

Edelman is the founding editor of *Science Fiction Age* magazine and, since 1996, he has also been editing *Sci-Fi Entertainment*, the official magazine of the Sci-Fi channel. In 1997, he received his second consecutive Hugo nomination as Best Editor.

As the author reveals, "The first few lines of 'A Plague On Both Your Houses' popped into my head as I was driving home from the 1992 World Horror Convention in Nashville, Tennessee. Something had obviously been stirred up in my subconscious by my hobnobbing with the horror elite, and as I began my long drive back home in the dark of a late Sunday evening, my synapses were working overtime.

"I still have the notebook that rested to the right of my knee as I drove north. I had scribbled dozens of ideas in a near illegible hand, writing as I drifted through the night – short story ideas, novel ideas, anthology proposals, and one title that turned into the piece you are about to read. I wrote the first draft furiously over the following week, and when I was done, I realized that I had once more done exactly what I had so often done before – written a bizarre freak of a tale so unique that it had no likely home.

"And for five long years 'A Plague on Both Your Houses' went unread by anyone but my friends and a few editors, one of whom rejected the tale with the remark, 'Sorry, but we don't like Shakespeare.' Frustrated by the failure of this piece to break through to the audience that I know is out there, I finally printed a small personal edition of the story as a Halloween card. That you're first reading this a half a decade later than you needed to do – *that's* a real horror story."

DRAMATIS PERSONAE

JONATHAN, *a gravedigger*
SAM, *a zombie, freshly risen*

VINCENT, *Mayor of New York City*
CARLO, *the Mayor's son*
EDDIE, *his friend*

LEOPOLD, *King of the Zombies*
DOLORES, *his daughter*
MARY, *her maid*

WOMAN REVELLER
MASKED PARTY GOERS

Scene. Manhattan Island. Sooner than you think.

PROLOGUE

A graveyard in lower Manhattan.

(*Enter* JONATHAN, *a gravedigger.*)

JON. Diseased New York, the setting for our play
Has lost its glitter, trading it for grue.
Cold dead come back, in graves they will not stay.
The living bear no young, and dwindle few.
I am an old man. I've seen many things:
A walked-on moon, democracy again,
The death of tyrants, privilege, nations, kings.
Now hope is weak. I fear the end of men.
I plant them deep, yet somehow they thrust up,
As if Spring's breath has touched their wint'ry souls,
Enticing them to once more grasp life's cup,
and mount the stage, demanding their lost roles.
Is this a fate mankind deserved to earn?
Watch, and listen, and perhaps you'll learn.

(SAM, *a zombie, speaks from the grave, his voice muffled.*)

SAM. Hello, up there! Hello, world I once knew!
Evicting dirt and worms from my parched throat,
I cry out loud. I call for you, yes, you!
Announcing, to the surface I must float!
JON. Dear friend, dead friend, are you so sure it's wise
To spurn God's gift of your eternal rest?
SAM. This second life has come as a surprise.
But who are you to judge for me what's best?

(SAM's *fist rises. His fingers uncurl like the petals of a flower.*)

JON. How dare I? I am he who oft' has dug
The beds for those who should have stayed below.
Thousands have I made forever snug,
Yet now, like you, they do refuse to go.
I'm one whom time has given weary arms.
My bones seem less mine each passing day,
'Till I myself desire death's own charms.
I'd take your grave if I knew I could stay.
SAM. Again, I say, you cannot speak for me.

Impertinence, is that thy Christian name?
Help me now. The sunlight I would see.
JON. My stomach will not let me play this game.
If you would live again, it's not my style
To interfere with what God means to be.
So though I think I'll rest with you awhile,
I'll watch, not interfere with fate's decree.

> (JONATHAN *sits atop the mound of the grave,
> setting his spade across his knees.*)

SAM. I wish, sir, if you're disinclined to help,
You'll stand, and hold me down not with your weight.
Assist or not the birthing of this whelp,
But please, sir, do not seek to bar the gate.

> (JONATHAN *sighs, and slowly rises to his feet.*)

JON. Quite right, dead friend, forgive my actions rude.
Old age has brought a torpor to my soul.
I'll strive to demonstrate a friendly mood
And do my best to aid you to your goal.

> (JONATHAN *begins digging in the loose earth.*)

SAM. I thank you, sir. You prove a kindly man.
JON. Kindness? No. No kindness in this flesh.
It's simply one man doing what he can
To help the live and zombie peoples mesh.
No longer are things as they once had been
When your kind ravaged mine, blind hate was strong,
And coming back from death was called a sin.
I'm just providing help to right a wrong.
My reticence was but resentment's trace
That my life's work has proven worthless now:
Unburied stay the children of your race.
SAM. I think not, friend, for to your skills I bow.
Long decades have you made your job the dead
As you have set them in the frigid earth.
But if those dead become a living mob,
Can you not act as midwife to their birth?

> (JONATHAN *pauses in thought, spade in hand. By now
> a growing pile of earth rests beside the grave.*)

JON. I never thought to find a new employer.

(SAM *sits up, his head and shoulders becoming visible out of the grave.*)

SAM. You've served the living, now you'll serve the dead.
Do not think of this plague as job destroyer.
Good men need never fear to earn their bread.
JON. Dear friend, dead friend, you are a man of wit.
  I feel much younger now, with you to thank.
Ennui has fled. I'm like a new-born kit.
Here, let me help you from your prison dank.

(JONATHAN *takes* SAM's *hand, and pulls the zombie up onto the stage.* SAM *brushes clumps of earth from his tattered clothing.*)

SAM. I'm glad, sir, that the captains of our race
Have made us into partners who can deal
With one another in this strange new place.
Time was you would have made my breakfast meal.
JON. If you in your new life are so relieved
Imagine how I feel. Your words have joyed
This one who surely would have felt aggrieved
To see myself as luncheon meat employed.
Times have changed. The world has made its peace
With how society transformed in decades past.
I'm pleased that you whom we do predecease
Now see us more as friends than as repast.
Let's celebrate the way the world has changed
From times of bloodshed filled with undead hate
To where our people's moods have rearranged,
So that we two can stand here and relate
How such a friendship could have come about
Amidst a world that did not value love.
SAM. Of love's transcendence there can be no doubt
Our God's transplanted heaven from above.

(JONATHAN *and* SAM *face the audience and speak the next lines jointly.*)

BOTH. Attend now as our players speak their parts
To see how hate must fade before true hearts.

ACT I

City Hall. Afternoon.

(*Enter* VINCENT, *Mayor of living New York City, with* EDDIE, *his son's closest friend.*)

VIN. Dear Eddie, you are like my second sun
Which warms the dark spots of this troubled life,
And Carlo long has known that you are one
Who'll be there if he needs you with your knife.
ED. Of late that fact it seems he does forget.
He acts not as the Carlo whom I knew.
Instead, his features tremble with regret,
And though I try, there's little I can do.
As weeks have passed, I've marshaled every skill
To draw my friend your son from out his shell,
Used travel, women, sports, food, drink and pill.
But nothing's worked to wrench him from his hell.
VIN. That's why we meet today. I need your aid
To lift his mind from what has brought him down.
And so I will announce a masquerade
Where we two joined will rob him of his frown.
ED. I fear his stupor's far worse than you think.
It won't be awed by song, nor gaudy masks,
Nor laughter, magic, dancing or strong drink.
Lord Mayor, you could have chosen simpler tasks.
VIN. And yet, it's ours, I'm certain that we must
Soon free my boy from what has captured him,
For someday age will my keen judgement rust.
Then Carlo must rule, or else life will turn grim.
ED. I'll try, sir, for my love of him and you
To breach the walls he's built to keep us out
And though there may be nothing I can do,
I'll swear to fight till his dark side I rout.
ED. Wait! Here Carlo comes, his head hung low.
No word to him of this, our secret plan.
ED. Let me to party preparations go.
Tonight we'll make your son again a man.

(*Enter* CARLO. *As he draws close by*, EDDIE *exits.* CARLO *is so lost in thought that he almost passes his father by. He pauses when he hears his father speak.*)

VIN. It's sad, my son, your father you pass by,
As if some loathsome stranger on the street.
You act as if this morning you did die
And post-death shambling zombiehood did meet.
CAR. O, father, dearest one, I could not bear
For you to think my love for you had fled.
Despondency does not mean I don't care
Or that this form before you's joined the dead.
It's just that life seems empty now, and sad,
And there seems little prospect yet of joy.
VIN. At your age (listen now, and trust your dad),
The world should seem to you a brilliant toy.
CAR. Speak not to me of "shoulds" in this mad globe,
Which cast off "shoulds" long years before my birth.
What "shoulds"? The dead should not shrug off death's robe!
Young men should always feel life's full of mirth!
A man should hand his son a better place
In which to build a life that should know peace!
There should be for each man a beauteous face
Which makes pain go away and madness cease.
No, "shoulds" you'll find won't sway me in the least.
I've learned should's just a senseless bitter word.
VIN. Calm down, son, you're a man, not mindless beast.
And now that I've your tortured anguish heard,
It's time you cast it off, became like old,
Became the son who caused a thousand sighs,
Who danced around our enemies so bold,
Dispatching those who dared again to rise.
Your mental pallor's gone on long enough.
You are my son. Someday you'll be the mayor.
So show the world you're made of sterner stuff,
And start once more to act as if you care.
CAR. "Care" is one more word with little weight,
For life's not black and white, but only gray,
and I care not for what might be my fate
and will do naught to grab one extra day.
No wine can get me drunk enough to care.
No woman make it worth the errant time
To run my fingers through her golden hair.
No staircase worth the effort of the climb.
I've seen it all, I've tasted every sin.

No longer do I care much if I lose,
No longer seems it worth my while to win.
It seems as if I wear another's shoes.

>   (CARLO *pauses, worn out by his own tirade.*
>   VINCENT *places a hand on his son's shoulder.*
>   CARLO *turns into an embrace.*)

CAR. For you, my father, I will try again
To find some satisfaction on this orb,
And join once more enthusiastic men
In seizing all life's gifts I can absorb.
VIN. I welcome back my first and only heir.
Let all your frozen fatal feelings fade.
Alive again you'll be and all things dare
Tonight once we commence the masquerade.

>   (*Exit* VINCENT.)

CAR. A masquerade? I know the man means well
And hopes to snare the stupor set in me,
But nothing's left to save me from this Hell
Nor magic spell my weary soul to free.
This night, I fear, may ruthlessly reveal
The very things he struggles to conceal.

ACT II

City Hall. Night.

>   (VINCENT *addresses the assembled masked party goers.*)

VIN. Welcome, friends, and friends-to-be! This ball
Does bring together all those not yet dead
Within the confines of a City Hall
Which centuries has stood while men have bled.
Let's take a moment, starting, to remember
How we are all that's left of what was life
And of our stand against those that dismember,
Destroy us, disembowel us, damn with strife
Our every human notion in this city –
The zombies, whose soiled name I spit as a curse.
Recall, as you peruse our world with pity
That only we can stop it getting worse.

Remember that humanity is ours,
That "let the dead stay dead" is our sole motto.
The zombies are as alien as Mars,
While we're mankind's last hope, a shining grotto.
So celebrate this gathering tonight
And raise a glass to what we represent.
CAR. If with those words my spirit he'd ignite,
He did instead aid in its dark descent.

> (VINCENT *waves happily to his son.* CARLO *raises one hand in response, a weak smile on his lips. A dance begins, and* CARLO *stands stage left and solemnly watches the roiling crowd.*)

CAR. Life! Damned life! Is this all life is for?
Stumbling clowns in masks who can't forget
They're born of ordure and must die in gore?
Whose days are made of fear and woe and fret?
Is that a life? I'll make no life of this.
Had I been born before my time – perhaps!
But now – no thrill, no battle, no secret, tender kiss
Would take the place of death's own milky paps.
If I could make my flesh just cease to be,
I'd do it! Question not what I would choose.
I'd cut the cord, and set my soul asea
And worry not that I'd a thing to lose.
I'd leave now, but my father watches near
To make sure that my lips have formed a smile.
I wonder if he knows he's seeing mere
Falsehood on a face etched full of guile?

> (EDDIE, *slightly drunk, stumbles over. His arm is around a masked* WOMAN.)

ED. Your father is a man of many graces,
Grand party-giving is his strongest point.
No better way exists to shed the traces
Of cruel despair in a life out of joint.

> (EDDIE *holds the woman's chin, displaying it for* CARLO.)

ED. Look at this fair one. Beauty, is she not?
More goddess true than any woman seen,
A form the womb of heaven has begot

To tempt me with the grandeur of a queen.
CAR. I've seen you drunk before, my good friend Eddie,
But never past beyond the point of truth.
Your words alone tell me that you are ready
To pick up coffee and set down vermouth.
ED. It's not the wine that speaks, it's just your friend
Who hopes your constant carping side to vex,
And bring this cruel charade to wise, just end
with help of sweet and tender female flesh.

(CARLO *shakes head sadly, denying the possibility.*)

CAR. No use, I fear. This thing has gone too far.
Your tools have not the power to appease.
Eddie, our clear friendship I'd not mar,
But send her far away – she does not please.
WOM. I never dreamt that you'd heap cruel abuse
On one whose sin was loving you too much.

(*The* WOMAN *leaves.*)

ED. I've never seen you wear a shorter fuse
Can not tonight you lighten up a touch?
CAR. Give up, my friend! No secrets here tonight.
My father planned this gloomy masquerade
In hopes to set my somber soul alight.
I'll have no part of this bereft charade.

(*Enter* DOLORES, *masked, attempting to pass for human. She pauses on the outskirts of the crowd.*)

CAR. And now, my last farewells to you I'll make.
Goodbye, my friend, for it is growing late.
Remember me when I was a young rake,
And hate me not for leaving. Farewell.

(CARLO *notices* DOLORES.)

Wait!
CAR. Who is that one who stands at party's edge
Warily watching all those who pass by?
As if she's made herself a solemn pledge,
As if my own intransigence she'd try?
Do you know her? Can you speak her name?
ED. Like all of us she hides beneath a mask.

CAR. Then find her out. You, hunter. She, the game.
Be quick!
ED. Your every wish becomes my task.

   (EDDIE *hurls himself into the crowd.* DOLORES *evades
   him while* CARLO *watches.* EDDIE *returns, crestfallen.*)

ED. I've failed you, Carlo. Find her I cannot.
It's just as if she's vanished like the dawn,
Just when you had changed from cold to hot.
I'd hoped to celebrate, and now must mourn.
CAR. You've done your best, as friends are meant to do.
In losing her you've earned yourself no blame.
Know that you've always been forever true.
Our friendship long has never witnessed shame.
Do one more thing for our long friendship's sake,
And leave me here to think on this awhile.
ED. I trust you still, and so your leave I'll take
And leave you with your thoughts as is your style.

   (EDDIE *bows to his friend, and vanishes into the crowd.*)

CAR. Where is she? Where's the one I thought I saw
Who changed without a word my night to day?

   (DOLORES *appears stage left, and watches him as
   he studies the crowd fruitlessly for her.*)

DOL. There stands the one my spirit wants to gnaw.
But heart says to my hungry spirit-stay.

            (CARLO *pauses in his search.*)

CAR. 'Twould torture be if one brief, blinding glimpse,
Was all of her I'd be allowed to taste.
She's vanished as if stolen off by imps,
This all too perfect vision, cool and chaste.
Until I saw her, I could not remember
What living my own life was really for,
But she's ignited some sad, sleepy ember
Inside of me, and breached my shuttered door.
I could have any woman who is here,
Or, for what it's worth, have any man.
My father's power sways all in this sphere
Who'd latch upon me for what gain they can.
But this fair one, who makes instead to hide,

Has something different in her form and soul
Than all those who would claim to take my side –
Only she can make me once more whole!

(DOLORES *moves forward and addresses the audience.*)

DOL. Beneath this mask is cold and lifeless flesh,
Beneath this breast a heart that's dry and still.
Yet seeing him my soul still wants to mesh
And disobey God's law as lovers will.
I am a zombie, and that one is man,
And there should be between us naught but pain.
Of intercourse between us there's a ban,
Each other's visage should bring dark disdain.
Enough of "shoulds"! It's shoulds that forged today,
A world dissolved to bloodshed and to war,
Escape from which no one can find a way.
Is this what our creator made us for?
So here I snuck, my father knowing not.
His daughter dear desires something new,
Unfettered by the world the plague begot,
Expecting not to see this princely view.

(DOLORES *sighs as she stares at*
CARLO *through the crowd.*)

DOL. But I was fool to come, myself to tease.
Nothing but tragedy can come of this.

(DOLORES *starts to go, but at this moment*
CARLO *catches up with her.*)

CAR. Lady! Tell me! How may I you please?
What must I do to from you earn a kiss?
DOL. Tempt me not, for I was fool to come.
'Tis better that we simply parted thus.
CAR. Say not those words which set me out of plumb.
I beg you of our meeting do not fuss,
Unless it is to say that by my side
You'll stay, ignoring what the world might do.
There's something in you close to what a bride
Should have. A shining spirit clean and new.

(DOLORES *speaks an aside to the audience.*)

DOL. He speaks of brides. Remembers he the rhyme?

How borrowed, blue, and old and new should be
Embodied in the bride at that rich time
She walks the aisle? How true those words for me.
Borrowed is my undead zombie soul.
Blue my skin, except where it is grey.
Old my bones which crack each time I stroll.
New my fleshly hunger every day.
How could a man in whom the blood still flows
See anything but monster in my form?
Leave him I must before the truth he knows,
To let him keep his fantasy of norm.

    (DOLORES *tries once more to leave*.)

CAR. Wait, my lady, why will you not speak
Sweet words to me? Instead you make to go.
I swear, my lady, my heart's blood will leak
Until your name I'm privileged to know.
DOL. If truth you knew, you would not make that wish.
If I leave now we've nothing to regret.
CAR. You make yourself as slipp'ry as a fish
But you tries to skip between a sailor's net,
But you will find in this case that the reel
Which seeks to pull you in won't let you go
As easily as that. So do not feel
I'll let you vanish 'fore your name I know.
I love you though I yet know not your name.
I love you though I've never seen your face.
In finding you I end the lover's game
I've played for years. For others I've no space.
DOL. If only love could keep such sure a course
And future promise anything but tears.
CAR. My vow I give that there'll be no remorse.
Just say you'll stay beside me through the years.
DOL. But no, it cannot be, this thing called love
Though I would wish some other fate were so.
CAR. Too late for flight, my pure, white, captured dove.
I'll take our future, whether joy or woe.

    (VINCENT *spins upstage and claps hands.*
     He moves downstage to speak.)

VIN. Friends old and new, I've watched you party well

And set yourself to celebration's task
Now time bids us to break the magic spell —
We're reached the hour where we all unmask.
DOL. Alas, kind sir, with that I really must
Say my farewell and from the party part.

(CARLO *seizes her hand.*)

CAR. Your fingers cool should never leave my own
'Till I have warmed them in the hearth of love.
DOL. No warming of this flesh can e'er be known
By wooer's hand, by heart, nor thickest glove.
CAR. Did not my words romantic buy your trust?
You have my mind, my soul, my life, my heart.
DOL. You have my hand.
CAR. I'll keep it 'till you tell
The holy syllables that make your name.
I'll keep it 'till I know your face as well
And both our hearts have merged into the same.

(CARLO *reaches for her mask.* DOLORES
touches his wrist with her free hand.)

DOL. Not here, surrounded by this drunken mass.
CAR. Name time and place and I will swiftly fly,
Will dare each mountain, cross each treacherous pass,
To see your face. Then gladly I will die.
DOL. It will not come to that, let us both pray.
CAR. Since we'll together stay 'till our last breath
Has left our lips, I do not fear the day.
In finding you I've lost my fear of death.
DOL. I fear not death, I fear what death may bring.
CAR. I fear the loss of you, and that is all.
Tell me where we'll meet, and make me king.
My life's begun the evening of this ball.
DOL. You know the graveyard at this island's tip?
Meet me at rosy dawn beside the gate.
CAR. To be with you to charnel house I'd skip.
For glimpse of you, I'd embrace any fate.
DOL. Now drop my hand.
CAR. You'll be there? Do you swear?
DOL. If swearing makes you drop my hand, I do.
CAR. Then here's your hand. Not easily I'll bear

The time till it is grasped again.
DOL. Ado!

(DOLORES *races through the crowd.* CARLO *follows her with his eyes.* DOLORES *pauses once and looks back over her shoulder before exiting.*)

CAR. Life! Grand life! My outlook she's reversed!
I feel as if a new life now begins,
Her blessings rescuing what was Carlo cursed.
True love absolves a man of many sins.
My gloom has gone, and now the future's bright
Bathing me in true love's cleansing light.

ACT III

The graveyard's main gate. Dawn.

(*Enter* CARLO *and* EDDIE, *stumbling on stage, obviously drunk. They are having a conversation which it is apparent they have been in the midst of for some time.*)

CAR. I tell you that she stepped from out of dreams
to drag me from this nighttime of my life.
ED. I must admit that your demeanor seems
Improved. But to already call her wife?
Who is this one on whom you pin so much?
Her face, her name, are secrets still to you,
And though I'm glad she's changed you with her touch,
How can you swear to be forever true?
CAR. Do not ask me to sense make of love's magic.
Why two hearts yearn can never be explained.
Cheer up, dear friend, true love is never tragic.
Start looking happy. Lose that look so pained.
I'm much too high to harbor any doubts,
So think you not to sway me with your fears.
I'll suffer all her frowns, moues, snits and pouts,
And gladly help her through all future tears.
ED. I've never seen your confidence so sure
At least not when it came to woman's sex.
Mayhap you'll marshall something to endure
And 'scape the often hidden marriage hex.
CAR. Love and marriage, laughter, children, age,
Welcome's the chance to put those garments on.

Now that this stranger's turned another page,
My book of life's less dreary. I'm less wan.
ED. But why her? What has she done to break down
The wall you've built around your secret self?
CAR. Seeing her, I saw myself a clown
Who'd put the best of me upon a shelf.
And though my friends did everything they could,
I heeded nothing of the things they said.
In seeing her I saw that I was good
And stirred myself back from the walking dead.
Tonight I'll see her while you stand your guard
Ensuring none disturbs us as we meet.
ED. I am myself disturbed that this foul yard
Should be the spot for lover's tryst discreet.
There is not love nor life nor safety here.
I wish that you had chosen other ground.
CAR. My love, not I, did choose the setting where
Together both our futures may be found.
I too admit that if I'd had the choice,
I would have picked less danger-fraught a spot,
But when she named the place I gave no voice
To my concern, just blessed my lucky lot.
I will protect her here, I make my vow,
Here or anywhere our fortunes trend.
An odd place to start off, I will allow,
But I care not what omens do portend.
Go now, and see that we are left alone
To worship here with Cupid's progeny.
ED. If any pass, with sword I will atone.
You'll have your time to woo her decently.

(*The friends clasp hands.* EDDIE *exits.*)

CAR. And now to wait, beside death's lit'ral door,
Praying that she comes to keep her word.
But wait! She is a lady at the core,
That she should fail a promise is absurd.

(*While* CARLO *paces the gate,* DOLORES *appears on stage
on the gate's other side. Her manner is subdued.*)

DOL. I'm here, my noble prince, as you have said,
To finish out this dance we've both begun.

CAR. More than my words. I hope our wills are wed,
And that your heart by my own has been won.
We stand on either side of this great fence
Which bars the dead from living. Come to me
And we will all our hopes and dreams commence.
Our fates are now entwined, you will agree.
DOL. This gate you see may be too hard to breach
And means more than you yet could even guess.
I think I may be ever past your reach,
And love is doomed, with no chance of success.
CAR. Your voice, so sad, it tears my very being.
Let me come close, the sadness I will steal.
DOL. Can it be true love that I am seeing?
Do you swear this love of yours is real?
This world has things that are not what they seem,
And beauty may be purely in your mind.
Will your true love vanish in a dream?
Once the truth is out, can you stay kind?
CAR. You talk as if you hide a wicked heart
Inside what seems to me an angel's form.
There's naught you could have done, for my own part,
Could make me lose sight of perfection's corm.
There's nothing you could say or see or plan
Could reach the roots of what today has found.
You are my woman, and I am your man.
Let our love in its rightful place be crowned.
DOL. He speaks so ardently, his words ring true,
And truth to tell, my ardor's also strong.

(DOLORES *slides between the bars of the gate.*)

CAR. The human angel entertains my view,
And now all will be right, and nothing wrong.
And now, your name! Dispel this empty void.
Speak quick the word to fill my hungry soul,
A name that means for me joy unalloyed.
End my ears' most unbecoming greed.
DOL. Call me Dolores.
CAR. Dolores are you called.
You're angel, and you bear an angel's name.
Your singing name does leave me more enthralled.
All other words than that will leave me tame.

Dolores! Three syllables which ignite
Within my spirit an infectious bliss.
And now, Dolores, set the world aright,
And grace this vagrant's lips with angel's kiss.
DOL. Alas, I fear my lips would leave you cold.
Other lips will have what you require.
CAR. You joke with me because I have been bold.
I'm sure your lips will set my soul afire.
Do you think I seek to toy with you?
I might have once, but now that's not my style.
Step closer now, I long for better view.
An inch away from you is like a mile.

(CARLO *extends a hand.* DOLORES *does
not move closer to grasp it.*)

CAR. You hesitate, Dolores, could it be
Your feelings fail to truly mirror mine?
DOL. No, Carlo, your heart and my own agree.
CAR. Why hesitate from making your lips mine?
DOL. I fear that our first kiss will be our last,
That but one kiss is all the fates allow.
CAR. Don't doubt my love. All other girls are past,
And this one seeks no more the earth to plow.
DOL. It's more than that. There's much you cannot guess
About what lies beneath this gaudy mask.
If I submit, our lives will be a mess.
CAR. Let us dare it, then, that's all I ask.

(*After a momentary pause,* DOLORES *takes* CARLO's *hand.*)

DOL. You swear that you will stay forever true.
CAR. I swear that you have bound my heart in chains.
I swear –
DOL. Enough. I pray we do not rue
This madness. Love conquers, and no sanity remains.

(DOLORES *leans forward to offer her lips. They chastely kiss.*)

CAR. Your lips, so cool. Your fine, fair cheeks like ice.
The touch of you relieves the lustful thirst
That's been in me since God did roll the dice,
And let me see you, and my notions burst.
My fever makes your own hot lips seem cold.

DOL. You would go on?
CAR. I would go on to Hell
To follow through this kiss with one more bold
Causing heaven itself to randy swell.
DOL. Curse God who has abandoned this poor world,
For letting pass the things that happen next.
CAR. Do you see me fight destiny unfurled?
Together, all despair will be perplexed.

(DOLORES *and* CARLO *kiss, more passionately this time, eyes closed.* DOLORES' *mask slips, but she does not realize it.* CARLO *opens his eyes first, and sees the pallor of her shredded face.* DOLORES *senses that something is wrong and opens her eyes slowly.* CARLO *backs away, puts a finger to his lips.* DOLORES *does not move, expecting the worst.*)

CAR. You're dead.
DOL. Yes, dead. And now what will you do?
CAR. I cannot do, I cannot even think.
I kissed your lips, and now your lips are blue.
DOL. My lips are blue. What's gray you'll find will stink.
CAR. You kiss me, but I always thought your race
Would eat me up without a second thought.
DOL. I'll eat you up, but first I would embrace
And eat you not the way that zombies ought.
I'd gobble you up as lovers often do
And press myself against your fresh, pink, skin.
Love makes me choose romance instead of grue
An act my people think a zombie sin.
I've said my piece. But you've not answered me.
You owe me that much, even if you're made sick.
CAR. Forgive my silent lips for what I see.

(CARLO *comes closer.* DOLORES *has not yet moved as she waits for his response.*)

CAR. Your kind has warred on mine since undead were.
No congress 'tween us save the rending blow.
But to me you are frankincense and myrrh.
To me you're poetry, all else is prose.
Your skin is different, eyes of color mottled.
Your smell is not my own, your flesh, it rots.
But with one look from you all doubt is throttled.

I love you, though no blood within you clots.
I love you still, it matters not your state.
Living or zombie, to me is meaningless.
As soon would I care about an ounce of weight,
As seek from Cupid's bow for some redress.
DOL. O, Carlo, I had dared not even hope
That our meeting could cause a valid bliss.
CAR. If you're my hangman, I accept the rope
Enough of words. Speak further in a kiss.

(*The lovers embrace. After a moment, a growing clatter can be heard from off-stage. Enter* EDDIE, *backing in, fencing with* LEOPOLD, *King of the Zombies, father to* DOLORES.)

ED. Begone, dead thing! You have no business here!
My friend and master's private in a tryst.
LEO. A grave your master's privacy will bear
Should here I find my daughter has been kissed.
CAR. Who speaks of daughter with a sword in hand?
DOL. My noble father Leopold comes near
King of all the zombies in this land.
If we don't fly, your future I do fear.
CAR. I cannot leave a true and trusting friend
To deal for my sake 'gainst the living dead.
I'll intervene and bring this to an end.
No man will ever battle in my stead.

(CARLO *draws his sword.*)

CAR. Eddie, you no longer fight alone.

(EDDIE *turns and for the first time notices* DOLORES *unmasked.*)

ED. A welcome sword you bear, but what is this?
You meet with that? Have your senses flown?

(*While* EDDIE *is distracted,* LEOPOLD *makes a mortal wound.*)

ED. To think I die so you a corpse could kiss.

(CARLO *catches* EDDIE *as he falls.*)

CAR. Speak not of death. Of death I'll not allow
A word from out your lips. Just lay and rest.

LEO. The devil a second death I will endow.
Beneath my heel I'll crush another pest.

(*As* LEOPOLD *lunges for* CARLO, DOLORES *interposes herself between father and lover.*)

DOL. Father, no, you cannot hurt this boy.
I love him, and he loves me back as well.
LEO. If love you have, it's something I'll destroy.
Before you two will love, you'll go to Hell.

(LEOPOLD *tries to reach* CARLO *with his sword as* CARLO *comforts* EDDIE, *but* DOLORES *is able to hold him back.*)

DOL. If me you love, you'll then do this at least,
One here's been killed tonight, so let the other live.
LEO. For you, my daughter, he'll not need a priest.
No last confessions will he have to give.

(LEOPOLD *storms off, dragging his daughter behind him.*)

ED. I thought I'd last far longer than this age.
Grow old, have kids, all life's treasure's hoard.
But now I'm being ushered from the stage,
One undead having slashed me with a sword.
CAR. Rest up, dear friend, it's far too soon to die.
We've many long, carousing years ahead.
ED. I know you far too well. Don't try to lie.
Before mere minutes pass I shall be dead.
CAR. Eddie, listen, let us hurry home,
Before from you more precious blood can ooze.
ED. Too late! Oh, God, I had so far to roam.
To think my life I could so early lose.
Goodbye, Carlo, I tried my very best
To be your friend through times best and times worst
And now it seems that I have failed the test.
My life is over and my spirit cursed.

(EDDIE *dies.*)

CAR. Wake up, dear friend, you go away too soon.
There still was much that we had both to do.
I thought my wedding day you'll play a tune,
When Dolores and I forged life of something new.
Who thought that true love could birth such distress?

Not death but rather, new life it should bring.
And now my neat world's been made such a mess,
Best friend slain by sullen zombie king.

> (CARLO *hefts* EDDIE *in his arms, and
> prepares to carry him home.*)

CAR. Forgive me, friend, your death and also this –
Regardless of the guilt brought by your fall
I love Dolores' cold, firm, undead kiss.
I love her still, submit to siren's call.
Dolores, I will have you or know why.
If your love can't be mine, I'd rather die.

ACT IV

> Dolores' bedroom. That afternoon.
>
> (DOLORES *tosses in bed while* MARY,
> *her maid, wrings her hands.*)

MA. I've kept your father's house for many years,
Since zombie plague made me be born again
And in that time I've witnessed many tears
Fall from your eyes due to the acts of men.
Love's not an easy game to have to play.
The rules are senseless if you're live or dead.
I'd hoped to be in heaven by today;
Instead we're still by Cupid's fever led.
DOL. It's not a fever; fevers are what pass,
And what I feel will never dare to fade.
MA. I know inside it feels that way, my lass,
But I am older. Listen to your maid.
I've loved many, obsessed on each in turn.
But now I swear I could not list their names.
Though once my body and my brain did burn,
My memories cast them off like childish games.
DOL. My heart sings true! Don't say that I'm a child,
Who's playing with a toy that she'll forget.
The feelings coursing through me aren't mild,
And father's turned my happiness to fret.
MA. Then tell me, child, what's brought you to this state,
And this old fool will help you if she can.

DOL. If you could aid my struggle with this fate
You'll stand beside me when they read the bann.
MA. A father's wishes must not be denied,
But I will lend a sympathetic ear,
For there's no pain as great as love denied.
So speak. Let me the situation hear.
DOL. I met him only yesterday, this man,
And though by now mere hours have been spent,
It seems that years are gone and that we can
Be sure that we are for each other meant.
MA. Who is this one who in you's made the change?
Where met you he who made your heart to fall?
DOL. This one whom my whole life did rearrange
I met last night at living Mayor's ball.
MA. You dared the ball against your father's will?
Torment swore he to any who dared go.
DOL. What will he do to me? He cannot kill
My form or heart. Inside me love does grow.
And I would risk my father's violent rage,
Or any punishments the Gods would bear –
For without my love, the world is but a cage.
Any pain's worth glimpse of Carlo fair.
MA. Carlo, no, you must not speak that name!
Is he the one who makes your heart to pulse?
Our enemy's fair son? Have you no shame?
He's living, and the mere thought does revulse.
DOL. I care not what you or my father feel,
What foolish rules my carefree heart does break.
The love that runs inside of me is real.
MA. My lass, I fear you do a grand mistake.
DOL. It cannot be. Who wrote these foul commandments?
Who said that those alive by us be eaten?
I say that love's a thing that perchance rents
The rules. Those foolish things can be beaten.

(*Enter* LEOPOLD.)

LEO. No! The thing that should be beaten wears your form.
You shall not mate with foul still-breathing thing.
I'll beat you 'till your limbs again are warm,
And remember once again that I am king.
Begone, Mary, this you should not see.

You are aware, I know, how discipline goes,
But as you are not fully family,
I'll not have you stand by to count the blows.
MA. Let me stay, I sad consequences fear
And severance of your love which should not pass.
LEO. Begone, my maid, what happens you'll not hear.
DOL. It's all right, Mary. Alone I'll drink his glass.

(*Exit* MARY.)

LEO. Now I will speak as fathers do, and warn
With stern pronouncements of what will transpire.
'Twill make you wish you'd not been once more born.
Unfailing service is what I require.
Need love and gratitude be requested
Of one whom I have brought through these mad times?
When I think of all I have invested
To raise you, and now this, it seems a crime.
Forget him. This first time I'll ask polite,
But then all niceties from my demeanor fade,
And if I do not see you are contrite,
As daughter you will know a failing grade,
And suffer all indignities within my power,
As I am suffering yours due to your tryst.
I'll let you think upon this for an hour.
DOL. No minute, hour, lifetime, I insist,
Holds time enough to from me love erase,
Or end this thing which you saw born last night.
LEO. I warn you, daughter, you must learn your place.
A world where your will conquers mine's not right.
DOL. Most noble father, I seek no fight with you.
My love for you has long known no extreme,
But now I've found a man as daughters do,
And I must go to him, as love's rules deem.
LEO. Ah, that's the problem. "Man" is what you said.
You've set your eyes on men when men are past.
Keep your love on a leash. Stay with the dead.
Of arguments let this one be the last.
DOL. If that be so, my father, it's your choice,
Of whether you will fight this happy thing,
Or join with me and Carlo to rejoice
That love, dear love, has made our hearts to sing.

(LEOPOLD, *enraged, slaps his daughter.*)

LEO. Don't speak of choices to one who's had none,
Who was pushed back to life to bond the dead.
I have no "choice" in whether war is done,
And in my presence I'll not hear this madness said.
The world exists, we cannot make our own.
The rules are written, which we cannot edit.
No feelings in a woman's tender zone
Can tip scales the direction that you credit.
DO. But, father –
LEO. No. "But father" I'll hear not.
The case is closed, with no room for appeals.
Carlo is alive, while you do rot,
And with that fact your love can make no deals.
No love can be between our races two.
Learn this well, your father does implore.
To change that fact there's nothing you can do;
Dolores shall see Carlo nevermore.

(*Exit* LEOPOLD. *Enter* MARY.)

MA. There, there, girl, that's it, give yourself to tears.
I've cried them oft' myself in years gone by.
Lovers are such flighty fickle dears,
That he'd have left you anyway to cry.
DOL. Not this time. Our true love is strong.
'Twill overcome whatever fathers say.
Our future bright together will be long.
Love's vibrant "yes" wins over parent's "nay."
MA. If only I'd your naïve confidence
When I was younger, it would have been strange
To see if I'd in my life's skein made rents,
Or my own father's will made any change.
DOL. You know then how it feels within my place.
Your heart was once a mirror to mine made.
Help this time the lovers win the race.
Help me to my man become a maid.
MA. Ah, lass, I wish there was a way to do
The acts of Cupid, but I have no bow.
Perhaps your only answer's to eschew
The very thing you wish. 'Twas ever so.

DOL. It will not be this time, that I do swear,
If it means end of me, of everything!
There's nothing that I would not gladly dare.
I'd fight the world to make the angels sing.
MA. You'd really for this Carlo risk it all?
DOL. If you've an answer, any price I'd pay.
MA. I think that I can help you vault this wall.
If you are unafraid there is a way.
DOL. What is it? Name it and it will be done.
MA. I'd hate to raise your hopes with crazy lie.
DO. I'll take lies if with them this be done.
MA. Then know what I have learned of those who die.
I've heard that we come back —
DOL. We all know that.
Those words bring nothing new to end my pain.
MA. Hear me out, girl, it is not that pat.
What I mean is that they come back again.
The living first come back to become us,
And that's accomplished through the worldwide plague
Involving not the slightest bit of fuss.
The manner that this happens is still vague.
But time to time I hear a silly rumor
Of dead instead of coming, going back,
And death is cut from their souls like a tumor.
DOL. Of how to do this thing you have the knack?
MA. I know the details not of how this works,
For there are some things it's best not to know,
And there are times I feel that madness lurks
In going places we're not meant to go.
But I know one for whom the things arcane
Are simple as to us our ABC's.
But he's an unforgiving one and I would fain
Become involved with him though he's the keys.
DOL. You must take me to him, give your word!
And having done so tell my father naught.
MA. That this should work is patently absurd.
And think if you are by your father caught.
DOL. I'm caught by Carlo. I so little care
For what another thinks that I am free
To fly to heaven like a bird in air.
In finding love, fear has no hold on me.

Say that you'll do it. Let us make to leave
And find this one who'll set all things aright.
MA. I'll do it for you though I fear I'll grieve
And with this thing unnatural turn day to night.
I'll send a message to him so we'll meet
And make you to the image of your love.
DOL. Tell him he should make himself be fleet
As eagles soaring through the skies above.
MA. Go now to your father with the news
That you your virgin senses have regained,
And hope that he your imprisonment eschews
So we can leave here to meet the mystic bard.
DOL. At this point if you feel that it is just
I'd tell falsehoods to King of Kings himself.

(*Exit* DOLORES, *leaving* MARY *momentarily alone*.)

MA. The girl is mad with love and that's a shame,
For love is surely the worst kind of madness.
I pray that once we're done there'll be no blame
For true love must too often end in sadness.

(*A handful of pebbles rattle off the wall.*
MARY *moves to the window*.)

MA. What's out there? Leave me shadow, with my fear
That anything I do will end with guilt.

(CARLO *answers from offstage*.)

CAR. Dolores, it is Carlo, my dead dear,
Ready to bury my sword down to the hilt
In anyone who stands between our lips.
MA. He thinks I am my lady. I will talk
As if I'm her and see if falsehood slips.
What brings you here? Visit you to balk?
CAR. I came, sweet love, because I have a plan
To end objections families may feel.
There's but one way together that we can
Disarm their hate so wedding bells can peal.
If we were both the same, we'd need not run
From hate, but rather towards our bliss.
MA. It seems that here two minds have thought as one,
And with true love there's nothing that's amiss.

CA. If both the same we could somehow arrange,
There'd be no need for war between our kin.
By making to one race another change
We'll rise above the earth's tumultuous din.
MA. You're right that you have nailed the only way
For happiness to be two lovers' fates.

(*Enter* LEOPOLD, *with* DOLORES *trailing*.)

LEO. Whom do you speak with? Hold there, villain! Stay!

(LEOPOLD *rushes to the window*.)

LEO. Look, he leaps like magic o'er the gates!
Who was that, maid, what did here just transpire?
Was that a brigand sent to bear my daughter hence?
Do you with living fiends tonight conspire
To undertake a brutal crime immense?

(MARY *falls to her knees*.)

MA. My lord, your every wish becomes my deed.
I've spent my second life here serving you.
Look not upon me as a weaker reed,
You've only but to say and I will do.

(DOLORES *studies* MARY *nervously*.)

DOL. I'm sure it was some creature of the night
Scounging for one last meal to stay alive.
And hearing us draw near it did take flight
Before we could its animal life deprive.
LEO. I guess you're right. Discord had made me jumpy.
I make each harmless creak into a threat.
Our path these past few hours has been quite bumpy.
We will have peace in this fine household yet.

(*Exit* LEOPOLD. DOLORES *pauses by the door
to make sure he has not remained to listen*.)

DOL. Bless your soul! To save me you did grovel.
My gratitude could not be more profound.
MA. A true love such as yours is something novel.
In my long life no other has been found.
DOL. So tell me, was that Carlo in the street?
It was, I know! What was it brought him here?

MA. He brought with him a brilliant plan that matches
The one that you and I have just contrived.
Like minds a like way out of sadness hatches.
Two start points have one destination arrived.
DOL. Then he will love me when I am as he?
MA. Your story cannot have another end.
A celebration out of this must be.
Love's reputation we hereby defend.
DOL. True joy awaits me, and my solid flesh,
Once rigor mortis leaves and I wax fresh.

ACT V

The interior of the graveyard. Night.

(*Enter* CARLO. *He wanders the graveyard, a shovel over his shoulders.*)

CAR. Where are your bones, friend? Sleeping time has passed.
This act alone cannot be carried through.
Though I'm the one who made you breathe your last,
I need your help to weave this strange skein through.
There's no one living I find I can trust,
So now's the time for me to you uncover,
And you to like a dog shake off death's rust,
So I can pleasure prove with lady love.

(CARLO *finds* EDDIE's *grave, center stage.*)

CAR. Ah, here you are, dear Eddie, noble friend.

(CARLO *digs.*)

CAR. Ashes to ashes, dust to dust, 'twas said,
But life's no longer guaranteed that end,
And dead rise up as if but out of bed.

(EDDIE *suddenly reaches up out of the grave to grab* CARLO's *ankle.*)

CAR. Impatient friend, I work fast as I can.
Forever waits, so try to patient be.
Awake again you'll be a diff'rent man,
And then I hope your new form will help me.

(CARLO *lends his friend a hand, and* EDDIE

climbs out of the grave.)

ED. So this is what death feels like. I once feared
The fetid breath of death upon my cheek.
I trembled as my last few moments neared.
All courage fled. I was left soft and meek.
But now that I have sliced the ebon veil,
I see how foolish were my moments tense.
By dying so, I've grasped the holy grail,
And suddenly the stuff of life makes sense.
CAR. I'm glad, friend, all makes sense from where you sit,
For you are where I do soon hope to be.
ED. You are not ready, Carlo. You're too fit.
No reason for you turning like as me.
CAR. My lady love's a zombie, such as you.
Fate has living flesh by zombies eaten,
But you'll help me escape the undead stew.
Tonight this madness by me will be beaten.
ED. I do admit in you I see a meal,
Though friendship bids me bypass this first bite.
CA. For myself you're thanked, and commonweal
Will surely thank you once they see the light,
For once they see the things that love can do
No longer will we one another kill.
With sacrifice I'll my fair maiden woo,
And make the waters of this world stand still.
ED. What is it that you ask in friendship's name?

(CARLO *passes the shovel to* EDDIE.)

CAR. Tonight, I'll die, and come back as another.
I'll kill myself, but to life's ember tame,
You'll to plant me in the ground, my brother.
ED. When I first living saw you with that girl,
I thought that you had given up your mind.
But now to me she seems a perfect pearl,
And you're the one who seems of the wrong kind.
I pledge my strength to with you disjoint mend.
You only speak the word. I'll meet your need.
CAR. My heart knew that on you it could depend.
Stand back, the time has come to do the deed.

(CARLO *plunges a knife deeply into his own stomach.*)

CAR. Such pain! It burns! But I will bear it well,
If agony will fair Dolores bring.
And now, I sleep, though just for but a spell.
O Death, hear I my dear beloved sing?

    (CARLO *staggers back, and tumbles into the grave.*)

ED. Rest well, I know the comfort of that bed.
It carried me hither from one life to next.
Now it's your turn to lie here in my stead,
To prove that death can be forever vexed.

    (EDDIE *scatters a handful of earth over* CARLO.)

ED. And now I leave my friend to where I'll wait
For his grand transformation to occur.
And once he's gained his lovestruck chosen state,
I'll see him wed, for True Love nothing can deter.

    (Exit EDDIE, *stage right. Enter* DOLORES, *stage left.*)

DOL. Here I return to where Carlo declared
Eternal love for me, so it is right,
That here the gap between us is repaired.
I'll drink magician's potion here tonight.
My maid waits yon so I may all alone
Contemplate incipient reunion
of two who now our race's hate atone,
and shatter any doubts. Love's no illusion.

(DOLORES *pulls a vial from her cloak and raises it overhead.*)

DOL. This drink will soon my barren flesh infuse
With stuff of life. I can no more postpone
The structures of my plague-like death to lose.
Soon this cold heart will ne'er more be alone.

    (DOLORES *drinks the potion. She grasps her throat
    and falls into the grave, vanishing from view.
        EDDIE returns once more to center stage.*)

ED. I thought I heard my lord and master stir.
Yet I sense nothing here that is amiss.
'Twas probably just the whining of a cur.
I'll go, and not return 'till lovers kiss.

    (EDDIE *exits. Within the grave, the lovers stir.*)

CAR. Is that my darling's hip close next to mine?
DOL. It is! Together we will be at last!
Has my skin at last a pallor that's like thine?
CAR. It must! Let's rise and take each other's cast.

(*Both* DOLORES *and* CARLO *stand. Their heads and shoulders now protrude from the grave. It can clearly be seen that* CARLO *has a grayish pallor, while* DOLORES' *skin is fair. They look upon their own hands first, and not each other.*)

DOL. The bard's wild potion worked. My skin is fair.
Memory hides from me when last was so.
CAR. I've joined the dead, but little do I care,
As long as down the aisle we soon must go.

(*They look at each other now. Shocked by what they see, they scramble from the pit. The grave yawns between them.*)

CAR. As zombie suitor I was to arrive.
Why have you gone and changed the other way?
DOL. But I thought we'd agreed I would contrive
To like a snake shed skin of blue and gray,
And join you in your world of living folk.
Why did you rather two steps backwards choose?
CAR. We tried to fix this thing, instead we broke
The sad machine of love. Must we then lose?

(*The lovers consider each other intently.*)

DOL. Love cannot lose. Do you so soon forget?
If you've a pulse or not to you I'm bound.
CAR. You're right, for looking, I still long to pet
The liquefaction of your curves so round.
Come to me, love, though places we did switch,
And let's forget our difference of race.
Beside the grand abyss of this death ditch
I swear your heart I love, not nature of your face.

(*The lovers embrace.*)

DOL. Let's to our fathers' hence and spread the news.

(*Enter* LEOPOLD, *stage right.*)

LEO. To me this treachery comes as no surprise.
How dare your father's kindness you abuse?

(*Enter* VINCENT, *stage left.*)

VIN. My son, it's time you shed this grim disguise.
LEO. Disguises both they wear, enemy foul.
It's time to wash them off and end this play.
To see my daughter like this makes me howl
My anger to the Gods. End this I say!
VIN. On this one point I'm with you, zombie king.
This travesty of love must not go on.
This tableaux pains me with ungrateful sting.
If you can't stop this I'll make war upon
Your zombie kin as you have never seen,
And find a way the earth of you to rid.
LEO. It's not my side that's birthed this madness mean.
It's you, you old buffoon, and your damned kid.

(*In their anger,* LEOPOLD *and* VINCENT *forget their children. The two men draw their swords and begin to fight.*)

VIN. Don't dare you in my sight defame my son.
Look homeward, blame your own deceitful bitch!
LEO. I'll kill you, man, and after you are done,
Cement you down! You'll never leave your ditch!

(*Enter* EDDIE.)

LEO. Prepare to die!
VIN. Prepare to –
ED. Stop this now!

(EDDIE *comes between King* LEOPOLD *and Mayor* VINCENT.)

ED. I've seen enough of violence this past day.
The races must become fast friends enow,
And end this mad desire to rend and slay.
VIN. It cannot end as long as they embrace.
Call off their love, and end this cruel charade.
LEO. Once they say goodbyes, we'll leave this place,
Once they have cleaned themselves and shut this masquerade.
DOL. They still don't understand what love has wrought
Nor comprehend our metamorphosis.
CAR. Their anger I fear will be ever taught.
I think that we will never vanquish this.
ED. I love you both. I'll end this impasse chill.

(EDDIE *reaches into the grave and removes the vial from which Dolores had sipped. He offers the vial to King* LEOPOLD.)

ED. King, surely your exertion raised a thirst.

(LEOPOLD *drinks.*)

ED. And you, Lord Mayor, I guess I'll have to kill.

(EDDIE *runs* VINCENT *through with his sword.*)

ED. All will be clear once you two are reversed.

(*As soon as* EDDIE *removes his sword,* VINCENT *tumbles into the grave.* LEOPOLD *grabs his throat, and follows.*)

ED. Let's leave this ground, and vanish 'till they wake.
Tonight we've more than made a match for you.
We're done that, but with our whole lives at stake,
Remodeled all our world to something new.

(*Exit* EDDIE.)

CAR. Come now, my love, our joyful future meet,
And from each other nevermore do part.
DOL. I need no more to make my life complete.
Between us two we do share but one heart.

(*The lovers kiss and exit. Enter* JONATHAN, *the gravedigger from the prologue, followed by* SAM, *the zombie.*)

JON. And so we reach the climax of this play,
Which in its five acts sought to fill you in
On how zombie and living reached this day,
Moving from enemies to accepting kin.
We've made our peace with how the plague has shaped
Our sordid world. We've ended all our wars.
Yet if you think that this world has been raped,
It's not a very different one from yours.
Our curtain falls. Go back now to your lives.
Take what you wish as you tonight return
To lovers, parents, children, husbands, wives.
Remember to be kind to those who yearn.
SAM. Living or dead, love lies in wait for you.
Begrudge it not. Or who knows what we'll do?

(*Exeunt omnes.*)

KARL EDWARD WAGNER

Final Cut

THREE YEARS AFTER his untimely death, Karl Edward Wagner's work continues to thrive. His final new stories have been turning up in various anthologies, and his novella "The River of Night's Dreaming" has been filmed as part of the Showtime TV series *The Hunger*, which has also optioned "Beyond Any Measure".

For nearly a quarter of a century, he chronicled the exploits of Kane, the Mystic Swordsman, in a series of superior novels and stories. Having trained as a psychiatrist, his short fiction often dealt with themes of psychological horror and bizarre eroticism. As a writer, editor and publisher he was a multiple winner of The British and World Fantasy Awards, and he continued to encourage new talent through his annual anthology series, *The Year's Best Horror Stories*.

Just prior to his death in 1994, Wagner finished compiling a fourth collection of his fiction, to be titled *Exorcisms and Ecstasies*. It was recently published by Fedogan & Bremer and I am proud to have had the opportunity to edit the volume, combining the author's original selection of stories with most of his uncollected work (including two never-before-published tales, one written when he was just 12-years-old), while such close friends and contemporaries as Peter Straub, Ramsey and Jenny Campbell, Brian Lumley, David Drake, David J. Schow, Francis Wellman, C. Bruce Hunter and James R. Wagner contributed personal memoirs of the man and the writer they knew. The book also features an extensive working bibliography of all Karl Edward Wagner's fiction published in the English language.

In his introduction to the following story in *Diagnosis Terminal*, editor F. Paul Wilson remarked: "This, I believe, is his last story. I think it's probably more truth than fiction (I'll let you guess who the psychiatrist might be). And I think Karl let more of his humanity slip through than he'd ever done before. A damn shame the title was so prophetic."

NO ONE GETS WELL in a hospital.

Dr Kirby Meredith had forgotten who had said that to him, but he hadn't forgotten the words. He was a prematurely aging attending psychiatrist at a large hospital in Pine Hill, North Carolina. He had graduated from the medical school here, gone through his residency, attained his present senior status. Talk was that he would go a long way, perhaps chairman of the department when the time was right.

Dr Meredith was a nonintimidating, rather dumpy man of thirty-something, with sandy hair and grey in his frizzy beard. He wore the same striped ties he had worn for years, button-down collar shirts, and cotton Dockers. Still wore tight black leather dress shoes, and he pulled on a rumpled tweed jacket whenever he thought the occasion called for it: weekly court commitment hearings, held here at the center; patient's family inquiring as to family member's progress. Shrinks do not wear white. Bad for patient rapport.

He hated wearing ties. If he ever set up in private practice, it would be T-shirts and maybe a sweater. A cardigan. No, just the T-shirt. Or some jogging sweats. Not that he ever jogged. Assume the air of informality. Patient at ease. Dream on.

Dr Meredith had just completed his rounds, was making medication adjustments to his charts, making mental notes regarding his students and staff, and considering journal club that evening, where he hoped his residents finally would be brought up-to-date on lithium therapy. There was a fine line between maintaining a manic-depressive and killing him, and the foreign resident who had confused q.o.d. with q.i.d. was going to speak at length upon the subject. In broken English.

"Dr Meredith." The nurse knew better than to interrupt him needlessly, and Meredith felt the tension. "He says he's your cousin, and it's urgent."

"Thank you." Meredith picked up the phone. He shouldn't be receiving personal calls here, unless from his wife or daughter. He worked hard, did not like to be interrupted. Once at home, he could find time for friends and family.

"Kirby!" said the voice over the phone. "It's your favorite cousin, Bob. I got a problem, maybe. Janice told me how to reach you at the hospital."

"What's the problem, Bob?" Meredith thought Cousin Bob sounded drunk. He'd rarely seen him sober. Bob Breenwood lived about half an hour's distance from Pine Hill and ran a small hardware business in a small town. They got together regularly to go fishing. Bob was always drunk. His wife and staff ran the business.

"Just started vomiting. Blood. Can't stop it."

Meredith froze for a moment. "How much blood?"

"I don't know. I was cooking a steak on the charcoal grill, and then it just started."

"Is it bright red, or is it sort of like dark and clotted, like it's coming from your gums or sinuses, and you've maybe swallowed it and choked it up?"

"It's bright red, and there's more of it coming up. All the time. Oh, shit! I got to hit the toilet!"

Meredith was very firm. "Have your wife call 911. Emergency. Get over here without delay. You're likely bleeding to death from ruptured esophageal varices. Do it now. I'll be here. For you. There's no time to waste. You'll be dead in an hour."

Possibly putting it a little too strong, but Meredith phoned 911 himself, with frantic details. Maureen Breenwood had already called. Meredith hovered about the Emergency Room, getting in the way, while explaining why an attending shrink was in the way. He was well liked, and the staff were ready when the ambulance arrived.

Bob's hematocrit was down to 10, for someone who liked to take down record lows. Typed and cross-matched, the units of blood finally flowed into his arm. He did not go into shock, by some miracle. A balloon was inserted past his esophagus, reducing the bleeding, and his blood pressure finally stabilized at 105/90 from 60/45. He should have been dead.

Dr Meredith observed, but stayed out of the way. He wouldn't want two or three other shrinks all giving therapeutic advice as he interviewed his patient, and he respected professionalism. Instead he made frequent visits to Maureen, who had left the waiting room for the chapel, and reassured her as she spoke with the priest. Dr Meredith was an atheist, but therapy was therapy. Janice was coming over to be with her.

Cousin Bob was fully stabilized by three in the morning and off to Intensive Care. Dr Meredith checked Maureen into a nearby hotel and promised to phone if there were any complications, then returned to his office in the psychiatric wing and fell asleep on his couch.

Meredith woke up about seven, very groggy but too concerned to go back to sleep. He brushed his hair and brushed his teeth, washed his face and sprayed his armpits, put on a fresh shirt and tie from his file cabinets. He wondered why he bothered to pay a monstrous mortgage for their home. He phoned his wife to see if she might stay with Maureen a few hours while Ashley was at school, and to say privately to Janice that things weren't going well – she knew that – and that he'd be home for dinner on time – she doubted that. Hell. This hospital *was* home.

Dr Meredith knocked back a cup of coffee at the administrative office, had another, tossed a buck into the coffee fund. He hated coffee. About time for morning rounds, and then he had group at 11. He wished he were as young as his med students, or even the residents. Youth and enthusiasm. Hell, he wasn't that old. He wished he had learned to play an electric guitar. Joined a rock band. Better the devil that you know. He poured another cup of coffee, then went to rounds.

Bob Greenwood was asking for him from the Intensive Care Unit as soon as they removed the balloon from his esophagus. Meredith delayed an outpatient appointment and went to see him instead of taking a late lunch. He wasn't hungry.

Cousin Bob was a year and a half older than Meredith, something he wouldn't let Meredith forget when they went skinny dipping together and Bob was growing hair on his crotch and Meredith was too young. Much later, Bob got him laid for the first time, double-dating in Bob's family's Nash Rambler with the fold-down front seat and a friendly high school girl and a convenient cemetery.

Meredith sat down on one of those uncomfortable plastic chairs at the bedside. Bad practice to sit down on the bed.

Maureen was sniffling, holding Bob's hand. She was a stout brunette with acne scars, but a good cook, which is why Meredith reckoned Bob had married her, because she couldn't keep house and the rest was none of his business.

Bob was as chunky as his wife: blue eyes, blond hair, rather short, no tattoos. Meredith had always thought them a good match. Happy, harmless couple. He was waiting for dozens of clueless offspring to appear.

Instead.

"Maureen," said Bob. "Could you let me talk to Kirby in private? Just for a few minutes. After all, he's a shrink."

"Sure." Maureen left the room.

Cousin Bob glanced around the Intensive Care Unit. There was fear in his eyes. Understandably.

"Liver's gone, they say."

Dr Meredith had read the charts. "Always a chance for a repair. This is 1973, after all."

"Kirby, they're saying I'm just a drunk. I don't think they really give a damn."

"I'm here for you. I'm staff."

"Did you know that I had TB years back?"

"No. You never told me."

"Friend of mine got it doing time in some shithouse reform school. We'd pass cigarettes and beers back and forth. They found some spots on my lungs after he'd been diagnosed. Put me on their two-drug therapy. Public health shits coming by to make sure I took all my pills. Isoniazid and something, I forget. Took them for ten years or so at their lawful command. Turns out that the combination wipes out your liver long-term."

"Shit." Meredith was familiar with the situation, but could think of nothing more profound to say. He wished he'd known about Bob in time.

"So now I'm here with a trashed liver, wiped out by the best medicine you can offer, told that I'm an alcoholic, serves me right. And they want to operate. Womak procedure, I think they call it. What do you think? I'm ready to walk."

Dr Meredith had read his cousin's chart. "Well, for whatever reasons, you are in liver failure, and you're bleeding internally. Very badly. It will start again and maybe not stop. I'm a shrink, and your surgeon can explain it far better. Basically they'll remove your spleen and the region of your stomach and lower esophagus where these varices – knotted-up blood vessels – lie. The liver can take a lot of abuse, and only a small portion need recover. There's work on liver transplants. I don't see it happening soon, but you're buying time."

"Then you think I should do it? The surgery?"

"I don't see any real choice. I mean, if you start bleeding again . . ."

Bob grabbed his hand, weakly. "Kirby, I'll go for it on your word."

It was a nonelective case, and surgery was under way by lunchtime the following day. Meredith bought a stale ham sandwich from a machine, munched on it, phoned his wife. She wasn't home. He fumbled around his desk and found some Maalox. By the time he'd had sessions with a few patients, it was growing dark and Cousin Bob had made it through surgery. Meredith spoke to him in the recovery room. He phoned his wife. She wasn't home. Meredith went back to his house. He microwaved a low-cal dinner, ate part of it.

Bob seemed to have come through it all very well. Maureen was at his bedside. Meredith persuaded Janice to visit with her when Janice could spare the time.

"I had a dream, Kirby," Bob told him two days postop. "I'm not sure it was a dream."

"Do you want to talk about it?"

"I'd climbed out of my bed, pulled out the IVs. I was fumbling my way along all these corridors. Lost. Just trying to get out. Go home.

"I was somewhere in the basement – I don't know how. I pushed open a door, thinking it led out. Only I was in the hospital morgue. Two doctors were doing an autopsy on a man. I think the man was me. I must have fainted, but I remember someone taking me back to my room. I'm afraid, Kirby."

Dr Meredith considered. He decided to be reassuring. "Near-fatal illness. Major surgery. Anesthesia. Pain medication. Not an uncommon sort of nightmare. Just rest and let your body heal. Just ask the nurse to call me if you have any more bad dreams."

He examined the charts, just in case, and found nothing out of the ordinary.

All of this was at the end of June. July brought in a new crop of interns, freshly graduated from med school and eager to excel. Dr Meredith lost a few of his residents, gained a few more, none of whom seemed promising, but that was his task – to bring them around. When he closeted himself in his office, he studied travel brochures.

Cousin Bob was now five days postop and starting to take semisolid foods.

He choked on the cherry Jell-O. Maureen pounded his back and shouted for help. By the time the nurse arrived, Bob's breathing passage was clear, but the spasms had opened some sutures, and this was causing pain and some bleeding. The nurse called for an intern.

The intern had only just arrived at the medical center, knew nothing about his patient, saw the postop abdominal incisions and fresh bleeding, obvious severe pain – and ordered a liberal injection of morphine to quell pain and agitation. He hadn't thought to check the charts for liver function, but he had been told that the patient in 221 was a hopeless drunk. Whatever. Who cares.

Cousin Bob died before Dr Meredith could rush over from the psychiatric wing. Janice came to be with Maureen. Meredith followed the body to the basement morgue. There would be an autopsy, although it was obvious to most idiots in white coats that a patient with minimal liver function had been massively overdosed.

"Shit! He's back again!" The chief pathologist was breaking in another pale and trembling med student. Meredith suspected he enjoyed this sort of thing or he'd leave this to residents.

"What do you mean?"

"Patient stumbled in here a few nights back. Guess he just couldn't wait."

"Nothing in his chart about that."

"One of your patients? Well, orderlies don't like to report a fuss when there's no harm done."

"No harm done."

"Looks bad for the hospital."

No one ever gets well in a hospital.

Dr Meredith wandered from the basement morgue, seeking his office.

The oppressive walls soaked with pain and rage pressed down on him. He thought of a thousand Cousin Bobs – slowly, painfully killed by the best efforts of modern unfeeling medicine. No one ever gets well in a hospital.

Tomorrow he would clear out his office.

Tomorrow couldn't come soon enough.

TERRY LAMSLEY

The Break

I HAVE NEVER BEFORE included two stories by a single author in the same volume of *The Best New Horror*. However, I am about to break that rule with Terry Lamsley.

Over the past few years, Lamsley has emerged as an undisputed master of the short horror story, and his work has recently graced the pages of such magazines and anthologies as *Cemetery Dance*, *Lethal Kisses*, *The Mammoth Book of Dracula*, *Dancing With the Dark*, *Dark Terrors 3* and *The Year's Best Fantasy and Horror*.

The following story, like the one that opens this volume, is taken from the author's impressive second collection, *Conference With the Dead: Tales of Supernatural Terror* and, as he explains, "'The Break' grew out of my memories of childhood holidays and of later experiences as a vagrant doing menial jobs in vast, strange, seedy hotels in various seaside resorts when I was in my teens. Happy days!"

You might not agree after you've read this . . .

INSTEAD OF GETTING UNDRESSED straight away, as Gran had told him to, Danny pulled aside one of the curtains she had drawn together and peered out again at the jetty, on the edge of the harbour to the right of him, to see what the men on the boat were doing. The little craft, a fishing smack, had docked five minutes earlier. He had watched with admiration as the men aboard had manoeuvred it into place as easily as if they were parking a car. The sky was getting darker and the sea was flat, black and shiny, except for the white lace of tiny waves tacked along the edge of the beach. He could no longer make out the shape of the hull of the vessel, but the jetty was built of pale, slightly yellow stone against which he could see, in silhouette, the top of the boat and the activities of the two sailors on board.

They had pulled a cumbersome object, a box of some kind, up from the deck with a winch operated by a third man, above them on the jetty. He had been waiting for them, staring out to sea, for some time before they had arrived. Danny had asked his Gran to open the top window because it was an oppressively warm evening and the hotel room had a flat, earthy smell, like the inside of a greenhouse in winter. Through it he could hear the rattle of the hoist's cranking chain as the box lurched into the air, and the barking shouts of the man operating it. He was a very big man, dressed in heavy, unseasonable garments that made him look like a bear. He moved like a bear as well, Danny thought, with rolling, lunging motions, and seemed to have trouble keeping his balance.

When the box rose to the level of his shoulders the man pulled it round with a rope attached to the top of the hoist, then slowly lowered it onto the jetty. It must have slipped its chains at the last moment because Danny saw it suddenly drop a few inches, and heard it land with a sound that made him think it was very heavy and made of wood. The bear-like man walked around it quickly, inspecting it, then shouted sharply down to the others on the boat. At once, a light came on in the cabin at the front of the smack. The engine started clunking, the third man cast off the ropes, and the vessel curved away out into the bay beyond, leaving a widening ark of crumpled tin-foil foam in its wake.

"Danny; please; it's *so* late, and you've not even got into your pyjamas!"

Gran didn't seem at all cross, as his mother would have been, but she sounded strained and disappointed in him. Danny hadn't heard her come in, but she always moved like that; so quietly and carefully, like a phantom. He dropped the edge of the curtain and, feeling slightly ashamed of himself, took the tray bearing a mug of chocolate and some toast she had brought him for supper, and set it down on the table beside his bed.

"I'm not tired, Gran," he lied, then yawned hugely, giving the game away. "I was watching the sea," he explained, somewhat inaccurately.

"You've got all week for that," Gran said, folding a triangle of quilt tidily back away from his pillow to display how temptingly comfortable the bed beneath it looked.

Danny said, "I like the boats. There's hundreds in the harbour. Will we be able to go for a trip on one?"

"I can't take Grandad, and I mustn't leave him behind, but perhaps you could go on your own, if I think it's safe."

"Is Grandad ill?" Danny asked, plugging the sink and twisting the taps to run water for his evening wash. When Gran didn't answer he turned back to her and added, "He looks all right. I can't *see* anything wrong with him."

"He's not exactly ill, like you were last winter, with your chest; it's just that, recently, he's got a bit . . . forgetful."

"Yes," Danny agreed, "I've noticed that," and saw his Gran's face darken. "I mean, sometimes, he looks at me as though he doesn't know who I am. When I met you both at the station, and you left me with him and went to get a magazine, he asked me what my name was."

"Oh dear," said Gran, poking nervously at the grey curl that dangled down over her right eye, "did he really?"

"Then, when I told him, he just shook his head, as though he'd never heard of me."

"I'm sorry."

"It's not your fault," Danny said generously. "He got my name right later." He began to brush his teeth.

Pleased to be presented with this enforced curtailment of the conversation, when she had been thinking how she could change the subject without arousing in Danny an alarming suspicion that her husband was worse than he really was, Gran decided to make an exit.

"Breakfast is at 8.30," she said, after kissing Danny goodnight on the top of his head.

"Can I go on my own, or must I wait for you?"

"No, you're big enough now to make your own way down, I think."

"Of course I am," Danny agreed. "I was last year, when we went to Brighton, but you wouldn't believe me."

Gran smiled, but she didn't seem to agree with him. "Into

bed now, Danny," she insisted. "I'll look in soon to make sure you're asleep."

When she had gone, Danny sipped the chocolate and pulled a face. It didn't taste anything like it did at home, when his mother made it. He poured the drink down the sink, ate the toast quickly, got into his pyjamas, then could not resist taking one more peep out the window before getting into bed. The man on the jetty was still there. He was pushing the big heavy box towards the shore with great difficulty. He was bending behind it, almost on all fours, looking more than ever like a fat black bear. Although obviously pushing with all his strength, he was only managing to move it inches at a time. After two or three strenuous efforts he stopped, leaned against the box as though exhausted, then strained to shove it a couple of times more. It made a harsh crunching sound as it moved, as if it was sliding across a surface scattered with broken glass. The box was still only a few feet from where it had landed. At that rate, Danny thought, it would take the man all night to reach the end of the jetty!

He could hear the box sliding and grinding along every now and then as he lay in bed, but it didn't sound as if it was getting any nearer. He felt sorry for the man. Why didn't he get someone to help him? He had looked somehow very lonely out there, and the way he had spoken to the men on the fishing boat, and they to him, had not sounded at all friendly. It occurred to Danny that it was likely that the man was not nice to know and had no friends.

When Gran peeped in twenty minutes later, she could tell from his breathing that he was asleep. She was closing the door again when she heard the sound of the huge box being moved outside, and went to the window. By mistake, she had only brought her reading glasses on holiday with her, but was just able to see what Danny had seen and, like him, watched and speculated about the man on the jetty. At that moment he was leaning on the far edge of the box and his white blob of a face was looking up towards the hotel, or seemed to be. He remained in this pose for only a few moments, then suddenly bent down, shuffled his legs back a little, and began to push. His body appeared to compress as he increased his effort then, though Gran's faulty vision could detect no movement, the box grated on the stone surface of the jetty as it jerked a few inches closer, and the figure behind it elongated. This happened three times, then the man stood up, stretched his back, arced his arms above his head, and glanced up towards the hotel again.

Gran stepped away from the window and closed her eyes for a moment as a harsh, cold light shone in on her. She realized it was the headlights of a car turning off the promenade, up into the town. She suddenly felt an unexpected evening breeze from somewhere, that made the edges of the curtains flutter, and caused her to twitch and clench her teeth and shudder.

Because of that, and because she didn't want Danny woken up by any noise, she shut the window before she left the room.

Someone knocked on the door. Danny opened his eyes, registered the dim daylight beyond the curtains, and waited. Gran never needed inviting. When, after a static silence, whoever it was knocked again, Danny sat up and called, "Come in." A young woman in a pale blue overall stepped sideways into the room. Still holding the door handle she showed him a sketch of a smile and said, "G' morning. Tea or coffee?"

Danny had not been expecting this. Hotels he had stayed in in the past had provided equipment for guests to make their own refreshments. He asked for tea and, while the girl was busy at a trolley he could see parked on the corridor outside, hauled himself up out of the last few yards of sleep, feeling obscurely embarrassed and slightly irritated.

The girl placed the tea by his bed and gave it an extra stir. She said, "Sleep well?" in a distant sort of way.

"Mmm; yes; very, thank you."

"Good," the girl acknowledged, and bent down over him and began fussing with his pillow. Danny made some effort to sit up. The girl must have thought he was having difficulty doing so, as she reached behind his head with her right hand and supported the upper part of his back. It was a gentle, helpful movement, but Danny didn't like it. The girl's fingers were thin and hard against his spine and there was something investigative about the way she touched him that made him uneasy, as though she was literally weighing him up, and testing the quality of the flesh beneath his pyjamas. He reared up away from her hand and shook his shoulders. The girl's thumb and fingers rested for a moment on the top of his arm, almost squeezing, before she turned away to open the curtains with a flourish, revealing rain-spotted windows and, beyond, the grimy, grey sky of the disappointing day outside.

"They say it will clear up later," the girl assured him, and the edgy smile shifted briefly across her face again. Danny couldn't understand why he didn't like her. There was nothing about her looks to upset him; she had a sharp, but almost pretty, face and she was obviously trying to be nice. She couldn't help having hard, bony fingers.

After she had gone, Danny snuggled down into the bed again until he remembered the man on the jetty the night before. He played a game in his mind, laying bets with himself about how far the man had moved the box. In the end, he decided there would be no sign of it. Someone would have been to collect it, and taken it away. He hopped out of bed to check, and saw the box still on the jetty, not far from where he had last seen it. A large sheet of dark green tarpaulin, tied in place with a strand of rope, had been draped over it. A puddle of rain had formed on top of it. There was no sign of the man. The jetty was otherwise empty.

Danny found that if he stood on tiptoe he could just see over the roofs of the hotels on the street below him onto the beach to the left of the jetty. It too was deserted now, except for piles of deckchairs and a solitary dog, jumping and jerking in the foam at the water's edge, tugging savagely at something, probably a strand of black seaweed, that glistened like a hank of wet, soapy human hair. From time to time the dog dropped the weed, held up its head, and snapped its jaws open and shut. Realising his window had been closed, because he couldn't hear the creature barking, Danny climbed onto the sill and opened it. Cold damp air straight off the sea surged into the room. He could hear the sloshing breakers of the turning tide, slightly baffled by the veils of wind-blown rain that were sweeping across the town, and the urgent, worried yapping of the dog, sounding much further off than it really was.

He washed, dressed quickly in a new T-shirt and jeans, and set out to find the dining room. The hotel was full of the smell of breakfast, and he hoped he could find his food by following his nose. He soon took a wrong turning, however, and wandered into a half-lit, grey painted room full of wheelchairs and pale-blue, uncomfortable looking furniture. There was a large mural on the wall depicting, in faded primary colours, what he thought must be Heaven, with naked sexless angels leading stooping elderly humans, in white togas, through an English rural landscape, drawn in such a way as to suggest a vast perspective. At the top of the picture, other angels, with tiny golden wings, flew through the sky, pulling strings of smiling old people along behind them. Yet more of the heavenly hosts, playing musical instruments, rested on cotton wool clouds beneath a beneficent, smirking sun, while a multitude of ancient mortals hovered around them, listening to their concert with obvious gratitude and appreciation.

At first Danny thought he was alone in the room, then he noticed, scattered along the walls, a number of elderly people, seemingly asleep in their seats and wheelchairs. They were lolling sideways, backwards, or forward, like inanimate puppets. One old man, his liver-spotted head quite bald on top, with an aura of pearly curls of unbrushed hair stretching up from the back of his neck to above his ears like coral or fungus, lay stretched out face down on the table in front of him.

Danny, chilled by the atmosphere of the room, froze on the spot for a few moments. Nobody moved or showed in any way they were aware he was there, until a voice to his left called out, "Nurse! Is it you? Can you prop me up? My cushion slipped; I've lost it."

Danny turned towards the sound and saw an incredibly thin old lady leaning at a sharp angle out of a wheelchair. She was resting on one arm, with her elbow in her lap, and stretching so far forward, she seemed to defy gravity. Her other arm dangled, limp as a bell rope, by her side. She had had to lift her head right back to see him, and her toothless mouth hung open wide, as dark inside as a railway tunnel. A pair of red-rimmed glasses rested slightly askew on her nose. Behind them, it seemed, her eyes were shut.

At the sound of her voice some of the other old people began to stir. A man's tremulous voice called out insistently, "I'm hungry." Someone started to cough and spit, another to moan, as though suddenly in pain, and a woman protested tiredly, "Mrs Grange has wet herself again. *When* are you going to do something about her?"

Danny stared at the floor below the person closest to the old lady who had spoken last, and saw, under her chair, a dark stain on the carpet.

The woman who had complained that she had lost her cushion repeated her plea for help, now sounding cross. Danny moved towards her and must have stepped into her line of vision because she said fiercely, "Who are you? You're just a boy! Are they sending children, now, to look after us?" Danny snatched up the cushion and thrust it towards the woman, who whined, "That's no good to me, unless you pick me up and pull me back. Can't you see that if it wasn't for the strap, I'd have fallen on my face? You can't leave me like this; I can hardly breathe," and her voice died away, as though she were indeed expiring. Danny saw she was held in place by a thick white belt tied tight around her waist and the back of her chair. She was so thin, the belt buckle on her stomach was only a couple of inches from the fabric of the chair against her spine. Danny placed his hand on the top of her chest, that felt like a bird cage under his palms, and tried to push her upright, but he was not tall enough, and must have done something painful, because she gave a shriek and shouted, "What are you doing, child? What are you doing? Let go, for God's sake; you're *hurting* me." Some of the other old people started to shout abuse at him then, and he felt his eyes flood and his throat constrict, and knew he was going to cry.

A man's voice, coming from just behind Danny, said, "What's the matter Betty? You *are* making a fuss. The young gentleman is only trying to help."

The scrawny woman said, "Where have you been Kelvin? Where's our breakfast? You're ever so late."

"No I'm not," the man said. "I'm just on time."

"You're a bloody liar," the woman suggested peevishly. "What do you mean by sending bits of kids to look after us?"

"He's not on the staff, Betty, he's a guest," the man explained, easily hauling the woman upright and adjusting her limbs so she sat in a comfortable, balanced position.

"Then why is he here? This is no place for kids."

"I don't know." The man, who was dressed in a white jacket, like the Chinese who worked in Danny's local chip shop wore, gave him a curious, slightly angry look that was only partly disguised by the shadow of a smile he managed to force across his face. He had a bony, narrow head, with dark hair brushed back tight against his scalp, and a large nose under which sprouted a pencil moustache. His smile reminded Danny of the girl who had brought him tea half an hour earlier, who had also seemed to find it hard to form her features into a good-humoured expression for more than a second. "I expect he's got lost," the man continued. "Is that right, young man?"

Danny, choking back tears, wiped his fingers under his nose and nodded.

"I expect you were looking for the dining room?"

Danny didn't stop nodding.

"This is the 'Twilight Lounge'. The room you want is on the floor below. You should have kept on walking, down another flight of stairs."

The man clasped Danny's shoulder unnecessarily hard and steered him out of the door. Two or three of the old people shouted, "Nurse, nurse!" in protest at being left alone again. "Back in a tick," the man yelled, with an edge of irritation. His voice was so loud, Danny looked up at him, startled. Noticing this the man explained, in a more moderate tone, "They're deaf, sonny; most of them are deaf," and led Danny to the top of the stairs and pointed the way to the dining room.

Danny, no longer crying, and bursting with curiosity now, said, "Those old people back there; they thought you were a nurse, didn't they?"

"That's what I am."

"But this is a hotel, not a hospital!"

"It's a bit of both," the man said, after a short pause.

"Oh," Danny said, totally confused.

Back in the lounge, the old people were cackling and calling for Kelvin, who gave Danny a horrible wink, that briefly distorted the whole of one side of his face, then retreated to join them. A portly woman pushed a heated trolley reeking of bacon out of the lift and across the corridor into the "Twilight Lounge". She was greeted with a tiny, ironic ovation from the residents.

Danny ran down to the dining room, which was almost empty. He had left his room at exactly 8.30, and the incident in the lounge had only lasted two or three minutes. He sat alone at a table close to a rain-flecked window that looked out to sea. He could see the box on the jetty, and, through a gap between two of the buildings below, a slice of the promenade and the beach beyond. The box looked bigger and somehow heavier from the lower level. The wind blew up under the tarpaulin draped across it, causing the hanging sides of the covering to flap mournfully. It looked as though someone inside the box was reaching about through holes in the sides with their hands, trying to find some way out.

When, fifteen minutes later, Gran and Grandad came to join him, Danny had almost finished breakfast. He wondered if he should have waited and eaten with them, but Gran said nothing about that. Perhaps she hadn't noticed; she had a preoccupied, anxious look on her face that Danny was getting used to seeing there. She kept half an eye on Grandad all the time, was aware of every move he made, and turned to give him her full attention whenever he spoke. Something about the way she treated her husband made Danny feel quite grown up, as though he and Grandad had changed places.

The room filled up with old people. Danny looked out for anyone his age, but there was only one girl, a couple of years older and four inches taller than him, who pulled a tight face when he smiled at her, and didn't look up from her plate again. When Grandad had finished eating, he asked Gran what day it was. She told him Sunday, but a little later he asked the same question and, when she tried to get him to remember the answer she had given him earlier, he said he hadn't asked her before, and if she didn't know what day it was, why didn't she just admit it? Gran put her hand on his arm and, very quietly, said she *had* told him, and not long ago. Grandad insisted she hadn't, in a high, strange voice, and Danny thought he looked worried, even frightened. A waitress came to clear the table and Grandad said to her, "My wife has forgotten what day it is; perhaps you can enlighten her?"

The girl arched her eyebrows, looked from Grandad to Gran and back, and tried to smile.

Why is it nobody at this place can smile for more than a second? Danny thought, and for the first time began to wonder if he was going to enjoy the holiday.

The girl looked unsure of how to respond to Grandad's request for such basic information, hoping, but doubting, it was a joke. To avoid her embarrassment, Danny looked out of the window, towards the box on the jetty. A big bird was standing on top of it. As Danny watched the bird started strutting backwards and forwards, half-opening and closing its long, slender wings. It was just some kind of gull, Danny supposed; it was that sort of shape; but he had no idea they could grow so big, and he had never seen one that dark before. Perhaps it had been caught in an oil slick? Suddenly, it launched itself off the edge of the box and soared into the sky.

Danny turned back to the table when the waitress said, "It's Sunday, of course; all day."

Grandad said, "Thank you very much," and gave Gran a silly, mocking shake of his head.

Anger, embarrassment, and some other indefinable pain registered on Gran's face. She got to her feet. As she did so, Grandad automatically rose from his chair, only more slowly, with less agility.

Danny jumped up to help him. "What are we going to do today?" he said. "It's raining. Do we have to stay in?"

"*We* will," Gran said, "for now. But you can go for a walk, to explore, if you want to."

"Definitely," Danny said. "It's *boring* here."

Gran gave him the first real smile he had received all day. "Don't catch cold though, and ruin your holiday."

"No problem; I'll be alright."

As Danny moved around the table to follow his grandparents, something moved out of the grey clouds beyond the window beside him, and descended towards him. The oversized gull he had seen landed on the balcony a yard from the window. It folded its wings with an air of deliberation and craned its neck. It turned sideways on awkward, stumbling feet; cocked its head at an angle, and stared at Danny down one side of its beak. The beak was grimy yellow, like a heavy smoker's teeth. The bird stretched forward and screamed, as though announcing its presence, then stood motionless, watching him. It was at least four times as big as any gull Danny had seen before, and he thought he had been right about the oil slick, because its inky plumage had a glossy sheen, like the wet tarpaulin on the box it had been standing on when he had first noticed it.

"*Danny!*"

Gran's voice. She and Grandad were waiting for him at the door. Everyone in the room turned towards him. They're all so *old*, he thought.

He knew Todley Bay was popular with elderly people, and owed its reputation to what it had to offer that age group; his mother had told him all that weeks ago, and explained that the holiday was intended as a break for Gran and Grandad, and that he had to be on his best behaviour all the time, and not give them any worries, so he knew the resort would be *their* sort of place, with probably not much going for kids; but he had not expected to see so *many* old people. Most of them looked really ancient. There was hardly anyone in the room under, what? he wildly guessed – seventy – eighty?

Except for the waitresses, and the girl he had noticed, he was the only young person present. He looked for the girl again, and saw she was watching him, like the others. She gave him a withering look that actually made him shudder. There was something about her, he decided, that set her among the old people; she looked used up, done in, worn out. Then he realized she was probably very ill, and felt sorry for her at once.

He hurried to the door, but looked back before stepping out. The gull hadn't moved. It was still there, glaring in through the window.

Danny was keen to get spending. He'd been saving up his pocket money for weeks and couldn't wait to drop some of it into slot-machines, or buy sticks of his favourite pineapple rock and things to play with on the beach. But the shops were disappointing. They were dingy and dark, with a lot of old stock that no one would ever buy, and the proprietors watched him all the time, as though they thought he were a thief. In one store down near the beach, the rock and other sweets were covered in grey dust, and looked shrivelled-up inside their wrappers. Danny bought a stick, because he had to buy *something*, but it tasted worse than the pencils he was in the habit of chewing at school, so he threw it in a bin. He wandered into the town, that sprawled almost perpendicularly up the hill behind the bay, in search of anything interesting, but soon got bored with endless rows of cream-painted houses advertising Bed & Breakfast or offering themselves as Residential Homes for the Aged. He passed a church that was open, with the bell ringing, but nobody went in or out. A gaunt and gloomy vicar with a lead-grey face was standing at the door, stiff as a waxwork, waiting to shake someone's hand.

It got tiring, climbing up the steep streets, so Danny turned back. His feet wanted to run down the sharp incline towards the beach, so he let them. The soles of his trainers slapped like clapping hands on the wet, empty streets, and he began to feel exhilarated, the way you should feel on holiday. The tide was on its way out and he ran without stopping right down the beach to the water's edge. It was cold down there, and a wind driving off the sea carried a miserable, almost invisible, mist with it, but Danny tried not to let that bother him. He threw some pebbles at a jellyfish, played tag with the waves, then trotted along until he was suddenly brought up short by the jetty, half of which still stretched out into the sea. It was about ten feet high, but there were steps up the side, which he climbed without thinking. As he reached the top, and looked across the harbour beyond, something called out to his right, towards the town. It sounded like the voice of a demented woman screeching his name. He turned and saw, five yards away, the box, and, hovering above it, with its feet stretching down, about to land, the enormous gull. It called again, almost dancing on the tarpaulin with the tips of its claws as it carved at the air with it wings to keep itself just in flight, then settled and became motionless and silent, like a stuffed bird in a museum. It was staring straight at Danny. There was something threatening about the creature's posture; it looked tense, as though it was ready to burst into furious action any second. Cautiously, Danny took a few paces towards it. It side-stepped once, adjusting its position slightly in a gust of buffeting wind, but showed no fear of him, or any sign that it was about to fly away. Its position on the box put it slightly higher than Danny's head, so its beak was just above his eyes. The beak resembled a scaled-down sword from a fantasy film. It was at least eight inches long, and the upper section curved sharply down in a cruel, hard, hooked point. Danny thought the bird would have no trouble opening up his skull with a weapon like that on its head. When he was a few feet away, and still beyond the gull's reach, he stopped; worried about his eyes, that suddenly seemed very vulnerable. He saw that the bird had a cold and crazy look in *its* eyes, that reminded him of snakes and alligators. Danny blew air out through his pursed lips, and shook his head. He realized he was afraid, and not just of the gull. There was more to it than that. The air around him felt charged and dangerous. Beyond the jetty, the town itself seemed to be watching him, poised and ready to tumble forward on top of him in a huge avalanche if he did the wrong thing. Something, he sensed, was in the balance.

For the first time he took a close look at the box. It was made of wood, bound with strips of greenish metal that could have been brass, and its unpainted surface was mottled with patches of dank, dark-emerald growth; probably some kind of marine weed. It stood in a puddle of its own making. The wood was waterlogged, which partly explained why the man he had seen pushing it had found the task such heavy going. The lid, if it had a lid, was under the flapping tarpaulin cover, but something about the box gave Danny the impression it was locked up very tight. It looked impenetrable! Briefly he wondered what, if anything, was inside it, then hastily closed his mind to the ugly images that were trying to crawl up out of his imagination.

All at once, Danny wanted to get back into the town. The jetty was narrow, but the box took up less than half its width. He could slip past it easily, but in doing so, he would put himself well within the reach of the gull. If it attacked him, he might fall off the jetty. It was a long way down to the beach, and there were flint rocks sticking out of the sand below. He took another look at the creature's beak. The gull glared back and nodded curtly once, as if to confirm his apprehensions.

"Look," Danny said, without having any idea why, "I don't want anything to do with this. I'm just here on holiday." Then he added, "I'm sorry," in a tone more of confusion than apology, and turned and fled back down the steps.

He didn't stop running when he felt the sand of the beach under his feet, but continued right up to the hotel. When he had almost reached it, just as he was trotting up the drive, the sun slid out from behind the clouds above him, and its light blazed down on all the town like a laser beam.

The rest of the day was showery, so the three of them didn't stray far from the TV in the hotel lounge. When he went to bed, Danny thought he could hear the box being pushed along the jetty again, but he was so tired, even though he had done nothing much all day, he fell asleep almost at once.

Next morning, when the girl came into his room, threw back the curtains to reveal a blue, cloudless sky, and came towards him with a cup of tea, he jumped up in bed at once, so she wouldn't have any excuse to touch him. Even so, she put one hand on his head and poked about in his hair while he sipped his drink, as though she was gently feeling for lumps. It seemed to Danny that her finger-tips were like cold, hard marbles rolling about on his scalp. He assumed it was a gesture of affection: he couldn't think what else it could be, and resisted the urge to duck away, but, when she sat down next to him, he jumped out of bed, ran to the sink and started washing.

In the morning, he spent an hour in a drab little sea-front café with his grandparents drinking banana milkshakes. After lunch, the three of them went down to the beach. Grandad, in a boyish mood, led the way. He looked as though he was wearing someone else's clothes, because he had lost so much weight in the last year, but Danny recognized the fawn trousers the old man had worn on the last three of their previous holidays together. Gran, Danny noticed, seemed more anxious than ever about Grandad when he was at all boisterous, as though she was scared his behaviour might get out of hand. As soon as Grandad had put his cap on backwards, and his face had taken on the now all-too-familiar clown's witless smile that had come to haunt it recently, Gran's features had responded by setting into a rigid, pained expression. She looked as though she had a bad headache. Grandad had wandered away from her twice, and the second time it had taken her half an hour to locate him. He had been with two men who were leading him away, or seemed to be. They had not spoken to her when she had reclaimed her husband, and she hadn't liked the look of them; they looked like muggers, she said.

Danny, feeling sympathy for both his grandparents, took care to be on his best behaviour when he was with them, but he wished they'd loosen up. He was now definitely beginning to wonder what kind of holiday it was going to be!

Gran decided it was too windy to sit on the beach, so she steered Grandad into a shelter on the promenade from where they could watch Danny doing the things children do on such occasions. He made a cake-like sandcastle without much enthusiasm, because he was beginning to wonder if he was too old for such activities, then stripped down to his trunks and sped towards the sea, now quite a long way out. In places, the surface of the sand had been formed into hard ridges by the action of the out-going tide. They ran along the whole length of the beach. They hurt the soles of his bare feet if he ran, and forced him to slow down and walk carefully. To Danny, it looked as though hundreds of endless fat worms lay paralysed just below the surface.

"Old Man Sand's got wrinkles," he said to himself, and laughed at the thought, though there was something not-very-nice about the idea that he found alarming and tried to shove to the back of his mind.

After paddling for a while in the shallow sea that was starting to warm in the sun, and taking a short, leisurely swim, he noticed he felt constrained and uneasy. Something was missing! Except for the sound of waves breaking on the shore, and the occasional scream of gulls (ordinary sized gulls, that was), the beach was strangely quiet. Conspicuous by its absence, he realized, was hubbub, pandemonium: he missed the sound of children yelling and shouting in excitement to each other, and telling their parents about what they were up to at the tops of their voices. The whole beach, the entire Bay even, though now more populated, was muffled; silent, and somehow static, like a painting. Danny looked about him at his fellow bathers.

There were not many. Within twenty yards of him, half a dozen elderly people, their trousers and skirts rolled or hitched up, wandered about ankle-deep at the water's edge. A beefy man with bulging eyes and purple skin, looking as though his whole body had been beaten into one huge bruise, occasionally hurled himself into deeper water further out and swam a few stiff, furious strokes. A woman in a lime-green costume, standing in the sea close to Danny, suddenly stooped, lowered herself to her knees, sat on her heels and bowed her head in a praying attitude. Her flesh oozed out around the edges of her costume like viscous liquid when she moved. Her skin was crinkled, like the brain in a bottle in the biology lab at Danny's school. She seemed uncomfortable in the position she had adopted and wriggled around so she could lay back on the sand. A wave breaking over her created the illusion that she was sliding feet first into the sea. Seconds later, when it withdrew, Danny imagined he saw something in the water, clasped around her ankles, tugging her away from the beach. This impression was so strong he walked closer to get a better look at her. The next wave was bigger, however, and submerged her completely. She did not, as Danny expected, start up when the water covered her face, but her body yawed slightly in the drag of the tide. Her eyes were shut and her mouth was open wide. She could have been shouting, laughing or even yawning.

Baffled and alarmed, Danny thought he ought to try to help the woman, though she gave no indication that she was at all distressed. He wondered if he should ask one of the other old people for their assessment of the situation, then saw that two of them were now also kneeling down. The red-skinned man who had been swimming had vanished, but Danny was sure he had not passed him on his way back to the beach. The last time he had seen him, the man had been in the act of lunging forward in a clumsy dive. Out in the area where the man had been standing, Danny noticed, for the first time, what looked like dark shadows under the waves. They appeared to be moving. He thought they must be weed-covered rocks, just visible at the bottom of the grey-green water.

One of the two people who were kneeling lay back in the water.

Danny suddenly looked down at his feet. He thought something had touched his right ankle. The sand next to it was disturbed, as though some fast-moving object had hurriedly dug down into it. He turned and ran a few yards out of the water, stood on the nearly dry sand, and looked back. The tide must be coming in fast, he thought, as there was no sign of the woman in the green costume. He could no longer see some of the other people who had been paddling, but a handful more had stumbled forward off the beach into the sea. He realized that none of them had nodded to him, or given him so much as a glance.

He shrugged, and jogged back to where Gran and Grandad were sitting in the shelter. Gran looked more relaxed, perhaps because Grandad was asleep. She held a finger to her lips to warn Danny to keep his voice down, and asked him if he was enjoying himself. Danny didn't want to upset her by telling the truth about how he did feel at that moment, which in any case would be difficult to explain, so he just nodded. He asked for money for an ice cream. As Gran fumbled in her purse, Danny noticed a man sitting on the bench on the other side of Grandad was watching him. He was heavily built, with a bald head and heavy jowls and was dressed in old, dark, working clothes. He could have been a fisherman. He had one arm along the bench behind Grandad's head. Two fingers of his hand rested on Grandad's shoulder. As Danny looked back at him, he lifted the fingers and curled them back towards his palm.

Danny got ice creams for himself and Gran, and hurried back. The bald man had gone, so Danny sat in the vacant place.

"Who was that man, Gran?" he asked.

"Which man?"

"The one who had his arm around Grandad."

"Danny; what do you mean? I'm sure he wasn't doing anything of the kind."

"He was," Danny insisted, and Gran, hearing the conviction in his voice, leaned forward and turned to look at him.

"This is a *funny* place, isn't it?" Danny continued.

"Todley Bay? Don't you like it?"

"Not as much as Brighton."

"I think it's very nice."

"There're no kids."

Gran smiled. "There must be some."

"I can't see any."

Gran pushed her glasses up her nose and looked around. "Not here, at the moment, perhaps," she conceded, "but on the beach . . ."

Danny swallowed the last of his ice cream and wiped his mouth. "No; it's all old people, everywhere."

"You're exaggerating. What about that girl who's staying at our hotel. She's about your age. Why don't you try to get to know her?"

"She's sick. I bet she never leaves the hotel."

"Um," Gran agreed thoughtfully, "she doesn't look well. I expect she's convalescing."

"I think she's dying," Danny said, matter of factly.

"Danny!" Gran said loudly, causing Grandad to twitch out of his doze, "I'm sure that's not true. What *has* got into you?"

"What's the trouble?" Grandad demanded. "What's got into who?"

"Danny, Harry, I don't think he's enjoying himself; he's in a very strange mood."

"Danny?" said Grandad, looking at his grandson as though he were a total stranger.

The grim look returned to Gran's face. She glanced at her watch. "Good heavens, look at the time, we'd better start back for the evening meal," she said, rising from her seat. Grandad rose up with her, like a Siamese twin joined to her at the shoulder.

Danny was surprised how easy it was to get lost in the hotel. The corridors and public rooms were decorated uniformly throughout, which made it hard to get your bearings, but even so, it didn't explain why he lost his way quite so often. He kept finding himself on the wrong floor! He'd carefully count the turns in the flights of stairs, so he was sure he knew exactly where he was, only to discover he was one, or even two, floors out. He noticed quite a few of the old people wandering around in even deeper bafflement than usual from time to time, which made him feel better, because it suggested he wasn't the only one experiencing this peculiar disorientation. A couple of times Danny bumped into Kelvin, the nurse with the walrus moustache, who told him how to get to where he wanted to go. He wasn't exactly unfriendly, but he must have been a very busy man, because he hardly stopped long enough to give the necessary directions before he blustered off again.

On the third night of the holiday, after leaving his grandparents in the TV lounge, Danny searched about down wrong corridors for ten minutes before he found his room. He complimented himself: he was getting better; the night before it had taken twice that long to get his bearings. As he was putting on his pyjamas, he heard the big box being shoved along the jetty. A shining mist, that had crawled up off the sea with the onset of darkness, had vanished when he looked out of the window. The air was clear, and he could see the man had nearly gotten the box to the end of the jetty. Danny was very interested to see what would happen next, because he knew there were two steps up from the jetty to the promenade and the street beyond, and he couldn't see how one man could possibly get the box up them without help. He got into bed and pretended to be asleep when Gran came, so she only stayed a moment. (He felt bad about it, but he had become fed up with her company that evening, because she was wearing herself out fussing over Grandad, who was definitely going ga-ga. They were both getting visibly worse daily: a lot of the time it was a *pain* being with them.)

When Gran had gone, Danny got up again and looked out the window. The box was about a foot from the steps, and the man had gone. He watched for a while, but nothing happened, so he slid back between the sheets, feeling let-down and disappointed, and fell asleep. Later, something woke him up. Noises, coming from the direction of the jetty. Different noises! He trotted to the window and looked out.

The man was back. He had set a lantern on the edge of the top step, and had placed a long metal tube or roller, four or five inches in diameter, at the base of the box, on the side closest to the steps. He was lifting the box with a jack. When it was the right height he kicked the roller under it on one side, let the box drop, then went around to the far side to repeat the process. When the roller was under the full length of the leading edge of the box, he went behind it and began to push. After a struggle, it moved a short distance towards the steps, and the side of the box above the roller rose a little higher. After giving three huge shoves the man got another, thicker roller from somewhere and laid it in front of the first one he had positioned. Then he went behind the box, and pushed and pushed. The front edge of the thing was soon higher than the bottom step and, in twenty minutes, after the man had put more rollers in place and done a lot more heaving, it was hovering a good distance above and beyond the top of the second. Then the man hit a problem. Because it was inclined at an angle, he was finding it increasingly difficult to move the box. He was having to push it up, as well as forward.

He seemed to give up then, and went and sat on the top step and stared down at the box. Danny watched the slumped figure for a while until he got bored. He thought the man might have gone to sleep. He was just about ready to return to bed when he saw movements on the beach below him. The tide was almost in, and a man was walking off the narrow strip of sand, diagonally out into the sea. The small, thin, stooping figure, dressed in dark clothes, was just visible against the inky water, moving slowly and regularly, as though setting out for a stroll on the ocean bed. When the sea was up to his waist he stopped, sank back into the water and disappeared from sight. Danny thought; no, he *knew*, the person, whoever he was, had stretched out on the sand, like the woman in the green costume he had seen the day before.

There were a few deckchairs left out on the beach, Danny noticed, spread about near where the now presumably drowning man had been when he'd first sighted him. To his amazement he could see shapes, that could only be people, sprawling in some of the chairs. Danny peered at his watch. It was almost midnight: it had been dark for almost two hours!

"They're moonbathing," he thought, and smiled uneasily in the dark, aware that the people didn't look at all funny.

As he looked back out the window, he saw something scuttle up out of the sea, across the beach, in among the parked deckchairs. It moved like a spider. It clung close to the sand, had no definite shape, and at first Danny thought it was dead seaweed, broken loose from its roots, washed ashore, dried in the sun, and blowing in the wind. Until he realized there *was* no wind to speak of; certainly not enough to set in motion anything more substantial than a scrap of paper. What he could see was moving of its own volition, and soon demonstrated that it had considerable strength! A section of its edge blended with the outline of one of the occupied chairs, which lifted and tumbled over on its side, tipping the person seated on it onto the sand. The figure lay motionless for as long as it took the mobile shape to dart around and attach itself to an outstretched arm, the part of the body closest to the sea. The body twitched once, then slid smoothly to the tide line and into the waves beyond, where it, and the thing pulling it, sank out of sight.

Then, for a time, nothing moved on the beach that Danny could see, though his eyes were alert for the slightest motion. It was a sound from the end of the jetty that grabbed his attention next; a loud grunt of pain or effort, or both. He turned just in time to see the bear-like man heave the box almost into the air and up onto the edge of the promenade. The action seemed to have spent the last of his energy: he flopped around picking up the rollers and tucking them under his arm like a man at the last extreme of exhaustion, then staggered off towards the harbour. Danny watched him shrink away into the darkness, then realised he was stiff with standing still, and crawled into bed. He fell asleep wondering what the man, who was awake most nights, did in the daytime.

It was very hot the next day. So much so, that Gran and Grandad sat on the beach for the first time. They couldn't walk far in the sand because of Gran's feet, so Danny put up deckchairs for them at the bottom of the steps that led to the promenade. He sat with them for a while, watching the beach fill with elderly holidaymakers then, for something to say because the old pair were not inclined to talk in the heat, he mentioned that he had seen people on the sands late at night.

"I expect they were workmen tidying up all the litter," Gran said.

"The tide does that," Danny said, "when it goes in and out. No, they were sitting in chairs, like we are, or walking into the sea."

"Danny, you were dreaming. They'd have caught their deaths of cold."

Danny wanted to say he thought they were dead, or looked it, but knew that Gran would say he was talking nonsense and get cross with him. Even so, he couldn't help saying, "I wish we *had* gone to Brighton. This place is *weird*."

"I think it's very pleasant," Gran said, "and restful. There's none of the noise and fuss you get at so many holiday places nowadays. And people are so nice and polite."

"You didn't like those men who walked off with Grandad," Danny observed.

"I was probably wrong about them. I expect they'd realized Grandad was lost, and were taking him to a policeman."

Danny didn't answer because he had just spotted, not far away along the beach, one of the deckchairs he had seen someone slumped in last night. He knew it was the same one, because it was in exactly the same position in relation to a stack of chairs next to it as it had been when he had seen it from his bedroom window. It was facing away from him but he could tell it was occupied because the canvas seat was bulging down and back. He was about to go and take a look at it and its occupant when something made him change his mind. There was a cloud of flies swarming above the chair, dozens of them, big black ones, he thought he could almost hear them buzzing. No one else had set up their deckchairs for a good distance all around that particular one, Danny noticed.

"Look at all those flies, Gran," he said.

"What?"

"Over there; look." He pointed. "Above that chair."

"I can't see *flies*, Danny, if they land on me. My eyes aren't good enough. I can only just see the chair."

For some reason this remark made Danny rather anxious. He felt suddenly isolated and vulnerable. Looking around he discovered he was, as far as he could see, the only child on the beach. He shut his eyes then, and pretended to sunbathe, but he couldn't settle; his mind was swirling with vague apprehensions. For the first time all week he found he was missing his parents. At first, he had been relieved to get away from them – they had been so grumpy and depressing recently – though they had continued to treat him as kindly as they had always done. Nevertheless life at home had been different since his father had received the letter telling him his job would no longer exist in ten weeks, and his parents had taken to endless grinding arguments about money.

Danny heard them late at night in the room below his, their voices rasping on like two blunt saws taking turns to cut through a particularly thick, hard log. They were worried about Gran and Grandad too, and Danny could understand why now. He realized that the whole family had problems. He had problems! Suddenly he wanted to talk to his parents very badly, but he knew he wouldn't see them until the end of the week.

After half an hour he went and got some drinks. Grandad insisted on coming with him, somewhat to Danny's relief. He tried not to listen to Grandad's talk, because he seemed to think Danny was someone he had worked with years ago in Canada. That was unnerving, but he felt glad he was not walking alone.

The way to the café took them past the huge, brass-bound box parked on the promenade. Even in bright sunlight it looked sinister, Danny thought, though other passers-by seemed unawed by it. The wood had dried out a lot, and was beginning to crack, and the mossy weed clinging to it had turned grey and ash-like. A heat-haze shimmered over the tarpaulin. There was no sign of the great gull but, when Danny looked up into the sky, he saw, very high up, a black dot that was growing larger as it descended fast towards the ground. Danny grabbed Grandad's hand to hurry him along. He had a vision of what the bird could do with its beak if it hit someone after descending at that speed from that height.

He made sure, when they returned to Gran with their drinks, they went a roundabout way along the beach, keeping well clear of the box. The route took them past the deckchair that had been shrouded with flies. It was empty now. Danny got the impression that a small group of youngish men in overalls, moving down the beach towards the sea, were carrying something they had lifted from the chair but, in the confusion of people, it was hard to be sure. He went quite near the chair and saw there were still a few flies on duty there, hovering over a wet, red-brown stain on the canvas seat.

It seemed to be a bad day for insects. Early in the afternoon, millions of tiny silver and brown flies with thin bodies and long legs appeared from nowhere on the beach. They hopped rather than flew, and got all over Danny's bare legs and arms. They were strangely dry and weightless, like the congregations of corpses that gather on window ledges in empty houses in the summer, and seemed almost without substance. They didn't bite or sting, they were just disgusting. Danny soon had enough of them. He asked Gran if he could go for a boat trip around the bay.

"You said I could, and if I don't go soon, the holiday will be over," he pleaded.

"There's still three more whole days," Gran said, but she agreed he could do as he had asked. They left their beach-bag and Danny's towels on their chairs because Gran said she was sure there were no thieves about, and the three of them made their way to the harbour.

One of the two boats that did trips was out beyond the headland, just visible in the distance, and the second was almost full and ready to go. It was a big, wide boat that Gran declared quite safe, so she gave Danny some money and told him to get on board. He found a seat at the front and waved at his grandparents with his handkerchief for a joke. Gran waved back, and Grandad copied her movements exactly, a sight that made Danny laugh aloud. A teenage boy in sun-bleached denim jumped onto the boat and began collecting money and handing out tickets, then a man stepped quickly down from the harbour, started the engine, and grasped hold of the wheel.

It was the bear-like man who Danny had seen moving the box. There was no mistaking his rolling movements, and he was wearing the same clothes as he had been the night before; Danny could tell by the shape of him. The only difference was that at night the man wore a cap and now had nothing on his bald head. Danny got a good look at his face and, not for the first time, he was sure the man had been sitting next to Grandad the day before, with his arm around the back of Grandad's chair and his fingers on the old man's shoulder.

Danny jumped up to get off the boat just as, with a grinding growl of the engine that echoed off the hill behind the town, it cut away from the harbour wall. The man glanced sharply at him and the teenager asked him to get back in his seat. Danny did so at once, and tried to make himself small and inconspicuous. The man, at the front of the boat, was facing away from Danny. He made an announcement about safety procedures as he steered the vessel out through the maze of moored pleasure-craft to the harbour mouth, then handed the wheel over to his young mate when they reached the open sea. He turned around, sat down, and lit a little cigar. As he blew out smoke, he raised his head and glanced quickly around at his passengers. When he saw Danny, he took another sharp drag at his cigar and seemed to shake his head slightly. The gesture had no clear meaning that Danny could interpret, but it frightened him because he felt he had been singled out, perhaps even recognized. He remembered that when he had been watching the man pushing the box along the jetty, he had got the impression that the fellow had looked back up at him on a number of occasions, though there was no chance he could really have seen a small boy standing some considerable distance away in the dark, half-hidden behind a curtain. Unless he had remarkable eyesight! He certainly had remarkable eyes, that stared through Danny as though they were focused on a point a million miles behind his head.

Danny thought of the huge black seagull then, that had been so high in the sky above the box when he had passed close to it with Grandad just a couple of hours earlier. The bird must have good eyesight too; it had dropped down at once when it had seen him approach, or so it had appeared to Danny. Why? Did it think he was going to do some harm to the box, that it seemed to be guarding? Danny couldn't believe that. He hadn't the means or strength to damage it, even if, for some crazy reason, he'd had the inclination to do so. He wasn't bothered about the box; he wanted nothing to do with it, as he had told the bird when he had come close to it on the jetty two days ago. At the time it he had felt foolish talking to a seagull, but not so now. He just wished he had said more: he was afraid he had not made himself understood.

When, after a quarter of an hour, the boat turned its prow into the Bay again for the return trip, Danny was glad the ride was half over. He'd been too confused and anxious to enjoy himself and imagined he was seasick, his stomach felt so queasy. He was very glad when the man, whose hard, unfriendly gaze had returned to him every few minutes, got up to take over the wheel again as they approached the harbour.

Gran was waiting for him on the promenade, holding onto a railing at the very edge of the harbour. Danny waved, but he knew she wouldn't see him. He doubted if she could even see the boat, but she knew what time he was due to return and was just *being there* for him. Grandad sat on a bench a few feet behind her, talking to a man seated next to him. His conversation was animated; he waved his arms and at one point stood up and made a gesture, incomprehensible to Danny, to illustrate some point he was making. Danny guessed he thought his companion was someone from years back in his past, when his life had been exciting, and that they were sharing some adventure together. As Grandad, in his enthusiasm, took a few steps away from the bench, another man, who Danny had not noticed but who must have been standing nearby, screwed up some paper he had been eating out of and tossed it into a bin. Then he sidled closer to Grandad as though he were on wheels, in a sliding, gliding movement that arrested Danny's attention completely and totally altered his understanding of the scene he was witnessing. The man on the bench got up, stood next to Grandad, and pointed inland to somewhere in the town. When Grandad turned to look, the man took his arm, and began, with a certain amount of force, Danny thought, to lead him away. The second man, moving as though he were sliding on ice, fell in behind them. Gran, still peering myopically out to sea, was obviously unaware of what was going on behind her.

The boat was coming in to dock now, and Danny could see her bland, smiling face staring out at the blur of the world in front of her. He half stood up and shouted at her, and made jerking movements with his hand intended to make her look behind. As he rose to his feet, some of the other passengers thought he was getting ready to disembark and also started to get up off their seats. Perceiving this, the man who was steering the boat turned and yelled something to his mate, who jumped onto a chair and called to everyone to be seated. In the confusion of people bobbing up and down Danny lost sight of Gran, but he was careful to keep an eye on Grandad, who was being led slowly uphill into the town. Not a purposeful walker at the best of times, Grandad liked to stop and start when the urge took him, and the two men were plainly having trouble getting him to go where they wanted him to and were making slow progress.

The boat bumped against the harbour wall and the teenager skipped ashore to fasten the ropes. The bear-like man took his place next to the couple of steps up the side of the vessel and helped his frail, nervous passengers onto dry land by steering them across the short gangplank, whether they wanted him to or not. Danny tried to squeeze forward in the queue, getting a few sharp comments from some old ladies as he did so. When his turn to disembark came he tried to avoid the hands of the man by almost running off the boat, but without success. He felt fingers like tentacles curl around his upper arm to stop him in mid-stride. The man lifted him effortlessly and half-turned him so they were face to face. Danny could smell cigar smoke on his breath, and other more strange odours that he had never come across before. There was a scrap of tobacco on the man's lip that must have irritated him, as he flicked it with his tongue, and spat it out over Danny's shoulder with a toss of his head. The action reminded Danny of squirrels he had seen in the park at home, standing on their hind legs and spitting out indigestible fragments of nuts they were eating. Not that there was anything cute or squirrel-like about the man's appearance: his heavily featured face with its sharp, down curving nose, and receding, almost horizontal, forehead was set hard in an ambiguous mask of contempt and vague curiosity, as though Danny were a not-very-fine example of something that, had it been of better or different quality, would perhaps have interested him. Either his head was unusually small, or it seemed so in proportion to the bulk of his vast, barrel-like body. His little gimlet eyes bore in on Danny's like nails: in the irises of each of them Danny could see tiny reflections of his own frightened face.

The man loosened his grip on Danny's arms and ran his hands down them to the wrists, pressing with his finger tips, feeling for the bones beneath the flesh. He held the joints of Danny's wrists between his thumbs and fingers and lifted them to the height of his shoulders, so the boy's hands hung in front of him like a half-animated puppet's. Danny squirmed and looked back over his shoulder. Gran was just behind him on the promenade. He could tell from the confusion and apprehension on her face that she was close enough to see what was happening to him. He tried to get away from the man's grasp, and yelled out, "Grandad's gone. They've taken him away again. Get after him. He's gone up into the town."

The man moved then, and held Danny out so that he was hanging by his wrists over the side of the boat next to the little gangplank. The vessel was about 12 inches from the harbour wall and rocking slightly, up and down and from side to side, in the wake of other boats passing beyond. Danny thought if the man let go and he fell he might be crushed between the wall and the side of the boat. The water below his feet, the colour of boiled cabbage, and marbled with rainbow tinted whorls of diesel fuel, looked deep, thick and viscous, like glue. Darker shapes moved below its surface. It somehow looked hungry too: Danny imagined his broken body being sucked down into it, dragged under the keel, and pulled out to sea by swirling undercurrents. He was only suspended thus for a few seconds before the man stretched out over the side of the boat and lowered him slowly onto the edge of the harbour and released him, but they were long seconds and terrible while they lasted. Some of the elderly people waiting their turn to go ashore thought the man had played an amusing joke on Danny, and squawked with laughter as he ran shouting to his grandmother.

By this time she had discovered her husband's absence, and, as soon as Danny's toes touched the ground, went stumbling away on her arthritic feet to look for him.

"Up the hill," Danny screamed, "they've taken him up the hill."

Gran turned to him with a hopeless look, already out of breath and concerned about her hammering heart.

"Don't worry," Danny said as he overtook her. "Wait here. I'll get him back."

The streets were full of old people drifting back and forth from the beach. They reacted too slowly to get out of Danny's way so he had to run a zig-zag course around them. He lost sight of Grandad from time to time but knew he must soon catch up with him because the trio had come to a stop half-way up the hill. They seemed to be arguing. They were standing just inside an alleyway between two decrepit looking red-brick Victorian hotels. The man who had been seated on the bench next to Grandad had hold of his sleeve; he wasn't actually tugging at it, but he was making it impossible for the old man to retreat. The other would-be abductor, with smooth, oily movements, was gliding around the pair of them, talking all the while, and making calming gestures with his outstretched hands. Danny could hear Grandad's voice. He was bellowing at the two men that he'd had enough of their nonsense. He was going to arrest them. Didn't they know he was a member of the Mounted Police? He was back in the past in Canada again. His face looked more worried than he sounded, but brightened when he saw Danny, who assumed he had been recognised for once.

The two men, following the old man's gaze, turned to see Danny running towards them. The one with peculiar movements detached himself from the tableau and slid towards Danny like a skater. He was dressed in a tight black jacket and shiny trousers, like a waiter's. Danny couldn't be sure, but it seemed that the man's feet, encased in narrow patent-leather shoes, hardly moved and never quite touched the floor; as though he were suspended a fraction of an inch above the pavement. Perhaps because he was, nevertheless, coming at Danny fast, his form seemed slightly blurred, his features indistinct. When they were almost touching, they both side-stepped to avoid each other in the same direction and collided.

Danny expected to get hurt. He heard himself shout to Grandad to get away as he made contact, then automatically shut his eyes to protect them. He felt a sensation as though he had run into a large, soft mattress that gave to the slightest pressure. There was no indication that what he had hit was anything like a human body that contained flesh and bones, and whatever it was gave way on contact and spread out alarmingly, as though it had come apart. Danny thought he had run right through it and somehow come out the other side. He opened his eyes and saw what looked like a two dimensional drawing of a bloated human figure expanding above and in front of him. It was floating away, and waving its flattened arms and legs slowly, like someone drowning in a dream, and clawing desperately at the air with its hands. Almost at once its fingertips appeared to grasp onto something invisible; a hard thin edge of reality, perhaps; and dug in and held on. Then, with an obviously painful effort, it *pulled itself back together*, it contracted, shrunk into itself, and reformed.

All this happened very quickly and, almost before Danny had time to think, the man was hovering in front of him again, with a mildly expectant look on his bland, undistinguished face, exactly like a waiter lingering at a table in expectation of an order. It was as though he were silently challenging Danny to believe that the astonishing metamorphosis he had just observed had indeed happened, and was trying to suggest, by his unconcerned expression and the shear ordinariness of his appearance, that it could not have done.

But Danny *knew*. He knew what he had seen. He knew a great deal all of a sudden and what he didn't know he guessed.

He flung himself at Grandad, latched onto his arm, and pulled the old man sideways down the hill with all his strength. They tottered along like the contestants in a three-legged race, barging into a number of ancient holidaymakers who they were not able to brush aside, and stumbling and almost falling on the steep incline. Gran was waiting for them on the promenade. She looked as though she was going to cry when she saw Grandad's face. It was blank and empty, like a paper mask before the features have been painted on it.

Gran said, "Where were they taking him, Danny? What did they want him for?"

Danny couldn't bring himself to say what he thought he knew. He pretended to be more out of breath than he was and stammered something about muggers. He could see Gran was terribly distraught, but knew this was because of the state her husband was in and because he had nearly been stolen from her. Thankfully, she could not have seen what occurred when he, Danny, collided with the man in the waiter's outfit, so he wouldn't be called upon to give an explanation of *that*. On the other hand, he realized, if she *had* seen, she would at least be more aware of what they were up against.

He looked back up the hill to see if the men had followed him, but there was no sign of them. Suddenly his stomach lurched, and he felt a surge of dizzying nausea, a return of the sea-sickness that had started half an hour earlier when he had been on the boat, now exacerbated by his recent experiences.

"Gran," he said, "I'm ill. Let's get away from here. This is a terrible place."

Misunderstanding him, thinking he merely wanted to return to the hotel, Gran nodded emphatically. She put her arm around her husband's shoulder and steered him away. The old man walked like an automaton, staring down at the pavement just in front of his dragging feet and saying nothing. Danny dawdled behind all the way to the hotel, to keep the couple in his sight.

Danny looked even worse than he felt when the three of them got together in the dining room for their evening meal. Gran led Grandad in by the elbow. His walk had developed an aimless, twisting tendency that had to be corrected every few steps, and his eyes looked empty and uncomprehending, like a blind man's, or someone concussed. The old man would eat nothing and Danny couldn't. Gran stuffed some meat into her mouth and made a show of chewing it to encourage him to do the same, but the smell and appearance of what was on his plate convulsed his stomach and he had to get up and away. Gran's face took on an even more concerned expression when he explained how sick he was. He hated to put this extra burden on her, but he had no alternative. She dug in her bag for some pills, instructed him on the dosage, and told him to get to bed. Danny said "good night" to Grandad, who made no response at all.

"He's lost his tongue," Gran said, trying to make a half-angry, desperate joke of it, but sounding instead, strangely, much younger than her years, and on the edge of tears again.

Danny dragged himself up the wide blue-carpeted stairs feeling dizzy and disorientated. The spaces around him seemed much wider than he knew they were, as though the hotel had expanded in all directions; a process that appeared to be obscurely continuing out at the edge of his vision. He counted flights from floor to floor grimly, passing hand over hand on the stair rail like a man hauling himself along a rope to safety. It occurred to him to take the lift, but he knew his stomach wouldn't stand for that. On the second floor corridor, he heard a confusion of hushed sounds behind him, and somebody called out sharply for him to step aside. Two men in white jackets were approaching him, pushing a grey painted metal stretcher bearer. On it was a slender human form half wrapped in a loose-knit white blanket. The lower part of the face of this person was encased in a plastic mask attached by a tube to a cylinder slung below the stretcher. A pink tube curled up from the blanket to what looked like a brown bladder on a stick one of the men was holding above his head. Danny realized the figure on the stretcher was the young girl he had seen in the dining room a few times. She was lying on her side with her eyes wide open. The transparent mask had a black rim that underlined and isolated her eyes. They looked like two shiny purple holes drilled into her almost bald head. Her little white ears stuck out like toadstools from the sides of her scalp that appeared as though it was made of scrubbed white wood. Danny realized that normally she must wear some kind of wig.

She stared at him hard as she passed, giving him an even worse version of the withering look he was used to seeing on her face, and rose up and turned as she passed to keep him in view. Danny found he was pressing his back against the wall to get away from her. The power of her gaze had a negative force strong enough to repel him physically. It felt like a protracted bomb blast. She struggled to keep her eyes on him, to keep up the pressure, and tried to sit up. As she did so, the blanket slid down from her shoulders to her waist and Danny saw what looked like black shadows, just beneath the skin, sliding down over the ribs of her flat white chest to take shelter under the blanket over her belly. It was as though they were afraid of the light. The shapes moved hastily, but with purposeful, controlled caution, like fish seeking the safety of deeper, darker waters. The girl kept her purple-black eyes on Danny until one of the men pressed her back down and pulled the blanket up to her chin. They stopped the stretcher at the service lift and Danny, released from the repulsive attraction of the girl, turned his back on them and staggered away.

He found his room at last, wriggled clumsily out of his clothes, pulled the curtains across the open window to hold back the early evening sunlight, clambered into bed and fell, sweating and squirming, into feverish sleep.

Suddenly, Danny was staring into the dark. His eyes had clicked open with a snap that was almost audible. His whole body was rigid with tension. His senses were as alert as a hunter's and, when at last he moved, he moved stealthily. He peeled the quilt smoothly back off the bed and stood up. As he did so, the sound that had woken him was repeated somewhere out beyond his window. It was a sliding sound similar to the noises he had heard earlier in the week, but not quite the same. It was a lighter, easier sound. The box was moving faster.

Danny crept to the window and edged the curtain to one side just far enough to give him a view of the section of the street visible between two hotels at the lower level. The sound seemed to be coming from down there. Seconds later he heard it again, as a long corner of shadow stretched out to his left along the street below. It was followed by the blunt black end of the box, which slid swiftly into full view and came to rest at a point half way between the hotels. But only for a moment: the bear-like man behind it hardly paused for rest before pushing it on out of sight. The box was only briefly visible, but Danny noticed that the tarpaulin had been removed from the top, and that an upper section seemed to be slightly askew, as though the lid had been lifted and not properly replaced.

Something has been taken out, or has come out, Danny thought: either that or the box has been opened in preparation for something that was going to be put into it. Or was going to get into it . . . For a second Danny had a dim vision of something huge and dark clambering out to make way for something frail and white that was desperate to clamber in. He shut his eyes and shook his head to shatter the fantasy, and went and sat on his bed.

He almost went back to the window to take a look at what, if anything, was going on on the beach, but decided against it. He was still feeling ill. He was weak and cold, though his skin was damp with sweat. The pills Gran had given him had helped, but their effect had worn off. But he knew she had more in her bag.

He went into the corridor, and tapped on the door of his grandparents' room. No answer. He tapped again, louder, then tried the handle. The door wouldn't move when he pushed it. It must be earlier than he thought, he decided, if it is locked. Gran and Grandad always went to bed at ten. They must be somewhere downstairs, probably in the TV lounge.

He set off at a trot along the corridor and ran down the stairs. It wasn't so easy to get lost going *down* into the hotel because you just kept on going until you reached the bottom, then you stopped. Or so he had assumed: it had worked before. Nevertheless, he misjudged where he was, and found he had wandered into the Twilight Lounge. It was pitch dark in there, but he knew where he was, because of the sharp, faint smell of urine. He stood for a moment just inside the door and heard a rustling noise, like paper being slowly crumpled, then someone sighed, and he thought he heard liquid dripping. A wheelchair creaked. They're waking up! Danny thought, and hurtled off without bothering to shut the door behind him.

When he found the TV lounge it was unoccupied. The big set in the corner was still on, filling the room with jumpy silver light and swirls of romantic music from the ancient black and white costume drama that was showing. Danny noticed the clock on the video player below the TV said 01:47. *In the morning*, that was. He'd never been awake at that time before, that he could remember. It wasn't surprising there was nobody about, but why weren't his grandparents in their room? In the past, Danny had often had a feeling that grownups did things after their children had gone to bed that they never talked about. It had only ever been a vague suspicion before, but now the idea played on his mind. Where were the adults, what *were* they up to? He would have to find out.

Whenever he had gone in and out of the hotel before there had always been someone at the reception desk, but now even that post was deserted. It seemed that the only people other than himself in the building were the ancient residents in the Twilight Lounge and, young as he was, Danny knew he couldn't expect help or advice from them. They had their own problems. His only hope of finding his Gran and her medication was to contact a member of staff, and ask them to take him to her. Then he remembered he had seen a big sign that said:

STAFF QUARTERS
Staff Only Beyond This Point
PLEASE

on a door at the rear of the hotel. Surely he would find assistance there! He ran down the silent corridor towards the kitchens, found the door, and saw with relief that it was half open. Beyond it, grey carpeted stairs led down to the basement. He could hear music thumping somewhere below, so someone must be awake down there. He glanced again at the off-putting sign on the door, then ventured cautiously onto the stairs. He felt that what he was doing was probably wrong, but guessed that if people were cross with him for venturing where he should not go, they wouldn't do him any harm, and would take him to his grandparents just to get rid of him.

Everything in the staff quarters was smaller and shabbier than on the floors above. The corridors were narrow, illuminated by dim, unshaded yellow bulbs, and the drab carpets were worn and hard. He passed lots of numbered doors, some of them split and cracked, as though the locks had been forced, or had been punched or kicked. He kept walking, without trying to rouse anyone who might be beyond them, because he could tell from the increasing volume of the music that he was getting closer to its source. In fact, when he turned the first corner, he walked right into it. Two doors, one marked STAFF and the other RECREATION, stood open wide and he found he had gatecrashed a party in full swing.

There were about two dozen people in the long, low-ceilinged room and most of them were sitting at a couple of trestle tables covered by white paper tablecloths. The air was murky with what at first he thought was smoke, then realized was a thin damp mist, like fog. A couple were dancing, away to one side, and a girl in a black, tight, silky outfit twirled somewhat awkwardly to the music, alone in the centre of the available space. She stopped when she saw Danny and stared at him as though he were an apparition. He recognized her as the girl who had brought him tea in bed each morning, and at once began to feel uneasy. The girl came and crouched down in front of him, on tip-toes, with her knees bent. She stayed like that for a while, without speaking or moving, weighing him up with her eyes. The calculating quality of her gaze chilled Danny's blood. He wanted to speak, but his lips had gone stiff and his tongue felt like leather. He was aware that other people in the room beyond had become aware of his presence and were also watching him. Someone with an old man's voice gave a creaky laugh that was echoed by a woman's shrill, mirthless cackle. A man, shouting over the music, said something he didn't catch, then most of them laughed. Danny was just thinking of running off when the girl reached out and took his left elbow in her hand. Then she said sharply:

"*What* are *you* doing *here*?"

As she waited for his answer, her thin fingers massaged the bones of his elbow and her thumb pressed painfully into his inner arm. He mumbled something about his grandparents that was inaudible to the girl, who shook her head to indicate she could not hear him. Then, desperately, he shouted, "I've lost my Gran. I want someone to help me find her." As he did so, the rock music tape that had been playing ended abruptly, and he found himself shouting into total silence. His voice sounded like a scream. It frightened him. The girl moved her head back slightly under the impact of it. She rose up again, still holding Danny's arm, and pulled him further into the room towards the tables. A man on a bench moved to one side to make way for him. The girl, by manipulating his arm, forced him to sit in the vacant space. The man next to him gave him a toothy smile. It was Kelvin, the moustachioed nurse who had rescued him from the people in the Twilight Lounge at the start of the holiday. He still looked reasonably friendly.

Danny recognized a few of the faces of the people seated around him. To his horror, he saw, opposite him across the table, the man in a waiter's uniform; the one with the strange, sliding locomotion, who had tried to lure his Grandfather away, and who Danny had run literally right into. The man looked very solid now however, and seemed amused to find Danny in his present predicament. Danny licked his dry lips and tried to avoid looking anyone in the eye by looking down at the paper cloth on the table in front of him. It was bare except for dishes of nuts and crisps, a couple of big cut-glass decanters almost full of what looked like tomato juice, and a quantity of glasses containing drinks of this liquid. The people around him lifted these glasses to their mouths from time to time to take a sip, then their eyes would roll and they pursed and smacked their lips with almost ecstatic satisfaction. It was obvious they relished their refreshments. Danny liked tomato juice himself, but he couldn't understand why anyone should make such a fuss about it – it was nothing special. Last Christmas, his father had drunk lots of it with vodka and there had been a row between his parents when his Dad had fallen from his chair when they had guests round, but there was no sign of any vodka on the tables now. Yet the people at the party, if that was what it was, seemed to think tomato juice was the finest drink in the world!

The man opposite him, the one dressed like a waiter, poured a fresh glass of the liquid and handed it to Danny. The drink had a funny smell, not a bit like tomato juice, that Danny detected as soon as he had taken the glass and he looked at it suspiciously. He raised it to his lips and sniffed. As he did so, the girl, who still had hold of his arm, increased the pressure of her grasp on his elbow. Danny saw, out of the corner of his eye, that the girl's face was flushed and excited and ... hungry looking. The tip of her tongue appeared briefly against her upper lip, and her brow arched up as her eyes stretched wide. He could tell she wanted him to try the drink. She wanted him to try it very much. And so did all the other people. They were all watching him with sharp, intense anticipation.

Danny held the glass a couple of inches from his mouth. His hand was not quite steady. "What is this?" he asked. "It's not tomato juice, is it?"

"Did we say it was?" someone said. "Did *anyone* say it *was*?" Everybody shook their heads.

"It's a fine drink," the girl said softly. "A rare old vintage; something you won't have tasted before. But once you've tried it, you'll want more of it; there's no doubt about that."

"I don't like the smell," Danny said nervously.

"Never mind that; it's not the taste or the smell that matters, it's what it does for you," the girl insisted.

Danny said nothing.

"It won't harm you," someone said. "We drink it all the time, and look at us. We're lucky here, we get plenty of it."

"The fine old stuff," the girl repeated, almost singing, as though she was quoting a popular song, "the rare old vintage."

Danny lowered his mouth to the glass and took a sip. The drink was thick and flat and metallic and slightly warm. It was neither good nor bad. He drank some more, and found he was suddenly thirsty. He emptied the glass slowly and put it down.

"Well?" asked the girl.

"It's okay," Danny said, unenthusiastically.

"Would you like some more?"

Danny was a polite boy. "Not at the moment, thank you," he said, and for some reason most of the people seated around him started to laugh. It was relaxed, good-humoured laughter. Danny noticed the girl had released her hold on his arm at last and, when the laughter had subsided, he repeated his request to be taken to his Gran. Someone made a joke that made no sense, about taking Gran to Danny, then Kelvin got up and told Danny it was too late to disturb Gran now, but he would take him back up to his room in the service lift. Danny would have to sort his other problems out in the morning.

To Danny's surprise, the entrance to the lift was at the back of the room they were in. Kelvin went and leaned on the button and, high up in the hotel, the lift lurched and groaned as it began unsteadily to descend. When it arrived, Kelvin had trouble pulling the slightly rusty, cage-like bars of the metal outer door open, then cursed as he bent to tug up the inner door that rose and slid back somewhere at the top of the lift. A cloud of the cold, steamy-looking mist Danny had noticed earlier wafted out of the lift shaft, surged across the floor, then floated up towards the ceiling on a cushion of warm air.

Danny saw at once that the lift was not empty. The huge brass-bound box he had seen so many times before was in there, taking up most of the space. It had been pushed up tight against one wall and there was just a narrow gap vacant to one side of it. Kelvin motioned to Danny to get in beside it. Danny shook his head and backed off a little way. He saw that the lid of the box was now in place, but could tell it was loose, unsealed. The dry wooden structure had finger-wide splits in it, and its sides were warped and slightly concave. In places, the wood had sunk away from the brass to reveal sections of the ancient, primitive nails that held it together. The seaweed that had been growing on it had shrunk, withered and turned colourless, like old wreathes in a graveyard.

Kelvin gave Danny a look that the boy recognised as the expression Todley Bay people sometimes put on their faces when they wanted to smile. It was probably meant to be encouraging, but Danny thought it had an impatient edge to it. Kelvin was in a hurry. Probably he wanted to get back for more of the red juice before the others drank it all.

Kelvin said, "What's the matter? Get in. I'll get you to your room in no time."

Danny pointed to the box. "What's that?"

"This?" Kelvin stepped forward and thumped the lid of the box with his fist. "Nothing for you to worry about. Not for a long time, anyway, I shouldn't think. You needn't trouble yourself about that."

"Is it empty?"

"I expect so." To placate Danny, Kelvin lifted the lid slightly and peered inside. He took a long, hard look.

"Are you sure?" Danny insisted nervously.

"Well," Kelvin said, lowering the lid, "it's not quite empty, but don't go bothering yourself about that."

"What's in there?"

"If you really want to know, sonny, I'll show you; I'll lift you up so you can take a look, if you think it'll make you happy, but I wouldn't recommend it."

"I don't want to see inside. I don't want to go near it. I don't want anything to do with it."

"You don't have to like it, son," Kelvin said, now definitely irritable, "but if you want me to show you to your room, you're going to have to ride up with it. So get in."

Danny waited for a long moment, and stared at the box. Something could be hiding in there, observing him; staring back at him through the cracks in the sides. But, if there was, he didn't feel it was necessarily out to harm him, it could be that it was just . . . curious about him. If there *was* anything in there, it wasn't him that it was after – or so, for no clear reason, he began to believe.

He decided to test his theory, since he could see no other option, and stepped quickly into the lift before he could think about his situation any more. He suddenly wanted to get to bed more than anything else he could think of.

Kelvin followed Danny onto the floor of the lift, shut the outer gates, pulled down the inner door, squeezed in along the side of the box beside the boy, and pushed a button. A stump of fluorescent tube set in the roof flickered and almost died. Something high in the building squealed as it took the strain. The sheet metal panels on the walls creaked all around them and the lift juddered – hesitated – lurched – then began to rise slowly, swinging slightly from side to side because it was out of balance. Danny kept as far away from the box as he could in the yellow green gloom that was almost darkness, and gulped to relieve his dry throat and mouth, that now seemed to be full of imaginary dust.

Kelvin saw him swallowing air and said, "What's the trouble?"

"I'm very thirsty," Danny admitted.

"Well, yes; you will be, it's only to be expected. But you'll get used to it. That's the way it is."

"I don't understand," Danny complained.

The lift shuddered to a halt.

"You will," Kelvin said, and stooped to pull up the door. He said something else as he tugged aside the doors of the metal cage, but Danny couldn't hear him over the clanging of the iron bars. Kelvin stepped onto the corridor and pointed to a door a little way away that Danny recognized at once as his own, leading to his room.

"You get to bed now," Kelvin ordered, "and don't go looking for your Gran anymore tonight."

In his room, Danny drank at least a pint of water out of the tap at the washbasin. It was warm and tasted slightly ferric, like the drink he had been given in the basement. He realized then that he hadn't felt at all ill since he had taken that crimson drink. In fact, it had made him feel very good: he was almost glowing with health inside. But he *was* tired out.

He flung himself into bed and slept at once.

Someone was moving quietly about in his room. Danny knew from the quality of the light it was early morning, so assumed the girl had let herself in to deliver his tea. Good, because he still had a thirst like an ache in the back of his throat. He didn't want to talk to her, however, for obvious reasons, so he kept his face under the quilt. Then, whoever was in the room sat down on his bed. Someone big and heavy: he knew this because the whole bed sank in the middle, whereas it had only dipped slightly when the girl had perched on it on previous occasions. A big person had come into his room, uninvited, and was sitting on his bed! An image of the bear-like man carved into his mind and filled him with fear. He's come for me or he's come for the box, or he's come for both, Danny thought, and he nearly stopped breathing.

Then the someone cleared his throat and said, "Danny, I know you're awake; it's me, don't worry." It was his father's voice.

Danny sat up with a jerk. "Dad! What are you doing here? What's wrong?"

His father's face was crumpled and tired, and his usually immaculately combed hair stuck up in bristles in a dozen places. His eyes looked sore and the flesh below them was flaky and grey. He was wearing his best suit over a white shirt that looked grimy at the collar, as though he'd worn it one day too many, and his tie was loose and askew.

"Danny, I'm sorry, but the holiday's over. Something's happened; so your mother and I came down here overnight. The car broke down. It's been very difficult, but we're here now, so..."

"Has something happened to Grandad?" Danny asked, thinking he could see the light. "Have they got him then? Has he disappeared?" He jumped out of bed, went to the sink, and drank more warm washing water from his tooth-mug.

His father looked confused. "No, he's okay; your mother's with him now. It's Gran, I'm afraid. You're going to have to know... I'm sorry Danny, but she passed away during the night."

"Passed away?"

Realizing that the euphemism was above and beyond Danny, his father explained that Gran was dead.

Three hours later, Danny, his parents, and Grandad were waiting in the hotel foyer for a taxi to take them to the station. The manager of the establishment, a razor thin, crop-haired woman in a black and white check blouse and grey suit, was commiserating with his mother, who was crying softly all the time that she was speaking. Danny heard part of the conversation, but didn't understand much of what was said.

"– terribly sad time – everything done that could be done – first rate staff who are used to dealing with death – see it all the time – we've taken care of the body – leave everything to us – unfortunately, another guest *in extremis*, even now, as I speak – and *so* young, just a girl – but of course, we prefer to deal with older people – the more mature person – ripe old age is our speciality – you . . . you understand?" The manageress sounded as though she had been reading from a publicity handout and had suddenly discovered that the last page was missing. She took a dive into sudden silence. Her sympathetic expression, set in stone, seemed only to effect her face below her eyes, which were empty and uninvolved. She and Danny's mother were seated on two gold-painted chairs, facing each other almost knee to knee.

"It was meant to be a break for them both," Danny's mother said, glad of a silence to break. She pushed her nose into her handkerchief and wiped her eyes. "She only had six months to live; that's what they told her, and she was so worried about leaving my father behind. He has Alzheimer's disease, so she was hoping to find somewhere here at Todley Bay where he could spend what time he has left in comfort. He could last years. She wanted to leave him in good hands."

The manageress nodded and clucked her tongue.

"She insisted on bringing the boy, because it would be their last chance of a holiday together though I didn't think it was right. But you can't argue with someone who's going to die soon, can you? Especially if it's your own mother, so I let him come."

The manageress nodded and looked about her for some excuse to get away. No obvious opportunity presented itself.

"It's so terribly sad, that she should be denied those last few months they promised her," Danny's mother said, and hid her face in her hands.

Danny was keeping an eye on Grandad. The old man was quite oblivious to his wife's death. He had a loopy half-smile on his face and was rubbing his hands together a lot, as though they were cold, or he were washing them. He kept strolling off, and Danny kept leading him back to his parents. Danny used these opportunities to buy soft drinks from a machine in the bar. He could feel them all sloshing about in his stomach but he still wanted more. Or perhaps he wanted something else. It was a funny kind of thirst he had, that would not be quenched, and there didn't seem to be anything he could do about it.

He had tried to explain his other worry to his father and mother, about the people who had attempted to lure Grandad away, but his mother had started to get angry with him and told him that this was no time for him to talk nonsense. It was obvious his father thought he was fantasising too. He had shaken his head at Danny when the boy had mentioned the man who travelled across the ground without moving his feet, like a skater. So Danny shut up. He realized there was no point in trying to get through to his parents, who were both up to their ears in troubles of their own, so he gave himself the job of protecting Grandad. He was delighted when his father told him the four of them were returning home by train at once, that very morning.

When the taxi came, Danny sat in the back with Grandad and his mother, who was now overwhelmed with grief. He held her hand, but got the impression she was unaware that he was there. Strangely, he had no feelings at all about Gran's death. It meant nothing to him yet. He was more concerned with the torrent of weeping beside him and was alarmed at his mother's inconsolable condition. He felt Grandad was safe now.

As the taxi drove along the seafront, Danny saw the great bulk of the box ahead of them on the edge of the promenade. Someone had started to push it back towards the jetty, but hadn't got very far. The oily-black, overgrown gull was perched on top of it, standing in perfect balance on one leg. Its head was set at an angle. It seemed to be carefully scrutinizing the traffic moving towards it.

The taxi, travelling slowly because a number of elderly people were dawdling and doddering across the road to get to the beach, came almost to a stop less than ten feet from the box. Danny slid down in his seat and turned away, trying to make himself invisible, just as the driver saw a gap ahead and accelerated into it, taking the vehicle some way beyond the box and the bird. Danny, thinking and hoping he had got by unobserved, couldn't resist turning around and sticking his head up over the top of the back seat to take one last look out the rear window at the gull.

The bird was riding the air a few inches above the boot of the taxi. Its beak dipped down towards the glass of the rear window, and it stared with one dead-reptile-eye straight into both of Danny's. It retained this pose for a moment, then broke away from the taxi with a single tug of its wings that took it soaring into the air. Danny expected it to follow the vehicle, but it didn't. It climbed up to a vast height at incredible speed, as though it had seen a hole in the sky it was afraid was due to close. Then it seemed to changed its mind. It plummeted back towards the town and disappeared behind the roofs to the right, ahead of the taxi.

Danny's father, sitting next to the driver, looked at his watch and remarked that they might miss the train. The driver shrugged, indicated towards the clutter of old people crossing the road ahead, and said he was doing his best.

When they got to the station there was no queue at the ticket office: even so, Danny's father had to write a cheque and seemed to take an age doing so. Danny bought a tin of Coke, gulped it down, then stood with the other two and a little heap of luggage at the ticket barrier, ready to assault the platform to get to the train the instant they were free to do so. When his father emerged, running with the tickets, Danny grabbed some of the baggage and shot past the ticket inspector right behind him. His father, with one arm around his still-distraught wife, scuttled awkwardly alongside the train looking for an empty compartment. They were half-way along the platform before Danny thought to look back to see where Grandad was. There was no sign of him.

Danny stopped and looked all around. Except for himself and his parents, the platform was empty. He shouted to his father, and felt the eyes of dozens of passengers on the train turn to stare at him curiously from behind the dusty carriage windows. His father understood what had happened at once.

"We've got to find him Danny. Go back. You take the right and I'll go left. He can't be far."

Danny shed his baggage and pelted back through the barrier again. He saw Grandad almost at once, standing by a newspaper kiosk, talking to the man in the waiter's uniform. The man was half-hidden in a doorway. His face was just visible, and only his arms protruded. They undulated in beckoning, luring movements, like the tentacles of an octopus. Grandad, shifting from foot to foot, was rubbing his hands and smacking his forehead in gestures of wild indecision. He also seemed to be laughing anxiously, like a donkey, with his mouth wide open. The man in the doorway slid back a few inches, like a man on roller skates, and Danny could see his feet were definitely *not* touching the ground. His body even seemed to float up a little way as he receded, and Danny remembered that he had no bones, no *substance*.

Danny shouted wordlessly at Grandad, who froze. The man in the doorway glanced at Danny, sneered, and vanished. He went out in an instant, like a fused light. Danny grabbed Grandad's arm and yanked him away, almost pulling the old man off his feet. He seemed to get the idea for once, however, and to Danny's surprise, started running quite fast. So fast in fact, the boy found it hard to steer him. He urged him in the right direction by pushing and pulling, a procedure that constantly threatened to entangle their legs and trip them both. The man at the barrier, who had watched the whole performance with some amusement, let them through and signalled to the guard at the far end of the station that the train could go. It started moving almost at once, sending Danny into a panic. There was no sign of his parents or the luggage, so he assumed that they had got on board. One of the doors of the nearest carriage was hanging invitingly open. Danny urged Grandad towards it, then trotted alongside as the old man climbed up the step to the corridor. As he did so, he glanced back and saw his mother struggling towards him clutching the luggage. Behind her, running desperately through the ticket barrier, was his father, his face purple with unaccustomed effort. Both his parents looked very angry.

For a moment Danny thought he was going to start to scream and cry in protest against the waves of confusion and frustration that were sweeping over him.

He turned to pull Grandad back. It was obvious that his parents would not reach the train in time to get aboard, since the carriage next to him was now moving at running speed. He shouted to Grandad to get down, then realized that it would be very dangerous if he did try to disembark. Nevertheless, the old man turned and appeared to make some confident attempt to get back off the step. As he did so, an arm reached out from the carriage door and the big hand at the end of it took firm hold of Grandad's shoulder and started to pull him in. A second hand emerged to take a grip on the other shoulder and Grandad was lifted up off his feet altogether and hauled into the darkness beyond the door. Then a figure leaned out for the handle of the door and quickly pulled it shut. Danny saw the hawklike nose and receding forehead of the bear-like man for just a second, peering out at him from behind the window at the upper part of the door, then the train gathered speed, retreated along the line, and snaked away out of the platform.

Then Danny did begin to scream and cry. He cried even louder when his mother caught up with him and started to blame him for what had occurred. Her face was a damp, white puffy blotch of grief and anger. His father, when he joined them, tried to calm things down.

"We can phone ahead, down the line, and get someone to go on the train at the next stop and bring him off," he said, but his wife didn't seem to hear him.

"He's senile," she protested. "He doesn't know where he is or what he's doing. He might just open a door and walk out while the train is moving. Anything could happen."

"It's not just that," Danny yelled, now quite beside himself. "One of those men was in the carriage. They've got him now. They've been trying to get him all week."

"What men, Danny?" his father said, trying to conceal his impatience.

"The ones I told you about," Danny said, "but you wouldn't listen."

On the very edge of anger, his father said, "And why would these men want an old man like Grandad, for God's sake?"

"For his blood," said Danny, "and some of them want his bones."

Then his mother dropped all the luggage that she was carrying and stepped very close to Danny. "How could you talk such rubbish?" she yelled, "at a time like this . . . ? On the day of my mother's death . . ." She spluttered to a halt, overwhelmed with indignation and rage.

A surge of intense and actually painful thirst, a craving for a drink that was not available, a liquid he could not obtain, cut into Danny and made him gag. He put his fingers into his mouth to touch his tongue to see if it was as dry as it seemed. It was. His father, alarmed by the expression on Danny's face, asked him what was wrong.

"I'm drying up inside Dad," Danny said, suddenly afraid to hear his own words. "I've got a terrible . . ." his tongue clicked against his pallet ". . . a terrible, awful *thirst*."

His mother regained her voice then. Her face was wet, wild, and dangerous, like a storm at sea. She howled at Danny wordlessly, and held her shaking hands, half-clenched like claws, in front of her face. "What are you trying to do to me?" she screamed at last. "How *can* you stand there and – talk – such – nonsense? After all that's happened, at a time like this, *you stand there whining about your thirst.*"

Danny, shattered, feeling quite alone, stood grey-faced and devastated by the injustice of it all. Something in his expression must have pushed his mother over the edge of her patience at that moment because, for the first time in her life, she slapped Danny hard across the face. Her ring cut the flesh of his cheek.

Danny broke away and ran. His mouth gaped open in a scream that only he could hear. Warm blood trickled down his cheek and into his mouth. The taste of it was at once familiar. It was like, but not quite the same as, what he was seeking; what he needed to quench his thirst.

Thinking about the dying girl back at the hotel, Danny ran right out of the station into the slowly moving holiday crowds passing back and forth along the front of Todley Bay. He darted through them like a wraith. Nobody seemed to notice him. He moved so fast, he thought he might be invisible.

He hoped the staff back at the hotel would understand and be kind to him.

When he got there, he found they were only too happy to receive him. They took him in, concealed him, and urged him to be patient.

The feast, they told him, though not of the rare old vintage of the night before, was almost ready. It would soon be served.

So, for the present, Danny had to content himself with that.

STEPHEN JONES & KIM NEWMAN

Necrology: 1996

The following writers, artists, performers and technicians who made significant contributions to the horror, science fiction and fantasy genres during their lifetimes died in 1996...

AUTHORS/ARTISTS

Walter M. (Michael) Miller, Jr., best remembered for his only-completed novel, the Hugo Award-winning *A Canticle for Leibowitz*, shot himself in the head on January 9th in Florida. Aged 73, he was despondent over his wife's recent death and his health had been failing for some time. In 1953 he scripted two series of TV's *Captain Video*, his story "The Darfsteller" won the Hugo in 1955, and in 1985 co-edited the anthology *Beyond Armageddon: Twenty-One Sermons to the Dead* with Martin H. Greenberg. Since 1989 he had been working on a sequel to *Canticle*, titled *St Leibowitz & the Wild Horse Woman*, which has been completed by Terry Bisson.

Sam Merwin, Jr. (W. Samuel Kimball Merwin, Jr.), who edited such magazines as *Thrilling Wonder Stories*, *Startling Stories*, *Fantastic Story Magazine*, *Wonder Stories Annual*, *Fantastic Universe* and *Satellite SF* during the late 1940s and early '50s, died of complications from a fall on January 13th, aged 85. He also wrote a number of science fiction and mystery novels, the screenplay for *Manhunt in the*

Jungle, and a series of Gothics under a variety of pseudonyms.

Composer **Les Baxter** died on January 15th of a massive heart attack due to kidney failure, aged 73. Best known for his scores for such AIP movies as *Fall of the House of Usher*, *Black Sunday*, *Pit and the Pendulum*, *Master of the World*, *Panic in Year Zero*, *Tales of Terror*, *The Man with X-Ray Eyes*, *The Raven*, *Black Sabbath*, *The Comedy of Terrors*, *Beach Blanket Bingo*, *Pajama Party*, *Sergeant Deadhead the Astronaut*, *Dr Goldfoot and the Bikini Machine*, *Dr Goldfoot and the Girl Bombs*, *The Ghost in the Invisible Bikini*, *Wild in the Streets*, *The Dunwich Horror*, *Cry of the Banshee*, *Frogs* and many others, he also scored *The Black Sleep*, *The Invisible Boy*, *The Bride and the Beast*, *Pharoah's Curse*, *Voodoo Island*, *Macabre* and *The Beast Within*.

Kaye Webb, who edited the Penguin children's imprint Puffin from 1961-79, died on January 16th, aged 81.

Comedy scripwriter **Philip Rapp** died on January 23rd, aged 88. His movie credits include *Wonder Man* and *The Secret Life of Walter Mitty*, both starring Danny Kaye, plus the *Topper* TV series.

Burne Hogarth, illustrator of the *Tarzan of the Apes* comic strip for many years, died on January 28th in a Paris hospital after spending the weekend as Guest of Honour at the 23rd International Comic Strip Festival in Angoulême, France. He was aged 84.

The same day, **Jerry Siegel**, who co-created Superman in a fanzine with Joe Shuster in 1933, died of heart failure, aged 81. As a teenager he published the fanzines *Cosmic Stories*, *Cosmic Stories Quarterly* and *Science Fiction* with Shuster (who died in 1992). They signed away all rights to the Superman character to DC Comics in 1938 for just $130, until a major popular opinion campaign mounted in the mid-1970s forced the company into making a financial and legal settlement for life. However, even in later life, Siegal admitted that the sight of a Superman comic book still made him feel physically sick. He was also the co-creator of such other comic strip characters as the Spectre, the Star Spangled Kid and Robotman.

Elsie B. Wollheim, who co-founded DAW Books in 1971 with her husband, Donald A. Wollheim, died on February 9th after a five-year battle against cancer. She was 85, and was scheduled to be an honoured guest at the 1996 World Science Fiction Convention in Los Angeles.

Irish-born SF author **Bob (Robert) Shaw** died on February 12th of heart failure, ten days after suffering a cardiac arrest complicated by pneumonia and liver and lung cancer. He was 64 and had recently returned to Britain after marrying US fan Nancy Tucker two months previously. In the late 1940s and early '50s he wrote humorous articles for *Hyphen*, the main Irish fanzine, finally becoming a full-time writer in the mid-1970s after working as a cab driver, structural engineer, journalist and public relations officer. He began selling short stories in the mid-1950s and his first novel, *Night Walk*, appeared in 1967. Later books include *Orbitsville*, *Orbitsville Departure* and *Orbitsville Judgement*, *The Ragged Astronauts*, *The Wooden Spaceships*, *The Fugitive Worlds* and the collection *Dark Night in Toyland*. He won numerous awards, including two Hugos as Best Fan Writer.

Brian (C.) Daley died of cardiac arrest on February 18th, after a long battle with pancreatic cancer, aged 48. He scripted the *Star Wars*, *The Empire Strikes Back* and *Return of the Jedi* radioplays, and his many books include *Doomfarers of Coramonde*, *The Starfollowers of Coramonde*, *A Tapestry of Magics*, *Requiem for a Ruler of Worlds*, *Jinx on a Terran Inheritance*, *Fall of the White Ship Avatar*, the novelization of *Tron*, and the first *Star Wars* novelizations to make the *New York Times* Bestseller list: *Han Solo at Stars' End*, *Han Solo's Revenge* and *Han Solo and the Lost Legacy*. As half of the "Jack McKinney" writing team (with James Lucendo) he wrote more than twenty novels in the *Robotech*, "Sentinels" and "Black Hole Travel Agency" series.

Canadian-born **H. (Horace) L. (Leonard) Gold**, the founding editor of *Galaxy* magazine, died of arteriosclerosis on February 21st, aged 81. He became a writer, selling to the science fiction pulps during the 1930s, and went on to work in editorial positions at Standard Magazines during the following decade. Throughout the 1950s he edited *Beyond Fantasy Fiction*, *Galaxy*, *If* and the line of *Galaxy Science Fiction Novels* in paperback. Winner of the Hugo for best professional magazine in 1953, Gold retired in 1961 after a debilitating car crash. His best fiction is collected in *The Old Die Rich*, and he collaborated with L. Sprague de Camp on a fantasy novel, *None But Lucifer*.

American artist **Richard (Michael) Powers**, who revolutionized science fiction cover art in the 1950s and early '60s, died from a stroke while visiting Spain on March 9th. He was 75.

Evangeline Walton (Evangeline Ensely), recipient of the 1989 World Fantasy Award for Life Achievement, died of pneumonia on March 11th, aged 88. She had undergone surgery for lung cancer the previous year. Her books include *The Virgin and the Swine* (aka *The Island of the Mighty*), *Witch House* (published by Arkham House in 1945), *The Cross and the Sword* (aka *Son of Darkness*), *The Children of Llyr*, *The Song of Rhiannon*, *Prince Annwn* and *The Sword is Forged*.

Novelist **Richard (Thomas) Condon**, whose books include *The Manchurian Candidate* (which he also scripted), *Winter Kills*, *The Final Addiction* and *Prizzi's Honor* and its sequels, died of kidney failure on April 9th, aged 81.

British-born film historian, archivist, author and teacher **William K. Everson** died of prostate cancer in New York on April 14th, aged 67. We always looked forward to his annual Christmas presentations at London's Gothique Film Society (from his own collection of 4,000 films), and amongst his nearly twenty books, *Classics of the Horror Film* is a cornerstone study of pre-1950s horror films. A belated follow-up, *More Classics of the Horror Film*, is less successful in covering recent material, but his other ground-breaking volumes include *The Bad Guys* and *The Detective in Film*.

Christopher Robin Milne, who was immortalized in his father A.A. Milne's Winnie-the-Pooh books, died on April 20th, aged 75. He spent his life trying to live down the unwanted fame and wrote three autobiographical volumes about his family.

TV and movie scriptwriter **Albert E. Lewin** died of heart failure on April 23rd, aged 79. His credits include *Alice in Wonderland*, *My Favourite Martian* and *Alfred Hitchcock Presents*.

Children's writer **P. (Pamela) L. (Lynwood) Travers O.B.E.**, the creator of Mary Poppins, died on the same day in London. She was aged somewhere between 90 and 96. Born Helen Lyndon Goff in Queensland, Australia, she followed her successful first novel with various other fantasy works, six sequels, plus *Mary Poppins in the Kitchen: A Cookery Book with a Story*. She had successfully blocked any follow-up to the 1964 Walt Disney movie, stating that "It's taken great strength of mind to live with that film . . ."

TV scriptwriter **Robert Hammer**, whose credits include episodes of *Voyage to the Bottom of the Sea*, *Star Trek*, *Lost in*

Space, *Time Tunnel* and *Planet of the Apes*, died on April 25th, aged 67.

Former Disney advertising executive turned writer-producer **Stirling Silliphant** died of cancer after a long illness in Thailand on April 26th, aged 78. His many credits include *Village of the Damned* (1960), *Charly*, *In the Heat of the Night* (for which he won an Academy Award for his script), *Marlowe*, *The Poseidon Adventure*, *The Towering Inferno*, *The Killer Elite*, *Telefon*, *Shaft in Africa*, *The Swarm*, *The Silent Flute* (aka *Circle of Iron*) and the TV miniseries *Space*. As the creator of TV's *Route 66* he also scripted the classic spoof horror episode, "Lizard's Leg and Owlet's Wing".

David Lasser, who edited such pulp magazines as *Science Wonder Stories*, *Air Wonder Stories*, *Wonder Stories Quarterly* and the last three issues of *Amazing Detective Tales*, died on May 5th, aged 94. He helped found and was the first president of the American Interplanetary Society (later the American Institute of Aeronautics and Astronautics) and wrote the 1931 non-fiction book *The Conquest of Space*.

Vera Chapman (Vera Ivy May Fogerty), one of the first women admitted to Oxford University, founder of the Tolkien Society in 1969, and the author of such Arthurian fantasy novels as *The Green Knight*, *The King's Damosel* (filmed as a cartoon by Warner Bros.) and *King Arthur's Daughter* (all collected as *The Three Damosels*), died on May 14th. She was 98, and didn't turn to writing until she was in her seventies.

Willis Conover, an early fan and correspondent with H.P. Lovecraft, died of lung cancer on May 17th, aged 75. The editor of the 1936 fanzine *Science-Fantasy Correspondent*, in the mid-1970s he published a collection of letters, *Lovecraft at Last*, and a booklet of Lovecraft's revisions to his *Supernatural Horror in Literature*. In 1955 he became host of the Voice of America *Music USA* programme, broadcasting jazz to thirty million listeners in Eastern Europe and 100 million around the world. In 1993 the American House of Representatives passed a resolution praising him as one of the country's greatest foreign policy tools.

Highly respected British SF editor **Richard (Clay) Evans** died on May 26th, aged 46. Still recovering from a long illness in 1994, he returned from a business trip to New York with pneumonia. He thought the pains in his chest were from straining to lift a suitcase, and by the time he entered hospital it was too late. While working at Fontana, Arrow, Macdonald/Futura (where he helped create the Orbit imprint), Headline and, finally, as senior Editorial Director of SF at Gollancz, he launched and nurtured the careers of many writers.

British actor **Jeremy Sinden**, who appeared in *Star Wars*, died of cancer on May 29th, aged 45.

Sixties guru and counterculture hero **Timothy (Francis) Leary** died of prostate cancer on May 31st, aged 75. In the 1970s he was jailed for possession of marijuana and was later a fugitive from justice in Algiers. He was paroled in 1976. An enthusiast of cyberpunk and new technology, his ashes were launched into space, along with those of Gene Roddenberry and nearly thirty others, in October 1996.

Children's author **Leon Garfield** died on June 3rd of cancer of the oesophagus, aged 75. His first children's book was *Jack Holborn*, a pirate adventure published in 1964. He followed it with *Black Jack*, *Mister Corbett's Ghost* (filmed in 1986), *The Restless Ghost: Three Stories*, *The Ghost Downstairs*, *Garfield's Apprentices* and *The Ghost Beneath the Sea*, the latter a collaboration with Edward Blishen that won the 1970 Carnegie Medal.

Long-time Scottish SF fan **Ethel Lindsay**, who published the fanzines *Scottishe* and *Haverings*, and for more than thirty years was the UK agent for Andrew Porter's US magazines *Algol*, *Starship* and *Science Fiction Chronicle*, died of cancer on June 16th, aged 75.

Superman comics artist **Curt Swan** died of a heart attack on the same day, aged 76. He began his career at DC Comics in the mid-1940s and, beginning the following decade, he drew the Man of Steel better than anybody else for three decades. He also worked on such classic characters as Batman, The Flash and Adam Strange.

Mystery writer **Collin Wilcox**, who created southwestern investigator Marshall McCloud, died of cancer on July 12th, aged 71. His other series characters included clairvoyant reporter Stephen Drake, San Francisco detective Frank Hastings and eccentric theatre director Alan Bernhardt.

Claudia Peck, author of the 1991 horror novel *Spirit Crossings*, died of breast cancer on August 1st, aged 43.

Charles O'Neal, screenwriter and the father of actor Ryan, died on August 29th, aged 92. His many credits include *The Devil's Mask*, Val Lewton's *The Seventh Victim*, *Cry of the Werewolf* and *I Love a Mystery*.

Longtime Minnesota fan **Eric Arne Carlson**, who co-edited the semiprozine *Etchings & Odysseys* from 1971 to 1987, died on September 6th, apparently of heart failure. He was 52.

French publisher, author and translator **Élizabeth Gille** died of cancer on September 30th, aged 59. She was responsible for the Présence du Futur series at publisher Denoël.

Frank H. (Herbert) Parnell, author of *Monthly Terrors: An Index to the Weird Fiction Magazines*, died on Hallowe'en, aged 79. Credited with having one of the most impressive collections of SF, fantasy and horror magazines in Britain, he also contributed a few stories to *New Worlds* and *Science Fantasy* under the names "Gregory Francis" and "Francis Richardson".

Tomi Lewis (Cheri Lynn Lewis) who, with her husband Doug, established Denver, Colorado's Little Bookshop of Horrors and the award-winning Roadkill Press, died of cancer on November 8th, aged 44.

Award-winning children's author **Eleanor F. (Frances) Cameron** died in California on November 10th, aged 84. The Canadian-born writer was first published in 1950 with *The Unheard Music*, her only adult book, while her novels for children include *The Wonderful Flight to the Mushroom Planet*, *The Court of the Stone Children* (winner of the 1974 National Book Award), *To the Green Mountains*, *The Beast With the Magical Horn*, *The Terrible Churnadryne*, *The Mysterious Christmas Shell*, *A Room Made of Windows*, *A Spell is Cast* and *Beyond Silence*.

British-born novelist and playwright **Derek Marlowe** died on November 13th in Los Angeles, aged 58. He suffered a brain haemorrhage after a short illness with leukaemia. His books included *Dandy in Aspic*, *Memoirs of a Venus Lackey* and *Nightshade*, and he also worked as a scriptwriter for TV and films. His only short stories appeared in *Vogue* and the anthologies *Darklands* and *Darklands 2*.

Liz Knights, publisher of UK imprint Victor Gollancz, died of cancer on November 14th, aged 41.

Author, playwright, actress and lyricist **Diana Morgan** died on December 9th, aged 88. She co-scripted the Ealing ghost movie *The Halfway House*.

Planetary scientist, astronomer, SF novelist and Hugo Award-winner **Carl Sagan** died of pneumonia on December 20th after two years fighting a rare bone marrow disease/immune disorder. He was 62. In 1980 he hosted the popular and award-winning documentary TV series *Cosmos*, and he received a then-record $2 million advance for his 1985 novel *Contact* (filmed in 1997).

ACTORS/ACTRESSES

Fearless Nadia, the Australian-born swashbuckling heroine of such Indian films of the 1930s to the 1950s as *Hunterwala* (aka *The Lady Hunter* – a series role as a masked avenger), *Diamond Queen*, *Jungle Princess* and *The Magic of Baghdad*, died on January 9th.

Francisco M. Garcia, leader of the pop quartet Cannibal and the Headhunters, best known for their 1965 hit "Land of 1,000 Dances", died on January 21st, aged 49.

Hollywood actor/dancer/choreographer/director **Gene Kelly** (Eugene Curran Kelly) died from a series of strokes on February 2nd, aged 83. His numerous credits include *Ziegfeld Follies*, *Anchors Aweigh* (in which he danced with Jerry the cartoon mouse), *The Three Musketeers* (1948), *On the Town*, *Singin' in the Rain*, *Brigadoon*, *What a Way to Go* and *Xanadu*. He won a special Academy Award in 1951.

Character actor **Martin Balsam** was found dead in a Rome hotel on the same day, aged 77. His numerous film and television roles include ill-fated private investigator Milton Arbogast in Hitchcock's *Psycho*, *The Bedford Incident*, *Seven Days in May*, *The Six Million Dollar Man*, *The Sentinel*, *Murder in Space*, *Two Evil Eyes*, *Cape Fear* (both versions), *Silence of the Hams*, *Alfred Hitchcock Presents*, *The Twilight Zone*, *Way Out* and *The Man from U.N.C.L.E.*

The star of TV's *Wild Bill Hickok* from 1951–58, **Guy Madison** (Robert Ozell Moseley), died of emphysema on February 6th, aged 74. He also starred in such movies as *The Beast of Hollow Mountain*, *On the Threshold of Space,*, *Superargo* and *The Faceless Giant*.

Egyptian actor **Adel Adham**, known as the "prince of evil" for his portrayals in more than 300 films since he became an actor in 1964, died on February 7th in Cairo. He was 68.

Child star **Tommy Rettig**, who played Bart in *The 5,000 Fingers* *of Dr T*, died on February 15th, aged 54. After appearing in *Lassie* on TV for four years, he later became a drug dealer, computer programmer and drug counsellor.

Christian Haren, who received a contract with MGM in the mid-1950s and appeared in print ads as the Marlboro Man in the early 1960s, died of AIDS on February 27th, aged 61. He owned a famous gay bar in Palm Springs and educated young people about AIDS and its prevention.

British stage and screen actress **Brenda Bruce**, who appeared as a prostitute in *Peeping Tom*, died in February, aged 78. Her other film and TV roles include Hammer's *Nightmare*, *Doctor Who*, *The Mad Death* and *Alice Through the Looking Glass*.

Haing S. Ngor, who starred in *The Killing Fields* and survived Cambodia, was shot to death by a mugger in Los Angeles in February. He also appeared in TV's *Highway to Heaven*.

Leading man **Lyle Talbot** (Lysle Henderson) died on March 3rd, aged 94. He appeared in more that 150 (often low budget) movies, including *The 13th Guest*, *A Shriek in the Night*, *The Dragon Murder Case*, *Trapped by Television*, *Return of the Terror*, *Strange Impersonation*, *Batman and Robin* (as Commissioner Gordon), *Atom Man vs. Superman* (as Lex Luthor), *Fury of the Congo*, *Jungle Manhunt*, *Glen or Glenda?*, *Mesa of Lost Women*, *Untamed Women*, *Commando Cody*, *Tobor the Great*, the legendary *Plan 9 from Outer Space*, *Torture Ship* and *Sky Dragon*, among many others.

American character actor **Whit** (Whitner) **Bissell** died on March 5th, aged 86. On TV, he played General Heywood Kirk in *Time Tunnel* (1966–67), and his many credits include *Lost Continent* (1951), *Creature from the Black Lagoon*, *Invasion of the Body Snatchers*, *I Was a Teenage Werewolf*, *I Was a Teenage Frankenstein*, *Monster on the Campus*, *The Time Machine*, *The Manchurian Candidate*, *Seven Days in May*, *Soylent Green*, *Psychic Killer* and *The Fantasy Worlds of Irwin Allen*.

Tom McDermott, who starred as Permes Lykos on TV's *Captain Video* in the early 1950s, died of prostate cancer on March 6th, aged 83.

Veteran vaudeville comedian **George Burns** (Nathan Birnbaum) died on March 9th. He was 100 years old. He married his partner Gracie Allen, and together they appeared on radio and TV and in movies until she died in 1965. In later years he made an amazing comeback, winning an Academy Award at the age of 80. His many films include *International House* (with Bela Lugosi), the titular character in *Oh God!*, *Oh God! Book II* and *Oh God! You Devil*, *Sgt. Pepper's Lonely Hearts Club Band*, *18 Again!* and *Radioland Murders*.

TV's Dr Ben Casey, actor **Vince Edwards** (Vincento Eduardo Zoine), died from pancreatic cancer on March 11th, aged 67. He also appeared on TV in episodes of *Alfred Hitchcock Presents*, *Tales from the Darkside*, *The Highwayman* and *Knight Rider*, and in such films as *City of Fear*, *The Mad Bomber*, *Sole Survivor*, *Return to Horror High*, *The Seduction*, *Cellar Dweller*, *Space Raiders* and *The Fear*.

Kim Dibbs, who starred as Buck Rogers in the 1950s syndicated TV series, died on March 28th, aged 78. The actor also appeared in *Riders to the Stars* and *Abbott and Costello Meet the Mummy*.

McLean Stevenson, best remembered as Lt. Colonel Henry Blake in the first three years of TV's *M*A*S*H*, died from a heart attack following surgery, aged 66. He was also in Disney's *Cat from Outer Space*.

Anglo-Irish leading actress **Greer Garson** died in Dallas on April 6th from heart failure. She was 92. Her films include *Mrs Miniver* (for which she won an Academy Award), *Madame Curie*, *Julius Caesar* (1953), *The Singing Nun* and *The Happiest Millionaire*.

Veteran character actor **Ben Johnson** died from an apparent heart attack on April 8th, aged 77. A favourite of director John Ford, his many credits include *Mighty Joe Young*, *She Wore a Yellow Ribbon*, *Shane*, *The Wild Bunch*, *The Last Picture Show* (for which he won an Academy Award), *The Savage Bees*, *The Town That Dreaded Sundown*, *The Swarm*, *Terror Train*, *Red Dawn*, *Radio Flyer* and *Cherry 2000*.

Egyptian-born actor **Alex D'Arcy** (Alexander Sarruf) died on April 20th, aged 88. His films include *The Prisoner of Zenda* (1937), *Topper Takes a Trip*, *Horrors of Spider Island*, *Way Way Out*, *The St Valentine's Day Massacre* and *Blood of Dracula's Castle* (as the Count).

Italian actor **Luigi Pistilli** committed suicide during a stage flop on April 21st. He was 66, and his films include *Illustrious Corpses*, *For a Few Dollars More* and *The Good the Bad and the Ugly*.

American actor **Adam Roarke** died of a heart attack, aged 58, on April 27th. He appeared in *Women of the Prehistoric Planet*, *Cyborg 2087*, *Psych-Out*, *Hells Angels on Wheels* and *Frogs*, as well as such TV shows as *The Man from U.N.C.L.E.*, *Star Trek*, *Alfred Hitchcock Presents* and *The Six Million Dollar Man*.

TV and film actor **David Opatoshu** died after a long illness on April 30th, aged 78. His credits include *Tarzan and the Valley of Gold*, *The Dybbuk*, *Conspiracy of Terror*, *Americathon*, *Beyond Evil*, the voice of Thun in the animated *Flash Gordon The Greatest Adventure of Them All*, *The Twilight Zone*, *The Outer Limits*, *Voyage to the Bottom of the Sea*, *Cloak of Mystery*, *The Man from U.N.C.L.E.*, *Star Trek*, *Buck Rogers*, *Alien Nation* and numerous others.

Tubby American character actor **Jack Weston** died of lymphoma on May 3rd, aged 71. His films include *The Incredible Mr Limpet*, *Mirage*, *Wait Until Dark*, *I Love a Mystery* (1973) and *Short Circuit 2*. During the 1950s he was a regular on TV's *Rod Brown and the Rocket Rangers* (as Ranger Wilbur Wormser) and also appeared in episodes of *Bewitched*, *The Twilight Zone*, *Thriller* and *The Man from U.N.C.L.E.*

British comedy actor **Jon Pertwee** (John Devon Roland Pertwee), much loved by generations of children as TV's third *Doctor Who* (1970–74) and the living scarecrow *Worzel Gummidge* (1979–81; 1987; 1989), died of a heart attack on May 20th, while on holiday in America. He was 76, and his many film and TV credits include Hammer's *The Ugly Duckling*, *Carry on Screaming*, *The House That Dripped Blood* (as a vampire) and *One of Our Dinosaurs is Missing*. In later years he recreated his role of the Doctor on stage and in two radio plays.

1940s cowboy star **Lash LaRue** (Alfred LaRue), known as "King of the Bullwhip", died of heart failure on May 21st, aged 96 (although he claimed to be twenty years younger). He made his debut in the 1945 serial *The Master Key* and the same year originated his trademark of dressing all in black and wielding a 15-foot bullwhip as the Cheyenne Kid in *Song of Old Wyoming*. In 1953 his films were edited into TV's *Lash of the West* and during the mid-1980s he came out of retirement to star in *The Dark Power* and *Alien Outlaw*. Seven months after his death, his widow Marion claimed that Forest Lawn Memorial Park had lost his body.

British character actor **Patrick Cargill** died of cancer on May 23rd, aged 78. On TV he starred in the long-running sit-com

Father Dear Father and in episodes of *The Avengers* and *The Prisoner* (as Number 2).

Leading British stage and screen actress **Dorothy Hyson** died of a stroke the same day. She was 81, and appeared opposite Boris Karloff in the 1933 movie *The Ghoul*.

British-born character actor **John Abbott** died on May 24th, aged 90. Rare Hollywood starring roles included the patriotic killer in *London Blackout Murders* and as an unlikely 400-year-old vampire in *The Vampire's Ghost*. His other credits include *Jane Eyre, Cry of the Werewolf, Pursuit to Algiers, The Woman in White*, and TV's *Thriller, The Munsters, Star Trek, Wild Wild West, The Cat Creature* and *Sherlock Holmes in New York*.

Italian actor and producer **Walter Brandi** died on May 28th, apparently from leukaemia. He starred in such films as *The Vampire and the Ballerina, The Playgirls and the Vampire, Slaughter of the Vampires* and many others during the 1960s.

Actress **Jo Van Fleet**, who appeared in Roman Polanski's *The Tenant*, died on June 10th, aged 76.

German silent star **Brigitte Helm** (Eva Gisela Schittenhelm), who will always be remembered for her portrayal of the sexy robot Maria in Fritz Lang's classic *Metropolis* (1926), died the same day, aged 90. She also appeared in both the 1928 and 1930 versions of *Alraune*, and as Antinea, the Queen of Atlantis, in the 1931 version of *L'Atlantide*. She retired from the screen in 1939 to marry a wealthy German industrialist. After the war, she and her family moved to Switzerland, where she died.

Singer and entertainer **Ella Fitzgerald** died on June 15th from diabetes complications. She was aged 78.

Chinese actor **Kwan Tak-Hing**, who portrayed martial arts hero Huang Fei-Hung in more than eighty features, many with magical elements, died from cancer of the pancreas on June 28th, aged 91.

British actress **Pamela Kellino** (Pamela Ostrer), who was married to James Mason, died on June 29th aged around 80. A columnist and TV personality, she also appeared in such films as *Lady Possessed, Pandora and the Flying Dutchman, Sex Kittens Go to College, The Navy vs. the Night Monsters, Wild in the Streets* and *Everything You Always Wanted to Know About Sex* *But Were Afraid to Ask*.

Actress and former model **Margaux Hemingway** was found dead under suspicious circumstances on July 1st, aged 41. The star of *Lipstick*, *Killer Fish*, *Killing Machine* and *Inner Sanctum* (1991) had apparently been depressed for some time.

British comedian and character actor **Alfred Marks** died the same day, aged 75. In 1969 he portrayed harassed Detective Superintendent Bellaver opposite Price, Lee and Cushing in *Scream and Scream Again*.

Attorney **Melvin Belli**, who appeared as the alien Gorgan in the 1968 *Star Trek* episode "And the Children Shall Lead Them", died after a long illness on July 9th, aged 88.

Actress and cartoon voice **Dana Hill Goetz** died on July 15th from diabetic complications. She was 32.

Randy Stuart, who portrayed Louise Carey, the wife of *The Incredible Shrinking Man*, died on July 20th, aged 72.

American actress **Luana Anders**, who appeared in such Roger Corman productions as *Pit and the Pendulum*, *Night Tide*, *Dementia 13* (aka *The Haunted and the Hunted*), *Games* and *Easy Rider*, died of breast cancer on July 21st, aged 54.

British character actor **Wolfe Morris** died the same day, aged 71. He appeared in the 1950s BBC-TV serial *The Creature* and the Hammer film version, *The Abominable Snowman*, as well as such movies as *The House That Dripped Blood* and *Screamer*.

American actress **Jean Muir** (J.M. Fullerton) died on July 23rd, aged 85. Her films include the 1935 version of *A Midsummer Night's Dream* and *The Lone Wolf Meets a Lady*. She was blacklisted in 1950 and fired from the TV series *The Aldrich Family*.

American character actress **Virginia Christine** died of heart complications on July 24th, aged 76. She was married to Fritz Feld and was Mrs Olson on the Folger's coffee commercials for more than twenty years. Her film credits include Universal's *The Mummy's Curse* (as Princess Ananka) and *House of Horrors*, plus *Invasion of the Body Snatchers* (1956), *Billy the Kid versus Dracula* and TV's *Daughter of the Mind*.

Director Jesús Franco's favourite actor, Swiss-American **Howard Vernon** (Mario Lippert), died the same day, aged 82. He created the role of Dr Orloff in Franco's *The Awful Dr Orloff* (1961), and reprised the mad scientist for *Only a Coffin*, *The Invisible Dead*, *El Siniestro Dr Orloff* and *Faceless*. He also worked with Fritz Lang in *The Thousand Eyes of Dr Mabuse* and for Jean-Luc Godard in *Alphaville*, and portrayed Dracula in Franco's *Dracula Prisoner of Frankenstien* and *La Fille de*

Dracula. His many other films include *The Diabolical Dr Z, Succubus, Night of the Blood Monsters, Mrs Hyde, A Virgin Among the Living Dead, The Erotic Rites of Frankenstein, The Demons, Seven Women for Satan, Zombie Lake, Blood of Dr Jekyll, Revenge in the House of Usher, Howl of the Devil* and *Delicatessen*.

Actor **Bryant Halliday**, who starred for producer Richard Gordon in such British-made movies as *Curse of Simba* (aka *Curse of the Voodoo*), *The Devil Doll* (1963), *The Projected Man* and *Tower of Evil* (aka *Horror on Snape Island/Beyond the Fog*), died of a stroke in Paris on July 28th. He was 68.

French-born Hollywood star **Claudette Colbert** (Lily Claudette Chauchoin) died at her Barbados home on July 30th, aged 92. Her many films include *The Sign of the Cross, Four Frightened People, The Hole in the Wall, Cleopatra* (1934), *Maid of Salem* and a TV version of *Blithe Spirit*. She won an Academy Award in 1935 for *It Happened One Night* and by 1938 was Hollywood's highest-paid performer. Married to actor/director Norman Foster, she retired in the early 1960s.

German silent star **Camilla Horn**, who starred in the 1926 version of *Faust*, died on August 14th, aged around 90.

Actor **Greg Morris**, who played electronics expert Barney Collier on TV's *Mission Impossible* (1966–73), died of cancer on August 27th, aged 61. He also appeared in the movie *The Sword of Ali Baba* and in episodes of *The Twilight Zone, Wonder Woman, Fantasy Island, War of the Worlds* and *Superboy*. At the time of his death, he was apparently very bitter that he wasn't asked to appear in the big-budget *Mission Impossible* movie.

Actress **Bibi Besch**, who played the mother of Captain Kirk's son in *Star Trek II The Wrath of Khan*, died of cancer on September 7th, aged 54. Born in Vienna, her other credits include *The Pack, Meteor, The Beast Within* and *Tremors*.

Louise Fitch Lewis, who appeared in such 1950s movies as *The Vampire, I Was a Teenage Werewolf* and *Blood of Dracula* (aka *Blood is My Heritage*), died on September 11th, aged 81.

German-born British stage and screen actress **Jane Baxter** (Feodora Forde) died on September 13th, aged 87. She appeared in *The Clairvoyant* (aka *The Evil Mind*), *The Man Who Could Work Miracles* and *All Hallowe'en*.

Actor/dancer/director **Gene Nelson** (Leander Berg) died on

September 16th, aged 76. He starred in *The Atomic Man* and the TV series *Men Into Space*, and also directed *The Hand of Death* and episodes of *Star Trek* and *Get Smart*.

American leading lady **Dorothy Lamour** (Mary Leta Dorothy Kaumeyer) died on September 21st, aged 81. Best known for the series of seven *Road* movies with Bob Hope and Bing Crosby, her other films include *The Jungle Princess*, *My Favorite Brunette*, *The Lucky Stiff*, *Pajama Party*, *The Phynx*, *Creepshow 2* and TV's *Death at Love House*.

British actor **Mark Frankel**, who starred as vampire leader Julian Luna in the short-lived TV series *Kindred: The Embraced*, was killed in a motorcycle accident on September 24th. He was 34.

American stage and screen actor **William Prince** died on October 8th, aged 83. He appeared in such films as *Dead Reckoning*, William Castle's *Macabre*, *The Stepford Wives*, *Network*, Hitchcock's *Family Plot*, *The Cat from Outer Space*, *Vice Versa*, *Spontaneous Combustion* and *Steel and Lace*, along with numerous TV shows.

British comedienne and character actress **Beryl Reid** died of pneumonia on October 13th, aged 78. She appeared in such films as *The Assassination Bureau*, *The Beast in the Cellar*, *Dr Phibes Rises Again*, *Psychomania* (aka *The Death Wheelers*), *Yellowbeard* and *The Doctor and the Devils*, as well as TV's *Doctor Who*.

American silent screen actress **Laura La Plante** died on October 14th, aged 92. She starred in the 1927 version of *The Cat and the Canary* and *The Last Warning* (1928), both for director Paul Leni.

French-Spanish actress **Maria Casares** (Maria Casares Quiroga) died on November 22nd, aged 74. She personified Death in Jean Cocteau's classic *Orphée*, and also appeared in *Les Enfants du Paradis* and *Le Testament d'Orphée*.

American actor **Mark Lenard**, aged 68, died the same day from multiple myeloma. Best remembered as Spock's father Sarek in the *Star Trek* series and various spin-off movies, he also played Urko in the *Planet of the Apes* TV series and appeared in the film *The Greatest Story Ever Told*.

British-Peruvian comedian and founding member of The Goons, **Michael Bentine**, died of prostate cancer on November 26th, aged 74. The creator of the 1954 TV puppet show about aliens, *The Bumblies*, he also wrote a supernatural novel, *Lord of the Levels*.

Suffering from heart disease, **Tiny Tim** (Herbert Buckingham Khaury) died on November 30th, aged 71. He married 17-year-old "Miss Vicky" on Johnny Carson's *Tonight Show* in front of twenty million viewers in 1969 and was a regular on TV's *Rowan and Martin's Laugh-In*. Doctors had warned the ukulele-playing falsetto singer, who appeared in such films as *You Are What You Eat* and as a psychopathic clown in *Blood Harvest*, that he would kill himself if he sang again. But he defied them in September, singing his 1960s hit "Tiptoe Thru' the Tulips With Me" one last time before collapsing from a heart attack while on stage in Massachusetts. He never recovered.

American actor **Willard Parker** (Worster van Eps), who appeared in the 1939 serial *The Phantom Creeps* and the 1964 movie *The Earth Dies Screaming*, died on December 4th, aged 84.

British humorist, author and cartoonist **William Rushton** died on December 11th, aged 59. Co-founder of the magazine *Private Eye*, he played Dr Watson to John Cleese's Sherlock Holmes on TV, wrote a sequel to *War of the Worlds* entitled *W.G. Grace's Last Case*, and voiced the stop-motion characters in TV's *The Trap Door* (1994).

Italian leading man **Marcello** (Vincenzo Domenico) **Mastroianni** died of cancer in Paris on December 19th, aged 73. His many films include *La Dolce Vita, Ghosts of Rome, 8½, The Tenth Victim, Ghosts Italian Style, What?, La Grande Bouffe* and *Bye Bye Monkey*.

Veteran Hollywood actor **Lew Ayres** (Lewis Ayer) died on December 30th, aged 89. A popular leading man during the 1930s, his career suffered when he announced he was a conscientious objector during World War II. He later became a regular guest star in TV shows and movies. His numerous credits include *All Quiet on the Western Front*, MGM's *Dr Kildare* series, *Fingers At the Window, The Dark Mirror, Donovan's Brain, Earth II, She Waits, The Questor Tapes, Battle for the Planet of The Apes, End of the World, Damien Omen II, Battlestar Galactica* and *Salem's Lot*.

Actor **Jack Nance** (Marvin John Nance) was found dead at his home the same day, aged 53. Los Angeles County Sheriff's department believe the 53-year-old star of *Eraserhead* and TV's

Twin Peaks was killed by being punched in the face during a brawl with two men in a donut shop the day before. His films included *Ghoulies, Dune,* the remake of *The Blob, Wild at Heart, Blue Velvet, The Demolitionist, Voodoo* and *Lost Highway.* Nance's wife Kelly Van Dyke hanged herself in 1991 after her husband decided to divorce her.

Thin character actor **Wesley Addy** died in December, aged 84. He appeared in such films as *Kiss Me Deadly, What Ever Happened to Baby Jane?, Hush. . .Hush Sweet Charlotte, Seconds* and *Network.*

Dario Argento's daughter **Fiore**, who appeared in *Demons* and her father's *Phenomenon*, was killed in a car crash in 1996.

FILM/TV TECHNICIANS

Virgil W. Vogel, who directed *The Mole People, The Land Unknown* and *Invasion of the Animal People*, died on January 7th, aged 77. An editor on such films as *Mystery Submarine* and *This Island Earth*, he also directed episodes of *Fantastic Journey, Man from Atlantis* and *Quantum Leap* for TV.

TV director **Don Richardson** died on January 10th of heart failure. He was aged 77, and his many credits include *Don Juan in Hell, Get Smart,* and numerous episodes of *Lost in Space.*

Hollywood producer **Don Simpson**, best known for such boxoffice hits as *Top Gun, American Gigolo, Beverly Hills Cop, Bad Boys, Crimson Tide* and others, died on January 19th from a probable heart attack, the result of his extreme lifestyle. He was 52.

Chinese director **Lo Wei** died from heart failure on January 20th, aged 76. His films include two early Bruce Lee vehicles, *The Big Boss* and *Fist of Fury*, plus *Dragon Swamp* and *The Golden Sword.*

Pioneer Walt Disney animator **Shamus Culhane**, whose credits include *Betty Boop, Krazy Kat, Popeye, Woody Woodpecker, Gulliver's Travels*, the "Heigh-Ho" march in the 1937 *Snow White and the Seven Dwarfs*, and the 1940 *Pinocchio*, died on February 2nd, aged 88.

William Claxton, who directed the giant killer bunny movie, *Night of the Lepus*, died of a stroke on February 11th, aged 81.

Producer **Josef Shaftel** died of cancer on March 9th, aged

76. His films include *Goodbye Gemini*, *Alice's Adventures in Wonderland* and *The Spiral Staircase* (1975).

Former actor turned producer **Ross Hunter** (Martin Fuss), died of lymphoma on March 10th, aged 75. His many movies include *Son of Ali Baba*, *Midnight Lace* (1960), *Portrait in Black*, *Pillow Talk*, *Thoroughly Modern Millie*, *Airport* and the misjudged musical version of *Lost Horizon* (1973).

Cult Italian director **Lucio Fulci** died in Rome on March 13th after a long battle with diabetes. He was 68. His films include *Don't Torture a Duckling*, *The Psychic*, *Zombie Flesh Eaters*, *The Beyond*, *City of the Living Dead*, *The House by the Cemetery*, *Manhattan Baby*, *Conquest*, *Rome 2033*, *The Black Cat* (1980), *Ghosts of Rome*, *Voices from the Beyond* and *Cat in the Brain*. At the time of his death he was preparing to direct *Wax Mask* for Dario Argento.

French director **René Clément** died on March 17th, aged 82. His films include *Purple Noon*, *Is Paris Burning?*, *Rider on the Rain* and *The Deadly Trap*.

Producer/financier **Irving H. Levin** died of cancer on March 20th, aged 74. His credits include *The Beginning of the End*, *Poltergeist* and *Romancing the Stone*.

Industrial film-maker (Harold) **Herk Harvey** died on April 3rd, aged 71. His sole feature, the cult favourite *Carnival of Souls* (1962), was shot in an abandoned ballroom and amusement park. The producer/director himself played the leader of the pasty-faced corpses.

Producer/director **Paul Leder** died of lung cancer on April 8th, aged 70. Among the films not listed in his *Variety* obituary were *A*P*E*, *I Dismember Mama*, *My Friends Need Killing*, *Sketches of a Strangler*, *Vultures* and *Body Count*.

Maverick director **Donald Cammell**, aged 57, shot himself in Hollywood on April 23rd, allegedly because his last film, *Wild Side*, was taken away from him and re-edited. His troubled career included *Performance*, *Demon Seed* and *White of the Eye*.

American designer **Saul Bass** died from non-Hodgkin's lymphoma on April 25th, aged 75. Known for his remarkable titles sequences, Bass had a single feature director credit, *Phase IV*. He also won an Academy Award for his short, *Why Man Creates*. His claim to have directed the shower murder of *Psycho*, on which he was a visual consultant, has been disputed by many, including Janet Leigh. His other credits include *Vertigo, Bunny Lake is Missing, Seconds* and *Cape Fear* (1991).

MCA executive **Jennings Lang**, who produced such films as *The Beguiled, Play Misty for Me, Earthquake* and *Airport 1975*, died of pneumonia, aged 81, on May 29th.

Producer **Saul David** died on June 7th from complications of congestive heart failure. He was 74, and his films include *Our Man Flint, Fantastic Voyage, In Like Flint, Skullduggery, Logan's Run* and *Westworld*.

The same day, **Max Factor, Jr.** died at the age of 91. With his Polish-born father, he made Max Factor one of the top cosmetic firms in the world, as well as creating specialist make-up for films from 1914 onwards. The firm received an Academy Award in 1928 for its Panchromatic (Pancake) make-up and worked on such early Technicolor features as *Doctor X*. The company was eventually sold in 1973 for $480 million.

Architect **Frank Israel**, who also designed the sets for *Star Trek The Motion Picture*, died of AIDS on June 10th, aged 50.

American-born **Albert R. ("Cubby") Broccoli** (Albert Romolo Broccoli), who produced the James Bond series from *Dr No* (1962) through to *Goldeneye* (1995), died on June 27th from severe heart problems. He was aged 87. In 1968 he also produced a film version of Ian Fleming's children's fantasy *Chitty Chitty Bang Bang* and in 1982 won the Irving G. Thalberg Award for "continued production excellence". He also apparently claimed that one of his uncles introduced the vegetable his family was named after into the USA in the 1870s.

Veteran Hollywood producer **Pandro S. Berman** died of congestive heart failure on July 13th, aged 91. His films include *Top Hat, The Hunchback of Notre Dame* (1939), *The Picture of Dorian Gray, The Three Musketeers* (1948) and *Jailhouse Rock*.

Disney animator **Robert W. Youngquist** died on August 2nd, aged 90. His career began in 1935 and he worked on such classics as *Snow White and the Seven Dwarfs, Cinderella* and *The Sword in the Stone*.

Film editor **Tony Martinelli** died of a heart attack on August 15th, aged 86. For more than twenty years he worked at Republic Studios on such serials as *Dick Tracy vs. Crime Inc., Spy Smasher, Perils of Nyoka* and the feature *The Vampire's Ghost*.

Walt Disney animator **Albert Bertino**, who worked on *Fantasia* and *Pinocchio* and helped create Disneyland's Country Bear Jamboree, Mr Toad's Wild Ride and the Haunted Mansion, died on August 18th, aged 84.

Clair Weeks, another veteran animator for Disney, died on August 26th. His many credits include *Snow White and the Seven Dwarfs*, *Bambi*, *Alice in Wonderland* and *Cinderella*.

German-born *Alfredo B. Crevenna*, who directed more than 140 Mexican movies, died in August, aged 82. His many credits include *The New Invisible Man*, *Bring Me the Vampire*, *Aventura al Centro dela Tierra*, *Dynasty of Dracula* and several of Santo's later adventures.

TV producer/writer **Leonard Katzman**, nephew of legendary serial producer Sam Katzman, died of a heart attack on September 5th, aged 69. He was a producer on *Wild Wild West*, *Hawaii Five-O*, *Fantastic Journey*, *Logan's Run*, *Dallas* and *Walker Texas Ranger*, and he wrote and directed the low budget 1965 movie *Space Monster*.

American cinematographer **Joseph F. Biroc** died of heart failure on September 9th, aged 93. His many credits include *It's a Wonderful Life*, *Bwana Devil* (in 3-D), *Donovan's Brain*, *Red Planet Mars*, *The Bat*, *The Amazing Colossal Man*, *13 Ghosts*, *Hush . . . Hush Sweet Charlotte*, *I Saw What You Did*, *What Ever Happened to Aunt Alice?*, *Escape from the Planet of the Apes*, *Shanks*, *Blazing Saddles*, *The Towering Inferno* and *Airplane*.

Federico Fellini's regular cinematographer **Ruggero Mastroianni** died of a heart attack on the same day, aged 66. His credits include *Juliet of the Spirits*, *The Tenth Victim*, *Satyricon*, *Amarcord* and many others. He was the younger brother of actor Marcello.

Japanese director **Masaki Kobayashi**, who made the ghost story anthology *Kwaidan* in 1963, died on October 5th from cardiac arrest. He was 80.

American director and former editor **Francis D. Lyon** died on October 8th, aged 91. He edited *Red Planet Mars* and directed *Cult of the Cobra*, *Destination Inner Space*, *Castle of Evil* and *The Destructors*.

Make-up artist **Harry Thomas**, best remembered for working on Ed Wood's films in the 1950s, died on October 21st. He was in his mid-80s and his numerous other credits include *Frankenstein's Daughter*, *Killers from Space*, *Missile to the Moon*, *The Navy vs. the Night Monsters* and *She-Freak*.

Producer **Edwin Carlin**, whose films include *Blood and Lace*,

The Night God Screamed, *The Evil*, *Battle Beyond the Stars* and *Tanya's Island*, died on October 24th, aged 64.

Marcel Carné died on Hallowe'en, aged 93. One of France's great directors from the late 1930s to the mid-'40s, with such titles as *Le Jour Se Lève*, *Les Visiteurs du Soir* and *Les Enfants du Paradis*, his career later went into a decline.

Walt Disney animator **George "Nick" Nicholas** died on November 23rd, aged 85. His credits include *Cinderella*, *Sleeping Beauty* and *The Phantom Tollbooth*.

American cinematographer **Jordan Cronenweth** died on November 29th of Parkinson's disease, aged 61. Diagnosed with the disease in 1978, his many credits include *Brewster McCloud*, *Rolling Thunder*, *Altered States*, *Blade Runner* and *Peggy Sue Got Married*.

Oscar-winning art director **Edward Carfagno**, whose films include *Ben Hur*, *The Wonderful World of the Brothers Grimm* and *Soylent Green*, died on December 28th, aged 89.

USEFUL ADDRESSES

ORGANIZATIONS

The Australian Horror Writers is a national support group for authors, artists, editors and fans of horror and publishes the quarterly magazine/newsletter *Severed Head*. Joining Fee is AUS$15.00 plus a further AUS$10.00 renewal each year on October 31st. Add AUS$5.00 for overseas memberships. Bank cheque/money order in US or AUS dollars only made payable to "The Australian Horror Writers" and sent to PO Box 7347, St Kilda Road, Melbourne, VIC 3004, Australia.

The British Fantasy Society (http://www.djb.u-net.com) began in 1971 and publishes *Prism UK: The British Fantasy Newsletter*, plus various magazines and organizes the annual British FantasyCon. Yearly membership is £17.00 (UK), £20.00 (Europe), $35.00 (USA) and £25.00 (the rest of the world) made payable to "The British Fantasy Society" and sent to The BFS Secretary, c/o 2 Harwood Street, Stockport, SK4 1JJ, UK.

The Ghost Story Society publishes *All Hallows* magazine three times a year. To join, please send $23.00 (USA), £14.50/$25.00 (the rest of the world) or Cdn $29.50 (Canada), to joint organizers Barbara and Christopher Roden at The Ghost Story Society, PO Box 1360, Ashcroft, British Columbia, Canada V0K 1A0.

Horror Writers Association (http://www.horror.org/HWA) was formed in the 1980s and is open to anyone seeking affiliate membership or qualified authors wanting voting membership. The HWA publishes a regular *Newsletter* and organizes the annual Bram Stoker Awards ceremony. Yearly subscription is $55.00 (US/Canada) or £35.00/$65.00 (overseas), made payable to "Horror Writers Association" and sent to Nancy Etchemendy, HWA Membership, PO Box 50577, Palo Alto, CA 94303, USA.

Thee Vampire Guild (vampire. guild @ zetnet.co.uk) describes itself as Britain's fastest growing vampire society. With a quarterly journal, *Crimson*, film nights, Goth music, events, merchandise etc. Send a s.a.e. to Thee Vampire Guild, 82 Ripcroft, Southwell, Portland, Dorset DT5 2EE, UK for more details.

The Vampyre Society, formed in 1987, publishes a quarterly magazine, *The Velvet Vampyre*, and organizes regular meetings, special events and merchandise. Membership is £16.00 (UK/Europe) or £20.00 (USA) per annum to The Membership Secretary, P.O. Box 68, Keighley, West Yorkshire BD22 6RU, UK.

MAGAZINES

Cinefantastique is a monthly SF/fantasy/horror movie magazine with a "Sense of Wonder". Cover price is $5.99/£4.50 and a 12-issue subscription is $48.00 (USA) or $55.00 (Canada and overseas) to PO Box 270, Oak Park, IL 60303, USA.

Interzone is Britain's leading magazine of science fiction and fantasy. Single copies are available for £3.00 (UK) or £3.50/$6.00 (overseas) or a 12-issue subscription is £32.00 (UK), £38.00/$60.00 (USA) or £38.00 (overseas) to "Interzone", 217 Preston Drove, Brighton, BN1 6FL, UK.

Locus (http://www.Locusmag.com) is the monthly newspaper of the SF/fantasy/horror field. $4.50 a copy, a 12-issue subscription is $43.00 (USA), $48.00 (Canada), $70.00 (Europe) to "Locus Publications", PO Box 13305, Oakland, CA 94661, USA.

Necrofile (http://www.necropress.com) is a quarterly review of horror fiction. $3.00 a copy, a 4-issue subscription is $12.00 (USA), $15.00 (Canada) or $17.00 (overseas) in US funds only to "Necronomicon Press", P.O. Box 1304, West Warwick, RI 02893, USA.

Science Fiction Chronicle is a monthly news and reviews magazine that covers the SF/fantasy/horror field. $3.50 a copy, a 12-issue subscription is $35.00 (USA), $42.00 (1st class and Canada) and £29.00 (UK). Make cheques payable to "Science

Fiction Chronicle" and send to Science Fiction Chronicle, PO Box 022730, Brooklyn, NY 11202-0056, USA or payable to "Algol Press" and send to Rob Hansen, 144 Plashet Grove, East Ham, London E6 1AB, UK. Write for details about foreign subscriptions available in Australia, Canada and Germany.

SFX (http://www.futurenet.co.uk/sfx.html) is a monthly multi-media magazine of science fiction, fantasy and horror. Single copies are £2.95 or a 12-issue subscription is £24.00 (UK), £42.00 (Europe) or £62.00 (rest of the world) to Future Publishing Ltd, Freepost BS4900, Somerton, Somerset TA11 7BR, UK.

Starburst is a monthly magazine of sci-fi entertainment. Cover price is £2.75/$4.99 and a yearly subscription is £29.00 (UK), $49.00 (USA), £34.00 (Europe) or £46.00 (rest of the world) from Subscriptions, Visual Imagination Ltd, PO Box 371, London SW14 8JL, UK or for USA and Canada: Subscriptions, Visual Imagination Ltd, PO Box 156, Manorville, NY 11949, USA.

Video Watchdog (http://www.cinemaweb.com/videowd) is a bi-monthly magazine described as "the Perfectionist's Guide to Fantastic Video". $6.50 a copy, a 6-issue subscription is $24.00 (USA)/$45.00 (overseas). US funds only to PO Box 5283, Cincinnati, OH 45205-0283, USA.

BOOK DEALERS

Cold Tonnage Books offers excellent mail order new and used SF/fantasy/horror, art, reference, limited editions etc. with regular catalogues. Write to Andy Richards, 22 Kings Lane, Windlesham, Surrey GU20 6JQ, UK. Tel: 01276-475388.

Ken Cowley offers mostly used SF/fantasy/horror/crime/ supernatural, collectibles, pulps etc. by mail order with occasional catalogues. Write to Trinity Cottage, 153 Old Church Road, Clevedon, North Somerset, BS21 7TU, UK. Tel: 01275-872247.

Dark Delicacies (www.wavenet.com/~darkdel) is a friendly store specialising in horror books and merchandise that also publishes the annual Horror Writer's Calendar. Contact them at 3725 West Magnolia Blvd, Burbank, CA 91505, USA. Tel: (818) 556-6660.

DreamHaven Books & Comics shop and mail order has new SF/fantasy/horror, art, reference, magazines, collectibles etc. with regular catalogues. Write to 912 West Lake Street, Minneapolis, MN 55408, USA. Tel: (612) 823-6070.

Fantastic Literature mail order offers new and used SF/fantasy/horror etc. with regular catalogues. Write to Simon G. Gosden, 35 The Ramparts, Rayleigh, Essex SS6 8PY, UK. Tel: 01268-747564.

Fantasy Centre shop and mail order has mostly used SF/fantasy/horror, art, reference, pulps etc. at reasonable prices with regular catalogues. Write to 157 Holloway Road, London N7 8LX, UK. Tel: 0171-607 9433.

MARKET INFORMATION

DarkEcho is an excellent service offering all the latest news and gossip in the horror field every week on the Internet. All you have to do to subscribe is contact editor Paula Guran on darkecho@aol.com or you can also find it on the Omni Online web site at http://www.omnimag.com/darkecho

The Gila Queen's Guide to Markets (http://www.pacifier.com/alecwest/gila) is a regular publication detailing news of new markets for SF/fantasy/horror plus other genres. A sample copy is $6.00 and subscriptions are $34.00 (USA), $38.00 (Canada) and $50.00 (overseas). Back issues are also available. Cheques or money orders should be in US dollars and sent to "The Gila Queen's Guide to Markets", PO Box 97, Newton, NJ 07860-0097, USA.

Scavenger's Newsletter is a monthly newsletter for SF/fantasy/horror writers with an interest in the small press. News of markets, along with articles, letters and reviews. A sample copy is $2.50 (USA/Canada) and £2.40/$3.00 (overseas). An annual subscription is $17.00 (USA), $20.00 (Canada) and £18.00/$26.00 (overseas). *Scavenger's Scrapbook* is a twice yearly round-up, available for $4.00 (USA/Canada) and $5.00 (overseas). A year's subscription to the *Scrapbook* is $7.00 (USA/Canada) and $8.00 (overseas). Make cheques or money orders in US funds payable to "Janet Fox" and send to 519 Ellenwood, Osage City, KS 66523-1329, USA. In the UK contact Chris Reed, BBR Distribution, PO Box 625, Sheffield S1 3GY, UK.